SCARLET FEATHER

Also by Maeve Binchy

Light a Penny Candle
Echoes
London Transports
Dublin 4
The Lilac Bus
Firefly Summer
Silver Wedding
Circle of Friends
The Copper Beech
The Glass Lake
Evening Class
Tara Road

Cross Lines (short stories)
Aches and Pains

SCARLET
FEATHER

Maeve Binchy

ORION

First published in Great Britain in 2000 by Orion,
an imprint of the Orion Publishing Group Ltd, Orion House,
5, Upper Saint Martin's Lane, London WC2H 9EA

A CIP catalogue record for this book is available
from the British Library

Typeset by Deltatype Ltd, Birkenhead, Wirral
Printed in Great Britain by
Clays Ltd, St Ives plc

To my dearest Gordon, with all my love.

New Year's Eve

On the radio show they were asking people what kind of a New Year's Eve did they *really* want. It was very predictable. Those who were staying at home doing nothing wanted to be out partying, those who were too busy and rushed wanted to go to bed with a cup of tea and be asleep before the festivities began.

Cathy Scarlet smiled grimly as she packed more trays of food into the van. There could hardly be anyone in Ireland who would answer the question by saying that they really and truly wanted to spend the night catering a supper party for a mother-in-law. Now that was the punishment posting tonight, feeding Hannah Mitchell's guests at Oaklands. Why was she doing it then? Partly for practice, *and* of course it would be a good way to meet potential customers. Jock and Hannah Mitchell knew the kind of people who could afford caterers. But mainly she was doing it because she wanted to prove to Hannah Mitchell that she could. That Cathy, daughter of poor Lizzie Scarlet, the maid who cleaned Oaklands, who had married the only son of the house, Neil, was well able to run her own business and hold her head as high as any of them.

Neil Mitchell was in his car when he heard the radio programme. It annoyed him greatly. Anyone looking at him from another car would have seen his sharp, handsome face frown. People often thought they recognised him; his face was familiar from television, but he wasn't an actor, he just turned up on the screen so often, pushing the hair out of his eyes, passionate, concerned and caring, always the spokesperson for the underdog. He had the bright burning eyes of a crusader. This kind of whining and moaning on a radio show really drove him mad. People who had everything, a home, a job, a family, all telephoning a radio station to complain about the pressures of life. They were all so lucky and just too selfish to realise it. Unlike the man that Neil was going to see now, a Nigerian who would give anything to have the problems of these fools on the radio programme. His papers were not in order due to bungling and messing, and there was grave danger he would have to leave Ireland in the next forty-eight hours. Neil, who was a member of a lawyers' group set up to protect refugees, had been asked to come to a strategy meeting. It could go on for several hours. His mother had warned him not to be late at Oaklands, it was an important party, she said.

'I do hope that poor Cathy will be able to manage it,' she had said to Neil.

'Don't let her hear you calling her "poor Cathy", if you want your guests to get any food,' he had laughed.

It was idiotic, this nonsense between his mother and his wife; he and his father stayed well away from it. It was obvious anyway that Cathy had won, so what was it all about?

Tom Feather was going through the property section of the newspaper yet again. A puzzled look was on his face. He lay across the small sofa – there was never room for his long limbs and big frame unless he draped himself somehow over the whole thing. If he could put a chair at one end for his feet to rest on, it was fairly comfortable; some day he would live in a place where there was a sofa big enough to fit him. It was all very well to have the broad-shouldered rugby-player's build, but not if you needed to sit down and study the Premises Vacant ads. He shook out the newspaper. There had to be something he hadn't noticed. Some kind of premises with a room that could be made into a catering kitchen. He and Cathy Scarlet had worked so hard to make this happen. Since their first year at catering college they were going to set up Dublin's best home catering company. The whole idea of serving people great food in their own homes at reasonable prices was something that fired them both. They had worked so hard, and now they had made contacts and got the funding, all they needed was somewhere to operate from. Cathy and Neil's little town house in Waterview, though very elegant, was far too small to consider, and the flat in Stoneyfield where he lived with Marcella was even tinier. They had to find somewhere soon. He was half listening to the radio programme. What would he really like to do on this New Year's Eve? Find the perfect place for their company to set itself up, and then he would like to stay at home with Marcella and to stroke her beautiful hair as they sat by the fire and talked about the future. No, of course that wasn't going to happen.

Marcella Malone worked in the beauty salon of Haywards store. She was possibly the most beautiful manicurist that any of the clients had ever seen. Tall and willowy, with a cloud of dark hair, she had that kind of oval face and olive skin that schoolgirls dreamed of having. At the same time, she had a quiet, unthreatening way about her that made older, uglier, fatter people take to her despite her beauty. The clients felt that some of her good looks might rub off on them, and she always seemed interested in whatever they had to say.

They had the radio on in the salon, and people there were talking about the topic. Clients were interested and joined in the argument, nobody really got what they wanted on New Year's Eve. Marcella said nothing. She bent her beautiful face over the nails that she was doing and thought how lucky she was. She had everything she wanted. She had Tom Feather, the most handsome and loving man that any girl could want. And even more, she had been photographed recently at two events with very good connections. A knitwear promotion and at a charity fashion show where amateurs had modelled clothes at a fund-raiser. This looked like the year it could all happen for her. She had a very good portfolio of pictures now, and Ricky, the photographer who had taken them, was giving a very glitzy party. A lot of media people would be there and she and Tom had been invited. If things worked well she would have an agent and a proper modelling contract, and she would not be working as a manicurist in Haywards by this time next year.

It would have been lovely for Cathy if Tom could have come with her to Oaklands. Moral support and company in that kitchen, which held so many bad memories for her, and also it would have halved the work. But Tom had to go to some do with Marcella, which was fair enough, it was going to help her career. She was so beautiful, Marcella, she just made people stop and look at her. Tall and thin, with a smile that would light up a night. No wonder she wanted to be a model, and it was amazing that she wasn't established as one already. But then Neil had said he would help and also they had hired Walter, Neil's cousin, to be barman. And she had kept it fairly simple, nothing too tricky; she and Tom had slaved on it all morning.

'It's not fair, your doing all this,' Cathy said. 'She's not going to pay us, you know.'

'It's an investment . . . We might make a rake of contacts,' he said good-naturedly.

'There's *nothing* in this lot that could make anyone sick, is there?' Cathy begged him.

She had a vision of all Hannah Mitchell's guests going around holding their stomachs and groaning with some terrible food poisoning. He had said she was getting sillier by the hour, and he must be mad himself to have such an unhinged business partner. No one would have lent them money if they realised how the cool-looking Cathy Scarlet was actually a bag of nerves.

'I'll be fine with real people,' Cathy reassured him. 'It's just Hannah.'

'Give yourself plenty of time, go there early, fill the van with swirling music to calm yourself down and ring me tomorrow,' he soothed her.

'If I survive. Enjoy tonight.'

'Well, it's one of those noisy things at Ricky's studio,' he said.

'Happy New Year, and say it to Marcella too.'

'This time next year – imagine . . .' he said.

'I know, a great success story,' Cathy said, looking much brighter than she actually felt.

It had been the way they got by. One being over-cheery and optimistic when the other was in any way down or doubtful. And now the van was packed. Neil wasn't home, he had to go to a consultation. He wasn't like an ordinary lawyer, she thought proudly; he didn't have office hours or large consultancy fees. If someone was in trouble, he was there. It was as simple as that. It was why she loved him.

They had known each other since they were children but had hardly ever met. During all the years that Cathy's mother had worked at Oaklands, Neil had been away at boarding school and then hardly home during his college years. He had moved out to an

4

apartment when he was called to the Bar. It was such a chance that she should have met him again in Greece. If he had gone to one of the other villas, or she had been cooking on another island that month, then they would never have got to know each other and never fallen in love. And wouldn't Hannah Mitchell have been a happier woman tonight? Cathy told herself to put it out of her mind. She was still much too early to go to Oaklands, Hannah would just fuss and whimper over things and get in her way. She would call and see her own parents. That would calm her down.

Maurice and Elizabeth Scarlet, known to all as Muttie and Lizzie, lived in the inner city of Dublin in a semicircle of old, stone, two-storey houses. It was called St Jarlath's Crescent, after the Irish saint, and once the dwellings had all been occupied by factory workers who were woken by a siren each morning to get them out of bed. There were tiny gardens in front of each house, only ten feet long, so it was a challenge to plant anything that would look half-way satisfactory.

This had been the house where Cathy's mother had been born and where Muttie had married her. Although it was only twenty minutes from Cathy and Neil's town-house, it could have been a thousand miles, and maybe even a million miles from the rarefied world of Oaklands, where she was going tonight.

They were delighted to see Cathy turn up unexpectedly with her white van. What were they doing to see the new year in, she wondered? They were going out to a pub nearby where a lot of Muttie's associates would gather. The men he called his associates were actually the people he met up in Sandy Keane's betting shop, but they all took their day's business very seriously and Cathy knew better than to make a joke about them.

'Will there be food?' she asked.

'At midnight they're going to give us chicken in a basket.' Muttie Scarlet was pleased at the generosity of the pub.

Cathy looked at them.

Her father was small and round, his hair stood in wisps and his face was set in a permanent smile. He was fifty years of age and she had never known him work. His back had been too bad, not so bad he couldn't get up to Sandy Keane's to put something on a cert in the three-fifteen, but far too bad for him to be able to work.

Lizzie Scarlet looked as she had always looked, small and strong and wiry. Her hair was set in a tight perm, which she had done four times a year in her cousin's hair salon.

'It's as regular as poor Lizzie's perm,' Hannah Mitchell had once said about something. Cathy had been enraged – the fact that Hannah Mitchell, who had expensive weekly hair appointments at Haywards store, while Lizzie Scarlet was down on her hands and knees cleaning Oaklands, should dare to mock her mother's hairstyle was almost more than could really be borne. Still, there was no point in thinking about it now.

'Are you looking forward to the night, Mam?' she asked instead.

'Oh, yes, there's going to be a pub quiz with prizes, too,' Lizzie said. Cathy felt her heart go out to her undemanding parents who were so easily pleased.

Tonight at midnight at Oaklands, Neil's mother would have a mouth like a thin hard line and would find fault with whatever Cathy produced.

'And have they all rung in from Chicago?' she asked.

Cathy was the youngest of five, the only one of Muttie and Lizzie's children still in Dublin. Her two brothers and two sisters had all emigrated.

'Every one of them,' Lizzie said proudly. 'We were blessed in our family.'

Cathy knew they had all sent dollars to their mother as well because they sent the envelopes to her address rather than to their parents' home. No point in driving their father mad with temptation, letting him see American money when he knew sure-fire winners were waiting up in Sandy Keane's betting shop dying to gobble it up.

'Well, I'd like to be with you tonight,' Cathy said truthfully. 'But instead I'll be disappointing Hannah Mitchell with whatever food I produce.'

'You took it on yourself,' Muttie said.

'Please be polite to her, Cathy, I've found over all the years it's better to humour her.'

'You did, Mam, you humoured her all right,' Cathy said grimly.

'But you won't start making a speech or anything, not tonight?'

'No, Mam. Relax. I agreed to do it, and if it kills me I will do it well and with a smile on my face.'

'I wish Tom Feather was going with you, he'd put manners on you,' Lizzie said.

'Neil will be there, Mam, he'll keep me in control.' Cathy kissed them goodbye and practised her smile as she drove to Oaklands.

Hannah Mitchell had contract cleaners these days, now that there was no more Poor Lizzie to terrorise. Twice a week four women swept in, taking no nonsense from anyone, vacuuming, polishing, ironing and bringing their own equipment in a van.

They charged time and a half for working on New Year's Eve. Hannah had protested at this.

'Up to you, Mrs Mitchell,' they had said cheerfully, in the knowledge that plenty of other people would be glad to have their house cleaned on a day like this. She gave in speedily. Things were definitely not like they used to be. Still, it had been worth it, the house looked very well, and at least she wouldn't have to lift a finger. That Cathy with all her grand notions *was* in fact able to serve a presentable meal. She would be coming shortly in that big white deplorable-looking van: even the women who came to clean the house twice a week travelled in a far more respectable vehicle. She would come into the kitchen huffing and puffing and throwing her weight about. Poor Lizzie's daughter, behaving as if she owned the place. Which, alas, she probably would one day. But not yet, Hannah reminded herself with her mouth in a hard line.

Hannah Mitchell's husband Jock stopped on the way home from his office to have a drink. He felt he needed one before facing Hannah. She was always nervous and tense before a party but this time it would be magnified many times – she so hated having Neil's wife Cathy doing the catering for her. She had refused to accept that the couple were happy, well suited and unlikely to leave each other no matter how she schemed. Cathy would always be Poor Lizzie's daughter, and somehow a villain who had seduced their son in Greece. She had always believed that the girl had got pregnant deliberately to trap him, and been most surprised when this had proved not to be the case.

He drank his single malt Scotch thoughtfully and wished that he didn't have to worry about this as well as everything else. Jock Mitchell had been severely disturbed by a conversation with his nephew Walter today. Walter, an idle layabout, the eldest son of Jock's brother Kenneth, had revealed that all was not well at The Beeches, his family home. In fact, things were very far from well. Walter said that his father had gone to England just before

Christmas, and had left no indication of his whereabouts. Walter's mother, not known to be a strong character, was reacting to this turn of events by a heavy reliance on vodka. The problem was their nine-year-old twins, Simon and Maud. What was happening to them? Walter had shrugged; he really didn't know. They were managing, he implied. Jock Mitchell sighed again.

As she arrived at Oaklands, Cathy heard her mobile phone ring. She pulled in and answered.

'Hon, I'm not going to be there to help you unload,' he apologised.

'Neil, it doesn't matter, I knew it would go on a bit.'

'It's more complicated than we thought. Listen, ask my dad to help you in with all those crates, don't go dragging and pulling just to show my mother how wonderful you are.'

'Oh she knows *that*,' Cathy groaned.

'Walter should be there . . .'

'If I were to wait for Walter to help me unload and set up, the party would be halfway through . . . Stop fussing and go back to what you have to do.'

Cathy told herself that there were only six hours or so of this year left, only six hours or so of being nice to Hannah. What was the very worst that could happen? The very worst was that the food was awful and no one would eat it, but that could not happen, because the food was terrific. The second worst thing was that there wasn't enough of it, but there was enough in this van to feed half of Dublin.

'There are no problems,' Cathy said aloud as she looked down the tree-lined drive to the house where Neil had been born. A gentleman's residence, a hundred and fifty years old, square and satisfying somehow, with its four bedrooms above the large door and the bay windows on either side of it. Ivy and virginia creeper covered the walls and in front lay a huge gravelled circle where tonight twenty expensive cars would be parked. A house as different from St Jarlath's Crescent as you could imagine.

Shona Burke often stayed late in her office up on the management floors of Haywards – she had her own key and code to get in and out. She had listened to the programme on the radio and was wondering if she really and truly had a choice about how she would spend New Year's Eve. Long ago in a happier life there would have been a celebration, but not in the last few years. She had no idea what her sisters and brothers would do, and if they would go to the hospital. Shona would make the hospital visit out of duty, of course, but it was pointless, she wouldn't be recognised or acknowledged.

Then she would go to Ricky's party in his studio. Everyone liked Ricky. A pleasant, easygoing photographer, he would gather a lot of people and make a buzz for them all. There would be a fair crowd of poseurs and empty-headed types dying to see themselves in the gossip columns . . . She was unlikely to meet the love of her life or even a temporary soulmate, but still Shona would dress up and go there simply because she did not see herself as the kind of person who would sit alone in her apartment in Glenstar.

The question nagged her, what would she *really* like to be doing tonight? It was so hard to answer because everything had changed so much. The good days were over, and it was impossible to imagine doing something that would make her really happy. So in the absence of that, Ricky's would do fine.

Marcella was painting her toenails. She had new evening sandals which she'd bought at a thrift shop. She showed them proudly to Tom. They had been barely worn; someone must have bought them and found they didn't suit.

'They must have cost a fortune new,' she said happily, examining them carefully.

'Are you happy?' Tom asked.

'Very,' she said. 'And you?'

'Oh, very, very,' he laughed. Was that strictly true? He didn't want to go to this party at all. But just looking at her did make him happy. He couldn't really believe that such a beautiful girl, who could have had anyone she wanted, really found him enough for her. Tom had no idea that he was attractive, he thought he was big and clumsy. He honestly believed that all the admiring glances they got as a couple were directed at Marcella alone . . .

'I heard a radio programme saying people were never happy,' she began.

'I know, I heard it too,' Tom said.

'I was just thinking how lucky we were; poor Cathy and Neil can't do what *they* want tonight.' Marcella stood in her thong and picked up a tiny red garment from the back of a chair.

'Yeah, Cathy will be there now, at her mother-in-law's house, laying up the tables. I hope she keeps her temper.'

'Well she'll have to, it's work, it's professional. We all have to at work,' said Marcella, who had bent over too many imperious hands already in her life, and wanted her day in the sunshine, walking down the ramp as a model.

'Neil will be there and that pup of a cousin he has, so she should be all right.' Tom still sounded doubtful.

Marcella had put on the red outfit. It was actually a dress, short and tight, clinging to her and leaving nothing to the imagination.

'Marcella, are you really wearing that to the party?'

'Don't you like it?' her face clouded over immediately.

'Well of course I like it. You look beautiful. It's just that maybe I'd like you to wear it here, for us, not for everyone else as well to see you.'

'But Tom, it's a party dress,' she cried, stricken.

He pulled himself together at once.

'Of course it is, and you'll be the success of the night.'

'So what did you mean . . . ?'

'Mean? I meant nothing. I meant you were so gorgeous I didn't want to share you with people . . . but take no notice. I didn't really mean that at all.'

'I thought you'd be proud of me,' she said.

'I am so proud you'll never know,' he reassured her. And she *was* a beauty. He must have been insane to have had that sudden reaction.

Hannah Mitchell stood in her navy wool dress, her hair hard and lacquered from her New Year's Eve visit to Haywards. She always dressed as if she were going out to a ladies' lunch. Cathy never remembered her wearing a pinafore or even an old skirt. But then, if you did no housework, what was the point of wearing things like that?

Hannah watched Cathy carry in all the boxes and crates, one by one, standing in her way and fussing and blocking her journey. She offered to carry nothing at all. Instead, she was hoping the crates wouldn't mark the wallpaper, and wondering where would Cathy put the van so that it would be out of the way when people came. Grimly, Cathy marched to and from the kitchen of Oaklands. She turned on the ovens, laid her tea towels on the backs of chairs, placed her bag of ice in the freezer and began to sort out the food. It would be useless asking Hannah Mitchell to leave her alone, to go upstairs and lie down. She would stay put, fuss and irritate until the guests arrived.

'Will Mr Mitchell be home shortly?' Cathy thought she might ask him to help her unpack the glasses.

'I don't know, Cathy; really, it's not up to me to police Mr Mitchell about what time he comes home.' Cathy felt her neck redden in rage. How dare this woman be so offensive and patronising. But she knew she stood alone in this resentment. Neil would shrug if she told him. Her mother would beg her not to annoy Mrs Mitchell any further. Even her aunt Geraldine, who could normally be relied on for encouragement and support, would say what the hell. It just proved that Hannah Mitchell was an insecure nobody, not anyone to waste time worrying over. Cathy began to peel the foil from the dishes she had prepared.

'Is that fish? Not everyone eats it, you know.' Hannah had her very concerned face on now.

'I know, Mrs Mitchell, some people don't, which is why there's a choice, you see.'

'But they mightn't know.'

'I think they will. I'll tell them.'

'But didn't you say it was a buffet?'

'Yes, but I'll be behind it serving, so I'll tell them.'

'Tell them?' Hannah Mitchell was bewildered.

Cathy wondered was there a possibility that her mother-in-law was actually a halfwit.

'Like asking them would they like fish in a sea-food sauce, or herbed chicken, or the vegetarian goulash,' she said.

Mrs Mitchell tried but found it hard to find fault with this.

'Yes, well,' she said eventually.

'So will I just get on with it now, do you think?' she asked.

'Cathy, my dear, may I ask who is stopping you?' Hannah said with her face hard and unforgiving at all this confidence in Poor Lizzie Scarlet's girl.

Neil looked at his watch. Every single person in this room had some kind of New Year's function to go to except the student that they had all gathered to protect. They would be finished soon, but nobody must be seen to hasten away. It would be terrible for the man whose future hung in the balance if he thought that the civil rights activists, the social workers and lawyers were more interested in their own night's fun and games than they were in his predicament. He was trying to reassure this young Nigerian that there would be justice and a welcome for him in Ireland. Neil would not let Jonathan spend the dawn of a New Year on his own.

'When we're through here, you can come back to my parents' house,' he said. He was already late, but it couldn't be helped.

The big sad eyes looked at him. 'You don't have to, you know.'

'I know I don't have to, and a barrel of laughs it won't be, but my wife is doing the catering so the food will be good. My parents' friends are ... well, how will I put it ... a bit dead.'

'I'm okay, Neil, truly, you're doing so much for me and all this has delayed you from it already ...'

'We'll go through it once more,' Neil said to the meeting, 'then Jonathan and I will go and party.' He saw them look at him in admiration. Neil Mitchell really went the distance. He felt a bit guilty at not being there to help Cathy as he had promised, but this was much more important – she'd understand. Cathy would be fine. His father and his cousin Walter would be there to help her by now ... Everything would be fine.

Hannah still hovered, which meant that Cathy had to talk, answer inane questions, pat down unnecessary worries and even bring up topics of conversation, lest she be considered moody.

'It's nearly seven-thirty, Walter will be here any minute,' Cathy said desperately. She could have got things done far faster had she not been under the scrutiny of the most critical eyes in the western hemisphere. Fingers could have been used more often than they were, things could have been flung into places rather than placed elegantly.

'Oh, Walter! Like all young people, I'm sure he'll be late.' There was a sniff of disapproval and resignation.

'I don't think so, Mrs Mitchell, not tonight. It's a professional engagement, he's being paid from seven-thirty until twelve-thirty. That's a five-hour booking. I'm certain he won't let us down.'

Cathy wasn't at all sure of this; she had no evidence that Walter Mitchell was reliable. But at least it was going to be known what his terms of business were. And if he didn't turn up, then his own relations would have been made aware of his shortcomings. She heard someone outside.

'Ah, that must be Walter now,' she said. 'I knew he'd be on time.'

It was in fact Jock Mitchell, who came into the kitchen rubbing his hands.

'This looks just great, Cathy. I say, Hannah, isn't this an amazing spread?'

'Yes,' said his wife.

'Welcome home, Mr Mitchell. I thought it was Walter. He's actually working for me tonight,' Cathy said. 'Did he leave the office at the same time as you, by any chance?'

'Ages earlier,' her father-in-law said. 'Boy keeps his own time. I'm getting a bit of stick from the partners over him, as it happens.'

Hannah Mitchell hated family business being discussed in front of Cathy.

'Why don't you come upstairs and have a shower, dear? The guests will be here in half an hour,' she said crisply.

'Fine, fine. Don't you want any help, Cathy?'

'No, not at all. As I say, my wine waiter will be here shortly,' Cathy said.

'And Neil?' he asked.

'At a consultation. He'll be along when he can.'

She was alone in the kitchen. So far she was surviving, but it was only fifteen minutes before eight o'clock. There were hours and hours to go.

Ricky's party was only starting at nine, and they would go much later, so Tom Feather had plenty of time to go up to his parents and wish them a Happy New Year. He caught the bus from outside the door of Stoneyfield flats, and it went directly to Fatima, his mother and father's house, weighed down with statues and holy pictures. He longed to call Cathy and ask how it was all going, but she said she had better not bring her mobile into the house – it seemed to irritate Hannah Mitchell beyond all reason. She would leave it in the van. Cathy would not appreciate being telephoned and called to the hall at Oaklands. He would have to leave it.

Tom sat on the bus, his heart heavy. He was so stupid to be upset by that skimpy dress Marcella was wearing. She was dressing up for him; she loved only him. He was so mean-spirited to grudge the hour it took to go and sit with his parents in their cluttered sitting room. It was just that they were so pessimistic, so willing to see the downside of things, while he had always been the reverse. He was a fool to be upset because they hadn't found premises for the new company yet. They would: it took time, that's what everyone said, and then the right place would come along.

Tom's mother said they had heard nothing from Tom's brother Joe, nothing at all even on Christmas Day. There were phones in London, he could lift one of them. Tom's father said that there was an article in the paper saying that the building industry was going to go through the roof, and yet Tom Feather was chasing after moonbeams trying to set up a catering company instead of entering a ready-made office. Tom was pleasant and cheerful, and talked on and on until his jaw ached, hugged them both and said he must go back.

'I don't suppose you'd make an honest woman out of Marcella next year. Could that be your resolution?' his mother asked.

'Mam, I wanted to marry Marcella about twenty-five minutes after I met her. I must have asked her at least a hundred times . . .' He spread his hands out helplessly. They knew he was telling the truth.

Walter Mitchell looked at his watch in the pub where a group of his friends were having a New Year's Eve drink.

'Shit, it's eight o'clock,' he said.

Cathy would be like a devil over this, but still, Uncle Jock and Aunt Hannah would stand up for him. That was the great thing about being family.

There was no sign of Walter, so Cathy unpacked the glasses, filled thirty of them with a sugar lump and a teaspoon of brandy and laid them on a tray. Later, once the guests arrived, she would top the glasses up with champagne. That boy was meant to be doing this while she got her trays of canapés ready. Cathy caught sight of herself in the hall mirror – she looked flushed and uneasy. Wisps of hair were escaping from the ribbon that tied it back. This would not do.

She went into the downstairs cloakroom and smoothed a beige liquid make-up over her face and neck. She dampened her hair and tied it more expertly back. This is where she needed Marcella, to put something magical on her eyes. Cathy hunted in her handbag. There was a stubby brown pencil, and she made a few stabs at herself with that. She put on her clean white shirt and her scarlet skirt. It looked a *bit* better, she thought. How wonderful if she got a lot of business for the company out of this party! But Cathy knew

14

she must be careful. Any sign of touting for business, or giving a card, would be frowned upon by her mother-in-law. Please may it be a success, otherwise days and days of effort, and money they could ill afford, would all have been wasted.

Ricky's studio was in a basement, three rooms opening into each other, drink in one, food in another and dancing in a third. You didn't so much come in, you made an entrance by walking down a big staircase which was brightly lit.

Tom and Marcella had left their coats on the ground floor, and he felt every eye in the room was on Marcella in her little red dress as she walked gracefully ahead of him down the stairs, with her beautiful long legs and the gold evening sandals that she was so proud of. No wonder they looked at her. Every other woman seemed suddenly drab by comparison.

Marcella never ate or drank at these functions. She might have a glass of fizzy water. But she genuinely wasn't hungry, she said, with such sincerity that people believed her. Tom, however, was dying to see the food, to compare it to what he and Cathy would have done. For a party like this they would serve a choice of two hot dishes with a lot of pitta bread, something like the chicken in herbs and the vegetarian dish that Cathy was preparing at her in-laws' house. But Ricky's caterers seemed to have endless plates of insubstantial and tired-looking finger food. Smoked salmon already drying and hardening on bread, some kind of pâté spread sparsely on unappetising-looking biscuits. Cocktail sausages congealing and allowed to cool in their own fat. Bit by bit he tasted and examined, identifying a shop paste here and a bought biscuit base there. He ached to know how much they had charged a head. He would be able to ask Ricky eventually, but not tonight.

'Tom, stop tearing those unfortunate things to bits,' Marcella giggled at him.

'Look at them, will you – soggy pastry, far too much salt . . .'

'Come and dance with me.'

'In a moment. I have to see what other awful things are lurking here,' he said, poking around the plates.

'Would you like to dance with me?' A boy of nineteen was staring at Marcella in disbelief.

'Tom?'

'Go ahead. I'll come in and drag you away in a minute,' Tom grinned.

It was considerably later, and after three glasses of inferior wine, that he found his way to the little dance floor. Marcella was dancing with a man with a big red face and big hands. The man's hands were spread over Marcella's bottom. Tom moved up to them.

'I've come to drag you away,' he said.

'Hey,' the man said, 'fair's fair, find your own girl.'

'Oh, this *is* my girl,' Tom said firmly.

'Well have some manners, then, and let us finish the dance.'

'If you don't mind . . .' Tom began.

'Let's just finish this dance,' Marcella said. 'And then I'll dance with you, Tom, I *have* been waiting for you.'

He moved away, annoyed. Somehow it was now *his* fault that this lout had his hands all over Marcella. He saw Shona Burke, nice girl from Haywards, one of the many people in Dublin who had been asked to look out for premises for the new catering company.

'Would you like me to get you a glass of red ink and a piece of cardboard with a scrape of meat paste on it?' he offered.

Shona laughed. 'Now, you're not going to get anywhere by bad-mouthing the opposition,' she said.

'No, but this kind of thing really does annoy me. It's so shoddy,' Tom said. His glance went back to Marcella, who was still talking to and dancing with that horrible man.

'It's all right, Tom, she has eyes for no one except you.'

Tom was embarrassed to have been so obvious. 'I meant the food. It's really outrageous to charge Ricky for this. Whatever he paid he was robbed.'

'Sure you were talking about the food,' Shona said.

'Would you like to dance?' he said.

'No, Tom, I'm not going to be any part of this. Go and get Marcella.'

But by the time he came over, another man had asked her to dance and the man with the big face and the big hands watched her approvingly from the sidelines. Tom went off to have another glass of the unspeakable wine.

Walter arrived at eight-thirty, when there were ten guests already installed in the sitting room of Oaklands. He came in cheerfully kissing his aunt on both cheeks.

'Now let me give you a hand, Aunt Hannah,' he said with a broad smile.

'Such a nice boy, isn't he?' said Mrs Ryan to Cathy.

'Indeed,' Cathy managed to say.

Mrs Ryan and her husband had been the first guests to arrive. She was totally unlike Hannah Mitchell; a humble woman, who was full of admiration for the canapés and had plenty of small talk for Cathy.

'My husband will be annoyed that we were here first,' she confided.

'Somebody has to be first. I think it's nice to be one of the early arrivals.'

Cathy wasn't concentrating. She was looking at Walter, small and handsome like all the Mitchells, and she was trying hard to keep her temper under control. He was being praised and fêted by people like her mother-in-law and stupid guests for having turned up one whole hour late. She was barely listening to what the apologetic Mrs Ryan was saying about being a poor cook herself.

'One thing they always wanted was apple strudels, and I just wouldn't know where to begin.'

Cathy brought her mind back. The woman was having some business friends of her husband to coffee and cake next week. Was it possible for Cathy to deliver something to the house and not stay to serve them?

Cathy looked carefully as her mother-in-law left the room, then she took down Mrs Ryan's phone number.

'It will be our little secret,' she promised.

It was their first booking. Not even nine o'clock, and she had got a job already.

'Do you intend to stop dancing with strangers at all tonight?' Tom asked Marcella.

'Tom. At last,' she said, excusing herself with a smile from a man in a black leather jacket and sunglasses.

'But maybe I'm not good enough to dance with,' he said.

'Don't be such a fool, put your arms around me,' she said.

'Is that what you say to all the lads?' he asked.

'Why are you being like this?' She was hurt and upset. 'What have I done?'

'You've lurched around half naked with half of Dublin,' he said.

'That's not fair,' Marcella was stung.

'Well haven't you?'

'It's a party, people ask other people to dance, that's what it's about.'

'Oh, good.'

'What's wrong, Tom?' She kept glancing over his shoulder at the dance floor.

'I don't know.'

'Tell me.'

'I don't *know*, Marcella. I realise that I'm a spoilsport, but would you come home?'

'Come *home*?' she was astounded. 'We've only just got here.'

'No, of course. Of course.'

'And we want to meet people, be seen a bit.'

'Yes, I know,' he said glumly.

'Do you not feel well?' she asked.

'No. I drank too much very cheap wine too quickly and ate five strange things that tasted like cement.'

'Well, will you sit down until it passes over.' Marcella had no intention of leaving. She had dressed up for this; looked forward to it.

'I might go home a bit before you,' he said.

'Don't do that; see the new year in here, with all our friends,' she begged.

'They're not really our friends, they're only strangers,' said Tom Feather sadly.

'Tom, have another cement sandwich and cheer up,' she said to him, laughing.

Cathy tried to show Walter how to make the champagne cocktails. He barely watched her.

'Sure, sure, I know,' he said.

'And once they have started to drink the red and white with the supper, can you collect all the champagne flutes and get them into the kitchen. They need to be washed because champagne will be served again at midnight.'

'Who washes them?' he asked.

'You do, Walter. I'll be serving the supper . . . I've left trays out here ready for—'

'I'm paid to help pass things around, not to be a washer-up,' he said.

'You're being paid to help me for four hours to do whatever I ask you to do.' Cathy heard the tremble in her voice.

'Five hours,' he said.

'Four,' she said, looking him in the eye. 'You got here an hour late.'

'I think you'll find . . .'

'When Neil comes, I think you'll find that we'll discuss it with him. Meanwhile, please take this tray out to your uncle's guests.'

Cathy lifted the trays of food from the oven. This night would end, sometime.

Shona Burke watched Tom Feather standing moodily in a corner. She knew she wasn't the only woman in the room looking at him. But the place might as well have been empty for all that he saw of them.

'I think I'll go home,' he said aloud to himself. Then he realised that was exactly what he was going to do.

'Will you tell Marcella, if she notices, that I've gone home,' he said to Ricky.

'Not a lovers' quarrel on New Year's Eve, please.' Ricky always put on a slightly camp accent. It was part of the way he went on. Tonight it irritated Tom greatly.

'No, not at all: I ate five things that disagreed with me,' Tom said.

'What were they?' Ricky asked.

'Search me, Ricky, sandwiches or something.'

Ricky decided not to be offended. 'How will Marcella get home?'

'I don't know. Shona might give her a lift – that's if the man with his two big shovels of hands which he has all over her doesn't take her.'

'Tom, come on. It's under an hour to midnight.'

'I'm in no form for it, Ricky. I'm only bringing other people down. My face would stop a clock.'

'I'll see she gets back to you safely,' Ricky said.

'Thanks, mate.' And he was gone, out into the wet, windy streets of Dublin where revellers were moving from one pub to another, or looking vainly for taxis; where closed curtains showed chinks of light from the parties behind them. From time to time he halted and wondered was he being silly, but he couldn't go back. Everything about the party annoyed him; all his insecurity that he wasn't good enough for Marcella would keep bubbling back to the surface. No: he must walk and walk and clear his head.

Eventually Neil got away from his meeting. He and Jonathan drove through the New Year's Eve streets of Dublin and out onto the leafy road where Oaklands stood, all lit up like a Christmas tree, he saw that Cathy had tidied her big white van as far out of sight as possible. He parked the Volvo and ran in the back door. Cathy was surrounded by plates and glasses. How could anyone do this for a living and stay sane ...

'Cathy, I'm sorry things took longer, this is Jonathan. Jonathan, this is Cathy.'

She shook hands with the tall Nigerian with the tired face and polite smile.

'I hope I'm not causing you additional problems by coming here,' he said.

'No, heavens no, Jonathan,' Cathy protested, wondering what her mother-in-law's reaction would be. 'You're most welcome and I hope you have a good evening. I'm glad you both got here, I thought I'd be singing Auld Lang Syne to myself.'

'Happy New Year, hon.' Neil put his arms around her.

She felt very tired suddenly. 'Will we survive, Neil, tell me?'

'Of course we will, we've covered all the options, they're not going to move on New Year's Day, are they Jonathan?'

'I hope not, you've given up so much time for this,' the young man smiled gratefully.

Cathy realised Neil thought she had been talking about the extradition. Still, he was here, that was the main thing.

'Is it going all right in there?' Neil nodded towards the front rooms.

'Okay, I think, hard to know. Walter was an hour late.'

'Then he gets paid an hour less.' To Neil it was simple. 'Is he any help to you?'

'Not really. Neil go on in and take Jonathan to meet people.'

'I could perhaps help you here,' Jonathan offered.

'Lord no, if anyone needs a party it's you, after all you've been through,' Cathy said. 'Go on in, Neil, your mother's dying to show you off.'

'But can't I do anything here for—'

'Go distract your mother. Keep her out of the kitchen,' she begged.

She could hear cries of excitement as people welcomed the son and heir of Oaklands, and told him they remembered him when he was a little boy. Neil moved around the room easily, talking, greeting and kissing here and there. He saw Walter having a cigarette by the piano and talking to a woman who was about twenty years younger than the average age.

'I think you're needed in the kitchen, Walter,' he said briskly.

'Surely not,' Walter said.

'Now, please,' Neil said, and took over the conversation with the vacant-looking blonde woman.

Tom Feather didn't go straight home to Stoneyfield flats. He walked instead up and down little streets that he had never walked before, lanes, mews and even backyards. Somewhere in this city of a million people there was a place which he and Cathy could find to start their catering company. All it really needed was someone with the patience and the time to go and look for it. And he had plenty of time tonight.

The phone rang in the hall of Oaklands.

Hannah Mitchell hastened out to answer it; she felt she needed time to collect her thoughts. She was so confused: Neil had brought this African man to the party without letting them know. She had nothing against the man at all, of course. Why should she? But it was annoying that people kept asking who he was, and she didn't really know. One of Neil's clients, she said over and over, adding that Neil was always so dedicated. But she felt she had been getting some odd looks. It was a relief to escape.

'I'm sure that's Amanda phoning from Canada to wish us a Happy New Year,' she trilled. Her face showed that it was not her daughter who had phoned.

'Yes, well, that's all very upsetting, but what exactly do you think ... Yes, I know ... Well, of course it is hard to know what to do, but this isn't a good time. Look you'd better talk to your brother. Oh, I see. Well, your uncle then ... Jock, come here a moment.'

Cathy watched the little tableau.

'It's Kenneth's children, apparently they're in the house on their own tonight. You talk to them, I told them Walter was here but they didn't think he'd be any help.'

'Too damn right,' grumbled Jock Mitchell.

'Well, well, well, tell me the problem,' he said wearily down the phone.

Cathy moved among the guests, passing little plates of a rich chocolate cake and a spoonful of fruit pavlova on the side, giving them no time to dither and make a choice when everyone knew they wanted both.

She saw Jonathan standing alone and awkward at the window while Neil went around the room greeting his parents' friends. She spoke to him as often as she could without making it look as if she was trying to mind him.

'I could work in the kitchen, I'm good at it,' he said pleadingly.

'I'm sure you are, and it would probably be more fun, but honestly, it's not on – for my sake. I won't let Neil's mother say I wasn't able to do it by myself. I have to prove it – do you understand?'

'I understand having to prove yourself, yes,' he answered.

Cathy moved on and found herself within earshot of Jock on the phone.

'That's fine then, children, I'll put Walter on to you and I'll come round tomorrow. Good children, now.'

Neil had just managed to galvanise Walter into doing some work when Jock removed him from the scene again. Cathy listened as the boy talked to his brother and sister, who were over ten years younger than he was.

'Now *listen* to me, I will be home, I'm not sure what time, I have to go somewhere when I leave here but I *will* be there sometime, so not one more word out of you. Just go to bed, for heaven's sake. Father hasn't been there for ages and Mother never comes out of her room, so what's so different about tonight?'

He turned round and saw Cathy watching him.

'Well as you will have gathered there's a crisis at home, so I'm afraid I'm off duty.'

'Yes, so I hear.'

'So suppose I just take what's owing to me . . .'

'I'll ask Neil to give it to you,' she said.

'I thought you prided yourself on this being your own business?' He was insolent.

'It is, but Neil is your cousin, he'd know how much you're owed. Let's go and ask him.'

'Four hours will do,' he said grudgingly.

'You haven't even been here for three hours,' she said.

'It's not my fault that I have to—'

'You're not going straight home, you're going to a party somewhere. But let's not fight, let's ask Neil.'

'Three hours then, cheapskate.'

'No, that's what I am most certainly not. Come, let's not do it in front of the guests, come into the kitchen.'

Her heart sank when she saw the washing-up, including the champagne glasses that would be needed at midnight.

'Goodnight, Walter.'

'Goodnight, Scrooge,' he said, and ran out of the house.

Tom stood by the canal and watched two swans gliding by.

'They mate for life, swans, did you know that?' he said to a passing girl.

'Do they now? Lucky old them,' she said. She was small and thin, he noticed; a druggy prostitute with an anxious face.

'Don't suppose you'd like any casual mating yourself,' she said hopefully.

'No, no, sorry,' Tom said. It seemed rather dismissive. 'Not tonight,' he added, as if to say that normally he would be utterly delighted. She smiled a tired smile.

'Happy New Year anyway,' she said.

'And to you,' he said, feeling hopeless.

The doorbell rang at Oaklands.

Hannah teetered out on her high heels, wondering who else it could be, arriving so late. Cathy leant against a table at the back of the hall to support her tired legs and to see what new confusion was arriving now. A late guest wanting a main course?

It appeared to be two children in a taxi which they didn't have the money to pay for. Cathy sighed. She almost felt sorry for Hannah. A Nigerian student, and now two waifs – what else would the night throw at her?

'Please get Mr Mitchell immediately, Cathy,' Hannah ordered.

'Is that the maid?' the little boy asked. He was pale and aged about eight or nine. Like his sister, he had dead straight fair hair and everything looked the same colour – his sweater, his hair, his face and the small canvas bag he carried.

'Don't say "maid",' the girl corrected him in a hiss. Her face was frightened and there were dark rings under her eyes.

Cathy had never seen them before. Jock Mitchell and his brother Kenneth were not close; the nearest they had ever come to solidarity was in the apprenticeship of Walter in his uncle's office, something that hadn't proved to be entirely successful, Cathy gathered.

Jock had come out anyway to see who was at the door. He was not enthusiastic at the sight of them.

'Well?' he began. 'What have we here?'

'We had nowhere to go,' the boy explained.

'So we came here,' said the girl.

Jock looked bewildered.

'Cathy,' he said eventually, 'these are Walter's brother and sister, can you give them something to eat in the kitchen?'

'Certainly, Mr Mitchell, go back to your guests, I'll look after them.'

'*Are* you the maid?' the boy asked again. He seemed anxious to put everyone in a category.

'No, actually I'm Cathy, married to Neil, your cousin. How do you do?' They looked at her solemnly. 'And perhaps you might give me your names?' Maud and Simon, it turned out. 'Come into the kitchen,' she said wearily. 'Do you like herbed chicken?'

'No,' said Maud.

'We never had it,' said Simon.

Cathy noticed them lifting some chocolate biscuits and putting them in their pockets.

'Put those back,' she said sharply.

'Put what back?' Simon's eyes were innocent.

'There'll be no stealing,' she said.

'It's not stealing, you were told to give us something to eat,' Maud countered with spirit.

'And give you something I will – so just put them back this minute.'

Grudgingly, they put the already crushed and crumbly biscuits back on the silver tray. Swiftly Cathy made them sandwiches from the cold chicken and poured them a glass of milk each. They ate hungrily.

'In your lives so far did anyone mention the words "thank you" at all?' she asked.

'Thank you,' they said ungraciously.

'You're most welcome,' she said with exaggerated politeness.

'What will we do now?' Simon asked.

'Well, I think you might sit here – unless you wanted to help me wash up?'

'Not really, to be honest,' Maud said.

'Should we be inside at the party, do you think?' Simon wondered.

'Not really, to be honest,' Cathy echoed.

'So will we sit here all night until we go to bed?' Maud asked.

'Are you staying here?'

'Where else would we go?' Maud asked innocently.

Hannah came into the kitchen, with her tottering, tiny steps which always set Cathy's teeth on edge.

'Oh, you're sitting here, Cathy, I think people's glasses need—'

'Of course, Mrs Mitchell, I'll go and see to it. Walter, who was meant to be seeing to glasses seems to have disappeared, and I was, as you asked, giving supper to Walter's brother and sister...'

'Yes, well, of course,' said Hannah.

'So I'll leave you to make all the arrangements with Maud and Simon, then,' said Cathy on her way to the door.

'Arrangements?' Hannah looked alarmed.

Cathy paused just long enough to hear Maud asking in her bell-clear voice, 'What rooms will we have, Aunt Hannah, we've brought our pyjamas and everything...' Then she circulated the party refilling glasses.

'Are you finding it all insane?' she asked Jonathan.

He smiled his weary smile. 'At school I was taught by Irish priests. They told me all about Ireland, but I didn't expect New Year's Eve to be quite like this.'

'It's not meant to be, believe me,' Cathy grinned at him.

She moved on, topping up glasses here and avoiding people's eyes there. That nice Mrs Ryan had had quite enough already. To her surprise, she saw that Maud and Simon had joined the party easily as if it were their natural place.

Cathy worked and worked. She removed plates, picked up scrunched-up napkins, emptied ashtrays, kept things moving. Soon it would be midnight and things might begin to wind down. Most people here were in their late fifties and sixties; they wouldn't have the stamina to party on until dawn. She looked towards the window where she had left Jonathan to fend for himself. He was talking animatedly to someone. Cathy looked again. The twins were in deep conversation with him.

'Jock, *what* are we going to do with them?'

'Calm, Hannah, calm.'

'They can't stay here.'

'Well, not for ever, no, certainly not.'

'But for how long?'

'Until we get them settled.'

'And how long will that be?'

'Soon, soon.'

'So where . . .'

'Put them in Neil's and Mandy's rooms, or wherever. Haven't we a house full of bedrooms, for heaven's sake?' He was clearly irritated and wanted to get back to the party. Hannah went over to the ill-assorted group at the window.

'Now children, don't annoy Neil's client, Mr . . . um . . .' she began.

'Oh, but they're not annoying me at all – delightful company,' Jonathan begged. They were, after all, the only people who had talked to him normally all night. Certainly the only people he had ever met who had asked him whether or not his tongue was black and if he'd had a lot of slaves amongst his friends.

'Are you staying in this house?' Maud asked hopefully.

'No, no indeed, I was very kindly asked for supper,' Jonathan said, looking at the ashen face of Neil Mitchell's mother.

'Time for bed, anyway,' Hannah said.

'Can Jonathan come round for breakfast?' suggested Maud.

'I'm not sure that . . .' Hannah began.

'Very nice having met you both – we might meet again but sometime, not tomorrow,' Jonathan said hastily and the children left with reluctance.

Hannah ushered them up the broad, sweeping staircase of Oaklands before any more invitations could be issued; she showed them their bedrooms and said they were to remain there quietly in the morning, since the house didn't wake too early on the day after a party.

'Are your nerves bad? Like our mother's nerves are bad?' Maud asked.

'Of course they're not,' Hannah snapped. Then, she recovered herself. 'Now it's all been very upsetting for you but it will get sorted out. Your uncle will see to that,' she said firmly, attempting to distance herself.

'Which is my room?'

'Whichever one you like.' Hannah pointed to the corridor where Amanda and Neil's old bedrooms still held souvenirs they had never collected for their new lives. There was a bathroom in between.

'Goodnight, now, and sleep well. We'll talk about everything in the morning.' She went downstairs with a heavy sigh. Her shoes were very tight, Neil had brought an African man and left him for everyone else to entertain and Cathy was being insufferable – who ever said it was easy giving a party? Even if you did have a caterer?

'Which room will you have?' Simon asked. They had done a complete tour.

'I'd like the one with all the coats in it,' Maud said.

'But she didn't say . . .'

'She didn't say *not* this one either,' Maud was determined.

'It could be their own bedroom, look, it opens into a bathroom, I don't think you should sleep here, Maud.'

'She said wherever we liked. We could put the coats on chairs.' They stood for a while in Jock and Hannah Mitchell's large bedroom.

'There's a television in this one.' Simon was sorry he hadn't found it first.

'Yes, but I have to move all these old coats and scarves and things.' Maud felt that made things equal. They pushed the coats on to chairs and, mainly, on to the floor.

'Look, she has all this make-up that mother used to have on her dressing-table before her nerves got bad.' Maud picked up some lipsticks.

'What are the black things?'

'They're for eyebrows.'

Simon drew heavy dark eyebrows and then a moustache. The sudden ringing out of bells and celebratory shrieks startled him and the pencil broke, so he used another one. Maud put on a dark red lipstick and then used a pinker shade to make little spots on her cheeks. She picked up a cut-glass atomiser and began to spray.

'Hey, that got in my eye,' Simon said, picking up what looked like a large can of hair lacquer in retaliation. It turned out to be some kind of mousse. It went all over the dressing-table. 'What on earth is that?' he wondered.

'It could be shaving cream,' Maud thought.

'That must be it. Imagine her wanting that.'

There were long earrings which Maud tried on, but they were for pierced ears, so she went to the bathroom and found some elastoplast. She admired herself. Simon had found a short fur jacket and put it on with a man's hat. They were bouncing happily on the two large beds with white counterpanes when two women came in.

They gasped when they saw the clothes on the floor; and one of them screamed when she saw Simon wearing her recently remod-elled mink jacket. Her screams frightened Maud and Simon, who screamed back and Hannah and Jock came running up the stairs – followed by a small crowd – to find out what had happened.

Neil was in the kitchen.

'What in the name of God's that caterwauling upstairs,' he asked.

'Stay out of it, if you investigate, you'll only become part of it,' Cathy grinned.

'But listen to them!'

'Keep well out of it,' she warned.

'We'll give Jonathan a lift back when the time comes, okay?' Neil said.

'The time won't come for me until everyone else is gone. You should take him home yourself and let me come back under my own steam in the van.'

More voices were raised upstairs.

'I'd really better go and see what's happening,' Neil said, and he was gone.

Jonathan brought some ashtrays into the kitchen and wiped them.

'Terrible smokers, the older generation,' Cathy smiled at him.

'I'd like to slip away now, do you think I could get a taxi?'

'Not on New Year's Eve, but Neil's going to drive you home anyway.'

'I don't want to put him out any more.'

'It won't put him out at all, but he won't be able to go for a while. Do you want to use that bike out in the back?'

'Do you think I could?' His eyes were full of relief.

'Certainly. It's an old one. It used to belong to Neil. Go now, Jonathan, while the third world war is being fought upstairs.'

'I suppose I could make things worse and ask if I could have a bed for the night,' he said with a grin.

'Now, that's something I'd like to see,' Cathy said.

'Who are the children anyway?'

'A long story, cousins, children of Neil's very hopeless uncle and aunt. It's their first night here.'

'It could very well be their last.'

Tom walked on up from the canal, and over and through the Georgian streets and down a lane he had never been down before. And that's where he saw it. A wrought-iron gate leading into a cobbled courtyard, and what looked like an old coach house that had been converted for some business. He pushed open the iron gate and went up to the door where there seemed to be some kind of notice. It was a piece of cardboard where someone had written For Sale. There was a phone number to contact for details. Bells were ringing all over Dublin, it was midnight, a new year had arrived. Tom peered through the windows. He had found their premises.

Mrs Ryan told Cathy that she was a little the worse for wear. Cathy said the solution was three glasses of water and three small slices of very thin bread and butter, never known to fail. Mrs Ryan ate the bread and drank the water dutifully and pronounced herself fine. Cathy filled the champagne glasses for midnight, and as the bells rang over the city they all toasted each other and sang Auld Lang Syne. Hannah Mitchell looked almost pleased with it all. Cathy decided to let her have her moment, and moved quickly and quietly away from the circle of entwined hands.

She cleared and washed and dried in the kitchen, she packed crates and neatly arranged several little dishes of goodies for Hannah to discover the next day, in the refrigerator. She moved in and out between the kitchen and the van; the bulk of the work was done. Now all she had to worry about was serving more wine, and more coffee. She could scoop the coffee cups away later. She felt tired in every one of her bones. She heard the telephone ring, thank God. Neil's sister had finally called them. Then she heard Hannah say in tones of disbelief, 'Cathy. You want to talk to Cathy?' She moved to the hall. Her mother-in-law stood there holding the receiver as if it might be transmitting a disease.

'It's for you,' she said, astounded.

Please let it not be bad news from home, Cathy prayed; may it not be her mother or father taken ill having chicken in a basket at the pub. Or some terrible phone call from Chicago where all her sisters and brothers had gone to live so long ago.

'Cathy,' said Tom, 'I've found it.'

'Found what?' she asked, not sure whether to be overcome with relief that it wasn't bad news, or with rage that he had phoned her here.

'The premises,' he said. 'I've found the place where Scarlet Feather is going to live.'

Chapter One

JANUARY

The year began in different ways in different houses.

Tom Feather woke in Stoneyfield flats with a pain in his shoulders and a stiff neck . . . The armchair had not been at all comfortable. He got some cold orange juice from the fridge, and fixed a flower to the glass with some sticky tape. He marched straight into the bedroom.

'Happy New Year to the most beautiful, saintly and forgiving woman in the world,' he said.

Marcella woke and rubbed her eyes. 'I'm not saintly and forgiving, I'm furious with you,' she began.

'But you haven't denied that you are beautiful, and I have totally forgiven *you*,' he said happily.

'What do you mean? There was nothing to forgive *me* for.' She was very indignant indeed.

'Quite right, which is why we will say no more about it. I should thank you instead, because last night I found the premises.'

'You what?'

'I know it's all due to you: if you hadn't behaved so badly and forced me to leave that party, I'd never have found the place. I'll take you to see it as soon as you're dressed so drink up that beautiful elegant drink I've prepared for you and—'

'If you think for one moment that I'm going to leap out of bed and—'

'You're so right. I do not think that for one moment. Instead I think *I'm* going to leap *into* bed. What a truly great idea.' And he had his crumpled clothes off as he spoke.

In Neil and Cathy's house at Waterview the phone rang. 'It's your mother, saying all the guests are dead from salmonella,' Cathy said.

'More likely to be some shrink saying that you've been committed to a mental home for advanced paranoia,' Neil said, reaching over to ruffle her hair.

'I suppose we *could* leave it?' she said doubtfully.

'When do we ever?' Neil replied, reaching down under the bed where the phone was nestling. 'Anyway it's probably Tom.'

It wasn't Tom, it was about Jonathan. Neil was half out of bed.

'Tell them I'm on my way,' he was saying.

Cathy put on the coffee as he dressed.

'No time,' he was protesting.

'Listen, I've put it in a flask. Take it with you, you can drink it in the car,' she said.

He came back, took the flask and kissed her. 'I'm very sorry, hon. I *did* want to go and see this place with you this morning, you know I did.'

'I know, this is more important. Go.'

'And don't sign anything or accept anything until we've had someone take a look at it.'

'No, Mr Lawyer, you know I won't!'

'Now of course I *do* have the address in case this thing ends early. I could come straight there.'

'It won't end early, Neil, it will take all day. Go and save him before it's too late.'

Cathy watched him from the window. As he put the flask down on the frosty ground in order to open the car door, he must have known she would be watching. He waved up at her. Jonathan was lucky that he had Neil Mitchell in his corner. Neil would worry at the case like a dog with a bone, just as he would get a colleague to examine the title deeds of this place, which looked like the perfect premises at last.

JT and Maura Feather woke up in Fatima, a small red-brick house in a quiet road. They used to be workers' cottages, but the Feathers had noted with disapproval that a lot of trendy younger people were buying. Attracting burglars to the area.

'I never thought we'd live to see another year, JT. The Lord must

31

have spared us for some purpose,' Maura said. She was a tall, thin woman with a long, sad face permanently set in the lines of a sorrowing Madonna bent low by the wickedness of the world.

Her husband was big and broad-shouldered, made strong by years of hard physical work in the building trade. His weather-beaten face had looked the same always.

'It's not that we're really all that old in terms of years, but I know what you mean,' JT agreed with her. He turned on the tea-making machine between their beds. It had been a gift from Tom. Maura had thought it was more trouble than it was worth, what with remembering to wash the pot and get fresh milk, but it was handy enough not to have to go down to the cold kitchen.

'Another year begun and not a sign of either of them wanting to do a hand's turn in the business,' he sighed heavily.

'Or settling down in marriage as God intended,' Maura sniffed.

'Ah, marriage is a different thing,' JT said. 'Anyone can marry or not marry, but no two other boys from this area have a ready-made business to walk into, and you have Joe making girls' dresses over in London and Tom making cakes and pastries. It would drive you to an early grave.'

Maura hated it when he got grey with worry. 'Haven't I told you to stop getting your blood pressure all het up over him,' she warned. 'He's like all young people, just looking out for himself. Just wait until he has a couple of children, then he'll be round to the door pretty fast wondering can he work in the business.'

'You may be right,' JT nodded, but in his heart he didn't think that he was ever going to see either of his boys ask him to put the words Feather and Son over his builder's yard.

Muttie Scarlet woke with a start. Something good had happened last night, and he couldn't remember what it was. Then it came back. He had drawn a horse in the pub sweepstake. That was all. Most people would be pleased about this. But to Muttie, who was a serious betting man, there was no skill or science in that kind of thing.

You just bought a ticket for a raffle and then twenty-one people got a horse, you couldn't even choose your own animal. He had something called Lucky Daughter. No form, nothing known about it, total outsider, probably had three legs. Lizzie didn't understand it at all. She had been pleased for him, said he'd have all the thrill of the race without having to put a week's wages on a horse.

Poor Lizzie. It was awful trying to explain anything at all about horses to her. And she was very sure that nothing *she* earned ever ended up at the bookmaker's. But to be fair, she *did* put the food on the table and didn't ask him for much from his dole money. Muttie hadn't known a week's wages for a long time. He had a bad back. But still and all, it wasn't too bad to get out of bed and bring Lizzie a mug of tea. She'd be going out to people's houses later to clean, to clear up their New Year's Eves for them. Lizzie was a great support to them all, the children in Chicago and to Cathy. Muttie smiled to himself as he often did over the fast one that their Cathy had done, grabbing Neil the son and heir of Oaklands, Hannah Mitchell's pride and joy. Even if he hadn't liked the boy, Muttie would have been overjoyed at that marriage. Just to see the hard, hate-filled face of Hannah at the wedding was vengeance enough for all that she had put poor Lizzie through up in that house. But Neil himself, as it happened, was a grand fellow. You couldn't meet a nicer lad in a month of Sundays. It was odd the way things turned out, Muttie told himself as he went to make the tea.

Hannah and Jock Mitchell woke at Oaklands.

'Well,' said Hannah menacingly. 'Well, Jock, it's tomorrow now. You said you'd decide "tomorrow".'

'God that was a good party.' Jock groaned. 'I feel it not exactly in my bones, more in the front left-side of my head.'

'I'm not surprised,' Hannah was terse. 'But there's no time to talk about your hangover. We are talking about those children. They are not staying another night in this house.'

'Don't be hasty,' he pleaded.

'I'm not being hasty. I was very patient when you and Neil said they had to stay last night. I was a saint out of heaven, not breaking every bone in their bodies when I saw the wreckage they had achieved in here. That jacket of Eileen's will never clean, you know, never. God knows what they managed to smear into it . . .'

'Best thing if it doesn't. Makes her look like a vole,' Jock whimpered.

'You've done enough for Kenneth over the years . . .'

'That's not the point.'

'It is the point.'

'No, it's not, Hannah. Where else can they go? They're my brother's children. He seems to have abandoned them.' He winced with pain.

'It's too much,' Hannah protested. 'And they were very rude, both of them, no apology, saying I'd said they could have any room and they had chosen this one. Enough to crucify anyone at what was meant to be a party, a celebration.'

'You didn't over-indulge yourself?' He had a faint hope that she might also have a hangover, which might tolerate the thought of a Bloody Mary at breakfast.

'Someone had to keep an eye on things,' she sniffed.

'Well, didn't Cathy do that very well. I heard a lot of praise for—'

'What do men know of what needs to be done?'

'She left the place like a new pin.' He tried to defend his daughter-in-law.

'Well, at least some of the training I gave her poor mother must have paid off eventually.'

Hannah would say nothing good about Cathy. Jock gave up. Some things weren't worth fighting over, especially with this hammering in his head.

'True,' he said, feeling he had somehow let that hard-working girl down. But Cathy of all people would know how it was easier to take the line of least resistance with Hannah.

'And then running off at the end because she got some phone call in the middle of the night about premises for this crackpot idea of hers.'

'I know, ridiculous,' said Jock Mitchell, getting up to get a painkiller and feeling like Judas.

Geraldine had been up since seven o'clock. She had been alone in the Glenstar swimming pool: usually she would have had the company of half a dozen other Glenstar residents, who loved the amenity of their swimming pool. But New Year's Eve had taken its toll. Geraldine did her twelve lengths, washed her hair and went through the arrangements again for today's big charity lunch. She had advised a group to have their function on January the first, since it was often a flat day when people were eager to recover in company. And indeed, the response to the invitation list had been overwhelming. She had been wise to leave that photographer's party early last night. There had been nobody that interested her to talk to, a lot of them much younger than she was. She had slipped away quietly before midnight. She had seen Tom Feather and his dizzy girlfriend there but couldn't get to meet them across the room. Cathy and Neil would have been there, but of course Cathy

34

had been catering the Mitchells' party last night; Geraldine hoped that it had gone well and that there had been a chance to make some useful contacts. Cathy hated that woman so much it was really important that the night had been some kind of success for her in terms of business. Geraldine wished they could find premises soon. She had agreed to back them for the loan when the time came, as had Joe Feather, Tom's rather elusive elder brother. All they had to do was find the place. And then brave, gutsy Cathy wouldn't have to nail a smile on her face and work in the kitchen of her mother-in-law's house, something she hated with a passion. One of the advantages of being single was that there were no mothers-in-law to cope with, Geraldine thought as she poured more coffee.

In a different part of the Glenstar apartments, Shona Burke woke up and thought about the year ahead. Many other women of twenty-six would wake today with a comforting body on the other side of the bed. In fact, she was sick of people asking her when she was going to settle down. It was so intrusive. Shona would not ask people why they didn't have a baby, or when they were going to have their facial hair seen to. She never queried why people drove a car that was falling to pieces, or stayed with a spouse so obviously less than satisfactory. How dare they speculate openly and to her face about why she hadn't married?

'It could be because you look too cool, too successful. Fellows wouldn't dare chat you up and go home with you,' a colleague had suggested helpfully.

Last night's party at Ricky's would have provided plenty of people who might have chatted her up and come back to the Glenstar apartments with her; in fact, she had had one very definite offer and two suggestions. But these would not have been people who would have stayed. Not anyone she could trust or rely on. And Shona Burke was not one to trust easily. She would get up soon go out to Dun Laoghaire for a brisk walk with a neighbour's dog, come back and get ready for the charity lunch. Because she was considered the very public face of Haywards, she was often asked to such things. Haywards was *the* store in Dublin. It had survived take-overs, makeovers and the passage of time. And today it would give her the chance to wear the new outfit which she had bought at a discount in Haywards. Ridiculous to have so many nice clothes at twenty-six, and not enough places to wear them.

'Neil, is it all right to talk?'

'Not really, father, we're in the middle of something...'

'So are we, we're in the middle of those two children taking the house apart brick by brick.'

'No, I mean what I'm in is really serious. I can't talk about Maud and Simon now.'

'But what are we going to do?'

'Father, we're going to look after them, it's as simple as that. We'll help you, Cathy and I, but now, if you'll excuse me...'

'But Neil...'

'I have to go.'

Jock Mitchell hung up wearily. The twins had unpacked all the desserts Cathy had left in the fridge and eaten them for breakfast. Simon had been sick. On the carpet.

In a garden flat in Rathgar, James Byrne was up and at his desk. Ever since he had retired six months ago he had continued the routine and habits of working life. Breakfast of a boiled egg, tea and toast, ten minutes' minimal tidying his three-room apartment, and then a second cup of tea and twenty minutes at his desk. It had been such a useful thing to do when he worked in the big accountancy firm. Cleared his head, sorted his priorities before he got into the office. Now of course there *were* no priorities. He didn't have to decide whether or not to oppose some tax scheme on the grounds that it was evasion. Other, younger people made those decisions. There was less and less to do, but he could always find something. He might renew a magazine subscription, or send for a catalogue. To his surprise the telephone rang. Very few people telephoned James Byrne at any time, and he certainly hadn't expected a call at ten o'clock in the morning on New Year's Day. It was a girl.

'Mr Byrne? Is it too early to talk?'

'No, no. How can I help you?'

The voice was young and very excited. 'It's about the premises, Mr Byrne, we're so interested, more than you'd believe. Is there any chance we could see them today?'

'Premises?' James Byrne was confused. 'What premises?'

He listened as she explained. It was the Maguires' old place, the printing works they hadn't even entered since the accident. He knew that they had been listless and depressed. They had been unwilling to listen to any advice. But now, apparently, they had disappeared, leaving a For Sale sign on their gate and James Byrne's phone number. In years of business James had learned that he must never transmit any of his own anxiety or confusion to a client.

'Let me see if I can find them, Miss Scarlet,' James said. 'I'll call you back within the hour.'

Cathy put the phone down carefully and looked around her in Tom's apartment, where the little group had been following every word of the conversation. Tom leaning forward, like her father always did to a radio when he wanted to hear who was winning a race. Marcella in an old pink shirt of Tom's and black jeans, her dark eyes and clouds of black hair making her look more and more like the top model she yearned to be. Geraldine, crisp and elegant, dressed for her smart lunch but still giving time to be present for the great phone call and what it might deliver.

'He's not an estate agent, he's an accountant, he knows the people who own it and he'll ring us back in an hour,' she said, eyes shining. They could hardly take it in.

It felt like three hours, but Geraldine told them it was only thirty-six minutes. Then the call came. This time Tom took it. James Byrne, ex-accountant, had been in touch with his friends in England. They reported they really did intend to sell. They had made their decision over Christmas, and had gone away to England yesterday now that it had been made. James Byrne had been asked to set it all in train. And as quickly as possible. Cathy looked at Tom in disbelief. It really was going to happen, *exactly* the kind of place they wanted. And they were the first potential buyers, they were in there with a chance. Tom was thinking the same thing.

'We are very lucky that you made this enquiry for us, Mr Byrne, and now if you would like us to let you know—'

The voice interrupted him. 'Of course you will understand that my first loyalty lies with the Maguires who own the premises. They will have to be represented by a lawyer, an auctioneer, and I will have to try and get them the best price possible.'

'Yes, of course,' Tom sounded deflated.

'But I am very grateful to you, Mr Feather, for bringing this to my notice, otherwise it might have been some days . . .'

Geraldine was scribbling something on the back of an envelope and showing it to him.

'Is there any chance you could show us inside the place, do you think?' Tom asked.

There was a pause. 'Certainly,' the man said. 'That would be no problem. In fact, the Maguires were anxious to know what kind of people had discovered the notice so quickly; they only put it up yesterday before they went to the airport.'

'Yesterday?' Tom was astounded. 'But it looks as if the place has been abandoned for a long time.'

'It has; the family had a lot of trouble.'

'I'm sorry. Are you a friend of theirs?'

'In a way. I did some work for them once. They trusted me.'

It was a sober sort of thing to say. Tom hoped that they could get back to the bit about letting them in. Then Mr Byrne cleared his throat.

'Suppose we meet there in an hour?' he suggested.

The city was still partially asleep, but James Byrne was wide awake. Small and rather precise-looking, wearing a navy overcoat and gloves, with a silk scarf tied around his neck, he was a man in his sixties who might have been cast in a film as a worried bank manager or concerned statesman. He introduced himself formally and shook hands with everyone as if they were in an office instead of standing in the bitter cold on the first day of the year outside a falling-down printing business. At first Cathy was pleased to see him take down the ludicrous cardboard notice while tut-tutting at the amateur nature of it all, but then he explained again that the place would of course have to be sold professionally, maybe even at auction. It could still be snatched from them. They sensed somehow that he wasn't going to tell them anything about the Maguires and what sorrows or confusion there had been in their lives. This was not the time to enquire.

They walked through in wonder. The place that could be Scarlet Feather's new home. First home.

All this middle section could be the main kitchen; this would be the freezer section, that would be the staff lavatory and washroom, and they would have storage here. And a small room where they could greet clients. It was almost too perfect: everything was what they had hoped. And it was so desperately shabby and run-down; perhaps others might not realise the potential. Cathy was aware that she had clasped her hands and closed her eyes only when she heard James Byrne clear his throat. He seemed to be concerned that she might be too happy about it all, too confident. She knew she must reassure him.

'It's all right, James, I do know it's not ours. This is only the first step of a very long journey,' she smiled at him warmly.

They had been talking to this man for forty-five minutes, calling him *Mr* Byrne all the while. He was a stranger, twice their age and she had called him James. She felt a slight flush creep up her neck. She knew exactly why she had done this; subconsciously it was part of her wish never to feel inferior, never to crawl and beg. But perhaps she had gone too far this time. Cathy looked hard at him, willing him not to take offence. James Byrne smiled back at her.

'It might not be too long a journey, Cathy. The Maguires are very anxious to get all this over; they want a quick sale. It might move much more quickly than you all think.'

Cathy did not go home. She didn't want to sit alone in the house while her mind was racing – and there were very few other places she wanted to be either. Tom and Marcella would need time to be on their own together. She couldn't go to St Jarlath's Crescent and hear a detailed description of their night at the pub when she ached to tell them the excitement in her life. There was no way she would go near Oaklands. In that big house at this very moment, there would be a terrible war raging. Those strange children, with their solemn faces and total disregard for anyone else's property or feelings might well have wrecked the place by now. She knew very well that sooner or later she and Neil would have to take some part in their care; but for now it would seem the wisest thing to stay away from Oaklands.

Hannah Mitchell would be on the phone to her friends, laughing and groaning or complaining to her husband that their daughter had not telephoned from Canada. She would not yet have discovered the neatly covered plates in her fridge with perfectly labelled chicken, vegetables and desserts. Cathy knew she would never be thanked for these. That wasn't part of any deal. The best she could hope for was that Hannah Mitchell would leave her alone.

No, that wasn't true. The very best thing would be if her mother-in-law fell down a manhole. Cathy was restless, she needed to walk, clear her head. She found that she was driving south, out of the city towards Dun Laoghaire and the sea. She parked the car and walked on the long pier, hugging herself against the wind. Many Dubliners with hangovers seemed to have had some similar notion, and were busy working up a lunchtime thirst for themselves. Cathy smiled to herself; she must be the soberest and most abstemious person here, one half-glass of champagne at midnight and nothing else. Even her mother who claimed that she didn't drink at all would have had three hot whiskeys to see the New Year in. It was probably wiser not to speculate on how many pints her father might have had. But there was nobody else walking this pier on this, the first day of the New Year who was nearly as excited as Cathy Scarlet. She was going to have her own business. She would be self-employed. Joint owner of something that was going to be a huge success. For the very first time since the whole thing had started she realised now that it was not just a dream.

They would paint the logo on the van, they would turn up in this funny mews every morning, the premises would have their name over the door. Nothing violent or loud that would be at odds with the area. Perhaps even in wrought iron? Already she and Tom had agreed that they would paint the two doors the deepest of scarlet red. But this was not the time for hunting down fancy door handles and knockers. No money could be spent on a detailed image at this stage. They had gone over so many times how much they could afford. They would not lose their business before it had even begun. One of those men at the Mitchells' party last night owned a big stationery firm; perhaps Cathy could go to him about a quote for printing brochures and business cards. They needn't accept it or anything, but it would remind the man and his rather socially conscious wife of their existence.

There were a million things to do; how could they wait now until they heard from these strange people who had apparently locked up a failed business and without making any arrangements about fixtures and fittings disappeared overnight? If it had not been for the calmer manner of James Byrne, Cathy would have feared that they were dealing with mad people who might never agree to the sale being closed. But there was something reassuring about this man. Something that made you feel safe, and yet who kept well at a distance at the same time. Neither she nor Tom had even dared to ask him where he lived or what company he had been with. They had his phone number from the strange cardboard notice, but Cathy knew that neither she nor Tom would telephone to hurry him up. They would wait until they heard his news. And in his perfectly courteous but slightly flat voice he had told them he was very sure that it would be sooner rather than later. Cathy wondered whether he had gone back to his house where his wife had prepared a lunch for him. Or would he take his family out to a hotel?

Perhaps he had no family, and was a bachelor catering for himself. He had looked slightly too well cared-for: polished shoes, well-ironed shirt collar. It might take for ever to know such information about him. But after James Byrne had introduced them to the strange, elusive Maguires, then they would probably never see him again. She must take his address sometime, so that when Scarlet Feather was up and running she could tell him that he had been in there at the very start of it . . . It *would* be a success, Cathy knew this. They hadn't spent two whole years planning it for it to end up as one of those foolish statistics about companies that failed.

And Cathy Scarlet, businesswoman, would be able to take her mother shopping and to lunch in a smart restaurant. And soon the consuming wish to kill Hannah Mitchell would pass, and she would be able to regard her as just another ordinary and even pathetic member of the human race. Tom Feather badly wanted it to succeed for all of his reasons, and she wanted it even more badly for all of hers. Which were very complicated reasons, Cathy admitted. Some of them very hard to explain to the bank, to Geraldine and even at times to Neil. There was a general feeling that life would be much safer if Cathy Scarlet was to bring her considerable talents to work for someone else. The someone else taking the risks, paying the bills, facing any possible losses. Usually but not always Cathy was able to summon up the passion, the enthusiasm and the sheer conviction that she was totally sane and practical. Cathy at top speed was hard to resist.

Sometimes during a wakeful night she had doubted herself. Once or twice when she looked at the opposition she wondered could she and Tom ever break into the market. At the end of long hours working in one of Dublin's restaurants, she was sometimes tempted to think how good it would be to go home and take a long bath rather than spend a couple of hours with Tom trying to work out what the food would have cost to buy, and how they might have cooked it better, presented it more artistically and served it more speedily.

But last night when she had seen the premises, and today when she had realised that they might possibly be within their grasp, she had no doubts at all. Cathy smiled to herself with all the confidence in the world.

'Well there's *someone* who had a nice New Year's Eve, anyway,' said a voice. It was Shona Burke, the very handsome young woman who was the head of Human Resources or whatever they called it at

Haywards. Always very calm and assured, she was a friend of Marcella and Tom's and had been very helpful in trying to seek out contacts for them. She was being tugged by an excited red setter, who wanted to go and find other dogs or bark at the sea – anything except have another dull conversation with a human being.

'What on earth makes you think that?' Cathy laughed.

'Compared to everyone else I've met, you're radiant. They are all giving up drink for ever, or they've been abandoned by their true loves or can't remember where they're meant to be going for lunch.'

'They haven't begun to know hardship . . . They weren't catering a party for Hannah Mitchell.' Cathy rolled her eyes. Shona would know the dreaded Hannah, always the stalwart of fashion news and Valued Customer evenings at Haywards.

'And you're still alive and smiling.'

'I wasn't smiling over the party, believe me. You don't sell any untraceable poisons in that store of yours, I suppose? Where were *you* last night, anyway?'

'I was at Ricky's party. I met Marcella and Tom . . . Well . . . Tom just for a bit.'

Cathy paused. She would like to have told Shona their news, but they had all agreed nobody would know until there really *was* something to know. Geraldine and Marcella had agreed to be silent, so Cathy must say nothing. Nor did she ask why Tom had only been there for a bit.

'What was the food like?' Cathy asked instead.

'Not you too. Tom practically had a forceps and swab out examining it.'

'Sorry. I know we're very boring.'

'Not a bit, and the truth is the food was very dull. Not only did I ask them for a brochure which I'll send you, I also asked Ricky how much he paid them and you'll be stunned . . .'

'Stunned good or stunned bad?'

'Good, I imagine – I know what you two could do for that price. Sorry, this animal's going to have me in the harbour in a minute.'

'He's never yours, how do you keep something that size in Glenstar apartments?'

'No, I just borrowed him to get me out for a walk before lunch.'

Cathy realised that she knew nothing at all of Shona Burke's private life. Maybe everyone worked too hard these days to *have* a private life. Or more likely, maybe they worked too hard to have any time to speculate about anyone else's.

'I swear I'm keeping my eyes open for a place for you. You will find one when you least expect it, believe me.'

Cathy felt shabby thanking her. But a promise was a promise. She looked into the faces that passed her by. Some people might never be their clients in a million years, but others might well need Scarlet Feather some time in their lives. There would be birthdays, graduations, weddings, anniversaries, reunions – even funerals. People no longer thought that caterers were the preserve of only the rich and famous. They had given up the nonsensical superwoman image of pretending that they had cooked everything themselves while holding down a job, looking after their children and running a home. In fact, nowadays you were considered intelligent to be able to find someone else to take part of a compartment of your life. Some of these people taking a morning walk and watching the waves might well be sending for the brochure that she and Tom would soon get ready. The brisk couple with their two spaniels might well be booking a retirement party or a thirtieth wedding anniversary. The well-dressed woman who looked so fit might need to organise a ladies' lunch for fellow golfers. That couple holding hands might want a drinks party to announce their engagement. Even the man with the red eyes and white face, who was vainly hoping that fresh air might work miracles on whatever damage he had done to himself last night, might be a senior executive who was looking for a firm to run his corporate hospitality.

The possibilities were endless. Cathy hugged herself with pleasure. Her father used always to say that it was a great life just as long as you didn't weaken. Not that her father had ever shown much get up and go except to Sandy Keane's, or Hennessy's the bookmaker's. Poor Da: he would fall down if he knew how much she and Tom Feather were prepared to pay for these premises. And her mother would go white. Mam would be apologetic to the end of her life that somehow the maid's daughter had snared the great Hannah Mitchell's only son. It had been a terrible crime – ten thousand times greater than taking a half-hour off for a mug of tea, a smoke and a look at a quiz show on television. There was no changing her. In the beginning, Cathy had tried to force the two women to meet socially but it had been so painful, and Cathy's knuckles would clench every time her mother leaped up from the table to clear away the dishes at Oaklands any time they were invited there, that she had given up the attempt. Neil had been relaxed and indifferent about it.

'Listen, nobody sane could get on with *my* mother. Stop forcing *your* unfortunate mother to do things she hates. Let's just go and see your family on our own, or have them to our house.'

Muttie and Lizzie were as welcome at Cathy and Neil's house as any of the young lawyers, politicians, journalists and civil rights activists who moved in and out. And Neil dropped in occasionally to see his parents-in-law. He would find something that interested them to tell them about. Once he had brought a young man that his own mother would have called a tinker but Neil called a traveller, to see the Scarlets. Neil had just successfully defended the boy for horse-stealing and asked him to come and have a pint to celebrate. Shyly the boy had said that travellers were often not welcome in pubs, and when no persuasion had worked Neil had said that he must come and meet his father-in-law: they would bring half a dozen beers and talk horses. Muttie Scarlet had never forgotten it, he must have told Cathy a thousand times that he was happy to have been of service to Neil in the matter of entertaining his prisoners. Cathy's father always called them prisoners, not clients.

Gradually her mother began to relax when Neil came to visit. If she started to fuss, throw out his cooling tea or sew a button on his coat, or, as she did on one terrible occasion, offer to clean his shoes, he just got out of it gently without the kind of confrontation that Cathy would have started. Neil found the whole scene seemingly normal. He never saw anything odd in the fact that he was having boiled bacon in an artisan's cottage in St Jarlath's Crescent with his in-laws, who were the maid and her ne'er-do-well husband. Neil was interested in everything, which is what made him so easy to talk to. He didn't show any of the fiercely defensive attitude that Cathy wore like armour. To him it was no big deal. Which, as Cathy told herself a hundred times, it was not. It was only her mother-in-law who made it all seem grotesque and absurd. Cathy put the woman out of her mind. She would go back to Waterview and wait until Neil came home.

Their house at number seven Waterview was described as a town house. A stupid word that just added several thousand pounds to the small two-bedroom house and tiny garden. There were thirty of them built for people like Neil and Cathy, young couples with two jobs and no children as yet. They could walk or cycle to work in the city. It was ideal for Neil and Cathy and twenty-nine similar couples. And when the time came to sell there would be plenty of others to take their places. It was a good investment according to Neil's father, Jock Mitchell, who knew all about investments.

Hannah Mitchell had delivered herself of no view about Waterview, apart from heavy sighs. She had particularly disapproved of their having no dining room. Cathy had immediately decided that the room should be a study, since they would eat in the kitchen from choice. The study had three walls lined with bookshelves and one window looking out over the promised water view. They had two tables covered with green felt, and they worked on them in the late hours together. One would go and get coffee, then later the other would decide it was time to open a bottle of wine. It was one of the great strengths they had, the ability to work side by side companionably. They had friends who often sparred and complained that one or the other was working to the exclusion of their having a good time. But Cathy and Neil had never felt like that. From the very first time they had got to know each other out in Greece, when he had ceased to be that stuck-up boy at Oaklands whose mother had given everyone such a hard time ... When Cathy had stopped being nice Mrs Scarlet's brat of a daughter, they had had very few misunderstandings. Neil had understood that Cathy wanted to run her own business right from the start. Cathy had known that he wanted a certain kind of law practice. There would be no short cuts for Neil Mitchell, no ever-decreasing office hours like his father had managed to negotiate; no pretending that he was somehow doing business by being out on a golf course or in a club in Stephen's Green. They would talk late into the night about the defendant who had never had a chance because the odds were stacked against him, how to prove that he was dyslexic and had never understood the forms that were sent to him. Or they would go through the budgets yet again for Scarlet Feather, and Neil would get out his calculator and add, subtract, divide and multiply. Whenever she was downcast he would calm her and assure her that one of his father's partners, a man who lived and breathed money, would advise them every step of the way.

Cathy let herself into number seven Waterview and sat down in the kitchen. This was the only room where they could really see the pictures on the walls. There was no room for paintings in the study because of all the books, files and documents. The hall and stairs were too narrow, you couldn't really see anything they hung there,

45

and the two bedrooms upstairs were lined with fitted wardrobes and dressing tables. So there was no room there.

Cathy sat at her kitchen table and looked up at their art collection. Everything there had been painted by someone they knew. The Greek sunrise by the old man in the taverna where they had stayed. The prison cell by the woman on a murder charge that Neil had got acquitted. The picture of Clew Bay in Mayo by the American tourist they had met and befriended when his wallet had been stolen. The wonderful still life by the old lady in the hospice who had an exhibition three weeks before she died. Every one of them had a history, a meaning and a significance. It didn't matter to Neil and Cathy whether they were great art or rubbish.

A telephone in a quiet house can sound like an alarm bell. Somehow, from its very tone, Cathy knew this wasn't going to be an easy phone call.

'Is Neil there?' her mother-in-law snapped.

'I'm afraid he's out with Jonathan. There was an attempt to hustle him out of the country this morning.'

'When will he be coming back?' Hannah's voice was a rasp.

'Well, when he's finished, he won't know when.'

'I'll call his mobile . . .'

'He turns it off at meetings like this, he couldn't . . .'

'Where *is* he, Cathy, he has to come here at once.'

'Has there been an accident. . . ?'

'There has indeed been an accident, and most of the kitchen ceiling has come down,' Hannah cried. 'They left bath taps running and the weight of the water . . . I need Neil to get those children out of here to wherever they're going to be sent. We haven't had a moment's peace – and as for you, Cathy, those children have eaten entirely unsuitable rich desserts and have been sick. I need to talk to Neil. Now.' Her voice was by now dangerously high and shaky.

'I can't contact him for you, I really can't. But I know what he'd say.'

'If you're going to tell me to calm down . . .'

'He'd say we'll take them here. So that's what we'll do.' Cathy sighed.

'Can you, Cathy?' The relief in Hannah's voice was clear. 'They've been allowed to run wild – they need professionals to look after them, to try to bring them back to normal. And I don't want Neil to say I put them on to you . . .'

'It won't be like that.'

'No. But get him to ring me the moment you can.'

Cathy smiled. She had now what her mother called her-meat-and-her-manners: she had offered and been refused – even if she had only offered because she could see it coming anyway. She dialled Neil's mobile phone to leave the message.

'Sorry to disturb you with trivia, but the twins have apparently brought down the ceiling in Oaklands. Ring your mother soonest. Hope it's all going well for Jonathan.'

Then she went to the spare room and made up two beds. The twins would be there before nightfall.

Tom rang to say he wanted to borrow the van and would that be all right.

'I want to go up into the mountains, I think. It's just I can't think or talk about anything else and I'm afraid I'll drive Marcella demented. Do you want to come? Is Neil bearing up?'

'He's still out fighting the good fight. I'd better not come with you, though, we have another horror-story brewing. Remember the twins from hell who turned up at Oaklands last night?'

'Have they burned the place down yet?'

'They might have by now. But they're probably packing their things and getting ready to come to Waterview as we speak.'

'Cathy, they *can't*!' Tom was aghast. 'You don't have room, apart from anything else.'

'Don't I know it, but as my father would say, even money we see them here tonight.'

'So what are you doing?'

'Nailing things down, mainly. Removing anything breakable. You know, the usual.'

'I'll just sneak into the courtyard and take the van away,' Tom said.

'Don't even look up at a window, they could fire something at you,' she said with a laugh.

'Just one word of warning, Cathy and then I'll shut up about it all. Don't let Neil take them on and then go off saving the world and leaving them to you.'

She sighed. 'And will you take one word of warning from me. Drive carefully, we haven't half-finished paying for that van and when you get excited you take your eyes off the road and your hands off the wheel.'

'When the business is successful, we'll get a tank,' he promised.

Cathy made yet another cup of tea and thought about Tom. They had met on her first day at catering college; with his shock of thick, light brown hair he had an artlessly graceful way of moving. His enthusiasm and the light in his eyes had been the keynote of their years on the course. There was nothing Tom Feather would not attempt, suggest, carry out.

There had been the time he had 'borrowed' a car from one of the lecturers because it had been left in the college yard for the weekend and Tom thought it could take six of them to Galway and back. Sadly, they'd met the lecturer in Galway and it could have been very difficult.

'We brought your car in case you wanted to drive home,' Tom had said, with such brio that the lecturer had half-believed him and almost apologised for the wasted journey since he had a return ticket and a girlfriend with him.

There had been the picnics and barbecues where Tom insisted they must be true to their calling and insisted on marinating kebabs when others would have been content with burned sausages. Cathy could almost smell those nights full of food and herbs and wine on the beaches around Dublin, and the winter evenings in the ramshackle flat that Tom shared with three other guys.

Cathy had envied him the freedom. She had to go back to St Jarlath's Crescent every night and, even though Muttie and Lizzie had allowed her a fair amount of freedom, it still wasn't the same as having your own place.

'You could come and live here,' Tom had told her more than once.

'I'd only end up doing their ironing and lifting their smelly socks off the floor.'

'That's probably true,' Tom had agreed with reluctance.

He had never been short of girlfriends but took none of them seriously. He had a way of looking at people that seemed to suggest no one else in the world existed. He was interested in the most trivial things people told him and he was afraid of no one. He was kind to his rather difficult parents but it never meant that he missed any of the fun. When they all wanted to go to a black tie event in one of the big Dublin hotels, none of them could afford to hire dress suits; but Tom had a friend who worked in a dry-cleaners. It had been dangerous and dramatic and at least four jobs were on the line, but as Tom said cheerfully, nobody lost and everybody won.

They had been talking about Scarlet Feather from the earliest days. No other form of catering had interested either of them; while their friends wanted to do hotel work, work on cruise liners, be celebrity restaurant chefs, write books and be on television, Tom and Cathy had this dream of serving top-grade food in people's homes. As Ireland became progressively more affluent, they felt sure this was the right way to go.

They worked together in restaurants to get the feel for the kind of food people liked. Cathy was amused at how casually Tom took the compliments and the come-on glances directed his way. Even the stern Brenda Brennan in Quentin's was sometimes heard to say she wished she were twenty years younger.

Had Cathy fancied him herself in those days? Well, yes, of course, in a sort of way. It would have been impossible not to. And it might well have come to something. She smiled at the recollection.

They had planned to go to Paris on a very cheap flight. They had listed the restaurants they would visit: some to admire from the window, one to tour the kitchens because a fellow student had got a job there; and two where they might actually eat dinner.

They had never been to Paris before. They discussed it, heads close together over maps, night after night. Once they got there, they would walk here, take the Metro there; this museum would be open, that one closed – but it was mainly the food they were going to investigate.

They hadn't exactly said that this was the trip when they might become lovers. But it was in the air. Cathy had her legs waxed and bought a very expensive lacy slip. They had been all set to leave on a Friday afternoon and then that morning three things happened.

Lizzie Scarlet fell off a ladder in Oaklands while hanging Hannah Mitchell's curtains and was taken to hospital by ambulance.

Tom was offered a weekend's work at Quentin's because Patrick's sous chef had let them down.

Cathy was called to interview for a job cooking in a Greek villa for the summer.

They told themselves and each other that Paris would always be there.

Cathy went to the Greek island to cook and met Neil Mitchell, a guest in the villa who kept putting off his return home to be with her.

And Tom met Marcella Malone.

And even though Paris was always there, it remained unvisited by Cathy Scarlet and Tom Feather.

She sometimes wondered about that weekend and what would have happened. But if they had been lovers, even for a short time, it would have been hard to forget once they were serious business partners in a thriving enterprise. And this way they brought no history with them. Nothing that could make either Neil or Marcella in any way uneasy.

Cathy heard a key turn in the door.

'Where are the twins?' she called.

'They're in the car,' Neil answered sheepishly. 'You knew they were coming? Mother said you did, but I didn't really believe her, to be honest.' His face was alight now, as if he had expected a protest. 'And you don't mind?'

'I didn't say that. But you had to bring them. How was Jonathan?'

'It looks as though it's going to be okay.'

'Well done.'

'It was a group effort, teamwork,' he said, as he always did. 'I'll get the twins – you're a hero.'

'For a few days I'll be one – they're not too easy to handle, are they? Did it get sorted out at Oaklands?'

'No way, a big shouting match with Mother before they left, right down to the "someone has to look after us" line, which is only too bloody true, poor things.'

'Wheel them in.'

She watched them coming up the steps, muttering to each other that it was a much smaller house, asking each other if Neil and Cathy had children, wondering was there a television in the bedroom. Cathy forced herself to remember that they were nine and frightened. They had been abandoned by their father, mother and brother, their aunt had thrown them out.

'This is the Last Chance Saloon,' she said pleasantly as they came in. 'You have one small bedroom between you with no television. We have a very stern policy on bathrooms here, leaving them clean but not overflowing for the next person, and there's an endless amount of please and thank you going on but apart from that you'll have a great time.'

They looked at her doubtfully.

'The food is terrific, for one thing,' she added.

'That's for sure,' said Neil.

'Did you marry her because she was a good cook?' Simon asked.

'Or did it just turn out that she was a good cook?' wondered Maud.

'And my name is Cathy Scarlet. I am married to your cousin Neil so from now on I won't be referred to as "she" or "her", is that very clear?'

'Why don't you have Neil's name if you're married to him?' Maud wanted everything cleared up.

'Because I am a woman of fiercely independent nature, and I need my own name for my work,' Cathy explained. This seemed to satisfy them.

'Right, could we see the room?' Simon said.

'I beg your pardon?' Cathy was icy.

He repeated it; she still looked at him questioningly.

He got it. 'I mean, please can we see the room. Thank you.' He looked pale and tired; they both did. It had been a long day: there had been nothing but dramas and recriminations. Their parents had disappeared, their future was uncertain, the boy had been sick all over the carpet in Oaklands, they had destroyed the kitchen ceiling and they would never be allowed back there again.

'Come on, then, I'll show you,' she said.

'How did you get on today,' Neil asked eventually when the children were asleep and they had time to talk to each other. She was by now almost too tired to tell him about it.

'It was exactly what we want – perfect place, perfect location, room to park the van . . . But we have to wait. Patience is what's needed apparently.'

The days crawled by after that. They waited and waited. And then finally, 'James Byrne here, Ms Scarlet.'

'Mr Byrne?' They were being formal; she was too nervous to call him James.

'I said I would try to come back to you within four days, and I'm very pleased to say that I have.' He sounded well pleased with himself.

'Thank you so much, but—'

'Mr Feather's answering machine was on, and you did say that it was fine to call either of you.'

'Please, is there any news?' Cathy wanted to scream at him for his slow, precise way of talking.

'Yes, I have been authorised to act for the Maguire family.'

'So?'

'So, they are going to accept your offer, subject to—'

'They're not going to go to auction ... They might have got more at an auction.'

'They and I have discussed this, and with the estate agents too, but they would prefer an immediate sale.'

'Mr Byrne, what do we do now?'

'You'll tell Mr Feather, I imagine, Ms Scarlet, and then you both get your lawyer and your bank, and then we go to contract.'

'Mr Byrne?' Cathy interrupted.

'Yes Ms Scarlet?'

'I love you, Mr Byrne,' Cathy said without pausing. 'I love you more than you will ever know.'

And everything began to move very quickly after that. Too quickly. Cathy looked back on the first three days of the year as if they had been in slow motion. Now she realised that there were not enough minutes in any hour to cope with all that had to be done. And she usually needed to be in three places at the same time. When she was sitting with Geraldine and the bank manager, she should have been meeting Tom and his father at the builder's yard. When she was making the four apple strudels for Mrs Ryan, the nervous woman she had met at Oaklands, she should have been having a medical at the insurance company, and when she should have been at the solicitor's going over every clause of the contract of sale, she was making spaghetti bolognese for Maud and Simon Mitchell, who were proving to be a nightmare.

At this of all times she appeared to have taken charge of a boy and a girl that she had never met before. Cathy, who knew all her uncles and aunts and cousins in great depth, barely had time to wonder why Kenneth and Kay weren't part of the extended family scene.

'He's got no visible means of support,' Neil said. 'He says he's in business, but no one quite knows what it is.'

'You mean like *my* father going to work, as he calls visiting the bookies, and meeting his associates, as he calls the others who hang out there?'

'No, nothing as straightforward as that, and I think she likes the vodka a little too much when he goes abroad. So that's the problem: no one quite knows where he is at present, and she's been taken away to hospital for not knowing where she is herself.'

He was unfeeling about the situation, not judgemental but not involved. Perhaps that's how you got to be a good lawyer.

It couldn't have happened at a worse time. *Why* had she agreed to take those monstrous children into Waterview for three nights because of some vague marital disharmony in their home? There was marital disharmony in every home in the Western world at the beginning of January. And suppose their father had gone walkabout and their mother retreated back into a psychiatric home then why couldn't their big brother Walter look after them? Why bother asking that question? Walter wouldn't have known where to find their cornflakes in the morning, that was supposing he was ever home by breakfast. And Hannah had made it quite clear that her brother-in-law's children were finding no substitute home at Oaklands.

They were pale, solemn-looking children, who asked disconcerting questions . . .

'Do you have a drinking problem, Cathy?' Simon asked when they first came into the house.

'Only problem is getting enough time to drink these days,' Cathy said cheerfully. Then she remembered the danger of being ironic with children.

'Why exactly did you wonder that?' she asked, interested.

'You seem kind of anxious,' Simon explained.

'And there's a big bottle of brandy on the kitchen table,' Maud added.

'Oh! I see . . . No, that's actually calvados, it's for putting in Mrs Ryan's apple strudels and then glazing across the top, that's not for drinking. It's too dear. And anxious because I'm buying a business. I don't think it's all drink-related. But what do I know?'

'Why are you buying a business?' asked Simon. 'Doesn't Neil give you enough money?'

'Why don't you stay at home and have children instead?' Maud wondered.

Cathy paused and looked at them. With their pale, straight hair and pasty little faces they lacked their elder brother's charm, but they also lacked his selfishness. They did genuinely seem interested in her predicament, and she must answer them truthfully.

'Neil would give me half he has very willingly, therefore I'd like to have something of my own to share with him. So that's why I want a business,' she said.

They nodded. This seemed reasonable.

'And Neil and I may well have children sometime, but not just now because I'll have to be out so much and working such long hours. Maybe in a few years . . .'

'Wouldn't you be too old to have children then?' Maud didn't want any loopholes in the plan.

'I don't think so,' Cathy said. 'I did check, they say I'd be all right.'

'Suppose they came earlier, by accident. Would you give them away?' Simon frowned at the thought.

'Or worse.' Maud wasn't a fool about such things.

'We arranged that they won't arrive until we're ready for them.' Cathy had the bright strained smile of a woman who has a hundred things to do that are more important than this conversation.

'So you'd only mate about once a month, is that it?' Maud suggested.

'That's about it,' Cathy said.

Tom was sympathetic about the twins, but the day they were going to see the lawyers he became suddenly anxious.

'I wonder can we leave them anywhere else today, Cathy. I know you take them most places, but honestly . . .'

'Where, Tom, where? They're barred from Oaklands, Walter won't mind them. What can I do with them?'

'Could Neil. . . ?'

'No, he couldn't. Could Marcella. . .?'

'No, she couldn't.'

'Jesus, Tom, I can't leave two defenceless children in a house on their own all day.'

'Are you suggesting that they come and negotiate some of the finer points of the contract with the solicitor?'

'Tom, stop picking on me. You're nervous, I'm nervous, it's too much money, it's too much risk. Let's take it easy.'

'I'm not nervous, and you're not nervous about it at all. The only thing that's causing any grief is those two time bombs you've installed in the van.'

'Where else can I take them?'

'Take them to your mother and father's.'

'And have my dad take their pocket money to put on something with three legs?'

'Tell them about your dad, warn them. Cathy, we *can't* take them to the lawyer. He's some posh friend of Neil's, believe me, they would not expect or appreciate those two with their sticky fingers all over the corporate furniture.'

'All *right*.' Cathy gave in. 'But remember, Tom, today is *your* tantrum for getting nervous; tomorrow or the day after is mine.'

'It's a deal,' said Tom.

'How are you, Simon?' Muttie gave a manly handshake.

'What's your name?' Simon was suspicious.

'Muttie.'

'Right how 'ya, Muttie,' Simon said.

'Or even Mr Scarlet, possibly,' Tom suggested.

'Muttie's fine,' said Cathy's father.

Simon looked triumphant.

'And this is Maud. You're very welcome, child.'

'All right, what are we going to do today?' Maud asked ungraciously.

Cathy thought to intervene but left it. It wouldn't be for long.

'I thought we'd take a little walk the three of us,' Muttie began. 'You see, I have one or two things to do, and maybe I could persuade you ...'

'No, Da,' Cathy cried. 'And kids, remember what I told you, hey?'

'I know he's an addict,' Simon said.

Cathy closed her eyes.

'A what?' Muttie asked.

Simon was clear on his instructions. 'You can't help it, it's like being a drug addict. You think if someone has a pound you need it to put on a horse, and Cathy says we have to buy magazines or sweets as quick as we can if you suggest it.'

'Thanks, Cathy,' her father said.

'You know I didn't put it quite like that, Da.'

'Exactly like that, Muttie,' grinned Tom, who had always called him Mr Scarlet before but wasn't going to be outdone by young Simon.

'But on the other hand, if you think of anything lucky for *me* today, the day we sign the contract, then can you put this on his nose?' He handed Cathy's father a ten-pound note.

'You're a gentleman, Tom Feather, I always said it.' Muttie shook his hand warmly.

As they left for the lawyer's office Cathy heard Simon asking her father casually, 'Do you have an addiction to drink too, Muttie? My mother has, she can't help it, you see.'

Cathy leaped into the white van. 'I want to be out of here before we hear him inviting the twins down to a good pub on the docks to start the outing with a pint.'

'On balance, that would be better than having them in the solicitor's office.' Tom had reversed the van and they were speeding along to their appointment.

'Better for whom?' Cathy wondered.

It went so smoothly at the lawyer's that Tom and Cathy were worried. There should have been some hold-up, something unacceptable.

'The other side are being remarkably accommodating; they have given specific instructions for a quick sale, and so of course we need to do a very intensive search in case there's something to conceal.'

'Of course,' Cathy and Tom agreed through gritted teeth. Why couldn't barristers or solicitors ever believe that people might just be telling the truth, that these Maguires were so anxious for their money, and to forget their old life, that they wanted to sell? But they knew it had to be done by the book no matter how slow and laborious. There was one message each on their mobile phones when they got back to the van. Cathy was to ring her aunt Geraldine. Urgently. Tom was to ring his father. They stood at either end of the van, talking. They finished and came back to sit down, both in good humour.

'Well, you first, *was* it a crisis?' he asked.

'Absolutely not. It was great news, she knows a restaurant selling up a rake of kitchen equipment, cookers as good as new, an enormous chest freezer. We can go over there after we've visited *your* Dad and look at them today.'

Tom said nothing.

'And you?' Cathy asked.

His father had agreed to do the building job but it involved putting someone else on hold. If Tom went round to sort that out and kept the name of Feather looking good, then it was a deal.

'He's around at the premises already, with two lads. There's an authorisation in from the Maguires; they want their equipment moved out and sold, so Da and the others are clearing the place. You can go there, can you?'

'Sure.' Cathy hoped they wouldn't mind talking to a girl about it.

'He thinks talking to me about building is *worse* than talking to a girl,' Tom said ruefully.

'But he needs you to do something more important?'

'Yes; talk nice to some architect and persuade him that my father and the team aren't a pack of cowboys.'

'What will you say?' Cathy was interested.

'I'll tell them the truth. It's amazing how often that works; tell them that the young Feather has a chance to do well. Might even pick up a bit of business for us – you never know.' He had such an engaging grin, Cathy knew it would work out.

JT Feather was a man very anxious that things should be done right. That no short cuts be taken, that the authorities never be offended in any way.

Cathy parked the van and noted with pleasure the way the place was being cleared out. The men had been working hard.

'You know it's very irregular, doing all this before the contract is signed.'

'You have their fax, Mr Feather. They want it this way.'

'But all my life I've worked on the principle that you don't touch a place until it is legally yours.' He frowned a lot.

'We're getting equipment this week; we have to have somewhere to plug it in.'

'Ah, not this week, Cathy, be reasonable. The floors have to be done, the walls hacked out and made good, there has to be a full paint job . . . There are a hundred details that have to be sorted out.'

'We'll talk about the details later. Tom told you, Mr Feather, we have to be up and running at the end of the month.'

'That boy was always a dreamer, will you look at the notions he had about this and that. You're never taking his timetable seriously, a sensible girl like you?'

'Oh, believe me, it's my timetable too, and we have a reception planned for the last Friday in January.'

'There's no rush, girl, the job must be properly done.'

'No, there isn't *time* to have it properly done. Three more catering firms will have opened and taken the business unless we get in there quick.'

'But the regulations, Cathy . . .' He was pale with anxiety.

Was this better or worse than her own reckless father, who

would have put the deeds of the house on the next race if her mother hadn't kept them well hidden?

'I won't delay you, Mr Feather, I have to take some measurements for equipment that I'm going to buy today.'

'Today?' She could hear him gasp but she took no notice. Instead, she took out her metal measuring tape and moved past him into the room, which was looking emptier by the minute as the bulky machinery was being moved out into trailers. Cathy knelt down to see how much room there was for the freezer. Geraldine had said it was enormous but hadn't been specific. She was busy writing the measurements into her notebook when she saw Tom's father coming in, opening the top button of his shirt so that he could breathe more easily.

'Tell me they're not coming today.'

'Oh, not at all. I'm only going to *see* them today. The auction is tomorrow, they'll come at the end of the week. I'll have the details about where we'll need sockets before the day is over. Can you have the electrician here as early as he can make it tomorrow morning, do you think?'

'The world has changed totally,' said Tom's father.

'Tell me about it, Mr Feather,' said Cathy, and was gone.

Tom called. 'I daren't ask, but how are things going?'

'Not too bad. And your end?'

'I bought the time, told them we were wonderful and that we'd send them a brochure. Just give me the address again of that place with the freezers and cookers and I'll meet you there.'

Her friend June rang to know would they go to a wine bar.

'I may never go to a wine bar again for the rest of my life,' Cathy said, crawling out from behind a particularly complicated measuring job.

'Great load of fun *you're* going to be when you're a businesswoman,' June said sourly, and hung up.

Neil rang. 'How did it go with the lawmen?'

She told him there seemed to be no hitches or problems.

'There are always hitches and problems with the law. That's what most of them get paid for,' he countered.

'Well not so far.' She was anxious to believe that it might, for once in life, be plain sailing.

'Well, you're with the best people,' he said.

'What time will you be home?' she asked.

'Lord, I don't know. Why?'

'No reason. It's just with the kids . . .'

'Oh, God, I'd forgotten about them. Where are they now?'

'In St Jarlath's,' she said.

'You never left them with your parents!' He seemed astonished.

'I had to leave them *somewhere*, Neil. I couldn't take them with me to the solicitor's, could I? Or here, which is like a builder's yard full of rubble, and on to inspect appliances at an auction which is where *I'm* going now.'

'But Cathy . . .' he began.

'But what?'

'Nothing . . . nothing. See you later.'

There were very few people looking at the kitchen equipment. It was almost exactly what they wanted.

'Isn't it kind of sad?' Cathy said in a whisper.

'I know,' Tom agreed. 'I was just thinking that. Someone else's dreams gone up in smoke.'

'It won't happen to us.' She sounded braver than she felt.

And all day their mobile phones kept ringing. Something else the lawyers needed, some further problem JT Feather had unearthed, Marcella wondering would they all go to an early film, James Byrne looking for another detail. At none of the places they visited was there ever any proper parking. Nobody they called was ever at a desk or could be located. At four o'clock they were very hungry but there was no time to stop, so Tom got them two bars of chocolate and a banana each. Somehow they got through the day, and Cathy realised guiltily as she drove to St Jarlath's Crescent that she had left those children there for far too long, and that she hadn't bought anything for them to eat that night. They would pick up a takeaway on the way home. Fine way for a caterer to behave, she thought.

It was still an odd feeling to drive up this small street of two-up, two-down houses, where she had been born and brought up. Her father had always told her proudly how he had moved their belongings in using a handcart, and now Cathy would drive in casually in her white van or her husband's Volvo. Like looking at your past from a great distance, where everything had changed and yet in other ways nothing had changed at all. A place where her mother still strove to please the unpleasant Hannah Mitchell, even though she had long since ceased to work for her. Where her mother even at this stage would be in some kind of awe of these terrible poor children because their name was Mitchell. Oh, please may nothing awful have happened. May her mother not have cleaned their shoes, or her father cleaned them out of their pocket money.

The twins were alone in the kitchen, staring at the oven. The table and all their own clothes seemed to be covered with flour. They had made pastry, they said, because that was all there was to do here, and Muttie's wife had helped them make a steak and kidney pie which they were going to take home with them because the shoemaker's children were never shed.

'Shod,' corrected Cathy.

'Shed, shod, yeah, whatever,' Simon said.

'Did you enjoy it?' Cathy asked.

She had loved standing at that very table, helping her mother to cook.

'Not much,' Simon said arrogantly.

'He thinks it's not men's work,' Maud explained.

'It's just I didn't expect to be doing this. We don't do this at home,' Simon complained.

'It's always good to learn things,' Cathy said, wanting to slap him. Her kind mother had taught them to make a pie, and all he could do was complain. 'What did you learn today?'

'I learned you need sharp knives to cut up the meat. Have you got any sharp knives for your waitressing business?'

'Catering business, actually. Yes, I do have sharp knives, thank you Simon.'

'Muttie's wife has a great way to put salt and pepper in the flour,' Maud began. 'You shake it all up in a paper bag together, did you know that?' she asked Cathy.

'Yes, Mam taught me that too,' Cathy said.

'I never knew that before,' Simon said, as if it were somehow a suspect way of doing things.

'You never made pastry before until Muttie's wife showed us,' Maud said scathingly.

'Oh, for Christ's sake call her Lizzie,' cried Cathy, at the end of her tether.

'We didn't know her name, you see,' Maud explained, startled.

'She told us she used to work for Aunt Hannah as a sort of servant or cleaner or something,' Simon said. 'And we told her that we hated Aunt Hannah and that she hated us.'

'I'm sure your aunt Hannah doesn't hate you, you must have got that wrong,' Cathy murmured.

'No, I think she does, otherwise why would we be at Muttie and Lizzie's place making steak and kidney pie, instead of Oaklands?' Simon spoke as if the whole thing were totally obvious.

'Anyway,' Maud added, 'we told her that this is better in a lot of ways than Oaklands and we said that we could come again tomorrow.'

Cathy looked at them in disbelief. What amazingly self-possessed, confident children. They were sure of their welcome anywhere, free to criticise and comment. That's what being a Mitchell did for you. They watched her face as if trying to read her expression. She must remind herself that they were only nine, that their father had left home and their mother had been taken into a psychiatric hospital. Their brother was hopeless. This wasn't the best of times.

'We did say it to them,' Maud said.

'Say what?' Cathy asked.

'That we were going to keep coming here until things got back to normal at The Beeches,' Simon explained.

'And what did they say?'

'Muttie said that he didn't have any problem with it, and his wife Lizzie said that it would all depend on Aunt Hannah.'

'Where are they now?' Cathy asked fearfully. Was there any possibility that these two demented children had driven her unfortunate parents so mad they had left home?

'Muttie said he was slipping out to the shoemaker . . .' Maud began.

'Bookmaker,' Simon corrected.

'Well, some kind of maker anyway, and his wife Lizzie is upstairs on the phone because her daughter telephoned her from Chicago.'

Cathy sat down in the kitchen. It could be a lot worse, she supposed.

'You must not interrupt us, we have to watch as it goes golden brown,' Simon said.

'Who is the bookmaker, and why was he never shod?' Maud wanted to know.

'Is he coming to dinner with us? Is that why we made the pie?' Simon wondered.

Cathy felt very, very tired, but she remembered asking her aunt Geraldine things years ago, and the really satisfying thing was that Geraldine had always tried to answer her.

'It's a sort of saying, really. What Mam meant was that in a shoemaker's house the man is making so many pairs of shoes for other people that he never has time to make any for his own children, and they go barefoot.'

'Why don't they get shoes in the shops?' Maud asked.

'But is he coming to dinner or is he not?' Simon insisted on knowing.

'Not tonight,' Cathy said wearily. 'Sometimes the shoemaker will come to dinner, I hope, but not tonight.'

Neil's court case was all over the papers; the fight had been won for the moment. Prominent civil rights leaders had come to court, there was talk of a big protest march, a stay had been given for three months, which was longer than they had hoped. Cathy had time only for a quick glance at the evening paper as she settled the children in the kitchen with instructions on how to set the table, and grabbed a shower. Neil had left a note saying he had gone out for wine and ice cream. She was just pulling on a clean T-shirt and jeans when he came into the bedroom.

'Those two told me they had made a pie – are they serious?'

'I think my mother made it, actually. Well done, I saw in the paper you're a hero. Was he delighted?'

'He was more stunned than anything else I think, but the great thing is we've mobilised a lot of support. It won't be so easy for them the next time, they can't bundle him out overnight any more.' Neil's face was animated and excited. He would have talked for ever. Cathy hung her head slightly. Her own day seemed suddenly very trivial in comparison.

He stroked her cheek. 'You look lovely, you know. What a pity we don't have time to . . .'

'I don't think we'll have time for that sort of thing in the foreseeable future. By the way, Maud told my mother that we mate once a month.'

'God, did she? What an extraordinary thing to say.'

'That's one of the mildest things they've said. Let's not even think about it, let's go and eat dinner and drink a great deal of wine and celebrate your win.'

Simon had the table set. 'Are we sure the shoemaker isn't coming?' he asked, slightly worried.

'The shoemaker?' Neil paused in drawing the cork from the bottle.

'Don't ask, please don't ask,' said Cathy.

'Were the cookers suitable?' Geraldine wanted to know next morning.

'Perfect, we're going to take two plus a fridge, a freezer, a deep-fat fryer and a lot of saucepans.'

'Great stuff, was Tom delighted?'

'Thrilled, we put reserve prices on things, they'll ring tonight. I can't go today as I have to be with the electricians. Feather and Company finally found an electrician who gets out of bed before midday, so I'm meeting him there in a few minutes. Tom's out with other suppliers.'

'Have you time for lunch? You could come to the hotel, they have some foreign chefs doing a buffet, you could steal a few ideas.'

'I'd love it, Geraldine, but I haven't a minute, we have to meet the insurance broker again, fill in a planning application, change of nature of premises, and there's a good January sale on. I thought I might have a quick hunt for curtain material before we meet James Byrne again up at the premises.'

'You're killing yourself.'

'Early days, busy days.' Cathy sounded cheerful.

'And why are these awful children not going back to their own people?' Geraldine was disapproving.

'There *are* no own people, their father has been sighted in Leeds, and this has sent their mother back to the funny farm.'

'And what in God's name do my sister and her capable, energetic husband do with the twins from hell all day?'

'You know Mam, she'll get neighbours to keep them entertained when she's out working, and she's teaching them to cook.'

'That sounds sensible, they'll need someone to cook if they're to go back to that house,' said Geraldine.

'I *know*, Geraldine, but what can we do?' Cathy wailed.

'And what does Neil say? They're *his* responsibility.'

'He says we can't let them go into a home.'

'So they're in your mother's home instead.'

'And ours at night,' Cathy said with spirit.

'I bet that's a barrel of laughs,' Geraldine said.

63

'Neil finds it very hard to work while they're there. Don't worry, Geraldine; it's not going to last for ever.'

'Mr Feather not with you?' James Byrne asked when Cathy arrived to meet him, as agreed, on site in the late afternoon. The noise of drilling was loud in their ears.

'I wonder, could you call him Tom?' Cathy knew that she sounded tired, and hoped that the bright smile somehow compensated for it.

'Certainly, if you wish,' the voice was polite.

'It's just that we have so much on our minds that when you say Mr Feather, I immediately think you're talking about his father, who's inside worrying his guts out in case the Maguires will fly back from England in a helicopter and settle on his head with all kinds of restraining orders.'

'I have put his mind at rest about that.'

'How on earth did you do that?'

'I let him talk to the Maguires in person on the phone.'

This was more than Cathy and Tom had been able to do. But she knew better than to cross-question this strange, reserved man.

'Good,' she said briskly. 'That explains all the activity in the background. Now, would you like to see what we've done so far?'

'And Tom Feather?'

'Will not be here today. We have to divide the work up as we can't both be everywhere. Is it all right if it's just me?'

She looked tired and wan. Unexpectedly he leaned over and patted her hand. 'It's just fine, Cathy,' he said.

'Mam, I really owe you for this,' Cathy said, falling into a chair at the kitchen table in St Jarlath's Crescent.

'Not at all, they kept your father out of the betting shop.' Lizzie poured them mugs of tea.

'You mean he took them out for the day?'

'To the zoo, no less. They'd never been there, could you credit it?'

'And Da took them there with his own money?'

'There was a bit of a good flutter yesterday, apparently.'

'And do they have any more manners today?'

'Not really. But Cathy, you wouldn't need to go commenting on that in front of the Mitchells.'

'Where are they?'

'Drawing away, there's not a word out of them.'

Muttie had given them paper to draw their favourite animal at the zoo. Simon had ten drawings of snakes with their names printed underneath them. Maud had done six owls.

'Muttie says he sees no reason why we couldn't have an owl at home,' she greeted Cathy.

'He doesn't? Maybe he could explain it to your mother and father when they get back to The Beeches.'

'They might never be back,' Simon said cheerfully. 'But Muttie says that there might be more of a problem with snakes.'

'There might be, all right. But excuse me, what do you mean, exactly, they might never be back?'

'Well, there's no word of our father, and our mother's nerves are pretty bad this time, I think.'

'I see.'

Cathy went back to her mother in the kitchen. 'What am I going to do, Mam?'

'I'll tell you one thing, a couple of days here and that is fine, but long-term you're not doing yourself any favours taking those children in. Can't you see it's showing her up as well . . . as well as everything else?'

'What do you mean, Mam? "As well as everything else?"'

'Well, you know I've said it a thousand times already to you, all this setting up a business. People like that, Cathy, you know they expect you to be grateful and glad you married so well. You should be staying at home and making Neil a good wife.'

'Oh, Mam, for God's sake.'

'No, listen to me for once, Cathy, I'm not as bright as you or as educated. I can't talk back to people like you do, but I do know them. I've cleaned their floors, yes, but I listen to them talking and they're not like us, we're not like them.'

'We are better than them, far, far better.' Cathy's eyes blazed.

'Now don't start . . .'

'It's you that started, Mam. Tell me what's good about an old cow like Hannah Mitchell, pointing to the legs of chairs with her umbrella and making you go down on your hands and knees, throwing tea bags into a sink you had just cleaned, using good clean towels you had just washed and folded to mop up floors. Tell me what's good about her, one thing good about a woman who won't even take two unfortunate brats who are part of her husband's family.'

65

'Shush, Cathy, keep your voice down.'

'No I will *not* keep my voice down, I hate that woman for the way she turned her back on them and I despise her husband, they're his flesh and blood after all. I know they're monsters and they're both as daft as brushes but they're not the worst, and it's not *their* fault that everyone has abandoned them and nobody wants them.' She broke off because of the frozen look on her mother's face. It was indeed as she suspected. Simon and Maud stood behind her open-mouthed in the doorway, having heard every single word.

'Hi, Lizzie. It's Geraldine.'

'Sorry, Ger, she's just left.'

'Who?'

'Cathy. Didn't you want to talk to her?'

'No, I wanted to talk to you. How was she, by the way?'

'Terrible, she lost her temper with me and started giving out about the Mitchells in front of those two harmless children. They heard it all.'

'What did she say?'

'She said that she'd explain it all to them in the van going home. God alone knows what she'll explain, she'll make it worse you can be sure.'

'You're not taking them again tomorrow?'

'Of course I am, where else can they go?'

'And what will they do in your house, if I can ask?'

'They're going to bring their washing in a big bag and I'm going to show them how to use the washing machine and hang their clothes on the line . . .'

'You're not?'

'And then I'm working most of the rest of the day up in the flats, and they can have a swim in the pool. The place is empty in the day. I don't suppose you would—'

'No, I wouldn't do whatever you were supposing. I rang you about Marian.'

'Marian?'

'Listen Lizzie, have you gone soft in the head? You have a daughter called Marian, in Chicago, and she's coming to stay with you soon. She wants to know can she sleep with her boyfriend.'

'She wants to what?'

'You heard.'

'Why does she want my permission if she's going to? They all do what they like nowadays over there, anyway.'

'Not in Chicago, in Dublin when she comes to stay in your house.'

'She's ringing you from Chicago to ask *you* this?'

'She said I was to ask you tactfully if she and Harry could share a room in your house when they come over, so I'm doing that. Asking you tactfully.'

'I don't know, Ger, it's one thing turning a blind eye, it's another when it's in your own home. I don't know what Muttie would think . . .' She was riddled with doubt.

'Muttie will mainly be thinking of what to back at Wincanton,' Geraldine said.

'It's very blatant, isn't it?'

'Will I tell her yes, that of course they can have the room?'

'I don't know.'

'And that you don't know whether you're going to do it up in pale green, or a sort of beige pink?'

'What?'

'What colour? I think green myself, and I'll tell Marian to bring you a nice set of dark green towels to go with it. Americans love bringing towels as a gift, but they need to know the colour.'

'But Ger, who'd paint it? You *know* Muttie has a bad back.'

'Oh, yes, I know that, you'd paint it and I would, and if we still have that child labour force hanging around the place they could hold things and carry things for us, before we send them up and down the chimneys.'

'Ger, you're ridiculous.' But Lizzie was laughing. The battle was won.

The white van stopped for an ice cream. Cathy bought three cones and they settled down companionably to eat them in the van. 'I always think an ice cream is just as good in the winter,' she began.

'Why do you hate our father and mother?' Simon asked.

Cathy shrugged. 'I don't hate them at all, I've hardly met them. In fact, they didn't even come to our wedding.'

'So what were you shouting at Lizzie about?'

'You heard what I was shouting about. I hate your aunt Hannah. I don't hate your mum and dad, believe me.'

'Why do you hate Aunt Hannah?'

'You hate her too, you've often said so,' Cathy said defensively. coming down to their level.

'But you're not meant to hate her, and anyway, you're married to Neil.'

'That's the problem, she doesn't like my being married to Neil, she thinks that my family and I have no class. That annoys me, you see.'

'Do you want to have class?' Maud wanted to know.

'No, no way. I don't give three blind damns what she thinks about *me*, I've plenty of class. But she looked down on my mother, and I can't forgive her for that.'

'Do you want us not to tell?' Simon's eyes narrowed at the wonderful opportunities and power that lay ahead.

'Tell what?' Cathy asked, wide-eyed.

'All this about what you said, and about our father roaring round and our mother getting drunk to help her nerves.'

'But that's the way it is, isn't it?' Cathy looked from one to the other, bewildered.

'Yes.' Simon was on less firm a footing now. 'But do you want us not to tell about your hating Aunt Hannah?'

'Tell anyone if you want to, I don't tell her *you* hate her, it's just a matter of being polite, really. But it's not a secret, is it?'

Simon saw his vantage point disappear. He gave a last try. 'Suppose we told Neil?' he tried.

'Neil is sick of hearing it, Simon, but if you'd like to tell him again, please do. Now let's go and buy some supper, since you didn't make us a pie today.'

They finished their ice creams and drove off. Cathy allowed herself a small smile.

In the Chinese restaurant the children studied the menu carefully. 'Are you and Neil rich or poor?' Simon asked.

'Tending to be more rich than poor, but if you don't mind my saying so, it's not a question you ask people . . . Just so that you know.'

'But how would you ever find out, then?' Maud was interested.

'Sometimes we have to face it that we can't know everything.'

'I needed to know.'

'You did?'

'In order to know how many dishes we could order,' Simon said, as if it were the most obvious thing in the world.

'Oh, I see. Well, there's four of us.'

'We could have Imperial Menu A for five,' Maud said.

'Let's have it. I'd love Imperial Menu A.'

'Don't you want to check up the price of items first?'

'No, Simon, I don't.'

'You must be very rich indeed, richer than your father.'

'What?' she was exhausted.

'Muttie, your father. Do you hear things in your head, like he does?'

'I didn't know he heard things in his head.'

'Yes, all the time. The sound of hooves, thundering hooves.'

'Oh, like the races, I see.'

'He says they go at the same rhythm as your heart. Did you know that, Cathy?' Maud wanted to share any new things that she had learned.

'I'm not sure I did.'

'*And* Muttie says that the sound makes your blood run faster in your veins and gives you a better life.'

'Oh, it does? we must try that then,' she said as she grabbed the price list and ordered Imperial Menu A for five.

'I don't think it's something you try.' Simon was doubtful.

'You have it or you don't. We both have it, as it turns out,' Maud positively smirked with pride.

'I'm very sorry if you do, very sorry indeed,' Cathy said.

'Why?'

'Because you'll spend the rest of your lives deafened by the hooves, and have no time or money for anything else,' she said grimly.

Back at Waterview the twins set the table, washed their hands and sat down politely, 'Would you like a can of lager?' Simon offered.

'God, no. Thank you all the same, Simon.'

'It's just that Muttie says it relaxes him.'

'I'm totally relaxed as a matter of fact,' Cathy said.

The phone rang, it was Tom. 'All going okay?' he asked.

'I'm hanging in there, Tom.'

'Kids are still with you, I gather?'

'Absolutely.'

'So I won't ask you, did everything else go all right?'

'Amazingly it did, no problems at all. And at your end?'

'Good, tiring but no disasters,' he said.

'I'm sure it was,' she sighed.

'You'll have a day off next week, I'll organise it.'

'I know you will. Glad it all went well. Good luck, Tom.' She hung up and came back to the table.

'Is Tom doing a waitressing job tonight?' Maud asked.

'Catering,' Cathy corrected.

'Yes, is he?'

'Sort of, yes. What's the black bean sauce like?'

'A bit salty but okay. Can we finish this?' Simon was spooning it out of the containers.

'Sure, I've enough, and I've left Neil's in the oven.'

'And the shoemaker isn't coming?'

'No, Simon, he's not.'

'I hope he never comes,' said Simon. 'You always get upset when you talk about him.'

'They go back to school next week,' she told Neil that night in bed.

'Should make it a *bit* easier, I suppose,' Neil said.

'Tell me something, Neil.'

He put down the copy of the law reports he was reading and turned to face her. 'I know the question you are going to ask, and the answer is none.'

'What am I going to ask?' Cathy laughed.

'What plans did I make for the twins today?' he smiled ruefully. 'Honey, it was a desperate day.'

'I know; mine was fairly filled, too,' she said.

'I know, I know, and then I was late home, but Cathy, I can't work while they're here, I just sat in a café. It's terrible to be kept out of your own home because children keep asking question after question.'

'I suppose it's what kids do,' she said.

'I'm going to get them made wards of court,' he said simply. 'I'll start proceedings tomorrow.'

She looked at him, shocked. 'But they'd have to go into care, a home, a foster family, total strangers.'

'We were total strangers a few days ago . . .' he began.

'But they're family,' she said.

'Not yours and mine.' Neil was trying to sound firm and in control. 'I can't *have* this,' he said. 'I met that little shit Walter down at the Four Courts today, and he's as cool as a cucumber about it all. He has to work, he has to see people, he has to go skiing, there's nothing *he* can do.'

'Well, would you trust them to him for two hours?'

'But it's not just my work alone, it's your work too. I'm just not going to *let* this happen to us now. We've put too much in to let it be wrecked by children.'

'I suppose that's happening all over the world.'

'People's own children *might* be different, though I must say this has proved to me once and for all that we are totally right not to want them. Just looking at Maud and Simon makes me realise that very clearly.'

'Our children wouldn't look like Maud and Simon,' she giggled.

'We're not going to find out,' he said grimly. 'And truly, Cathy, I'll get them out of your hair. There has to be *some* money there, we'll mortgage The Beeches, something to borrow against, we could still keep an eye on them.'

'You know we'd have no say in where they're sent. Leave it for a few days until we know more.'

He reached out for her. And she lay awake with her eyes open for a long time afterwards.

Geraldine still got to her office before eight o'clock. In the mornings, she herself handled only the public relations and publicity for the hotel group, but three others looked after the list of clients that she had built up when she opened a private company of her own. She flicked through the list of projects to see was there anything that might be channelled in Scarlet Feather's direction. Haywards the store were doing a fashion show some months down the line, but they wanted to book a hotel, nothing for Cathy there. Quentin's the restaurant were doing a presentation of cookery prizes, but that was obviously in-house. Makers of garden furniture greatly wanted a presentation, possibilities there, but first she would have to examine the location, no point in sending those two into some awful place full of lawnmowers and rakes where nobody would see and appreciate their food.

By the end of the week, a lot of things had changed. The electrical appliances had all been installed, the shelves were painted and Tom and Cathy were waiting for the rest of the equipment. The window frames and door had been painted a vivid red. James Byrne had spoken to them gravely, as if he were interpreting from some aliens on another planet, that the Maguires had professed themselves satisfied with everything. Tom and Cathy's solicitor said it was the nature of the law that things must take their time, but that nothing untoward was showing up in the search on the company title. Marcella was being supportive and begging to be allowed to help. Geraldine was already coming up with names of contacts for future events. Cathy and Neil had decided that there was now no way they could immediately abandon Simon and Maud, but that living permanently in Waterview was proving too much of a strain, and that they did need a bit of space from them. Lizzie and Muttie, on the other hand, seemed perfectly content with them, and found endless jobs for them to do around the house. Next week they would be going back to school. It was a compromise. Neil had told them that an unofficial carer's allowance had been arranged by his father. In fact, it was guilt money put up by Jock and Hannah until the situation sorted itself out. The arrangement was that Muttie and Lizzie would get a fixed amount for minding Simon and Maud in St Jarlath's Crescent after school, and they would sleep alternately in Waterview and St Jarlath's. Two homes instead of one. Maud and Simon said okay, it would suit them.

'Manners, Maudie,' said Cathy's father. There was a way that Muttie could correct the worst excesses of the twins without appearing ever to have taken offence.

'I'll never be able to thank you, Mam,' Cathy said to her mother.

'Don't go on like that, Cathy, doesn't it give Muttie some shape to his days. He's very fond of them.'

'He can't be, they're pig rude at times. Make sure they make their beds and wash up and everything. They left wet towels all over the floor of the bathroom in Waterview. Neil nearly lost his mind.'

'No, no, that's all fine,' her mother reassured her. 'And Neil is giving us so much money, I can give up Mrs Gray.'

'The one who's as bad as Hannah?'

'Oh, poor Mrs Mitchell was a walking saint compared to Mrs Gray,' Lizzie Scarlet said with a laugh.

Neil had been so good about going to St Jarlath's Crescent that Cathy felt she must visit Oaklands in return. Surely there must be other women in the world who had to sit down and think up a reason before calling to visit their mother-in-law? Cathy didn't want to talk about the excitement of the business, the way the premises were leaping ahead because Hannah was so obviously against the whole undertaking. Nor did she want to go into detail about the fact that Jock Mitchell's nephew and niece were currently residing partly in St Jarlath's Crescent with her ex maid and what she always referred to as the unfortunate maid's ne'er-do-well husband. She couldn't say she had done those apple strudels for Hannah's friend, the nervous, edgy Mrs Ryan because she would be accused of having touted successfully for business at the New Year's party. Mrs Mitchell showed no interest in what she and Neil had done with their house in Waterview, which was probably just as well, since she had done so little recently. Still, she owed it to Neil to keep the channels open.

She forced the white van up the drive of Oaklands at four o'clock one afternoon, knowing that Hannah's sniff of disapproval could be directed equally against her daughter-in-law or the vehicle. But Cathy was ready to ignore it and talk pleasantly for as short a visit as she could manage, without it appearing that she had just dropped by to deliver something. She brought her mother-in-law a sturdy-looking fern, one that couldn't die even in the tropical central heating of Oaklands, and knocked at the door.

'Cathy.' Her mother-in-law couldn't have been more astounded if a troupe of tap dancers stood on the step.

'Yes, Mrs Mitchell, I did send you a card saying I hoped to drop by and see you today?'

'Did you? Oh, you may have indeed . . .'

'But if you're with somebody?'

'No . . . no, it's amazing to see you, please come in.'

'I brought you this. It might . . .' Cathy handed over the little fern. The woman must be deranged, imagine saying that it was *amazing* to see your daughter-in-law, who had sent you an advance note about her visit!

'Thank you so much, dear.' Hannah Mitchell didn't even look at the plant, just left it on the hall table. 'Now that you're here, I suppose we should go into the kitchen, we'd feel more at home there,' she said, preceding Cathy down the hall.

Cathy seethed. And wondered if she could feel a tic in her forehead, or was she just imagining it? Mrs Mitchell rarely welcomed anyone into the kitchen. Guests, family, anyone at all who called would be received in the den. Cathy saw the subtlety and grinned at herself in the mirror. Her reflection startled her; she looked drawn and tired, her hair greasy and stuck behind her ears. When she got the show on the road she would really have to smarten herself up, she thought. She would frighten possible clients if she looked like this.

'You look very badly,' Hannah Mitchell said on cue.

'I think it's just one of those twenty-four-hour flu things,' Cathy said, saying the first words that came into her head. She saw Hannah physically draw away, as if fearing to catch some dreadful germ. 'Not contagious, of course,' Cathy said cheerfully. The conversation was painful. Cathy enquired about Amanda in Canada and heard there had been something wrong with the Ontario phone system, and Amanda worked in a really old-fashioned carriage-trade business that didn't have faxes or e-mail. Cathy allowed no muscle on her face to change as she listened. Either Amanda or her mother was spinning a story. Whichever one of them it was, the whole thing was just very sad. Remember that word 'sad', and she would survive.

Lizzie Scarlet, who had scrubbed this floor and the legs of the table for years was sitting at this moment in St Jarlath's Crescent serving a glass of milk and home-made shortbread to Simon and Maud, before helping them do their homework. Later they would play a game on the video, and tonight the children were going to learn ironing as a great treat. There would be speculation about whether this horse might be held back on Saturday to let his stablemate win, and there might be neighbours dropping in. There would be plenty of activity. Cathy knew that her aunt Geraldine was going to a dinner party at an Embassy tonight, and had bought herself another stunning dress at Haywards. Her two married friends, Katy and June, had asked Cathy to a party they were having but she had said no, she wanted a proper dinner alone with Neil in Waterview, and they might even get a chance to mate more than once a month. Maud's definition of her sex life was looking uncannily prophetic. Shona Burke had a date with a man she met last week, a man that she thought would never call her again. Tom was also taking a night off from Scarlet Feather and was taking Marcella out to one of the clubs where she might get noticed. Ricky the photographer friend said there were a lot of big fashion-mag people in town. Mr and Mrs JT Feather were going to an Irish Tenor concert, and the silent James Byrne had mentioned that he was going to the theatre. And on this cold, wet January night Hannah Mitchell, patting her hair and smoothing her fine wool skirt, had no one to meet and nowhere to go. Cathy reminded herself of this as she forced the polite, interested smile to stay on her face.

Somehow a great many more things than they expected got done. They read all the hygiene regulations, put in an application to become regulated. They got the logo painted on their white van. One big, waving red feather. The name and phone number underneath. They went to a printer's to get the business cards, the brochures and the invitations printed.

'I know that address, it's where Maguire's the printer's used to be,' said the old man behind the counter when Tom and Cathy had gone to arrange the lettering.

'Yes, indeed, we've just bought the premises. Did you know them? Were they good printers?'

'Ah, the best at one time, but then everything changed, they didn't, and there was all that other business.'

'What other business?'

The man looked from one to the other and decided against it. 'I don't know, I can't really remember.'

'They're in England now,' Tom said helpfully.

'God be good to them wherever they are,' said the old man.

She was very quiet in the van. 'We'll never know, Cathy. Stop trying to puzzle it out,' Tom said.

'We knew there was something odd, and of course you'd never in a million years get it out of James.'

'It doesn't matter,' Tom said.

'Don't you want to know? Men are very incurious sometimes.'

'Practical, maybe. Let's go out tonight and have a coffee and make a list.'

They had taken to doing their Scarlet Feather work away from home. It wasn't fair on Neil to have his whole study commandeered, nor on Marcella to keep her out of her own sitting room or kitchen. It was not that Neil and Marcella had been in any way critical – neither of them had made a murmur of complaint – it was just that they hadn't any time to help. Neil was involved in committees and consultations almost every night of the week; Marcella had signed on for a fourteen-day course of aquarobics to tone up her already perfect body. They said they'd love to help if only there were time.

And indeed, one evening saw Neil up a ladder painting; and

another evening Marcella helped hem the curtains. And then there was the evening Neil and Marcella had fallen about laughing over the ventilation regulations. Giggling over phrases like 'steam-emitting appliances' and 'mesh size 16 maximum pore size 1.2 millimetres essential to be fly-proof'. Cathy and Tom were familiar with such phrases from catering college, and just shrugged at all the mirth. And their main backers too had been very undemanding.

'If I didn't believe you could both do it, I wouldn't have invested my hard-earned money,' Geraldine said simply.

'How *did* she earn enough to be able to give us a whack like that?' Tom wondered.

'No idea. I used to think once that she was old Mr Murphy's fancy woman, but apparently not. Just invested it well, I think.'

'Up to now, anyway,' Tom had said, touching wood.

Joe Feather had written from London.

'Why does he never stay at home with your parents, they'd love to have him . . .' Cathy asked.

'I don't know,' Tom said. 'Selfish, I think.' There was something in the way he spoke that made Cathy look at him suddenly. The world was full of mystery, Cathy told herself sadly as they began to make the list for their launch party.

'Ricky knows good contacts,' Cathy began.

'I behaved like a horse's arse to Ricky on New Year's Eve,' Tom said sheepishly.

'If you did, and it's unlike you, I don't suppose he'll remember,' Cathy soothed.

'He might.'

'Go on, if I were the one that had said that, you'd tell me I thought the whole world revolved around myself.'

Tom laughed. 'Yes, you're quite right, of course we'll ask Ricky for contacts, and Shona, of course, and a couple of the guys we knew back at college. But mainly I think we should have friends and family, don't you?'

'Of course I do, though it has to be said hardly any of *my* family and friends will put any business our way, not much demand for caterers down on the morning shift in the bookies, with my dad's betting associates, as he's inclined to call them.'

'Nor mine,' Tom said. 'But that's not the point.'

'Can we do a quick deal, the pair of us? If you don't ask your in-laws, I won't ask mine,' Cathy pleaded.

'I don't *have* any in-laws, as you very well know, and you *have* to ask yours, as you also very well know.'

'It's just a wish,' Cathy sighed. 'She'll make it a misery for everyone there if she does come, and she'll sulk for six months if she's not asked.'

'And what does Neil say?'

'What do you think he says? He says it's up to me. As if that was any proper answer at all.'

'So we ask her?'

'I'm afraid so. Does Marcella have any hateful people who might destroy the evening for us?'

'No, not that she's mentioned.'

'Okay, then I'm the only one inviting a big bad wolf,' Cathy said. 'Let's get on with the list. Will we ask any famous people? They just might come.'

'Definitely let's ask famous people.' Tom was eager, and the shadow of Hannah Mitchell hung over them no longer.

'What will we do at the party?' Maud asked.

'I don't think you'll be there,' Cathy said.

'But where else would we be?' Simon asked, as if it were all arranged.

'You see, Simon, it's really for older people.'

'Yes, well, people of all ages I'd say.' Simon had thought about it.

'Sure, but not people who are just nine, actually,' Cathy said, trying to keep her voice steady.

'But where would we go? You're going, Neil's going, Muttie and Lizzie are going, Aunt Hannah and Uncle Jock. There won't be anyone left to look after us.'

'Muttie was saying when he picked us up from school that we'd be going.'

Cathy felt yet another urge to give her father a very hard kick for his helpfulness. But then she remembered that he did walk up to those school gates and wait for the children, which was more than any Mitchell seemed to be prepared to do. She must think, she must not panic.

'Walter, your big brother Walter will look after you.' Cathy felt very pleased that she had pulled this rabbit out of the hat.

'No, he's talking about going skiing,' Maud cried triumphantly.

'We could take the coats. Muttie thought that might be a good job for us,' Simon said.

'Did he now?' Cathy asked. 'And did he also by any chance suggest what I myself should do during the party, or was it only your work he had planned out?'

'No, he didn't say,' Simon answered solemnly. 'I think he thought you would probably *know* what to do, what with it being your own waitressing business and all.'

'Catering business,' Maud corrected primly.

And Cathy heard a sudden hysterical tinge in her own laughter.

The Feathers had wondered to Tom whether they should have replied formally to the invitation.

'Did you keep your temper?' Cathy was working on the choux pastry.

'With extreme difficulty,' Tom admitted. 'And it's so stupid, I could hear the sarcasm in my voice, asking them did they think they wouldn't be let in.'

'They're not used to parties, any more than mine are,' Cathy soothed.

'Well at least yours won't be fingering the walls and telling people that everything really needed another coat, but it was such a rush job that there wasn't time . . .' Tom wouldn't be consoled.

'No, but my mother wanted to wear a yellow nylon coat and wash up in the back kitchen. We've had three scenes about that, and my dad says that he's bringing his own beer because fancy wines give him a headache.' Cathy had finished the tray of little pastry cases and was setting the timer.

'But then you *have* got Geraldine working the room for us, and talking us up to everyone.' Tom was jointing the chickens expertly as he spoke.

'And you've got that sexy brother of yours to keep all the women happy. Let's hope he goes into one of his charm routines, I love to watch him in action, it's amazing the way they lap it up.'

'I was always afraid at the start that Marcella would fall for him when she met him, but mercifully she didn't,' Tom said.

'Marcella? Fall for Joe when she could have you?' Cathy laughed.

'He is very smooth, though.' Tom had a hint of worry.

'Very obvious, you mean, and your Marcella's too bright for that.' Cathy was confused by Marcella in these last days before the great launch. She had been extremely helpful behind the scenes, coming on from her work at Haywards, changing into jeans and taking out her rubber gloves to protect her hands: she did all the menial jobs anyone could give her. But she utterly refused to serve and help at the party. She had what seemed to her very good reasons.

'Listen, Cathy, you should understand about having a dream and a goal. You and Tom have got yours now. I haven't yet. I want to be a model. I know I can do it, I believe I'm as good as anyone else, I've spent a fortune on courses and portfolios. I just *can't* be seen in public as a waitress or that's all I'll ever be, a manicurist and a waitress.'

'You could be worse things.' Cathy had been curt.

'And you could have been a typist or a shop girl, but you wanted more,' Marcella had answered with spirit. She had refused to take the coats. She would be there only as a guest. She would work with them afterwards, clearing up, she promised, but her public face was to be an invited person. There was no moving her so Cathy didn't try. After all, she had yet to explain to Tom that the terrible twins might be part of the night. Partnership was all about give and take.

James Byrne said yes, he would come to the party. Cathy was somewhat surprised, but pleased.

'And of course if there's anyone else that you'd ... um, like to ... um, bring with you,' she said hesitantly.

'Thank you, but I'll come on my own.'

They were finally on first-name terms with each other, not that it seemed to sit easily with the older man. He was so courteous and old-fashioned. And so extremely reticent. The business with the Maguires seemed to be almost concluded now. Yet Cathy and Tom knew as little about the family of printers who had sold them the premises as they had known on New Year's Day. They did, however, know a little more about James.

He lived in what he called the garden flat of one of the big Victorian houses in Rathgar. He had been an accountant in a large provincial town for most of his life, and had only come to Dublin in the last five years. He was now retired. They couldn't ask him what he did all day, and if time was heavy on his hands these days. They didn't dare ask him had he any family. Their conversations, though warm and relaxed, were always professional. One day Tom had asked whether he might know someone who would act as a bookkeeper for them. They told him that they assumed that maybe one morning a week would be enough at this early stage, or possibly they didn't even need that. Perhaps he might have come across someone.

'I'd be very happy to do it,' he said.

'To find someone?' Cathy wasn't sure what he meant.

'No, I mean to act as your bookkeeper, if that would suit you. Two hours a week should be adequate at the start.'

'But Mr Byrne ... I mean James ... we couldn't ask *you* ...' Tom began.

Cathy sensed he was lonely and had nothing else to do. 'But of course, if you would take us on a trial period we would be delighted,' she had said firmly. And an unaccustomed smile came across James Byrne's face, making him look handsome. Still grave, despite the smile, but definitely very handsome.

'I've got your mother a dress, *and* I've booked a hairdo for her,' Geraldine said.

'You'll be bankrupt,' Cathy protested.

'Not on the kind of place your mother insists on going to have her hair done in, that's when she does go at all.'

'But the dress?'

'It came from Oxfam.' Geraldine looked at her with clear, lying blue eyes.

'It didn't. It came from Haywards.'

'And what makes you think that?'

'Shona Burke told me she met you getting it.'

'Busybody,' Geraldine said, laughing.

'If my mother knew she was wearing a dress from Haywards she'd have to be in the next bed to my one in the nervous hospital, as Maud keeps calling it. Oh, Geraldine, *what* am I going to do with those children?'

'There must be someone in St Jarlath's Crescent, some neighbour.'

'Of course there are a dozen people, but Ma has reservations about all of them, and I don't want her like a hen on a hot griddle all night wondering are they all right.'

'All right, all right, give them to me,' Geraldine said. 'I'll get them into the child-sitting service at Peter's hotel.'

'What does that mean?'

'In their case, chicken nuggets and chips, suitable video and a swim in a heated pool if they want one.'

'Would you really?'

'Of course I would, and remember that I do have to protect my investment tomorrow night, don't I?'

'It's nothing to do with an investment, it's a lifeline that you've given us and always have,' Cathy said.

But Geraldine would hear none of it. 'It's just that you're overtired, but tomorrow will be a roaring success, believe me,' she said. 'And if the backers are confident, then everyone is confident. Take me through the menu again.'

'You're going to a hotel tomorrow evening,' Cathy told Simon and Maud.

'I'd be just as happy to go to the do,' Simon said.

'To help you,' Maud explained.

'I know, and I do appreciate it, but honestly there's not all that much room in the premises, and you'll have a great time there.'

'Is Walter going to your party?' Maud wanted to know.

'Yes, I think he is. He didn't reply, but I'm sure he will be there.'

'Will he be working for you and Tom?' Simon asked.

'Not if all the guests were lying writhing on the ground parched with thirst, pleading and roaring for a drink will Walter Mitchell ever work for me again,' Cathy said cheerfully.

'It doesn't sound much of a party,' Simon said to Maud. 'I think we'd be better off in the hotel, to tell you the truth.'

Neil was up and dressed when Cathy woke with a start. 'God almighty, what time is it?'

'Relax, it's not even seven yet.'

'Why are you up?'

'This is the big day,' he said.

Lord, she had forgotten. Today Scarlet Feather would be a reality, the launch party, the brochure out, the whole company up and ready for business.

'I know, I can hardly believe it.' Cathy stood there in her stripy nightshirt. She rubbed her eyes and shook her hair back.

'I know he's only a junior minister, but it's very big for him to come to the breakfast, and he's crazy about publicity so it'll give the whole thing some attention.'

She realised that it was a big day for Neil because a group of them had managed to get a government minister to meet them about prisoners of conscience.

'I hope it's a great success, anyway,' she said in a flat voice.

He looked at her, startled at the tone, but she said nothing by way of explanation. 'So I must run . . .' he said eventually.

'See you tonight,' she said.

'Oh yes, of course, the do. It will be great, honey, don't have a worry in the world about it.'

'No, of course not.' Still the same flat voice.

He came back and gave her a quick hug. 'I'm very proud of you, you know,' he said.

'I know, Neil,' she said. But she wished that it were much more important to him than a quick hug and a pat on the back.

Ricky sent one of his photographers down to the premises an hour before people were expected. Just to do a few food shots, to see the buffet before it got all clogged up with people. Cathy's friends June and Katy were well kitted out in their white shirts with the scarlet feather logo. They all posed beside the plates of dressed salmon, long, oval dishes of roasted peppers, colourful salads and baskets of bread.

One moment there seemed to be nobody except the staff standing around nervously, and the next the place was teeming with people. The front room, which would later be their little reception office, looked terrific tonight. How right they had been to have old-fashioned sofas and chairs. Their new filing system was cleverly hidden in elegant drawers. It was a peaceful place where they hoped that customers would sit and discuss menus. Nothing of the precision shining white and steel of the kitchens here: that was all beyond the door, and they had cleared spaces for people to stand and later to dance. Tonight the front room was acting as a cloakroom with two great rails. And a ravishing-looking redhead who worked in Geraldine's office but did not think helping at a party was beneath her, gave people tickets for their coats and hung them neatly on the rails.

Then June and Katy, her two great friends through everything from schooldays long ago, stood with trays of welcoming drinks leaving Tom and Cathy free to greet and welcome and to listen to the praise and admiration for their new premises.

Neil was not among the early arrivals. Cathy planned to place him very near to the door, so that he could cope with his mother whenever Hannah chose to make her entrance. Cathy's own parents were there, totally amazed by it all, awkward and out of place. Her father twisting his cap that he had inexplicably refused to surrender at the cloakroom, and roaming the room with his eyes looking for someone he might talk to. Her mother in a soft, flattering green wool dress that had set her sister back a small fortune at Haywards and with her hair nicely styled, had no idea how well she looked. Instead, her eyes scanned the room for somewhere to hide.

'Mam, you look beautiful,' Cathy said, and meant it.

'No indeed I don't, Cathy, I'm a disgrace. I shouldn't be here with all these people at all. I wonder, is . . .' Why did they feel so ill at ease, as if somehow they were going to be found out, pronounced unacceptable and sent home? Cathy had been down this route, had asked herself these questions so often that she knew it to be totally fruitless. But of course Tom had to put up with it too. JT and Maura Feather didn't look as if they were having fun either. Now there was an idea. She excused herself from talking to a pleasant man who ran a house-cleaning service. They had been saying that there were ways in which they might well work together, one would recommend the other. Expertly Cathy made the introductions. In one way it didn't really work: instead of being moral support to each other, they made each other more nervous. But they each drew some strength and solidarity from realising that the other couple was also full of doubts. Tom's father said that if anyone wanted to know what he thought, then he thought that it wasn't worth spoiling the ship for a ha'porth of tar, and they should have given it more time. And Lizzie Scarlet said she was afraid they had bitten off more than they could chew. Maura Feather said there was a perfectly good living for Tom in his father's business and he needn't even get his hands dirty – he could have sat in an office and brought in clients. Like these people who were all dressed to kill, and would have plenty in the bank to build extensions and maybe even second homes. Muttie said that if his Cathy and their Tom were such great cooks, then if they went to work for other people without putting their money at risk they would save a small fortune in no time, but of course nobody ever listened to the voice of experience.

The mood was getting more relaxed by the moment. Cathy caught her aunt's eye and in seconds Geraldine was in there talking and enthusing and broadening the circle. The noise level was much higher now. Cathy noticed, and she allowed herself to take a couple of normal breaths and to accept that it was all going very well. She even looked around her at the guests. James Byrne had phoned at the last moment to say he couldn't come. Marcella looked just exquisite in a beautifully cut silk jacket and long black skirt. She wore no jewellery, even though anything at all around that long, slim neck would have looked good. Somehow she had great style the way she was. She was the centre of admiring glances, and Tom looked on proudly. Cathy was glad that this was not one of Marcella's rather over-sexy nights; she had seen Tom's face too often on such occasions.

In and in they came, and then she saw Neil's parents arrive. Jock with his handsome if marginally vacant face had the slightly affected manner of always appearing to think he should be somewhere else. Good-natured and bewildered, but not entirely convincing. And beside him was Hannah. She wore a harsh, dark purple dress that somehow drained the colour from her face. She looked affronted before she even came in the door. There was nothing here that she could fault, Cathy thought triumphantly. Nothing at all. There were even a few minor celebrities from the stage or television. But in general it was just a well-dressed, well-behaved crowd of people who might form a pool of future clients. She had, however, known Mrs Mitchell since her early childhood, for too long not to be able to read her face. The woman was spoiling for a fight. She would not have one with Cathy.

They all seemed to love the food: it had been worthwhile showing off their wares. Cathy noticed her father deep in conversation with a sports journalist, and her mother sitting happily with Mrs Keane, a neighbour of theirs from Waterview on two chairs a little away from the general throng. To Cathy's surprise, Hannah Mitchell approached them.

'Ah, good to see you, Lizzie; give me that chair, will you, like a dear, and get me a plate of mixed bites, nibbles, whatever they call them . . .' She spoke imperiously, as someone who knew she would make it happen. And it would have happened, had Cathy not been near at hand. Poor Lizzie Scarlet stumbled to her feet and apologised. She was still Mrs Mitchell's cleaner, and she had been caught sitting down and talking in an overfamiliar way with the quality.

'Yes, Mrs Mitchell, sorry Mrs Mitchell, what exactly would you like, a little of everything?' Cathy's resolutions were out of the window. She had never been so angry. This woman had now crossed over every boundary of behaviour and good manners. In an icy voice, she ordered her mother to sit down and not to abandon Mrs Keane in mid-conversation. Out of sheer shock Lizzie did just that, and with a combination of shoulder and arm Cathy moved and manipulated Hannah Mitchell to the other side of the room. Out of the corner of her mouth she hissed at June that she needed a stool, and at Kate that she wanted a plate with a small selection. Then she seated her mother-in-law in an area where she could see everyone.

'There was no need to push me across the room, Cathy, really.'

'I know, isn't it just terrible when places become so crowded? But you wanted a chair and I wanted to make sure you got one.' She smiled until the sides of her face hurt.

Hannah Mitchell was not fooled. 'I had a perfectly good chair where I was.'

'Sadly no, that was my mother's chair, but can I leave you for a moment? I do hope you like the premises.' And she was gone trembling and shaking.

Neil, who had noticed nothing amiss, was talking to his cousin Walter, jumpy and restless as ever. Cathy saw Joe Feather come in; he had brought them a kitchen clock with pictures of old-fashioned cooking utensils on it.

'Figured you didn't need any more food and drink in this place. What a great, great job – you've done it, I smell success everywhere.' Tom and Cathy beamed at him, he had such a knack for saying the right thing, and was a strange magnet immediately for people. He didn't even have to move towards them, they came to him.

They turned the background music level down slightly. It was time for the speeches. Tom and Cathy gave each other the thumbs-up sign. They had rehearsed these for ever. No long Oscar-style lists of thank-yous. No boasting of how successful they would be. Even before they had got the premises they had been trying them out on each other. It would be an absolute maximum of two minutes each, and then fade up the music. People could continue their conversations without feeling seriously interrupted, and it worked just as they'd planned. It was much too good a party to interrupt for more than four minutes, plus applause. When it was over, they looked at each other. Had they really said what they meant to? Neither could remember. They were congratulated on all sides, and could hardly take it in. Some early leavers were beginning to get their coats, but the hard core would be there for much, much longer.

'What a pity we didn't think of having a tape recorder!' Cathy said.

'I did.' Geraldine was beside her. 'And you were both brilliant.'

'Is Ma all right?'

'She is. Stop fussing.'

'You're lucky you can speak to Cathy like that, Geraldine. I try to, but she bites my head off,' said Tom.

'Ah, family gives you great privileges,' Geraldine said, and was gone.

Cathy saw JT and Maura Feather leaving. 'I don't think they've even *seen* Joe, he's been over on the other side of the room,' she began.

'Leave it, Cathy. Joe will find them if he wants to.'

'But wouldn't it be a shame . . .'

'It's always been a shame, but that's the way he is, he doesn't do anything that bores him and going to Fatima bores him, so he never goes.'

'He's going to meet them tonight,' Cathy insisted, and raised her voice loudly. 'Joe, I think your parents are leaving . . .' He had to meet them then. Cathy saw how their faces lit up with pleasure at the sight of their elder son. Joe put up a good show of being delighted and surprised to see them: he admired his mother's dress, and praised his father for the work that had been done and swiftly he got them to the door. At no stage had Cathy ever seen such joy and enthusiasm on their faces when they were talking to their son Tom, who went to see them regularly and looked after their every need. But then, when had life been fair?

Geraldine had arranged a taxi, which would collect Muttie and Lizzie and take them to the hotel to pick up Simon and Maud. But by the time it came, neither of the Scarlets wanted to leave. Muttie was going to meet the sports journalist at the next big race meeting and was to be invited into the press box. Lizzie was going to visit Mrs Keane in Waterview to look at this new mop she had. Apparently you didn't need to kneel down on the floor nearly so much these days, and Lizzie's knees were a bit achy. It had begun as a conversation about cleaning equipment, but it was now almost a social visit. Cathy looked at her mother with a wave of love. The day would come, she swore it would, when Lizzie Scarlet would never again have to clean a floor for anyone other than herself. Just as the Scarlets had got to the front room, Hannah moved in on them again.

'There you are, Lizzie, get my coat for me, will you, dear?'

'Certainly Mrs Mitchell, is it your fur?'

'Of course not, Lizzie, to a place like this. No, it's my black cloth coat ... Oh, but maybe you weren't with me when I got it. You might have left by then.'

'Do you have a ticket, Mrs Mitchell?'

'I don't have an idea what I did with the ticket, find it for me quickly like a dear, will you, I don't want to hang around here longer than I have to.'

Cathy moved in quickly. She nailed a smile to her face. 'Mam, your taxi is getting restless, I'll get Hannah's coat for her.' Together with Geraldine she got her parents into the taxi. Which was far from easy.

'And listen, thank you both for coming and for talking to everyone. You're marvellous, both of you, and thank you so much for looking after the little Mitchell children. I really don't know what they would all have done without you.' The last bit very loudly.

'Gently, Cath,' whispered Geraldine. 'You might need Hannah and Jock some day.'

'For what, exactly?'

'All right, but still gently.'

'Right, thanks Geraldine.' Cathy walked over to the gorgeous red-headed cloakroom girl and pointed out her mother-in-law's coat. 'That dame is pretending to have lost her ticket. Can I have that black one, please?' She held it open, but Hannah made no attempt to put it on. So Cathy laid it on a chair. They were alone in the foyer at this stage.

'You've gone too far, Cathy Scarlet. You'll regret your behaviour tonight, mark my words.'

'And I very much hope that you will regret yours, Mrs Mitchell, trying to humiliate my mother as a way to annoy me. Yes, it worked for you in that it *did* annoy me, but you couldn't humiliate her, it's impossible. She has a decent, generous soul, and because she took your money for years for hard, menial work she thinks she still owes you.'

Hannah was white at the insolence. 'Your mother, limited as she is, is worth ten of you.'

'I agree with you. And she's worth a hundred of you, Mrs

Mitchell. I said it to her the other day. She wouldn't listen, of course, but it's still true.' Hannah Mitchell gasped and Cathy went on. 'Believe me, I'm actually glad that we are having this conversation, and I want you to know that my days of being polite to you are over.'

'You were *never* polite to me, you common little . . . little . . .' Words failed Hannah at this point.

'When I was young and came to play in the garden, if Mam was working at Oaklands, I wasn't polite, that's true, but when I married Neil I was, I tried very hard. I didn't want to make things difficult for him and actually I was sorry for you. Yes, I was, because you were so very disappointed in the wife he brought home.'

'*You* were sorry for *me*!' Hannah snorted.

'And I still am in ways, but there will be no pretence any more. There's something you have not understood: I was never in my whole life afraid of you. You just don't have any power over me. Your day is gone, Hannah Mitchell. It's a new Ireland, a country where the maids' children marry who they bloody well like, and where the nobs like your brother-in-law, if he's aware of anything at all, are very glad to have Muttie and Lizzie Scarlet going down in a taxi to the best hotel in Dublin to pick up his children and take them back to St Jarlath's Crescent where it looks as if they might spend the next ten years—'

Hannah interrupted her. 'When you apologise, Cathy, as you will, I assure you, I am not going to forgive you or put it down to overexcitement because of all this . . .' Hannah looked around her and sniffed.

'Oh, no, I will never apologise, believe me, I meant everything I said,' Cathy spoke icily. 'If you, on the other hand, apologise about the way you insulted my mother twice tonight, I will consider it and ask Neil what he thinks. Otherwise we will behave courteously to each other in public and communicate not at all in private. Now, you can either come in and join your husband or leave. Suit yourself.' And Cathy turned and went, head high, back to the party. Inside, she saw Geraldine looking at her anxiously.

'She still has a pulse, Geraldine, don't worry.' Cathy Scarlet had her first drink of the night. A very large glass of red wine. She realised now that Hannah had two ways to go. She wished for a moment her father were here to tell her the odds. But as Muttie often said, there are times when there are no odds, when you have to go by instinct. And her instinct was that Hannah would say nothing. Reporting the insolence of her daughter-in-law would mean putting the spotlight on her own behaviour. Hannah wouldn't risk it. So there would be no need for Cathy to explain anything at all. She smiled at the thought that she had won, she had really and truly won. It was somehow nearly as good as this launch.

'I don't like you sitting alone drinking wine and laughing to yourself,' Geraldine said disapprovingly. The music was louder. Tom moved to hold the beautiful face of Marcella in his two hands and began to dance with her. Cathy's two friends June and Kate were both quite reached by drink and dancing already. Dreamily, Cathy put out her hand towards Neil and they held each other tight. Over his shoulder she saw Jock Mitchell look around for his wife and eventually go out of the door to find her. She saw Joe Feather leave quietly and watched Walter put a bottle of wine under his arm before leaving. And Cathy Scarlet closed her eyes and danced with the man she loved.

'What are you thinking about?' he asked her, but there were too many things even to begin to tell.

Chapter Two

FEBRUARY

'Tell me that we cleared the place up,' Tom asked Marcella sleepily next morning. 'Tell me that we didn't just walk out and leave everything as it was.'

Marcella laughed. 'Surely you remember the way you said to everyone that you were calling two taxis in half an hour, and the place had to be perfect.'

'You know what? I thought I remembered that, but I was afraid I just dreamed it.' Tom said.

'You had us all running in and out like a fast-forward film, and by the time the taxis came everything was covered with cling film and put into the right places and the dishwasher was turned on.'

'I'm a genius,' Tom said happily.

'Of course you are. You did say, however, that there would be about a hundred more glasses to do, but you were very proud that all the litter bags were tied up and the floor was clean.'

'I really laid into the wine, I'm afraid.' He was contrite.

'Not until the end. You and Cathy must have drunk a bottle each in ten minutes and you deserved it, but you'd had nothing to eat or drink all day.' She stroked his forehead and began to get out of bed.

'You're never leaving me alone in the morning of my triumph and my slight hangover, are you?' He was very disappointed.

'Tom, it's my dance class,' she said.

'Of course.' He had forgotten. Marcella didn't need this two-hour class in movement every Saturday morning; she didn't need the other classes she took either. She was a lithe, gorgeous girl who turned heads. But she was convinced that these were all part of her apprenticeship, and worked hard for the extra money. She spent hours after work and early in the morning shelf-stacking in the Food Hall at Haywards. Only the staff saw Marcella Malone doing a menial job like that. And they didn't matter, as Marcella always said, because they were not the ones who were going to discover her and give her this break in modelling. The rest of the public saw her either as a beauty therapist in Haywards' salon, or as a beautiful party animal much photographed at press receptions and at the clubs.

Tom understood entirely why Marcella could never work as a waitress for them in Scarlet Feather. It would mean the end of the dream for her, admitting that there would be no starry future ahead. He wasn't totally sure that Cathy understood; sometimes he thought he saw a flash of impatience pass over his business partner's face when he said that his life partner would not be helping them out. Cathy's own husband Neil never minded carrying heavy trays or loading the van, if he was around. But then he seldom was, and anyway, he *could* do that because he was already somebody, a successful and known young barrister, his name and photograph often in the newspapers. He had already made his way. Marcella had yet to make hers.

Tom knew he should go into the premises and get the glasses done, check that the food really had been properly put away, but it was early still and they had been rushing so much in the run-up to last night, he deserved another cup of coffee. He looked out on the wintry scene, the leafless trees and wet courtyard surrounding Stoneyfield. Tom's father always said that it was a disgrace leaving that ground to go to waste when they could easily have fitted three more units into the space. It wasn't even as if it were a proper garden with lawns or anything. In vain would Tom try to tell him that the kind of people who came to live here had no time to mow lawns. But they did need places to turn and park cars, and for the athletic like Marcella, chain their bicycles in elegantly disguised sheds. JT Feather, builder, from an earlier time when more was good, would never understand it in a million years. Any more than he would take in the amount of their earnings that he and Marcella put into the mortgage. Better not to weigh his father down with details like that. As was increasingly becoming the case, Tom sighed to himself.

This thought led him to think of his brother. Joe had said he would call before he left for the airport, but then Joe was spectacularly vague about family. Tom dialled his hotel.

'You thought I'd forget to phone you,' Joe said.

'You? Forget to phone your family? Never.' Tom laughed at him good-naturedly.

'I would have, mainly to say that you've a great set-up there, it's very professional, really it is. Geraldine and I think our investment is one of the best we've ever made, we told each other several times.'

'She's a real looker that woman, isn't she? Loads of style. She's not there with you, by any chance?' Nothing was unlikely with his brother Joe.

'No indeed, she's not. Let's say *she*'s not.'

'I don't know how you do, it Joe.' Tom shook his head. Imagine, Joe had picked up someone at their party last night and persuaded her to go back to his hotel!

'Only because I'm a sad old man without a lovely wife of my own like you have.'

'She's not my wife yet.'

'I know, but she might as well be for all the looks she gives towards anyone else.'

That pleased Tom, as Joe knew it would. 'Anyone I know from the party?'

'Aha,' said Joe.

'Is she there with you? Now?'

'In the bathroom at the moment. Any time for a drink before I get the plane?'

'I have to go round to the premises ... I really do not want Cathy coming by and doing it.'

'Right, I'll see you round there in half an hour,' Joe said.

Tom was ready to leave in minutes. The van wasn't outside the door, it was in Waterview at Cathy's place. He'd get a taxi on the street. There was something he wanted to talk to Joe about too. Like was there any hope that he might actually *do* something in terms of their mother and father, come and see them even for very short visits. It would mean so much to them, and take so little out of Joe's lifestyle. And it would lift a great deal of the burden from Tom's back.

The van was there when he arrived. Tom was annoyed; not only had he not beaten Cathy to it but now he wouldn't be able to talk to Joe. Perhaps he could take him out for a coffee. He would make it up to Cathy later. Tom hoped that Neil would not be there, it would point up how much more involved the two of them were, Marcella at her dance class and Tom about to slip out with his brother. But no; Cathy was not with Neil. She was with those bizarre children that she seemed to have taken under her wing. Solemn-eyed, self-centred, intense and appallingly bad mannered, although there had been a bit of an improvement in their behaviour recently.

'You're late,' said Simon.

'Where's your girlfriend?' asked Maud.

Cathy came out and gave him a hug. 'Wasn't that a night to remember,' she said. Then, looking at the children, she said in an entirely different voice, 'Tom is not late, we are only here for two minutes, and his girlfriend Marcella is at her dance class, and what did I say about greeting people?'

They lowered their eyes.

'No, stop looking down at the floor. How do we greet people in a civilised society? Tell me this minute.'

'We say hallo and pretend to be glad to see them,' said Simon.

'We use their name if we know it,' added Maud.

'Okay. Sorry Tom, could you go out and come in again, it wasn't a civilised society for a moment but it will be when you come back.'

Tom went back outside, irritated. There was little enough time as it was, and now he was playing ridiculous games in a vain attempt to teach these monstrous children manners.

'Good morning,' he said as he re-entered.

Simon, with a nightmare rictus grin on his face, came out to shake hands. 'Good morning Tom,' he said.

'You are most welcome, Tom,' Maud said.

'Thank you . . . um . . . Maud and Simon,' said Tom, gritting his teeth at being welcomed to his own premises by these two children. 'Thank you so much, and to what exactly do we owe the pleasure of your company?' They looked at him without an idea of what he was talking about.

Cathy explained. 'My mother isn't all that well this morning.'

'Too much wine here last night,' Simon explained.

Cathy interrupted, 'and so I thought it would all be for the best if they came to help me here . . . And if you have no objections, they are about to unload and load the dishwashers very carefully now.

Now,' she barked suddenly at the children, who scuttled away to get on with it.

'Sorry,' she whispered to Tom. 'I really had to. I've never seen my poor mother so shook. She never goes anywhere where there's drink, and it's all my fault. I hated that old bitch Hannah Mitchell so much I kept tanking poor Mam up so that she wouldn't hear your woman patronising her.'

'Cathy, whatever you want, believe me, it's just . . .'

'It's just what?' Her eyes were bright and searching his face for what he was trying to say.

'Well it's just that I don't seem to do as much as you do. I was going to meet Joe here and have a chat with him, so now we might slope off and that's not fair on you . . . And also it's just . . .'

'Oh, go on, say it Tom. Ask are they going to be living with us until Neil and I are old and grey, and the answer is I don't bloody know. I just know that we can't abandon them. And they will do this, you know, so go off with Joe and for God's sake stop saying you're not pulling your weight. You do far more than me.'

'It *was* a great night last night,' he said. ' I really do think we're going to be all right, don't you?'

'I think we'll be millionaires,' said Cathy, just as Joe came in through the open door.

'That's what I like to hear,' said Joe Feather. He took Cathy up in his arms and swung her round in a circle. 'Well done, Cathy Scarlet, you and my little brother here have really got the right touch.'

She was pleased, Tom noted, as every woman that Joe Feather looked at seemed pleased.

Maud and Simon peered out of the kitchen at the sounds. 'Good morning, I'm Maud Mitchell and this is my brother Simon. You're very welcome.'

'Would you like me to take your coat?' Simon asked.

'I'm Joe Feather. Delighted to make your acquaintance,' Joe said.

'Are you Tom's father?' Simon asked, interested.

Cathy's face fell.

'Not quite, more his brother,' Joe said agreeably.

'And do you have children and grandchildren of your own?' Maud wanted to be clear on everything too.

'No, I'm a bachelor, that's a man never lucky enough to marry,' said Joe as if he were being interviewed on radio. 'And I live by myself in London in an apartment in Ealing. I go to work by the

Central line every day from Ealing Broadway to Oxford Circus, and I walk down to the garment district, where I sell clothes.'

Tom hadn't known any of this. He knew his brother's post code, but he hadn't known it was Ealing . . . He didn't know about the tube journey, either.

'Do you sell them in a shop or in a street?'

'It's more an office really. You see, they come in to me and then I send them out again,' Joe explained.

'Do you improve them before they go?' Maud asked.

'Actually, no. No, they go the same as they arrive,' said Joe.

'Terrible waste then, isn't it, them going to you?' Simon said.

There was a silence. 'I suppose it is in a way,' Joe agreed. 'But it's the system, you see. It's how I earn my money.'

There was another silence. 'Are we talking too much?' Simon asked Cathy.

'No, truly, but why don't you go into the kitchen again and sort the cutlery? Like now,' Cathy shouted so that they all jumped. Maud and Simon went out immediately.

'They're extraordinary,' Joe said.

'Mixed blessing,' Cathy said.

'Who are they?' he asked.

'You don't have time. Go off and have a coffee somewhere sane, and we'll do this place.'

Tom thought that Joe was reluctant to leave. His brother was such a womaniser and always had been. Tom hoped against hope that Joe hadn't suddenly taken a fancy to Cathy. Life was never uncomplicated, but all he needed now was something like this to happen, for his brother, who seemed to be able to get the entire female population of Ireland to fancy him, to move in on the happiest marriage in the Western world – that of Cathy and Neil Mitchell. Whatever else happened, this must not even be allowed to get to first base. 'Come on, Joe, we'll go to Bewley's,' Tom said, and they left.

'What does Geraldine do for a living?' Joe asked when they were seated with their sticky almond buns and coffee.

'She's got a PR agency, you know that.'

'No, I meant how did she get the money to set it up, and how can she match me pound by pound?'

'Funny thing,' Tom said. 'Geraldine asked Cathy the same question. She wanted to know where *you* got the money.'

'And what did Cathy say?'

'She said that she didn't know, and as far as she knew that I didn't know either.'

Joe said, 'So what do you want to know? Ask me, I'll tell you.'

'I suppose I don't know exactly what you do. You don't ever say.'

Joe leaned on the table and looked across at him without the usual jokey smile. 'God, you *know* what I do, Tom. I rent two rooms in the garment district in London. I get stuff made up out in the Philippines. I import it, I show it to retailers, they buy it and I get more stuff made up in Korea and I show it to more retailers and they buy it.'

'And that's it?'

'Of course it's bloody it. What did you think it was, stealing old ladies' pension books, selling hash in pubs?'

'No, of course not.'

'But what then? You know what I do. There was never any mystery. When you went to work in those restaurants I knew what you were at. I didn't say to myself, I wonder what Tom is doing in Quentin's? I knew you were an apprentice learning how to cook with that chef Patrick, what's his name?'

'Brennan. Patrick Brennan.'

'Yes, I know. I often go in there, his wife Brenda is something else. When you went on the catering course, I knew what it was about. Ask me anything you like if you can't understand what it is I'm doing,' Joe grinned at him.

'I know, it does sound like the Special Branch. Sorry.'

'It sounds worse, it sounds like the Inland Revenue,' Joe said with a look of mock terror on his face.

'Talking about that, Joe, we have a very upright bookkeeper . . .'

'I get your drift,' he laughed.

'No, I mean he really does ask toughish questions and, you know me, I like the canvas to be uncluttered with little problems.'

'I have one really spotless account, believe me. Any support comes from that one.'

Tom decided to go no further down the road on that one, in case he heard of accounts which were not spotless and learned more than he wanted to know. 'And do you ever go out to these places in the Far East to see them making your clothes?' he asked.

'As little as I can. I know you think I'm a capitalist pig but I actually can't bear to see how poor they are and how little they're paid, I just prefer to see stuff arriving in a warehouse.'

'Oh, I can't talk about people being capitalist pigs now, I've joined them,' Tom said ruefully.

'I know, the Feather brothers taking over.' Joe grinned at him. 'Talking of that . . .'

'Yeah?' Joe was wary now, as if he knew what was coming.

'Joe, I don't want to preach but couldn't you just go sometimes to see Ma and Da. You *never* see them and I have to keep on . . .'

'No, Tom, you don't have to keep on doing anything you don't want to. I met them last night, for God's sake.'

'For thirty seconds at a party.'

'You want me to spend hour after hour listening to Ma telling me I'll burn in hell because I don't go to Mass, Da complaining that my name isn't on the sign in the builders yard . . . No, Tom, I have a life to lead.'

'So do I, and I have to live yours for you too . . . Where is he, why doesn't he stay in touch.'

Joe shrugged. 'Say you don't know.'

'I do say it, and it's the truth. I *don't* know. I don't know why you who are so good with people can't send them the odd postcard, make the odd call.'

'If I go to Manila I'll send them a card, is that a deal? Will you get off my back now?'

'A card from London would be exotic enough for Ma and Da,' said Tom, but he knew when he had to give up.

Tom and Cathy sat for hours dreaming up menus for the christening, the first night party and the business lunch. All of them desperately important in their own way. The christening would have a very flash, moneyed crowd at it, people who could spend. They would have to do it right, lay out a bit more on the actual presentation. The theatre party was on a very low budget; what they wanted was something much nicer than sausages and crisps but at the price that sausages and crisps would cost. It needed a lot of thought. If they got on well with the theatre crowd it would really stand to them, there would be contacts for all kinds of events from now on. Cathy had been endlessly patient trying to think of cheap food that would seem more upmarket. Crostini, maybe? And lots of dips and pitta. But since people actually *did* like sausages, maybe they should have some, with a redcurrant and honey glaze.

She knew there would be no profit in it but that it was very dear to Tom's heart. So he wanted to help her also with the business lunch. Cathy's dream was that they would get into some of the banks or money houses in the financial centre, where they would serve light, exquisite lunches to the companies' clients as part of corporate hospitality, and have the ability to pick up further business at every meal they served. It would mean more daytime work, too.

Cathy had asked once if Marcella would consider helping to serve this first one, just to start them off. Nobody would ever forget Marcella pouring their mineral water and smiling her dazzling smile. Tom hated having to say no at the outset. He knew that Marcella just would not do it, and it would be unfair to ask her.

'She must have a stab at this modelling, you know, no matter how hard she pushes herself. I hardly ever see her.'

'I know what you mean,' she shrugged. 'But you're going to have to get used to it when she does become a model, because she'll be off at shows somewhere all the time.'

Tom realised with a shock that he had probably thought Marcella would never make it. He had somehow seen a future where Scarlet Feather became very successful and they could put in a manager. A future where he and Marcella would marry and have two children. But perhaps he was just fooling himself.

'Where will we be in ten years time, do you think, Cathy?' he asked her suddenly.

'I'd say we'll still be here working out this bloody menu, and the child will be nearly grown-up and walking round a pagan because he never got christened at all,' she said. 'Come on Tom, let's cost it out, salmon *and* a chicken dish, they want it done right, and judging by your figures, they're not likely to have a big family and lots of other christenings to follow.'

'It'll be too dear, it's the rich who always carp about the prices ... you know that,' Tom said.

They were back in business. Sitting arguing in their shiny new premises, drinking coffee from the marvellous mugs which said *Scarlet Feather*. A gift of six of them from Marcella, who had them painted specially. Cathy's friend June who had helped last night came in to say that she would love to do the odd night waitressing, and could they just show her a few of the finer points.

'I'm not sure we know them,' Tom said. 'But we'll try anyway.'

June was a small, jolly girl who had been at school with Cathy. She had got pregnant when she was sixteen and the great thing about that, she said, was that she had her family reared now and she was free to do what she liked. According to Cathy, she sometimes felt a little bit *too* free to do what she liked, or that's what her husband said, anyway. But June just laughed and said that she had to go dancing and to clubs nowadays: she had missed out on all that when she was seventeen and eighteen, pushing prams and minding babies.

'I'll try not to be too forward or anything,' she promised Tom, 'and if you tell me how to pronounce the things each time, I'll be great altogether. Well, I'll be cheerful anyway, and a lot of these ones you meet at functions look as if they have a poker up their arse.'

'Yes indeed,' Tom had said.

'But of course, if *they* fancy *me* then I can't help that.'

'No indeed,' Tom said.

'When's that brother of yours coming back to town? He's nearly as good-looking as yourself, but he's a real goer, isn't he?' June ate one of the crostini.

'June, stop that, you're eating the profits,' Tom said firmly. 'Oh, Joe comes and goes, he never stays. You just hear he's here, then you hear he's gone.'

'Dead exciting,' June said.

It flashed across Tom's mind that June could have been Joe's companion, the woman who had gone back to the hotel with him after the launch party. But no, surely not June. Her interpretation of having a bit of freedom could hardly have extended to staying out all night. She did have children at home. Then of course, he realised, it couldn't have been June, she had been here dancing at the very end, when Joe was long gone. But she could have gone on and joined him there later. Sexy little thing, in her way. Not something he would ask Cathy. What he really needed were those two Mitchell children. They'd get to the heart of any story. For some reason, nobody seemed able to refuse to answer their questions.

Cathy and Tom had been trained on the catering course to do their accounting very carefully, pricing their ingredients, labour and staff very precisely. They had to work out portion control in advance *and* take out the hours they worked afterwards. On the theatre job they lost a total of £76. Tom was shaken to the core.

'It's a one-off,' Cathy soothed. 'It's buying goodwill. We should put part of that under the promotional budget.'

'We don't *have* a promotional budget. The launch party saw to that,' Tom wailed in despair.

'It will lead to other things,' she pleaded.

'No, Cathy, it won't, it was to please my theatre friends, that's all. They asked half the audience in, so no future business in that crowd ... and we were hours getting the place right.'

'*And* we had to send June home in a taxi, which was miles,' Cathy agreed.

'*And* we had to pay her two extra hours because she worked them. I had no idea it was going to go on so late.' Tom was contrite.

'Okay, three jobs this month and we lost seventy-six pounds on the first. I wonder what we'll end up losing? If we did it spectacularly enough they could use our books as an exhibit on some marketing course. How *not* to go into business.'

'We'll have to *get* bloody books, you know, otherwise we'll end up in jail as well as bankrupt. It all looked so simple in theory, didn't it?' Tom sounded less cheerful.

'What we need just now is one of those strokes of luck we kept saying that we were having,' Cathy said.

The phone rang. Cathy was nearer.

'Oh, yes, James, how are you?' Tom watched as Cathy frowned.

'Yes of course, James, it would be a pleasure.' She put the receiver down. 'You'll never guess what James wants.'

'Nothing would surprise me these days. It's not one of those strokes of luck we were looking for, is it?'

'I don't think so,' Cathy said slowly. 'He wants us to teach him to make a supper for two people, three courses. He says we are to buy the ingredients and come to his place. He's costing our time at fifteen pounds an hour. Minimum four hours, including the shopping.'

'When does he want it?' Tom asked. 'We're very busy this week, we're going to . . .'

'No, it's ages away, but he's going to pay us in advance to book us, he says it's proper professional practice and he insists upon it,' Cathy said, knowing well that James was only trying to put some money into their very meagre bank account.

'That's okay. Sixty quid will nearly make up the deficit on the theatre party.'

'Listen, he said fifteen pounds an hour *each*.'

'He's going to pay a hundred and twenty pounds to make a dinner? He's off his skull.'

'I suppose it's for some woman, he did say that discretion was to be a part of it,' Cathy said.

'Good. Then let's not let Simon and Maud know; they'd have it on the six o'clock news,' said Tom happily.

Once a month Neil and Marcella cooked a meal for them all. They were both utterly hopeless at cooking, and Tom and Cathy itched to get up and do it themselves. It would have taken half the time, and been so much better. But they had to sit through the endless fussing, sauces burning, meat shrivelling and salads being drenched in dressing. It was a ritual.

Tom thought to himself that if they were giving a lesson to poor James Byrne, perhaps they should include their partners as well. But it wasn't something you could suggest. It would look too critical of all that had gone before. But unexpectedly, it was Marcella who suggested it. When she heard about the lesson she said that she and Neil had been thinking of going secretly to Quentin's restaurant to ask Brenda and Patrick for a lesson. Could this be the solution, here on their doorstep? A rehearsal for Mr Byrne? This month it was to be Stoneyfield in their own flat. Perfect.

'If you were as old as James and he was trying to seduce you, what would you like him to serve you?' Tom asked Marcella.

'She mightn't be old, she might just be a young one,' Marcella said.

'Well, what?'

'Oysters, grilled fillet of sole, French beans and fresh fruit salad with no sugar.' Marcella spoke with certainty.

'But that's because you've been on a diet since you were nine,' Tom complained. 'She might be a big fat lady dying for steak and kidney pie and apple pie to follow.'

'Yes, but she wouldn't like it on a date, she likes to be treated as if she were fragile, even if she isn't.'

Tom thought this was a good idea, and so did Cathy. 'We should put Marcella down as our group psychologist,' she said approvingly. And, as always, Tom beamed at the compliment for his girl. He loved people to praise Marcella, as he sometimes feared that they didn't know her well enough to realise how much she cared about the enterprise.

The cookery lesson was much discussed. Tom and Cathy had to accept that Neil and Marcella were even more hopeless than they had suspected. Everything was going to take three times as long as it should have; they would get flustered and confused. Even the very language of cooking, the simplest terms, seemed to upset them. Tom and Cathy had presented them with the instructions, which had proved far from clear. They didn't know what it meant to 'reduce' something. Neil was in a rush to leave, and he read the list briefly.

'I suppose reduce means you throw half of it away?' he said absent-mindedly as he hunted for his papers.

'I can't believe that anyone thinks you are an adult,' Cathy laughed. 'Of *course* it doesn't mean that, why would you make twice as much and throw half away?'

Neil shrugged. 'It's all very odd, anyway. See you tonight at their place.' He kissed her and was gone.

Cathy wanted to shout that he mustn't be late, Marcella was giving up a dance class to be there. But somehow it sounded trivial, so she didn't. Tom reported that Marcella thought to reduce something meant you had it wrong and should start again with fewer ingredients.

'We have an uphill job,' he said sadly.

Cathy drove past a house where she knew her mother would be working. Lizzie's face lit up when she saw her.

'Well now, isn't that a wonderful surprise,' she said, settling into the van. 'I feel like a great lady driving in this. I hope they all see me.'

Cathy looked at her fondly. She met so many people who would have looked askance at getting into a big white delivery van, but to Lizzie Scarlet it was a treat.

'Did the others like cooking at home when they were young, or was it only me?' Cathy asked.

'Marian was quite good. She's so efficient about everything she touches, it came automatically to her, but the others didn't have the feel that you do. They didn't have much time, really; they all left so young. What was there to stay for, when there was all that fortune to be made over there?'

Lizzie sighed. Ever since the first boy had emigrated to Chicago to his uncle's house, and told the youngsters about the wages that could be earned in Illinois, her children could barely wait to be eighteen and out at the airport. They had been amazed when Cathy had never shown the slightest interest in leaving. Her mother looked tired, as well she might after a day's cleaning.

'Are those kids too much for you, Mam?'

'No, I tell you, I like their company and your dad is great altogether with them. He'll take no guff from them. I'm inclined to be a bit more . . .'

'I know you are, Mam. You're too kind to everyone.'

'And it's *nice* having children around. I was always getting ready to look after babies again when you and Neil . . . that is, if you and Neil . . .'

'Mam, I told you lots of times there isn't any possibility of that, not for ages yet, if ever. We're far too busy now.'

'God be with the old days when you didn't have any choice in the matter,' her mother said.

'Now you sound just like Tom's mother, talking about the good old days. They were *not* good old days, Mam, you had eleven in your family and Da had ten in his. Where was the chance for any of you?'

'We did all right,' Lizzie's voice was small and tight and she had taken offence.

'Mam, of course you did, and you did so well by all of us, but it wasn't easy for you, that's all I'm saying.'

'Yes. Yes, I see.'

They had arrived at St Jarlath's Crescent. Her mother was still hurt by the thoughtless remark.

Cathy looked at her pleadingly. 'I don't suppose there's a hope you'd make me some tea?'

'Well of course, if you have the time.'

'And would there be any apple tart left, do you think?'

'Oh, come on Cathy, stop behaving like a five-year-old.' Lizzie was rooting for her key and dying to put the kettle on. Forty-five seconds, the longest sulk she had ever known her mother to hold. Cathy felt a prickle of tears in her eyes.

They gathered in Tom's flat in Stoneyfield. All the ingredients were out on the table and Marcella was looking at them doubtfully. There was no sign of Neil yet.

'Should we start?' Tom wondered. Neil and Marcella made such heavy weather out of everything, they might not eat until midnight otherwise. Patiently Tom and Cathy explained, and industriously poor Marcella struggled to follow their instructions. Then Cathy's mobile rang. Neil was tied up, he'd be there in an hour, could they start without him.

'Traitor,' called out Marcella from the other side of the room.

'Swear to her I'll be there and do my share,' he begged.

But Cathy had taken too many of those calls to make any such promise. They ran out of wine, and Neil, who was meant to be looking after that side of things, still hadn't turned up. Cathy knew he might easily forget so she called him. The background noise was a pub.

'Sorry honey, I'm on my way.' He sounded annoyed to be nagged.

'Just to remind you about the wine,' she said coldly.

'God, I'm glad you did. I forgot totally, can you open what you have there just in case . . .'

'We have,' she was brisk.

'All *right*, Cathy,' Neil said.

He was in Stoneyfield an hour later, exactly two hours after the time they were meant to start. He had brought a bottle of expensive wine which he opened and poured for them. Marcella had fumbled her way through a starter and a chicken with wine main course, and she was exhausted.

'You're to do the dessert Neil,' she said, collapsing in a chair.

'Of course I will, *and* the washing up.' Neil smiled them all into good humour.

'Tell me what was this reducing business, anyway? I asked someone at the meeting and they thought it had to do with calories.'

They explained. 'Well why don't they use proper words like . . . well, make a concentrate?' Neil objected.

'Or like boil the divil out of it?' Marcella said.

Tom and Cathy took notes on the cookery lesson. It would have to be radically altered before they presented it to James Byrne. The salmon mousse was beyond them, they would have to take that off the list. The coq au vin was fine, but it took them all day and all night. The tiramisu looked and tasted disgusting. Tom couldn't see why, but it was soggy and bore no relation to what they had been asked to do. The food was terrible, but somehow the evening was not ruined. Cathy noticed that Marcella ate practically nothing and only sipped at her wine. Neil offered to keep his promise of washing up but Tom and Cathy knew they would be there until dawn if they let him, so they cleared the place up at high speed.

'Cleans up a treat, doesn't it?' Cathy admired their handiwork.

Tom looked around the flat. 'It's very practical, but I wouldn't want to live here for ever. It's like as if we're passing through without leaving any mark at all.'

Once he had mentioned it, the place did look very minimalist. Clean white walls and empty surfaces. No pictures on the walls, not many books on the shelf, no ornaments on the mantelpiece or window ledge. A little like a hotel suite, in fact.

'I know, I feel the same about Waterview sometimes. Move Neil's books out in one van load and it's just the way we got it. But then would you want it like St Jarlath's Crescent, where there isn't a space to put anything down?' she asked.

'Or Fatima. I know,' Tom agreed.

The happy medium was something that eluded the world, they all agreed.

They had no idea how hard it was to make contacts. People either didn't consider themselves in the league which hired a caterer, or if they did then they already knew someone who was doing just fine. Geraldine and Ricky gave them names, but they drew blank after blank. Tom was determined not to be downcast.

'Listen, we'll do leaflets and get some kid to deliver a thousand or two.'

If Cathy thought it was useless she didn't say so. Sometimes, after a fruitless day of searching for work, she would say that it was only Tom's enthusiasm that kept her going. And it was sincere, he really believed it. He wasn't just trying to keep her spirits up. They were so good, they had such imaginative ideas and worked so hard. It was only a matter of time until everyone realised this and recognised them for what they were. But Tom never sat back and just waited for things to happen: he was always on the move looking, asking and hunting.

'I hate breaking into your time, Geraldine, but could I come and spend just thirty minutes going through your client list again? You *know* we're good, it wouldn't be compromising you to recommend us.'

'It does my street cred good to have a handsome young man like yourself come to the apartments,' Geraldine said. 'Come round on Sunday morning and we'll see what we can find.'

The Glenstar apartment block was immaculately kept. There was regular landscape gardening, all the outside woodwork was repainted every year, brass gleamed everywhere and a smart commissionaire stood in the hall. Tom wondered how much they paid a year in services charges. Then he reminded himself not always to think in terms of how much things cost and how much they might bring in. It was the way his parents went on, and he certainly didn't need that. It was just that these sessions with James Byrne had been exhausting and worrying.

He had organised a filing cabinet and installed proper ledgers for them, warned them thunderously about keeping every receipt, and details of every piece of equipment bought so that its eventual depreciation could be properly noted. He explained how they must bill separately for waiters or waitresses asking clients to pay them directly; this way they avoided tax problems. It had been fascinating to hear James Byrne talk. It made Tom feel that anything was possible, and that they were safe from all the minefields of being prosecuted over VAT or any other kind of tax. Three jobs in February wasn't *too* bad. Was it? But he was out on the hunt for more work. And he had a Sunday-morning appointment with Geraldine O'Connor, so that she could go through her list of clients and decide who could be approached and with what angle. Geraldine looked magnificent: she wore a dark green velvet tracksuit, her hair was still slightly damp from swimming in the Glenstar pool. The smell of coffee filled her big sitting room. The Sunday papers were scattered over the big, long, low table in front of the sofas.

Geraldine got down to business at once, and they spent an hour at her dining table seeing where any opportunity might lie. 'Peter Murphy's hotel is useless, of course, since they have all their functions there and are catered by themselves. The garden centre never wants to spend any money, they serve thimbles of warm white wine and that's that.' The estate agents might, only might, let them send menus and a letter, saying how much it would enhance any future function to have unusual and memorable canapés served. 'Let's put it this way, it might give people *something* to remember from their dreary dos.'

Tom looked at her with admiration. She was afraid of nobody. Where had she got this confidence?

'But Tom, these now are a bit more lively . . .' She gave him the address of an import agency. 'They take a lot of clothes, even some from your brother, he was telling me the other night. The sky's the limit with these lads. And they're totally legal now, no more black economy. I'll tell them they should get better known. They need an upmarket party. I'll promise them buyers from Haywards if they come.'

'And Haywards themselves?' Tom said hopefully.

'No, not a chance. Shona Burke and I have talked about it over and over. She's done her very best but they have a café, you see, so it doesn't make any sense for them to bring in an outsider.'

'I know, that's true. It's just that it would have been such a feather in the cap for Scarlet Feather,' he said wistfully.

What Tom really meant was that it would have been good for Marcella too. If her fellow was doing the high-profile catering it would make her look good by association. But it wasn't to be. They went through the list of names. The pharmaceutical people possibly, the educational project no way, the people who organised the big literary competition were attached to a brewery and had their own contacts, the cross-border cooperation people had no money. Tom admired the matter-of-fact way Geraldine went about her business. She spoke affectionately, even discreetly about her clients, she emphasised to Tom that this was all in confidence, but she was in no way impressed by any of them. She told him that they had to have this conversation in her home rather than at her office as she would not want the staff to know she was divulging the secrets of the filing cabinet. She looked so at ease with herself, unlike any other woman he knew. Not like her sister, Lizzie, who worried and apologised; unlike Cathy, who was driven to show Hannah Mitchell that she was a career woman in her own right. Not like his mother, who saw only the bad side of everything and relied on the power of prayer. Not like Shona Burke, who always had this faraway, sad look on her face. He remembered Joe asking how Geraldine had got the money together to buy this agency, but it wasn't a question he would ever put to her, even though the great splendour of her apartment and her readiness to back them in this enterprise sometimes did make him speculate. But he frowned to himself. He would *not* become obsessed with money like so many people were nowadays.

'What on earth are you making faces about, Tom?' Geraldine didn't miss much.

'I was thinking about money, actually, and why it mustn't be a god itself but if you don't keep an eye on it you go down the tube,' he said.

'I know what you mean. Money itself is not important at all, but in order to make it and to get the life you want you have to pretend that it is for a while, just so as to keep it rolling on in.' Her face looked hard for a moment.

Tom said no more on the subject. He gathered up his notes to leave. When he took his coffee cup into the kitchen he saw ingredients for a lunch set out there. 'Have you a busy day?' he asked.

'A friend to lunch,' she said briskly. 'Which reminds me, find a few canapés that freeze well and give them to me, then I can talk you up all round the place.'

'Of course, but why don't you let us *do* a lunch for you, any time, it's the very least we can do.'

'I know, Tom, so Cathy already said. You're both sweet, but the kind of guys I entertain like to think that I cooked everything for them with my own fair hands.'

Shona Burke was getting out of her little car, and she called out to him as he left. 'Do you have your brother's phone number in London?' she asked.

'No, not you too. What do you all see in him?' he groaned.

'Purely business,' she said. 'Anyway, you're much better-looking than he is. They're doing a young people's promotion in Haywards in late spring, and he told me that he might just have a line of what he called fun clothes. Swimwear, lingerie, you know.'

'Sorry, Shona.' He took out a Scarlet Feather card and looked up Joe's London phone number for her in his diary.

'You don't know it?'

'Hey, no, I've no memory for numbers,' he said.

She nodded.

For some reason Tom said, 'Anyway, I don't call him that much or he me, I don't know why it is. Have you got sisters and brothers?'

Shona hesitated. 'Well, yes, in a way I do.'

It was an odd response but Tom let it go. Some people hated to be interrogated about their families; Marcella did. Her mother was dead and her father, who had married again, just wasn't interested, she said, and wanted it left like that. Cathy, on the other hand, had something to say every day about her parents: she loved Lizzie and Muttie, in spite of her mother's humble, grateful attitude to life. Cathy would also go on about her mother-in-law Hannah's innate viciousness, and about the sisters and brothers in Chicago, particularly Marian, the eldest, who had done well in banking but poorly in her love life until recently, and was now going to marry a man called Harry who looked like a film star. And look at his own brother Joe, who had not a family bone in his body. Tom got into his van waving her goodbye. She stood there taking no notice of the light rain that had begun to fall, not covering up her hair as most women would, still looking oddly lonely and vulnerable. She was a handsome girl, not strictly beautiful. Marcella always said that Shona Burke could look much better than she did if she wore more make-up and got her hair changed from that old-fashioned style. Her hair did look dull and flat. But she had a lovely smile. He wondered for a moment if *she* had been Joe's companion back in the hotel after the party. Why not? They were both free. She didn't have to tell anyone about it. Then he pulled himself together. He must stop speculating like this. She was saying something; he opened the van window to hear properly.

'I was only saying that you're very restful, Tom, a peaceable, handsome person,' Shona said.

'Not a word about the killer instinct that's going to make me a force in the land?' he called.

'Oh, that goes without saying.' She laughed.

Marcella came home from Haywards beauty salon the following evening and told Tom amazing news. This woman had come in to book a hairdo, manicure, a facial, the works, and said she was going to a drop-dead-cert smart christening party on Saturday, and she had actually said there were going to be fancy caterers at it. Tom could hardly believe it. Already people were talking about them and they hadn't even got properly started! He couldn't wait to ring Cathy. But tonight she and Neil were taking those children to see their mother in some drying-out place. He would tell her tomorrow.

'Will we celebrate?' he asked Marcella.

'Ah love, I'm just off to the gym,' she said.

'Couldn't you ... Just for one night ... To raise a glass to posh people in Haywards referring to us as fancy caterers?'

'Tom, we *agreed*. The subscription costs so much, the only way to make sense out of it and get any value is for me to go every day.'

'Sure,' he said, then knew he must sound a little warmer. 'You're absolutely right,' he said. 'And as soon as we really are a fancy caterers, then you'll come to every classy, fancy thing we do as a guest and get yourself photographed all over the place.'

'It will happen that you'll be a great big success ... you do know that, don't you?' she said, and he thought he saw tears in her eyes. 'I'm not just saying that ... you really know.'

'I know.' He *did* know. She had wanted the best for them from the start. 'Of course I know,' he said, and he held her close to him before she went to pack her leotards, trainers and body lotion. Tom looked out of the window until she waved up at him from the gates of Stoneyfield, as she always did. He wondered had she any idea how beautiful and endearing she was already, without having to punish herself with all this ruthless regime.

Ricky rang. He had the pictures they needed, six black and white arty studies of food which they were going to put up in the premises. He could bring them around tomorrow if the picture rail was up, and did Tom want the measurements. Tom did, and he got his paper and pencil.

'I was going to give them to you tonight at the do, but I figure it makes us look idiotic talking work at a party,' Ricky explained.

'Party?'

'Yeah, you know, the new club?'

'No, I never heard about it.'

'Well I told Marcella, she said you'd both be there.' Ricky was puzzled. Tom could feel his heart beating faster.

'Misunderstanding of some sort,' he mumbled.

'Sure. Now they're all portrait-format. I'll give you the top-to-bottom measurements first, then the side-to-side. Your father's getting a rail made, isn't he?'

Ricky went on and on with his specifications and Tom wrote down lists of numbers of centimetres on his pad, but his mind was on autopilot. He could not believe that she had just left pretending to go to the gym, and was in fact heading off to something without him. And how would she account for her late arrival home? He felt such a shock at the betrayal that he could hardly hear Ricky's words.

'Right, I'd better go and put on my going-out gear. Crazy idea having a party at this time. No one's properly awake yet. See you over at the HQ tomorrow, okay.'

'Okay Ricky, thank you a million times,' Tom Feather said to the cheerful photographer who had just broken his heart.

*

He needed to give his father the measurements. The pictures were to be suspended from a pole that would have grooves cut in it at a specific number of centimetres apart, and JT had been asking when anyone would inform him of what he had to do, so that it would not be yet another botched job. With fingers that seemed the weight of lead he dialled his parents' number, realising that first he must cheer him up before his father would agree to write down the measurements. Please may it be his da – he couldn't go through the whole cheering-up process twice if he got his mother.

But it was neither of them. It was a woman with a bark that nearly lifted him off the phone.

'Yes,' the voice said.

'Sorry,' Tom began, 'I've got the wrong number. I was looking for the Feathers.'

'This is the Feathers. Who's that?'

'Tom, their son.'

'Great bloody son you are, wouldn't you think you'd have left your number beside the phone for them?'

'But they *know* my number,' Tom cried, stung by the injustice of this.

'They don't know it now,' shouted the woman.

'What's happened. . . ?' This was a new kind of fear. Tom could hear voices in the background. Something must have happened. Eventually, and only when he had assured her that his phone number was at the top of a list in a plastic-covered notebook which for some reason his mother kept in the kitchen drawer, did the woman with the barking voice agree to tell him what was going on, and he learned that his father had chest pains and his mother had run out into the street to get help. Almost all the neighbours in the small street had come into Fatima, and someone had gone to the hospital when the ambulance came, and others had stayed making tea with poor Maura, who wasn't herself at all and couldn't cope with what was happening.

'Can I talk to her?'

'Why don't you just *get* yourself there?' said the woman with the unpleasant voice. Which made sense. He wished he had been nicer to his father, less impatient. Tom grabbed up his car keys and coat. He paused for a moment to consider writing a note. He and Marcella often communicated by letters left to each other on the table. But he didn't want to tell her about his father. And moreover, he couldn't forgive her for lying to him. And he knew she had. She had looked too excited going out to the gym, she smelled too well, there had been tears in her eyes over something. But then, she must not think he had run away either. 'My father's not well, gone to see him, hope you enjoyed the party,' he wrote. That would show her. He drove to the hospital.

Unless his father had another heart attack tonight the prognosis was fairly good, they told him in Intensive Care. Competent, calm young men and women his own age who knew about valves and arteries. A nurse asked him gently if he would perhaps like to take a seat outside. Tom realised that he must have been standing right in everyone's way.

'He's resting now, he's fine.'

'I know. Thank you,' Tom smiled.

She smiled straight back at him, a big, open smile. She was a square, freckled girl with a country accent and slightly messy hair. Tom recognised the look she gave him; it was the kind of look that almost every woman in Ireland gave his brother Joe. Interested, aware and slightly fancying. He looked back at her with a hollow heart. A perfectly nice girl, with a white cardigan over her uniform. But of course he could not fancy a woman like that in a million years. Compared to his Marcella, this girl was like something from a different planet. A totally separate species. He went out into the cold night to get some fresh air and telephoned his mother on his mobile.

'He looks fine, Mam.'

'What do you mean, he looks fine? Didn't I see him with my own two eyes clutching his chest, fighting for his breath?'

'But he's sedated now, Mam, he's breathing normally.'

She gave a whimpering sound and he heard her neighbours comforting her.

'I'll ring you in an hour.'

'Why?' she wanted to know.

'Just to tell you that he's still fine.'

'He's finished, Tom, you know he is. He shouldn't be up ladders at his age, he was just desperate to get that place right for you.'

'It has nothing to do with being up ladders, they said. It's looking good, everyone says that here.'

'Oh, so you know all about medicine, a boy who wouldn't even stay on in Sixth Year. Someone who couldn't go into business with his own father to help him out. You suddenly know what's causing heart attacks, do you?'

'Mam, I'll ring you back.'

It was freezing out here, but it was better than the heat and noise and medical smells of the hospital. He went to a bicycle shed and sheltered there against the wind, huddled in the corner and willed his father to get well. And when he *was* well, he would talk to his father man to man, and not leave until the conversation had gone somewhere beyond a series of shrugs. He would from now on insist that his parents came up regularly to Stoneyfield to visit them. He would cook things *they* liked, roast chicken, shepherd's pie. He would beg Marcella to talk to them about things that would interest them. Marcella. He remembered with a shock. He stood and watched people arrive and leave in their cars from the big ugly-looking concrete car park. What a hideous place. But to be fair, if money were to be spent on hospitals he would prefer it spent on machinery that would monitor his father's heart than on attractive landscaping for the grounds. He saw someone very like Shona Burke locking a car and then walking purposefully towards reception wearing a raincoat and carrying a shoulder bag. It was Shona. He moved forward to talk to her, then he moved back. He didn't want to tell her about his father before he knew what there was to tell. Also, he didn't want her to ask about Marcella. It would be normal for someone's live-in girlfriend to be there when there was a question that his father might die. But then, what was normal with Marcella? But Shona had seen him and called out.

'You look shivery, Tom.'

'I know, but still it's too hot inside there.'

'Oh, don't I know all about it, I come here quite a lot...'

'I'm sorry, is it...?'

'It's all right, Tom.' She spoke gently, letting him know that there would be no discussion on who she was visiting. 'But still, you look badly. Come on inside for a bit.'

'Right.' He walked in beside her.

At first, neither of them asked each other. Then she turned to him.

'Is it something bad?'

'I don't know. My father, chest pains, angina. It all depends on tonight – if he makes it through till tomorrow he'll have a great chance.'

'Poor Tom, when did it happen?'

'I just heard about it over an hour ago. All hell broke loose; my mother is so upset I think she should be in the next bed to him.'

'You mean you've only just heard?' Shona asked.

'Yes, it hasn't quite sunk in.'

'That means Marcella doesn't know yet, does she?'

'No,' his voice was flat.

'Oh, poor Marcella. I offered to drive her home from the gym but she said no, she was getting a bus, buying you a potted plant as a surprise.'

In front of everyone in the reception area, Tom Feather kissed Shona Burke and gave a whoop of delight. 'She was at the gym?' he cried. 'Tonight?'

'But you *know* that, Tom, she told me you wanted her to stay at home and celebrate that people were saying you're classy caterers.'

He drove home so fast he was amazed that there wasn't a police siren following him the whole way. He let himself in the door and she was sitting there at the table, a big fern in a pot beside her.

'Marcella!' he said.

'How is your father?' Her voice was icy.

'He'll be fine, it's all under control . . . You were at the gym?'

'As I told you I was going to be.' Her face was like a mask.

'Marcella, if you knew . . . you see, I thought . . .'

'What did you think, Tom?'

'I supposed you'd gone to a party, to a club . . .'

She put her head on one side as if asking a question.

'You see, Ricky said he'd asked you.'

'He did, yes. But I didn't want to go, because you're too busy and too tired, and I knew you'd hate it, so I went to the gym as I told you I was going to do.'

He couldn't stop the tears that came to his eyes.

'I'm so sorry. You see, I didn't think . . . I didn't think you could love me enough to give up something like that for me.'

'I did, yes of course I did.' Her voice was very level; she did not appear to see how upset he was.

'You do love me, I know it now.'

'No, Tom. I said I did, not I do.'

'It hasn't changed. Surely?'

She picked up the note and passed it to him. 'You are the most bitter, mistrustful man I ever met. How could anyone love you?' She stood up and went to the bedroom.

'Marcella, you're not leaving.' He was ashen-faced now.

'If you imagine that I could stay a night here with you when you think I'm a liar.'

He stood at the bedroom door looking at her.

She had taken off her clothes, and reached for one of those micro-skirts he hated her to wear. She picked dark tights from the drawer and moved towards the bathroom.

'Where will you stay?'

'I have friends. I'll find somewhere to stay.'

'Please, Marcella.'

She phoned a taxi to pick her up and then closed the bathroom door. Later, when she heard the doorbell ring, she came out.

'I am so sorry,' he said.

'So you should be, Tom, seriously sorry, because I have *always* told you the truth, and if you think it's possible to lie to anyone you love, then you're in deep trouble.'

And she was gone. Eventually the phone rang. It was his mother.

'You said you'd ring in an hour, I had to ring the hospital myself.'

'Is he all right, Mam?'

'A fat lot you care, Tom.'

'Mam, please.'

'He is for the moment. Tom, what will we do if he dies?'

'I'm coming round to Fatima, Mam,' he said.

Before he left he had two things to do. He rang his brother Joe in Ealing. He got an answering machine.

'Joe, this is Tom. Dad's had a coronary. I'll give you the number of the hospital. All you need to do is say you're his son and they'll tell you what's to be told. I hope you'll do something, Joe, but it's your life, not my life, so I'll just leave it at this.'

Then he sat down to write a note to leave on their table.

'I hope and pray you come back, and if you do, darling, darling Marcella, just know that I didn't know the meaning of love before I met you, and that I can't see much point in life without your love.'

Tom kept his mobile phone on all night, and not long after dawn he stopped at another builder's yard to make the pole with the notches to hang the pictures on, and drove to the premises. Cathy was there already.

'What does the other fellow look like?' she asked.

'What?'

'It's a joke, it's what you say to somebody who's been in a fight. You hope that someone else came off worse.'

He looked at her blankly.

'God, Tom, it was a joke. You're worse than Simon and Maud. Were you on the whiskey or something?'

'No, I've been up all night with my father. He had a coronary and Marcella has left me.' He said it in a very strange tone, as if he were just recounting two unimportant events.

Cathy looked at him, exasperated. 'What really happened, Tom?'

She was both kind and unbelieving at the same time. Tom was about to lose it, to break down and sob helplessly with his head on the table, when Ricky arrived with the pictures.

'Jesus but did you miss a wild night,' Ricky said, holding his head. 'You were the very wise one not to come along to that particular party, my friend.'

'That's me, Mr Wise Guy,' said Tom Feather sadly taking out the pole that his father had not been able to do because he had gone into heart failure before he got the measurements.

'You're nearly over twenty-four hours, Dad, so that means you're going to be fine,' Tom said to his father the next afternoon.

'If you knew what it was like, Tom, it was like two hands squeezing your ribs.' His father looked a lot better today. 'They tell me you were here all night?'

'Where else would I be?'

'But Marcella, you know?'

'She sent you her love, Da.'

'I know she did, and she's a grand girl, I heard from one of the nurses that the pair of you were hugging and kissing in the hall when you heard I was going to be all right, I'll never forget that.'

Tom looked at him blankly.

'Oh, that nice girl Catherine, she said she was very disappointed to know you had a ladyfriend. She was on duty and she told me everything.'

His father was patting his hand and Tom smiled at him. The nurse in the cardigan had seen him kissing Shona Burke when he had discovered that Marcella had really been to the gym.

The christening was what Cathy said should be called The Function from Hell. They had been asked to cater for fifty, but they could see as the room filled up that there were at least seventy people there. They hadn't cleaned the kitchen properly so Cathy, June and Tom had to spend the first twenty minutes wiping surfaces and putting down a disinfectant. When they opened the kitchen windows to let out the medicinal smell the baby's father came in and said the whole place stank like a urinal. When they tried to set up the buffet, the two small dogs of the house began a game of pulling the tablecloths.

'People who don't like animals are really not my kind of people,' said the baby's mother, who was three gins in before they had left for the church.

The ceremony had been forty minutes shorter than Cathy and Tom were told, so their bar wasn't ready.

'I was told you were top-drawer,' said the baby's father. 'We're in business just as you are, and we don't pay for what we don't get.'

They had ordered kedgeree served from a hotplate as a starter. It was a good choice, but before it got under way, the baby's mother began telling everyone, 'Don't bother eating all this rice and fish stuff, they have a proper roast coming later.' So a lot of people obediently put down their half-finished starters. Tom and Cathy looked at each other, wild-eyed, in the kitchen. Their only hope was that people would stock up on the kedgeree. Now they were waiting for the miracle of the loaves and the fishes.

'What in the name of God will we do?' Cathy asked him.

'Get them drunk,' Tom suggested.

'It's not fair on them, it means they will have to pay for all that extra wine.'

'What's fair, Cathy, tell me, what's fair about anything? What's fair about my father who worked hard all his life lying in hospital? What's fair about you having those kids that don't belong to you, ballsing up your life and your parents' lives? What's fair about that guy that Neil was trying to save being thrown out of Ireland? And what is fair about these two beauties telling us they were having fifty people when they have seventy-five? Get them drunk, I say.'

And they did. Spectacularly.

Before they started on their mission, Cathy Scarlet approached the baby's father firmly.

'Can I suggest something? Your guests seem to be enjoying themselves enormously, and you have chosen some particularly good wine.'

'Yes, yes, what?'

'And in case there's any doubt about the wine you would like us to serve, can I ask you to sign permission to bring out more?'

'We thought a half-bottle a person?' He was a small, fat man with small, piggy eyes.

'Yes indeed, that is what we suggested, but it's all going so well here, we would like your permission to bring out—'

'Do what you want.'

'And is it all to your satisfaction so far?'

'Yes, it's okay . . . just keep getting the drink round.'

'Thank you. You are a wonderful host,' Cathy said through tightly clenched teeth.

Nobody had ever told them it was going to be like this. Tom eased his way through the crowds of guests, smiling and telling them that the kedgeree was delicious.

'You're pretty delicious yourself,' said a woman with chocolate smeared over her face. She looked silly, and was about to become sillier. Tom thanked her for the compliment.

'You've got such a lovely dress,' he said. 'Is it from Haywards designer room?'

'Yes, it is.' She was stupidly flattered.

'Come here to the mirror, you've got some kind of mark on your face.' He offered her a tissue, and she looked at herself. Then, appalled at the reflection, she wiped the smears away hastily.

'That was nice of you to do that,' Cathy said.

'Come on, Cathy, it's only those clowns giving the party who are the villains here. I wish I knew where I saw that guy before, he really annoys me. The poor eejit with the Walt Disney designs on her face isn't doing anyone any harm.'

'No, you're right. God Almighty, there's more of them arriving at the hall door. They'll be eating the wallpaper.'

'What does he do for a living? I've met him somewhere, I *know* I have.'

'Probably some bar we worked in once. Listen, give June a hand over there. I'll ring my father and get him to provide taxis.'

'Muttie? Taxis?'

'Have we time to start looking up taxis at this stage? Half the people my father bets with drive taxis.'

'You're brilliant, Cathy! Maybe there's something we can salvage from this after all. Listen, am I going mad or something, or is that man Riordan looking at me as if he's fallen in love with me or something?'

'Well you don't realise it, but you are quite good-looking. Why shouldn't Mr Riordan try his chances like everyone else?'

'Excuse me?'

'Yes, Mr Riordan?'

'Don't we know each other?'

'Well, Mr Riordan, I'm the caterer . . .'

'Stop pissing about, we met at a party a couple of months ago, New Year's Eve . . .'

'Oh, yes?' Tom wasn't really listening, he was watching the room, seeing where he was needed.

'I remember now. I just wanted to say that this sort of thing rarely happens, it was the drink, I felt very odd after it. I think they deliberately mixed the drinks there. Some photographer fellow, very irresponsible of him.'

Then Tom remembered him. He was the man who had been pawing Marcella at Ricky's party.

'Oh, yes, yes indeed, Mr Riordan, of course I remember you.'

'You did from the beginning,' Larry Riordan said.

'No, not until this minute.'

'Come on, you've had a load of attitude since you came in the door, you knew you had one over me.'

'I knew you had made a mistake about the number of guests you had invited. I didn't realise until now you were the happily married man I met on New Year's Eve,' Tom said. He seemed to grow taller and broader as he spoke. Larry Riordan shrank in front of him.

'The whole thing was a total misunderstanding, of course . . . due entirely . . .'

'We know what it was due to, Mr Riordan.'

'What I wanted to say was that if there was any offence . . .'

'Oh, there was great offence at the time.'

'But not now, I hope.'

'Now I shall continue to do this job professionally for you and your wife, with whom I have no quarrel. Despite the fact that you told us there would be fifty people and there are over seventy in the house.'

'That was also a misunderstanding.'

'There *have* been a lot of them . . . I *was* going to ask your wife . . .'

'No need to ask her anything. Just ask me.'

'Relax, Mr Riordan, I was only going to ask her did she think we should arrange some taxis for later; many of your guests will have to leave their cars behind.'

'Do whatever you like,' said the host, loosening his collar. 'But believe me, that was all totally out of order, that incident, and I hope it had no repercussions. I mean, that everything is all right in so far as . . .'

'Everything is fine, Mr Riordan.'

'Very fine, beautiful young lady . . . I apologise again.'

'Thank you, now if you'll excuse me there are quite a lot of people need attention.' Tom moved away. This man would never know that Marcella had left him.

Cathy had busily recycled the kedgeree, adding mushrooms and chopped potatoes. She told Tom that she knew all that crowd would need it later as blotting paper, and they certainly did. They gave everyone in sight their business card, and tidied the house to within an inch of its life. When those people woke up next morning, they would find their place looking immaculate. They would find one cold bottle of champagne and a carton of orange juice in their fridge. They lined the bottles up in the back garden in ranks like soldiers, so that there would be no dispute about the number ordered and drunk, and said they would collect them the following day when they called in the afternoon to present the account. Muttie had sent five taxi-driver friends to the scene. They did a shuttle service all evening, and were well rewarded for their efforts. Tom and Cathy paid June an extra three hours, and her taxi home, before they got back to number seven Waterview.

'Come in,' Cathy said.

'No, it's late, Neil will be . . .'

'Neil'll be one of three things: out, asleep or happy to pour us a drink,' Cathy said, and they went up the stairs.

Neil was sitting at his big table with papers all around. 'Oh, good, Cathy I . . .' Then he saw Tom, and momentarily his guard fell.

'Oh, Tom,' he said, disappointed and then recovered quickly. 'How was the function? Come and tell me.'

'No, honestly Neil, it's late.'

'Come in now that you're here.'

He got three beers and they sat down.

'Tell me all about it,' Neil asked politely. His heart wasn't in it; Tom gave the briefest of descriptions and drained his beer. Before he could leave there was a tap on the door.

'Are you drunk?' Simon asked with interest.

'Not yet,' Tom said.

'Where's Marcella?' Maud wanted to know.

'Not here,' said Cathy.'

'Should I not have asked? I was just being interested, as you said I should.' Maud was confused.

'No problems.' Cathy was tight-lipped.

There was a silence.

'Would you prefer us to go back to bed now?' Simon enquired.

'Yes. It is the middle of the night, actually,' Cathy said.

Maud and Simon departed swiftly, detecting a hint of steel somewhere.

Tom let himself into the van and drove home through the dark, empty streets. Those two really worked hard – few other couples were still earning a living at this time of the morning. And it couldn't be easy for Neil having those odd, awkward children there half the time. And your wife out all hours working as well. Cathy had been wonderful. She had asked everything about his father and nothing at all about Marcella, who had left him, had refused to accept his calls into Haywards and had not even come back to collect her clothes.

'Is there anything wrong, Neil?' Cathy said. 'Your mind was a million miles away when we were telling you about the party.'

'Sorry,' he said, 'but honestly, those children, I couldn't do a thing all night. They kept coming in, asking about this and that. Homework, and where they should do their washing.'

'Well that's an advance, when they first came they just threw it on the floor.'

'They can't keep coming here. We'll have to increase what Muttie and Lizzie get.'

'They don't do it for the money, we agreed to give them a bit of a break.'

'But who is giving *us* a break? There's so much to do and discuss, and we haven't one minute to talk.'

'Okay, we have a minute now.'

'No real time.'

'Well, okay, I'm happy to talk now, it's kind of unwinding, but if you're tired . . .'

'There's this job . . .'

'The big case next week. . . ?'

'No, not a case. A job. I could . . . Now, it's not definite but I hear that I *could* be offered this amazing position . . .'

She looked at him open-mouthed as he told her about a committee that worked in connection with the UN Commission for Refugees.

'Now it's not an actual UN appointment, it's part of a group under the umbrella . . .'

She interrupted him. 'Sorry, I don't understand. Are you trying to tell me that you would consider taking a job abroad now?'

'Not immediately.'

'When then?'

'In about five or six months, I imagine. That's if it comes to anything, but it's only fair to tell you about it now.'

'Is this a joke?'

'No, I was amazed when I heard it myself. Usually you'd have to have much more experience, but they think that—'

'You're not asking me to throw up everything and follow you out to Africa because you got a *job* out of the blue?'

'It's not necessarily Africa. It could be Geneva, Strasbourg, Brussels.'

'You *have* a job. You're a barrister, that's your job. Defending people, rescuing them, representing them. That's your job.'

'But this is something—'

'That was never on the cards, Neil, never part of any plan.'

'You don't know anything about it yet. And you'd love it, you've never had a chance to travel.'

'Oh, but I have travelled. To Greece, didn't I, where I met you.'

'But that was only a holiday.'

'It may have been a holiday for you. It was a job for me. I was cooking in that villa.'

'Oh, but honey, that was only a Mickey Mouse summer job as a chalet girl,' he said.

Her face hardened. 'But I don't have a Mickey Mouse job now, I have a company,' she said.

'Yes, but you can't expect to think—'

'Think what?' she asked.

'It's not the right time to talk now, it's too late.' He stood up.

'One sentence isn't finished. You said I can't expect to think . . .' She looked up at him.

'Please, this is how fights start.'

'No, leaving sentences unfinished is how they start.'

'I didn't know how it was going to end,' he said, anxious to be out of it all.

'Well, will I finish it for you?' She sounded calm, too calm.

'No fights, Cathy.'

'Absolutely not. I think we'll end it like this: we can't expect to think that you'd ask me to give up my whole life's work and dream any more than I would ever expect you to. Was it something like that?'

'It needs a lot more thought and discussion,' he said.

'You're right,' she said, and they went to bed, where they slept so far from each other that not even a toe touched, and Cathy pretended to be asleep when he left Waterview early next morning having totally ignored his promise to take the twins to school.

At the premises Tom was in better humour – his father was definitely on the mend. His mother had apologised for her somewhat hasty words; it had been the shock. The Riordans sent a message that the account was all in order and the bill for the christening would be paid in full this afternoon. There had been a note from Marcella saying that Shona had told her of Mr Feather's heart attack, and she sent her sympathy and hoped that he was getting on well. All that news was good. The bad news was that Marcella had asked him please not to get in touch for the time being. There had been no word of response from Joe Feather, whose father could well have died and been buried. And when Tom told James Byrne that Mr Riordan, the baby's father, wanted to pay for the christening in cash, the accountant was not happy.

'Not good to hear,' James Byrne said crisply.

'I know this, James, but what do we do?'

'We present an invoice for *our* records, and receipt it when we get the money.'

'But suppose . . .'

'You're paying for my advice, so don't suppose,' James said.

'Mr and Mrs Riordan, I hope it was all to your satisfaction.'

'They loved it,' said the wife.

'Full of praise,' echoed her husband.

Tom didn't milk it, he did not want to make the man squirm any more.

'Our accountant actually prefers us to be paid by cheque.'

'Sure, it's sometimes that people like cash to avoid the tax,' said Larry Riordan.

'Which we wouldn't want to do.' Tom never lowered his gaze.

'No, of course.'

'Will we all go into the other room while I get my chequebook,' Larry Riordan suggested. He was obviously terrified to leave Tom alone for a moment, in case he began to tell tales.

Tom took out his calculator and his invoice book. 'The wine is all accounted for, the taxis and extras paid. It's just a small matter of . . . Are you sure you had the numbers right? You see, our waitress kept counting the plates and—'

'My wife says there was a mistake. She thinks we were well over fifty, actually.'

'How well over?' Tom's eyes were cold.

'Nearer to eighty, she thought.'

'Perfect,' said Tom, and signed a receipt for them.

Back in Stoneyfield he put on the Lou Reed record he loved because it showed other people had lives as confused as his own. There was a ring at the door. He answered it, and it was Marcella.

'You have a key,' he said quietly through the intercom.

'I wouldn't use it unless . . .' Her voice faltered.

'Unless what, Marcella?' He was still very quiet.

'Unless you wanted me to come in and talk.' He pressed the buzzer. But she didn't come in. 'I mean, really talk,' she insisted.

'Well, I've been just waiting for you all those days, hours, minutes, seconds, however long it's been,' he said.

'You know I know, come on, we both know how very, very long it's been,' she said simply.

'So, Marcella, are you going to come up here to me, or what?' He hardly dared to hope.

'Tom, I wanted to know how the christening went, and to tell you that I do know you love me, and that we both made silly mistakes along the way.' There was a silence. 'Would that let me come home, do you think?' He knew she was crying, and he didn't care if she knew that he was crying too as he ran down the stairs to bring her back home.

Next morning there was a call from the woman at the party whose face Tom had rescued. She said that she wanted to thank them for their courtesy and splendid food, and to book them for a silver wedding party weeks ahead. Geraldine booked them a lunch for a group of estate agents who wanted to get into the villa market, and would like a buffet with a Spanish theme. The hospital called to say that Tom's father was now well on the mend, and that Mr JT Feather would be going home today. There was a message from Joe in Manila saying that somebody had eventually caught up with him with the news about their father, and could someone now fax him back since he had to be in the Philippines for another two weeks. James Byrne left in a note confirming the date of his cookery lesson, and saying that he always paid in advance and always by cheque, being someone who disapproved strongly of the black economy. Cathy got an e-mail from her sister Marian in Chicago, asking Scarlet Feather to cater for a lavish Dublin wedding in August. The theatre wrote to say that there just *might* be another gig. Apparently everyone had been very pleased with the last one, they said with some surprise. They were sure Tom could oblige again. Cathy had received a letter from Hannah Mitchell marked 'personal', in which her mother-in-law had suggested a little lunch in Quentin's to clear up any outstanding difficulties. And when Cathy rang Tom to tell him this last and most amazing of all the amazing pieces of information that day, the phone was answered by Marcella.

'Oh, Tom, you were so right to be optimistic. You just kept us all afloat. I'm so happy for you, so very happy,' Cathy said with a lump in her throat when Marcella passed the phone to him.

'I *know* you are,' he said, and he smiled at Marcella as he said it.

Chapter Three

MARCH

Cathy was early at Quentin's.

'Coming to steal our ideas?' Brenda Brennan asked.

Both Cathy and Tom had worked as waiters and in the kitchen here, in what was often described as Dublin's best restaurant.

'Oh, we've stolen all those already,' Cathy admitted cheerfully. 'Those little tomato and basil tarts go down a treat.'

Brenda smiled, she had little to worry about in the way of competition from home caterers. People came to Quentin's for the atmosphere as well as the food.

'Where will I put you, Cathy?' she asked.

'Where does my mother-in-law like to sit?'

'Nowhere very much, hard lady to please.' Brenda Brennan knew the score.

'Don't start me off, I'm trying to be nice today,' Cathy pleaded.

They chose the table least likely to annoy Hannah, and Cathy sat down to wait. She had told nobody about the meeting, not even Neil. They had an armed truce at home now, where normal conversation was carried on and meals were eaten, but the great thing that hung between them was only skirted around. They had agreed to give it a cooling-off period and then they would approach it in a saner way than at two-thirty a.m. in a small town house that was also home to Simon and Maud. Perhaps Hannah knew all about the job. But that was unlikely. She would wait until her mother-in-law showed her hand, and after all, the woman *had* put 'personal' on the envelope. Possibly Cathy's outburst had hit home, and Hannah really did want to apologise. If so then she should have the dignity to do so without thinking that there was an audience out there waiting to know the details. Perhaps it was about Maud and Simon? Apparently there had been some form of contact made with their father. Perhaps one of Hannah's friends might need a caterer? There had been some talk of Amanda coming back for a visit from Canada. Hannah might need a reconciliation just for appearances' sake? No point in speculating, Cathy told herself. She would know in just over an hour when the main-course dishes were cleared away, when they would both refuse dessert and ask for coffee.

In the private booth of Quentin's James Byrne sat with his guest, Martin Maguire. The great thing about this particular table was that you could see out while others found it difficult to peer in.

'Lean forward just a little, Martin, and you'll see her. That's Cathy Scarlet on her own over there.'

The other man looked in the direction he had been shown, and saw the fair-haired girl reading the *Irish Times*.

'She's very young,' he said in a low voice.

'They all are these days, Martin.'

'No, she's never able to run a business, too much stress and strain.'

'She's about twenty-six, that's not young by today's standards.'

'That's almost the same age as Frankie.'

James Byrne looked at the tablecloth, searching desperately for words. Eventually he just said, 'Frankie's at peace.'

'How do we know?' asked Frankie's father.

'Because God is good,' James Byrne suggested.

The Riordans, who had given the christening party, recognised Cathy also.

'Didn't think they were up to this kind of place,' sniffed Molly Riordan.

'Well they sure as hell know how to charge. Why wouldn't they be able to afford it here?' asked the husband, who was still anxious that Tom Feather might blow the whistle on him.

At that moment Hannah Mitchell came in, hair freshly done, new heather-coloured wool suit, carrying parcels in Haywards bags, fussing about her fur coat, wondering very oversolicitously if the table was all right for Cathy. And eventually sitting down.

'God, that's Jock Mitchell's wife, they *do* move in high circles,' said the husband, very surprised.

'I've always wanted to meet her. Hannah Mitchell runs these charity bridge dos. They're always photographed in the papers and magazines. I might just drop past the table later,' said the wife.

'Oh, leave it out ... They're nobodies, those caterers. We don't need an introduction *that* badly,' said the husband, who greatly feared ever having to meet Tom Feather ever again.

'Mrs Mitchell, Ms Scarlet,' Brenda greeted them in her calm, measured way.

'You *know* my daughter-in-law?' Hannah annoyed as always that she had not been able to make the introduction.

'It's always a pleasure to see both of you,' Brenda murmured as she left them the menus. She had not mentioned that Cathy had washed plates in the kitchen, served tables and was far better known in this establishment than the elegant Hannah would ever be. Mrs Mitchell was special only for habitually changing her table, sending food back or querying the bill. Cathy had carved for the entire restaurant the night that Patrick the chef had burned his hand. Cathy had found fifty pounds in the ladies' cloakroom and had managed to give it back to the woman who had left it there without letting her husband see. Cathy had been there the night the drains packed up. It was no contest as to who was the favourite customer.

'It is nice to have time to have a little chat like this,' Hannah Mitchell began.

'It's very kind of you, and a lovely break for me, certainly,' said Cathy, who had told herself twenty-five times already that there was no point in going to this lunch at all unless she remained calm and courteous. The shouting bit was over, the confrontation had taken place. She had not spoken to her mother-in-law for weeks until she had made the phone call to confirm this lunch date with her. She must listen now, listen and not react.

'Possibly you work too hard. You should have a few more breaks,' Hannah said.

'Possibly indeed.'

'So you agree you might be overworked, a little tense, ready to fly off the handle, then?'

Cathy saw now where her mother-in-law was coming from. She, Cathy, was going to be cast in the role of screaming neurotic, up to high doh over her little business, unable to control herself at functions. A-ha ... It was good to see the way the land lay.

'Funnily, Neil and I were saying this the other day, at our time of life we all have to work so hard running just to keep up, that by the time we get to your age and Mr Mitchell's, our life will be so much calmer.'

'You were saying that?'

'Yes. We were noting the way Mr Mitchell can spend so much time on the golf course, and you have all these hours to give to charity lunches. Our day, for all that, will come too.' Cathy smiled broadly.

Mrs Mitchell was put out. This was not the way she had intended the conversation to go. 'Yes dear, but don't you think you might be ... how shall I put this ... directing too much energy into one channel?'

Cathy looked at her, confused. 'One channel?' she asked.

'Well, this waitressing business.'

Cathy laughed aloud. 'Yes, that's what we call it too, like Simon and Maud. They *are* funny, aren't they. So solemn, and yet total babies at the same time.'

'I don't know what you mean.' Hannah was genuinely perplexed.

'I'm sorry, it's just that they call our catering company a waitressing business too because they don't understand ... I assumed you were quoting them.' Her eyes were hard and her voice harder still.

Hannah made a decision. 'Yes, of course I was,' she said.

'I knew you were, but to go back to your point, Mrs Mitchell, you're probably right. I am devoting a lot of energy to the new company, and so is Tom Feather, but that's natural. Once we get it off the ground we hope to relax a little more, have two or three nights properly off a week.'

'But my dear, that's ludicrous, isn't it? What about your life, your real life ... With Neil, for example.'

'Neil's working almost every night too, either at home or at some consultation. It's just the way things are.'

'I think it's just the way you've let things become, dear.'

Cathy remembered that tone. It was the way Mrs Mitchell had spoken to her mother. 'Sorry, Lizzie dear, I don't think we were terribly thorough cleaning the bath, were we?' Cathy had wanted to kill the woman then. The feeling was hardly less strong now. She crumbled some olive bread in her fingers and reduced the substance to a fine powder as she did so.

'Do explain what you mean, Mrs Mitchell.'

'It's just that I'm asking myself, *why* does Neil go out so much for work, why do you not have a social life, give dinner parties, go to clubs? I mean are *you* a member of *any* clubs, tell me? It's just, I worry when a young couple don't have a healthy social life. One begins to wonder why.'

'We both work fairly hard, and I think we can safely say that Neil cares hugely about his clients and about justice being done, so this naturally takes up a lot of his time. I think that must be it, don't you?'

'Well, yes, of course, of course, that goes without saying, it's just that I wondered, perhaps if you were to . . . Well if you were to try and . . .' She seemed to lose the words.

'If I were to what, Mrs Mitchell?' Cathy was genuinely interested now. What on earth was the woman going to suggest? That Cathy should learn some new and devastating sexual techniques, or give dinner parties twice a week inviting politicians and the media? She waited with interest.

'Well, that you should smarten yourself up a little.' Mrs Mitchell was diffident. But once she had said it she was sticking to it. 'It's just that possibly you've been so busy with work and everything . . . that you haven't had time to stop and take a good long look at yourself.'

Cathy did not know whether to feel humiliated or amused. It was so patronising for one woman to tell another that she needed to clean up her act. Yet this advice was being given by a woman aged sixty, with her hair scraped up into a style that was ten years out of date, squeezed into a wool suit one size too small, wearing a nail colour that had not been seen outside pantomime for decades. Hannah Mitchell whose hard, over-made-up face and mink coat made her a caricature, was daring to offer Cathy advice.

'And where do you think I should start?' she asked in a level voice.

'Well, your hair, of course, and to show you how much I really mean it I've got you a token for Haywards.' Mrs Mitchell pulled out an envelope.

'I can't possibly accept this,' Cathy began.

'But you *must*. I don't think I gave you a proper Christmas present, and let this be it. You did such a delightful job catering for our New Year's Eve party, a lot of people have spoken of it so well since. The very least I can do is start you off on some kind of makeover.'

Cathy stared glumly at the envelope.

'And do get your nails done at the same time, have nail extensions maybe, won't you? There's a good girl. If there's anything a man likes to see on a woman it's long, groomed nails.'

'You know, Mrs Mitchell, I'll certainly think about the hairdo but if you don't mind, I think I'll pass on the nails. You see in our job nail extensions would be a bit dangerous – we could lose them making pastry, for example.' Cathy tried to be light-hearted. It was the only alternative to doing what she really felt like doing, which was standing up and pushing over the dining table into her mother-in-law's lap.

'Well.' Mrs Mitchell sounded sad and disappointed, as someone who had done her best but failed in the end, thanks to Cathy's gross stupidity.

'But truly I am grateful for your kindness, Mrs Mitchell. And for this lunch.'

They had just put the fish in front of them, and Hannah was looking at it suspiciously. 'Is it properly filleted?' she asked the waiter.

'I hope so, madam. Very often a tiny bone escapes, but I think you will find great care has been taken.' Cathy winked at the waiter as Hannah peered at her plate. She knew him well from her nights working here. He kept a solemn face. Brenda Brennan ran a tight ship at Quentin's. He didn't want to be spotted mocking the customers.

James Byrne approached the table with an elderly man.

'Ms Scarlet, I wouldn't dream of interrupting you, but I hoped you might just meet Mr Martin Maguire, from whom you brought your premises. He is only in Dublin for a few hours.'

Cathy leaped up. 'I'm so pleased to meet you. Would you come round and meet Tom Feather there this afternoon? We'd love to show you how happily we've settled in, and excuse me, may I introduce Mrs Hannah Mitchell, who is taking me to lunch here?'

Hannah stared. She could never accustom herself to the fact that her maid's daughter introduced her with ease to two well-dressed men older than herself. Where had this confidence come from? Mr Maguire promised to come to the premises for coffee at four o'clock, and they were gone. Sensing the older woman's irritation, Cathy changed the subject.

'I must tell you that my sister Marian is getting married. Do you remember her at all from the old days?'

Hannah Mitchell's eyes narrowed as the old days were mentioned. 'No, your mother didn't bring any of the children except you.'

'Oh, Marian's the bossiest of us all.'

'Out in Chicago. That's where I think they went. I remember your mother saying.'

'They love it there. I've been out to visit. Have you been there at all, Mrs Mitchell?'

Before Hannah had time to shudder her disapproval of any city where Poor Lizzie's children had ended up, Cathy saw that they were being approached again, and to her horror she saw that it was the terrible couple who had given the nightmare christening party. Again she made the introductions, but this time Hannah Mitchell offered some information.

'I'm actually Cathy's mother-in-law,' she said. This was a personal first.

'And is er ... Tom ... your son, then?' Molly Riordan asked, gushing.

'Oh, no, no, not at all. My son is a lawyer, a barrister actually,' Hannah said.

They left eventually, the couple having given their card to Hannah and assured her of substantial sponsorship at the next charity do.

'Sorry about that,' Cathy apologised.

'No, I'm amazed. If your poor mother could see you here with these people ...'

'Mrs Mitchell, it's very, very good of you to take me to lunch here and to offer me this expensive hairdo, and I am touched and grateful, but can I ask you as a personal favour not to refer to my mother as my *poor* mother. She is far from poor, she is happy and content and has children and a husband who love her.'

'Yes, of course ... I only meant ...'

Cathy waited.

After a long time Hannah Mitchell said, 'I only meant she doesn't have your confidence.'

'Oh, confidence isn't everything, Mrs Mitchell.'

'It seems to get people quite far, though.' The mouth was narrow.

Cathy saw Geraldine being ushered to a nearby table with Peter Murphy, the managing director of the hotel where she did the public relations. Their eyes met, and Cathy gave a barely obvious shake of her head. Geraldine got the message and didn't acknowledge her. To be greeted by a third customer at Quentin's would put Cathy in an intolerable position. She had already shown her mother-in-law too much of this confidence thing. It was time to listen to the wisdom of having a regular facial and not let the muscles get saggy. Cathy listened, and wondered to herself as she had so often before how this empty, sad, envious woman and her pleasure-loving husband had given birth to Neil. Neil, who was at this moment fighting another no-hoper's case, Neil who would be mildly interested that she had met his mother for lunch but who would never understand in a million years how outrageous it was to be patronised like this. Cathy almost wished they could have gone back to the days of straightforward hostility. It was far easier to cope with.

Peter Murphy and Geraldine O'Connor saw them leave.

'God, isn't that a tiresome poor woman?' he said.

'She's pretty difficult as a mother-in-law, let me tell you,' Geraldine said.

'And how on earth would you know?' he asked.

'That's Cathy Scarlet, my niece, walking out the door with her. She has the bad luck to be in that role.'

'Yes, I *did* know that. She married the young lawyer, right?'

'*And* has set up a very good catering company I keep telling you about, which you keep telling me is of no interest to you.'

'No indeed, it is not of any interest only in so far as it's competition. She can't hate her mother-in-law so much if she's having lunch with her.'

'She does, believe me.'

'And why didn't you say hallo to them?'

'Cathy frowned at me not to,' Geraldine explained.

'I'll never understand women,' said Peter Murphy, who had nonetheless made considerable efforts to do so by having affairs with many of them. Including Geraldine, some years back. But that was all over now. Today they were just very good friends.

'I wish I hadn't agreed to go back to the old place,' Martin Maguire said to James Byrne as the two men strolled through Stephen's

Green and fed ducks with the bread given to them by Brenda Brennan as they left Quentin's.

'No, believe me it's a good idea. You'll remember it like this now, the way they have it all shiny, and different,' James reassured him. They watched in silence as a mother duck rounded up her ducklings for the new source of food.

'Look at that.' Martin Maguire was amazed. 'Look at the way they love their parents and trust them. It's not like that with humans.'

'Don't punish yourself. Please, Martin, there's no point.'

'There's not much point in anything. Are you sure you didn't tell them?'

'I told you I didn't.'

'They must have wondered why I was so eager to sell so quickly. They must have asked.'

'It's your story, your life, Martin. Of course I didn't tell them,' said James. 'Anyway, those two were so anxious to get their business up and running, they never asked. Believe me.'

'I can't go,' Martin Maguire said. 'It's as simple as that. Will you tell them, James?'

'Of course.' James Byrne nodded gravely.

'Imagine, she's their daughter-in-law and she's only got a real ordinary accent.' Molly Riordan was astounded.

'I could have told you that she wasn't married to that tall eejit Tom with the face like some kind of teenage idol,' said Larry, sounding aggrieved.

'I thought he was cute,' she said.

'Well I tell you, he's not going for a lady barrister. No, his line is a bit of stuff, believe me.'

'How on earth do you know?' Molly asked.

'I heard,' he nodded sagely.

Molly shrugged. 'Well, all our friends thought he was a doll. Why did you take such a dislike to him?'

The husband couldn't remember. Just one of those instant things, he thought.

Brenda Brennan was having a cup of coffee in the kitchen when lunch was over at Quentin's.

'Patrick, we should try and put a bit of work in Cathy and Tom's way, it's very hard at the start.'

'What do you suggest?' he asked.

'You know the way people often ask us to do funerals . . . and we can't get away so end up sending them over a dressed salmon.'

'You're right, next one we'll recommend them. Get them to give us a card.'

'They already have,' said Brenda.

Tom and Cathy had coffee and shortbread ready at four.

'What were you doing at Quentin's anyway?' Tom asked.

'Penance for all the many sins I committed in my life,' she said.

'What did you eat?'

'I can't remember. I was with Hannah.'

'Is there blood all over the place?'

'No, she just wanted to cut my hair,' said Cathy.

Tom found this increasingly puzzling. 'But she didn't?' he said eventually.

'She did.' Cathy tapped her handbag. 'She gave me a voucher for it, so I'll be in Marcella's domain one of these days. Tom, do I need my hair cut?'

'I don't know. Do *you* want to?'

'No, not particularly.'

'Then don't.' It was simple. Simple for men. Simple for anyone who hadn't taken Hannah Mitchell's money.

At that moment they heard James Byrne and Martin Maguire arriving.

'Remember, we must not sound as if we are too grateful or he'll take it back,' Cathy fussed.

'It's all signed and sealed, Cath, it's only a social call,' Tom whispered, and they opened the door. James Byrne was alone.

'I'm very sorry. He decided not to come after all, so I came along to give you his apologies.'

They were very disappointed. 'Whatever made him change his mind?' Cathy asked, and as soon as she spoke she knew that James Byrne would not tell her.

'I just said I'd tell you that he was sorry.' He looked sad himself.

'Well, maybe it was too soon for him; he might come another time,' Cathy said.

'He might indeed. He'll be glad to know that he didn't cause any fuss.'

James Byrne left.

'We'll never know,' Cathy said.

'Nobody'll ever know our secrets from him either,' Tom said.

'We don't *have* any secrets,' she laughed. 'Though actually I do. I'm going to give this hairdressing voucher to June.' She waved it gleefully.

'How much is it for?' asked Tom and when she showed him he pretended to reel around the premises. 'Do people really spend that much money on hair?' he asked.

'Apparently.' Cathy laughed.

'Marian was on again about the wedding entertainment,' Cathy said to her mother.

'They get terrible notions over there,' Lizzie said.

'No, it's dead easy. Nothing we can't provide: *Ave Maria* and *Panis Angelicus*.' Cathy was casual.

'It's amazing you even know the names of the hymns, it's so long since you darkened a church.'

'Stop it, Ma, I tell everyone how tolerant you are . . .'

'How tolerant I *have* to be,' sighed Lizzie.

'They want a pageboy and a flower girl, Mam. That's a bit of a poser.'

'Well they can't have them,' Cathy's mother said. 'Marian's going to have to be told, it's not all posh Chicago notions here, we don't have anyone that age in the family.'

'We have Maud and Simon,' Cathy said thoughtfully.

'Oh, no, that wouldn't do at all,' Cathy's mother said immediately.

'Why not?' Cathy asked. 'If they're still here, and it looks as if they will be, then wouldn't it be nice for them? Marian would love them.'

'Cathy, stop filling their heads with such nonsense, you know *she* wouldn't stand for it, not for a moment.'

'Well *she* has nothing to do with it, Mam. Let's discuss it with Maud and Simon. They loved Riverdance,' Cathy said.

'Everyone loved Riverdance, but they won't learn something like that and anyway, I told you. She wouldn't hear of it.'

'Mam, *she* is not important. Let's ask the kids.'

'They're not here,' Lizzie said.

'Of course they're here, Mam, they're always here, listening, spying, stealing food. That's what they do all day, isn't it?'

'That's not fair, Cathy, you sound as if you hate them, they're only children who didn't have a proper home.'

'No, I don't hate them. I've got to like them a bit more recently. But they still steal food. It's because they're not sure they'll get any more. *And* they listen at doors. Don't you, Maud?'

'I was just passing by,' said poor Maud, and Simon raised his eyes to heaven.

'Tom, it's June. Can I ask you something?'

'Anything, as long as it's not asking to cry off the next job.'

'No ... It's just ... is Cathy sound in the head? She's given me *the* most amazing token...'

'Take it, use it, splash out with it.'

'But won't she be sorry?'

'No, it was from Neil's mother. She doesn't like the lady, so go get the hair done, Junie baby.'

'I was thinking of very bright purple streaks, highlights, you know, but they have to be well done otherwise they look a mess.'

'Go for them June,' said Tom, and he hung up.

There was just so much time you could spend talking about hairdos.

'I'm not being a pageboy at *anyone's* wedding,' said Simon.

'I'd like to have been a flower girl. I don't think anyone else would have let us be part of anything,' Maud said.

'Lots of people at school are learning Irish dancing, of course,' Simon said. 'It would be a way to learn it free.'

'How do you mean, free?' Maud wondered.

'Well, Father and Mother aren't there to pay for anything any more,' Simon said sadly.

'But Muttie hasn't any money to pay for lessons,' Maud protested.

'How do you know that?'

'Well, he has holes in his shoes, he hasn't a car or a chequebook or anything,' Maud said.

'So we won't get dancing lessons then.'

'Would you like them, Simon?'

'I wouldn't mind,' he said.

'We'll just wait and see. Let's wait for them to start talking about it again.'

'It's a pity they knew we took food,' Maud said.

'We don't from Muttie and his wife Lizzie now, only from Neil and Cathy, and that's because we weren't sure,' Simon agreed.

'I know, and Cathy *did* say she likes us more now.' Maud was always hopeful.

'Only a *bit* more, that's all she said.' Simon was more watchful.

'And what on earth is this,' Muttie said when they came in and saw a huge lump of pastry in the centre of the kitchen table.

'It's Beef Wellington,' Simon explained.

'Is it now, and where did it come from?' Muttie asked.

'I think Cathy nicked it for us from people who paid her in her waitressing business,' Simon was helpful.

'Stand up, Simon, and leave the room,' Muttie said.

'What did I say, Muttie? You asked, I told you.'

'That's not the truth. My Cathy never nicked anything in her life, in fact the only people that ever nicked *anything* in this house are you two, nephew and niece of the famous Mrs Mitchell that Lizzie spent her life cleaning up after. Those are the only thieves we ever had here.'

'Please Muttie, it was only four sausages and a couple of packs of cornflakes just in case,' Simon said.

'In case what?'

'In case there would be no more,' said Simon, ashen-faced, as Maud sat with the tears trickling down her cheeks.

'I had lunch with Cathy today,' Hannah said to Jock.

'That was nice, dear.'

'It was actually, much nicer than I thought.'

'Good, good.'

'She knew absolutely everyone at Quentin's. Isn't it amazing, when you think of poor Lizzie.'

'But that was a different age, dear.'

'So it would appear,' she said.

'And what did she say about Neil's plans?'

'Plans? What plans?'

'No, no nothing dear, something else. You know my mind's always miles away.'

'Indeed it is,' Hannah said sadly.

'A quick yes or no: do you want the dancing lessons? Do you want to be part of this deal for Marian's wedding? Answer now,' Cathy said.

'It's a bit complicated,' Simon said.

'No it's not, it's very simple . . . It costs this number of pounds to get you taught three numbers to dance, it costs about twice that to pay real dancers to do it. But we thought you should make the choice.'

'Why?'

'Because you're family,' Cathy said simply.

'We're not really.'

'How often must I tell you, you live here in the house where Marian was born, you are the nephew and niece of my husband. Just a yes or no, and we'll go ahead and book the real people.'

'Will we be coming to the wedding anyway, you know, as guests,' Maud asked.

'Doubt it,' Cathy said.

'But you said we were family,' Simon wailed.

'Not all that close, come to think of it.'

'Why are you being so horrible, Cathy?' Simon asked.

'Because *you* are both horrible. You told my dad I nicked that Beef Wellington, which I did *not*. I made it specially for him to thank him for looking after you, because you make Neil's life a misery and he can't get on with his work and because you have no manners and I wish your mother and father would come and take you straight back to The Beeches. Now is that a good answer?'

Cathy's mother came in at that point. 'We'd all like Mr and Mrs Mitchell of The Beeches to be well in themselves and run their own home again, but until that point Simon and Maud are very welcome here,' she said looking around her, 'and I hope that everyone here knows that.'

'I'm sorry Mam,' Cathy said later.

'Sure you should be, taking it out on innocent children.'

'Lizzie?' Simon knocked at the kitchen door. This was another great improvement; up to now they had stormed in everywhere. 'Lizzie, we'd like to do the dancing please,' he asked.

'It might not be possible, child. *She* might not like it.'

'She doesn't know us yet,' Simon complained. 'She can't hate us already.'

'She surely can't take against us without meeting us,' Maud protested.

'No, we're not talking about Marian, Mam is talking about your aunt Hannah, aren't you, Mam?'

'Well I was, Cathy but not here, not like this, not in front of, can't you wait until. . . ?'

'It's all right,' Simon reassured her. 'We know all about Aunt Hannah, we know that Cathy hates her.'

'I don't any more,' Cathy said. 'I quite like her. I had lunch with her today, as it happens.'

'You never did.'

'I did indeed. We went to Quentin's.'

'But why?'

'Search me, Ma, but it had something to do with cutting my hair.'

'I wish you'd be serious for a moment.' Cathy's mother beckoned her out to the scullery to get away from the twins.

'Is there any word on the children?' she whispered.

'She never mentioned them once,' Cathy said cheerfully, well aware that Simon and Maud had crept towards the door to listen.

'But talking about Marian,' Cathy continued, 'I think in a way I'm glad she wants child dancers. She might well go for it, she seems to be having the full works from what I hear. Fireworks, jugglers, lions and tigers.'

The children's faces lit up. 'Tigers at the wedding! Isn't that *great*,' said Simon. Again Cathy remembered too late her resolution not to be ironic in front of the children.

'I had lunch with your mother today,' Cathy said that evening when she got into Waterview.

'Oh, good.' Neil didn't look up from his papers.

'Aren't you surprised?'

He was still reading a whole sheaf of something, but at her tone he looked up and kept his finger on the paper so that he wouldn't lose his place. 'What?' he asked.

'It's not a usual occurrence. I thought you'd wonder why.'

'Well, why then?'

'Don't know.' Cathy shrugged.

'Listen Cathy, you told me you had to work out a silver wedding menu and a Spanish buffet tonight, so I took all this stuff home . . .'

'What stuff? Is this about Africa?'

'No, of course not, I told you that all that about the job was on hold until we had time to talk about it seriously.'

'So?'

'So you said you were working, and I've two things to do here. I told them I'd get this paper together on a writer.'

'Sorry.'

'No, don't be like that.'

'I *am* sorry, you're quite right, I did say that . . .'

She meant it, she wasn't even sulking. They did tell each other in advance what their plans for the evening were. He was justified in being put out. Yet this was so huge a fact she had just told him, and he wasn't even mildly interested. His own mother, who had waged war on her for years, had invited her to Quentin's for God's sake. Neil had not even registered it.

'No, I'm sorry I was a bit short with you . . . It's not just the unfortunate Nigerian writer. There's another bloody complicated thing, and we'll be in court over it tomorrow. I'm for the tenant who broke his back on a faulty stairway, and the landlords will have a top team saying they did all the proper repairs. Problem is, my fellow talks and looks like a gangster, and the landlord is mild and articulate and concerned, so it's all stacked against my client. I have to look up and list all these decisions . . .'

Cathy held up her hands. She really was contrite. 'I'm going out, anyway. I just came in to leave the shopping. I'll be back in a couple of hours and we'll have supper.'

'You don't have to, honey,' he said.

'I do,' she said, and she was gone.

Cathy hadn't intended to go out, she had planned to have a long bath and then sit down and go through some files and cookery books to think up dishes in a leisurely way. She had even thought about making a paella to rehearse for the Spanish buffet, but she knew the mood was wrong. Neil would just think she was killing time waiting until he was free. Better to pretend to be busy and go out. But where?

She couldn't go to Tom's; he and Marcella were going to the theatre tonight, a possible photo opportunity for Marcella since it was a first night. Cathy drove to Glenstar apartments and dialled Geraldine on the mobile phone from the van. The answering machine was on. Stupid to have come all this way without ringing first, Cathy thought, and then by chance she looked up at her aunt's flat and saw the curtains being drawn. There were two figures in the room. Geraldine was entertaining someone. A man. She was just about to pull out of the parking bay when she saw someone waving. It was Shona Burke from Haywards.

'I saw your van . . . Well, who could miss it?' Shona laughed. 'Do you want to come in for coffee?'

Cathy looked around as Shona got out the coffee machine. Similar to her aunt's flat, but not nearly as big and totally different furnishings. A lot of brightly coloured rugs and embroidered cushions. There were no family pictures on the wall, two shelves of books on management and business, a small, neat music centre and no television set. Cathy wondered what kind of people Shona entertained here, and how she could afford the rent or the mortgage. These apartments were not cheap. Of course Shona had a very good job at Haywards. Still. Perhaps she came from rich people. Shona Burke would never tell. She was very adroit at taking the conversation away from herself.

'You're very far away,' Shona said coming back to join her.

'I was thinking about Maud and Simon,' Cathy lied.

'Who are they?'

'Neil's nephew and niece. We appear to have adopted them, my mother and I.' She laughed a little grimly and explained the background. To her surprise Shona didn't find any of it funny or endearing. Nor did she shrug at the hopeless inevitability of it all and praise them like other people did. She just listened, with no expression at all on her face.

'So that's it,' Cathy finished. 'Neil and his father got some kind of order, oh, I don't know exactly what, but it's about releasing money from trust funds, and some of that goes to my mam and dad, and I suppose some even comes to us if we need it.'

'And what about their social worker?'

'She's happy enough with the set-up, she knows they're well looked-after. The mother isn't getting any better, and the father isn't showing any signs of coming back home. We're holding the fort.'

'It's terribly unfair on the children,' Shona said.

'Life's unfair, Shona. Of course I'd prefer them to have a nice Mummy and a nice Daddy who knew who they were, and who read them bedtime stories and cared for them, but they don't, so we have to pick up the pieces.'

'And then they go back to hopeless Mummy and Daddy, and what then?' Shona asked.

'I wish I knew, but if I were Tom Feather I would say miracles happen, because he genuinely believes they do,' Cathy said wistfully.

Cathy drove home with a sense of depression that she couldn't quite shake off. She didn't know why it was there. She was not annoyed with Neil for being somewhat brisk with her – he was perfectly right, she *had* said she would be working. Her mother-in-law's crass criticisms hadn't the power to get beneath her skin any more, it wasn't that. Her own mother's craven humility was something Cathy had lived with for ever, this was nothing new. They had always *known* that Maud and Simon would have to go into care, that wasn't any great shock. Scarlet Feather was doing well these days, with lots of things booked ahead. Its books would look healthy enough at the end of this month to make James Byrne feel reasonably calm. Whatever it was it wouldn't lift.

At traffic lights on her way back to Waterview, Cathy was startled as two very dishevelled-looking people knocked urgently at her window. A man and a woman in their thirties, with empty eyes. Her first instinctive act was to make sure her door was locked. They looked rough and aggressive. Neil Mitchell would probably have pulled into the side and asked them what had happened. Tom Feather would have given them the price of a meal, and convinced them that good times were around the corner. Cathy felt ashamed that all she wanted was for the traffic lights to change and that she could be away out of there, away from their haunted, disturbed faces. She could hear them calling out. 'You have a good life, you have everything you want, please, *please*.' The lights were for ever red. She told herself that the social services were good these days, those people did not *have* to beg in the streets. There were centres, hostels, rescue teams on the streets. These must be winos, drunks or druggies. She must stare straight ahead as if she didn't see them, if she opened the window it could be dangerous. 'Please,' she heard the woman cry, 'you've got everything, a lovely van with a picture on it, a home to go to, just give us something.' It was the van with the picture on it that softened her heart. Cathy indicated and pulled to the side of the street. Out of her bag she took a ten-pound note. She opened the window a fraction and handed it to them. They looked at her in disbelief. It was five times what they might have hoped for. The woman looked younger close up, maybe younger than Cathy, her hair was matted and her face dirty.

'You deserve all your good luck, missus,' she said eventually.

'I don't,' Cathy said, grimly thinking, 'Nobody *deserves* good luck, it's just handed out. Very unfair, as a matter of fact.' The lights changed and she drove on. It was all such an accident, every bit of it when you stopped to think. Why was that girl standing there in the rain begging from cars at the traffic lights? Why was she, Cathy, driving a van with a picture on it to an expensive town house in Waterview? Why were Simon and Maud going to have to live with strangers? None of it made any sense at all. When she let herself into the house Cathy found a folded note. Her heart sank. He couldn't have been called out *again*. This was a workman's compensation case, for heaven's sake, not a political prisoner matter. She opened it and read: 'Sorry Cathy – back 11-ish, don't wait up.' She didn't.

Tom said that the whole trick for the estate agents' reception was setting up the Spanish atmosphere. Cathy said that was all very well certainly, but they must have a whole range of tapas to start. Followed by a knockout paella with all the right flavours. Tom was so busy chasing up Spanish hats, castanets, a guitarist and a flamenco dancer that he never seemed to have time to discuss the menus. Cathy worked out that they should have two paellas, one with shellfish and one less authentic one without. She knew how much the estate agents would love to see Marcella Malone moving among them, but she didn't even think of suggesting it to Tom. Instead, June was given instructions about hiring a Spanish outfit and learning to say 'arriba' at appropriate times. Cathy wanted little labels on the individual plates of tapas showing how typically Spanish they were; Tom begged her to believe that all they wanted was the feel that they were actually in Spain already which the sangria, Rioja and the click of the castanets would give them. They were showing off to potential clients and the press. But she wanted it to be right, there would be *some* people there, surely, who would know and recognise the real thing.

'Would it be educational for us to go to it, do you think?' Simon wondered the night before.

'No,' said Cathy briefly, and saw their two disappointed faces. 'Thank you for suggesting it, but actually it would be boring and depressing for you. Have I ever told you a lie?'

They paused to consider this question. 'No,' they said at exactly the same time. 'Will there be leftovers, do you think?'

'Not at St Jarlath's tomorrow, Maud. Your aunt Hannah is

coming to Waterview tomorrow, tomorrow night, to supper with Neil and myself.'

'Are you going to poison her?' Simon asked.

'Of course not, I'm going to serve her and your uncle Jock some delicious Spanish food and try and make my hair look good.'

'Why would she want to see your hair?' Maud asked.

'Believe me, Maud, I'm not sure, but she does, and often when people want things that are quite easy it's probably best to do them, it saves trouble in the long run.'

'Where did you learn that . . . Was it at school?' Maud wondered.

'No, my aunt Geraldine told me, years ago. It's a very useful piece of advice.'

The estate agents loved the lunch. None of them mentioned the food; they all talked about the atmosphere.

'Right again, Tom,' Cathy said, genuinely admiring. He got things so right, he had known all along they were selling the mood, not the gourmet dishes of Spain. A lot of these people wouldn't even venture into proper Spanish food when they bought their villas out there.

'They needed good food as a back-up. If it hadn't been as good as it was, we would have heard the complaints,' he reassured her as they packed up the leftovers. Some were going to Fatima, where Tom's father, now home from hospital was well on the mend. There had been a huge basket of fruit delivered there, courtesy of Joe who was still in the Far East. Tom didn't say much about it, but Cathy knew he was very pleased. Cathy was packing two separate boxes, a small one for the twins who would be hoping for something, and another to provide most of the meal tonight when the Mitchells were coming to Waterview. Please may Neil not be late again. Please may Jock not know any of the estate agents here today who might have mentioned they were at a Spanish lunch. And please may Hannah Mitchell not get into a temper because she hadn't used the hair voucher.

The Mitchells were in good time, and of course Neil wasn't home. Cathy had laid out little dishes of black olives.

'Thought we'd be getting these,' Jock Mitchell laughed his bluff, loud laugh.

'Ran into a couple of lads from the golf club and had a drink with them. They said you had done this slap-up Spanish meal, and I said to Hannah on the way over here what's the betting we get the taste of old España tonight.'

Cathy's face took on a set look. 'Ah, but I hope you didn't have *real* money on it because you'd have been wrong, Mr Mitchell,' she said triumphantly. 'Just these lovely fat olives. I thought I'd save a few for you.'

He seemed disappointed. Hannah was busy hanging up her coat and looking around disapprovingly at their house, as she always did. She hadn't seen Cathy properly since she came in.

'Oh, dear, Cathy, no time to get the little job done on the hair yet?' she said, more in sorrow than in anger.

Cathy felt that she wanted to put on a raincoat and start running in any direction, miles and miles from these people.

'Alas no, Mrs Mitchell, but I have given it a lot of thought,' she said.

Neil came in at that moment. 'Hey, that smells good,' he began. Cathy put her finger over her lips and then spoke in a high, unnatural voice.

'Neil, *great* you're back. I have to do just five minutes' work and send something by taxi somewhere. Your parents are here, can you entertain them for just a minute?'

'Sure,' he said agreeably.

But before he went in she whispered in his ear, 'We are not eating Spanish food, not, repeat *not*.'

'Of course not.' He shrugged, puzzled.

She called her local taxi firm and wrote a note to Brenda Brennan at Quentin's.

'This is Last Chance Saloon. Can you send me with this taxi driver four portions of anything at all on God's earth that I can give my bloody mother-in-law. Only thing, *nothing* Spanish. I will pay whatever you want, whenever you like or work it off for you in the kitchen. Love from a distraught Cathy.'

Then she went back and talked nonsense and rubbish to them all for forty-five minutes until the taxi returned with a wondrous steak and kidney pie, a bowl of salad, mashed potatoes and garlic bread. She managed to get it all on the table without any of them seeing, and called them in blithely to their dinner.

'This is lovely,' Hannah said, and Cathy smiled serenely. 'I knew it wouldn't be reheated Spanish food,' Hannah continued. 'Jock can be way off-beam sometimes.'

'Sorry,' said Jock. 'Should have realised I was dealing with a professional.'

And Cathy knew she shouldn't be so pleased about it all, but there was no way of hiding it. Afterwards when they were washing up she admitted it to Neil.

'It was touch and go but it worked,' she said, delighted with the little victory.

'Sure,' he said.

She knew that he was patting her down. 'But seriously Neil, wasn't it brilliant?'

'It wasn't necessary, hon.'

'It was essential,' Cathy said with total conviction.

'What are you trying to prove?'

'That she hasn't won.'

'But you proved that, Cathy, long ago.'

'No I haven't.'

'I married you, didn't I? What other battleground has she got to fight on?'

Tom was a great audience next morning when Cathy told the tale of the taxi takeaway from Quentin's. They sat companionably drinking mugs of coffee and trying out his new date and walnut bread.

'Tell me how did they not see it coming in.' He sat like a huge child on his high stool, wrapped in his scarlet apron.

'I put a big screen near the door.' She was gleeful about it all.

'And the containers, all the foil, didn't they notice?'

'No, Quentin's sent proper dishes, all I had to do was put them straight on the table.'

'And what did you do with the Spanish food?'

'I asked the same taxi driver to take it straight round to St Jarlath's. I don't care *what* it all cost, it was worth it, Tom, it was so worth it.'

A pinger sounded on the kitchen wall, so Cathy reached into the oven to take out more bread and screamed with pain. Tom leaped up to take the tray from her.

'I've told you a hundred times to put on those long gloves,' he fussed.

'I know, it's just that I was trying to be quick.'

'That's what you always say, and is it any quicker? Here, let me see.'

He held her two arms under the cold-water tap and let the water flow over the red patches.

'It's nothing, Tom, stop clucking like a hen.'

'Someone has to cluck or you'll be as much use as the Venus de Milo.'

'What?'

'The one with no arms. It was a joke.'

'I know, you eejit, it's just that Hannah and Jock were only talking about it last night.'

'What cultured conversations you have with your in-laws.' He had patted her arms dry and was rubbing the cream in gently.

'I wish. It was an argument between Neil and his father. Jock had bought some sculpture for his office, Neil said it was showy and a waste of money. Jock said that if Neil got a present of the Venus de Milo tomorrow he'd only stick a pair of arms on it and sell it to raise funds for tinkers and foreigners. *That* kind of cultured conversation.'

Tom laughed as he stuck the gauze on loosely, leaving room for air to get into the burn, and put things away in their first-aid cabinet. 'And what did you and Hannah talk about?'

'My hair,' Cathy said simply.

To her rage, she felt tears in her eyes. Cathy didn't *want* to be as obsessed with her body as Marcella was, but she wanted to look well.

'Oh, Cathy,' he said.

'Tell me, Tom, is it stupid or something? I don't know.'

'Is this serious?' he asked, astounded.

'Of course it is. If that awful woman gave me a king's ransom to get it changed, then it must be frightening the dogs in the street.'

'But if Neil tells you it's lovely...?'

'He'd say anything for an easy life.'

'No he wouldn't, and it's gorgeous.'

'What's it like? Go on, close your eyes, tell me.'

Tom closed his eyes. 'Let me see, it's fair, sort of honey fair, very thick and it's tied behind your back, and little bits curl over your ears and it smells of shampoo and it's just fine.'

Peter Murphy called Geraldine in the office.

'Awkward thing to ask you,' he began.

'My speciality, awkward things,' she said.

It was easy for her to sound so suave and cool. She knew already the awkward thing he was going to ask. Peter Murphy's estranged wife had died that morning, Geraldine had already been told this. It would be either asking her to attend the funeral or not to. It was a matter of indifference to her, whichever Peter wanted she would do. They were old history now as a couple; there had been many ladies in his life since she had been there. They were truly just good friends now. She listened and made what she hoped were the appropriate and non-committal sounds of regret, coming as they did from an ex-mistress. It turned out that Quentin's wouldn't do the catering for the funeral, they were passing such work over to Scarlet Feather. Would this be embarrassing for Geraldine?

'Absolutely not, I'm just delighted they can help you, and I'm sure they'll do it very well,' she said, still in her concerned, sympathetic voice.

'It will be on Saturday morning ... um ... at what is ... was ... well, her house ... The children ... Her friends would expect ...' Geraldine had never known Peter Murphy at a loss for words before. For years he had been able to live exactly the life he wanted to. Only by dying had the sad, rich, plain wife whom he had always managed to ignore satisfactorily even slightly inconvenienced him.

'Yes, Peter, and what would be best...?' She waited. He was unwilling to decide, she would second-guess him. 'Perhaps I shouldn't come to the house. I didn't really know her personally, after all.' She could hear his sigh of relief, echoed by her own. Geraldine had no wish to be seen as a false sympathiser. Yet she *would* like to know who turned up. This way she could work behind the scenes, peer out and see everything without being seen herself.

'I've got a question for you Simon,' Lizzie said.

Simon's face lit up. 'Is it about Muttie's Yankee today? Did it work, then?' He was very excited.

'Yankee?' Lizzie said.

'It's a bit complicated, it's a way of increasing your stake,' Simon explained helpfully.

'I know only too well what it is, thank you Simon, it's just that there was an agreement that such a thing as a Yankee was never, ever going to happen with household money.' Lizzie's face was thunderous.

'I'm sure it wasn't with household money,' Simon said swiftly.

'No, I'm sure it wasn't. It must have been from his own personal income, his stocks and shares and dividends,' she said vaguely.

'Oh, good, that's all right then,' Simon said, relieved.

Lizzie looked at him in despair. 'That wasn't the question,' she said. 'It's that you and Maud have to say yes or no to Marian's wedding today. If you say yes, then you get dancing lessons and outfits. If you say no then that's fine. It's got to be your decision, the pair of you.'

'Then I say no,' Simon said.

'Right.' Lizzie was leaving it at that.

'What do you mean, right?' Simon could be very imperious.

'Just that you got a choice, you said no. Maud will be disappointed, she said yes, she wanted to dress up.'

'Well I don't,' he said.

'Fine. Cathy will be relieved.' This was part of a plan.

'Why?' He didn't like playing into Cathy's hands.

'She says you'd have been no good. Muttie and I didn't agree, and it would have been a great day out but there, it's your choice.'

'I suppose I *could* do it, I mean, if Maud wants it so much.'

'Yes or no today.'

'Oh, all right then, yes.'

'And you do have to learn the dances and wear a kilt?' Lizzie was making sure there were no grey areas.

'Well, I suppose. There's not going to be anyone from school there, after all.' He was talking himself into it.

And then came the clincher. 'And of course the tigers? Will there still be tigers?' He had remembered Cathy's chance throwaway remark, just as he would remember Lizzie saying sourly that Muttie had stocks and shares.

'I don't think so, I think there was some kind of a problem getting the tigers into Dublin.'

'But *why*, Lizzie. Why?'

Lizzie finally spoke. 'I beg you, Simon, don't ask me the answers to any more questions. I don't *have* any answers. Why does Muttie throw away everything he gets? Why does Geraldine live like a millionaire? Why isn't Cathy grateful to Mrs Mitchell for everything that woman gives her? Why does Marian want some of the Mass to be in the Irish language at her wedding? Why do women I clean houses for leave such terrible rotting things in their fridges? I'll tell you, I really and truly don't know.'

'Do you know when the wedding is, Lizzie?' Simon asked in a level voice.

'Yes, it's in the summer,' she said glumly.

'I suppose we *could* learn to dance in four months,' said Simon, who had discovered that life threw something new at you all the time.

'Listen, can I help you out Saturday at the Murphy funeral? What I want to do is be in the kitchen out of sight, buttering bread and washing dishes.'

'Why?'

'Because you're a businesswoman. Where will you get a better offer, a pair of hands free for four hours?'

'No, you're doing this for some horrible reason.'

'Only pure curiosity. I used to have a fling with the grieving widower, as you well know. I'd like to see at first hand how many people turn up and who they are.'

'I'm not in favour of it,' Cathy said.

'I *could* approach your partner, Mr Feather.'

'How will we get you in?'

'I'll come in with you when they're all at the church.'

'The kitchen might not be big enough to hide you.'

'It is,' said Geraldine, who had after all been there when it was a joint family home, but when the deceased lady was not in residence.

This was their first funeral, and they must do it right. Brenda Brennan at Quentin's, who had given them the job, said there was a lot of work in that area. You just had to be terribly nice and considerate to the family concerned, and keep everyone else fed and supplied with drink. The problem, of course, was that nobody could tell them how many people to expect. Certainly not Mr Murphy, who seemed highly embarrassed about it all.

They would cook two hams, Tom decided, baked and dressed, just produce one and carve it in the dining room, keeping the other in reserve. This way it wouldn't point it up if there was a very small attendance, much less than had been anticipated. They would have salads ready to make on the premises, a selection of Tom's breads ready to warm up in the oven, Cathy's home-made chutneys and pickles served in the big white pots with their Scarlet Feather logo. There would be warm asparagus quiches and big plates of Irish cheese served with apples and grapes. Desserts might make it somehow too festive and party-like. *Inappropriate* was the word they kept using to each other. And yet it was very odd and inappropriate to be looking for approval and new business and success just because some wealthy, unloved woman had died and her guilty, remorseful relatives were trying to give her a good send-off.

'Very big house, isn't it,' said Cathy as they climbed the steps with the first load of boxes.

Geraldine sniffed as if she could tell a lot of stories about this house but would not be drawn. June said that she might meet a rich fellow here today. Walter, who was being the barman once again, said it was ridiculous for one woman to have lived in a huge place like this on her own. Tom said it was great that there was lots of space, because he was so big he took up the whole kitchen in some houses. Cathy said nothing but just scurried back to the van for the next lot of trays. A lot of things were puzzling her. Why was Geraldine coming here, anyway? The place must have nothing but bad memories for her. Why was June talking about meeting a fellow? She had *met* a fellow years ago, for heaven's sake, and had two children with him. Why was Walter so bitter? He had everything going for him. All right, so two very dysfunctional and at present disappeared parents. But he had never been involved even when they *were* around. How could he resent anyone who had anything? Including a dead woman whom he had never even known. And lastly, how could anyone else on earth be so unfailingly optimistic as Tom Feather? They had three loose cannons on board with them today. They didn't know whether there would be thirty or two hundred people turning up today. And *still* he was able to see something good about it all, like he would have a big kitchen. She smiled to herself as she ran up the steps again.

'Don't get into a good humour on me, Cathy Scarlet . . . That's when you usually burn yourself or cut yourself,' he warned.

'Right,' she said. 'Grim-faced from now on.'

The family of the late Mrs Murphy were back at the house first. Cathy took their coats and hung them on her mobile coat rack which was set up in the back of the wide hall. Then Walter offered them a drink, and they moved into the big and seldom-used drawing room.

'Should we help with the food?' one of the daughters offered grudgingly.

'No, no, it's all under control, and you'll see we have set up a buffet here in the back room.'

They looked around. In all the years that she had lived here their mother would never have entertained like this. And the big rooms looked so well today; these caterers had added small touches, and certainly managed to show the place at its best. How sad that the first time their mother's house, their own family home, should be seen in its glory was at her funeral.

'It must be very poignant for you all,' Cathy said. 'So many memories all coming together.' They looked at each other, surprised. 'I'm sure she would have been very pleased that you opened up her lovely house to everyone . . . It will be a lovely way to greet her friends,' Cathy went on. She saw them relaxing, and yet again she blessed Brenda Brennan at Quentin's saying that you can never be too sympathetic. Tom kept looking out of the window and giving a running commentary.

'They're coming very slowly, but I think there's just enough to take the bare look off the place. No, wait, there's three more cars pulling up outside, we might have a decent house after all.

'Oh, dear, there are people already checking their watches, they mightn't stay long. June, go in and take up your stand behind the buffet. Is Walter there, or has he gone off to have one of his fifteen-minute reads in the gents?'

'He's still in the hall. I've got my eye on him,' Cathy said.

'Geraldine, do we sympathise with Mr Murphy or not?'

Geraldine paused in her work, which was spreading pâté on small round biscuits, and garnishing each of them with a speck of tomato, parsley and crème fraiche. 'I think the words "Upsetting day for you" should cover it perfectly,' she said briskly, and peered again through the little service hatch. 'That's interesting, hardly anyone here from Peter's hotel, I don't suppose they know what the protocol is.'

The lunch party didn't last long, and soon people were saying goodbye to the daughters of the house. Peter Murphy had left, kissing each of his girls on the cheek. He didn't need to come into the kitchen; he never knew that Geraldine was there. The invoice would be presented to his hotel and the cheque in payment for it written immediately. Cathy wondered whether Geraldine was pleased or disappointed by the small turnout at the funeral of the woman whom she must have hated at one time. Geraldine had been involved with Peter Murphy for several years. But it was impossible to know: Geraldine gave little away, she just commented that the daughters had several of their friends there, but that there were hardly any of Mrs Murphy's own cronies out in that room . . .

'Possibly she didn't *have* many friends,' Cathy suggested as she counted the plates. They could only charge for forty-two people.

'Everyone has friends, specially if they live in a big house like this,' said June, as she packed the cutlery into the mesh baskets.

'Not necessarily,' Tom said, as he carefully wrapped up the unused ham. 'I think people get isolated in big places like this. Not that I know, or will ever know,' he grinned.

'It's got nothing to do with the house,' Geraldine said. 'She was in an impossible position. No man, so no escort, and people are afraid of women who lose their men, they think it's catching. And then no job either, nothing to talk about, so she must have been as dull as ditchwater.'

'That sounds very hard, Geraldine,' Tom said, wagging his head at her mock disapprovingly.

'Life *is* very hard, Tom, you had better believe me.' And it was as if a hard mask had come over her face for just a few seconds.

'Will we freeze the ham, or wheel it out again out for Mrs Hayes, do you think?'

Tom and Cathy had dropped Walter off at the top of Grafton Street, where he was going to spend his pittance, as he called his three hours' wages. They were driving June back with them to the premises. Her pittance was for five hours, since she was to stack the dishwashers and help tidy up.

'Mrs Who?'

'The lady that had chocolate all over her face has given us a very nice job, as it happens, for her silver wedding, just because I rescued her.'

'Oh, yes, of course, you're great with the charm. No, let's freeze this fellow, I say. They want gooey things, lots of creamy sauces. A nice lean ham would be much too healthy for them.'

Cathy looked at him questioningly and he nodded. They were, as so often, in agreement; Tom had the label written and dated and the ham placed on the right shelf of the freezer. They turned on the answering machine: three requests for brochures, one girl asking if they had any vacancies, since she would like to pursue a career in catering.

'Pursue!' Cathy laughed. 'Why do kids talk like that?'

'Because they think it makes them sound as if they weren't kids,' Tom suggested.

Then there was a booking, a ladies' lunch for eight, just to deliver and leave for the Riordans.

'No address, no phone number. Great. Really, people are so thick,' Tom fumed.

'Come on, Tom, we *know* them. We've been there.'

'We have?' he looked at Cathy in puzzlement. They hadn't been to all that many houses. Not so many that he could afford to forget the names of clients.

'*You* know, we did the christening there, you kept referring to him afterwards as Mr Bloody Family Man.'

'Oh, *him* yes indeed. I've blanked his name deliberately from my mind,' Tom said.

'Well mercifully we haven't blanked them out of the computer,' Cathy said. 'What will we give them?'

'A lecture on the subject that there ain't no good in men,' Tom offered.

'No, silly. To eat. And anyway, that's not true. There's plenty of good in men. My father's buying a puppy for the twins to keep in St Jarlath's Crescent, though he'll have to do all the work training it and cleaning up after it. My husband has got us two great tickets for the opera tonight, even though he doesn't really like it. James Byrne's going to give up his Sunday morning to do the books for us just because we couldn't meet him today. My business partner, also a man, is going to stay here and lock up on his own for me, so I haven't one thing against men at the moment,' she laughed at him.

'Why am I going to stay and lock up, remind me?' Tom asked.

'Because the love of *your* life is going to be at the gym all evening while the love of *my* life is busy thinking up reasons why we might not go to Lucia di Lammermoor, and I'd better be home to head him off at the pass.'

There was a note on the table. 'Now I *know* you'll think I'm trying to wriggle out of culture, but when you hear what's happened you'll agree . . .' A perfectly legal advice bureau was being threatened, and the solicitors said that the presence of a barrister would definitely make the authorities think again. There might even be a press conference ... He was sorry ... very sorry. He would make it up to her. The tickets were on the table. Could she find someone else? Cathy was furious. Could she find someone else to dress up and go to the opera with her at five o'clock in the evening? What world did he live in? She could feel the start of tears of annoyance and disappointment, but she fought them back. This wasn't a major-league thing. Not like all the real battlefields she had been on before ... Not like the times that Hannah had sneered at her and said that she would only marry Neil over the dead bodies of herself, her husband, anyone who knew them. This wasn't as big as Hannah laughing loudly behind her back in a voice intended to carry, patronising her, saying she was the poor cleaner's daughter. This wasn't like wanting to take a job and live overseas. It was only about a night out.

However, who else could she ask at this late notice? June? At the Opera? Forget it. Geraldine? Geraldine with her active social life was sure to have a date on a Saturday night. Cathy pulled the phone towards her. She'd call Geraldine.

'Geraldine?'

'You have another job for me, is that it?'

'Would you like to stand in for Neil at the opera tonight? I have a spare ticket.'

'I'd love it. Is it sad?'

'Pretty hopeless set-up, yes. Heroine marries a guy she doesn't love, she kills him. The guy she *does* loves kills himself. That sort of thing, low in communication skills, fairly typical of opera.'

'Fairly typical of life, I'd say,' Geraldine said crisply.

'I'll take you to Quentin's for supper afterwards.'

'It's a deal.'

They laughed with Brenda Brennan about the whole steak and kidney adventure. They saw Shona Burke having dinner with two of the senior Haywards people.

'I wish that girl would smile more,' Geraldine said.

'She's got quite a bit to smile about. Apartments at Glenstar don't come cheap; good job, good looks. Tom said he saw her up at the hospital visiting someone when his father had that heart attack. I did ask her about it, but she sort of clammed up on me.'

'She's good at her job but no warmth there,' Geraldine said. 'You did a fantastic job, today. I was very proud of you.'

'No, don't try to slip out of it. Were you pleased not to see a big crowd there, before?'

'No, I was indifferent really, just objectively interested, that's all.'

'But if you loved him once, you can't have been totally indifferent. You must have ... felt something.'

'I never loved Peter Murphy,' Geraldine said simply.

'But weren't you...' Cathy's voice trailed away.

'Certainly I was ... for over five years, but that doesn't mean I loved him.'

'At the time it must have seemed like love,' Cathy said.

'No, not for me.'

'Then what ... Why...' Cathy stopped again. 'I'm sorry Geraldine, it's none of my business.'

'No, I don't mind ... I was having a nice time with a pleasant companion who also introduced me to a lot of people and helped me build my business up. And why? I suppose I'd just say why not? *And* he got me the apartment in Glenstar.'

Cathy looked at her. 'He *got* it for you?'

'You're a big girl now, Cathy, you have your own business, stop being the round-eyed innocent with me.'

Cathy spoke with spirit. 'I'm not playing the innocent. I'm just surprised that you'd take a present, well, like a luxury flat from a man. That's all.'

'If people want to give me presents, I should throw them back?'

'Of course not, but a *flat*, Geraldine.'

'It was the same builder who was putting up Glenstar at the time as he was doing his hotel extension, and it didn't cost him as much as it would have cost other people. It was very generous, though, and as you know, we have always remained good friends.'

'But he doesn't think he can come round and ...'

'No, of course he doesn't, Cathy. Please.'

'But wasn't it an odd thing for him to do? I mean, most men don't do things like that, do they?'

'I find that most men do,' Geraldine said, giving the matter some thought. 'People do give me things. I got the car as a present, and that CD player you admire so much.'

'You got all those things from different men at different times? I just don't believe you! You're having me on.'

'Not at all. Why would I make a joke about something like this? It's a fact. Do you think less of me?' Geraldine asked.

'No, *no*, of course not,' Cathy said emphatically. But she did.

Greatly less. The aunt that she had so much admired, the gritty woman who had made it all on her own from a working-class background to a position of power and elegance turned out to be no more than what in the past was called a courtesan. She was getting presents for sex. It was one small step away from being paid for it.

'Good, I'd hate you to get all pious on me.'

'Me? Pious? Never,' said Cathy with a weak grin.

Geraldine had paid for a secondary education which Muttie and Lizzie thought to this day was a scholarship. Geraldine had bought the school uniform and listened sympathetically when Cathy said she wanted to learn the catering trade from the bottom up, and then provided the fees for the catering course when the time came. Geraldine had been her ally when she had come home from Greece with the amazing news that she was in love with Neil Mitchell, son of the hated Hannah, and had helped her calm Lizzie down . . . It was Geraldine who had been guarantor for the Scarlet Feather loan without hesitation. There was no way that Cathy was going to go all pious on her aunt. She sought to change the subject, and looked down at Geraldine's wrist.

'Hey, is that a new watch? It's gorgeous.'

'It *is* nice, isn't it.' Geraldine twisted it to make it catch the light. 'It's a lovely little setting, tiny seed pearls and a nice gold bracelet. That nice estate agent, Freddie Flynn gave it to me last week. It was very sweet of him.'

'Was it good . . . all the screeching?' Tom asked early on Monday morning.

'What? Oh, great, just great.'

'And did Neil catch any sleep at all while he was there?'

'No, he wouldn't dare,' Cathy said. Why had she lied and pretended Neil had been there? It wasn't a lie exactly. It was more a matter of loyalty. It would have been very complicated to explain to Tom just how hard Neil worked, and how much he had regretted having to pull out of the opera. Easier to let it be. It was an unimportant white lie which would never come to light.

They had all the food they could freeze for the silver wedding ready.

'I might even buy you a beer just to get us out of here . . .' Tom began, as someone knocked on the door. He went out to answer it. It was Neil.

'I was in the area, so I thought if I offered my wife lunch she might forgive me for standing her up at the opera,' he called out.

Cathy came out to the front room.

'So will you forgive me?'

'There was nothing to forgive, I *told* you that. There wasn't even a row, Neil, none of this is necessary.' She was so mortified she could hardly speak.

'It *is* necessary. I promised something I didn't deliver. Can I deliver a lunch instead?'

'Go, Cathy. Go to one of the posher places and steal ideas,' Tom urged. 'See are there any exciting breads out there, ask to see the whole breadbasket and take one of everything, anything new, bring it back. Okay?'

She took off her Scarlet Feather overall, put on her jacket and got into the van.

'Won't we take the car, maybe?' he suggested.

'It's pure advertising, Neil, we can park it somewhere down near the quays where everyone will see it. See you, Tom.'

They sat opposite each other in a very trendy place. They only got in because it was a Monday, and gradually she got over her annoyance. It wasn't his fault. He really *did* feel badly about letting her down. She insisted that she had enjoyed her dinner with Geraldine.

'And now I get to have lunch with you as well, so I won out as it happens,' she said cheerfully.

'What did Geraldine have to say?' Neil asked.

'Not a lot, we just rambled on about everything.'

Cathy wondered why she hadn't told him about Geraldine's extraordinary lifestyle. Normally she told Neil everything. She decided yet again that it had something to do with loyalty. She wondered did this mean she would be lying constantly from now on.

'They've heard from the missing Uncle Kenneth.'

'I don't believe it, where is he?'

'On the high seas coming home, apparently.'

'And what about Aunt Kay in the funny farm?'

'Getting stronger by the minute, I hear.'

There was a lump of lead in Cathy's chest. 'It doesn't mean they'll be in any shape to take Maud and Simon back?' she asked fearfully.

'Well, not this very moment I'd say, but of course they will have to go back sometime Cathy.'

Cathy was aware of her very mixed feelings. It would be wonderful not to have to worry about Simon and Maud any more. Yet these people were not going to look after their children properly. She had taught them some manners, some fear of upsetting others, her Mam and Dad had taught them love and friendship. It seemed a terrible waste to see it all washed away when Kenneth and Kay came back for whatever time suited them. The return of the prodigal parents had always been something for which she had devoutly hoped. Now that it was beginning to be a reality, Cathy was not so sure.

'They're okay, the parents, do you think?' she asked Neil.

'As good as can be expected,' he said. 'Anyway.' He was changing the subject. She looked at him. 'Anyway, none of that is really important. You and I have to talk about the job,' Neil said.

'Tom, it's Walter. Can I come in and have a word?'

Tom swallowed the sandwich he was eating and pressed the buzzer to let him in. The boy was basically harmless, Tom thought. No hard worker, a little over-swift to find his jacket at the end of a job rather than help carry the plates and glasses out to the van. A little snobby towards June and her pronunciation of words. Still, it suited them at the moment to employ him as a barman. He was reasonably personable, charming to the younger women and if he could only concentrate more, remembering who was drinking what, then he would have been fine. They had decided not to ask him to do the Hayes silver wedding. Instead they were going to try out a barman they had met, a red-headed boy called Con with a friendly smile, who managed to give the impression that he loved what he was doing.

'Cathy not here?' Walter looked around him, hand in pocket. Slightly quizzical, almost as if he had been let down. Tom remembered that he and Cathy had agreed in a whisper that Walter had this slightly annoying body language, as if he were conferring some kind of favour and wished the whole thing could be dealt with as quickly as possible.

'No, but she'll be back soon.'

'That's Neil's car in the yard?'

'Yes, he'll be back soon too. Can I do anything for you in the meantime?'

'This gig, this do ... whatever ... What time's it at?'

'I'm not with you,' Tom said.

'The big function on Wednesday. I want to know, is it dinner jacket for me to wear, and what time should I turn up?'

'I don't think we made any arrangement...' Tom began.

'It's just that I was hoping you could give me something in advance now ... Towards getting geared up and all.'

Cathy would *not* have booked her husband's cousin without telling him. In fact, she had been more vehement against Walter than he had been. She had been quite outraged that he had called his wages a pittance. There had to have been a misunderstanding here. It was tempting to say that they should wait until Cathy came back to sort it out. But Tom knew he couldn't do that.

'We didn't book you for Wednesday,' he said, much more confidently than he felt.

'What?'

'Just that. We didn't book you, Walter, so there's no question of any advance, I'm afraid. I'm sorry if you got the wrong end of the stick.'

'Don't talk to me about wrong ends of sticks, you told me all about it, you spoke about it in front of me – what was I meant to think?'

'What are *we* meant to think, Walter? You describe the wages we give you as a pittance, you don't enjoy the work. How were we meant to be inspired with the idea that you want to work at the Hayes silver wedding?'

'Oh, this is what it's all about. It was a joke, it's what people do, they make jokes. They don't expect people to take a light-hearted remark seriously. But now I see it's a matter of bowing down to the ground and thanking you from the bottom of my heart for the privilege of being allowed to work with you.'

Tom thought that Cathy had been gone for an age, how long could one lunch take? Was she ever coming back?

In the restaurant, Cathy looked at Neil across the table.

'The job? The one they were going to offer you abroad?'

'Yes, and still are. You and I sort of got started on it the wrong way. I wanted to tell you what it's all about.'

'Do,' she said.

'No, not if you're going to put on that clipped tone with me.'

'Neil, I said tell me about it.'

'Please don't let's begin by being so hostile about it.'

'I have no idea how to ask you to tell me about this job without apparently insulting you or offending you, so why don't you just please *tell* me all about it?'

Just then, of course, they had to order. Neil was uncaring about what he ate, but Cathy wanted to taste different things, so she spent time making the choices.

'It doesn't matter,' he said when the waitress asked if they would like a cocktail.

'I'd love one of those silvery things over there with the frosting on the glass,' Cathy said.

'Why do you want that?' Neil was amazed.

'We're doing this silver wedding. You know, I told you all about it. This drink might be just the thing,' she said.

And she waited while he told her about the chance to change the whole thrust of immigration law. It was new and exciting, and it would be so great to be in on the ground floor when it was happening, and it mattered so much. And when all came to all there was only so much individuals could do on the ground in their own countries. What was needed was a proper policy up and running in the international institutions, not something that was controlled by politicians whose own interests could change, but by lawyers and social workers who cared. Cathy listened. Too often countries with perfectly good records on civil liberties looked the other way when there was oil involved, or if they were selling arms to the area, or if they were conscious of votes at home depending on the number of foreigners you let into your country. This agency would be above all that, it would be international, it would change the thinking of the world.

'Where from?' Cathy asked.

'Initially The Hague,' he said.

'You want us to live in Holland?'

'There will be travel, of course, and you can come with me, that's all agreed. You'll see places, Cathy, places that you never dreamed of.'

'What will you do every day, Neil? Try to give me a picture of how the day would break down.' Her voice felt disembodied; she needed to buy time to think about this. He really and truly did want to go, and expected that she would drop everything and go with him. She didn't listen as he struggled to paint a picture of how he saw their days shaping out. She wondered instead if anyone truly knew anyone else. This man opposite her who had defied his parents with icy indifference to their arguments when they had objected to his marrying her, now wanted to uproot her from the business she had slaved to form and take her away to be some kind of diplomat's wife. She heard words somewhere around her in the air as she tasted the bread which was ordinary and the tomato butter which was over the top. The silvery cocktail was a disaster – they would not even suggest it for the Hayes celebration.

'You're very quiet,' Neil said eventually.

'I'm thinking about it, letting it all sink in.'

'I knew you would, if we had time. Back in Waterview you had boxing gloves up in the air in confrontation, your-job-my-job sort of thing. It's not about that, it's about our life.'

'Yes, yes.' She spoke almost dreamily.

'What do you mean, Cathy?'

'Well, you're right, it is about life. Would you go without me, on your own, to live your life out there, just suppose I couldn't go?'

'But that's not what we're talking about. You can go if you want to,' he was bewildered.

'I'm trying to work out how you see your life. Would you go alone?'

'No, I wouldn't do that. You know that, don't you?'

'I'm just asking. So you'd stay here and go on with the way things are?' she insisted.

'Yes, but, well ... Yes, I suppose.'

'I see.'

'But it's not like that, Cathy. You can go, and believe me, I know you'll love it. They want you to come out with me for a week. Very soon, just to see first-hand where we'd be living and the kind of work that's involved. Cathy, you *love* a challenge, it's written all over you ...'

'We need a lot more discussion about this. A lot more,' she said, her voice still sounding unreal in her own ears.

'Of course we do.' He patted her hand.

Neil seemed to think the conversation had gone well. He called for the bill and they left. Cathy had parked the van precariously on a corner. She saw a traffic warden looking in its direction, and raced her to the vehicle.

'I won,' she laughed, clambering into the driving seat.

'What's Scarlet Feather ... is it a mattress?' the traffic warden asked.

'It's the best catering company in Ireland,' Cathy said, and got the van into gear and away from there at speed.

To their surprise, Walter was installed at the premises and Cathy noticed that Tom was looking hassled.

'Hey, are you better?' Neil asked Walter.

'Yeah, I'm okay,' Walter said, shrugging.

'What was wrong?' Cathy asked.

'He had a fall and hurt his back,' Neil explained. 'Dad was telling me this morning. He's been out of the office a week.'

Tom and Cathy looked at each other. They knew there had been no fall, but they said nothing. At that moment the phone rang. It was Mrs Hayes. They had decided they wanted two waiters for Wednesday. One to stay entirely behind the bar, the other to go round and refresh drinks. Would that be any problem?

'No problem at all, Mrs Hayes, it will be done straight away.' Tom hung up. He turned round to look at Walter. 'Usual pittance Wednesday, Walter, turn up here at six-thirty to help stack the van, no money up front, no need to hire a dinner jacket, you already have one. Okay?'

'Okay,' Walter said smiling. 'I knew you really meant me to work.'

'No we didn't, the situation just changed. We have Con, who is our waiter for Wednesday, you're just the back-up. That's if your own back will be all right by then?'

'Are you going back to the Four Courts?' Walter asked his cousin Neil. 'If you are, I'd love a lift.'

'Are you back at work then?' Neil was confused.

'No, but I have to see someone down that area.'

Tom was relieved that Walter was going to go. 'Did you two have a good lunch?' he asked.

'No. Breads we tried, and boy did we try them ... Weren't anything compared to yours, Tom,' Cathy said cheerfully. And Neil muttered agreement.

'Great news.' Tom was pleased. 'The show can stay on the road for another few weeks, then.'

When they were gone Cathy sat down and looked at him. 'Sorry, Tom.'

'About what? We know Walter's a little shit, but they *want* two ...'

'Not about that, about lying to you, about saying Neil *was* at the opera when he wasn't.'

'Oh, that . . .' Tom appeared to have forgotten it totally.

But she went on. 'It was stupid, but you knew how much I was looking forward to it and I suppose I just . . . didn't want you to think he'd let me down.'

Tom seemed to think she was making heavy weather of it all. 'Poor Neil couldn't face all the screeching when it came to it, was it? Can't say I blame him.'

Muttie had planned the surprise for weeks. And he wanted as many people to witness it as possible. So he asked Cathy and Neil if they could drop in about six o'clock on Tuesday, and Geraldine. It didn't really suit anyone, but they all made an effort. The little black Labrador puppy was going to be in the house already hidden on newspapers up in the bedroom. And then the conversation would be brought around gradually to dogs. Maud and Simon would say yet again how much they'd love a puppy, and Muttie would say excuse me, I think we *do* have one for you. Lizzie would say that it's nonsense, there couldn't possibly be a dog in the house without her knowing, and then Muttie would produce the little fellow . . .

It didn't suit Cathy because she and Tom had to collect their dishes from the Riordan ladies' lunch in order to use them again for the Hayes silver wedding. Sometime they would have enough china and ovenproof dishes not to have to call everything in, but not yet. It didn't suit Geraldine because Freddie Flynn said he might be able to call round to the Glenstar apartment for an hour or two after work. But there was something magical about the thought of Muttie and this pedigree dog which had cost him over a hundred pounds. So they all tried to fit it in. Lizzie would hurry back from her last cleaning job of the day. Geraldine told Freddie that she'd be a little delayed but would be back at the apartment by 6.45. Neil said he'd try to be there, but he'd have to be out of St Jarlath's Crescent by 6.30, just so long as everyone knew. Cathy said that she and Tom could call there for a while before they went to pick up the dishes at Mrs Riordan's.

'Is something happening?' Simon asked when they all sat down at the kitchen table.

'Why do you say that?' Lizzie asked.

'Well, everyone here's sort of waiting,' said Simon.

'No, Simon, we're sitting round a table having tea.'

Cathy continued her attempt to improve the twins' manners. 'And making general conversation rather than centring everything on ourselves. That's what people do, you see.'

'Is everybody all right for sugar and milk?' Maud said obediently.

Muttie cleared his throat. 'There's nothing better than a family sitting down round a table,' he began. 'All over Dublin there's people sitting down to their tea now, watched by their cats and their budgies and their dogs.' He looked around him proudly, as if this was a perfectly normal remark to make out of the blue . . . He waited, but the children said nothing. They looked at him solemnly.

Tom felt he had to fill in the gap in the conversation. 'You've got a point there, Muttie, a family could be watched by all kinds of things, a hamster, a rabbit, well, from its hutch if the angle was right, and a dog, of course.'

Still not a word from Maud and Simon.

Muttie was desperate now. 'But there was never a dog in this house, of course, not having been in the past a family of dog lovers.'

'No, that's right,' Lizzie shouted as if reading lines from a play. Then the twins leaped up.

'It *is*,' cried Simon.

'I *knew* it,' shouted Maud, and they were out of the room in a flash and up the stairs towards the main bedroom. There were sounds of barks and screams and snuffles, and then they arrived carrying the puppy. It looked like a toy, all black fur and wagging tail and panting breath.

'It's beautiful,' said Maud.

'It's a he, I looked.' Simon was holding the puppy and looking again in case there should be any misunderstanding.

'Is it for us?' Simon asked, hardly daring to hope.

'It's for the pair of you,' Muttie said gruffly.

'To keep for ever?' Maud said, unbelieving.

'Sure, of course.'

'We've never had an animal, a real animal,' Simon said.

'There was a tortoise at The Beeches but he went away,' Maud said. 'And you know we were hoping you might get a dog. And only today . . .'

'We heard it whimpering inside the door,' Simon took up the story.

166

'And I said maybe it was a puppy.' Maud wanted to show how bright she had been in identifying the dog.

'And I said yes, Muttie *could* have got himself a puppy, but also it could be just some old person groaning and grunting on the floor of Muttie's bedroom and we'd better not go in.' Simon also needed praise for the great control that he had shown.

'But we never knew it was for us,' Maud said.

'For ever,' Simon said.

Cathy realised that this was the moment when the twins actually changed their personality. And everyone else seemed to think the same. The way they stroked it and laughed aloud at its antics would melt the hardest heart. They had the little animal on the table now, flopping about on its fat little paws. Tom put a newspaper under him, just in time, and people hastily took their cups of tea and biscuits away.

'He just beautiful,' said Maud again.

'And he's very intelligent, too. Did you find him on the street or somewhere?' Simon asked innocently.

'Aw, well, I sort of went out and chose him, you see, he's yours now, he's for the two of you,' Muttie said, beaming all over his face.

'Dad went out to a kennels and bought him for you,' Cathy said proudly.

'And Lizzie went out to work so that she could pay for the vet's fees for injections and everything . . .' said Geraldine.

'And we'll show you now how to train him,' said Lizzie.

'You just keep pulling the newspapers nearer the door every day, well, that's what they used to do at Oaklands.'

'And what are you going to call him?' Tom wanted to know.

The puppy looked up as if interested to know as well. 'Hooves,' said Simon, and Maud nodded eagerly. There was a silence.

'Hooves Mitchell,' Maud elaborated, in case they hadn't understood.

'Yes Maud, but normally dogs don't get called by their surname, so he'll just be Hooves for most of the time, okay,' Cathy said.

'Okay,' said Maud.

'And . . . umm . . . why exactly did you think of this . . . um . . . interesting name?' Tom voiced everyone's thoughts.

The children were surprised that they didn't understand something so obvious. 'It's what Muttie always says is the best thing in the world . . . the thundering hooves that match your heartbeat,' said Simon.

Muttie blew his nose very loudly.

'And when they're off . . .' said Maud, 'then the sound of those hooves touches your soul.'

Neil called Cathy on the mobile just as they were leaving.

'I'm so sorry.'

'It doesn't matter, Neil, nobody expected you to be there, and it was great, they just love the puppy . . .'

'That's what I was calling about, Cathy. They can't go on living in this fool's paradise. Uncle Kenneth is back cleaning up The Beeches, Kay is getting out of hospital at the weekend . . . This can't last here, all this make-believe.'

'It's not make-believe, it's a home. What kind of a home is that uncle of yours making for children?'

'According to Dad and Walter, who've been dragged in to help, not too bad a fist of it. Walter even suggested that they get some food from you for the freezer.'

'I'll tell them what to do with food for the freezer,' Cathy said.

'Cathy please, we'll talk later.'

'Sure.'

Geraldine was leaving then too.

'Sorry I can't stay longer, Cathy, Freddie's coming round for a drink. I was going to cook an elegant dinner for him tomorrow night – he usually drops by on a Wednesday, but he has to go to some do, poor love.'

'No, *I'm* leaving too. Listen, do you want some posh canapés? I have a box in the van.'

'You're an angel, just the thing.'

Geraldine was gone in minutes, her smart red car taking the corner of St Jarlath's Crescent sharpish.

Tom came out then, and they got into the van. 'Wasn't it fabulous to see their faces,' he said.

'Yeah.'

'What is it?'

She told him.

'The courts, the social workers?' Tom began.

'Love the biological parents, apparently.'

'Even if they're fruitcakes?'

'So it seems.'

'You'll miss them,' he said simply.

'I'll miss them, certainly – but can you see Muttie walking that floppy hound called Hooves round for the rest of his life? He'll be devastated.'

'Won't they take it with them? The dog?'

'No – those two would freak if they had to cope with a dog as well as children.'

'But surely they'll go on visiting St Jarlath's Crescent a lot?'

'Kenneth Mitchell's son, going to a working-class area? Never! They'd be afraid they'd learn a common accent *and* get fleas!'

'It's just not fair,' Tom said. They were driving up to the Riordans' house as he said this. There were definite sounds of a party.

'There's another thing that's not fair,' Cathy said. 'They swore they'd be finished by five o'clock, *now* what will we do?'

'Leave it to me,' Tom said.

'Oh, I'll leave it to you willingly, but you're not going to go in and take Mr Riordan by the neck and shout at him about being Mr Family Man, are you?'

'No, this is a different task altogether. Stay in the van, have a sleep. It might take half an hour.'

She heard Tom rummaging in the back of the van for something and then saw him running up the steps with a package. Cathy closed her eyes. It had been a long, upsetting day and she was nervous about tomorrow's silver wedding. Still, this *was* her choice, she must never forget that.

Mrs Riordan came to the door. She looked at him guiltily. 'Oh, God, is that the time?' she said.

'Must have been a wonderful party.' Tom nailed his happiest, most enthusiastic smile to his face.

'What? Yes, they're all in good form.'

'Can I go in and say hallo to the ladies, I brought them a gift,' he beamed at her.

'What? Yes, of course, come in.'

'Good evening, ladies,' he said pleasantly to a group of eleven women who had drunk too much wine but who had also, he was pleased to see, eaten almost all the food provided. 'I thought you'd like . . .' he began.

'A stripper!' screamed one of the women happily.

'Sadly no,' he said hastily. 'I've hurt my back. I wouldn't be able to give you a proper performance at all, but I *did* come with a gift of petits fours and chocolates to thank Mrs Riordan for using our food ... So here's a box to divide among you.'

They thought this was wonderful, and even though they said he was terrible to be giving them things that contained four hundred calories a bite, they ate them all the same.

'And while I'm here, why don't I give you more room to enjoy things?' Adroitly he started to clear the table. The women rushed to help him, and they scraped the plates. In the kitchen, they saw him begin to stack them in the crate.

'We must wash them first,' Mrs Riordan said.

'No, no, we do that back at base, all part of the service,' he said. But they insisted. A sinkful of hot, soapy water, another for rinsing, two ladies drying. The party was in the kitchen now.

'Your back doesn't look all that bad to me,' said the woman who had hoped Tom was a stripper.

'Wait till I'm on real form,' he said to her roguishly, and she blushed with excitement.

They helped him carry the boxes down to the van, where Cathy leaped out in disbelief and began to stow them away. At that moment Mr Riordan's car came into the drive.

'Thank God the place isn't looking like a bomb-site, you're a pair of angels,' said Mrs Riordan, pushing two twenty-pound notes at them. 'Go on, go out and have a drink on me.'

Mr Riordan nodded at them. 'Looks as if it was all a good lunch,' he said grudgingly.

'Oh, the food was all right but I think they rather liked me as a stripper for most of the afternoon.'

'You're making this up,' the man spluttered.

'Well, you're never going to know, are you, Mr Riordan? After all, they're obviously going to say it didn't happen, aren't they?' Cathy and Tom laughed all the way to the city.

'Will we drop in on the reception after Neil's lecture? There'll be warm white wine and cold sausages provided by one of the faculty wives,' Cathy said.

'Sure, will I call Marcella? She should be home by now, we could pick her up on the way, she might like an outing too.'

'Great idea.'

They spent the forty pounds in a Chinese restaurant. Cathy noticed that Marcella had three prawns, no rice, no stir fry, no sweet and sour pork. Tom noticed that Neil was concerned because the Chinese waiters were probably not in trade unions. They told the story of Hooves.

'Isn't The Beeches a big house with a garden?' Marcella asked. 'They might be able to have it with them there.'

'Not until it's trained, it would run straight out on the road and be killed,' Cathy said.

'But maybe they won't be going back there for ages.'

Neil said that it would be much sooner than anyone thought; the law actually did move quickly in restoring children to their homes.

'It seems a pity if they're happy where they are,' said Tom, who had been touched by the family scene in St Jarlath's.

'That's not the point.' Neil was very strong on that. 'Years ago, children were always being taken from their homes and given to people who would so-called improve them ... At least nowadays the importance of the birth parents is actually recognised.'

Cathy thought that this was being over-recognised in this particular case. But she said nothing. There were so many other things to be discussed with Neil, and a rare meal out for the four of them was not going to become a battleground over Simon and Maud.

The Hayes household was up to high doh when they arrived at six-thirty. Two discontented sons who lived at home were hanging around, unsure of what to do. An equally discontented daughter attached to what looked like a young man mightily disapproved of by her parents was saying that it was inconceivable and intolerable that there was no way she could use the ironing board in the kitchen, where it had always been used. Mrs Hayes said they were to call her Molly, and her husband was Shay. He was a plump, somewhat anxious man, who was obviously a hard taskmaster at the business he ran, and felt the need to bark out orders on this occasion as well.

'Shay, can I make us all a quick cup of coffee and briefly run through the agenda with you?' asked Tom.

Meanwhile, Cathy had switched on the kettle, asked June to help get the ironing board and iron up to the spare room, got the boys to put the two Persian cats into a place with a litter tray and a bowl of food, a place from which they could not emerge and eat the trifle or shed hairs on the salmon. By the time the kettle had boiled Cathy had persuaded Molly that the main thing was for her to go upstairs and rest with her feet slightly raised. Cathy had even brought her a cold mask for her eyes, it worked wonders, she said.

'But setting everything up. . . ?' Molly begged.

'Is exactly what you are paying us well to do, and believe me we will do it,' Cathy said firmly.

She heard Tom telling Shay that they had a chain of command, a checklist, a routine to follow and it was wise if they were left to themselves to do it. He had always thought it good for the family to come down at seven-thirty, half an hour before the first guests arrived, so that they could examine everything and check it was all in order. Shay nodded, it made sense. And soon the Hayes family, fuelled with coffee, had all gone to their rooms. Tom and Cathy got into action, the food was unpacked, the conveyor belt for canapés was under way with June and her friend Helen. The buffet tables were set up. The ashtrays were placed in the conservatory where smoking was allowed, the cake was unwrapped and placed on a silver stand. The creamy dessert which needed to have the number 25 written on it with toasted almonds was produced, the salads were filling up the great glass bowls that had been rescued last night from the Riordans. It was all going according to plan. At exactly seven o'clock the two barmen arrived. Con, the cheerful redhead they had spotted in a pub, and Walter, sulkier and moodier than ever.

'They'll be having champagne cocktails to start,' Cathy explained.

'How naff,' Walter said.

Cathy's face was hard. 'I'm never sure exactly what that word means. You know how to do them, and fill them up very shortly before the guests arrive with champagne.'

'Or what passes for champagne,' said Walter, lifting up a bottle and letting it slip back again into the case.

Cathy now addressed herself entirely to Con and not to Walter. 'I'd like you to get forty glasses ready in this way, and can you see that Walter opens twelve bottles of white and twelve bottles of red, the white goes into the big ice box outside the kitchen door, and after they're down to four then open the bottles in fours from then on, and . . .'

'Excuse me, Cathy, do you have a problem talking to me? Perhaps you don't want me here. Should I leave?' He looked so supercilious she wanted to hit him. He knew that she couldn't let him go now. Not just before the guests arrived. He could be as rude as he liked. Or could he? Neil was at home tonight – in a real emergency he would certainly come and help. She moved slightly away so that Con, the new boy, would not hear every word of the family row.

'Either change your attitude or get your coat,' she said crisply.

'I don't think you are in a position—'

'I'm in every position, I'm hiring you.'

'And where will you get a replacement at this hour?'

'Your cousin,' she said simply, and took out her mobile phone.

'Neil? You wouldn't.'

She began dialling.

'Okay, sorry, I was out of order.'

'No, I'm sorry, Walter, I can't rely on you. This is a big job for us.'

Suddenly he realised that she meant it. She really was going to ask Neil Mitchell the barrister to put on a dinner jacket and serve booze to these people. His uncle, who was also his boss, would kill him. His recent returned father, who was also his only other means of support, would kill him.

'I beg you, Cathy, you have my word,' he said.

'It had better be a very good word,' she said, and went and left him.

'Walter's actually doing some work for once,' Tom said admiringly, watching the wine bottles moving swiftly as requested.

'I put the frighteners on him,' Cathy said, with some satisfaction. 'The other boy's good, isn't he, we'll have him again. This is the last of Walter.'

'Will that not cause family strain?' Tom asked.

'No, probably prevent it, in that it will stop me killing Walter with my bare hands and messing up the kitchen,' Cathy said.

'Cooking is meant to have great elements of patience and calm about it,' Tom marvelled. 'You haven't a calm, patient cell in your body.'

'Cooking is also meant to have a certain fire about it, and I'm full of that,' said Cathy.

Just then the Hayes family all appeared downstairs. The fussing was going to start again.

'We have a little tradition, which is to take a family photograph before everyone comes, while the whole place is peaceful, and coincidentally when the food looks at its best,' said Tom, and he posed them next to the cake by the buffet table, accepting their first champagne cocktail of the night.

They saw the hosts beginning to relax, and by the time the first visitor arrived they had agreed that the house looked beautiful, and the food, and that it would be a good evening. Only an hour in they knew it was going to be a roaring success. Even Walter was moving swiftly from group to group, topping up drinks and talking pleasantly. 'Fantastic, these things,' said Shay to everyone about the trays of roast beef and Yorkshire pudding. It was in fact little choux pastries each filled with horseradish sauce and cream and a small slice of cold rare beef. People couldn't stop eating them.

'Did you invent these, Cathy?' a man asked her.

It was Freddie Flynn, her aunt's friend. Mrs Flynn was there, small and jewelled. Cathy looked at the woman's wrist; her watch was plain compared to Geraldine's. She smiled at them both.

'Mr Flynn, Mrs Flynn, thank you so much, no, alas I didn't invent them, but I did see them somewhere and remembered them! Is that as good?'

'Certainly,' he said. He had a nice smile. 'Darling, this is Cathy Feather, she's a sort of cousin of Geraldine, you know, who does our PR. Be nice to Cathy and she might just do more work for us, and Cathy, this is my wife Pauline.'

'You might do *our* silver wedding when the time comes,' the woman said.

'Oh indeed, we'd be honoured. It was wonderful to meet you, now excuse me, I must see that everyone . . .'

She moved away, seething. He was darlinging his wife at every opportunity. They were going to have a silver wedding party. And according to Geraldine, this was meant to be a dead marriage. So poor Freddie was perfectly entitled to have his fun elsewhere, since there was nothing for them at home. God, it would make you sick.

The party went better than anyone could have hoped. Molly had said wistfully that she thought they would all feel too old to dance, but Tom had brought the *Best of Abba* for them just in case. First he put on Leo Sayer 'When I Need You' and then, 'Don't Cry For Me Argentina' and 'Mull Of Kintyre'. Nice and low but insistent in the background, and when he heard people humming and joining in the choruses and when the desserts had been cleared away, he let rip with 'Mamma Mia' and they were all on their feet.

Tom and Cathy paused to have a coffee in the kitchen. Around them the dishes had been collected and stacked. The two barmen had skilfully retrieved the Scarlet Feather glasses and replaced them with those that belonged to the house. Soon it would be midnight, time to pay them their five hours. Shay Hayes had also left an envelope for the staff, so there would be good pickings tonight. Cathy had brought a silver polish cloth with her to shine up the four solid-silver ladles that Molly Hayes had insisted on using. They had been a wedding present, she said, they must be shown off.

The van had been filled, the ashtrays had been emptied, open bottles left on the tables, the kitchen was immaculate and only a hard core of ten people remained to celebrate still further. Tom could pick up the CDs when he came round tomorrow to finalise things and present his account. Con asked if he could speak to Tom for a moment. The boy drew him away a little.

'Very awkward, this,' he began.

'What?' Tom hoped that Con wasn't going to ask for more money; he had been such a good waiter all night. They need never have that young pup Walter again.

'It's just that . . . This is a hard thing to say . . . but I think you should have a look at that sports bag over there if you know what I mean. God, I hate saying this . . . but I have to.' The boy looked really distressed. Without pausing to ask more, Tom unzipped the bag. There on top of Walter's sweater and jeans were four silver ladles, two silver cruets and an ornate photo frame. His throat constricted with fear.

'Thanks,' he said. 'You go off now, quick as you can. I found this bag myself, do you understand, and thank you again, we'll be in touch.'

'I'm sorry, Mr Feather.'

'So am I,' said Tom.

Cathy came back into the kitchen and took off her Scarlet Feather apron. 'Tom, you're a genius, how did you know that was the kind of music they wanted. It's working like a dream, look at them all leaping about to "Dancing Queen". God, I hope we'll be able to do that at their age.'

'Cathy, Walter stole the silver. His sports bag there, filled with their stuff, look for yourself.'

The colour left her face. He hated to do this to her, but there was no other way. He couldn't act until he knew what she would do. Walter was part of Cathy's family set-up, not his.

'Where is he?'

'Still in the dining room, chatting up Molly and Shay's daughter, being glowered at by the girl's boyfriend.'

Cathy took out her mobile.

'What are you doing?' he asked.

'Getting a taxi for June and Helen, there's a taxi rank a couple of minutes away, I took its number.'

'And then?'

'We sort this out here, get the guards if necessary, if he denies it.'

'What would Neil say?'

'I don't know, but I'll let Walter ring him, he's going to need a lawyer over this.'

'You're not going the distance on this?' Tom was amazed at her courage.

'If I can I will.'

'Walter, can I interrupt you for a moment? I need you in the kitchen.' Tom spoke in a low voice.

'Hey, my hours of servitude are over, I'm here on my own time now.'

'Straight away, please.'

When he saw the open bag, Walter began to bluster. 'How *dare* you root in my private things . . .' he began.

'An explanation, Walter.'

'I didn't put them there, *you* did. You both hate me.'

'We haven't touched them. The guards will be here shortly and will tell us whose fingerprints are on them.'

'You're never going to call the guards?' His face was white, but he still thought they were bluffing.

'It's what you have to do in a case of theft.' Cathy lifted her mobile phone again.

'You're going to call them now?'

'No, I'm going to wait for you to call your cousin first because you're going to need someone to speak for you, Walter. It might as well be Neil, that's if he takes you on.'

He looked at her, unbelieving.

'Go on, make the call.'

'I don't know the number.'

'It's pre-set. You just dial one.'

They sat and watched him as he waited until Neil answered. The kitchen door was closed; they could hear both ends of the conversation.

'Neil, sorry . . . sorry for ringing you, it's Walter.'

'What is it? Is Cathy all right, what has happened? Was there an accident?'

'No, actually I'm in a bit of trouble.'

'Where's Cathy?'

'She's here beside me ... Do you want to talk to her?' Cathy shook her head. 'No, sorry Neil, I have to talk, apparently.'

'Talk then,' the voice said crisply.

'Well there was a bit of a misunderstanding ... We're still at this house, you see, and Tom went rummaging in my private bag and he found or he says he found some silver there ... belonging to the house, as it were ...' Walter paused but there was no response so he had to go on again. 'And now, Neil, they're talking about calling the guards, Tom and Cathy are. Uncle Jock will kill me, you have to help me ...' Still silence at the other end. 'What will I do?'

'Take off your jacket.'

'What?'

'Take off your jacket and hand it to Tom.'

'I don't think that's going to be any help. What's the point ... ?'

'Do it, Walter.'

He did it. There was a rattle as he struggled out of his dinner jacket and passed it over to Tom. Tom shook it again. There were silver teaspoons in the pocket, a watch and a paper knife.

'Is it done?' Neil asked.

'Yes, there seem to be ...'

'I was sure there might have been,' Neil said.

'What happens now?'

'Not up to me, I'm afraid.'

'Who is it up to?' Walter asked fearfully.

'Cathy and Tom and the people whose silver you stole. Do they know yet, by the way?'

'No, and I didn't really steal it, you know.'

'Of course not. Good luck, then.'

'What do you mean, good luck, aren't you going to help me?'

'No, I most certainly am not.'

'Neil you *have* to. I'm family.'

'No, listen to me ... Cathy's your employer, you stole from her. You could have had her prosecuted, you stupid little shit.'

'Cathy's here, Neil, let me pass you over to her ... Please, Neil, beg her, beg her.' There were tears running down his face.

'Cathy and Tom run their business, Walter. They had the bad

luck to employ a thief. Anything they do is fine with me.' And he hung up.

Tom and Cathy looked at each other. 'Your trouser pockets,' Tom said.

There was a cigarette lighter and some more spoons. He wept and begged, but they spoke as if he weren't there.

'You call it, Tom.' She was very calm.

'No, I won't. I'm not taking on that emotional stuff. Truly I'm not. You wouldn't want to do it if he were Marcella's cousin.'

'That's fair.' There was a silence. 'I want him done for this, every bit of me wants that. There are just two things against it.'

'I'm family,' Walter begged tearfully.

'Shut your face about family,' Cathy said. 'It's that I don't want to spoil Molly and Shay's evening, and I don't want to look those children in the eye and tell them I was the one who put their brother in jail and added to all the problems the unfortunates already have.'

'So you'll not call the guards?' He grabbed at the lifeline he saw. 'Tom?'

'I'm with you,' Tom said.

'Give me back your wages,' she said.

Walter hurried to find them for her.

'No,' Tom said. 'Keep them, you did five hours' work, so you're being paid for it.'

'Thank you Tom,' he looked at the ground.

'Go now,' he said.

'I'm sorry, Cathy.'

'You're just sorry you were caught, Walter.'

'No, funnily enough I was beginning to enjoy it tonight for the first time, seeing the whole operation get under way.'

He spoke with an odd sincerity. 'Why did you do it, Walter? Jock pays you plenty.'

'I'm in debt,' he said.

'Well, look on the bright side . . . At least you're not in the Garda station,' she said.

'I'll never forget this, Cathy.'

'Sure.'

He left. Cathy sat there, very still.

'You were great,' Tom said. 'And Neil was great too.'

'I knew he wouldn't defend Walter,' Cathy said.

'I didn't.' Tom was thoughtful. 'I thought he'd see him as the underdog.'

'No, *we* were the underdogs, Neil could see that straight away. Our entire business could have gone under because of his little cousin.'

'He has an extraordinary sense of justice,' Tom said admiringly.

'So do you,' Cathy said. 'I'd never have given him tonight's wages, not in a million years. And yet you're right, he *did* earn them before he started nicking things.'

'Come on, let's go home,' he said, and began to drive the van back to the little town house in Waterview where Neil would be waiting up to talk over the night's events with Cathy. And then he would drive himself back to the flat in Stoneyfield where Marcella would also be waiting to know how this, their biggest booking ever, had gone.

'Do you get the feeling this night went on for days and days?' Cathy asked wearily.

'I do, weeks and weeks actually.'

They drove on in silence, then Tom said, 'But compared to a lot of the all-time losers we met tonight, I think you and I are fairly lucky. Or is that me being too over-cheerful?' he asked.

Chapter Four

APRIL

Molly Hayes said at lunchtime the next day that she had never enjoyed anything so much, and all her friends had rung to congratulate her. It had been an evening that could so easily have ended differently.

They had worked hard this morning, and it was good to have a little breathing space. They decided to visit Haywards mid-season sale. They found some white blinds with a discreet scarlet trim, and extra lighting strips. The preparations were all done for the two delivery jobs ... a fancy bridge tea for twelve people, tiny sandwiches and little cakes to go to a private house. They had been ages working out how you put recognisable hearts, diamonds, clubs and spades on each as a motif, but between radishes and black olives as fiddly little decorations they had come up with something acceptable. They also had to sneak a supper to a woman who was pretending to her in-laws that she had cooked this meal herself. She had given them her own dishes, paid in advance – the only rule was that they just leave simple easy-to-follow instructions and never tell anyone that they had been. They would leave her a big jug of spinach soup, a slow-cooked casserole and a lemon tart. It was extremely puzzling to them, but then there was no point whatsoever in criticising her. She was part of the way they earned their living. They felt like children stealing time out of school as they sat down to have a coffee after their buying spree. Cathy saw Shona Burke, sitting alone and reading a book; she was eating a small salad and drinking something from the health juice bar.

'She's an odd mixture, isn't she . . . friendly one minute, shutting you out the next.'

'Yeah, maybe she has a sugar daddy tucked away,' Tom said.

'Why do you say that?'

'How else could she afford a flat in Glenstar?'

'It's only a studio flat, Tom, and they're all like little boxrooms, anyway she could be old money.' Cathy didn't want living in Glenstar being associated with sugar daddies or having gentlemen giving you gifts.

Shona looked lonely. And rather prim. She finished her lunch, closed the book, looked at her watch and was about to go back to her work when she spotted them. She looked a totally different person when she smiled.

'Aha, Scarlet Feather undercover in our café,' she said.

'Your breads are rubbish compared to mine,' Tom teased her.

To his surprise she nodded. 'You're absolutely right, that's what I was saying last Friday at a meeting, lovely soups and salads here but just the plainest and dullest of bread. You know, *that's* how I'm going to get you in here. They can put up a notice saying that the breadbasket is by Scarlet Feather. Listen, there's a meeting tomorrow at ten-thirty. Can you let me have a selection of your best, and I'll suggest it.'

They talked about prices and presentation and quantities and delivery. The enthusiasm was enormous. Shona became anxious about it.

'Don't be too disappointed if it doesn't work, I'll give it my very best shot for you both, I think it would be really good for the restaurant too.'

'You're a star, Shona,' Tom said, gathering up his bags of light fittings.

'Are you back to the kitchens to start baking now?' she laughed.

'No, now I'm going to see my father. I'll go into the premises tomorrow, early. You're not going to get one-day-old bread for your demonstration . . . It's going to be the real thing, fresh-baked, about five different kinds . . .'

'How *is* your father?' Shona always asked.

'Oh, he's fine thanks, Shona, you were very kind to me that night at the hospital. He's taking it a little easier, which is no harm. My mother thinks it's all to do with some prayer she said . . . A bit wearing, but if it works for her . . . why not?' Tom shrugged.

Cathy agreed. 'It's not doing anyone any harm, and she prayed like mad that our business would survive, so won't you be sure to tell her how well we're doing?'

'I will, of course. Listen, I'm going to run up to the salon and see Marcella for a quick word before we go.'

'Don't say anything yet about the bread business,' Shona warned.

'No, of course not. Cathy, will you pay for the coffee out of office funds, and I'll see you in the van in ten minutes.' He was gone. The two women watched him, and saw the admiring glances as he moved like an athlete through the tables, smiling his apologies if he had to push past people.

'He has absolutely no idea the effect he creates,' Cathy said. 'They're all mad about him wherever we go; the young ones are delighted to know that he's not attached to me, and of course all these old dears, they love him to bits and he just hasn't a clue.'

'When he and Marcella go anywhere together they're just like film stars, the pair of them,' Shona said, getting up to leave. 'Listen, let me look after your coffee for you.'

'No, no,' Cathy protested.

'Cathy, please. This time tomorrow you may well be official suppliers – you're certainly entitled to a cup of coffee.'

Cathy accepted, and as she picked up her parcels said, 'Tom said you had family in the hospital when he went to see his father?'

'Yes, that's right.'

'And is it all right ... for them too?'

Shona looked at her. 'No, no, it wasn't all right, in this case she died.'

'Oh, I'm very sorry to hear that.'

'Thank you, Cathy.' Very flat, very unemotional.

'And was it anyone close?'

There was a pause. 'No, not close, not close at all.'

Marcella was sitting at her little table doing nail extensions for a very elegant woman who was busy holding out her hands and admiring them. She was delighted to see Tom, and jumped up to greet him. She looked so gorgeous in her short white uniform with the blue Haywards logo, her long slim legs in dark navy tights and her cloud of dark hair like a halo around her tiny face. Sometimes he could hardly believe how beautiful she was, and that she might love only him. He saw everyone in the salon admiring her.

'Will I get a video, or would you like to go out?' he whispered.

'There's a book launch,' she said.

'Let's hit that, then,' he said with a good-natured shrug. He knew not to ask Marcella whose book and on what topic. A book launch was a photo opportunity. Someone might take a very glamorous picture of Marcella, which could appear in the Among Those Attending column. It would be clipped from the newspaper and added to the growing file in the portfolio. He took the name of the bookshop and the time and said he'd see her there. No point in suggesting dinner afterwards. Marcella hardly ate dinner, and anyway, she'd be going to the gym.

'Could I drop you off at Fatima and then take the van tonight?' Cathy asked him when they had fitted the two blinds, and realised that the light installation needed an electrician. Tom said it was fine, he was meeting Marcella later in the city centre, he'd take a bus back in from his parents' house.

'Are you sure? I could go home and get the Volvo,' Cathy said. 'Where are you off to?'

'To see some of the further adventures of Hooves the wonder dog, and to try and reassure those two kids that their life isn't totally over if they do have to go back to their barking-mad parents.'

'But wouldn't you be a little bit relieved, in a way? Go on, be honest with me, I'm not family.' He smiled at her.

'I've never *been* more honest . . . I think it would be so wrong for them to have to go back to that set-up. We've just got some manners on them, some small appearance of normality, they have a dog, they have two happy homes to live in; what makes those selfish clowns think they can wake from their drinky, dysfunctional lives and take them straight back?'

'You won't be relieved then, I take it?'

'No, I'll be heartbroken, as it happens.'

'How'ya, Dad?'

His father sat at the table reading an Irish Heart Foundation publication about avoiding stress.

'Tell me how on earth can anyone avoid stress? If you're in business you can't do it, that's what business is about. How do *you* avoid stress, Tom?'

'Well Da, there's a lot of people who say I never even achieved any stress, let alone have to avoid it.'

'Well it's true, you *have* had an easy business life compared to the building trade, but surely you must worry about ... will this job do well, or will you get that contract?'

'Sure Da, every day. Today I'm worrying about whether the bread I make tomorrow will be good enough for Haywards to sell ... I just try to put it out of my mind when I'm not actually doing it.'

His father grunted. 'Yes, yes, that's what they say here, but of course yours isn't really a business worry in the proper sense of the word.'

'No, Da,' said Tom, who wondered if his father had any idea at all of the years spent having to work night after long night in bars to make the fees for catering college, to borrow huge sums of money for the company, to ask people to be guarantors for the loan, to look at Marcella and know that she was the most beautiful person on earth, and surely someone with style and class would take her away from him. And his father still thought he knew no stress.

'Marcella sent her love,' he lied to his father.

'I know she did, a grand girl no matter what your mother says.'

'What exactly is she saying these days?'

'Ah, you know, the living as man and wife bit ... the usual ... nothing new.'

'Wouldn't you think she'd have got used to it by now, Dad?' Tom looked at him helplessly.

'People of your mother's frame of mind never get used to it, son, sure you only have to look at Joe to know that.'

'Joe? What do you mean?'

His mother came in just then. 'He's on the mend, isn't he, Tom? What were you saying about Joe just then?'

'I was saying it was nice of him to send Da that basket of fruit, that's all I was saying,' Tom said hastily.

'Huh,' said his mother.

'Marcella was saying it's a great present to send people, far healthier than sending them a bottle of wine or chocolates or something. Oh, and she sent you both her love.'

'Huh,' said his mother again in exactly the same tone.

'You must be delighted that Dad's so fit.'

'Well of course it's all thanks to Our Lady.'

'Sure Ma, and the hospital and everything.'

'The hospital could have done what it liked, it wouldn't have been able to cure your father if Our Lady hadn't intervened.' She nodded her head several times as if she were agreeing with other people who also held this view. Her husband and son looked at her at a loss. There was a silence.

'Was it the Thirty Days' Prayer?' Tom asked eventually.

'Fat lot you know about prayer. There wasn't *time* for the Thirty Days' Prayer, you eejit. I had to get something much quicker.'

'And she found it in the *Evening Herald*.' Tom's father knew what to say.

'Oh, laugh away, the pair of you.' She was huffed now.

'Maura! Am I laughing?'

'No, but you would if you had a mind to. It was a Never Known to Fail prayer, and all you have to do when you get your wish is publish it again in the paper so that someone else will see it and know how very powerful the Holy Virgin is in times of crisis, and . . .'

'That's pretty clever of the newspapers. It means they get columns of prayers in the classifieds,' Tom said admiringly.

Maura went on as if Tom had not spoken. 'And the other thing Our Lady asks is that we just sit down for five minutes with a non-believer and explain how her Son so loved the world that . . .'

'Yes, well, Mam, but I was only really dropping in to see how Dad was . . .'

'We could do it now, Tom.'

'But Ma . . .'

'Please son,' his father asked.

Tom sat obediently and listened while his mother told him of Our Lady's personal distress about a variety of subjects. 'Why can't you believe it, Tom? Just tell me,' his mother asked in the tones of one who would be able to sort it out immediately if she knew the exact point of disagreement.

'It's not that I *don't* believe,' he began.

'But what's the problem then?'

'Mam I've *told* you, it's not like that. I don't *not* believe things,' he began, imploring her to understand.

'But what *do* you believe Tom? What exactly?'

'Well, I believe there's something . . . something out there to make sense of it all.'

'But you know what's out there, Tom.'

His father's eyes were on him. 'I suppose I do, Mam.' He let his mind drift on to the kind of baskets he would use to present this bread tomorrow, and whether they should wrap them in the good

Scarlet Feather napkins. He nodded gravely at everything his mother had said, and gave her longer than the five minutes she had sought. She was pleased now that the bargain with Our Lady had been kept. And went out to the kitchen head held high.

'Thanks Tom,' his father said.

'But Dad, *you* don't have to go along with all this . . .'

'I do, Tom, it's called give and take . . . Your mother gives a lot to me, so I give her this bit of listening, that's all there is to it.'

'No, there's much more to it, you have to put on a whole act about things you don't believe.'

'You'd do the same for Marcella now, son, wouldn't you?'

'Well, I suppose I go along with all these nights she spends at the gym when she's already perfect, but I wouldn't pretend to believe something I didn't believe. I wouldn't do that.'

'You might, you know,' his father said. 'In times to come you might well pretend just for an easy life.'

The twins were doing their homework in the kitchen when Cathy arrived at St Jarlath's. Her mother had begun making their wedding outfits, and had the sewing machine whirring away. Her father was out in the back painting the kennel that one of his pals from the bookies had made for Hooves. Another friend had given him an old horseshoe which he was going to nail over it for luck. The puppy sat on a newspaper quivering with pleasure in the warm kitchen.

'You're welcome, Cathy, but this is a house of hard industry at the moment. Everyone has to be kept at their work until after six-thirty, if you know what I mean.'

Cathy knew exactly what she meant. She meant that it was hard enough to get Muttie to paint and the children to do their school work without having a welcome interruption like a visit to cope with.

'I'm just going to do my accounts at the table,' she said quickly, and sat down opposite Maud and Simon. 'Hallo,' she whispered, as if she too were just a fellow hater of homework.

'Should we make tea?' Maud hissed hopefully behind her hand. Simon looked up eagerly.

'No, not until half past six,' Cathy whispered, and they all went back to work. She didn't even see the figures, they were just a blur. She had phoned Neil just before coming here. Simon and Maud's mother and father were very grateful to these people who had done so much when they were unavoidably absent, but everything was now fine again. They were looking forward to seeing their children again, and were expecting them to come home at the weekend. And tonight he was meeting someone who would let them know about the timescale.

'Timescale?' Cathy had asked.

About the job; apparently this guy knew how long it could be held open for Neil.

At half past six they all went on a tour of inspection of the snow-white kennel.

'It's beautiful,' Simon said with awe.

'A palace for Hooves,' said Maud.

'But of course he can't get into it until the paint is dried,' Muttie explained.

'Or he'll come out looking like a Dalmatian, all white spots,' said Cathy.

'Dalmatians are actually white with black spots,' Simon corrected her. Then he remembered that you didn't correct people. 'At least, what I meant to say was . . . that some of them are white with black spots. Of course, they *could* be the other way round, too.'

'Good boy, Simon,' Cathy said with sudden tears in her eyes. They had taught these children so much, they were almost human beings now, and for what? So that they could be sent back to these dysfunctional parents?

'Are you crying?' Maud asked with interest.

'Sort of. People of my age do cry sometimes, quite unexpectedly. It's a nuisance,' she said matter-of-factly and blew her nose.

'Our mother used to cry like that in the hospital, and she didn't know why either,' Maud said kindly, as a sort of reassurance.

'But in her case it was really due to her bad nerves.' Simon was anxious always to be fair.

She hadn't realised just how very much she was going to miss them. It was nonsense to say that they *belonged* with this ridiculous couple, Jock's brother Kenneth and his wife.

'Come on kids, let's take Hooves for a walk. I know he's not mine but I feel very close to him, even though I don't live here.'

'It won't be much of a walk, it's more a waddle,' Maud said, and ran for the lead. Up and down St Jarlath's Crescent they went, telling the people that they met about the puppy. They divided the time meticulously between them.

'I never thought we'd have a real puppy of our own, I thought we'd be able to play with someone else's, but not one of our very own, living in the house,' said Simon when it was Maud's turn to hold the lead.

'Sure, and he'll always be yours. The actual *house* where Hooves sleeps isn't all that important, not as important as the fact that he belongs to you.'

Simon looked up at her, troubled. 'Why do you say that?'

'Well, you know,' she shrugged vaguely.

'I know now,' he said. The old solemn look was back.

'What do you know?' she asked fearfully.

Maud had joined them, and was looking from one to the other.

Simon spoke very slowly and deliberately. 'Father has come back from his travels, Mother is coming out of the nervous hospital and we'll be leaving Muttie and his wife and we're going back to live with them and leave Hooves behind us.'

Maud looked up, stricken, waiting to hear it wasn't true. 'We're to call Muttie's wife Lizzie,' she corrected. 'Remember.'

'Yes,' Simon said flatly. 'Sorry, I forgot. Yeah, it's Lizzie all right.'

There was a silence. 'It's your turn with Hooves,' Maud said to Simon.

'I don't want him, Maud. Thank you all the same,' Simon said, and walked ahead of them back home. His shoulders were hunched and his head was down. Cathy let him go. She knew that he was trying very hard not to show how upset he was.

'Are we really going to be leaving St Jarlath's Crescent and you and Neil, Cathy?' Maud's face was paler than ever.

'It's not really *leaving*, you know friends don't leave each other, you'll be coming back to us and to Dad and Mam and who knows, maybe things are much better now and you can take Hooves with you.'

'You didn't know Mother, did you?'

'No, not really *know*, so to speak.'

'Her nerves would never let her make a home for Hooves,' Maud said sadly.

Marcella was talking earnestly to Ricky, but her face lit up when Tom came into the bookshop.

'You'll never guess what Ricky's going to try and get,' she said excitedly.

'No, tell me.' Tom was tired. His mother had worn him out, the passivity of his father had depressed him, he feared they hadn't costed the breads right for tomorrow's demonstration. Cathy had rung him on the mobile to say that St Jarlath's Crescent was plunged into gloom and the only person giving her the time of day was the black puppy, who had peed several times into her shoe.

'I just wondered if you felt like a cheering drink,' she had asked.

'I'm on my way to have one, come and join us. We might make a pitch for the bookshop trade as well,' he offered.

'Will I get in? I wasn't invited,' Cathy wondered.

'I'd say they'll be out in the highways and byways dragging people in off the street,' he said.

'Tom, don't look now,' Marcella warned, 'but that woman over there in the hat ... She's the editor of the new magazine I was telling you about, well, Ricky thinks he could sell her a picture story. Big, hunky photos of you ... wearing a *much* classier sweater than that ... Huge publicity for Scarlet Feather, too ... you know, at home and at work or wherever.'

'Yeah, I mentioned it to her, she seems to be interested, but you know they never tell you yes or no. Still, I think she'll bite.'

'You do, Ricky?' Tom's eyes lit up. This would be truly wonderful. Everyone who was ever going to hire a caterer read this publication. He could see Cathy and himself taking the tray of bread into Haywards, the van with its jaunty little logo. Maybe they could give a recipe, and get a perfect picture taken of the completed dish. Like the scallops and ginger Cathy did so well, that would really show up well. They would never in a million years be able to get this kind of coverage. Wasn't Marcella *great* to talk Ricky into this. Ricky would persuade the woman in the silly hat.

'He's going to ask her to come over and meet you in a minute – give her your biggest smile,' Marcella begged. She looked so beautiful, but extra lively and happy tonight in a very smart short, dark grey and white dress he had never seen before.

'New?' he asked admiringly.

'Tom darling, you are so wonderful but you know nothing about clothes. This would cost seven hundred pounds if you were to buy it.'

'So how did you ...'

'Joys of working in Haywards. Someone returned it to the designer room, a flaw in one of the seams or something. All I pay for is the dry-cleaning.'

She was like a toddler at a birthday party she was so thrilled with it all. Just then he saw Cathy. She looked bedraggled in her raincoat, and instead of a bright ribbon holding her hair back she had an elastic band. She wore no make-up, and she had lines under her eyes. He would not have noticed except that the room was filled with overdressed women and he had just turned away from the immaculately groomed Marcella in her designer outfit.

Cathy smiled. 'Lead me to the cheapest red wine and let me loose on it,' she said.

'Not if you're driving the company van, no way,' he said.

'No, I parked it up at the premises. It's all tucked up there waiting for the dawn baker to arrive.' She was as tired as he was. Where did all these other people get the energy to yap so much to each other?

'My God, look at Marcella! She's utterly dazzling in that dress. Bet it cost a few quid.'

'Don't ask,' he said.

'Oh dear, domestic rows on this matter?'

'No, I meant don't ask because it's off Haywards rail tonight and back tomorrow, I understand.'

'No harm done then.' Cathy was cheerful. 'Lord, but this is truly dreadful wine, I'll be glad when I've had enough!'

The woman in the silly hat approached and was introduced by Ricky. 'This is the celebrated Tom Feather I told you about,' Ricky said.

'Mmm,' she said, looking Tom up and down.

'I hear the magazine's doing really well,' he said.

'And your business too.' Again she seemed to let her eyes run all over Tom's body slowly and appreciatively.

'Yes, well, let me introduce you to the other half of the business, half of Scarlet Feather, Cathy Scarlet.'

'Great to meet you,' Cathy said pleasantly.

The woman looked somewhat puzzled. 'How nice,' she said.

'We'd be very happy to cooperate in anything . . . everything,' he said with his huge smile.

'Well *that* sounds like the best offer I've had all night,' she said. She had a strange manner, this woman with the hat. Full of innuendo, as if a very obvious pass was being made to her and she was being coy and flirtatious about it. Cathy thought she was grotesque. But she had gone now, so it was immaterial.

'Marcella . . . you look stunning.' She was genuine in her admiration.

'You're sweet, Cathy, it's just fine feathers, borrowed feathers actually.'

'Wait till you know what's going to happen, thanks to Ricky.' Tom couldn't wait a moment longer.

'What?' Cathy had rarely seen him so excited.

'That woman who looked as if she was wearing two building blocks stuck to a coat hanger on her head. She's the head of the new magazine we couldn't afford to advertise in, and wait for it, there's going to be a photo feature about Scarlet Feather in it.'

'Well, Tom . . .' Ricky began.

'*No*! You're not serious.' Cathy was utterly delighted but apprehensive. She was going to have to do so much, finally change her hairstyle, borrow some clothes, get a professional make-up . . . But it would all be worth it.

'When do they want to do it?' she asked, as excited as Tom was.

'Well you see, actually . . .' Ricky began looking ill at ease.

Marcella explained. 'Ricky was telling me she's a very difficult woman, she blows hot and cold, we won't really know when or what form it will take for quite some time.' She seemed to be looking very directly at Ricky as she spoke.

'Sure,' he said eventually. 'Marcella tells it as it is. Stay in this part of the room, honey. I'll get one of the guys from the Sundays to come over to snap you.'

'Photographers always use that word "snap" as a joke. It's like people calling the radio a wireless . . .' Marcella said.

'Why did Ricky change his tack so suddenly? A few minutes ago he was saying it was in the bag. I can't understand it.' Tom was puzzled and annoyed.

The woman with the hat was leaving. She waved at him. ''Night, Tom, be good now. We'll be in touch soon. Ricky knows everything,' she said and was gone.

'*Now*,' Tom was triumphant. 'I'm going to find Ricky and tell him.'

'Please Tom, don't.' Marcella spoke seriously. Cathy looked up at her tone. 'There's been a misunderstanding.' Marcella looked awkwardly from Tom to Cathy as if unsure where to start or which of them to tell.

'Go on Marcella,' Cathy was gentle.

'Ricky was selling her a feature for a kind of Glamorous Couples thing . . . you know, you the big, gorgeous gourmet cook, me the model, our home, pics of us coming out of Stoneyfield together, you serving a meal to me, me at the gym, you piping cream on a dessert . . . Me doing the charity modelling show for that children's home . . . That kind of thing . . . So you see . . .'

'It's not about Scarlet Feather at all.' He was bitterly disappointed.

'Well, of course it is in part . . . after all, it's going to say what you do for a living, people will get to know your name.'

'But it's all a fake. I don't cook you meals, Marcella . . . you don't *eat* any meals.' Tom's face was red with indignation.

'Oh, come on, Tom, I thought you'd be delighted. She said you were gorgeous-looking. She told Ricky that when he showed her a picture he had taken of both of us. This is the chance I need. Why are you being so difficult? They can't *have* a feature on the business alone, that would be just advertising and the other catering companies would all go mad.'

'And what about all the other models or future models, won't they go mad also if it's about you?'

'About *us*, Tom, not just me, it's you too, how else are you going to get Scarlet Feather mentioned? I thought you'd be so pleased.'

Cathy saw this argument going nowhere except sharply downhill. 'I think it's great, Tom, this is the very best way that we could get publicity you know, it's *exactly* what we want.'

Marcella looked at her, a quick, very grateful glance.

But Tom had yet to be persuaded. 'I think it's silly. I'm not a male model, strutting about for knitting patterns, dressing up in a posh sweater or serving something in a cream sauce that you wouldn't eat in a million years . . .'

'Tom, stop the dramatics. How else are we going to get Scarlet Feather that kind of publicity? Tell me.'

'*You're* not being asked to behave like an arsehole.'

'And neither are you . . . I'd do it for the company. I would in a flash if I looked the part, and if Neil's bloody job would let him take part. But you know the way those barristers go on . . .' She had defused it.

'So do you really think. . . ?'

'Well of course I think . . . But listen, in the end it's all up to you and Marcella to fight about it. I'll leave you now to get on with it. Just know that I put on the table the view that it would be great for business.' She turned to go away, and saw herself reflected in a glass door. Of course it had been ridiculous to think that a glossy magazine would have wanted her in it. She had been even more idiotic than Tom.

'Don't go, Cathy, you wanted a drink and to be cheered up.'

'Well I *am* cheered up, very.' Her eyes were very bright, over-bright. 'We've got a load of great publicity ahead of us and all you have to do is smile.'

'I'm sorry. I thought it was the two of us.'

'I'm not ... I'm totally relieved,' and she was out of the bookshop.

'Do you think Mother will let us come back here to St Jarlath's?' Maud asked Simon hopefully.

'I don't think so, do you?' Simon had no idea.

'Not really. Her nerves might not be able to take it,' Maud said.

There was a silence. Eventually Simon spoke. 'I suppose it will be all right being back at home again. In a way.'

'Yes.' Maud was glum.

'At least we don't have to change schools again. Neil got that sorted for us,' Simon said.

'I suppose we'll just get ourselves home ... I mean, Muttie and Hooves can't come and collect us any more.'

'No.' Simon was very sure on this.

'It's a pity Mother's nerves got better so soon in a way, isn't it?' Maud said.

'And that Father was found,' said Simon.

They looked at each other guiltily. But it had been said now, and it couldn't be taken back.

Cathy was around at the premises at dawn the next day.

'I'm not here to interfere ... just to make coffee and tidy up after you ... This is your show,' she explained.

Tom was overjoyed to see her. 'God, I'm glad to see you. I'm having awful second thoughts about the fruit and nutty bread.'

'But everyone loves that,' Cathy protested.

'They love it when they've paid for it in advance, when it's in their house and they can't give it back,' Tom wailed, 'but will they love it if they have to pay so much a slice and wonder why if it's sweet they aren't buying a slice of gooey gateau instead. I think it was a stupid idea.'

'It's in the oven, isn't it?' Cathy checked.

'Yes, but—'

'I think it's a great idea ... Come on, strong, strong coffee and lots of backbone ... Which was Geraldine's great advice to me when I was a teenager. How's Marcella?' He had stopped worrying about the bread now.

'I proposed again last night. I said to Marcella that if we have to do this idiotic photo shoot let's make it an engagement celebration, but she won't hear of it.'

'Proper order. What an unromantic proposal!' Cathy said firmly.

'No, it's not that at all; she says she won't marry me until she's successful, until she believes that I'm getting as good a bargain as she is.'

'She's amazingly direct and straightforward, isn't she,' Cathy said with admiration.

'She is the only person I know in the whole world who has never told a lie,' Tom said.

'Hey, come on, what about me?'

'You lie from morning to night, as do I. We *have* to, we tell people their houses are terrific when they're terrible, we tell them this Chardonnay is better than that depending what price we get it for, we thank the butcher and tell him he's terrific to chop the meat for us even though he doesn't do it properly but at least he waves his cleaver at it. We're telling lies all day.'

There was a ping on the oven timer and the bread came out. It all looked perfect as it went onto the wire trays. Cathy shook Tom's hand formally. 'It's bloody great, Tom, I can't believe they won't take it. I *know* we're into Haywards today, I just know it.'

They delivered the baskets to Shona just before the big meeting. Shona looked so elegant in her dark suit and pale pink blouse, slightly severe but very much in control. You didn't stay in a senior job at Haywards just by looking pretty.

'It smells utterly magical, but you know it's not down to me. I can only hope for you,' she said, and she was gone.

They would meet in the café at noon to hear the result. They had the time planned down to the last second: they would go to the market to buy the ingredients for James Byrne's cookery lesson that evening. They would price little breadbaskets in the market too. Just in case they got the Haywards job ... They would check on a new laundry, what it would cost to do their tablecloths; they would walk around the new Eastern Delights delicatessen with notebooks at the ready, looking for more ideas. That would certainly fill up all their time until Shona was able to tell them the news.

Shona came running into the café, thumbs up in the air. Not only had they bought it as an idea, they had eaten it all at their coffee break. There had been little dishes of butter on the tray as well, to encourage them. They could start next week on a six-week trial period.

'Can we use our name?' Tom asked.

'Yes, but a bit smaller than you wanted . . . They'd like "baked fresh every day especially for Haywards", and then your name . . . But we can put your logo on, of course, and make it whatever size we like.' Shona was as eager as they were.

Cathy flung her arms around the girl. 'We'll never be able to thank you,' she said, her voice choked.

Then Tom folded Shona in a bear-hug. 'I swear I'll make it a success, for your sake as well as ours.' He was gruff with gratitude.

'You'll be responsible for putting two inches onto the hip measurements of Ireland,' Shona said. 'You should have seen the way they went at it, and they want double the order of the fruit and nut one.'

'And they accept the price?' Tom was beaming all over his face.

'Yes, they think it's fair, but don't be appalled when you see what *they* charge, they didn't get to be rich by having a small mark-up,' she apologised.

'We'd take you out to dinner tonight to thank you properly, but we have a job,' Cathy said.

'No need, believe me, I'm the flavour of the month after that feeding frenzy upstairs!'

Tom and Cathy looked at each other in disbelief.

'Back to the market,' she said.

'To buy the breadbaskets,' Tom said with a great whoop of joy that turned every head in his direction.

James Byrne had explained to them that he wanted three cookery lessons. And that he would need to master a starter, a main course and a dessert at each lesson. Then he could mix and match, and when the time came he could serve whatever he liked best or possibly whatever was easiest. They didn't ask him what was the time that was going to come. You didn't ask James Byrne anything personal like that.

It was a big house, back from the road, with a well-kept gravelled space for cars. The house was probably in four large apartments. James Byrne had said to ring the Garden Flat bell. It was a basement with iron bars on the window. Fairly typical of his cautious behaviour. Assume the worst. Be prepared for burglars, clients with laundered money, random tax inspections, people clamping your car, stolen credit cards. James Byrne was someone who did not automatically believe the best of people.

He opened the door to them and smiled his usual grave smile. Dressed formally – no sweater and sloppy corduroys for James Byrne at home. They carried in their bags of ingredients though a dark narrow hall. On the right was a sitting room, on the left a kitchen and straight ahead what must have been a bedroom and bathroom. It was mainly a dark muddy-brown colour, and even with the April sunset peeping through the dark curtains there was nowhere that the light seemed to land on a cheerful corner. The kitchen had various storage cupboards, all of different heights, and an awkward table, an old-fashioned oven, a sink that was impossible to reach and a fridge that took up a great amount of room, and which held a bottle of water, a carton of orange juice, half a litre of milk and a packet of butter. Cathy ached to get it all torn out. A phone call could have had two of JT Feather's men round in half an hour, then they could order fittings. She and Tom knew places who would deliver and install in a day. But this was not going to happen. This man would live with these hopeless, outdated appliances for ever. How old was he now? About sixty-something. He had never said if he was single, married, divorced or widowed. His flat gave absolutely no sign of any lifestyle. You would not know what chair he sat in in the evening to watch television. Or if he ever did watch it. A small set stood at an inconvenient angle. A low table had a pile of neatly stacked newspapers and magazines on it. Were they waiting to be read, waiting to have things clipped from them, or just pausing before going to a waste-paper bank? Pictures on the walls were of mountains and lakes. Dull prints, no life in any of them. Old, inexpensive frames. Just two shelves of old books. They looked pretty undisturbed. A desk with some papers on it and an old-fashioned blotter, although nobody had written with ink for years. A plastic mug held all James Byrne's ballpoint pens. Cathy saw that Tom was looking around him, probably making similar judgements. She shook herself.

'Right. The lesson starts here, James: put on your pinny.'

'I don't think I have one . . .' he began.

'I didn't think so either, so I brought you one of ours!'

Triumphantly she produced a Scarlet Feather apron with its big red logo around the edge. He seemed bashful as he tied its strings around his waist.

'That was very nice of her, wasn't it, Tom?' he said. 'Trust a woman to have a nice little touch.'

'Not a bit of it, James; don't ever let the females think they have a monopoly on little touches. Look what I brought you, a great big oven glove so that you won't burn your arm to a crisp like some people I know.'

He was very pleased with this and tried it on, flexing his arm up and down. 'Looks as if it's all going to be much more intensive, not to say more dangerous, than I thought,' he said.

The conversation sounded so normal. Why did they feel they couldn't ask him why he was paying them all this money to learn how to make a meal? Who was he going to serve it to and why? But they knew that this was not a question that could be asked, nor would be answered.

They did a smoked mackerel starter in little ramekins. Cathy flaked the fish expertly and added the thinly sliced mushrooms and cream.

'The cheese for the top is nicer if freshly grated,' she said, 'but you could use a shake from the packet of Parmesan.'

James Byrne looked doubtful.

'I always use the packet myself for small things like this,' Tom lied.

'Oh, you do?' Cathy said, laughing.

'Indeed I do. Saves you that little bit of time just when you need it, I always say.'

'It seems a very easy thing to make.' James Byrne was suspicious.

'It tastes as if it were very difficult to make, I assure you.' Cathy patted him down.

'I've had it in restaurants, and you know I thought there was an awful lot of cooking in it, and now it's only tearing up a cold smoked fish and pouring cream on it.' He shook his head in wonder.

'Wait till we deconstruct chicken tarragon for you, James,' Tom laughed. 'You'll never trust a cook again.'

They sat and ate together, the three of them. Cathy had written out everything step by step. James said it was all quite delicious, and what's more, he thought he could do it on his own. They talked easily about the theatre, how Cathy and Tom had once seen every play that was on every stage in Dublin, and now they never made time to go at all.

'Do you go to the theatre much?' Cathy asked.

It turned out that James did, almost every week. Why did neither of them feel able to ask if he went with a group of friends or on his own or with a companion? They touched on a lot of subjects: politics, prisons, drugs and eventually opera. James said he used to go a lot to the opera when he was a student, but somehow since then . . . His voice trailed away. Neither of them asked why he couldn't go now. Or indeed, in the years in between.

'Do you listen to it here at home?' Cathy indicated the rather old-fashioned music centre.

'No, not for a long while. You have to be in the mood to set it all up.'

'No, James, of course you don't, you just put it on . . . it creates its own mood. I put it on doing the washing-up if I'm alone. Let's put on something when we're doing the washing-up here tonight.'

'No, please, I don't have anything suitable,' he said a little anxiously.

She drew back. 'Sure,' she said easily.

She had seen tapes of operas piled high in his sitting room, but he obviously didn't want to play them.

'Come on then, let's do the washing-up without an aria.'

'No, no, you must not feel . . .' he began.

'Rule one. *Never* refuse an offer of washing-up. Right, Tom?'

'Absolutely, and be quite sure to let your guest help do the washing-up if she offers,' Tom added.

'Why do you think it's a she?' James asked.

'Because a mere man wouldn't care what he was being offered if he came round to dinner, and probably wouldn't notice. Believe me, I've cooked for them, I know,' said Tom, cursing himself for being so tactless.

Cathy looked at him admiringly. 'Too true,' she said. 'No, James, the first thing is to have a dish of hot soapy water to stick the cutlery into after each course, and a place to scrape away the leavings. Then it will take two minutes.'

'I don't have a dishwasher, you know,' he said anxiously, in case there had been any misunderstanding.

Cathy looked around the kitchen that had no electric beater, liquidiser or proper chopping board. Of course the man wouldn't have a dishwasher. 'No need for one, hands are just as good. Take us five minutes at the outside, what do you say, Tom?'

'Six if we do it thoroughly,' Tom said, starting on the frying pan.

Joe rang at the door of Fatima. He carried a bottle of sweet sherry and a tin of fancy biscuits. He could hear his mother grumbling as she came to the door. 'It's all right, JT, I'm going to get it, whoever it is at this time of night.' It was seven o'clock on an April evening, hardly the middle of the night. He must not allow himself to become annoyed.

'How are you, Ma?' he said with false good humour.

His mother looked him up and down. She looked old and tired now, not like she had in January when he had seen her briefly at Tom and Cathy's launch party. Then she had worn a green tweed suit and a white blouse with a green cameo brooch at the neck. Tonight she wore a faded pinafore and shabby slippers. Her hair was flat, grey and limp. When he saw what women her age could do with themselves, Joe's heart felt heavy. Maura Feather must be fifty-eight at the very most. She looked as if she were well over seventy.

'And what brings you here?' his mother asked.

'I came to see you both, and to know how Da is getting along.' He kept the smile on his face.

'You know how he's getting along. We sent you a note to thank you for that basket of fruit.' His mother's face was hard.

'Yes, yes, indeed. It was a very nice letter.' Joe knew that Tom had written it, typed it, made it up for them. Anything to keep a lifeline open between them all.

'Anyway, now that I'm here, Ma . . .' He began to take a step over the doorstep.

'Who asked you to come in, Joe?'

'Well you're never going to send me away?' He held his head on one side, the way of pleading that rarely failed. But he was at Fatima now.

'What makes you think you're welcome in this house? You often come to Dublin, and never come to see us. I saw you one day myself out of a bus, laughing on the corner of a street. Why should we welcome you here?'

'I suppose any man who wants to see how well his father has recovered from a heart attack is welcome in his old home,' Joe said.

The legendary Joe Feather charm was not finding its mark with his mother.

'I've had to live with the results of your selfishness year after year, your father having no one to lift a hand to help him at his work.'

'Ma, I was never going to work in Dad's business, you know that.'

'I do not know it, and a fine example you were to your brother, too . . .'

'Tom was never going to work in it either, Ma . . .'

'Not good enough for you, only good enough to pay your school fees and buy you clothes and football boots and a bicycle, but not good enough—'

'Could I see Da, do you think?' Joe cut across her.

'What makes you think you can walk in here after all this time, and that your father will be pleased to see you?'

'I had hoped that you both would,' he said.

There was a tic in his forehead. Why was he doing this? One more refusal and he would leave, but he just had to see the old man before he went. He moved gently but firmly past his mother to the room where his father sat in the chair, straining to hear every word. The man looked white and papery. But there was a welcoming light in his face that Joe hadn't seen in his mother's.

'Joe, good to see you, lad.'

'And you, Da, I know it's been a day or two but I wanted to make sure that you were as good as they say.'

'They?' His mother sniffed from the door.

'Well, Tom for one, Cathy Scarlet for another, Ned in the yard for a third. People who care about you.'

'Huh,' said Maura Feather.

'Look, I'm so glad to see you well, and you looking fine too, Ma. I'm just rushing through Dublin and I haven't been back here since you were in hospital, so I thought it would be good for us to meet just for a few minutes.'

'It is indeed, Joe.' His father reached out for Joe's hand.

Joe pretended not to see the gesture because he could sense his mother's hostility towards any hand-grasping.

'I brought us a quick small drink and a sweet biscuit, and maybe the next time I come Ma would make us a cup of tea and a scone . . .'

He didn't look at her, instead he opened the sherry and found glasses on the sideboard.

'I hope the next time will be soon. If you knew how tough it is over in London...'

'I can't remember anyone forcing you to go there.' Maura Feather was not won over yet.

'I liked it when I was young and foolish, Ma, everyone likes a big bad place then ... But people aren't really happy there, like they're not in any big city.'

'What do you mean?'

'Well, you know yourself. You can see it in Dublin too, though of course London's much bigger. People are restless. They're looking for something to explain what it's all about...'

They looked at him blankly.

'You know, when I went to London first the churches were empty ... Today there are people going into them at lunchtime, in the evenings looking up, everyone looking for answers.'

'How would *you* know?' Maura Feather asked.

'I know because I go sometimes, and into a temple or a mosque or a synagogue ... There's not just one God, Mam, not like there was when we were young.'

'There's only one true God,' she snapped.

'I know, I know, but honestly nowadays it's much better than it used to be, isn't it, people respecting everyone's beliefs.'

'It's very little belief you respected, Joe Feather, when we last saw you.'

At least she had used his name. It was an advance. He poured the sherry and smiled at them. His professional smile. He didn't care for them himself – they were strangers, a weak man, a bitter woman. True, he had felt a tug of pity when he heard that his father had been fighting for breath in the hospital. Joe's own inclination would have been to continue sending the occasional long-distance gift. But he had promised Tom he would make the effort. And somehow he owed Tom.

Tom had been right, he hadn't helped the business of being a son of Fatima. He had been of little help in sharing what he saw as the burden of elderly and tiresome parents. He would keep smiling and talking about searching for more meaning in life and pouring sherry. He saw that his mother had relaxed and his father was touchingly pleased at his efforts. Joe thought he had put much, much more work than this into selling a line of coordinated tops and shorts to a tough Northern businessman. He would stay another half an hour.

The photo shoot was endless. Tom just could not believe that grown-up people spent such huge amounts of time doing something so trivial. Marcella had taken two days off work and arrived home with a selection of Haywards garments for both of them. The sweater and jacket she had chosen for him were astronomically expensive.

'It's all with Shona's blessing ... It's as good as an unpaid advertisement for them. And you are so gorgeous to look at I'm going to have trouble beating them all off you, the make-up artists' the hairstylists, the lighting people ... And that's only the men,' she laughed excitedly.

It was beginning to happen for her. The work dream coming true, as it had for him earlier this year. Tom would do his utmost to smile and look rugged, or whatever they wanted that would help Marcella's career.

The man who was meant to know the timescale of everything hadn't known it, according to Neil. It was a new posting, it was all up in the air, it was not fixed to any date. There was plenty of time to talk.

'Good,' Cathy said.

Muttie and Lizzie whispered in the dark bedroom.

'They'll be gone at the end of the week,' she said.

'I know, and I was just getting to like them,' Muttie said.

Neil said that Kenneth and Kay Mitchell were now installed, and everything was in place; they were ready and waiting.

'I told the social worker that it would be a bit hard on the kids to go straight back in, and she agrees entirely. She's very nice, by the way, you'll like her; her name is Sara. Anyway, Sara says that we should bring them to visit their parents once or twice before leaving them there. She'll come with us.'

Cathy felt an unreasonable twinge of jealousy. This was *her* call, hers and her kind parents, who had put themselves out for the children when nobody wanted them. Now it seemed that everyone wanted them – mad, runaway fathers, mad, drunken mothers, bossy social workers called Sara.

'Okay, I'll fix a time to take them over to the House of Horrors,' she said.

'Don't even whisper that name in front of those two. You know the way they pick up on everything,' he warned.

'You're right. I'll see when I can snatch an hour and take them.'

'Well, we'll have to coordinate when you're free, Sara's free and I'm free.'

'But Neil, that could be next year. This isn't a conference call that we're setting up, it's my taking those kids back to where they're going to be living from now on without frightening them to death. It's about putting some kind of mad appearance of normality on it, not about checking everyone's diaries.'

'Hon, I *know* what you're saying, but in these kind of things it's best to do it by the book, keep the social worker on board, then if anything goes wrong we're all in the clear.'

'But we know exactly what will go wrong ... Eventually Kenneth will hear the sounds of distant excitement in far-off lands and Kay will smell a vodka bottle and we're back to where we were.'

Tom had never seen Ricky at work before. He had only seen him as the relaxed man who watched everything and knew everyone. He had no idea of the preparation that went into taking what would result in five or six photographs in a magazine. Tom's face was a picture. He felt sure there had been some mistake, and that this was a multimillion-dollar movie that was being made in the small apartment in Stoneyfield. What he could not begin to understand was Marcella's sense of calm throughout all of this. She served endless coffee and ice-cold mineral water. When asked to smile, she did so with a radiance he could hardly believe. It didn't matter how many times she had to do it, the same smile was delivered as fresh as if it had come from the heart. She sat motionless as they applied yet more make-up, touched up the lip gloss and lacquered her already perfect hair. Tom, on the other hand, made jokes, clowned around, felt awkward, knocked things over and apologised again and again. He thought the day would never end. No night working in a noisy pub, no back-aching hauling of food up flights of stairs, no squeezing through tiny narrow corridors without upsetting trays of food had ever been half as exhausting as this. When they were finally alone in jeans and T-shirts, with all today's finery at the dry-cleaner's and tomorrow's hung up in readiness, Tom lay down on the sofa with his head on her lap. She stroked his brow. Still fresh as a daisy, and her eyes dancing with the pleasure of it all.

'Thank you, dear, dear Tom. I know you hated it,' she said softly.

'I didn't *hate* it, exactly, but it was very stressful. I was hopeless, I'm afraid.'

'You were wonderful. They all said so.'

'Marcella, how have you the patience?'

'I ask you always how have *you* the patience to do all that fiddly work. Those little perfectly shredded garnishes, and rolling up those tiny bits of sushi . . . I would go mad rather than do it, I tell you.'

She stroked his brow and he wanted to go to sleep there and then. 'That's because you don't eat,' he said, smiling up at her. 'You've never had a lust for food like other fatter folk.'

'Oh, I might have had a lust for food once upon a time,' she said.

But he knew that she never had. Any of the few pictures of her childhood that he had seen showed a little waif-like girl. Marcella had never been a foodie.

'I have to go, alas,' he said, dragging himself up.

'Surely not? After all the work you put in already today?'

'We have a do. Cathy's been working on it all day while I've been posturing here. I have to go and help her serve it.'

'Sure you have to go. Though your posturing, as you call it, may well get you lots more business.'

'Marcella, be serious!'

'I was never more so. What is it tonight?'

'Our Lady's Ladies.'

'*What?*'

'I don't know. Some past pupils' group. They're all twenty years left school this year, and apparently two decades ago they swore a mighty oath that if they were alive today they'd have a party.'

'They're not really called that, are they?'

'Something like that. Anyway, off I go. Am I too casual, do you think?'

'I'd say Our Lady's Ladies will just about tear you to pieces,' said Marcella admiringly.

'Jesus, Cathy, what a day I've had: I'm so sorry for leaving all this to you.'

'No problem, Mister Cheesecake . . . I was glad to be distracted, I have to take those kids to meet some terrifying Nazi called Sara tomorrow, and ease them back to the madhouse … I preferred making salmon *en croute*.'

How they got through the night, they never knew. Tom, who was nearly dead from smiling at cameras for over seven hours and with the thought of the same thing again the following day, smiled and laughed and told the women that there must be some mistake, none of them could have left school twenty years ago. Cathy, who was nearly dead worrying about how to handle the horrific social worker Sara without putting anyone's back up managed to weave and duck around the room as the women shrieked and remembered funny things from years ago. Almost everyone had turned up, they told Cathy, only three had cried off. Janet who was in New Zealand, Orla who was in some kind of weird cult in the West of Ireland and Amanda who was in Canada running a bookshop with her lover. Was that Amanda Mitchell by any chance, Cathy had wondered, too much of a coincidence. Yes, it was, apparently! They were annoyed about Amanda, she always had plenty of money, her family owned that big house, Oaklands, so she could well have come back. It wasn't as if any of them were going to be worried one way or another about her lover.

'And who is he?' Cathy had asked politely.

'Aha, it's not a he at all, it's a she. Imagine! Amanda Mitchell is the only girl in a class of twenty-eight females who fancied a woman, what does that do to statistics?' asked the woman who had set up the party.

Cathy sat down in the kitchen. Her sister-in-law was a lesbian. What else would the day bring?

'They were a nice lot,' June said as she helped to pack the van.

'And they seemed pleased with it all,' Tom yawned.

'They gave me a good tip, too. And four of them asked me where I got my streaks done.'

'Did they like them?' Cathy was still doubtful about the startling violet sections of June's hair.

'They loved them, they were dead impressed that I could afford Haywards. Thanks again, Cathy, it was a great gift.'

'That bit was nothing, it's my hair we have to worry about with Hannah,' said Cathy.

They left June at a taxi rank. 'You know, I have a great life because of you two,' she said, and trotted off.

They drove in silence towards the premises.

'I didn't know it was all going to be so bloody exhausting,' Cathy said.

'Nor I. The food's no trouble, it's just the people who are a pain,' Tom agreed.

They spent one hour and forty minutes unpacking the van, loading the dish-washing machines, wrapping and freezing the leftovers and preparing the kitchen and ovens for the morning bake. They worked companionably, and didn't waste one unit of energy by speaking to each other. When they were through, Tom drove the van slowly out into the street.

'I'm like a zombie,' he said. 'Can you watch me in case I fall asleep?'

'Well, the very thought of you doing that might keep *me* awake, anyway,' Cathy said.

'It will be May next month,' Tom said.

'That's true.'

There was a silence.

'Why did you tell me that?' Cathy asked eventually.

'I can't remember,' Tom confessed.

'Are we becoming geriatrics, do you think? We don't actually *say* things any more.' Cathy sounded worried.

'No, there's not much to say except that my brother has turned into a major pain in the arse,' Tom said.

'And it seems that my sister-in-law is going to give a few people at Oaklands a few major surprises,' said Cathy. She looked at Tom's face. 'You don't need to know now. Anyway, as you say, it will be May soon. I've a feeling that this means something.'

'Something good or bad?' Tom wondered.

'Jesus, Tom, if I knew that ... wouldn't I be able to run the world,' said Cathy Scarlet, who then fell asleep until Tom drove her into the courtyard of Waterview.

Chapter Five

MAY

They told Hooves that they were only going out for a visit, and that they would be back later on.

'I know it sounds silly, but I think he does understand,' Maud said.

'Why wouldn't he understand? Isn't he a dog of pedigree?' Muttie asked.

'Do people have pedigrees too?' Simon wanted to know.

'No,' Cathy said, a little overemphatically. 'All people are born the same, they make their own pedigrees.'

She saw her parents looking at her and realised the futility of her statement. She could not accept that Neil was right to insist they be returned to their natural parents. Nothing would make her believe that this was the just or fair thing to do. But she had to go along with it.

'Come on, kids, into the van, and take me to see your house. I want to know where you were as babies.'

'Could Muttie and his wife come too?' Maud hung back.

'One day they'll come to see it, but today it's just us,' said Cathy, refusing to look at her parents watching the children leave.

The Beeches was in a road where a lot of other properties had been sold as apartment blocks, but it stood there in its own grounds ... A large, shabby, ill-kept house a hundred and fifty years old, a gentleman's residence which had seen better days. Not as imposing as Oaklands – there was no great sweep of a drive coming up to it – but attractive, with good proportions and creeper growing among the windows. A disused tennis court and a broken garden shed showed how grand it must have been at some stage. Before the parents of Walter, Simon and Maud lost interest in the business of keeping up a normal home. The children looked at Cathy anxiously as they drove in, watching her for a reaction.

'What a lovely house,' she said with a hollow feeling in her heart. 'It must have been a nice place to grow up.'

They looked at their home doubtfully. 'I'm sure St Jarlath's Crescent was nice to grow up in, too.'

These had been such horrible children, stealing food, referring to Cathy as a servant, throwing their clothes on the floor only a few short months ago, and look at them now! Cathy tried to keep the break out of her voice.

'It was indeed, Simon, thank you for saying that, it was a nice place to grow up. Now let's go and find your father and mother.'

Kenneth Mitchell welcomed them in as if they were the most honoured guests, rather than the two children he had abandoned and his nephew's wife whom he had never acknowledged before.

'How perfectly splendid,' he said as Cathy arrived with the children.

'Hallo Father,' Simon said.

'Simon, good chap. Good boy,' his father said, 'and Maud too, of course, excellent.' He looked at Cathy vaguely as if trying to place her. He was quite like his brother Jock in appearance, but he had not run to fat. Being on the road, or however he described it, meant that he had no paunch. There was no sign of his wife. She decided to address him by his first name.

'Well, Kenneth, as you say, it's all splendid. Shall we wait for Kay and Sara before we do the tour?'

'Tour? Sara . . . um, Kay?' He was bewildered.

It was now Cathy's turn to be bewildered. 'Kay, your wife?'

'Oh, yes, she'll be here in a moment, she's getting ready.'

No welcome, no warmth, and in the case of their mother, not even an appearance. Maud seemed to feel uneasy as well.

'What time is Sara coming?' she asked.

Kenneth Mitchell looked confused. 'Sara?'

'The social worker,' Cathy said in a level voice.

'But I thought *you* were the social worker,' he said.

'No, Kenneth, I am Cathy Scarlet, daughter of the people who have been looking after your children while you were abroad. I am also married to Neil, who is your brother Jock's son. The social worker is Sara, who is expected to meet us here . . .'

His embarrassment, if he had any, was spared by the sound of the bell ringing. They heard Kenneth out in the hall welcoming the social worker with great charm and even greater confusion. She looked as if she weren't seventeen or eighteen, a very tall, handsome girl with flaming hair and big laced boots. She seemed altogether too confident.

'Hi Maud, Simon, everything okay?' she asked.

'Well, Sara, you see . . .' Simon began, and Cathy felt a tug of jealousy.

'I mean, have you been to the bedrooms to check all your things are there?' She was so casual, so unafraid of Kenneth Mitchell, so out for the twins.

'We haven't been here very long, you see,' Simon said.

'We haven't even seen Mother yet,' Maud added.

'Okay, go and check the rooms and then come back to me.'

They scampered up the stairs obediently. Sara began to roll a cigarette.

'I'll smoke in the garden if you prefer, Mr Mitchell,' she said with such a threatening frown that Kenneth began to panic again.

'No, no, good Lord no, please, I mean, as you like . . .'

'How'ya, Cathy. I believe you hate my guts,' Sara said companionably.

'I'm sure in your job you must know how kids exaggerate,' Cathy grinned.

'*And* your husband? He seemed to think you had problems with their returning home.'

'No, Sara, I don't think I have any problems with it at all.' Cathy's voice became serious. 'I brought them along here for a visit, their father, who is my father-in-law's brother, thought that I was the social worker, which was a little startling and their mother wasn't here to greet them, which I found odd.'

'Neil says that you and your family have bonded with them to an extraordinary extent.' Sara watched her carefully.

'*Someone* had to bond with them,' Cathy said, exasperated. 'Listen, I'm doing everything by the book. They're here for their visit. Why don't you go and inspect the visit and leave me out of it? I'm going to be out of it anyway when they come back here.'

Kenneth Mitchell had looked from one to the other as if he were watching a tennis match. When they had stopped talking he asked would anyone like tea, and seemed surprised by the abrupt refusal from Cathy and Sara.

'I did prepare a tray,' he said in an aggrieved tone.

'Very hospitable of you Kenneth,' said Cathy in a tone which made Sara look up again.

'And where is Walter?' Sara asked, looking at her notes.

'Walter?' asked Kenneth vaguely.

'Your son,' Cathy said helpfully.

'The whole family was meant to be here,' Sara said.

'I expect he's at work.' Kenneth looked anxious to be helping in an ever more confusing world. He was constantly being rescued by other people's arrivals. The children came in at that moment, holding their mother by the hand. Kay Mitchell looked frail and as if a wind would blow her away. She had a nice smile.

'Hallo, how nice to see you,' she said to Cathy.

'You look much stronger now,' Cathy said.

'Do I? That's good. Did you come to see me in hospital?'

'Yes, from time to time, but the important thing was the children's visit.' Cathy slid a glance at Sara, to hope that she was taking this on board.

'So much of it took place in a sort of fog, as if it were all happening to someone else.' She beamed around at them all.

'Any sign of your brother Walter?' Cathy asked the children.

'He sort of made the beds for us,' Maud said.

'But he didn't really, it was just the sheets and pillowcases left at the end of the beds, and actually . . .'

'They were very damp, so Mother has been helping us put them into the hot press,' Maud explained.

'That wasn't really work for Walter. Isn't there a Mrs Thing to make beds?' Kenneth was puzzled.

'Mrs Thing doesn't start until next week,' Cathy explained sarcastically.

'Mrs Barry, I see from my notes,' Sara corrected.

'So now it's only Walter we're waiting for, is that right?'

'He's meant to be here,' Sara said disapprovingly.

'I'm sure . . . There must be a misunderstanding, should he be telephoned, do you think?' Kenneth wondered.

'Might be best.' Sara wasted no words.

'Well, does anyone . . . I mean where . . . exactly?' Kenneth began.

'Your brother's office, Jock Mitchell's law firm.'

Cathy tried to hide the sarcasm in her voice. But Sara didn't miss it; there was a hint of a smile. Nobody helped with all the fumbling and looking up in the telephone directory. It turned out that Walter was on his way, he would be here shortly.

'And Walter lives here? This is his home?'

'Well, he's an adult man of course, he doesn't have to check in every night.'

'I see he sometimes stays with friends.' Sara was writing notes.

'But his room is here ... For him, of course.'

'Locked,' said Simon.

'How do you know?' Sara was interested.

'We had a rocking horse and an old black and white telly. I thought maybe Walter had borrowed them when we were staying with Muttie and Lizzie ... which would have been fine with us.' Simon's voice was straight and clear. He didn't want to get anyone into any trouble.

'Odd to lock a bedroom in a family home,' Sara said.

'When will we be coming back here for good?' Maud asked.

'Whenever you like,' her father beamed.

'The sooner the better,' her mother's smile was wide.

'When all the paperwork is complete,' Sara said.

'And Cathy, were you able to explain properly to Sara all about Hooves visiting, and the wedding of Lizzie's daughter to that man that she's sleeping in the same bed with in Chicago?'

'I say ...' Kenneth began.

Yet again he was saved from having to say anything by the arrival of Walter. Dishevelled and out of breath, Walter had come on a bicycle.

'Hi kids, Mother, Father, Cathy.' He nodded to them all, then he put on the Mitchell smile.

'And you must be Sara? Aren't you terribly young and, um, gorgeous to be doing this job?'

Cathy looked at him in despair. *Please* may Sara not fall for it, the little-boy-lost bit, the hair in the eyes, the naked admiration.

'You were meant to be here forty-five minutes ago.' Sara was stern.

He tried to smile it away. 'But happily I'm here now,' he said.

Sara called the meeting to order with a cough. 'If Maud and Simon are coming back here to live, can we run through the arrangements, please?'

'Well, what arrangements exactly?' Kenneth was finding all this above him. 'I mean, I'm here, and their mother is here and these, er ... kind people who looked after them when I was unavoidably away and Kay was ill have delivered them home. That's it, really, isn't it?'

'No, Mr Mitchell, it's not it. You know this. We've been down this road before, they are our responsibility, something which will not be given up until we know what's best for Maud and Simon and their future. So can we start with school.' Sara had her notes in order.

'Last September there was a problem with school for the twins. They needed to be driven there and people weren't really about to drive them. They missed a lot of days. But since they went to stay in St Jarlath's Crescent they have been doing well in their new school. You are content that they continue where they are, they have made friends and there is a bus journey if nobody can collect them.'

'Good to become familiar with buses,' said Kenneth.

'Quite. And meals. Will you do the cooking, Mrs Mitchell?'

'Well of course I will, and there's a Mrs ... Mrs ... Somebody who is coming to help with the awful things, isn't she?'

'Yes, a Mrs Barrington, darling,' Kenneth intervened.

'Mrs Barry,' Cathy and Sara said together with one voice.

'Silly of me, easy mistake.'

'Quite. Now about their sleeping arrangements. You say there are damp sheets on the beds.'

'Which will be aired, of course, by the time they come home,' Kay said.

'Yes indeed. And there's a matter of a missing rocking horse and a black and white television set.'

'I didn't say they were missing. They might be in Walter's room.' Simon wanted things to be clear.

'Which is locked.' Cathy added.

'I've every right to lock my room, everyone has.'

'Sure, but can we go and see if the kids' things are in it?' Cathy's eyes were narrow. She could sense his fear. There was something in that room that Walter didn't want seen.

'Excuse me,' he said, 'are you running this suddenly, Cathy? I thought it was Sara's job.'

'Do you know anything abut a rocking horse and a television set?' Sara asked him levelly.

'Oh, those. They were very old and past their sell-by date. I gave them away to friends ages ago. Sorry, you're both much too old for a rocking horse. I didn't know they were still needed.'

Cathy knew he had sold them.

'We're not too old for a television set, though,' Simon said.

'And I liked the rocking horse, too,' Maud complained.

'Well, perhaps Walter has some gifts for you instead in his room. . . ?' Cathy suggested.

'Listen to me, Sara, is this a witch-hunt or what? You're here to make sure this is a fine family scene for Simon and Maud to come back to . . . and then suddenly it's down to me to show off whether I've made my bed in my room or not. Now come on . . .'

He looked so genuinely upset and put upon that Cathy could see that Sara was falling for it.

'Of course we don't want to examine your room, but we do want to know what contribution you can make to your brother and sister's return.'

Walter paused to give a slow, triumphant smile in Cathy's direction. There would be no inspection.

Then he turned to Sara. 'What I hope now that our family is reunited is that we should all get to know each other better. That I should learn about their interests and concerns . . . Like I don't want to go giving away rocking horses again. Do I, Maud?'

'Or television sets,' Maud said.

Cathy loved her with a passion at that moment. There were many more points also answered very vaguely by the children's parents, and with warmth and enthusiasm by their elder brother. Time now to take Maud and Simon back to St Jarlath's Crescent. There were no hugs; Kay kissed them both on the cheek and looked at them vaguely and proudly. Sara and Walter were outside, comparing bicycles. Sara's was the folding type.

'Handy for taxis when you get tired or drunk,' she explained.

'Why don't I give you a lift back to the office? I've got the van, your bike can go in the back,' Cathy said suddenly.

'Oh, I couldn't,' Sara said.

'She's not drunk yet,' Simon noted.

'No, but she could be fairly tired, and this way we can go by St Jarlath's Crescent and you can introduce her to Hooves.'

'I've seen St Jarlath's Crescent, and I am totally aware of the splendid care your parents have been doing as a stopgap,' Sara said.

'You haven't seen Hooves yet, Sara. Come on, and Simon and Maud would love to show you their outfits.'

'That's a great idea, Cathy,' Simon approved as they climbed into the van. 'This way she'll see the really important things.'

Cathy and Sara exchanged glances. And spontaneously they both started to laugh.

James Byrne's second cookery lesson was on Thursday.

'Did he say what he'd like?' Tom called out to Cathy in the kitchen of the premises.

'No, he's leaving it up to us. Oh, *shit*.'

'Have you burned yourself again?' He came running.

But this time she had cut her finger on the jagged edge of a can.

'Serves you right for using cans anyway. We're not meant to be a convenience-food outfit.'

'Tell me how to add tomato pureé to something without opening a can of it?' She held up her finger to be inspected.

'You don't need a stitch, come on and wash it. By using a tube and squeezing it, or if you have to have a tin, then by using the electric thing on the wall instead of going at it with a stone-age can-opener.'

'I was in a hurry.'

'Sure you were, and now you'll be wearing Elastoplast. Great advertisement for the company,' he grumbled to himself as he bound up her finger. 'Come into the front room and sit down to get over the shock,' he said.

'I'm not in shock,' Cathy protested.

'No, but I am. Come on.'

'There you go again, a broody old hen cluck-clucking,' Cathy said.

'You can stem your own pouring blood next time,' Tom said good-naturedly.

They loved a chance to sit down in their front room and relax in the big chintz sofas that Lizzie had covered for them. Cathy put her feet up on the low table with its elegant cookery magazines.

'Someday we'll have time to read some of these,' she said.

'Food will be out of date then,' said Tom.

It was pleasant to sit here and look up at the plates on the shelves, and see their discreet filing system looking for all the world like an elegant desk in a gracious home. Joe had found that for them at an auction, he said. They worried about it once or twice.

'I know he has a bit of an aversion to paying tax, but I don't think he deals in stolen goods,' Tom had said at the time.

'Of course he doesn't,' Cathy had stroked it lovingly – it was just right.

One of Muttie's associates was in carpet pieces, so they had got a perfect piece for the floor. It gave off such a good feeling when anyone came in to see them. If only a few more people would turn up, they would be less anxious about it all.

'What will we do with James?' Tom asked.

'We did smoked fish and chicken tarragon last time ... something redder, more violent this time, I think.' Cathy pondered.

'Parma ham and figs to start, fillet steaks in mushroom and cream sauce?' Tom wondered.

'He'll say the starter's too easy, and he'd fuss too much with the steak,' Cathy was shaking her head.

'No he wouldn't, he's much less of a fusser than he used to be since you told him you can always lift the pan off the heat. Apparently he never realised that before. Imagine.' Tom was amazed.

'I wonder did he ever have children?' Cathy said.

'Why do you say that?'

'I don't know, it's a funny thing but I get the impression that he's not doing this dinner for someone he fancies ... More for some young person that he wants to prove something to ...'

'I don't know where you get that notion. Perhaps you should bring a crystal ball to the next party we do.' Tom often thought women were complicated, but this was ridiculous.

'No, think about it. You know it's something like that, he's doing something to show someone he cares, which is hard for him because he's so buttoned up.'

'You're so non-buttoned up, why don't you ask him straight out?' Tom challenged.

'You know I can't do that, Tom,' she said. 'I think I've spent so long dinning politeness into Simon and Maud I've sort of caught some of it myself. I hope it's not destroying my personality.'

'No sign yet, I assure you. But I'll keep an eye out in case it does.'

'Eejit,' said Cathy. 'What will we give him as a pudding?'

'Brown-bread ice cream,' he suggested.

'Okay, now all I have to do is sell it to him.'

'Come on, Tom, injury time over, back to work,' Cathy said, and went back into the kitchen for the telephone.

*

James Byrne objected to every course, but they held fast.

'It sounds too simple, as if it were bought in a shop,' he complained.

'Listen, we have to show you how to cut the figs, how to arrange the ham.'

'But steak. It's too ... too ...'

'It's a huge treat, and you can have small steaks. Wait till we show you the sauce.'

'She'll think I bought the ice cream in a delicatessen,' he said.

At least they defined it *was* a she. That was some advance.

'Not when you can tell her how you made it, and honestly, it's great fun,' Cathy begged. She had a lot on her mind; she didn't want their accountant starting to grizzle about a perfectly reasonable menu. Her finger was throbbing, she was sick at heart about Simon and Maud, Freddie Flynn and his wife had asked them to do a dinner, she owed Hannah Mitchell a lunch. She had no idea what they were going to do as a great feast for her sister Marian's wedding in just over two months' time. She couldn't bear the thought of her poor father walking that hound to the betting shop every day and tying him up outside the door. Her hair looked awfully flat and dull. Hannah Mitchell had been right. She was not going to listen to one more word of James Byrne's fears that this was not a good dinner.

'James,' she said in a voice like the crack of a whip. Tom looked up from the dough in alarm. 'James. Do we question a balance sheet? No. Do we say that we don't think this input or output VAT return will work? No, we don't, we say James is the particular expert that we are paying for this advice. We are the particular experts that *you* have paid for our advice. Yes, good. See you on Thursday, James.'

She hung up with a loud noise. She knew without looking that Tom was looking at her open-mouthed. 'Well?' she asked belligerently.

'Well indeed,' he said.

'Meaning?'

'Meaning that you most certainly haven't altered your personality,' he said.

She laughed and he crossed the room to hug her. He was such easy company, and defused so many situations for them both.

'Tom, I need your advice.'

'Of course you do, you sound as if you actually need a heavy tranquilliser, but my advice will have to do.'

'How am I going to entertain Hannah? I'm trying to build a hedge of olive branches, but I'm no good at it.'

'What does Neil suggest?'

'He asks why bother? He shrugs. He's a man.'

'Big disadvantage, we know that. Right, is it just the two of you?'

'Yes. I can bear an hour and thirty minutes being patronised; I couldn't stand her doing it to someone else.'

'Do you want her to enjoy it, or do you want to show off to her?'

'Good question, but actually I'd quite like her to have a good time.'

'Okay, why don't you ask her here?'

'Here, to the premises?'

'Sure, ask her for lunch next Monday. We've nothing on, it will be nice and quiet. I'll serve you, then put the phone on answer and leave.'

'She'd think that very low-class.'

'No, she wouldn't: posh place that we are, nearly six months surviving. She gave it six days, I remember, the last time she was here.'

'Oh dear, yes, the opening. I sort of forgot the words we had then.'

'Bet she hasn't, though. Really, Cathy, this would be real olive-branch territory. Go on, ring her now. Ask her.'

'I'm not sure, Tom.'

'What did I just hear you saying about people taking professional advice? Ring her, Cathy.'

'You're not a professional in this area.'

'Like hell I'm not! We've been hearing you on the subject of Hannah Mitchell since we were at catering college. Call her now.'

'Absolutely fair. Pass me the phone.'

Hannah Mitchell accepted. It was a lovely idea. Quite a lot of her friends had heard of Scarlet Feather now. They would be very interested to hear what it was like inside.

'It looks as if Maud and Simon are going back to base next week,' Cathy said.

'Yes, thank God, what a terrible episode for everyone, and wasn't poor Lizzie wonderful to step into the breach so well.'

Cathy allowed the silence to last for many seconds. Long enough for Hannah to remember.

'Ah, yes, what I meant to say was wasn't it great that, er, Lizzie and, er, Muttie were so helpful when poor Kenneth and Kay had such problems . . . That's what I meant.'

'Did that go all right?' Tom asked.

'Yes, better than I dared hope.'

'Say thank you Tom, then,' he said eventually.

'Thank you Tom,' she said.

It was extraordinary not to be afraid of that woman after so many years.

Tom went to pick Marcella up from work.

'Your brother was in today,' she said.

'He's never back in Ireland twice in a few weeks. What's it all about?'

'He said he's setting up this show . . . Feather Fashions . . . He wants trade to come to it as well as the public. He's full of ideas, he's here to see Shona and I think he's going to meet Cathy's Geraldine about doing extra PR.' Marcella sounded very excited.

'Is he going to come and see *us* at all, do you think?' Tom felt an unexpected stab of jealousy that his only brother was in town contacting almost everyone except him.

'Of course he will, he just called to see me . . . because . . . Tom, you won't believe this, he's putting in a serious word that I should do some modelling during the show.' Her eyes were dancing.

Tom had said nothing in months that had pleased her as much as this.

'Just let me tell you that I hope and pray he gets you this job, with all my heart,' he said.

'I'm sorry I wasn't able to get up to The Beeches, the case went on for ever,' Neil apologised.

'No, that's okay, I didn't expect you.' Cathy was in the kitchen preparing supper. 'Things often turn up.' She spoke without any annoyance. In his life things *did* turn up. 'And anyway, you couldn't have done anything to help . . . they behaved like the family from hell, but still they're getting the children back. That's showbiz and social workers for you.'

'Did you meet Sara, she's great, isn't she?' He sounded very enthusiastic.

'Yes, she is actually. I thought she was going to be boot-faced, but she doesn't miss much. Walter took her in, though.'

'I was very impressed with her, I must say, and she's going to help on this homeless project. It's good to have a social worker on the team, she has all the statistics from her end . . .'

Neil was excited about it in a way that slightly turned Cathy's heart. She had been going to tell him all about Walter's locked bedroom, about her plans to entertain his mother at the premises, about the menus they were dreaming up for the Chicago-style wedding in July. But they all seemed very trivial and like tittle-tattle compared to the project for the homeless. The one where Sara with the big boots and the hand-rolled cigarettes was being co-opted onto the committee. A long time ago Cathy would have gone to those meetings, taken notes and typed letters; that was before she had a proper career of her own.

But by Saturday Cathy felt well cheered and able to cope with all that lay ahead, like taking the children back on a visit to their real home. She drove to St Jarlath's Crescent to collect them.

'Mam, how old is Geraldine this autumn?' Cathy asked when the children had gone out with Hooves, and so were way out of hearing.

'Let's see, I'm the eldest, and then . . . Well now, she'll be forty next birthday. Imagine, the baby of the family forty!' Lizzie was smiling at the thought.

'I wonder, would she like a party?' Cathy mused.

'Don't you know her better than anyone, what do *you* think?'

'I don't know her all that well, Mam, I haven't an idea what she'd like in lots of areas. But would she like it mentioned that she was forty, that's what I don't know.'

'But aren't you in and out of each other's houses all the time?' Lizzie was surprised.

'Used to be, not so much these days. Mam, was she gorgeous-looking when she was young?'

'She certainly was, and wild! You wouldn't believe it . . . When we were married first Muttie and I couldn't come back into my mother's house without getting a list of complaints as long as your arm about Geraldine – she was out till all hours, never doing her homework . . . Dressed like a tramp . . . I wish my poor mother had lived to see the way she turned out in the end. The perfect lady, mixing with the highest in the land.' Lizzie spoke with admiration and amazement but no jealousy.

'And when did she change?'

'Oh, she had this fellow, I can't remember his name. Very posh anyway, and a good bit older; she began to smarten up her act to go out with him. Then after he was gone she went back to school again. My poor old ma used to think she was trying to educate herself so that Teddy – that's his name, Teddy – would think she was more top-drawer, but I said it was a bit late for that now. Anyway it didn't work out and there was no mention of him again. Teddy! I haven't thought of him in years.'

Cathy wondered if this was also true in Geraldine's case. She was going round there later, once she and Sara had made their second visit to the twins' family home. What she had said to her mother was true. There were many, many ways in which Cathy knew absolutely nothing about the glamorous, groomed, self-confident woman who took cars and jewelled watches and even an apartment from married men. She didn't even know whether Geraldine would want her fortieth birthday highlighted or buried.

This time the tea tray was on the table when they arrived. Kay poured from the heavy teapot with a frail, shaking hand. Kenneth seemed to be more aware of his surroundings and of the fact that his children, whom he had abandoned for months, were not automatically being returned to him. He knew that he had to put on some kind of a show.

'Two charming ladies *and* my beloved twins as well . . . Too much happiness,' he said.

The children looked at him, startled. This was even more effusive than last time.

Sara spoke first. 'Can we run through a few outstanding matters, Mr Mitchell,' she said briskly.

'My dear lady . . . anything, anything.'

Kay came running in at that moment. 'I made scones,' she cried triumphantly.

'But Mother, you don't . . .' Simon began.

Cathy frowned a terrible frown at him, and he stopped in mid-sentence. Cathy looked at the small shop scones which the woman had heated up in her attempt to make this look like a normal home. She felt a lump in her throat. Kay *had* given birth to Simon and Maud nine years ago. They must mean something to her, even in her confused state of mind. She had looked so poorly when they visited her in hospital; Cathy had never seen the day coming when she would be in charge of a home again.

'Your nephew Neil was telling me about your financial arrangements last night,' Sara said. 'Apparently his father has arranged for this house to be mortgaged and has set up a trust.'

'Very good of Jock, sorted it all out,' Kenneth nodded and beamed eagerly.

'He gave me these figures, and it's agreed that this proportion goes towards their clothes, school needs, books, bus fares, and so on, and that there was a figure towards the upkeep of the house, including Mrs Barry three times a week and a gardener half a day once a week to keep the place in check.'

'It all sounds wonderful,' Kenneth said.

'And how much do you think Walter will contribute to the household?' Sara's face was expressionless as she asked the question that she must have known was futile.

'Oh, poor Walter doesn't have any ready money,' his mother said with a little laugh.

'But his room and board? After all, he does go out to work and earns a salary,' Sara was dogged.

'He must be quite poor because he sometimes works in Cathy and Tom's waitressing, I mean catering, business as well,' Maud said helpfully.

'Not recently; he won't have that as a source of income any more,' Cathy said in a tone that left no doubt whatsoever.

Sara looked up with a smile. She was really pretty when she smiled. Her funny spiky hair and her big boots were outside the frame.

'You could of course let his room if he weren't here?' Sara's eyes were mischievous.

'Oh, no, it's the boy's home,' said Kenneth. 'By the way, he left you a note about his room . . .' He offered her a letter without an envelope, 'One that all were meant to see.'

Sara read it out. 'Dear Sara, sorry that I can't be here today to meet you. On your last visit my cousin's wife seemed to be suggesting that I was unwilling to show you my bedroom. I would hate it if my little brother and sister's return home were to be delayed by any misunderstanding over something so irrelevant. I have tidied it up, ready for inspection. Please feel free to go in as you please.'

They all listened as she read. 'No need to, of course, but very courteous of him,' Sara murmured.

'No need now,' said Cathy, half under her breath. Whatever Walter had been storing in his room, whatever stolen goods he was fearful that they should see, had been moved. They did a tour of the house, checked the bedrooms, saw that the linen had been aired, the bathroom properly cared for. Sara was very thorough; she checked that the washing machine worked and went through the food cupboard and examined the dates on items in the freezer. She asked practical questions about what work Mrs Barry would do, ensured that there were cleaning materials and even checked the garden shed.

'Nothing to cut the grass with,' she observed.

'We used to have a big motor mower,' Kenneth was startled. 'It was quite new, actually. Do you remember it, darling?'

Kay thought hard. 'Not really, not since last summer ... Children, do you remember a motor mower?'

'Walter took it to be mended,' Simon said.

'When was that, Simon?' Cathy asked.

'Ages ago, when we were living here,' he said. 'I think it was a secret.'

'Why do you think that?' Cathy was gentle.

'I don't know. I thought he had broken it himself, you see, cutting the grass, and he wanted to get it mended before Mother and Father found out.' Simon's face was so innocent that Cathy wanted to cry.

'When was this, can you remember at all?' Sara wondered.

'Oh, last summer, a long time ago,' said Simon, who had never wondered before why the machine had never been returned to the shed, and wasn't even particularly worried now.

'Will we wait until Neil gets here before we agree that they can come back?' Sara asked as she and Cathy walked through the wilderness of the garden.

'Neil?'

'Yes, he said he'd be here.'

'Oh, sure.' Cathy was actually sure that he wouldn't be here. She had left him back at Waterview still on the telephone about some other crisis.

'Walter sold the grass-cutting machine. And the kids' things,' she said.

'We've no proof whatsoever of that, Cathy.'

'Would you believe it if Neil said it?'

'But surely he doesn't think. . . ?' She seemed aghast.

'Let's ask him, Sara, when he gets here,' Cathy said.

In her heart she thought, 'If he gets here.' But she was wrong: when they got back to the house he was there, just as businesslike as Sara.

'Uncle Kenneth, have you been through the house to make sure that nothing went missing while you were away?' he asked crisply.

'But how could it have? I mean, Walter was here.'

'You know how hopeless young people are. Any items like clocks, or maybe any silver?'

'I did wonder had we put away the little carriage clock so carefully that we couldn't find it,' poor Kay trilled.

'And I can't seem to see those silver brushes I had,' Kenneth seemed puzzled.

'Maybe we should make a list,' Neil said.

'Oh, do you think so?'

'I do.' Neil was very firm.

'You see, when we were assessing the value of your estate, we took all the possessions into account. We'll have to assess downwards if some things turn out to be missing, and anyway we'll need to give a list to the police if you're to claim on your insurance.'

'And to show to Walter also, Neil,' Cathy suggested, 'because quite possibly he may have taken some of these items to have them mended.'

'Mended?' Neil asked.

'Yes, Simon here was telling us that Walter kindly got the new motor mower mended, took it off with him at the end of last summer . . . And it hasn't been mended yet, apparently,' Cathy said.

He nodded. 'You've understood all this, Sara?' he asked.

'Totally,' she said.

'Right, we'll go round the house and see what's not where it should be . . . Can you help, Maud and Simon? Your sharp young eyes will be terrific, and it will make it into a sort of game.'

'I think that the marble chess set isn't where it used to be . . . I can't see it, anyway,' Simon offered as information.

'Can I have a board like Sara's to write on?' Maud asked. 'Please, if it's possible, I mean,' she added.

Sara immediately ripped some pages off and handed the clipboard and pad to the child. Neil smiled at her in gratitude, and

Cathy then saw the look that Sara gave him in return. It was naked admiration.

'Cathy, it's Geraldine.'

'People always say this, but I was just thinking about phoning you five minutes ago.'

'You weren't thinking about Sunday lunch tomorrow, by any chance?' Geraldine asked.

'No, but you're very welcome. It would force us to cook something instead of just picking, and we'd love to see you. That would be great.'

'I meant here, it's a working lunch ... I really think it's time someone did something about Marian's wedding. Their hotel accommodation is booked, but nothing else ... We should have a council of war.'

'Well, we have the hall. Should Tom come too, do you think?' Cathy asked.

She hated breaking into his weekend as she did into her and Neil's. There was so little free time for any of them these days. She was relieved when Geraldine said not to disturb him during his weekend.

'It isn't necessary now, not at this stage ... This is really only talks about talks. Shona's coming, she's a great help at things like this, and Joe Feather will be here about something else, it's a fashion show he's setting up but he might have a few ideas about the Chicago party as well.'

Cathy felt tired. There was too much to think about. Her mind felt full of problems, like swarms of bees.

'That would be great, Geraldine. Can I bring something with me?'

'No, no.' It didn't sound convincing.

'I can go into the premises, take something out of the freezer,' she said.

'Well, if you did have a dessert ... I certainly wouldn't say no.'

'Chocolate roulade?' Cathy suggested; she had plenty of those in the freezer.

'Great, see you tomorrow, notebooks at the ready.'

Cathy wondered whether Tom knew that his brother was setting up a fashion show, and more importantly, whether Marcella knew. But it was a Saturday night, let it go, let it go. Enough drama in her own family. Why get involved in other people's?

*

'That's twice in a month Joe came to see us, Maura, the boy's heart must be in the right place,' JT said as they had their Sunday lunch.

'I did offer him a dinner today, but he had somewhere fancy to go.' Maura was not yet totally won over.

'He's setting up a fashion show, Maura; he has to have lunch with the people who will help him.'

'They shouldn't be working on the Sabbath day,' she said.

'I don't imagine it's *working* as such, more talking, I'd say.'

'What would *you* know, JT, about fashion shows, and whether they're working or talking?' she asked.

'What indeed? But don't I have a proper life for myself, a great wife, a fine home, a decent business and a grand Sunday dinner on the table? Isn't that better than anything Joe has?'

He was rewarded. Maura returned to the kitchen and cut him an extra slice of beef off the very overdone roast which had been in the oven for several hours. She was gradually coming round to the son who had hurt her so much over the years by ignoring his family and abandoning his faith.

'No love, I can't go,' Neil said.

'Okay.'

'No, Cathy, don't be like that . . .'

'Neil . . . I said okay. I suppose I'm disappointed not to have you there, and I thought we might go to the pictures afterwards . . . But if you have too much to do then I understand.'

She called Geraldine to tell her there would be one less, but the number was engaged. What the hell, she'd tell her when she got there.

But when she got to the Glenstar apartment the table was only set for four.

'Joe not coming then?' Cathy asked as she placed the roulade on one of Geraldine's plates.

'No, he's on his way. It *is* set for four, isn't it?'

'Yes, of course.' Cathy was puzzled.

'You, me, Shona, Joe?' She came out of the kitchen and counted, and looked surprised that Cathy had thought it would be otherwise.

'Did Neil ring you then?' she asked, surprised.

'Neil? No, why?'

'To say he couldn't come. He was very sorry . . .'

'I didn't expect him to come...' Geraldine said.

'Well it turned out all right. My mistake, I thought...'

'Of course he was invited, but he never turns up at things, does he?' Geraldine said, going back to the kitchen.

'Ah, he does, Geraldine, he was marvellous out with the twins yesterday, you'd be amazed at him. He was just like a dog with a bone, nothing would deter him. He *does* go to things.'

'And if I wanted a lawyer for any cause whatsoever, he'd be first on my list, that's without a doubt.'

'But this wasn't a case, it was family.'

'*His* family, Cathy. He's too busy for other things.'

The buzzer went and Shona had arrived, followed minutes later by Joe. They were sitting down making plans. Cathy had to drag her mind back to the conversation. Why hadn't she forced Neil to come today? He would have if she had told him that she needed him. Cathy wondered was she getting flu; she had been feeling tired and slightly weepy for a few days now. Suddenly a terrifying thought came to her. There was no wild possibility that she could be pregnant? She grabbed her diary to see where she had put the little x's to show when she expected her period. It was three days late. But it often was, Cathy told herself firmly, and forced herself to listen to ways they could publicise a fashion show. As soon as this was over they would help her to organise her sister's wedding. And she'd think about the other thing later. There was no problem.

Hannah stood at the hall door of Oaklands and looked on with annoyance as Jock Mitchell put his golf clubs in the back of the car.

'I didn't know you were going to play on *Sunday* as well,' she complained.

'You haven't arranged anything?' he asked. Jock was a sociable man; he didn't like to think that guests would arrive at Oaklands and find him missing.

'No, but...' Hannah bit her lip.

'That's fine then. See you when I see you.'

'When will that be?'

'I wish I knew.' He was vague.

'But food, Jock? Will you be back for lunch?'

'Lord no, it's a competition. Sometime in the evening. Bye now, dear.' He was gone.

Hannah went back into the house. She would get the Sunday papers and sit in the garden and read. She got little joy these days from sitting under a tree on the well-kept lawn at Oaklands. She hated to admit it to herself, but she was very lonely. What had happened to this house where once Lizzie had been polishing and scrubbing, and Neil tumbling in and out with his friends, Amanda bringing girls home from school and all Jock's colleagues and friends dropping in for a drink? If she had invited people to lunch, Jock would not have run off to the club. But he wouldn't stay at home if it was only Hannah. Perhaps she should ask Cathy about simple things to have ready in the freezer. Yes, she'd do that tomorrow. She thought about Jock's brother Kenneth and his unstable wife. Hannah was glad that she had kept out of all their messy affairs. She could well have been landed with those children. She looked around the big, empty garden.

'Neil? It's Simon. Do we have any money of our own anywhere, you know, pocket money or anything like that?'

'Don't you get something every week?'

'Yes, but it's only a pound and that's not enough.'

'Enough for what, actually, Simon?'

'We wanted to buy a present for Muttie and his wife Lizzie to say thank you when we leave.'

'Oh, they don't want that at all . . .' Neil reassured them.

'That's not it, it's that we'd *like* to give them a present, they've been very nice and they bought Hooves and he cost real money, all Muttie's winnings one week.'

'Yes I know, but they realise you don't have any money . . .'

'We've got *much* more money than they do, haven't we got a huge house, Neil? And money in the bank and everything. St Jarlath's Crescent is very small.'

'Simon, you're not going to buy them a new house, are you?' Neil laughed.

'No, they like this house. We wanted to buy Muttie a good pen for his work at the bookmakers', it would be about two pounds, and we wanted to get Muttie's wife Lizzie leggings.'

'Leggings?'

'She has pains in her knees and she thinks it's the cold and damp, so if she had red woolly leggings they would keep her warm and stop the pains.'

Neil gulped a bit. 'The leggings cost four pounds, and then we'd like to get a present for Cathy too, she did an awful lot of driving us around. Maud says she needs hair lacquer, it's a kind of glue that holds your hair together. They're different prices. We'd like a kind of middle-price one, about two pounds.'

'So that's about eight pounds altogether. Is this what we're looking at?' Neil asked.

'About that, yes.' Simon sounded doubtful.

'You sound as if there's something more. Let's have it.'

'We'd like to leave a tin of dog food for Hooves, and to give you something too. I know you didn't do all *that* much, but we thought you should have a present, a small one.'

'Well, that's very nice indeed,' Neil said, trying not to be annoyed.

'So what do you think?' Simon wasn't going to lose the main clause.

'I think twelve pounds should see you right, with some over.' Neil said firmly.

'That sounds just right, thank you, Neil.' Simon, who would have settled happily for ten, was delighted.

'So it's a question of transferring the funds.' Neil took it all very seriously.

'What does that mean, exactly?'

'Well, you don't have bank accounts, so I can't send you a cheque. It will have to be a cash transaction, I'd say.'

'An envelope of money, do you mean, Neil? That would be great.'

'No problem, it's owing to you. I'll get it to you today.'

'Will Cathy drive it over? You see, we don't want her to know . . .'

'She's not here. I'll tell her nothing and I'll drive it,' he promised.

He hung up the phone and sat thinking about them for a while. They were funny little things, certainly, and Cathy had done wonders with them. But they were a full-time job. It had made them both realise what a wise decision they had made about their future. Be marvellous to other people's children, but don't have any of your own.

Joe Feather was very focused at the lunch. He never lost sight of what they were trying to do, not for one moment. He had a very quick mind, which was good in business but he said that he lacked broad sweeps of imagination, and also he was totally out of touch with the clothes scene in Dublin. First he needed to know the rivals in his field, then where they were succeeding and failing. He needed to identify trends in the ready-to-wear market, which might be different in country towns from Dublin. He wanted to be sure why Haywards thought it a good idea to go downmarket when they had designer rooms and a very wealthy clientele. He listened intelligently while Shona explained that Haywards was busy encouraging the younger shopper, women in their twenties who would buy three or four outfits for summer or a whole holiday wardrobe rather than those who paid a fortune for two items. Geraldine went through different types of PR plan, one very expensive indeed, involving lunches with fashion journalists and buyers and interviews with the financial press on the mechanics of getting the clothes to Ireland.

'Too expensive and too many awkward questions asked.' He grinned at her.

'You're right,' Geraldine agreed.

'But I had to show you what could be done. Right. This is what I suggest.' And she reeled through plans for a press party before the fashion show, advance photographs taken by Ricky and sent to papers and magazines so that each would have a different one, models, make-up, hairdressing. Joe Feather took quick notes, agreeing to this, arguing that. It took half an hour and one glass of wine each.

'You have my yes please on that at this moment, but I'm only a third of the company on this lot so could you bear to talk to my two partners if they were to call you?' Joe said.

'Of course I'll talk to them,' Geraldine said, 'but let me do out a proposal and e-mail it to them first so that we all know what it is we *are* talking about; it will take less of everyone's time. They'd have this tomorrow by eleven. Is that all right, Joe?'

'Super-efficient.' He raised his glass to her.

'Oh, and Joe, you should put yourself all out to talk to the press. Very difficult prima donnas, some of them are. A personable man like yourself, with an Irish accent and well able, would go down a treat.'

'Me?' He was genuinely surprised.

Cathy smiled. The Feather brothers had no idea how good-looking they were; it added to their charm.

'She's right, Joe, I don't go for your kind of looks at all, but you have that superficial, attractive charm that makes them fall off their branches and roll over for you,' Cathy said, laughing.

'Ah, Cathy, you wound me ... I'm superficial ... You don't go for my looks, what else are you going to hit me with?' He pretended to be offended.

They were unexpectedly helpful, it turned out, on the subject of the Chicago wedding. Cathy wished that Tom were here to share the ideas and the conversation that went backwards and forwards. Her hand raced across the notebook writing things down, as Joe had been doing about his fashion show earlier. Joe wanted to know all about the hall they had hired ... It was an old church hall attached to a parish where James Byrne knew the parish priest. The priest had been happy with the thought of any money whatsoever for the parish, so the price was reasonable. Cathy and Tom had been to inspect it, and thought it was fine. It could be used as two areas, one for the reception and drinks and the other for the food, then the first one would be cleared for dancing. It would hold a hundred people comfortably, had fair kitchen space and cloakrooms. They could decorate it as they liked – Marian had suggested she would like an Irish-American theme, and maybe flags. Joe said that he thought it was over the top to drape the hall with US and Irish flags. Shona said it wasn't over the top at all, it was exactly what they would like. The Americans were travelling many thousands of miles for a ceremony; it must be marked. Geraldine asked was there a budget, and Cathy said yes there was, but of course they would go over it for Marian's sake. Joe debated buffets. He thought they were far better, you didn't get stuck with anyone. Geraldine said that the point of this was for people to get to know each other, and perhaps it should be a carefully thought-out seating plan. Shona said the thinking nowadays was not to mix up the families but let each side sit with its own. Geraldine had been at a smart wedding recently where everyone changed seats after each course – all the men moved to the next table – it meant that everyone got to know more people. Joe had been to a wedding where the receiving line was on a little stage surrounded with flowers. Cathy thought that Marian would prefer it to be as traditionally Irish as possible; people often thought like that when they had left home. Of course, it depended what you meant by traditional.

'You're the only married person at the table, Cathy,' Joe said. 'What would you like, what was your own wedding like...?'

'You don't want to know about my wedding, oh, believe me, you don't,' Cathy said ruefully.

'It wasn't *that* bad,' Geraldine said.

'Well, that was only thanks to you,' Cathy said, grateful always to her aunt for having saved the day. 'We had the reception at Peter Murphy's hotel, lovely salmon I remember, my mother had to be sedated, my father bribed, Neil's parents stayed for thirty-five minutes. The priest we had was very decent, by the way. He said the right thing to everyone, it was just that no one was listening. Hannah's nose got further up in the air and my mother's head nearer the ground.'

The others laughed at the image, but Cathy was serious. 'No, if you only knew, it's quite true. We wanted to get married quietly, in London maybe, and go back to Greece, but we thought we owed it to them. Neil was the only boy in the Mitchell family and I was the only Scarlet left at home. We didn't want to short-change them. Boy, were we wrong!' Her face was set hard.

Geraldine lightened the mood. 'Well as far as we know Marian's doing what she wants, not what she thinks whole groups of the previous generation want.'

'But does she *know* what she wants? She thinks Ireland is coming down with Irish dancers leaping up into the air and that two of them are called Simon and Maud. She's probably told all the Americans that the place is like Maureen O'Hara in *The Quiet Man*.'

'Well give it to her,' Joe said as if it were obvious.

'The customer's always right,' said Shona.

'The atmosphere is more important than the food, I've always said that,' Geraldine said.

'Well thanks for the vote of confidence in the caterers,' Cathy laughed.

'No, silly, you know what I mean.' Geraldine was brisk. She summed up all the arguments for and against every suggestion they made. No wonder she had got on so well in business, she had a very clear mind. Cathy finally had a proper plan in front of her.

They cleared the table in minutes between the four of them and shortly afterwards, Shona and Joe left to go back to work. Cathy watched them from the window. Geraldine was sitting on one of the sofas when Cathy turned away from the window. She had poured two glasses of wine.

'I'm not sure . . .' Cathy began.

'Sit down please, Cathy.' The voice was firm; it wasn't an invitation, it was more a command.

'Sure.'

'What is it, Cathy? Tell me, please.'

'What do you mean?' she blustered.

'Don't insult me. I've known you since the day you were born, I skipped school and went in to see Lizzie in the hospital. You were already terrifying her with your roaring and bawling ... So you won't go on pretending that's everything's all right, we have been down too many roads together to lie to each other at this stage. It's one of two things: either I have offended you or annoyed you by something I did or said, or else it has nothing to do with me and you're in some bad trouble.' She sat there on her sofa, her legs tucked underneath her, looking ten years younger than her age. Always immaculately groomed, dressed today in a navy and cream outfit as if she were going to Quentin's instead of hosting a working lunch.

'Which would you like it to be, Geraldine?' Cathy said eventually.

'Well obviously I'd prefer it to have been something I said or did, then I could explain it and apologise if necessary. Naturally that's what I'd want, rather than to think you had an illness or your marriage had problems.'

Cathy said nothing.

'So can I ask you again, which is it?'

'It's neither and both in a way.' Geraldine waited.

'All right,' Cathy said eventually. 'You're going to think this silly, but I was upset when you told me you took presents from men.'

Geraldine looked at her. 'You're not serious.'

'I'm very serious. It's only one degree away from taking cheques ... it's so tacky, Geraldine. You don't need that. You're the icon for us all, you're the role model, for God's sake.'

'And you've changed your opinion of me since I told you that Freddie bought me this watch ...'

'Well, yes, and that Peter gave you the flat and that someone else gave you that sound system, and the rug, and for all I know everything here.'

Geraldine's face was cold. 'You actually think less of me. Me, your friend, because I accepted gifts.'

'Yes, I do, it's so tacky, and it's so unnecessary. You don't love these men who fancy you, Geraldine, you haven't loved any of them, they're just ... they're just ... Well, I'd say a meal ticket, but you don't need a meal ticket, you have your own business.'

'Go on.'

'I shouldn't have started this, I feel much cheaper than I am accusing you of being, sitting here throwing back all your generosity to me and to my family . . .'

Geraldine just sat, calm and motionless.

'You forced me to say it. I see now why you didn't feel upset being in Peter Murphy's house . . . you never cared about them, not one little bit, it was all for this . . .' She made a sweeping gesture around the room and its style. Her face was red and upset. Geraldine seemed unmoved. 'So what do you have to say to *me*? You said you wanted me to tell you and now I have. Is it going to be a stony silence?'

'No, Cathy, but nor is it going to be one word of apology, not one.'

'You're proud of all this?'

'I'm neither proud not ashamed, it's a way to live.'

'And you never loved any of them, that's right, isn't it?'

'I loved Teddy,' Geraldine said.

'Teddy?'

'Oh, I loved Teddy and he loved me, but not enough to leave his wife for me.'

'But that was back a long time ago. People didn't then.'

'It was twenty-two years ago, not the Dark Ages, and people *did* leave home and start again, as Teddy said he would, and as I believed he would, particularly when I was pregnant.' Cathy stared at her. 'But it turned out not to be the case.' The voice was very flat. Cathy hardly dared to move. 'And we agreed that the timing was all spectacularly bad, I can't remember what, one of his children going to school or leaving school or hating school or loving school. Some bloody thing. Does it matter?' Cathy took a sharp breath. This was horrifying. 'But it meant that there could be no baby.' A long pause. 'I *could* have kept the baby. But then I knew I'd lose Teddy, so I lost the baby instead. A friend of his was a doctor, not a great doctor, as it happened, and I had left it too late so that complicated it, and I don't think this doctor was entirely sober at the time. So after that, no more babies, ever.'

'Geraldine.' Cathy was stricken.

'So after that, as you can understand, I was a bit low, but I thought I'd have Teddy to comfort me, but as it happened I didn't. He was nervous. I had become a loose cannon on the deck, and he took his family and went abroad. So, Cathy, it sounds very dramatic but I didn't allow myself to wallow too much in the luxury of love after that. The men I've known since and who have been my friends like my company and conversation just as much as my bed and my wearing lacy underwear. I have not been dependent on *any* of them for *any*thing. They can't offer me commitment or a home, so they give me watches and that silk rug on the floor in front of you. But I'm sorry if it *upsets* you and you think *less* of me and that it's, what did you say, *tacky*,' she repeated Cathy's accusations with great emphasis. 'That's all I can say. I'm sorry if it offends you, but it doesn't offend me, and it's my life.'

'I'm so ashamed I could die,' Cathy said.

Geraldine sighed. 'Leave it, Cathy. You had guts to say it, I give you that much. And what was the other thing that was upsetting you, the one that didn't have to do with me?'

Cathy spoke slowly. 'I don't suppose there could be any more inappropriate thing to tell you, but I think I might be pregnant, and it's the last thing on earth I want now.'

Chapter Six

JUNE

'What time is she coming?' Tom asked.

'Who?'

'Well excuse *me*, but I thought all this shining and polishing and getting out the best linen was to impress your mother-in-law,' Tom said.

'Oh, sorry Tom, I was miles away. Hannah's coming about half past twelve.'

'Let's get the skates on then, and go and make some soup,' he suggested.

Cathy leaped up guiltily. Tom had been here since five a.m., and she had been barely able to get in by nine. The bread had been delivered to Haywards, he had stopped at the fish shop on the way back, he had got all the vegetables and a huge lamb bone for a big soup order, he had already made her two cups of coffee and she had done nothing. Of course she hadn't told Neil last night. There had been no time. After the hours of crying in Geraldine's flat she had felt drained. Neil had been distracted, stuck in his books. And as Geraldine had soothed and consoled her over and over, it might be a false alarm. She must get a Predictor first, from the chemist, and then go to a doctor. Then and only then should she tell Neil.

'Tom, I'm so sorry. Here, pass me over the knife, I'll start chopping the basil and tomatoes.'

'She'll think it's tinned,' he objected.

'No she won't, so what, anyway?'

'*You've* got very courageous suddenly,' he said.

'No, I'm still terrified of her, but at least now I know there's no pleasing her, so that helps a bit.' Cathy's eyes were a little too bright.

'I don't think you should have a knife in your hand this morning,' Tom said. 'You'll be in ribbons by the time she comes. Leave the dangerous stuff to me.'

'Great. So what do I do?'

'Set the table, get some flowers.'

They had a great bank of flowerpots in a wheelbarrow in their courtyard. Whenever they wanted a table decoration they just lifted out a pot of primulas, pansies or begonias, cleaned it around the edges and placed it in a brass container. When the function or the need to impress was over, the plant went back outdoors.

'That doesn't sound very much,' Cathy said.

'And start practising your smile. Remember the last time Hannah Mitchell was here? You were shouting at her like a fishwife about her coat and your mother and assorted other topics.'

'Oh, we've all mellowed since those days,' Cathy said loftily.

'I think we'd need to have,' said Tom, who had already got the stock into the soup saucepan and begun the work.

'Imagine, we'll be going home on the bus today,' Simon said to Maud.

'By ourselves, no Muttie,' Maud said.

'He said he might happen to be walking by the school sometimes, and he'd walk us to the bus,' Simon said.

'But he's probably going to the shoemaker's or the bookmaker's, it's not really on his way,' Maud worried.

'How else will we ever see Hooves?' Simon said, and they looked at each other in concern. It hadn't been actually said, but they knew that social visits to St Jarlath's Crescent were going to be very few and far between.

'You're a very sweet girl, you know, Geraldine,' Freddie said as they had coffee together in her office. He had called in to discuss the Italian villa presentation, which would be upcoming soon. But they were also talking about his own party, for which Geraldine's niece and her partner were going to do the catering.

'I know I am,' Geraldine said. 'I'm totally delightful, but in what particular way at the moment?'

'You're as anxious as I am that the party Pauline and I are having will be a success,' he said in some wonder.

'But why ever not, Freddie? I don't want anything from you except what I have, your company, your interest, your concern, your wonderful loving . . . Why *should* I not be interested and wish it all well?'

'You're amazing. You really mean it.' Freddie Flynn had not come across such women before.

'You know what the French used to say about a mistress. She must be discreet, and never, ever do anything that would upset the man's family, his children and certainly not his property . . .' She laughed engagingly at him.

'You ask so little, Geraldine,' he said in a throaty voice.

'But that's not true, and truly I have so much.' She waved her hand around the office, the business that was hers alone. The hand that she waved had a jewelled watch on the wrist.

'So Cathy will come round to the house and set it all up with Pauline, will she?'

'Yes, Cathy or Tom, they take it turn by turn. He's just as good,' Geraldine said.

She hoped it would be Tom that made the visit. The way poor Cathy was behaving at the moment, she wouldn't be able to keep her eye on the ball at all.

'Nice to see you, Mrs Mitchell, and don't you look well.'

'Thank you, Shona,' Hannah patted her hair. 'I've just had a glorious hour in the salon. I'm going to have lunch with Cathy, as it happens. I thought I'd buy her a little gift. What do you suggest?'

'Well, now, if it were anyone else I'd say a loaf of that delicious bread that Scarlet Feather does for us, but you'll be having that anyway . . . Flowers are always nice, a fancy soap maybe?'

'The bread doing well, is it?'

'We can't keep it on the shelves or in the restaurant. I told Tom that we're going to have to make him an offer he can't refuse and come and work here full-time.'

'Imagine.' Hannah was surprised.

'Anyway, enjoy your lunch, Mrs Mitchell. Lots of people would envy you, you know.'

'Yes, I'm beginning to realise that,' Hannah said in a disapproving voice.

She still found it hard to accept that she was lucky to be getting a meal cooked for her by the maid's daughter. But she *must* not think like that, or else something would slip out as it so often did for absolutely no reason at all, and then everyone took horrific offence and Neil sighed and Jock sighed and Cathy went totally berserk. Don't say *poor* Lizzie. It was just an expression, but try telling that to Cathy Scarlet.

James Byrne had decided to cook a dinner that night. Not the real one, not the one he was rehearsing for, but just to see whether he could or not. And as it happened, Martin Maguire was going to be in Dublin. He would try it out on him. He took out Cathy and Tom's meticulous instructions – they had even typed out advice about the shopping. It was a Monday morning, he had nothing else to do with his time, he would go to the market that they had suggested with their list in hand. Martin Maguire would be very surprised indeed to be presented with such a gourmet meal. And it would be great practice for James. He had enjoyed those two evenings with Tom and Cathy enormously, and wished he could think of an excuse for more. But he must remember that this had been his undoing before. Becoming too fond of people, too dependent. It must not happen again.

'This house will never be the same,' Muttie said when the children had left for school. 'Those people won't get the children to do their homework the way we did.' He shook his head sadly.

'They'd know more than we do,' Lizzie said.

It had always worried her, looking after the children of the quality in her own home.

This was something that had never worried Muttie. 'It's a matter of discipline,' he said firmly. 'This house has proper rules and regulations.' And at that, he got out the paper and studied the racing pages, while Hooves laid his sad black head on his knee, and the woman that the children still called Muttie's wife got ready to leave a house that had proper rules and regulations to go out and clean the apartments and houses of the quality.

Joe Feather called his brother.

'Could I buy you a nice pint and a plate of sausages for lunch?' he offered.

'God, I'd love it Joe, but it has to be late. I'm setting up a lunch here for Cathy's mother-in-law!'

'Is it a big do?'

'No, only the two of them.'

'God, you've fallen on hard times, a lunch for two people. Have I invested in a Mickey Mouse company?'

'No, you fool, it's a social thing.'

They fixed a place to meet.

'Give Cathy my love. Thank her for everything yesterday.' Joe hung up.

'Hey, you didn't say you met my brother yesterday,' Tom said.

'Tom, I haven't said anything this morning. I'm like a zombie. I met him at Geraldine's, and he was a great help about the Chicago wedding. Actually he really was, I meant to tell you. I took lots of notes.'

'Geraldine's, no less?'

'Yeah, but they weren't thinking of withdrawing their funding or anything, it was about this fashion show he's putting on.'

'I know, Marcella's going to be one of the models, isn't it great?'

'Great,' said Cathy, wondering whether Tom knew that it was mainly lingerie that his girlfriend would be modelling.

'Come in, Mrs Mitchell.' Tom's smile rarely failed to hit its target.

'Oh, hallo, er ... Tom, isn't it?'

'It is indeed, Mrs Mitchell, and how well you're looking, if I may say so.'

She patted her hair again. It was so wise to go to a good salon regularly. Cathy was so foolish in this regard, as in so many things.

'I didn't know that we were all going to ... I mean ...'

'No, no, I'm just serving you and then making myself scarce.'

'I heard you do marvellous bread for Haywards.'

'Thank you so much, they're very kind about it. I've left you a little selection to try, and also a packet to take home.'

Eventually the Tom Feather smile had worked. Hannah Mitchell was smiling back.

'You are a kind boy,' she said, as so many middle-aged, middle-class matrons had said to him over the last few months.

Cathy stood waiting, in a pink and lilac summer print dress that did her no favours, her face as white as a sheet, her hair tied back with an elastic band.

'You're welcome, Hannah,' she said in a flat voice.

'It's a pleasure to be here, and my goodness doesn't the place look nice!'

She looked around, and Tom hoped that Cathy would respond warmly to her, otherwise all this would be in vain. To his relief, Cathy was smiling.

'This is our front room, where we sit clients down and persuade them to have much bigger parties than they intended,' she said.

'Very nicely done,' Hannah looked around her with grudging admiration. 'Nice colours, too.'

'My mother made the curtains and covers,' Cathy said proudly.

Hannah looked at them in disbelief. 'Oh, Lizzie was always . . . marvellous with her hands,' she said eventually.

Tom sighed with relief, poured them a sherry and went to the kitchen.

'Tom, will you either eat that sandwich or throw it away, but for God's sake stop analysing it,' Joe said, laughing at the way his younger brother was unpicking all the ingredients.

'Look at what they charge for that, Joe, no seriously, look at it. A tired tomato, a piece of plastic cheese, a dead leaf of lettuce, half a hard-boiled, discoloured egg . . . A smear of cheap salad cream . . . And they dare to call that a Summer Salad Sandwich. What do visitors to this country think, tell me what do they say. . . ?'

'Oh, shut up and eat something else,' Joe said good-naturedly.

'Like those cremated sausages you're eating? People have no standards,' he was still ferocious.

'What am I going to do about Ma?' Joe asked.

'What about her?'

'Well, I've been going up there a bit,' Joe began.

'I know you have, Joe, and honestly it does mean so much to them . . .'

'But they say you drop in every second day . . .' Joe said.

'When I'm passing I do, it's no trouble . . .'

'Come on, who ever passes Fatima on the way anywhere?'

'I've had to do it, Joe, it's no big thing.'

'I'm sorry I left it all to you.'

'Well, you were in London, and anyway you're doing your bit now, it lightens the load.'

'Okay, okay. So what'll I do about Ma? She wants to come to the fashion show.'

'Well, let her, can't you?'

'Of course I can't.'

'I'll keep an eye on her.'

'No, not that, the clothes. Ma can't see them.'

'But why not, she came to our launch party. I don't think she enjoyed it very much but she was glad to be there . . .'

'But Tom, the garments . . .'

'What about them?'

'It's swimwear, lingerie, half-naked girls all over the place . . . Mam would only drop stone dead.'

'It's not *all* that, is it?' Tom asked with a hollow feeling in his stomach.

'Most of it.' Joe looked at his brother's face. 'Marcella told you, didn't she?' he said.

Neil went into Quentin's restaurant and sought out the elegant Brenda Brennan immediately.

'I'm having lunch with a real gangster, Brenda, he's going to try to get me drunk. Can you just put tonic at the bottom of my vodka glass each time . . . so that he thinks I'm having a real drink?'

'It's not fair to charge him then, Mr Mitchell.'

'You'll manage something, take it off something else . . . You know all the ways around things.'

'I've been long enough in the business for that, it's true, so perhaps, Mr Mitchell, if you'd like to keep your eyes down I'll lead you swiftly to a table without your having to meet your father, who will be exiting from a booth fairly imminently.'

Neil followed her as directed.

'You should run the world, Brenda!' he said, just glimpsing his father leaving with a blonde half his age.

'I often think I do,' Brenda Brennan sighed.

'That was delicious. That tomato soup, very sweet taste, and my heavens, that's good, that bread . . . You hardly ate any,' Hannah said.

'Hannah, I'm eating it all day, and all night . . . Tom is so proud of it, and olive bread isn't enough for him these days, you have to have green olive or black olive . . . he's such a perfectionist . . .'

'And what do we have now?'

Was there a time when she had dreaded this woman? How long ago it all seemed. 'It's monkfish, I think you'll like it, and quite a small helping to leave room for dessert . . .'

'I brought you this.' Hannah spoke gruffly, and thrust across the table a gift-wrapped Haywards parcel.

Cathy knew she must open it, however ill-timed; the monkfish with its saffron sauce, the green beans with tiny lardons of bacon and toasted almonds, the potatoes and ginger were all wafting up their vapours at them. It was a time to savour the food, not to open presents. But she unpicked the elegant wrapping and opened the gift. From the paper came an overwhelming and pungent smell of incense. Cathy felt slightly weak.

'It's wonderful, Hannah, what exactly... ?'

'It's one of those new very powerful aromatic oils for the shower, apparently young people like them...' Hannah began.

It was too much, the heady smell of that and the food. Cathy clutched her stomach and ran from the table, and knelt vomiting into the lavatory pan. She heard her mother-in-law calling outside the door.

'*Cathy*. Cathy, let me in, are you all right?'

Marcella looked up from arranging bottles of nail colour and saw Joe Feather in the salon.

'You're very, very beautiful,' he said in an odd sort of voice.

'Joe?' she was alarmed.

'Sorry, I'm actually just saying this as a fact... it *is* a fact... but I sort of let slip to Tom that the lines you'll be modelling are fairly sexy ... And to be honest, I don't think he knew that.'

She looked at him, surprised. He began to wish he had never spoken.

'Now I'm getting out of it and letting you take it from here, Marcella ... okay?'

'Sure.' She was very calm.

'It's just that he adores you ... you see.'

'Of course.'

Joe shrugged. 'It's just, I don't honestly think Tom knew.'

'Thank you, Joe,' she said in a voice that made him feel small.

'I'm so sorry, Hannah, you'll have to forgive me, that's why I wasn't eating so much bread. You see, I've had an upset tummy.'

'But you should have said, you should have cancelled the lunch ...'

'No, *please* Hannah, look, I'm fine now.' Cathy forked herself a helping of the monkfish, which tasted like soap in her mouth, and forced herself to swallow it. She had moved the heavily scented bath oil to another part of the kitchen entirely. Eventually she felt her stomach return to normal. The conversation wasn't exactly easy. Every subject had a background; any chance remark, a history. They talked about the twins returning to The Beeches and how genuinely *good* Lizzie had been. Good and generous, all the right words. Hannah remarked that Cathy hadn't found time yet to go to the Haywards salon, and Cathy looked her in the eye, promising that she would go soon. They talked about Neil and how hard he worked, and how lucky Cathy was that Neil did not play golf like his father, otherwise she would be a total widow. And suddenly out of the blue Hannah mentioned Amanda.

'Cathy, can I ask you something . . . Do you think Amanda has some reason for not coming home to see us?'

This was a moment where Cathy could do some good or some ill; she had to be very careful. She barely remembered Amanda Mitchell, two years older than Neil, bossy, distant and didn't come to their wedding, but had sent a really great present . . . a top-class atlas and an expensive radio that got all kinds of frequencies and wave bands and a card saying, 'May you see the world and love it.' Cathy had thought that lovely of her. Although it might have been rather over-prophetic, if Neil still had it in his head that they should set off to see the world and love it full-time. She had often asked about Amanda. Up to now, her mother-in-law had been vague and dismissive; Amanda was too busy, too successful in Canada to keep in touch with a new sister-in-law whom she barely knew. Neil had been no help about her either. Manda was great, he said, her own person, great, no, of course he wouldn't telephone her, what would they say? It seemed very distant not to want to talk to your only sister about *something* . . . Cathy would prattle non-stop about her sisters in Chicago at any time. Now that Cathy had heard fairly authoritatively that Amanda was in a gay relationship in Toronto, what did she say or do?

'Perhaps she's met someone over there?' she suggested.

'I don't think so. Amanda was never particularly interested in men, she didn't bring boyfriends home when she was here . . . We always thought of her as a career woman.' Hannah was thoughtful.

'Maybe that's it, then, she's tied up in her career and the people she meets there, the other women who run the bookshop. Maybe that's her life now.'

It trickled away as other subjects of conversation had done. Soon Hannah made a move to leave.

'Won't you have more coffee?'

'No indeed, it was all quite perfect. I really enjoyed this lunch, and you look much better now, dear.'

'Yes, I'm so sorry . . . And thank you again for the beautiful bath oil.'

Even remembering the smell of it made Cathy feel slightly nauseous again, but she held on. She watched as Hannah left taking small steps across the cobbled courtyard. In all those years of fighting this woman with the small, pinched face, she never could have envisaged a day like today. A day when she would stand at the doorway of her own business and might very well be, as it happened, pregnant with this woman's grandchild.

Simon and Maud couldn't believe it. Outside the school stood Muttie and Hooves, waiting for them as usual.

'I thought you'd need to be settled onto that bus,' Muttie said simply. They looked at him, delighted. 'For the first day anyway, until you got the hang of it,' he said, and the little group headed off happily to the bus stop.

Sara was sitting in the garden rolling a cigarette when Neil arrived. He went to join her on the old wooden bench.

'How does it look inside?' he nodded towards the house.

'Okay . . . for the moment . . . but you get the feeling that your uncle could be poised for flight at any time; he's fairly unsatisfactory about his plans.'

'He always was,' Neil agreed ruefully.

'I'll keep an eye on it,' Sara promised. 'Just because kids live in a lovely big house like this doesn't mean that they still don't need someone to look out for them.'

'They should sell it and move somewhere much smaller, more manageable, but they won't hear of it. All puff and style and grandeur and nothing to back it up,' Neil said.

'You don't approve of him,' Sara said.

'He's never done a proper day's work in his life. My father takes it all fairly lightly, but he *has* put in hours in an office. Anyway, I think it's ridiculous in this day and age, one family living in all these rooms,' Neil looked back up at the house.

'You and Cathy don't have a big house, then?' Sara asked.

'Lord, no. Small place in Waterview.'

'Oh, I know those, they're nice. Still, not a place for a family, though, not like this place here is.'

'We don't have children,' said Neil Mitchell, proceeding to take the papers out of his briefcase and tell Sara the social worker where they needed her help for a report on the homeless that was going to be presented by an umbrella organisation. They pulled the old garden table up to them and worked away happily. From inside the house, Kenneth Mitchell watched them absently from one window, only mildly interested in these people in his garden. Kay Mitchell watched anxiously from another. It was nearly time for the children to come home, she had asked Mrs ... Mrs Barry to make sandwiches for them. Mrs Barry wanted to know should the crusts be on or off; Kay decided eventually that there should be two plates, one with, one without.

'Please come in, Muttie,' Maud begged.

'No, child, honestly. Hooves and I will get another bus back.' He was very insistent.

'But we want to show you our house.'

'Another time, son, not the first day.'

'And Hooves could go for a run in the garden, our garden ... *please*, Muttie.'

But he was firm. It wasn't sensible, not the first day, there would be people taking notes, he didn't want it to look as if he and Lizzie were trying to muscle in, get more than their fair share of the twins.

'You mean, like ... everyone wants us to be with them.' Simon was puzzled at this possibility.

'Of course we do, but the best thing is that your own mam and dad are back to take care of you, now that they're in a position to do so,' Muttie spoke with a heavy heart. Nothing he had heard from Cathy made him think that this was any fit pair to be looking after the children.

'But you will come in *some*time, will you, Muttie?' Simon begged.

'Of course I will, son, when you're more settled, when Hooves is more acceptable.'

'And we're definitely coming to St Jarlath's Crescent at the weekend, that's agreed with Sara,' Maud said anxiously.

'Of course you are, child, and Lizzie and I are looking forward to it greatly, so we are.'

'I wish . . .' Maud began.

'So in you go now, like a good girl,' Muttie said before anyone could say what they wished.

'Sandwiches!' Simon said, pleased.

'Thank you very much, Mother,' Maud said.

They sat down at the table and their parents watched them admiringly. Neil and Sara had come in from the garden.

'How many may we have?' Simon asked.

'Well, they're all for you, of course.' Kay Mitchell was proud to be seen to be such a provider.

'Yes, but won't it take our appetite away for tea?' Maud asked.

'Muttie's wife Lizzie always says only one biscuit each when we come in, otherwise it will spoil tea.'

'Well, this *is* tea,' poor Kay stammered.

'No, I meant *real* tea, you know, bacon and egg tea,' Simon asked.

'Or tinned beans or whatever,' Maud said in a small voice, as if realising that all was not entirely well.

Kay looked wildly from her husband to Sara. 'Nobody said anything about bacon and eggs, there was to be a tea ready and it's ready.' She looked about to cry.

'Well that's fine, Mother, we'll just eat them all now,' Simon said.

'It's enough for me, really,' Maud assured her.

Sara and Neil exchanged glances. Kenneth Mitchell looked out into the garden as if inspiration and solutions would come from the wilderness he saw.

'I had lunch with Hannah,' Cathy said to Neil that evening when they were both back at Waterview.

'Well done.' He went to the fridge to pour two glasses of Chardonnay.

'She was fine. She talked a lot about Amanda.'

'Sorry, she does drone on about her. Hey, have you gone all total abstainer on me? That's the second glass of wine you've waved away; you must be sickening for something.'

'I just don't want it now. Neil, did you know Amanda's gay?'

'No, I didn't. Did my mother tell you that? I just don't believe it.' He was open-mouthed at the very thought.

'Of course she didn't.'

'And since when?'

'I've no idea, but those women I did a reunion for the other day mentioned it, and I checked with another woman who knew her in Dublin when she worked in a travel agency, and this woman is gay herself and she said yes, it's true, and Amanda has this marvellous partner and they work in a bookshop together . . .'

'Well, imagine that! Manda, who would have thought it? Good luck to her, I say.'

'And so do I, Neil, I say good luck to her, and all our friends will . . . It's her mother and father who might not be so jolly about it.'

'No . . . you speak only the truth,' he said, grinning ruefully.

'So anyway, I thought you'd like to know,' Cathy said.

'Cathy, how did you try to tell this news to my mother? I've pleaded some pretty impossible cases in my time, but this one I must hear.'

She laughed. 'No, I didn't even get to first base. Listen, are you going to sit down with that wine, or are you going to take it to work with you?'

'I'm taking it to work with me, by which I mean next door. I have a hell of a lot to finish on this homeless thing . . . I met Sara today with the twins, by the way, and she's a lot of help . . .'

'Oh, how did it all go? I'm dying to hear. Sit down for a minute and tell me.'

Neil sat down. 'It was amazing, she explained that there *is* funding, but that no one can really get at it. It needs the right questions to be asked at the right time . . . She gave me lots of notes.'

'Funding?' Cathy was bewildered.

He explained at length about a European Union grant that might be available for the homeless, and how the ad hoc committee mustn't throw away this piece of information at once, they must keep it as a card to play later once they had got some muscle. Eventually, after a lot of listening to details of strategy, there was a moment when she could get in a word about Maud and Simon.

'Oh, they were fine,' he said, getting up to leave the table.

'No, sit down and tell me, Neil, did they have a welcome, any kind of a meal for them?'

'Yes, they had sandwiches.'

'Is that all?'

'The twins were so funny, they kept asking about their real tea. Sara took over, it's under control.'

And that was all she was going to hear. And it seemed it was not the night to tell him about anything else.

Tom was looking for the right way to mention the fashion show to Marcella. A way that would not reveal the sick feeling at the base of his stomach that she was going to be walking around half naked in front of strangers. He knew that this jealousy had nearly destroyed them before; he *must* keep it under control. She loved only him, he knew this, for heaven's sake. Why couldn't she just keep her clothes on and join him in the business? But he realised so well that this was destructive. It was impossible to fathom why someone as loving and happy in a relationship as she claimed she was still wanted to strut about in swimwear and lingerie. But he must be careful. This kind of suspicion and possessiveness was what had made her walk out before. He was walking on eggshells. To his surprise, she brought the subject up herself.

'You won't believe the colours that Feather Fashions have for the show, lime greens and fuchsias . . . *nobody* could want to wear that kind of underwear.'

Tom let his breath out slowly. At least she was telling him that it was lingerie.

'No, give me basic black lacy stuff any day,' he smiled.

'Just so that you realise it's all a bit of fun?' she said.

'Of course.' His heart was heavy. She was preparing him. 'And the swimwear, what colour is that?'

She seemed relieved that he knew about that much, anyway. 'The same, mad, wild colours, almost luminous . . . He either hasn't a clue what he's doing, or else he's got it just right . . . There's a very fine line between the two.'

He stared at her. She really was obsessed by the whole fashion business. It didn't have anything at all to do with stripping off in public. He would be mad to let that thought settle in his mind.

'Darling, you'll never believe who was just on the phone!' Kenneth Mitchell said to his wife as he came back from the phone in the hall.

'Who was it, dear?'

'Old Barty coughed up out of nowhere.'

'Barty . . . Our best man!' she cried, pleased.

'Yes, I told him he could stay. He's got a vintage car, or a veteran one, whichever . . . He's going to take it to some show.'

'What did he cough up?' Simon asked.

'Sorry?' His father looked at him vaguely.

'Was it blood?' Maud asked fearfully.

'Or a pint of stout. Muttie coughed up a pint of stout once, his wife Lizzie was very annoyed.'

Their parents looked at them, confused.

'Anyway, old Barty says he'll take us all for a spin in the car, Saturday. You kids too.' He looked at them, proud of the treat.

'But on Saturday we go to St Jarlath's Crescent,' Maud said.

'To see Hooves and Muttie and Muttie's wife Lizzie.'

'No, darling, you can go another day. Those people won't mind,' their mother said.

'No, we can't go another day, honestly they'll be getting ready. They're making a proper tea and everything, we asked for sausages.' Maud was almost tearful.

'Well telephone them and say it's off, that's a good girl.' Her father was brisk.

'Why do I have to do it?' Maud was now mutinous.

'Because I don't know them, my sweet child, and you do.'

'Why can't Simon do it?' Maud complained.

'Girls are better at that sort of thing, darling,' her father said.

'They'll be so upset,' Maud said to Simon.

'And I'm upset too,' Simon said.

'I wanted to see Hooves. I have a new trick to teach him.'

'It's not fair,' Maud said.

'It's not,' Simon agreed.

They looked at each other.

'Let's ring Cathy,' they both said at the same time.

Cathy said they were to leave it with her, just say that they had telephoned and found Cathy there and spoken to her as her parents weren't in.

'But that's not exactly true,' Simon said. 'We *did* ring you at Waterview.'

'Yes, but I could have been in St Jarlath's Crescent. I don't think we should worry about it, do you?' Cathy was brisk.

'A white lie,' Simon suggested.

'Hardly a lie at all,' Cathy assured him.

'Neil, this is *not* going to happen,' she fumed at him.

'Hey, peace, peace . . . I'm on *your* side, of course it's not going to happen.'

'So who rings your uncle and tells him, do you or do I?'

'I'll ring Sara,' he said. 'That's her job, and she'll tell them.'

'But she's not at work now, surely.'

'I have her mobile number,' Neil said, somewhat to Cathy's surprise.

As it happened, when old Barty turned up he didn't have his car at all, so the outing would never have taken place.

'Just as well the children went off to those people,' Kenneth Mitchell said.

'What people?' Barty asked as he sat down at the table and Kay fussed around vaguely, bringing in first a plate of bread, then a dish of butter, then removing the bread to toast it.

'Oh, some people who live up in some terrible place, but they've been very good to the twins . . .'

'Are they family?'

'No, or yes, in a way, through marriage. Very complicated . . .' Kenneth ended the discussion mainly in order to cover the fact that he wasn't entirely sure why his son and daughter had been looked after for months by a couple with the extraordinary names of Muttie and Muttie's wife.

'What did happen to your car, Barty?' Kay asked.

'Well, um . . . it's all a bit hard to explain . . . as old Ken here would say, it's all pretty complicated,' said Barty.

Kay went back to the kitchen to sort out what to do next. Barty explained to Ken in a low, urgent voice that he had actually lost the car in a card game, and wondered would his friend Ken help him win it back. Kenneth Mitchell explained in an equally low and urgent voice that things were not as they used to be. Today's world meant a budget, a tight budget worked out by Neil, that thin-faced nephew of his, and policed by people like this boy's wife and a social worker. Had to account for every single thing. His incomings, small as they were, from a couple of directorships and the rental of a property, went straight into some fund or trust, and a living allowance was paid out each month. Degrading to say the least. Old Barty hadn't given up hope. Could they borrow against next month's living allowance? Kenneth proved to be a changed man in this area . . . Things were too precarious, he said. Sorry, Barty old man, can't do.

※

'The dancing teacher's coming round tonight,' Lizzie told the twins.

'Oh, good, will we wear our costumes?' Simon wanted to know.

'No, I don't want them getting all messed up, I've made up cheap kilts and cloaks for you so you can get the swish of it all . . .' Lizzie's face was glowing with pride over it all. 'The teacher says you need a bit of practice; suppose you were to take a tape home with you and practise in your kitchen back there?'

'Yes . . . yes, we could I suppose,' Simon looked doubtful.

'Or would that not be too easy?' Muttie wondered.

Simon threw him a grateful glance. 'You see, it's Father . . . He can't understand fellows dancing, he says, and he doesn't understand it being a family wedding. I said it was for our cousins coming from Chicago, and he didn't understand that either.'

Simon looked embarrassed by having to explain all this, but Muttie hastened to reassure him. 'Oh, a man like your father, who'd have travelled and all, he'd not be in the way of knowing the way things have changed, fellows dancing and leaping all over the place there are nowadays,' he said cheerfully.

'But it *is* a family wedding, isn't it?' Maud was always anxious to have things straight.

'In a way . . . But of course . . .' Lizzie began. Humble again, and still not wanting to claim any kinship with the great Mitchells.

'It is *of course* a family wedding. Isn't Cathy the sister of the bride, and she's married to Neil, your first cousin. What on earth could be closer than that?' Muttie asked. This satisfied the twins totally, and they ran off to teach Hooves the new trick before the dancing teacher came.

Muttie and Lizzie looked at each other.

'We should never have taken them in,' Lizzie said.

'We should never have let them leave,' Muttie said.

Neil went into his father's office. The solicitors' firm was a busy one, long established and middle-of-the-road. They didn't send many briefs to Neil Mitchell, fiery defender of causes, but then he didn't need them. There was plenty of work coming in from elsewhere. Neil wasn't coming in about business; this time it was family. He saw Walter through an open door, and paused for a moment. By rights the boy should be brought in on it, but then he was much more likely to hinder than to help. Walter looked up.

'Neil?' he said without much pleasure.

'Glad to have the kids back at home?' Neil asked.

'What? Oh, yes, they're great,' Walter said unconvincingly.

'No problems with your parents or anything?'

'No, no, they leave me alone, I'm glad to say ... and of course I'm not always there.'

'I meant with them and the twins,' Neil said coldly.

'I see. Of course. No, I don't think so. Should there be?'

Neil gritted his teeth. What a self-centred little monster Walter had become. He thought only of his own entertainment, his own good time. Neil remembered suddenly that he had lent the boy his very expensive binoculars recently to go to the races. He had asked for them back twice when he was at the house.

'By the way, Walter, do you have those field glasses I lent you? You told me they were at the office.'

'You came all the way in here to get them back?' Walter's face was a sneer.

'Do you have them, Walter, please?'

'Keep your hair on.' He got up and went to a drawer which he pulled, but it was locked and wouldn't open. 'See, I did my best.' He looked so supercilious and unrepentant that Neil felt his knuckles clenching.

'Lock your drawers in the office as well as your room at home, I see?'

'Can't be too careful, I say,' Walter said cheerfully and picked up the telephone to show the conversation was over.

'Dad, we're going to have to give some thought to Kenneth and the whole set-up there,' Neil said.

'Are we?' Jock Mitchell was disappointed. It was a sunny day, and he had been hoping to slip away from the office in a few moments. He had his golf clubs already locked into the boot of the car, and was just waiting until the coast was clear in order to leave.

'Walk down to the car with me, Neil, we'll talk as we go.'

'No, Dad, I want you to write him a letter on your office writing paper.'

'What about?' Jock was testy now. He had carefully organised his clients and his associates into line with his plans; all he needed was to be disturbed by his brother.

Patiently Neil explained that Kenneth Mitchell was in actual danger of losing his children into care. A foster home, or even residential accommodation might be found if he continued to break the terms of the agreement.

'He's not doing that already, surely?'

'Well yes, he is, he's reneging on everything: no homework supervision, forgot pocket money, tried not to let them go back to the Scarlets' on Saturday, Cathy says there's no proper food there at all, they live on crisps, cornflakes and sandwiches.'

'Is Cathy taking too much on, do you think?' Jock asked.

'No, I don't think that at all, *and* they're trying to take holidays at the time of this wedding when the children are doing a dance, they've been learning the bloody two-hand reel for months.'

'At Lizzie's daughter's wedding?' Jock asked.

'Yes, at my sister-in-law's wedding as it also happens to be, and they're not missing it. Believe me, they are not.'

'Hold your horses, Neil.'

'And that's another thing, that bloody Walter keeps his drawers locked in his office, why's that? He borrowed my binoculars to go and follow the horses six weeks ago and says he can't get them out of his file cupboards.'

'That's nonsense, Neil, everything's on computer these days, you know that. There are no locked drawers here.'

Neil saw his father checking his watch. 'If you dictated the letter now, Dad, and got it signed, then we could all go about our business, whatever that business is.'

Very grudgingly Jock Mitchell took notes and called in a secretary. 'Sorry Linda, my son insists,' he said.

Muttie brought the children back on the bus.

'I don't mind it, honestly. I like the journey, you see, and it makes us independent if we're able to go to and fro on our own without annoying Sara or Cathy or Neil,' he explained to them.

'If you had been a wealthy person would you have had a car, do you think?' Simon asked.

'Indeed I would, I'd have had a big red Beamer.' Muttie smiled at the thought.

'What's that?' Maud wondered.

'It's a BMW. But no, to be honest, I'd probably have had a station wagon, a great big thing half the length of the footpath outside,' Muttie said.

'But there's only the two of you,' Simon objected.

'Ah, but just stop and think of all the people in St Jarlath's Crescent who'd like a lift somewhere,' Muttie said.

'You are very kind, Muttie,' Maud said.

'You really *deserve* an accumulator,' Simon agreed.

Walter came home on Saturday evening and found that old Barty was still in residence. The introductions were vague. There seemed to be a bottle of good whiskey on the table which was causing his mother some distress.

'Father, don't you think ... I mean, weren't we meant to ...'

'Nonsense, Kay knows well that she's not drinking and I'm not wandering off, we're here to give you a home.'

His father sounded quite reached already.

'The children will be home soon. They might have their private army with them,' Walter warned.

'That's a good point, let's put this bottle on hold for a while.' Kenneth tucked it away out of sight. 'And Walter, since we have you, if you're going to be out and about I wonder could old Barty have your room? He's in the small room on the stairs, it's rather like a boxroom,' Kenneth began.

'Oh, no, heavens no, I'm just fine where I am,' Barty began to bluster.

'Sorry, Dad. I'll be here for a few days but then I was hoping to go off to England to the races, I'll have my room right for you by then.' He smiled his warm Walter smile. Barty said nonsense, he'd be well gone by then. Kenneth said nonsense, where could Barty go, he'd even lost his beloved car in a card game. Barty said that would all be sorted out soon, he had plenty of chances to win it back. And Walter pulled up a chair at the table with them to discuss how and when ... It seemed a subject very dear to his heart.

This time the twins persuaded Muttie to come in and say hallo, very much against his will. But he needn't have worried about being out of place. Kay Mitchell was already in bed, and the three men at the table looked up, mildly and politely interested.

'You've had supper at ... um,' Kenneth said.

And as Maud and Simon began to tell about all the extra things they had with their sausages, the flat mushrooms and the filled baked potatoes, Kenneth Mitchell's interest flagged.

'You're so kind to look after them so well,' he said to Muttie, and shook his hand firmly. Muttie opened his hand. A pound coin was there, less than his bus fare home. Muttie's face flushed a dark red, and the colour went right around his neck.

'Thank you very much indeed sir,' he said with great difficulty.

Simon and Maud looked on, stricken. 'See you next Saturday Muttie,' Maud said. 'Thank you for a lovely time.'

'And for paying for the dancing lessons, Muttie, they can't have been cheap,' Simon added.

Muttie was backing out.

'Do you want to see our rooms, Muttie?' Maud asked.

'Another time, Maud, thanks all the same.'

'Or look at the garden where we could have a kennel if Hooves came to stay,' Simon begged.

'Honestly, next visit, Simon, thanks. Good luck to you all,' and he was gone.

The twins had thought they might do the reel tonight at home. They had a tape of the music with them. This would be a new audience. But they noticed a bottle of whiskey had come onto the table, and their father and brother and old Barty wanted to discuss something other than dancing. Everyone was waiting for the children to go to bed, on a bright summer evening when they had been hoping to be up for ages more. With brief goodnights the twins marched grimly upstairs. Mother's door was closed.

They missed sleeping in the same room as they had in St Jarlath's Crescent. Everything was different now.

Cathy said they couldn't possibly take on a sales conference lunch for thirty on the very same day as Freddie Flynn's party.

'It will be dead easy,' Tom pleaded. 'They're slave-drivers these people, no lingering and enjoying themselves for the employees, no drinking and getting messy like a real lunch. They'll be back working in that hall at two-fifteen and we'll be out in half an hour after that.'

'Stop smiling at me like that, Tom Feather, it doesn't work here,' Cathy said. 'We want to do the Flynn thing right, we're being silly taking on something else that might put it at risk.'

'And do we or do we not want to get this business up and running?' he asked.

'We do, but not by beating ourselves down onto our knees.'

'Aw, come on Cathy, I'll do the lunch with June and you and Con keep things ticking over here. We'll be back to you before three. Yes?'

'We're pushing ourselves,' she said.

'Stretching ourselves,' he corrected.

They looked at each other long and hard.

'It's easy money, it's a good contact,' said Tom. In his heart he was thinking that if he cleared a few pounds profit on this he'd take Marcella to one of those fancy hotels for a weekend, a place with a swimming pool and a health centre, a place she could dress up at night.

'We've always said people go under if they take on too much, their standards fall,' Cathy said. She was thinking that she truthfully could barely manage as things were, the nausea was still there, she didn't sleep properly and she still hadn't found or made the time to tell Neil. The Predictor from the chemist had said yes, but people knew they were often wrong, she had an appointment with the doctor next week. It might all be nothing, surely it was too soon to have morning sickness anyway, supposing it were true.

'Let's go to arbitration,' Tom said.

They took out of the drawer in the kitchen table the coin that they always used when they were at an impasse. Solemnly they watched as the coin spun round, and waited until it fell. Tom picked it up.

'So I won, but I promise you'll be glad.'

'Sure I will.' Cathy nailed the smile onto her face.

'Can we come to England with you on a holiday?' Simon stood at the door of Walter's bedroom.

'Of course you can't,' Walter said impatiently.

'But we'll have no holiday then,' Maud said.

'Aren't you back home ... *and* you'll have no school, that's meant to be a holiday, surely?'

'Muttie was going to take us to the country when we were living in St Jarlath's Crescent,' Simon said mutinously.

'You weren't living there, you were only staying there,' Walter complained.

'It felt like living there,' Maud said.

Walter went on packing his case. The twins didn't move.

'Muttie has been to the country a few times, he said you wouldn't want to spend too long there, though,' Maud explained.

'He found it was desperately quiet, and that you could hear birds roaring at you from trees,' Simon said wistfully.

'Kids, I'm sorry, I have to get on.'

'Are you going today?' Maud asked, disappointed. It was marginally more lively here when Walter was around.

'Tonight or tomorrow. I have some work to do with Father and Barty.'

'But Father doesn't *have* any work.' Simon was remorseless about getting things straight.

'Of course he does, Simon,' Walter was annoyed. 'He has meetings and responsibilities.'

'With Barty?' Maud wanted to know.

'Not always, but today, yes.'

'So if Father's out and Mother's going to stay in bed . . . what will *we* do?' Simon and Maud looked at each other blankly. There had been so many things to do in St Jarlath's Crescent. And so many people, including Hooves, to do them with.

'You could get a job,' Walter suggested.

'I don't think we're old enough,' Maud said.

'No, doing kids' jobs: stacking shelves, collecting trolleys in a supermarket, tidying someone's garden . . . those kind of things . . .' said Walter vaguely, having never attempted any of them.

'We might be able to wash up for Cathy and Tom,' Simon said cheerfully.

'Hard taskmaster, that one,' Walter said.

'Still, it's worth a try,' said Maud.

'Imagine, no more school until September,' Cathy said when she saw the two faces arrive at the premises.

'I don't mind school too much,' Maud said. 'You wouldn't want to say it there, but I don't.'

'No, I didn't either,' Cathy said. 'I felt I owed it to Geraldine to do well, and I got great pleasure out of getting good results.'

'Why Geraldine?' they asked, and Cathy remembered that the twins produced every single piece of unwanted information at the wrong time. She was meant to have won scholarships, all through. Geraldine's generosity was never mentioned nor even known in Lizzie and Muttie's home.

'I meant she always encouraged me to study for the scholarships, you see.'

'Were you brilliant to have won them?'

'Not bad,' Cathy said modestly, feeling slightly ashamed. She racked her brains to think of something that the twins could do to help, where they wouldn't be in the way and they couldn't do too much harm.

'Polish glasses?' Con suggested.

'No, they'd smear them,' she whispered.

'Chopping anything. . . ?'

'They're worse than I am, the place would be running with blood. I know, they can shine up the silver and count the forks.'

Maud and Simon were installed in what was eventually going to be called the second kitchen but for now was the storeroom. They chattered on happily; sometimes Cathy leaned against the door and listened. There were bits about Father's business with Barty, and how good Sara was at getting Mrs Barry to do the shopping from a list. Sara knew a place where they could learn tennis, but Father said it cost too much. Whether Muttie would ever come to visit them at their home again after what Father had done. Cathy sighed. She had resented them so much a few short months ago, mainly because she knew they were being passed on by Hannah and Jock. But everything had changed so much. Who could have thought it? Again and again she went over when exactly it must have happened. Neil would be furious. Why did it feel different now? Once it would have been unthinkable to keep something this important from Neil. It was still unthinkable. She would tell him tonight.

Tom and June came back from the sales luncheon in high spirits. Fifty people, all of them as obedient as mice, start eating, continue eating, finish eating, if only the whole world was run like this.

'But how awful to be part of it,' Cathy said, shuddering.

'Ah, but it was so easy, Cath, you've no idea, they'd have eaten a paper plate smeared with jam, believe me.'

'They must have been *very* hungry,' Maud said, shocked.

'Well *hallo*, we have help.' Tom was surprised and pleased.

'And great help they are. Tell them you were joking about the paper plates and jam Tom, otherwise they'll tell everyone it's our signature dish.'

'You don't give them enough credit, you know that was a joke, Maud, didn't you?' Tom said.

'I wasn't totally sure,' she admitted.

'Well it was, they'd never eat a paper plate, and what's more they wouldn't have a chance to. Why? Because we'd never serve anything on a paper plate, is that very clear?' He had a mock-ferocious face on. The children nodded furiously. It was clear, they said.

'We've been polishing your good silver,' Simon said.

'You could see your face in the punchbowl,' Maud said proudly.

'Well that's great, because everything we own, all the things we have been saving for are tied up in these four walls.'

'What, everything here is all you have?'

'Yes, our treasures are here, certainly,' Tom agreed.

'Is it all very valuable?' they asked.

June was stacking the dishwasher, and raised her eyes to heaven.

'Well, some of it is irreplaceable, like that punchbowl you just cleaned so beautifully,' Cathy said. 'I won that at a competition at college, it was first prize for a summer fruit punch, we use it everywhere now.'

'The Flynns don't want it tonight apparently,' Tom said thoughtlessly, after all Maud's hard work. 'Which means we have it ready shining and waiting for the next job, which is just *great*.'

Maud beamed with pleasure.

'And what's the next most valuable thing?' Simon wondered.

Tom, Cathy and June joked about whether it was the disk on the computer with all the recipes, the book of contacts, the double oven, or the chest freezer . . . They laughed as they listed all the things they had.

'We never thought we'd own such a huge amount of stuff,' Cathy said.

'Like Muttie thinks he'll never win an accumulator,' Simon said, eager to show he was on her wavelength.

'But he never will, Simon,' Cathy implored.

'People may well have said to you and Tom . . . that you'd never have any treasures,' Simon was fierce in his defence of Muttie's dreams.

'We worked for it, night after long night . . .' Cathy said.

'Muttie works at the bookmakers', he studies it, he learns about form and he lets the sound of hooves get in on his brain.'

'Of course he does,' Tom said gently.

'Are you insured, in case anyone came in and took all your treasures?' Maud worried.

Cathy made yet another resolution not to go down any road like this again with the children. 'Very well insured. James Byrne is like a clucking hen,' Cathy reassured her.

'What Cathy means is that James isn't remotely like a clucking hen: he is a marvellous man who made us take out a very big insurance policy.'

The twins seemed reasonably pleased with this, but Simon had one more worry. 'Do you lock up properly when you leave?' he wanted to know.

'Yes Simon, two locks, an alarm with a code and all.'

'And do you remember the code?'

'We had to make it simple for Tom,' Cathy said.

'Men find it hard to take complicated things on board,' June agreed.

'Do you have your birthday?' Simon asked. 'Or your lucky number?'

'No, they told us not to,' Tom said.

'So we have the two initials of Scarlet Feather instead.'

'Are you allowed to have letters?'

'No, the numbers, S is nineteen and F is six. If we forget, all we have to do is go through the alphabet. Even men can understand that, Simon.'

'I don't think that men are any more stupid than the rest of people, really,' Simon said thoughtfully.

'No, Simon,' Tom was contrite.

They agreed to drive the children back to The Beeches, since it was on the way to Freddie Flynn's house. Solemnly Simon and Maud watched as the alarm code was set.

'Brilliant idea,' Simon said.

'No one would ever think of that,' Maud agreed.

'Imagine, we're travelling with all the food for a posh party.' Simon was pleased.

'Yes, *and* all those nice shiny forks you polished as well.'

'Why do they not have knives?'

'Good question. They claim to have all the cutlery we need, but people never have enough forks. I went and checked; they don't have nearly enough forks.'

'You need to be quite intelligent for this work, don't you,' Simon said.

'You do,' said Tom as he counted and completed a checklist. 'It's all there, Cathy, ready to roll.'

'Okay Tom, okay June, ceremony of the keys.'

Simon and Maud watched fascinated as they hung the keys to the premises carefully on a hidden hook at the back of the van. 'Why do you put them there?' they asked.

'Whichever of us takes the van back needs to be able to open the place up, so we always have the ceremony of the keys . . .' Cathy explained.

They had arrived at the Beeches. The two children ran into the big house with the huge overgrown garden.

'Looks like a posh place,' June said.

'Yeah,' Cathy said, 'posh, dead sort of place.'

'They have to be with their own parents, their natural parents. Don't they?' Tom asked.

'To be honest, I've never exactly seen why,' Cathy said, and put the van into gear with a crash as they drove off.

Freddie Flynn was most welcoming when they got there. 'Now I know the drill, your aunt says you hate people saying to you this is the kitchen, this is the hot tap, this is the cold tap . . .'

'You wouldn't ever do that, Mr Flynn,' Cathy smiled up at him from under her eyelashes.

Tom let out a low whistle between his teeth when he'd gone. 'And you say that I put on the charm for the ladies . . . I never saw anything like that performance,' he teased her.

'I promised Auntie Geraldine he'd get the full treatment,' she whispered.

'Yeah, well.'

At that moment Freddie's small, plump wife Pauline came in. 'Freddie says I'm not to fuss, and I promise I won't, but somehow it seems like cheating to let you do it all,' she said.

Cathy felt a lump in her throat. This woman was being deceived by Frederick Flynn, important Dublin businessman, purchaser of diamond watches for Cathy's aunt. 'Not a bit of it, Mrs Flynn, you and people like you are providing Tom and myself with a generous living, we want to make it a huge success. Now your husband tells me you don't want anyone to take the coats. Have I got that right?'

'Yes, after all it *is* the summer, so they won't have that many coats . . . But you see, we got the upstairs all decorated, and I sort of hoped they might go up and see it so that I could show it off.'

'You are so right, let me see where I'm to direct them.' Cathy ran lightly up the stairs ahead of Pauline Flynn, and saw the magnificent bedroom which had been spoken of. It was in beautiful shades of pale green and blue, and there was an elegant white dressing table. It wasn't exactly a four-poster bed, but there was a ring with cascading curtains over the top; a white crochet bedspread and lace-trimmed pillowcases; doors opened on to a huge, luxurious bathroom with white fluffy towels alternating with others in baby blue. This place had all the appearance of an altar built to the god of pleasure. Cathy held her hand to her throat. Geraldine could not possibly know that Freddie's dead marriage involved this kind of decoration.

'Lovely room,' she said in a slightly strangled voice to Pauline Flynn.

'I'm glad you like it; I'm old and silly I know, but it's what I always wanted and Freddie seems to think it's nice too, and that's what pleases me most of all.'

Cathy ran downstairs quickly.

'Hallo Walter,' the twins were surprised. They thought he would have gone to England by now.

'Hallo,' Walter grunted.

'How was the business?'

'What business?'

'You said you were having a business meeting with Father and Barty.'

'Oh yes, I bloody was.'

'So it didn't work?' Simon was philosophical. 'Muttie always says that you win some, you lose some.'

'What does Muttie know about anything?' Walter asked.

'A fair bit,' Maud said. 'I think,' she added doubtfully.

There was a silence. 'We got a job like you said,' Simon said eventually.

'Good for you. Where?'

'With Cathy and Tom . . . They have a fortune in their premises, it's full of their treasures.' Simon wanted to impress his older brother.

'I'm sure,' Walter laughed.

'No, they do, all their worldly goods are there, they have two keys and a code lock in case anyone gets in.'

'Oh yeah, I bet the whole world is trying to get in there and steal catering plates and paper napkins,' Walter laughed.

'They have a solid-silver punchbowl, it's beyond price. They have loads of things,' Maud said.

'I'm sure it's very impressive, but do you mind moving off for a bit, I've a lot to think about now.'

'Okay,' Simon and Maud were good-tempered.

'And you're not whining for food or anything.'

'No. Cathy gave us something for the microwave.'

'What is it?' Walter asked with interest.

'Pasta. It will take four minutes on high,' said Maud. 'Do you want some? There's plenty for the three of us.'

'Thanks.' Walter was gruff.

They sat at the table, the three of them, Walter's mind a million miles away as the twins talked on happily about the party that Tom and Cathy were doing that night.

'They have money to burn, the Flynns do,' Maud said.

'I don't think they really *are* going to burn it though, I think it's only an expression that people use,' Simon explained.

'Yes, whatever.' She brought Walter into the conversation. 'Do you think we should get a burglar alarm here, Walter?'

'Nothing for a burglar to break in here for,' he said glumly.

'We could set it before we went out and disarm it when we got back.' Maud didn't want to let the notion go entirely.

'Yeah, can you see Mother and Father doing that? Can you see Barty coming to terms with disarming an alarm? It would be like a cops and robbers movie. We'd have the guards living here all the time.'

'But it's so simple,' Simon said. 'We know how to get into Cathy and Tom's premises just after seeing it once.'

'Sure, but do you have the keys?' Walter took his plate across the kitchen to the sink.

'No, but we know where they are,' Maud said.

Walter came back and sat down with them again.

The party up at the Flynns' was going very well. Twice Freddie put his head around the kitchen door to congratulate them.

'They're just loving it all,' he said. 'Well done.'

'Why is a nice man like that unable to look me in the eye and tell me he needs me to be a significant part of his life?' June wondered.

'Hard to know all right,' said Cathy as she piped out more crème fraiche on the little buckwheat pancakes that were disappearing with alarming speed from the platters.

'You'd never think that a woman like Mrs Flynn would be enough for him,' June said as she swept off with the new tray.

Tom and Cathy's eyes met. 'Funny old life, Tom, that's what I always say,' she grinned at him.

'Women are just riddled with intuition, Cathy, that's what *I* always say,' Tom replied.

Walter looked up the Flynns' address in the phonebook. It wasn't far away. He had been able to get the loan of a car from a night-owl friend for a few hours. He parked it beside the van and found the keys exactly where the twins had said. Through the windows he saw them all, Tom, Cathy, June and that creep Con moving about inside.

Geraldine moved restlessly around her apartment in Glenstar. Normally she never felt like this. She had been truthful in saying that she believed Freddie's private life was just that . . . private, and no concern of hers. It was just that . . . well, she hadn't planned to do anything tonight. She had taken work back to the apartment but she didn't feel like doing it, and there was nothing she wanted to see on television. In a million years she would not admit it, not even to herself. Geraldine was lonely. Then her telephone rang.

'I miss you,' he said.

She forced her voice to be bright. 'And I you. How's it going?'

'Fantastic. They're very talented, those kids, it's running like clockwork.'

'I'm so pleased for you, Freddie, truly I am.'

He hung up. A stolen moment away from his guests, his wife. It had always been like this, and this is what it was always going to be like from now on. So why was she complaining? Geraldine had known the score when she signed up.

Wearing black cotton gloves, Walter let himself in and used the code to disarm the alarm. Where were all these treasures the kids had talked about? He must be quick; he needed to get the stuff hidden in his garden shed, the key back into the van and the truck back to the friend who would be starting his evening at around ten p.m. It looked like it had always looked, a big ugly catering kitchen, a lot of stainless steel, coloured tea towels drying on the backs of chairs, shelves of inexpensive china, drawers of worthless cutlery. He pulled out possible items like a toaster, an electric grill, a microwave oven. But these things were peanuts. They wouldn't bring him a fraction of the money he needed. The money he had lost with that fool friend of his father's, old Barty, who knew a great game and had brought Walter along. On the table in the front

264

room, he saw the big silver punchbowl the children had spoken of. It wasn't solid silver at all, and he pushed it aside in disgust. There were boxes of supplies, unopened steamers and saucepans in the storeroom; they might make *something* if he could just unload them on the right person. And he needed something, even if he got a couple of hundred quid it would be a start. He began to drag the items towards the front of the premises, and knocked over a tray of glasses as he did so. The splinters of broken glass were everywhere. They wouldn't like that when they got back. Something welled up in him, and he swooped an entire shelf of plates onto the floor as well. It was somehow satisfying. He would do more later.

He worked for forty minutes, unscrewing and transporting what might possibly change hands in an iffy market he knew about. Then, with his elbow, he raised the end of one of the china shelves so that all its contents went in a great crashing slide to the floor. He pulled out the plug of the freezer and tossed items out of it at random. He noticed with annoyance that they had a very poor stock of alcohol, and remembered that they usually arranged for a wine merchant to deliver straight to the venue. Still, there was a bottle of brandy and some other off-looking liqueurs; it would keep the guy who owned the car cheerful. He remembered one day how they had been going on and on for ever about what message to leave on the answering machine, so he wrenched it from the wall and stood on it. He hit the light bulbs with a stick and leaped aside as the shattered glass came tumbling down. He packed the car, taking the punchbowl at the last moment. He might get £20 for it anyway, and these days that couldn't be laughed off. What fools to tell the children that these things were treasure! They were so bloody smug, those two. This would show them.

Chapter Seven

JULY

Even if they hadn't had to tell the story two dozen times, they would never forget the return to the premises that night. They were high with the success of the party at the Flynns'.

'We've got so much better,' Tom said as he reached for the keys.

'I hope so. Sometimes I think we've just got more confident, you know, papering over the cracks,' Cathy said.

'No, we *are* better,' said June. 'I met the Riordans there, remember, the people who had the christening . . . They said our food was in a different category altogether.'

Tom and Cathy loved the way June considered herself part of it all; even young Con was beginning to feel the same way. Then they opened the door. They had often heard that people who were robbed felt this strange sense of being violated. This was what it was like. When they walked into the front room, Cathy saw the clock Joe had given them lying on the floor inside the door, broken beyond repair. Tom saw the huge vase that Marcella had chosen with such care in three pieces beside the overturned table. And all their plates knocked from the shelves. June saw the drawers opened and their contents spilled and the telephone and answering machine dragged from the wall. Cathy saw that her punchbowl, the only prize she had ever won in her life, was gone from the table. They couldn't take it all in. Tom was the first to speak.

'Bastards,' he said. 'Total bastards. There's nothing to steal, and so they've destroyed everything we have . . .' There was a catch in his voice which released the tears. He clung to Cathy and June.

The guards were mystified. No sign of a break-in, no forced entry, nobody else had access to keys. They had no idea of anyone who harboured malicious feeling towards them. Had they? They couldn't think of anyone at all. Rivals over work, possibly? No, they weren't in the business in a big enough way, they explained. One of the young guards who had already asked twice about insurance mentioned it yet once more to Tom.

'Yes, I told you,' Tom said a trifle impatiently. 'Our accountant insisted we pay what we think is a huge premium, but that's not the point . . . That's not going to sort this out.'

'I know, sir. They can take it up with you themselves,' he said.

'Who can?' he asked.

'The insurance company, sir,' he said.

Neil was asleep when Cathy rang. 'Yes, Neil Mitchell,' he said sleepily.

'Neil, we've had a break-in.'

'Cathy?' He was mystified. He had thought she was beside him in their bed.

'Oh, Neil, burglars . . . the whole place is destroyed.' There was a catch in her voice.

'Anybody hurt?'

'No, but it's terrible,' she knew her voice was quivering.

She could see him swinging his legs out of bed as he had so often when phoned at night about a case.

'You'd like me to come in?' he said. His voice sounded resigned.

'The guards are here, it's very frightening, Neil.'

'I'll be there.'

'Do you mind?'

'Of course not.'

'Neil coming in then?' Tom said.

'Yes. Do you want to ring Marcella?'

'No, let her have her sleep, she'll know soon enough.'

Why had Cathy not done the same thing?

Neil arrived wearing a sweater and a pair of faded cotton trousers, but as full of authority as if he were wearing his full formal barrister's outfit and carrying a briefcase. The questions were endless and the leads seemed to be non-existent. The guards hadn't known of any gangs working in the neighbourhood, not anyone specialising in this kind of crime. Back and back they went to the keys and the access.

Finally the guard said, 'So all I can say is for you to take things up as best you can.'

'What do you mean, exactly?' Tom was barely paying attention. 'We *are* taking things up as best we can, aren't we?'

'With the insurance company,' the guard said.

'But what has this got to do with finding whoever did all this?' Tom waved his hand around despairingly.

Neil spoke suddenly in his crisp, barrister's voice. 'The garda is pointing out, Tom, that because there were no signs of a break-in or forced entry, the insurance company is going to have to look into the possibility of it being an inside job.'

There was silence in the room. Nobody thought that things could get any worse than they were, but they had now.

It seemed that all night they were cooking Tom's bread for Haywards partly in the small oven in Stoneyfield while Marcella helped and timed things and lifted out batches, and partly with the better facilities in Waterview with Neil and June helping.

'What will your Jimmy think about your being out so late?' Tom asked.

'He's had time to get used to it in the past; he'll think it's just another party,' June said succinctly.

The night ended, the bread was delivered and they were back at the premises.

Gradually and slowly they picked through the rubble, pausing to sigh or even cry over a broken treasure. Tom insisted that Cathy put on those big thick mittens they used to take things out of freezers.

'I can't feel anything with them on,' she complained.

'You'll cut your hands otherwise.'

'I won't.'

'Listen, Cathy, all we have left are your own good hands if we're ever going to get out of this mess,' he said.

The reality of it hit her. They might not get out of this mess. Whoever had done this to them had ruined their life's work, their dream, their one chance of running a business. She picked up a large, triangular piece of glass and took it to the heap outside. It had once been part of a corner cupboard in the front room. All the big coloured plates it had once held were broken, just as the ones from their old dresser had been flung to the ground.

She felt a great wave of sadness.

Good hands or no good hands they might never build this business up again; nothing would ever be the same. She wanted very badly to sit down and cry like a child.

They had fixed the telephone and it rang cheerfully from time to time, calls from people who had no idea into what devastation their call was being received. Molly Hayes wanted a supper for twelve. It was Shay's birthday.

'Can we come back to you on that one, Mrs Hayes, before the end of the day?' June asked in a bright, businesslike voice.

'Very busy, are you?' Molly asked.

'You wouldn't believe, it Mrs Hayes,' said June.

Cathy looked at June with pride. In six short months she had learned confidence and style as well as a lot of other little interests that her silent plumber husband would not have approved of. But she was no longer apologetic and afraid to tell the customers which was filo pastry and which was choux. June could discuss quail's eggs and langoustines with any of them now. And Cathy gulped thinking that June's career and future lay in ruins on the floor as well as their own. She watched Neil as he worked with them, helping with the clearing away: his face was grim at the outrage, his energy unflagging, even though he would have to be in court that morning. This was the man whom she had hoped to tell about the pregnancy, but that would have to wait. She paused and looked at him as he squatted in front of the cooker with Tom. They were trying to see how much of the actual fixtures and fittings had been destroyed. She couldn't hear what they were saying, but she saw him pointing and Tom pointing and the concentrated effort Neil was making to understand something unfamiliar to him.

Some of the frozen food still seemed very hard, but they couldn't take the risk of refreezing it. No one could know when the vandals had come in. It could have been any time after six p.m., and they hadn't discovered it for nine hours. By now the food might be twelve hours out of the freezer compartments. Impossible to know what to do.

When the rest of Dublin was beginning to wake up and go to work, they sent June home in a taxi, Marcella showered, changed and went to Haywards, put on her cool white coat and dealt with the nails of those with the money and time to pay for it. Despite the shocking events of the night, her heart was much lighter than usual. She wasn't going to be painting and shaping nails always. By the end of this month she was going to have had her first professional modelling work *and* an introduction to a model's agent. She could afford to smile and be charming to the customers. This life would not last for ever. Neil showered, changed, put on his lawyer's gear and went down to the Four Courts to represent two men in a wrongful dismissal case. Everyone said that he hadn't a chance, the two were troublemakers from way back, their case was full of holes. But Neil knew that the company who fired them was on very thin ice; it had an unhealthy history of being anti-trade union. He was going to win and confound them. Nothing to make legal history, and indeed his clients could well be described as highly unreliable, but it was the *principle* of the thing that mattered.

Back at the premises, Tom and Cathy looked at each other, red-eyed.

'They surely can't think it was an inside job?' she asked.

They had been asking each other this all the time.

'Apparently they could think we did it to get the compensation.'

'People would think *we* did this to *ourselves*?' She spread her hands out at the rooms.

'It's been done before, when companies were going down the tubes.'

'But we're *not* going down the tubes . . . James could tell them that for one thing,' Cathy said.

James! They had forgotten about him. Was it too early to ring him? They risked that he would be up on a summer morning just before eight o'clock.

'James Byrne.' He was crisp and matter-of-fact when he heard the news. He asked questions, one after the other. The safe? Opened and papers scattered around. Yes. Yes. The guards? Any likely leads? No, no. The plant, cookers and freezers, would Scarlet Feather be able to continue trading? Hard to say. Quite, quite. The insurance? Yes, he assured them, it was all in order and would well cover losses. Then they told him that there had been no break-in, no forced entry.

'I see,' said James Byrne.

'But you know that it wasn't an inside job, James,' Tom cried.

'Yes, I know. Of course I know,' was the answer.

'But you mean they mightn't?' Tom was hardly able to say the words.

'Let's say it may just take longer for them to pay up,' said James

Byrne. He was thoughtful and quiet. Last night by chance he had had a dinner with Martin Maguire, who had said that he wished those youngsters success in their premises, truly he did, but he felt that there was some kind of curse on the building. Something they would never be able to conquer and survive. James didn't feel it necessary to report this conversation. Those two had enough to put up with already.

Shona Burke got them permission to use Haywards' kitchens from now on to do the breads; in fact it worked so well they said it could be permanent. Tom worked until the store opened, and assured the management that he would not use their ovens for his own work.

'Getting back to normal there?' the management at Haywards asked him sometimes.

'Absolutely,' lied Tom.

Nobody could be told of the shambles that was the kitchens of Scarlet Feather.

Cathy did the entire birthday party, including a chocolate birthday cake for Shay and Molly Hayes in her own house, and no one was any the wiser. No one but Neil, who was more or less dispossessed and had to step over crates and boxes everywhere if he moved, so much so that he set up a table and chair in the bedroom to do his own work.

'I thought a town house was small, but it seems to have become a bedsitter,' he grumbled. He was out almost every evening, so they could work on without fear of annoying him further.

They had forgotten how impossible it was to prepare food in such a small space. There was simply nowhere to leave anything down. Every single chair, stool and even suitcase had been pressed into service and used as a surface to store the plates that had been done, but they were always knocking them over. There wasn't nearly enough room in the freezer or the fridge; ice melted, cutlery fell on to the floor. Each day was more like a nightmare than the one that went before.

June and Cathy worked on and on as they had never worked before. They did a picnic for Freddie and Pauline Flynn; they did two First Communion buffet-lunch parties on the same day, shuttling from one to the other with Con. They left Tom to deal with the business of putting the pieces back together. And this, they all knew, was something that was sheer hell. Men from JT Feather's builder's yard came in to clear the premises, but only after James Byrne had insisted on photographs being taken and a representative of the insurance company coming to view the waste and destruction. It was going to cost over two thousand pounds to get the cooking under way again, and this was before they bought a single replacement item for the hundreds of pieces of china and glassware that would need to be replaced. The frozen food had been given away that morning or destroyed; long weeks of work thrown out at just a stroke.

Among the very first people that they should have told were Geraldine and Joe, their backers, the guarantors who had invested in their company. But neither Tom nor Cathy wanted to tell them until it was under control. Not until they knew they were going to come out of this horrible thing. They had the sickening feeling that they were going to go under. It was not a feeling that could yet be shared. Cathy didn't want to tell Geraldine. To ask her aunt to dig deep again into those pockets lined by wealthy men of whom Cathy had disapproved, and said so. She didn't want Geraldine to hand over more money. Cathy's pride had always meant that it was a debt of honour to repay Geraldine's investment with interest. The aunt who had given her so much, wanting nothing in return except the satisfaction of seeing her do well. The aunt whom she had insulted and criticised about her lifestyle. That was one aspect of it. Another aspect was that she feared Geraldine might say they should pack it all in now, since Cathy was pregnant; that the timing might have been in an odd way appropriate. There was a minefield that she didn't want to walk into yet.

'Do you mind if we don't say anything to Geraldine for a bit?' she asked Tom.

'That's funny, I was just going to say the same about Joe,' he said.

He didn't explain because they didn't have to tell each other everything. Joe was the last person he wanted to talk to just now. Joe who had given Marcella this chance to strut nearly naked across a stage in front of half of Dublin. Joe who had filled Marcella's head up with the chance of meeting some model's agent who could put her on his books and get her jobs 'across the water', as he called it. Tom hated the phrase – if he meant London or Manchester why couldn't he just say so? He couldn't bear to hear his lovely Marcella parroting it all and talking about the opportunity of modelling across the water. Joe who had been so good and generous with his funding; Joe who had obediently become a regular visitor to their parents at Fatima, thus halving Tom's own need to be present; Joe who somehow felt guilty about this fashion show, would dive into his resources and find funds for Tom as a way of buying himself out of any unpleasantness. Tom didn't want Joe to know how very near the ropes they were.

So if they didn't want Geraldine and Joe to know, that meant they couldn't tell a lot of other people either. Shona was sworn to secrecy, and June was asked to keep quiet as well – there was no problem there. They couldn't tell Muttie and Lizzie Scarlet, nor JT and Maura Feather. Cathy longed to tell her mother, to go to that familiar kitchen and cry while her mother stroked her hair. But if you told one you had to tell all. There were no accounts of it at all in the evening newspaper, nor did they go on the television programme which tried to get the public to solve a crime. James Byrne had urged caution as he always did, and Neil Mitchell had said the big multinational insurance companies would not be allowed to shelter behind a lot of pious phrases. It was an issue he felt very strongly about. He would fight for them against nameless bureaucrats who always kept the little people waiting for their money. He was already looking up precedents about it, and he wouldn't let them get away with it. He was being supportive, but Cathy wished more than anything that he had been a different kind of help. That he would take her head on his shoulder and stroke her hair. Tell her that he loved her and that they would get through this. And then she could tell him about the baby.

'Are we going to have tennis lessons?' Simon asked at breakfast.

'Tennis?' His mother looked at him vaguely as if she had heard the word before and with time would place exactly what it meant. She poured the cold milk out on the cornflakes, far too much of it so that the cornflakes were soggy and there wasn't any milk left for their tea. 'This is nice,' she said.

'Yes, Mother,' Maud said dutifully.

'Sara said there would be tennis lessons,' Simon said.

'Oh, Sara, yes, poor girl,' his father said.

'That the lady in boots and a cap on backwards? Dear, dear,' Barty said.

'I have her phone number. I could ring her,' Simon said. 'She'll know when and where.'

Kenneth Mitchell sighed. 'I have the address somewhere here, no need to ring her, I think just ring them and start the lessons off whenever you like.'

'And Father, when I do book the lessons, who shall I say is paying for them?' Simon was worried.

'Don't concern yourself with that.'

'I'll ring Sara,' Simon said.

'Damn it, boy, I'll pay for the bloody lessons. Stop driving everyone mad, will you, we have things to think about here.'

Kay Mitchell began to tremble. She hated seeing Kenneth upset.

'I'm sorry, Father.'

'No, no, that's all right, get your racquets out of the shed and start practising a bit here on the lawn.'

The twins lowered their eyes. This wasn't the time to tell their father that the shed was locked and they couldn't get into it.

'Cathy, could we come round to the premises to work today, to polish the treasures and things?' Maud asked.

'No Maud, sorry, today's not a good day.'

'We wouldn't want money or pasta or anything,' Maud begged.

'Sweetheart, if I could I'd say yes. We'll do it another time, okay?' She hung up.

'She hung up on me,' Maud said alarmed.

'Did she sound cross?' Simon wondered.

'A bit. What did we do?'

'Maybe we should have written to thank her for the pasta,' Simon said. 'It's very hard to know.'

'Sara, I'm ringing from a public phone on the road, it's Simon. Does Father pay for our tennis lessons?'

'Yes he does, he knows that.'

'I think he's a bit short of money.'

'Not too short for tennis lessons, it's part of his allowance ... Start whenever you like, I'll keep an eye on it.'

'It's just that, you know ... he gets a bit ...'

'I'll be very tactful,' Sara promised.

'And Sara, our racquets are locked in the garden shed.'

'Walter?' she asked.

'I suppose so, but they're all in such bad tempers if you ask anything.'

'You don't have to ask anything, I'll do it ...' she said.

'Was *she* cross, like everyone else?' Maud wanted to know.

'Yes, she sounded cross, but not with us I think,' Simon said after some thought.

'Walter Mitchell? I'm Sara, Simon and Maud's social worker.'

'I know,' he smiled at her warmly. 'We don't get many like you visiting our house or our offices.'

But he was getting nowhere this time. 'Why have you locked your garden shed?' she asked.

'And what possible business is that of yours,' he said, smile now totally gone from his face.

'Look, I don't care if you have two thousand pornographic magazines stacked in there, just get those kids their tennis racquets.'

'You had to come all the way to my office to deliver that message? Why couldn't they just ask *me*?'

'Apparently everyone at the home I fought to have them rejoin is in a bad temper. They didn't want to make things worse.'

'So they rang you,' he sneered.

'Well at least I did something,' Sara said simply. 'Are you going to give me the key now, and I'll pick up their racquets for them, or . . .'

'I'll go back and get them,' he said.

'But your work?' she said.

'I'm my own boss. I can make my own decisions whether to go or stay.' He got up as if to leave.

'Thank you, Walter.'

'Don't mention it, Sara,' he said.

She noticed that he looked up and down the corridor as he left, and that he didn't go down in the main lift, but ran down the back stairs. Mr Walter Mitchell working in his uncle's office was not at all as secure as he would have people believe.

St Jarlath's Crescent had never looked so well. Smart new curtains, window boxes, the bedroom for the bride and groom filled with little touches.

'It's very empty, you know. I miss those children terribly,' Lizzie told her sister. 'And poor Muttie's distracted.'

'How often do they come over?' asked Geraldine.

'Every Saturday. They want to come more but it's not on, apparently.'

'Couldn't Cathy bring them over sometimes? She's able to get what she wants, and she's not afraid of any Mitchell,' Geraldine suggested.

'I haven't seen or heard from Cathy in days,' Lizzie said.

'I think she's got a lot on her mind,' said Geraldine, who wondered why Cathy hadn't phoned back to tell her about Neil's reaction to everything.

There was another rehearsal for the Feather Fashion show. Joe made it his business to talk to Marcella.

'Tom okay about everything? All this, you know . . .' He waved his hands at the half-dressed girls around him.

'Fine,' Marcella said.

'It's just that—'

'Just that what?'

'I haven't seen him recently, and I hope he's not pissed off with me for being part of all this.' He waved his hand around at the scene.

'No, no. Tom pissed off at you? Of course he's not, he's just very busy with everything, that's all. I hardly see him myself.'

'Hi Cathy, it's Geraldine.'

'Oh yes, Geraldine. Oh.' Cathy sounded distracted.

'Sorry, is this a bad time?'

It couldn't have been a worse time. The place was full of people and tension. James Byrne, Neil and the man from the insurance company were all walking in circles around the premises. She had been sitting with Tom and June going over it all for the umpteenth time.

'Not great. Why don't I call you?'

'I wonder.' Geraldine was terse.

'What?'

'I said, I too wonder why you don't call me, I've not heard from you since Freddie's do . . .'

'No, no.'

'And how did it go telling Neil the news?'

'I haven't.'

'But it's ages—' Geraldine began.

'Please, can I ring you back?' Her voice was near breaking.

'Certainly,' Geraldine said, puzzled, and sat and looked at the phone for a long time.

*

'It will be months before they pay,' Neil said when the insurance man had left. 'If we get it out of them by New Year we'll be doing well.'

'How much do we need, James?' Tom's face was hard.

'To get back to where you were when this happened, you need just under twenty thousand,' James said. 'Probably more because I'm basing that on a figure that's assuming you can get equipment marked down again, like you did before from the restaurant sale.'

'How much is that a week?' Cathy asked.

James Byrne told them what the repayments would cost at the bank. And that was if the bank were to give it.

'They'll give it because they know the insurance will pay in the end, and they'll get their money, but it's far too much,' Neil said.

'Neil, we wouldn't make half of that in a week, *and* we have all the other repayments, you know, on this place.' Tom's face was hard and sad.

James Byrne spoke. 'Before we make or reject any big decisions, will you give me twenty-four hours to prepare some figures, and then you really can see what your options are.' He seemed to know people wanted time to cool down; the hurt was too raw and the sense of failure too great for either Tom or Cathy to think rationally.

'I'm sorry, hon,' Neil said in the car as they drove home.

'Neil, are you going to be at home tonight?' She cut straight across him.

'You know I'm not, hon, you know I have to go to the homeless group, it will be the last and only chance to give them some points before I go to the conference.'

The conference! How *could* she have forgotten that Neil and four other lawyers were representing Ireland at an international forum on refugees, in Africa? He was leaving tomorrow evening.

'You can't go to that group tonight, I need to talk to you.'

'Talk to me in the car, hon, I can't let those people down.'

'Sara will explain to them, tell them what you want to say.'

'Cathy, be reasonable. Sara's a young social worker, she's not a lawyer.'

'What time will it be over?'

'How do I know, hon ... When it's over.'

'Don't go with them to some awful café talking and yammering all night, come back. *Please*.'

He was annoyed now. 'Cathy, I've spent all day, a day when I should have been getting my papers ready for the forum, down in your office sorting out the mess there. You know I'd do anything for you, but opting out of this thing tonight is not possible. And don't dismiss my work as going to some awful café yammering all night. I've never said anything like that about your work.'

'Neil!' she was aghast.

'No, I mean it, we made a bargain, we are partners in the very best sense of the word. We both care about the work we do and we help each other. In a few years' time we will settle down and take things more easily.'

'When?' she cried.

'Well, not tonight, obviously Cathy . . . Not until you have your business up and running again . . . Not until I have done something about all the things I wanted to do.'

'That could be five or six years,' she said.

'Well, that's what we always said, isn't it?' Neil Mitchell said. There was a silence.

'I don't want to fight with you Cathy, specially not before I go away.'

'I don't want to fight with you either.' She spoke in a small voice.

'We're upset, that's all.'

'That's all,' she agreed.

'I'll try to get away as early as I can. Promise.' He smiled at her.

'Sure.' She forced a smile back.

'And listen, when I come back from Africa we'll go down to Holly's, that nice hotel in Wicklow where we once went to lunch, and we'll have dinner and stay the night.'

'Great,' she said.

When he came in that night, she was lying awake in bed. If he showed any signs of being alert she would get up and tell him. He couldn't go away for nine days and not know. Through her eyelids she saw him pull off his shirt with a weary movement. He went into the bathroom, and through the open door she could see that he barely brushed his teeth and ran a face flannel around his neck and under his arms. She saw his face; he was tired and strained. When he slipped into bed beside her, he spoke.

'Sorry, hon, there *was* a lot of yammering after it, as you forecast.'

'You don't feel like a cup of tea?' she offered.

'Believe me, I couldn't keep my eyes open long enough to get it to my lips,' he said, and he was asleep beside her. Cathy got up and went to the kitchen. As the dawn came up she still sat there, no nearer a solution. This was a good, strong marriage, a partnership in every way. Was she afraid to tell him? *Afraid* to give him the best news of anyone's life? She heard him moving about. He had slept for five and a half hours; she had sat at the kitchen table for all that time. Even if he did have an hour to listen now, which was unlikely, she was too confused and too weary to tell him properly. When he had gone to Africa she would go to a doctor and have confirmed what she knew to be true from her pregnancy indicator. What a terrible, terrible piece of timing.

'You two are so tiresome, you do know that?' Walter said when he got back home to the twins.

Simon and Maud were sorry. 'We thought it would be easier. She said in any difficulty to contact her.'

'But you weren't in any difficulty, you could have waited until I got back from work.'

'We thought you were going to England, you don't tell us what you do,' Maud said defensively.

'Not that you have to, of course,' Simon said.

'Oh, shut up, I'll get you the bloody racquets, then you can call her and say you're set fair for Wimbledon.'

'Can't we go with you to see if there's anything else we need from the shed?'

'No,' said Walter. 'Sit down and shut up.'

'But how will you know our—' Maud began.

'He'll take all the racquets and we can choose,' said Simon, who hadn't at all liked the look he saw on Walter's face.

'You're learning, Simon,' Walter said. 'Slowly, but at least you're learning.'

Martin Maguire had gone back to England without discovering the fate that had befallen his old premises. This time James Byrne had not pressed him to go and visit the couple who ran it nowadays. Martin Maguire had known so much sadness in that place he didn't think he yet had the strength to see two young people in such a desperate state.

Geraldine had to ring Joe Feather about his press conference at the end of the next week. She needed copies of his speech.

'I prefer to speak off the cuff,' he said.

279

'So do we all, but we have to have something that the journalists can write in their papers, some kind of statement of intent, policy, patriotism . . .'

'Oh, come on,' Joe laughed.

'I mean it. How you had to come back to Ireland, how you love Irish women, how much more adventurous they are nowadays, how well they dress . . . How great the government is, encouraging this and that . . .'

'Are you serious?'

'Never more so.'

'You wouldn't write it for me yourself, Geraldine, by any chance?'

'Not today, I have to go out. You have a stab at it, fax it to me, e-mail it whatever you think, and I'll come back to you tomorrow morning.'

'Sure. By the way, have you seen anything of Cathy and Tom recently?'

'No, why do you ask?'

'It's just they seem to have vanished off the face of the earth. I've been trying to get hold of Tom. Marcella says he's fine, so why doesn't he return my calls?'

'If I find out I'll tell you,' said Geraldine, who then left her office and hailed a taxi. *She* was not going to hang about any longer. It was too much of a coincidence Tom not getting in touch as well as Cathy. Quite obviously something was wrong. She was going right up there to the premises to find out exactly what had happened.

The broken glass, china and woodwork had been cleared away. Well, more or less.

They were always finding some frightening reminder, like the broken glass at the back of the cutlery drawer. Like realising that the big platter they had thought was in good shape was cracked all over and disintegrated, taking with it an entire dressed salmon. It was all over the floor, nothing could be rescued; both food and china had to be swept into the bin.

'Hours of work,' wept June.

'We're getting there,' said Cathy in desperation.

But it had indeed been hours of work and now they were left with no main dish for a lunch party. Wearily, Cathy rang the fishmongers. Could they do one for her in two hours?

'It'll cost you, Cathy,' said the man apologetically.

'It would cost us more if we didn't deliver,' she replied. She saw Tom looking at her. They spent so much time cheering the others up, keeping the show on the road, they had hardly any time to talk to each other honestly.

'Will we survive, Tom? Will we?' she asked sadly.

'I know. There are times I think we won't, too,' he said. They looked at each other, frightened. If they were to panic, the lifeboat might sink. It was only their optimism that kept it afloat.

'Of course, it looks a lot better now than it did on Monday,' Cathy said.

'Even than yesterday,' Tom agreed.

The men from JT Feather's builder's yard had put a coat of paint on the place. Tom had told his father that it was very important that they told nobody about their misfortune; it didn't look good in business when a calamity like this happened. His father had nodded sagely and said he was right to keep his counsel. JT Feather never thought for one moment that it was a secret to be kept from Joe. When his elder son called to Fatima that afternoon, he got every last detail of the robbery.

'Why did Tom not tell me?' Joe was shocked.

'He said he wasn't telling business people because it looked badly,' JT said, shaking his head.

'I see.'

'But it's odd he didn't tell you, you're not business.'

'I suppose there's a way he thinks I am,' Joe said thoughtfully.

'What do you mean, son?'

'Nothing Da, I'm only rabbiting on to myself. Don't mention to him that you said a word; he'll tell me when he's ready.'

Geraldine got out at the end of the mews and walked slowly up. She let herself into the courtyard of the premises, through the gate she had oiled herself last January when they were frantically clearing everything up. There was nothing Cathy wouldn't have told her or discussed with her back then. How had it all changed? She looked through the window, where normally you saw the little square table with its silver punchbowl and flowers. The old coloured plates would look down from the wall, and the place was like a little haven before you opened the door into the bright, modern, busy kitchens. Geraldine had always admired how they kept the chintzy, welcoming feel with the deep chairs and sofa. Those two were very bright; they did a lot of things by pure instinct. Today it was totally different. There was nothing on the table, only a lot of broken implements like twisted egg beaters laid out in a line. Peering further in, she could see through the kitchen door that there seemed to be huge renovations going on inside. She couldn't see what exactly, but appliances had been pulled from the wall. What could have happened to this place since she had been here last? Tentatively she rang the bell and saw an exhausted-looking Cathy come to the door.

'Oh, Geraldine,' she said without enthusiasm, and with no attempt to invite her in.

'That's me,' Geraldine said, about to step inside.

'It's not a good time, as it happens,' Cathy began.

'It never is these days, which is why you always say you'll call me and never do.'

'Please, Geraldine, please. I'll come round to your place tonight and we'll have a chat. There's a lot to talk about.'

Geraldine looked past her. Everything seemed to have tilted somehow. And Cathy was doing everything except actually bar the door to her. Gently but firmly Geraldine pushed her way in.

'Excuse *me* Geraldine, aren't you the one who says nobody should ever invade anyone else's space ... You said that. I was never to call into Glenstar without telephoning in advance ... What's happened to all that now?'

It was too late, Geraldine was inside looking at the wrecked premises. 'Oh, my God,' Geraldine cried. 'Oh, my God, you poor child, you poor, poor child, who could have done this to you?' Cathy just looked at her, stricken. 'When did it happen? How long ago...?'

'The night of Freddie's do.'

'He never said.'

'He doesn't know, Geraldine, no one does.'

'Why on earth not?'

'We have to sort out what to do first, then I was going to tell you.'

'But Cathy, I'm your friend, you have no closer friend than me.'

'I know.'

'So why couldn't you tell me about this terrible thing ...'

'You know why ...' Cathy hung her head.

'I *don't* know why ... If someone had come in, done over my house or my office, I'd have told you immediately ... not keep it all a stupid secret.'

'I didn't pay for your office, you did pay for mine,' Cathy said, still looking downwards.

'But that's got nothing to do with anything. Who did this, Cathy, who could it have been? Do they have any idea?'

'They think we did it, Geraldine, that's what they think. That we trashed this place just to get the insurance money.'

Marcella put some special oil in Tom's bath. It was meant to take the ache out of tired muscles and bones, she said; a lot of her customers swore by it.

'Most of them don't get up at five o'clock to make bread in Haywards, then spend the day shovelling away great sacks and boxes of broken things in their place of work,' Tom said grouchily. As he spoke he heard his own tones, whining and self-pitying, the kind of person he normally loathed. He felt Marcella recoil a little too.

'I know,' she said. 'It's very hard on you, but I thought it just *might* make you feel a bit better.' She had spent her hard-earned money on this gift for him, and all he had done was complain.

'Is there any hope you might massage it into a boy's shoulders?' he asked.

'Of course I will, but the boy is actually meant to lie for ten minutes soaking it up first.' She was all smiles now.

'I have no problem with that.' He smiled back at her, and went to lie down in the bath.

Marcella came in and sat on the edge of the bath to rub his shoulders. 'Now you've had a quarter of an hour it must have done you a lot of good,' she said, and he prayed she would never know that he had lain there clenched for fifteen long minutes, wondering how he was going to bear all that lay ahead in his home life and his work life without actually cracking up.

'I think you'd like tennis, Muttie,' Simon said the following Saturday.

'Tennis isn't for the likes of me,' Muttie said.

'But can't everyone do everything?' Maud asked.

'I'm not sure. They should be able to, but it doesn't always work out.'

'Cathy used to say it did,' Maud explained.

'That one thinks she can do anything, fly off the top of Liberty Hall,' said Lizzie disapprovingly.

'Sure Cathy could move mountains,' Muttie said.

'We think Cathy's cross with us,' Maud confided.

'What on earth would make her cross with you?' Lizzie said. 'Cathy's mad about you, didn't she bring you here in the first place?'

'But she never brings us anywhere now,' Simon said.

'It could be because you're meant to be above in The Beeches big house,' Muttie explained. 'They've laid down all kinds of rules and regulations about where you're to be and not to be, she doesn't want to butt in.'

'We never see her. I think we did something to annoy her,' Maud decided.

'We hardly see her ourselves these days, child,' Lizzie said. 'That job she's taken on is huge, you know, she and Tom will be worn to threads by the end of the year if they go on like this much more.'

'Joe, have you heard about this business in Tom and Cathy's?'

They were working on his press release.

'Well, I heard, yes, but I wasn't told, if that's what you mean.'

'Neither was I . . . I think it was something to do with not wanting to involve us any further. Financially.'

'Yes, I got that vibe too. But I'm perfectly prepared to go in with a bit more myself. Are you?'

'Certainly I am, but they're very prickly, both of them. I think we have to wait to be asked.'

'Cathy's always on an even keel; I don't see *her* as being prickly.'

'She has her own problems, Joe, believe me.'

'That's rather bad news, because my little brother is as high as a kite about Marcella in this show. Honestly, sometimes I wish I'd never put in a word for her with those guys at all.'

'You can't say that, isn't it her big break?'

'Big nothing, Geraldine. Marcella's twenty-five years of age. She's far too old now to be a model. If she were going to make it she should have been out there at sixteen.'

'Does she know that?'

'If she's got an ounce of sense she must.'

'Come in tomorrow and see a rehearsal, Tom,' Marcella begged.

'No, I don't want to be in the way,' he said.

'You wouldn't, lots of the other girls have their friends in to watch. Eddie and Harry think it's good for us to have an audience.'

Tom didn't want to go. It would be bad enough to see it all on the night; he couldn't bear to go in and watch, an extra peep show. 'Love, if I can I will, but it's going to be a desperate day tomorrow.'

'But Tom, you'll actually be *in* Haywards anyway with the bread, all you have to do is come up to the fourth floor. I'd love you to be there.'

She was very anxious that he be a part of it. He was going to have to see it all on Friday next; why not please her? 'You're right, I'd love to get a sneak preview,' he said, and her eyes shone with the excitement of it all.

Shona came up to him next morning in the kitchen. 'Do you know that you really are Mister Popular here, Tom?'

'What did I do now?' Tom asked, alarmed, assuming that she was being sarcastic. But apparently not. The staff had been saying that it was great to get in to a kitchen that was already up and running each morning. Tom had coffee ready on the stove for them, and a loaf of his own bread to start their day. The restaurant staff had at first been a bit doubtful about letting an outsider into their territory, but it had worked out better than they could have dreamed.

'That's good to hear, Shona.' Tom's mind wasn't really on it; he knew he had to go to the fourth floor now and watch Marcella at what she saw as her new work. Shona hesitated.

'It's just that . . . Well, I don't know how to say this, but if you and Cathy sort of *don't* get back on the rails after this burglary, I thought you should know that there could well be a full-time job for you here.'

He swallowed hard before he spoke. Shona had no idea what she was saying. She was putting into words the great fear that Scarlet Feather might not survive. Something he and Cathy hadn't even dared to consider. And what was more, a lifeline was being thrown. Not to both of them, just to Tom. He scarcely trusted himself to answer.

'Shona, you are so good, and it would be a great honour, but you know how we're killing ourselves to try and get the show on the road back there.'

'And I'm sure you will,' she murmured diplomatically.

'You see, it's all to do with having this dream. I don't think you survive without one.'

'I don't know,' Shona said.

'Do you have a dream too?'

'I had once.'

'And did you get it?'

'Yes I did, I wished for my apartment in Glenstar,' Shona said in a small voice.

It seemed an odd, bleak thing to wish for. But then to other people his wish to run a catering company might not seem all that exciting either.

'And what about love?' he asked lightly.

'I gave up on that a long time ago,' she said equally lightly, but he thought she meant it.

A section of the fourth floor had been curtained off for the rehearsal. Tom hung around at the edge, unsure whether to go in. There were a lot of other people milling around equally vaguely. Some of them were involved in setting up lighting, a music track was starting and stopping, Ricky was there advising photographers about where to stand. There was no sign as yet of the girls or the garments. They must be in that area at the end, and would come out of that arched doorway each time. His stomach lurched again at the thought of his Marcella being part of this. He saw Joe in the distance but couldn't catch his eye. Then they were called to order for a run-through with music.

'We want a lot of hush now,' Joe was saying. 'It has to be timed fairly exactly, so if anyone falls or a light doesn't work just keep on going ... Right, we're going in ten seconds from now.'

Two men sat down beside Tom. He smiled and moved to make room for them. 'Thanks, mate,' said one. They must be Joe's associates from London, and there was also a man who owned a model agency who was looking in this week. Marcella had talked of little else. 'Mr Newton himself,' she kept saying, with a reverence that set Tom's teeth on edge. Maybe one of these guys with their London accents was Mr Newton himself. 'Mr Newton?' he asked. 'Over there, mate,' one of them said, nodding towards a small man leaning back in the kind of chair that movie directors used to sit in in studios over forty years ago. Tom Feather felt pleased to notice that Mr Newton himself looked like a disagreeable little pig. Tom sat and watched as one by one the girls came out, young and unformed many of them, almost schoolchildren in bathing suits. They danced along, hitting a beach ball one to another in time to the music, and there was Marcella bringing up the rear. Not dancing with the others, but walking haughtily through them as if she had tired of childish games. She wore a white bikini shaped like three shells one cupping each breast and one as a tiny G-string. Her flat, tanned stomach and long, tanned legs looked so familiar and yet so alien in this setting. He wanted to do nothing as much as cry. She had told him that Joe insisted she should have a starring role, that she wasn't part of any chorus line, and this seemed to be true all right. When the halter-top beach dresses were shown, there were rainbows full of pastel shades for the line of dancing youngsters, but Marcella was there in black with a cleavage that came down to her navel. The men beside him seemed to watch her with admiration. Tom had to say something.

'I know her. She's good, isn't she?'

'Gorgeous,' said one of them.

'Some guys get all the luck,' said the other.

'Do you think she might make it, big time?' Tom asked, trying to keep his voice neutral. He wanted so very much for this to be a success for her; he wanted that much more than the base wish that she be a spectacular failure and give up the dream.

'Aw, she's not in this seriously, she's only doing it for fun,' said one of the men.

'She's a friend of Joe Feather, he got her the gig,' said the other.

'I think she's hoping to do it as a career,' Tom said.

They shook their heads.

'No way,' said one.

'She's far too old,' said the other.

'She's twenty-five,' Tom said.

'Exactly,' said the man, and looked back at the catwalk where the girls were coming out now in nightdresses. Marcella could not have looked more naked if she had stood in front of them without a stitch of clothing on. The wispy garment that hit and missed her artistically just pointed up all the beautiful parts of her, as if she had been coloured in with dayglo pen.

He left her a note saying that she was marvellous, the show was a winner and he was so proud of her. Then he drove the van to the canal and sat and watched two swans for about ten minutes as they sailed up and down and arched their long, beautiful necks. He didn't realise that he was crying until he went to start the van again, and felt his tears splash on his hand. He must be going totally mad.

At the premises he found that two envelopes had been delivered by hand. Geraldine had sent a letter to Cathy; it was short and factual. She wanted to make another investment in the company, and believed Cathy to be short-sighted and not looking after the good of the investors by refusing it. However, if that was her intent, she enclosed some details on renting equipment, china and cutlery. It would be expensive, but at least there would be no initial outlay.

Cathy rang her aunt and left a thank-you message on her machine. 'Tom and I both think that's a great idea. If we only have to rent it for a few months it will all make sense. Thanks again, Ger. You're great.'

The other was from Joe Feather to Tom. He had heard by devious means that they had had a break-in and he wished to offer his condolences and some cash in hand. This was not a time to be filling in forms and VAT returns. Take this thousand now, and of course he'd pay the bill for the catering for the press reception in the handy folding money too. Tom rang his brother and left a thank-you message on his machine.

'Cathy and I want to thank you from the bottom of our hearts, we will take that thousand pounds joyfully and lodge it as a further investment, but alas, everything else has to be done straight up, and right through the books. If you knew our accountant you'd realise we are more afraid of him than anyone on earth. Thanks again though, Joe, you're great. Oh, and I went to the rehearsal this morning, show looks really good.'

'Does the show look really good?' Cathy asked.

'Why do you ask that?'

'Well, everything else you said to him was lies, you're not afraid of James Byrne, it's just we don't want hot money floating around.'

'It was okay, the show,' Tom said slowly. 'That's what it was.'

'But presumably you found a better word to describe it to Marcella?' Cathy laughed.

'I did, a few,' he grinned ruefully.

'Listen, how in the name of God are we going to do that reception with no equipment?'

'We start renting,' Cathy said, phoning the company. 'This will be our first real do inside Haywards. We don't want to borrow a plate or a glass from them; we gotta show them.'

'Did you really think it was good?' Marcella asked when she got home.

They had been having drinks, Joe and his partners, about finer points, and Mr Newton had joined them.

'Was that Mr Newton himself?' Tom asked, regretting his sneer the moment he had said it.

Marcella however had noticed nothing amiss. 'Yes, he's as nice as anything, and very easygoing to talk to. When you consider all the kinds of people he has handled in his career! He's just very normal and ordinary, it's like talking to anyone.'

'Imagine,' Tom said.

'I know, and he was very praising of everything about the show. Joe was thrilled.'

'Good, great.'

'It's all kind of unbelievable to think that it's all going to happen on this very Friday,' Marcella said.

He looked at her, mute with the fear that those two business associates of Joe might be right, that Marcella was far too old even to think about beginning a modelling career. 'And there's a real possibility that Mr Newton might get you a contract?' he asked her.

'Well, I don't want to be too hopeful, but it looks like it. Still, he's only seen two rehearsals today, and apparently it all depends on how you do on the night ... People can be fine in front of a handful of people and yet go to pieces in front of an audience.'

'You didn't go to pieces today, and there were lots of people there.' He was begging her to have confidence in herself.

'But there'll be three hundred and more on the night,' Marcella said, hugging herself. 'Still, I think I can do it, all those younger ones there in the group give me great confidence ... It's been great working with them.'

'Are they younger than you, then?' Tom asked, wide-eyed.

'Oh, Tom, will you shut up. Of course they are, some of them are at least eight or nine years younger than me, stop playing the fool.'

'I didn't see that they were, you looked so much the best ... But would Mr Newton not be looking for them, then, or are they too young?' he asked.

Marcella frowned. 'You know, I thought that too, that maybe he'd go for the younger ones for his books, but he said to Joe that he thought I'd be suited for a lot of stuff he has on hand.' Marcella hugged herself. 'It's all so wonderful, Tom, really, I can hardly take it all in.'

The letters, faxes and e-mails were coming in thick and fast from Chicago. Each one was headed simply *Wedding*.

'Nobody ever got married in the world before Marian Scarlet,' Cathy grumbled, looking at the latest message.

'So what are you complaining about? They want fancy, we give them fancy.' Tom was determined to be cheerful.

'No, wait till you hear.'

'Honestly, Cathy, it's just because she's your sister you're making all this fuss. That church hall where they've never had a wedding in their life, where you didn't want to have it, will become *the* place, believe me, Ricky's going to take pictures of it . . .'

'But you haven't heard . . .'

'The priest is delighted, and I think that we'll make a fortune out of it for us and for him too,' Tom said hastily. Cathy watched helplessly. 'My father's men have it all painted up already, the priest has got the parishioners to plant window boxes. It's going to look—' He broke off at the sight of her face. 'What is it?' Tom asked.

'They want a traditional Irish wedding, Tom, they want us to serve corned beef and cabbage.'

'What for, in the name of God?'

'That's what they think is traditional Irish food.'

'But Marian was brought up in St Jarlath's Crescent, she *can't* think that.' Tom was aghast.

'She's been a long time in Illinois,' Cathy shrugged.

'We are *not* going to serve them corned beef and cabbage,' Tom said.

'I know.'

'So who's going to tell her?' he asked menacingly.

'You have the better turn of phrase,' Cathy said.

'She's your bloody sister,' Tom answered.

'It's a question of what else we can persuade them is typically Irish.'

'But there are a thousand things, for God's sake. Wicklow lamb, Irish salmon, loads of lobster, mussels, we could have a centrepiece of Irish shellfish. I would have thought they'd have liked huge ribs of Irish beef. Isn't Chicago the sort of home of the stockyards and everything? They'd be used to big steer on their plates.'

'They don't want what they're used to. They want Irish dancers, shillelaghs, colleens saying top of the mornin' to them.'

'They don't?' Tom was aghast.

Cathy waved the letter at him again. 'Well it sounds very like it from this . . . All Harry's relations are so looking forward to the whole Irish experience, steeping themselves in another culture, experiencing the simple, unspoiled peasant cuisine.'

Tom put his head in his hands. 'Come on, Cathy, let's think what we'll offer them. Imagine, we once thought this was going to be an easy number.'

'There's no such thing as an easy number in this game,' Cathy said, with such a sigh that he looked up suddenly.

'Are you all right?' he asked, concerned at the expression on her face.

'Of course I'm not. We can't go on fooling ourselves. There's no way we can do this wedding.' She was bent double now, her head in her hands, her whole body shaking with tears. 'We can't possibly go ahead, it's ludicrous, we were mad to take it on . . .' she sobbed.

'Cathy, Cathy . . .' He got up from the chair in the front room and came to kneel down beside where she was hugging her knees and making no attempt to hide the tears or the fact that she had dropped her guard so completely.

'We'll think of something,' he said.

'But what is there left to think of,' she wept. 'Marian's gone mad, we should never have listened to one word she said, we should have told her we were done over and we couldn't cope, why do we have to keep on pretending and say that everything's all right when it's not.'

'Because that's the only way we stay in business.' He was very gentle and stroked her head soothingly.

'No, we don't have to pretend, we're finished, aren't we, we're never going to get back up and running . . .' She stood up suddenly, and looked at him, red-eyed and distraught. 'Can't you see we're only fooling ourselves, every step we take we're only sinking in further, it just makes it more difficult for us to get out, deeper and deeper in debt . . .'

Tom had stood up and now he pulled her to him in a big bear-hug.

'Now this is not going to go on, it's not, you have to help me. When I hear you saying all this, I half-believe you, do you hear?'

She cried in his arms as he stroked her hair over and over. It was a luxury not having to hold back, to keep a permanently false grin on her face in front of June and Con and anyone else who came in and out.

Her shoulders shook and he held her until the sobs died down. She mumbled something he couldn't hear into his sweater.

'What did you say?'

'I said it's over, Tom, we have to be strong and face it.'

'There's nothing strong about letting your sister down on the biggest day of her life.'

'Tell her to get some other leprechaun outfit.'

'There isn't one, we're the only leprechaun outfit in town.' He looked down at her face. It had worked a little. There was a half smile.

'You never thought of quitting?'

'No, not ever.'

'Right then.' She blew her nose loudly. 'Right then, if we're not quitting, then we'll have to redefine.'

'What, come up with something traditionally Irish that Scarlet Feather can actually live with?' He looked at her. She was better. They were back in business.

Their computer had escaped the vandalism by the sheer good luck of having been out for repair at the time. Cathy sat down in front of it.

'We'll send an e-mail, you come up with the creative, persuasive bit and I'll do the dear long-lost sister part.'

'We must make her think she's getting it just right,' Tom said thoughtfully.

'Whatever made us think that a catering business had anything to do with producing food?' Cathy laughed.

'It's only for the trade, Mam,' Joe Feather said to his mother for the twentieth time.

'But there was a thing in the paper saying it was for everyone.'

'Everyone in the rag trade, Mam, believe me I'd invite you if there was anything there you'd like to see.' He spoke the truth. His mother would not like to see her future daughter-in-law, of whom she already disapproved mightily, dressed in next to nothing. Nor would she like to see her son Tom's face as this was going on. Joe had seen him at the rehearsal, and had realised how hard he was taking the whole thing, and yet trying to face up to it as well. Which wasn't really necessary at all. Marcella hadn't a chance in hell of making it on the modelling circuit. Beautiful-looking woman, but wooden on stage and built so that you only saw her body, not the garments she was modelling. She wouldn't last five minutes in the big world out there. Surely Tom didn't take any of this business about finding work across the water seriously. Surely.

*

Cathy came back from the cash and carry and Tom helped her unpack the van.

'Just one message – Simon and Maud don't love you any more.'

'Simon and Maud? What have I done now?'

'It's what you've not done. They want to come and polish your treasures again.'

'But we don't *have* any treasures,' Cathy wailed.

'We never did, technically,' Tom said ruefully.

'They'll tell *everyone*, it's worse than having it on the nine o'clock news on television. They can't come here, they'll have Muttie and Lizzie up to high doh, the folks in Chicago will cancel, everyone would cancel if they knew what we were working out of.' She felt guilty about the twins, but she knew that she had total right on her side.

But Tom wouldn't let her get away with it. 'They think you've gone off them, they want to know what they've done.'

'Shit,' said Cathy. 'We don't need this now.'

Tom said nothing. He continued unpacking.

'All right, you win, to be fair they've enough to cope with, they don't need it either. I'll take them out somewhere.'

'I left their number there on the desk,' he said. 'Poor little devils, I'd say life is no bed of roses up in The Beeches.'

She went to the telephone.

The twins' father answered the phone. Cathy couldn't remember whether she called him Kenneth or Mr Mitchell.

'My name is Cathy Scarlet. I would like to speak to Maud Mitchell or Simon Mitchell, please.'

'Oh, yes indeed, um . . . er . . . we *have* met, if I'm not mistaken,' the voice said.

She could hear him saying 'extraordinarily rude woman' as he called the children. Cathy felt a moment of guilt when she heard their excitement.

'For us?' Simon was saying. Normally they wouldn't get any calls.

'Who is it?' Maud asked him, and got no reply, so she got to the phone first.

'It *is*, it *is*,' she called. 'It's Cathy.'

And Cathy felt a sudden rush of tears, which she beat back as she suggested they go on an outing.

'I thought we'd go to the cinema and have a burger, then I'll drive you home,' she offered.

'Will we come and pick you up at the premises?' Simon offered.

'*No*, I mean, no thanks, Simon, just get the bus in to O'Connell Street . . . and I'll see you there for the four o'clock show.'

'Come with us, Tom,' she suggested.

'No, only two days to the show. Marcella's nerves are frazzled, and she says she wants to talk this evening.'

'Right. I suddenly thought you could do with a relax too.'

'I could have,' he said. 'But these are stressed times, and you've not forgotten we're having a supper after the show?'

'No, indeed. Where are we going?'

'The little Italian place, Geraldine's coming. Ricky and Joe too, I think, if he can get away, Shona and half a dozen more. We'll be able to get away nice and early when the show is finished. No coming back here with the van or anything. Haywards says we can clear into their kitchens and just lock up. I'll cope with it when I get in to do the bread on Saturday.'

'You work too hard,' she said sympathetically.

'So do you. Was there a lot of standing and hanging around when you were up there at the cash and carry?'

She looked at him sharply. It had been exhausting, she had an ache in her back and some of the food she saw revolted her. She thought that the visit there would never end.

'Not too bad today,' she said. This would be another very hard conversation, the day she would have to tell him she would be taking maternity leave. But she would face it when she had to.

'And you're sure we didn't do anything bad?' Maud persisted.

They were having their burger after the movie.

'No Maud, remember what I told you about not being the centre of the world.'

'Yes, but we were afraid you thought—'

'I wasn't thinking about you at all, we've been very busy.'

'So how do you know when someone is really cross with you, or if they're just busy and not thinking about you?' Simon wondered.

'It's something that comes with time, you do get to know, Simon.'

'Were you older or younger than us when you got to know?' Simon asked.

'A bit older, about six months older, I think.' Cathy felt very tired.

The more the children talked on and on about some madman called old Barty and the strange food they ate, and Mother being in bed a lot during the day and Father out a lot at night, she knew it had been a great, great mistake to let those children go without a fight. Neil had given the wrong advice there. She knew it. It had nothing to do with flesh and blood. Muttie and Lizzie Scarlet sitting alone up in St Jarlath's Crescent would have made much better parents to these children than the ones who had actually brought them into the world.

'Why don't I take you up to see Hooves before we go home?' she suggested suddenly.

They looked at each other awkwardly. Embarrassed, Maud shuffled her feet and Simon looked out of the door of the restaurant.

'What is it?' Cathy looked from one to the other.

'Well, you know the bargain. We weren't to go back to St Jarlath's Crescent except on Saturdays,' Simon began.

'But the bargain was all about you being good children and going straight home from school. It's the holidays now.'

'Sara said it was the same term or holiday.'

'But it's just a drive, you're allowed to go out with *me*, can't I drive you where I want?'

'Better not, Cathy . . . Sara said that Mother and Father are a bit jealous of what a good time we had at Muttie and his wife Lizzie's . . . And they don't like us going back there . . . in case it shows that it's where we prefer.'

'And is it?' Cathy asked.

'You told us not to say anything about preferring one place to another. You told us that would be bad-mannered,' Maud said, confused.

'Did I? I must have been very intelligent back then.'

'It's not all *that* long ago,' Simon said. 'You couldn't have lost a lot of intelligence in such a short time.'

'I love you, Simon,' Cathy said suddenly. 'And I love you too, Maud. Right, if everyone's finished I'll take you home to your parents' house.' Cathy busied herself about the departure so that she wouldn't have to see the looks of total shock on the twins' faces. Nobody had ever said I love you to them like that before. They hadn't an idea how to cope with it. Back at the house, she was about to drop them at the door.

'Please come in,' they begged.

'No, truly, it's better not.'

'But you're not afraid of them like Muttie is,' Simon cried.

'And we could do our dance for you,' said Maud.

'Certainly I'll come in,' Cathy said, and marched into the house purposefully. 'Kenneth, Kay, thank you for lending me your magnificent son and daughter, we had such a nice evening, or I think we did.' She looked at them, waiting for the polite, enthusiastic response she had taught them that people expected.

'Terrific film,' said Maud.

'And Cathy paid for two burgers each,' Simon said.

'So they won't need any supper.' Cathy looked around to see any signs that someone had been preparing a meal for the children at eight o'clock on a summer's evening.

'There's some ham in the fridge,' Kay said defensively.

'Oh, I'm quite sure there is, Kay, and that you would have made a lovely supper for them, according to all the agreement and everything, but tonight I don't think they'd be up for anything at all.'

'No indeed, thank you,' said Simon.

'Can we get our shoes and the tape recorder now?' Maud wanted to know.

The parents looked on in bewilderment as Simon and Maud waited, toes pointed, until the correct bar of the music, and danced solemnly up and down the kitchen. They had improved greatly since the last time Cathy had watched it, with her hand over her mouth to hide the nervous laugh and to beat back the feeling that her sister Marian would kill her dead for allowing them to get up in public.

'And this is for a wedding, apparently?' Kenneth Mitchell said, having clapped because his wife and Cathy had done so with such vigour.

'Yes, my sister's wedding next month ... They'll be the star turn.'

'It's just that I'm not really sure ...'

Cathy clenched her hands. This fool was not going to try to renege again on the wedding. 'Oh, you *are* sure, Kenneth, remember your brother Jock told you all about it, part of the terms of the agreement?'

'Yes, yes, of course.'

'And talking about the agreement, I want you to know how reliable Simon and Maud are about everything. You see, I had forgotten that you only want them to visit my parents' house once a week. I was going to drive them up there briefly to visit their dog . . .'

'Well, come on now, it's not exactly *their* dog, is it?'

'Yes it is, very exactly their dog, my father bought it for them himself and looks after it for them with pleasure until their weekly visit, but you interrupted me. I was telling you how proud you should be of them; they reminded me of the agreement which I had forgotten. I think it's sad myself, but I do think they were splendid to be so up front about it all, since it's your wish.'

'Well . . . um, yes, it . . . of course . . .'

'So I thought I'd mention that since they are being so generous and observing the letter of the law as regards your wishes, you might be equally generous next month and let them make a few extra visits around the time of the wedding, so that they can meet everyone properly.'

'Well, we'll have to see . . .' Kenneth began.

'Of course you will, I knew you would.' Cathy beamed at the children. 'Your father is just as reasonable as I said he would be, and there will be no problem at all about the various wedding parties . . . As soon as Neil is back from Africa, he and his father will be in touch to firm it all up.' The children looked at her, bewildered. 'Thank you all so much, it's been a very pleasant visit.' And then she was gone. She slowed down a little just to hear what Kenneth Mitchell would say.

'Extraordinary woman,' he said, and without looking, she could see him shaking his head from side to side.

'Love, before you even speak a word let me tell you that you'll be a sensation,' Tom said.

But her face was troubled, almost as if she hadn't heard him. 'Marcella, what are you worried about? *Tell* me, you look lovely, you knock the others off the stage, you are stunning – it's just actor's nerves, I know . . .'

'No, that's not the point.'

'But it is in a way. You tell yourself that in a day and a bit, tomorrow night at ten o'clock all this will be over and life goes on as normal.'

'But that's just it. I can't go back, not now.'

'What do you mean, go back?'

'To the salon to do nails.'

297

'But there'll be more jobs once people have seen you . . .'

'There will be no jobs unless I get an agent.'

'You said Mr Newton—'

'Paul Newton *is* interested in representing me and arranging for me to go over the water for some try-outs . . . But it's not definite . . . it depends.'

'I know you were saying you're afraid you won't be good on the night itself, but you will, I tell you, I can see confidence in every bone of your body.' He begged her to believe him.

'These are tough, selfish guys, used to getting what they want.'

'He'll see you perform tomorrow night, he'll *know* you're what he wants.'

'It's a bit different.'

'What do you mean?'

'It's all in their court, they can make or break you. If you play according to their rules; you get to be part of it all, if you don't, you're not allowed to join.' She was twisting her hands uneasily.

He had no idea what she was trying to say. 'So what's the problem? If you do right tomorrow on that catwalk, as you will, then you will be part of it, or whatever you say the expression is.'

'They say we have to go and party with them tomorrow night,' she said, looking at the floor.

'Party?'

'Yes, back at their hotel.'

'But we *can't*, you know I've set up a dinner in the little Italian place, everyone's coming. You'll have to tell them we can't make it.'

'Not you, just me.'

He assumed she was joking and laughed. 'And what do you do for an encore?'

'No encore. If I do that, then I'm on his books and that's it.'

He realised it wasn't a joke. She was actually telling him that this guy had made her such a gross proposition. You come round to the hotel and party, or you don't get on my books. It was laughable.

'It's just because you *do* look so lovely it makes men lose their senses and say such ridiculous things.'

'He means it.'

'Well he can mean what he likes. *I'm* telling Joe he's not to come near the place tomorrow night and upset you like this.'

Marcella allowed herself very few cigarettes a day; she knew they dulled her skin tone and discoloured her teeth. But she lit one now. 'Could you stop making gestures for a minute. There's no question of telling Joe anything of the sort. Joe needs people like Paul Newton to get his clothes shown, you're not going to say one thing that would upset that.'

'So what are we talking about?' Tom asked.

'We're talking about what Paul Newton suggested,' she said simply.

He looked at her in disbelief. And then he began to laugh. It was a real laugh, not a pretend one. She *had* to be joking. But why was she not laughing back? 'You're not remotely serious, are you?' he said suddenly.

'Never more so, that's what I wanted to talk to you about.'

'Stop it, you're unhinged, you're not some high-class tart he can buy with the thought of a modelling contract.'

'It's not the thought, it's the actual contract,' she said.

'And you'd screw him for that?'

'It won't come to that, you know it won't. Just a party with girls and champagne, that's what they like.'

'Give us a break, you nearly had me fooled.'

'I have never in my whole life told you a lie or done anything to deceive you, why would I do so this time?' She spoke in that strange, almost robotic voice she had used once before, that time when he had thought she had lied and gone to a party instead of to the gym.

'He's only calling your bluff, don't fall for it. You're too bright for that, for heaven's sake.'

'No, it's one or the other.'

'Well let it be the other, the decision that involves telling him to get lost.'

'It's my choice, my future, I'm the one who has to do it or not do it, to get onto a proper bona fide model agency's books or lose the chance for ever.'

He looked at her and realised that she meant it. 'So we're not discussing this at all, you're telling me what you're going to do. Is that it?'

'It's not like that.'

'What's it like, then?'

'It's like my never going behind your back as I could easily do, or could have done.'

'I wish you had.'

'You don't mean that. We swore that we would be honest with

each other. I never knew that being honest would end up like this. It's meaningless, it's silly even thinking he's a hotshot.'

'Then why even contemplate it?'

'Because it's not meaningless to him. So where's the harm?'

'And you're telling me that you wouldn't mind, if for work's sake I were to do something similar?'

'We *have* to be nice to people in business. You do, every single day, and remember that awful woman who ran the magazine that did our photo shoot ... She was making great signs of fancying you. I thought you might have to go off and have lunches and parties with her; if you had to, then you had to.'

Tom laughed aloud at the very thought of it. 'You see, you say something like that and I'm ninety per cent sure you must be winding me up about all this.' Again he got no answering laugh. 'So you admit he fancies you?' he said.

'He admires me, and I'm nearer his age than the teeny-tots are. It's just a party, Tom. I tell you again, I wouldn't have minded if you had to go to a party with that woman.'

'Not if my life depended on it, let alone just a career.'

'I'm sorry about the Italian place,' she said.

What he said and did now was very important. It would affect his whole life. He must be very, very careful. He stood in the little sitting room where Marcella still sat at the table. The picture imprinted itself on his mind. The table had a pink crushed velvet cloth which Cathy had given them last Christmas. There was a shallow white fruit bowl with peaches and black grapes. The evening sunlight came in and touched the edges of Marcella's hair, giving it that strange halo effect. As if she were some kind of saint. She wore a floppy black cotton sweater and blue jeans; she looked about eighteen. Her enormous eyes searched his face for the response he was going to give.

'So, Tom?' she asked.

'So, Marcella?' he said.

'So what are you going to say to me?' she asked.

'As you said, it's your decision, your choice, your career. Nothing I say will change that.' He spoke gently and held her hand.

'But?' she continued for him.

'But it would break my heart for you to leap to his command as a party girl, and it would lose dignity and respect for both of us, and despite what you say you *don't* need to do this. And under normal circumstances you wouldn't consider it, but these are not normal times, you're so nervous about tomorrow night.'

He looked at her waiting for her to throw herself into his arms and thank him for his insight and understanding. There was a long, long silence. 'So, then, my love, you'll come to our party with all your friends who will drink to your success?'

'Thank you for everything, for not losing your temper and getting those wild ideas that I'd tell you a lie.'

'No, no, I know you wouldn't,' he soothed. But she still hadn't said yes or no. He *must* let her work it out for herself. She didn't want to go ahead with this party, and he had spoken as honestly as he could without getting up and smashing his fist through the door, which was what he felt like doing. She came round to his side of the table, put her arms around him and drew him towards the sofa. And they sat there in the summer sunset, with her head on his shoulder and holding his hand, for a long, long time.

A lot of the rented equipment had arrived, and was being installed at the premises. Men were backing in and out with the crates that held cookers and deep-fryers. The sheer volume of noise was frightening. Thinking about how much they were going to have to earn to pay for it all made Tom and Cathy feel weak. June and Cathy were supervising it while getting the finger food ready for the fashion show.

'Most of them won't eat at all, wannabe models like stick insects,' June complained.

'No, you're totally wrong, apparently people who are far too old and fat for the garments make up the main part of the audience. My mother-in-law will be there, for one.'

'And won't Hannah's eyes fall out of her head when she sees some of the items on display? Right, that's the second last tray – one more and I'll go out and start loading the van.'

'Okay, I'll get started on Mad Minnie,' June said cheerfully.

'Shush, June, one of these fine days she'll come in and hear you saying that,' Cathy warned.

Minnie was a woman whose husband thought she could cook, so every Friday she arrived for one fresh dish and five frozen suppers for two. Cathy had long ago offered to teach her to make the simple dishes she wanted, but no, she wanted them made for her in her own dishes. So every time they were making Beef Carbonnade or

Chicken Provençale, they remembered to spoon two extra portions into Minnie's red or green containers.

'What a desperate life they must lead the two of them, never having anyone in or ever going out,' Cathy said sympathetically.

'Does she think there are six days in the week?' June wondered.

'No, they have fish and chips once a week, her husband's little treat to thank her for all this baking.'

'He must be as thick as a plank,' June said. 'She's better off not telling him anything, the less you tell men the better, I always say.'

'But what kind of communication is that, lying to him over something as basic as the fact she's not making his dinner?' Cathy asked.

'Believe me, I've been over the hoops longer than you two,' June said. 'Say nothing, do what you like, that's my motto.'

Tom carried the trays out grimly. There was some truth in what she'd said, he thought. Suppose Marcella had said that there was a training course or a business meeting in the hotel or something. Of course he'd have believed her, and he'd never have known the horror of last night and the lingering possibility that she might still choose Mr Newton's party rather than the one he had so lovingly organised himself. When he came back, Cathy was looking with some dislike at the food in front of her.

'What's this?' she asked June.

'God, imagine you asking me. They're poussins, baby chickens, I'm just doing them for Minnie, are you losing your marbles or something?'

'You take them over there to the other side, will you? I don't really like looking at them, they make me feel sick, they're sort of, I don't know, human-looking.'

'Sure.' June was cheerful as she prattled on. 'You know, I think we should try and get some kind of Christmas menu ready way in advance, a pack of things for eejits to have in the house like canapés, and teeny mince pies . . .'

'Like we could deliver them in the van?' Cathy sounded eager.

'I'd love that, going round to these houses saying Merry Christmas, like Santa Claus. But will you still be working at Christmas?' June asked casually.

'What do you mean?' Cathy looked alarmed.

'I mean, when will you be taking leave, and everything? We'd need to know, wouldn't we, Tom?'

'Of course we would,' Tom said, understanding nothing.

'And by the way, were you ever going to tell us about this baby? I mean, were we meant to wait until you asked us to boil some water and time the contractions?'

At Haywards things looked very busy. Tom's stomach felt sick about almost everything, and tonight the opinion that people had of Scarlet Feather's catering was way the lowest worry on the list. He helped Con, June and Cathy set up the press reception and then slipped away and left a small bunch of roses in a vase in the dressing room. He put a card saying, 'Beautiful, lovely Marcella. Good luck on your first night and always.' His hand trembled a little as he left it there. The girls were on stage for a photo call; they would come up and mingle with the press later. Tom hung around the dressing room. He knew in his heart that the whole thing had been brought on by nerves, and that she wasn't going to mention the matter again except with embarrassment. He just wished he could get that strange, dead, mantra tone she spoke with out of his mind. She had sounded like someone sleepwalking. Someone slightly out of control.

The press reception went very well, three journalists took the Scarlet Feather card as well as the Feather Fashions press release. The brothers were photographed together, arm in arm.

Cathy had been shocked by this morning's revelation. She had spun them a good story; the whole thing was something she hadn't realised at all herself. She had only just been to the doctor and confirmed it, and she had not been able to tell Neil before he disappeared to Africa. *Now* could they understand the need for discretion. Or a total news blackout. They had realised the urgency and backed off admirably.

'Well, we always wanted another pair of hands around the place. As long as the baby starts work at six months, we'll not mention the matter again,' Tom agreed.

'Sure,' June had said. 'Let's keep it really quiet, let's just tell Maud and Simon, is that okay?'

Cathy knew that she could rely on them, and that she could *just* get through today, the press reception looked as if it was motoring fine, then there was this show which was obviously cracking poor Tom up, then there would be the finger food afterwards, stack the dishes in Haywards' kitchen and then, as if the day had not been long enough, she would have to go to the Italian restaurant to the party. Lucky old Neil with his bureaucratic red tape and his composite resolutions at a conference under African skies. He had nothing to worry about. He didn't begin to know what problems were!

Tom could hardly remember the show. He remembered a few gasps here and there and a lot of applause. He saw Joe look across at him and put his thumb up in the air a couple of times when Marcella was on stage; he forced a smile onto his face. It only took him seconds to see where Paul Newton was sitting, prime viewing area, without his cigar but sucking a pencil instead. He felt such a loathing for the man that he almost fell over. Please may Marcella stumble, he thought, or may she miss her cue, do it all wrong. Then immediately he felt guilty: what a terrible thing to call down bad spirits on someone's first night, especially the night of someone he loved. And then there was the applause, and the buyers from different parts of the country lining up for more details and information about stock in front of Joe and his friends, Brendan and Harry, and a watchful eye on it all being kept by Mr Newton himself. Tom worked like an automaton, passing filo-wrapped prawns here and Thai fish cakes there. 'Delighted you like them, we have a little recipe sheet there near the door if you're interested.' It had been one of his own ideas, give them a list of how to make half a dozen simple hors d'oeuvres that anyone could make really, and also add the names of about twelve more that were complicated but part of the repertoire. Phone, fax and e-mail of Scarlet Feather and you had a wonderful advertisement – they were all tucking them into handbags. He moved feverishly around the room, and felt a woman's hand on his arm. It was the woman from the magazine that had done their photo shoot, the hard-faced journalist fifteen years older than him, the one Marcella said fancied him.

'Oh, hallo, I didn't see you at the press reception,' he said.

'You were looking out?' she asked.

He fled. And saw Marcella smiling and waving her glass across the room. Would this evening never end? Gradually the crowd thinned.

'Don't fill their glasses any more, Con, they'll never go home,' he pleaded.

'Suits me, Mr F,' Con said, and began clearing up the empties.

'June, can you sort of amalgamate whatever food is left; the word's out we're finishing up now.'

'Most of this won't survive, Cathy, we can't recycle it.'

'I don't care if we plaster the walls of the ladies' cloakroom with it, we're not giving them any more,' Cathy said, with an insincere smile as she saw her mother-in-law approaching.

'What a delicious spread, you really *have* come on in such leaps and bounds.'

'Well, thank you so very much,' Cathy said, resisting with difficulty the urge to knock Hannah senseless on the floor at Haywards, ensuring that she and Tom never worked again.

'And a lot of my friends said so too, they said it was the only thing that made the evening worthwhile.'

'You didn't like the show?' Her face was bland and innocent.

'Dear me no, tacky and tawdry, not Haywards at all. I must have a word with that nice Shona Burke.'

'Neil will be back on Sunday,' Cathy said, intent on changing the conversation. 'Apparently it's very interesting out there.'

'Such a pity you two don't ever manage to be in the same place at the same time at all.' Hannah Mitchell used to sing a very different tune. Times had changed.

The dirty dishes had been stacked in the Haywards' dish-washing machine, and trays of glasses rinsed for Tom to cope with next day. Con and June had seen to this as well as emptying ashtrays and taking every last sign of litter away from the salon. Tom was rounding the little group up for the restaurant. Joe had said that Marcella was terrific, star of the show and he would love to come to Tom's supper, but he simply had to stay with his colleagues.

After ages they were ready, the restaurant was only minutes away. Tom begged Cathy to take the others with her, to order the house Frascati and get it all started. They were flashing the lights on and off in Haywards, a definite sign that it was time to go. Security men and caretakers were going around checking the big solid ash-filled containers where cigarettes might not have been fully extinguished. Tom knew a lot of them by name from his early-morning bread-making visits.

'I'm just running up to the dressing rooms, Sean,' he said to one of them. 'Got to pick up Marcella.'

'Nobody there, Tom, lights all out, they're all gone,' said the man.

'No, Marcella went back to change. She must be there.'

'Honestly, not a soul,' the man said.

His job depended on it, Tom knew he was right. He went downstairs, mystified. She must be going straight to the restaurant, but why hadn't she said? And here was Shona.

'Come on with me; they must be all there in the restaurant already.'

'I was just looking for Marcella,' he said.

'Oh, she left half an hour ago. She left with Joe, and his pals Brendan and Harry and that Mr Newton. They all have to go to some do back in the hotel.'

He felt as if he were going to pass out. 'Sorry, they went where?' he said eventually.

Shona looked at him with concern. 'I said to her that I thought we were all going to the Italian to celebrate her night, and she said that you *knew* she had to go to this meeting. You did, didn't you?'

'Yes, deep down I did,' said Tom Feather.

Chapter Eight

AUGUST

Tom let himself into the flat with a heavy heart. How had he managed to keep cheerful all night, talking about everything under the sun except the fact that Marcella hadn't come to her own party? The others were supportive, too supportive. They had taken in the situation immediately. It was *Hamlet* without the prince; the beautiful model hadn't thought they were good enough to come and have dinner with afterwards, she had gone with the important people. They had all tried to behave as if it was an acceptable thing to do. Of course she had to, very difficult to get away, part of the job. He had wanted to cry so much that he was astounded he hadn't actually broken down. But no, they all went on, fussing about which pasta to choose. And he urged them to stay longer to have wine, he didn't want to go back to that empty flat and wonder when she would be home. He couldn't remember what he had eaten or how much he had paid. The evening was bitter in his mouth and heart.

Cathy said as he was leaving, 'She's probably at home already, furious that she couldn't be with us.'

'I'd say that's where she is all right,' he said with what he hoped was a grin, rather than the beginning of a howl.

Of course she wasn't at home. It was one a.m., and Mr Newton's party would only be getting going. He sat down and drank a lot of cold water to try to get rid of the taste of whatever he had been eating. He nodded off at the kitchen table. And woke suddenly to hear the phone ringing. It was twenty minutes after three o'clock.

'Tom?'

'Yes, Marcella?'

'Tom, the thing is . . .'

'Yes?'

'The thing is, the party is only just getting going here. So I wanted to say I'd be later, and I'm sorry, but you know the way these things happen.'

'Of course I don't know the way these things happen. It's nearly four o'clock in the morning. You're not coming home, is this what you've phoned to tell me?'

'Not immediately, and in fact some of the girls were thinking we should get a room between us and maybe stay . . .'

'Please stay, Marcella,' he said.

'It might be more sensible, what with taxis and—'

'Goodnight,' he said.

'Are you cross?'

'No, that's not the word,' he said.

'Tom, please, tell me you understand that it's all for the job.'

'Stay there, please, Marcella. Please stay.'

'Not in that cold voice, not making me feel—'

'Stay there,' he said, hung up and took the phone off the hook in case she called again.

It was an extraordinary Saturday morning. Tom was busy, saying nothing whatsoever about Marcella not having come home last night, or Cathy's pregnancy and all it would involve for the company. He couldn't believe that Neil was still in Africa knowing nothing of this news, and he didn't like the lines of anxiety in Cathy's face when she had told them this. Cathy was busy saying nothing whatsoever about not having spoken to Neil, or Marcella's non-appearance at the supper last night and all it might involve in Tom's life. She couldn't believe that Tom hadn't known until the last moment that there was a business do Marcella had to attend, and she didn't like the pale, waxen look on his face all evening. So they talked instead about the Chicago wedding, which was running into murkier waters all the time and was now under three weeks away. How had August 19th crept up on them so quickly?

'Is Marian like you at all?' Tom wanted to know.

'I've no idea, I've hardly seen her since I was a child. She left when she was seventeen, and I've been over once and she's only been back twice. And I don't know *what* Harry is like, so we can't get any clues to their character.'

'Do we know anything about the kind of people they'll be asking from Chicago?' he tried.

'No, not a notion.'

'And the Irish contingent?'

'A few of Mam and Dad's sisters and brothers, their children, a couple of cousins, all of them anxious to have the ties off, the shirts open and get stuck into the pints.'

'What would they like?'

'Prawn cocktail, roast chicken and ice cream with chocolate sauce.'

Tom groaned.

'And the message from Chicago sounded a bit pissed off about the typically Irish fare.'

'Yes, a huff has been taken, not to me personally mind, but behind my back to Mam, and to Geraldine . . . The "wouldn't you think Cathy would know what's expected" sort of thing. It would sicken you.'

'Do you think we should just *give* it to them, for an easy life?' Tom looked very tired.

Cathy wondered had he slept at all, they might have had words when they got home. 'I don't really, Tom. I know what you mean, we don't need all this aggravation, doing something right when they want a load of old rubbish.'

'But what about the customer being right? And another thing, there's not going to be anyone there who'd know us, that we'd feel ashamed in front of . . .'

Cathy frowned. 'I know there's truth in what you say, but honestly, I want it to be right for them, all this crowd are going to be eating in restaurants in Dublin the rest of the time they're here, they'll be having a rehearsal party in one hotel and a recovery party in another, they'll *see* that no one except on St Patrick's Day cards in New York eats bacon and cabbage. They'll all be at desperately expensive places. Places that will rob them blind.'

'Heigh-ho,' Tom said. 'Have they booked?'

'Well. I'd hope so, they've been talking about them for six months.'

'We'd better send another e-mail,' he said. 'Should we try pushing a choice of glorious Irish lamb and Irish salmon, we could even send them pictures of that dressed salmon we did a few weeks back, it was gorgeous.'

'It's not draped in shamrocks and Irish flags,' grumbled Cathy.

He was standing beside her cutting vegetables. They had exactly the same stroke, the same rhythm, it was as if they were rowing a boat together. There was something companionable and calming about it all. Even their conversation wasn't demanding, but it was enough to take their minds off their worries; they couldn't brood about Neil and Marcella if there was work to be done, food to be sent out, bills to be paid and the wedding of the century to organise.

James Byrne came in to go over the accounts.

'How did the fashion show go last night?' he asked politely, and was surprised at the curt response.

'Fine,' Tom said.

'Great,' Cathy said.

James Byrne asked no more. He went through the prohibitive cost of renting equipment, and noted the slow progress of dealings with the insurance company, which was really dragging its heels.

'When will Neil be back from Africa?' James Byrne asked innocently.

'Tomorrow,' Tom said.

'Monday,' said Cathy.

Both answers were barked out in exactly the same way as the previous ones. James Byrne looked from one to the other, and hoped that his friend Martin Maguire had not been right when he said that there was a curse on this place. These two, Tom and Cathy, used to be great friends, and the happiest of young people to work with. Today they were like wild animals waiting to pounce.

'The reason I said Monday was it's just that we're going to a hotel tomorrow night,' Cathy said. 'In case you were planning to talk to him about the insurance company.'

'Sorry,' said Tom. 'It's not my business when he comes back.'

James Byrne was mystified. He turned to a different and hopefully less tense subject. 'I want to check that you have work upcoming that will be paid at the time; we can't afford to give anyone ninety days' credit at the moment.'

'Yes, my brother paid half in advance, and when he gets the final wine list on Monday he'll pay at once,' Tom said.

James noted it down.

'And then there's my sister's wedding, they'll pay on the dot too,' Cathy added.

'You both have very admirable families,' James murmured.

'Haywards pays for the bread by the month,' Tom said.

'Mad Minnie pays by the week, but it's only tiny.'

'We'll be doing two jobs at the studio for Ricky, about three hundred pounds' worth; he'd pay on the night if we asked him.'

'There's a funeral next Wednesday; Quentin's will get that money for us fairly quickly.'

'Good, good.' He nodded gravely at their list.

'Are you anxious, James?' Cathy asked suddenly.

'I'm always anxious,' he said with a weak smile.

'But no, is it serious, the cash flow, the situation?'

'Very serious,' said James Byrne. 'Very serious indeed.'

When Cathy got home at lunchtime there was a message on the answering machine saying that Neil's plane would be delayed on Sunday, but that he'd still love to go to the hotel in Wicklow. He'd ring from the airport when they got in, and he loved her.

When Tom got home at lunchtime there was an envelope on the mat. A note from Marcella saying she'd be back about noon, and maybe they might go out somewhere and have a nice cheerful lunch, that she'd ring him first. And that she loved him.

On Saturday lunchtime Geraldine got a phone call which was hard to understand.

'Hallo, is that the dry-cleaner's, it's Frederick Flynn here. I was meant to collect a jacket this afternoon but as it happens I won't be able to, I have to go away suddenly.'

'Freddie?' she gasped.

'Yes, thank you so much for understanding, can I ring you on Monday? Good, good, you've been most obliging.'

'What are you telling me, Freddie?'

He had been coming round in an hour's time. They were going to have two whole nights and a full day together. His wife was going to Limerick.

'Yes, thank you for making special arrangements for me, but I have to go to Limerick.'

'No, Freddie, you don't have to go, you said *she* was going.'

'Again, thank you for being understanding.' He hung up.

*

'Hallo, is that Mr ... er, Muttance Scarlet?'

'Muttie here. Who's that?'

'It's Mr Mitchell, actually.'

'Oh, is that Cathy's father-in-law?' Muttie asked.

'No, it's ... um ... it's ... er ... Simon and Maud's father.'

'Oh, good, how are you, Mr Mitchell? Lizzie and myself, we're here waiting for them to arrive any minute, but they're not here yet.' Muttie thought he wanted to speak to the twins.

'No, and they won't be there, I mean, they weren't able to go.'

'They're not coming?'

'No, I'm sorry, Mr Muttance. Very sorry.'

'And are they sick or something, Mr Mitchell?'

'Yes and no to that; let's say that their mother is not at all well, due to them, so they have to stay here and look after her.'

'And could I have a word with them, do you think Mr Mitchell?'

'That would not be at all appropriate.'

Walter came home to what he hoped might be a late lunch on Saturday. He saw his father sitting alone at the table.

'What's wrong, Father?'

'Just about everything, Walter.'

'Tell me.'

'Your mother's gone back on the drink, those twins have been dancing with things on their shoes all around the house all day driving her madder than ever before, old Barty got into another game and lost so much that he's gone into hiding.'

'But what had he to lose? Old Barty hasn't *got* anything to lose,' Walter said.

'Why do you think I'm so worried? I'm waiting for someone to come for the house,' said Kenneth Mitchell.

'No lunch?' Walter asked.

'Not unless you make some,' Kenneth said.

'Have the children gone out to those mad people in St Jarlath's Crescent?'

'No, I wouldn't let them go, it was their bloody tap-tap-tapping that sent your mother over the top.'

'So where are they?' Walter asked.

'Sulking in their room, I gather ...'

'Better be careful, Father, this army of women police will be after you if you break any of the rules.'

'They're my children, Walter. I've every right to say where they go for Saturday lunch.'

'Yes, Father.'

Walter looked pointedly at a kitchen table on which there was no sign whatsoever of a Saturday lunch being made for anyone.

Shona sat in her flat and read the letter for the thirtieth time. She was being invited to dinner on 19 August by someone she had never thought she would see again.

Lizzie said to Muttie that he must not disturb Cathy: the girl was the colour of a sheet these days. Muttie said you had to fight now or give up for ever. That man who had pressed a pound coin into his hand would walk over them unless they made a stand. Mark his words, the twins wouldn't be allowed to dance at the wedding if they gave in on this one. And the dancing teacher was waiting for them in the kitchen. He was going to ring Cathy this moment. She wasn't at Waterview, she wasn't on her mobile phone. He tried the premises.

Tom Feather had left Stoneyfield. He couldn't bear to stay there in case Marcella came back to check was he all right. He had to be out of the place immediately. He answered the phone. 'You missed Cathy, Muttie, she's taken herself off for the afternoon. On my orders; I told her that it had been too long since she had seen the sea, and she's never even visited James Joyce's tower, so I sent her out to Sandycove to see both and clear her head.'

'That was good of you. Lizzie's been saying she looks tired. It's just that I've a bit of a problem here.'

'Tell me the story,' Tom pleaded. Anything was better than being left with his own thoughts. He listened to the tale.

'I'll go and get them for you,' he said. 'Just give me the address.'

'We don't want to make any trouble,' Muttie said.

'Of course not,' Tom said.

'Good day, Mr Mitchell. I'm Tom Feather, come to collect the children to take them to St Jarlath's Crescent.'

'I'm sorry, I have no idea who you are.' He spoke arrogantly, and a small tic began in Tom's forehead.

'If your son Walter is here, he can verify who I am. I work with your nephew's wife Cathy. I'm sure my name has been mentioned to you, but in the meantime I'm collecting the children, their dancing shoes and their tape recorder as laid down in the terms of your agreement.'

'Agreement? We have no agreement with you, Mr ... er ...'

'With the courts, the social welfare department, with the Mitchell family.'

'I don't think this is any time ...'

'You're so right, there *is* no time, Mr Scarlet is paying the dancing teacher by the hour and there has been a delay already.'

'SIMON! MAUD!' he shouted.

The twins had been listening fearfully and came out into the hall. 'You should have been there ages ago,' he said, mock severely.

'But we couldn't go, we made Mother ill,' Simon said.

'By practising the dancing, you see,' Maud explained.

'Nonsense, of course you didn't. Right, get your shoes, hop into the van and we'll be off.'

'You have absolutely no right to barge into my house ...' Kenneth Mitchell began.

'Take it up with the social worker, and with Cathy and Neil when he gets home tomorrow. I'm only the driver,' said Tom, and slammed out of the house and into the Scarlet Feather van, which he revved up like a maniac. He saw Walter looking at him from behind a curtain at an upper window. 'Hi, Walter,' he shouted. 'Always to the forefront when you're needed, as usual, I see.'

Walter disappeared. The twins were running out, excited but anxious at the same time. It was so cruel and unfair to treat children like this. When he and Marcella had children, they would be loved and praised. He remembered that Marcella had not come home last night. And suddenly there was a taste of bile in his mouth.

'Can I get anything for you, Tom? Tea, coffee, a drink, you're so good to get the children for us.'

'No, I'm just fine thanks, Lizzie, just wanted to do something to take my mind off things.'

'That work is just killing the pair of you, Cathy's pale as a ghost.'

'No, it's not that at all, we both love the work ... it's just ...'

He paused. There were so many things he couldn't say. Like why Cathy was so pale. Like why they had to work so hard because the premises had been done over. Like his own life being in tatters.

'It's just one thing, Lizzie, what time do they leave to go back to that place?'

'Muttie'll take them, it's only a couple of buses, they have to be back before eight.'

'I'll come and pick them up at a quarter to.'

'We can't have you traipsing all over the city with—'

'No, please, it suits me,' and he was gone.

She stood at the window and watched him leave.

'He's had a row with your one, you know, the beautician,' Lizzie said.

'How on earth do you make that out?' Muttie asked.

'Phyllis down the road, she was at the fashion show in Haywards, she said you wouldn't see it in an X-rated movie and that your one, Tom's girlfriend, had hardly a stitch on her.'

'I'm very sorry we didn't go, now that you come to think of it,' said Muttie reflectively.

'I asked Geraldine about it and she said to keep you under lock and chain and not let you near it, so I didn't,' said Lizzie with some pride.

Cathy thought that when Neil came home she would drive him straight down to Holly's hotel in Wicklow, and that they wouldn't stop at Waterview. She took down all Neil's messages for him on the answering machine, she packed him an overnight bag. Now he would have no excuse to pause at home and be distracted. She drove the Volvo to the airport and waited as the arriving passengers came though the gate. There he was: slightly tanned, so there must have been *some* free time. His handsome, animated face was full of the conversation he was having with one of his colleagues. He barely paused when he saw her.

She knew one of his companions, a very earnest man with no sense of humour but an ability to wear the other side down. She recognised another as a politician with an eye to self-advancement; the fourth was a tall, grey-haired man whom she didn't know.

'Good heavens, you're Scarlet Feather!' he said. 'We were at a do you did for Freddie Flynn, simply superb affair, we kept your card. Now this is just the prompting we need ... Neil, why didn't you tell us you were married to this genius?'

'Because then you'd have taken your eye off the ball out there and talked about Cathy's food all the time,' he said. But he put his arm around her shoulder. He was proud of her, she could see. It would all be fine, she must not be so nervous about telling him. They walked hand in hand to the car park.

'I'm dying for a shower,' he said. 'We won't spend long at home, though we'll head straight down to Wicklow, a promise is a promise.'

Tom came out of one cinema in the big complex, went to the desk and bought a ticket for another. The blonde girl in the ticket office smiled at him.

'Glutton for the movies, aren't you?' she said.

'What?' Tom said, startled.

'That's the third you've got today. Are you catching up or something?'

He was so handsome, big shoulders, fair hair, a gorgeous smile. The kind of fellow you hardly ever met these days.

'Yeah, that's what I'm doing. Catching up,' he said.

She got the feeling he wasn't talking to her properly, that he couldn't really see her. She shrugged to herself. Maybe he was on drugs or something. When the cinema finally closed on Sunday there was still light in the sky. It must be the lights of the city causing a glow. Tom drove back to the premises and let himself in again. He wondered was the spy from the insurance company lurking somewhere, waiting for Tom to trash the place a second time. He wondered would he have anything to eat. After all, it was like a child in a sweetshop to be here. The rented freezers were stacked with food, or he could make a simple omelette. But food would taste like sawdust in his mouth. He sat down with his head in his hands. He lay down again on the sofa in the front office. He had slept here once before, in the run-up to the launch party last January. It had been cold then, and he had laid every coat he could find over him. Tonight was warm, and he needed nothing to cover him. He lay in the dark and looked at the ceiling. Soon he would sleep, and the awful, shocking hurt and jealousy would go away. But that hadn't worked at the cinema. The plots of all those movies had meant nothing to him. All he could see was Marcella. Talk to her, talk to her, he told himself. She might well be sitting up in Stoneyfield, anguished, waiting for him to come back. But what would be the use if they were not able to talk? What could he say, or she say that made any difference now? With horror Tom realised that there was nothing to talk about any more. They were way beyond that now.

'Any sign of Tom these days?' Joe asked his parents.

'Didn't you see him on Friday night at this trade fashion show?' Maura Feather sniffed. She still suspected that she had somehow been misled about the nature of that evening, and that neither of her sons had wanted her to attend.

'Yes, of course I did.'

'And isn't that only the day before yesterday?' his mother said.

'Is that all it is? How extraordinary.'

It seemed like a lifetime since the night his brother's great love Marcella had come back so unexpectedly to the hotel with Paul Newton to the party, instead of going to Tom's little dinner in the Italian restaurant. Joe didn't dare to think what Tom had made of it all.

Marcella telephoned four times on Saturday and was puzzled to find the answering machine on on each occasion. He had *known* she wasn't coming back on Friday night. She had *told* him, for heaven's sake. Why the sudden attitude? Maybe he was sitting waiting in Stoneyfield, brooding, sulking, looking like a little boy and needing to be cajoled and patted down.

'Tom,' she called as she went into the flat, but there was no reply.

The place was quiet, too quiet. Also tidy, too tidy. She realised at once that he wasn't at home. She looked around for a note, but there wasn't one. Marcella sat down and took out a cigarette. For a woman who claimed and believed that she didn't smoke, she was getting through rather a lot of cigarettes these days.

'I'm sorry if our dancing made you feel badly, Mother,' Maud said on Sunday.

'Dancing?' Kay Mitchell asked, confused.

'Father said the sound gave you a bad head and made you sick.'

'I don't remember,' she said.

'Could we get you a cup of tea or anything?' Maud wondered.

'That's very nice of you, dear, but why, exactly?'

'Well, you didn't come down for breakfast or lunch or anything, and we thought you might be hungry,' Simon explained.

'No, you are kind, but not at all,' she said.

Simon and Maud went downstairs. Their father was at the kitchen table in a very black humour altogether. Most of his rage was directed against old Barty, who had disappeared without trace, apparently. They knew from the past that it was unwise to ask about food when anyone was upset. So they took a tin of peaches and some bread out to the garden.

'Do you think they're sort of, you know...?' Simon asked Maud.

'You mean, Mother's nerves getting bad and Father about to wander?' Maud spelled it out.

'Something like that,' Simon was upset.

'Don't let him see you crying. Let's go into the shed.'

'It's locked, isn't it?'

'No, Walter went out earlier and left it open. I went in to see was there a skipping rope.'

Simon scooped up the peach tin and scurried into the shed. His father's lectures on behaving like a man and to stop this very poofy dancing were becoming increasingly hard to take.

Tom went for a long run. It was a warm evening, and if he had been able to take in some of the things he saw he might have enjoyed himself. But he didn't see very much. He let himself into the premises. At first he thought he saw someone watching near the courtyard, but decided he must be imagining things. He went in and slept on the big chintz sofa. He slept badly, but had he gone back to Stoneyfield he would not have slept at all.

The phone rang harshly beside her. This would be Freddie now. She would be very cool. It wasn't Freddie Flynn, it was her niece Marian, ringing in floods of tears from Chicago. Through all the sobs she could only understand one word, repeated over and over, and it seemed to be the word 'men', then she heard how useless and unreliable and hopeless they were. Geraldine sighed a deep sigh. Harry was obviously as bad as every other man. They didn't breed them better in Chicago than anywhere else. But gradually it became clear, Harry had *not* run off with someone else and cancelled the wedding. The wedding was still very much on, it was just that Harry and his family hadn't booked the hotels for the rehearsal party and the recovery party, and they were now absolutely at their wits' end about what to do. Geraldine made soothing noises.

'Maybe Cathy will come up with something, she's there on the ground ... She won't have an awful lot else to do, will she?' Marian snuffled and wept.

'Stop crying, Marian, it will all be all right.'

'Geraldine, you're so good at calming people down, how did you get to be a member of our family, answer me that.'

Geraldine stared dumbly across her expensive apartment and wondered about this also.

He reset the machine and left the apartment. He would not come back tonight, he had packed gear that would take him through the weekend. He would not be here to listen to her explanations. He did not want to listen to the fact that it didn't matter that the party meant nothing, and that she was being so good and honest about having told him that she should be getting a pat on the back for it all.

It had taken Shona Burke twenty-four hours to know whether she would accept the invitation or not. She didn't want to go, but the wording was very hard to refuse. She wondered how long it had taken to write. Days, possibly. She could not be expected to respond instantly. She would write her letter carefully too. When other people were out enjoying a summer Sunday, Shona Burke would spend the hours composing her reply.

Geraldine was also in her apartment in the Glenstar building. She could not believe that Freddie had done this to her. Called her in front of his wife and told her that plans had changed. Pretend he was talking to the dry-cleaner's. She would not accept that. Not from anyone. No matter how tense the situation might be at home, no matter how great the pressure from his wife, and possible suspicion, Geraldine was owed more than a travesty of a phone call like that. When Freddie apologised, as he would, when he tried to explain how it seemed the only option open to him, she would listen to him coldly. As Geraldine had told him, she always behaved perfectly, she was the ideal mistress, she wished only the same consideration in return. She turned her wrist so that the jewels on her watch caught the light. Yes, of course he had been considerate to give her this and other gifts, but that wasn't the point. She needed respect as well.

'Ah yes, but a hijack is a hijack. They have showers in Wicklow too. My only hope to get you to myself is if we go straight there . . .'

'But hon, my messages . . .' he wailed.

319

'They're in the glove compartment, all of them, and you can't call anyone on a Sunday anyway,' she said.

And in the afternoon sunshine they drove down to Wicklow, and he told her tales of the conference and the people they met and what had gone well and what had been stymied as usual.

Tom tidied up the apartment at Stoneyfield meticulously. He packed an overnight bag for himself and put it in the back of the van. The phone rang just as he was leaving. He listened to hear who it was. It might just be Marcella. Or it might not. But he would not pick it up. After the click there was a hesitant intake of breath, and then whoever it was hung up. He played it four times to see what he could decipher. It was definitely Marcella.

She was shocked that he had left the phone on the machine. After what she had done, she had expected him to be waiting and ready.

He wondered where she was calling from. He wondered why he had never got that call identify gadget that Cathy had ... What would it have told him? It would have identified which hotel his brother had booked for this thug who had bought Marcella. Would it make it better if he could exonerate all the other hotels in Dublin and just blame one?

Holly's hotel did a big Sunday-lunch trade, it was just the right distance from Dublin. People brought grannies and mothers-in-law there. It always reminded them of their youth, some kind of continuity in a changing world. It had an old-world charm, a lot of chintz and the same waitresses year after year. They checked in at the big, old-fashioned desk with all the keys to the rooms hanging there with their coloured tassels. People were moving to and fro in the hall behind them. Among them, Molly and Shay Hayes. There was a lot of shouting about what a small world it was.

'Having a little anniversary, are you?' Molly wanted to know.

'No, Neil has just come back from Africa, he was at a forum on refugees,' Cathy explained.

'Hope you sorted them out,' Shay said glumly.

'Well, we did our best, Mr Hayes, but you know, there was so much red tape, and these things go so slowly.'

'Still, as long as you put the boot in, we've quite enough of our own in need here, without letting in a lot of people who don't know our ways ...'

Neil's mouth was open in astonishment.

'We've got the room key, Neil, don't you think we should go on up?' Cathy said hastily.

'I don't exactly understand . . .'

'And neither do I, people speaking languages no one can understand getting free houses and filling up the place . . .'

'Mr Hayes . . . Molly . . . you'll have to excuse us, I haven't seen this man of mine for nine whole days. Do you mind if I drag him upstairs with me?'

'Not at all, I'm all for that sort of thing, there's not enough of it about these days,' Shay Hayes said approvingly.

They scampered up the stairs and burst into the big sunny room. Where they could let themselves laugh properly.

'He's a monster, that man . . . I don't know why we're laughing,' Neil said, almost ashamed of himself.

'Listen, you've met a thousand, I've met a thousand, but the hall in Holly's hotel isn't the place to fight it out,' Cathy pleaded. 'Forget him. Tell me all about it, I want to know what you did there from the moment you arrived.'

He sat down in one of their little chintz-covered chairs to tell her, the words tumbling out: the delegates who were expected and did not turn up, the surprise celebrities who came to give support, meetings that were cancelled, the others that started impromptu but grew to be more important. Cathy ordered a bottle of wine and a plate of sandwiches to be sent up to the bedroom as he told of what was being done and what an amazing amount there still was to do. Then he said he'd have the shower that had been promised.

He called out from the bathroom, 'Hardly any point my getting any of that clean gear on, is there? I mean, you'll only be tearing it off me, won't you?'

'Do put something on just for the moment,' she called back. 'And come and sit here, it's so gorgeous.'

He came out, damp and clean, glowing in the dark blue shirt she had packed for him. He was so attractive. No wonder they always wanted him on television as a spokesman. Neil Mitchell was so convincing about everything. She looked up at him as he came over to the table and poured a glass of wine for them both.

This was the time to tell him.

'There's something I want to tell you. I've been wanting so much to tell you.'

He came and sat opposite her and held her hand. He smiled at her. Perhaps he had guessed.

'What do you want to tell me,' he asked.

'Neil, I'm pregnant,' she said.

Neil looked at her stunned. 'Say that again.'

'You heard what I said.'

'You're not,' he said.

'Oh, I am.' She was smiling broadly but searching his face, wanting to see the answering smile and not finding it.

'How did this happen?' Neil asked.

'I think you know how it happened, like the way it always happens.' This wasn't the way she had thought the conversation between them would go.

'Don't play games, you know what we agreed.'

'Yes, I do.'

'So, then, how did this happen?'

'One night when I didn't put in my diaphragm. And when we thought it was a safe time of the month. We *did* discuss it.'

'Oh yes, I'm sure we did, long and logically.'

'Neil!'

'Sorry. I'm afraid that I just can't take it in.'

A small lump of fear began to grow in her heart. 'I thought you'd be pleased.'

'No, you didn't think that, this is not something we agreed.'

She was very frightened now. He had released her hands and pushed his chair back. He had got a great shock. Too great a shock. She knew she must be calm now, and speak in the same unemotional tones as he did.

'Some things are above and beyond agreement,' she said simply.

'No, that's not so.'

'It's the way it feels.'

'Not in an age when we can control fertility, not when two people agreed in Greece that we wanted to be together always, live our dreams despite any obstacles that would be put in our way and without children.'

'We never said permanently without children,' she said.

'No, you're right, but what we *did* actually say was that if we changed our minds we would discuss it, and we haven't discussed it,' he said.

'We are now,' she said, with a feeling of unreality.

He must come round to realising what was happening and how wonderful it was. He must.

'How far is . . .'

'About thirteen, fourteen weeks.'

'So there's plenty of time . . .' he began.

'For us to get used to the idea,' she finished swiftly.

'Why didn't you tell me sooner? You must have known a long time. Why didn't you say anything?'

'I wasn't certain . . .' she began.

'But even if you thought. . . ?'

'There was never time to talk. You always had to go somewhere, I always had to go somewhere . . .' She wanted to be sure to take equal blame for their having no proper time together in their marriage.

'But this is so big. You could have told me . . . surely?'

'I tried several times, but then we had the fuss about Simon and Maud, and you talking about this posting abroad, and then the break-in and all the hassle about that, then the night before you went away you had to go out . . . no, you *had* to go, I know you had. So the days passed. I mean, was I to send you an e-mail about it?'

'Please don't be flippant, I beg you not to do that.'

'Oh, no, I'm not, not in the least bit flippant. Why do you think I got you down here to tell you? I wanted us to talk calmly. I was terrified to try and tell you at home with all that goes on, I needed there to be no interruptions.'

'So nobody knows? Your mother and father or my parents?' he asked.

'Of *course* they don't know,' she said truthfully.

He nodded as if ashamed that he had asked. 'I know. I'm sorry, I shouldn't have asked you that.'

She felt guilty that he didn't know that she had already told Geraldine and that Tom and June had guessed . . . But it wasn't important, not nearly as important as the look on his face. She reached for his hand, but he moved away. Very slightly, but it was definitely withdrawing from her.

'It will take time to get used to it,' she pleaded.

'Time isn't necessarily something we have, hon.'

'What do you mean?' she asked in a voice that seemed to come from a thousand miles away; but she knew what he meant.

'Well, we have to make a decision, don't we?' He had never looked like this when he was facing the mighty Mitchells with the news that he was marrying the maid's daughter. He had never looked like this in the High Court.

'Decision?' she asked, to buy time.

There was a long silence.

'We agreed we wouldn't have children.' He was trying to sound calm.

'And we didn't intend to yet, but . . .' she said.

'But fortunately there's time to reverse this.' He looked at her, his face drawn, his eyes cold.

'You want me to have a termination?' she said.

'I want us to discuss it, yes.'

'We marched together in the Woman's Right to Choose demo,' she said. 'Do you remember the day?'

'Of course I do, and that's exactly what I'm saying. It *is* a right to choose.' Neil believed this passionately.

'The *woman's* right,' Cathy said in a small voice.

The pause seemed very long. He looked at her, shocked. 'You mean, we're not in this together, suddenly it's all what *you* want, not what *we* want? Where's my right to choose whether or not to be a father, tell me that?' He was trembling as he spoke.

'That's not the way it is, Neil.'

'But it *is*,' he cried. 'We agreed that night in Syntagma Square, that night we decided to be together for ever that we would not have children . . . We agreed it, nobody put a gun to anyone's head . . .'

'We didn't mean never,' she pleaded. 'It just happened, that's it.'

'We have time, plenty of time to decide now, with total safety.'

'I don't believe you.' She was aghast.

'I'm not a monster, we were in this together, years ago, that would have been it, an accident, and of course I don't blame *you* for it . . . It was down to both of us . . . But there is a chance to alter that, rectify things, and then if we do want a child at a later stage, then it should be something we would plan for together and agree.'

'Aren't you at all glad? Aren't you in any way pleased that . . .' She didn't trust her voice to say any more.

She stroked her stomach and he leaped up and went to the window. 'It's not fair, Cathy, it's not fair, it's not our child yet. Don't talk of it like that. This is only something that could *become* a child, you *know* that.'

She couldn't say anything. The tiny mouthful of sandwich she had eaten ages ago seemed lodged at the base of her throat, as if it might choke her. She felt almost dizzy at what was unfolding before her. He didn't even want to discuss how they would manage with the baby. Neil didn't want the baby at all. There was going to be no discussion. He seemed to be saying that because she wasn't agreeing instantly to a termination, she had somehow broken a promise.

'Say something, please, don't just sit there, say something,' he asked with his back to her as he looked out on Holly's hotel where people were walking in the late afternoon sunshine. But there was too much to say, so she couldn't speak.

'You know that the job they're offering me was dependent on us not having children?' he said.

'I don't believe you, that's not a moral or legal basis on which to offer a job or to accept one. You would be the first to say that,' she said with spirit.

'Let's put it this way, I had already told them that children were not in the frame, and so that was a deciding factor in my favour.'

The silence was longer this time.

'I need some fresh air, I'm going out to the gardens for a while.'

'Don't go, please,' she cried.

'I tell you, my head is bursting. I need to be on my own and walk a bit, get something into my lungs. I feel like I'm choking.'

'Don't leave me, not now, not just now.'

'I'm not leaving you.' He was irritated. 'I need to breathe, that's all.'

He came towards her and stroked her cheek. 'I wouldn't leave you, it's just I've had a shock. I need time to think about it. I'm not running away. I'll be back.'

He was gone. She saw him walking along the paths, past the monkey-puzzle trees, his head thrown back, biting his lips, so striking and handsome, even though he always laughed that away and said he was too small to be good-looking. He went as far as the kitchen gardens, and she saw him in the distance bending over something to read a label. She sat in the bedroom, which had seemed so beautiful when they had come into it less than an hour ago. The ice chinked as it melted in the bucket under the bottle of wine, and the tears fell down her face. She had not believed that this would ever be possible, but she knew that no matter how many hours of discussion they might have tonight when he came back calmer and more reasonable, she would not choose to give up this child that she carried. It could not have appeared at a worse time for everyone, but that wasn't the point. It just wasn't a theory any more, not a case or a constitutional amendment. It was her baby.

*

It seemed a lot darker outside when she heard the door of the room open. But she had no idea how long he had been gone. He seemed different somehow. Not bewildered, not shocked any more. As if this were one of the many crises and dramas that formed part of his everyday work and the kind of practice he had chosen at the Bar. He sat opposite her at the little table, and though he smiled in an attempt at reassurance, she felt a little as if they were lawyer and client.

'Cathy, if you have the baby, who will look after it?' he asked. Gentle, but very deliberate.

'Well I will, of course.'

'But the business?'

'Well, of course I'll make arrangements.' She knew her voice sounded flustered.

'You can't take a baby into the premises to lie there all day in the middle of your cooking.'

'No, but there will be ways ... We'll find them.'

'What ways? A nanny?'

'Well, yes, if we can afford one.'

'And where would she sleep?'

'I don't know, you can get people by the day.'

'But as I see it, most of your functions will be in the evening, so what happens then?'

'Well, the odd time I suppose you could ...'

'How can I commit myself to doing that? I have to work at night, too.'

'We'll work it out when it happens.'

'We can't do that. We have to plan now. I'll be away from home a lot, more anyway. Apart altogether from the big job, I will have to go abroad quite a lot.'

'We'll manage.'

'Like you've managed up to now?'

'I don't know what you mean.' She was alarmed.

'Like the business is in great debt and danger, like you are already worked off your feet paddling to keep up, like there's a new crisis every day. What do we do if there's a child to consider?'

'So you're asking that there should be no child to consider?' She spoke carefully.

He answered just as carefully. 'That is most definitely *not* what I'm asking, Cathy. I have no right, no right whatsoever to deny you a child, and I will not dream of doing so.'

He was very calm, cold almost. This is what his walk among the roses, hollyhocks and lupins of Holly's hotel had achieved for him. The kind of honest clarity that always stood him in such good stead in every cause he had ever fought.

'So there will be no discussion about whether we have the child or not?'

'You obviously want to have the child, and I am not going to stand in your way. It wouldn't be a moral or right thing to do.'

Too measured, too calm. She felt frightened. 'Will it always be like this, do you think, where you will be putting up with the situation, and having our baby there will be something on sufferance?'

'I don't think it should be like that at all. But if we are going to have another person in the house we must prepare, we must make contingency plans.'

'You sound very distant. Very remote.'

'Believe me, that's not what I mean to be, it's just that we *must* go into this with our eyes open ... Yes, of course I wish it had happened at a time when we were ready in every sense to give a child a better welcome ... a better lifestyle, but it hasn't, so we must decide what to do. Like how much maternity leave will you take?'

'Three months, like anyone.'

'And will Tom agree to this?'

'It's the law, but he would anyway, I'm certain.'

'We'll have to move house. Waterview is so unsuitable for a child,' he said.

'Not yet, not for a baby ... it doesn't matter where a baby lives ... Later we might think...?'

'But I have committed myself to work in my area, I'm not taking big insurance cases or conveyancing just to make money.'

'We don't need all that much money. We don't need a big house like Oaklands, we don't want one of those gigantic prams like you were reared in, we don't have to go to a big expensive fee-paying school. Children don't need all kinds of luxury or royal treatment, they need to be loved.'

'We have had a good start. If we have a child, we must give that child a good start too.'

'My mam and dad raised six of us in St Jarlath's Crescent, and did so with no money and no problems.'

'Well, hardly with *no* problems,' he contradicted.

'What do you mean?'

'You are always railing that your mother had to go down on her hands and knees to scrub my mother's floors and put up with dogs' abuse while she did it.'

'But I won't have to do that, and neither will you.'

'I suppose I'm just not ready,' he said.

'Neither am I. But loads of people haven't been ready, and look at the great fist they made of it.'

'I'm not a monster, why am I being made to feel like one?'

'I'm not making you into a monster.' She was gentle.

'It's just ... it's just...' He couldn't find the words.

She said nothing.

'Listen, I haven't even asked you anything about all this ... How do you feel? Have you been sick...?'

'It comes and goes...'

'And what do *you* want to happen?'

'What's happening now, for us to talk about it calmly and sanely without getting upset.'

'What's there to talk about ...? I mean it.'

'What do you mean?'

'Let's be logical, we didn't want children, now you're pregnant.' It was very chilly, very clinical, the way he said it.

'We have been missing each other a lot recently ...' he went on. 'I misunderstood the depth of your feeling about the company, and I thought that you'd eventually see sense about it, come abroad with me because it was such a great posting ... and you misunderstood. Once you were pregnant, you thought that I'd automatically come round to being delighted to be a father. We both got it very wrong.'

Suddenly she couldn't help it any more, the remorseless logic, the working out where praise and blame were due. She felt the sobs coming on and couldn't stop them. He watched her aghast as her shoulders heaved with the misery that went right through her. It was impossible to hear what she was saying; the words were drowned with all the sobbing.

'Please, Cathy...' He reached out to touch her. He hadn't expected this, he had been trying to sum it up as accurately as he could. He had been struggling not to blame her and say that he felt a sense of betrayal. He thought it was unjust that he had been somehow bypassed on their bargain, but the rights of a birth mother were obviously more important, so he had tried to concentrate on the practicalities, and now judging by her weeping that had not been right either. He wished he could understand what she was saying. And Cathy wept and wept, saying the same thing over and over. He didn't want the child. There was no instinctive, loving response to the thought of being a father. There was no way she could end this pregnancy, because even if she did, and suppose she got over it, she still would remember this day and how he had proved not to be a loving, caring, good person after all, only a selfish one determined to get all that he could achieve in his career. She wept more because she could not and would not believe this of Neil, the man she loved so much. He watched her, his eyes misting with confusion, he was doing his best for her, being as fair and just as anyone could be under the circumstances. His future was going to change because she had not kept faith and honoured straight dealing. He had agreed to go ahead with it, and then just sorting out a few details had reduced her to this state.

'I've never seen you cry like this before. Please, please stop,' he begged.

She made a great effort, and he passed her a box of tissues. She wiped her eyes and blew her nose.

'I'm not saying anything out of any badness, I just couldn't hear what you were saying,' he said. She blew her nose again. Tentatively he offered her some wine and she drank it. He moved her hair out of her eyes and put his arm round her shoulder.

'Cathy, hon?'

'Okay. I'm okay now.'

A determination as strong as she had felt all those years ago in Greece came over Cathy. They had been through too much, conquered so many problems, they would not fail now. Not now that the best part, a child, was on the way.

'When I told you I had something to tell you ... what did you think I was going to say?' she asked, sniffing a bit.

'I don't know,' he was evasive.

'Please tell me.'

'Well, I think I believed you were going to say to me ...' he hesitated.

'Tell me.'

'I thought you were going to say you'd decided to leave Scarlet Feather and come with me wherever I went,' he said.

And outside it was dark in the garden and the smells of cooking came from downstairs.

*

The man who was watching the premises thought that he had got lucky. The big guy who owned it was letting himself in. At this time of night, at a weekend. They had been totally right, it was, of course, all his own doing; he was going to do further destruction now. He crept up to the window to see it begin before he called for back-up. These insurance cases were all the same; they had to have heavy proof. He kept in the shadows; he wanted to watch it begin, but he didn't want to be seen himself and there might be more than one of them.

Marcella lay on the bed in Stoneyfield. He would have to come home sometime. So he hadn't wanted to go out to lunch; maybe she should not have suggested it to him. But he wasn't going to stay out all night, every night. This much she knew. Where would he go? He was too proud to go round to Ricky's studio apartment. He would never go to his parents in Fatima. He wouldn't want to go within a million miles of Joe at this time. He would come home. When she woke later and he still wasn't there, she began to worry. He was so headstrong, but he'd never have done anything foolish. Marcella couldn't sleep any more. She went out on the street and walked until she saw a cruising taxi. She asked it to leave her in a street near the premises, then she walked quietly down the lane and opened the gate into the cobblestoned yard. There was a man in a parked car outside, but he didn't seem to take any notice of her. She looked in at the window and, peering in the very early dawn, she saw a figure lying on the divan. Thank God. And how foolish of him. They would have to talk sometime; why keep putting it off? She rang the bell and he didn't stir. She could see that his eyes were open but he made no move. He must have known she was there. 'Tom,' she called. 'Please, Tom, don't leave me here. Tom, let me in.' He never moved. 'There was nothing else I could do,' she cried. And then finally, 'I never betrayed you. I told you everything, I was so honest with you. I can't understand why you won't talk.' After half an hour, cold and frightened, she left and got another taxi back to Stoneyfield.

The man who had been watching the premises was mystified. That big guy had not gone in to break the place up, he had gone in to sleep on a sofa, for God's sake. And what was more peculiar still was that one of the most beautiful women ever seen in Dublin had been hammering on the door trying to get in. Any normal man would have let her in straight away. This guy was weird.

Tom got up an hour later, went to Haywards and made the bread. Was it only two days since he had been in this building? Making the Saturday morning batch; clearing up after the fashion show while still half drunk and shell-shocked. It seemed like for ever, and yet he realised that he was only talking about a mere forty-eight hours. He was afraid that Marcella might try to confront him in the kitchen, but she wouldn't risk it. She couldn't afford a public scene so shortly after her triumph. It was strange, that whole business last night.

Back at the premises he was surprised to find Cathy already there.

'Was Neil delighted?' he asked.

'Yes I think he was,' Cathy said.

'Of course he was, anyone would be delighted to be having a baby with you,' Tom said.

'Yes, well, he was startled, that's for sure.' Cathy didn't catch Tom's eye.

It obviously hadn't gone well, this announcement. It was so much less than he had expected, Tom felt he should say something. 'I suppose it was a bit of a shock as well,' Tom was soothing.

She looked at him thoughtfully. 'Yes, it was a bigger shock than I realised.'

'But he'll be delighted when the shock bit dies down,' Tom reassured her.

'Of course he will,' Cathy said with a smile.

Tom might be right. Neil could well become excited about the baby. Eventually. He had been so kind last night in Holly's after her weeping fit, so gentle, and he had put away the interrogating manner. They had talked long and calmly last night, and got up very early to drive back through the sunshine of County Wicklow, getting to Dublin well before the traffic had started. Neil had driven leaning over to pat her arm occasionally. Yes, when the shock died down, as Tom said, it would be fine.

'We decided that we wouldn't tell anyone about it yet.' she explained to Tom. 'So you see . . .'

He understood immediately. 'So the two clairvoyants you work with will keep quiet, is that what you're saying?'

'For a bit. I would be grateful. And Tom, thank you *so* much for sorting Simon and Maud out on Saturday. Dad left a message on our machine about it; you really are a hero.'

'He's such a shit, that man Mitchell.'

'Oh, don't get me started on him, I've never wanted to hit anyone quite so much.'

'It's monstrous that they should have those children, but don't get *me* started on that either.' He paused, and she knew he was going to say something important. 'And since you don't ask, which is very good of you, I haven't seen Marcella since Friday and I might sleep here a couple of nights, if that's all right with the company.' He spoke lightly, but she could see his pain. Quietly, she put her arms around him.

Eventually, she said, 'That's fine with the company. Let's open up the e-mails and see what we've got.'

He moved away as she started up the computer, more grateful than he could ever say at her understanding and lack of questions at this raw time. Then he heard her scream.

'God Almighty, I don't believe this!'

'What is it?'

He came running. Together they read that Marian was throwing the whole wedding party on their mercy for a rehearsal and a recovery party because Harry and his stupid relations had not thought that you needed to book anything in Dublin. Sleepy little backwater Dublin, where nobody needed to make reservations. And they had to be booked into somewhere classy for a dinner and a lunch at the height of the tourist season, and they had to find the places in just under three weeks.

'It's impossible,' Cathy said. 'That's all there is to it. Great stupid eejits.'

'We'll have to cater them all ourselves,' said Tom. 'It's just as simple as that.'

'Now you're the one that's mad! We can't do that.'

'Why not? It'll make us some badly needed money, and it will take our minds off other things,' he said.

Walter was furious that they had played in the shed.

'It wasn't playing, it was dancing,' they said defensively.

'That's my shed, stay out of it,' Walter ordered.

'I didn't know it was your shed, Walter, honestly, I thought it belonged to all of us,' Simon said.

'Yes, well, you know now, and give over this dancing business, it's really annoying Dad. He might go away again.'

'Not over our dancing?' Maud was wide-eyed.

'No, but he keeps saying that old Barty's gone to England, and he might follow him.'

'And would he?'

'He just might.'

'And what about Mother?'

'Mother's been away with the fairies for days now, you must know that,' Walter said scornfully.

'And would her nerves get bad and she'd go to hospital again if Father went away?' Maud wondered.

'You can bet on it, so try to cut down on the dancing where anyone can hear you, will you? Okay?'

'Sure, Walter.'

'And no whingeing and whining to Sara, either. It was quite bad enough asking that Tom Feather to stick his nose in on Saturday.'

'We didn't ask him, honestly,' Maud said.

'Muttie rang Cathy and he took the message, that was all,' Simon said.

They were so obviously telling the truth that Walter left it. 'The only hope of keeping this place going at all is not to tell Sara long stories, do you understand?'

'Yes,' the twins said doubtfully.

Hannah Mitchell telephoned her daughter in Canada.

'No, Ms Mitchell has taken a long weekend with her partner.'

'Oh, she's a partner in the company. Now isn't that wonderful,' Hannah said.

'No, I mean she and her partner have gone to their chalet on the lake.'

'And when will she be back?' Hannah asked. She knew nothing of any chalet on any lake.

'Tonight I guess, tomorrow they're both back in the store.'

Hannah hung up, delighted with this news, and couldn't wait to spread it around. There had been so little about Amanda to boast about recently; in fact, so little communication at all.

Neil called into Oaklands on Monday at about six o'clock and told them about the conference in Africa. Hannah listened impatiently until she got a chance to deliver her own good news from abroad.

'Did you hear, Amanda has been made a partner in that bookshop,' she said.

'That's pretty big. When did that happen? Did she say?' Jock was pleased.

'Well, no, I didn't catch her herself, I called and they said she and her partner were taking a long weekend, and she must have got some kind of executive chalet by the lakes.'

Neil swallowed his drink hastily. He must head his mother off at the pass before she said anything further that would be seen as pathetic later. 'They're notorious in stores for getting things wrong. Let's wait till we talk to Amanda before we tell anyone,' he said.

'But the girl wouldn't have said—'

'You see, she might have meant with a partner, meaning her *partner*, a boyfriend, a girlfriend, you know the way people say partner nowadays.'

'But she meant in the bookshop . . . I know she did.'

'She may have a partner *in* the bookshop.'

'But if Amanda had a boyfriend she'd have told us.'

'Not necessarily, Mother,' Neil said. 'You have to be sure in your own mind, you have to be sure that everyone's ready to hear.'

'Well I'm always dying to hear about any boyfriends or partners or whatever they're called now. Where's all the secrecy?' Hannah was annoyed.

'Let's wait, Mother, I feel sure it's best.'

He saw his father looking at him quizzically, but Jock asked no questions.

It took them all day to find what they kept calling Suitable Venues. For the rehearsal dinner they would have the basement in Ricky's studio. For the recovery lunch they would use Geraldine's apartment. They checked their watches: it was six o'clock. Good time to contact Chicago. They would send menus later, in a day or two, but for the moment Marian and Harry were to consider it done. They faxed it off and decorated the writing paper with wedding bells and horseshoes and good-luck charms to cheer the couple up. Marian phoned about five minutes later, in tears of gratitude. Cathy was an angel, a saviour, an uncanonised saint, and undoubtedly Marian's favourite sister, and Harry's family were just dying to see the menus so that they could make their choice, and truly money was no object, so don't hold back . . .

'Do you get any message from that conversation, Cathy?' Tom asked when it had been repeated to him.

'Yes I do, I'm afraid,' she admitted.

They looked at each other and laughed as they both chanted together: 'They want the menus *now*.'

At six o'clock on Monday Geraldine realised that she and Freddie Flynn were now finally over. He had not called at all during the weekend, after his hurtful and devious message letting her know that he would not be joining her. She had steeled herself not to call him all day. She had forced herself to believe that the best course of action would be to be pleasant, cool and have no screaming recriminations. To prove that she knew how to behave.

Freddie called into Glenstar and pressed the bell. Nobody ever had a key to Geraldine's place.

'Freddie?' she sounded pleased but surprised.

'I was wondering. . . ?'

'You didn't telephone.' It was an unbreakable rule.

'No, but this time I thought we might . . . I mean, if it's not convenient I could . . .'

'Certainly. Come on up, Freddie.'

He sat down and twisted his hands. Pauline had been told that he was seen holding hands with a woman, and she had been impossible to console. He just had to go with her to Limerick. Prove the gossipmongers wrong, for one thing; to reassure her for another. Geraldine nodded distantly and pleasantly as if Freddie were talking about a different species. And then it appeared that when they were in Limerick, Pauline had said she was lonely and frightened that he might leave her and she wanted him to come home early after work every day. Geraldine nodded graciously to this request.

'So you see . . .' he said.

'I see, Freddie, please believe me, I see.'

He sat there awkwardly in the silence. She made no mention of the watch. That had been given at a time when he had thought she was the loveliest woman in Ireland and would not have cared if his wife had discovered. It was a gift from a different part of their relationship. It would be crass and commercial even to *suggest* that it might be returned.

'I can't tell you how I'll miss you,' he said.

'And I you, Freddie.'

'You deserve much better than me, of course,' he began to bluster now, trying to joke his way out of the situation, which was that he was telling her the affair was over. She remained utterly cool.

'Now don't say that, don't sell yourself short, and you'll always, I hope, be a wonderful friend.' She uncurled her legs from the sofa and stood up ... a sign for him to leave. Freddie Flynn moved to the door with an overpowering sense of relief that there had been no scene. She kissed him gently on the cheek.

'Good luck always, dear Freddie,' she said.

'You're a woman in a million, Geraldine. I just wish ...'

'Goodbye, Freddie,' she said softly, and went in, closing the door behind her swiftly. She stood in her empty apartment, tense and taut with rage and annoyance. Of all of them, she had liked Freddie best. He wasn't as bright as Peter Murphy, or as sophisticated as some of the others, but he was fun to be with. She thought he would be there always. What had made Pauline confident enough to get him back on her terms? Pauline had a lot of family, brothers and sisters, and of course she had Freddie's children. Pauline had respectability; the future, the past. It was, in the end, better than having great legs, a big flat in Glenstar and designer clothes. Disappointing, but true.

So when Tom and Cathy had phoned asking whether they could stage the ridiculous Day After party or whatever it was in Glenstar, Geraldine said yes. It would serve a number of functions. It would please her niece Marian, who seemed to be having a nervous breakdown in Chicago. And it would take her mind off the faithless Freddie Flynn.

Marcella didn't know what to do after work on Monday. She delayed as long as possible in the salon, but then she had to make up her mind. She went back to Stoneyfield eventually and went through the whole ritual, telephoning in advance and getting the answering machine, ringing on the apartment intercom and getting no reply, then going into the flat. He hadn't been back. It was Monday evening, and Tom Feather had not returned to his own apartment. He must be going to live at the premises from now on. This was idiotic. This was *his* place, for heaven's sake, his flat, and he had just abandoned it. Her note remained untouched on the table, the same carton of skimmed milk stood in the refrigerator. It was a cold, dead place. She shivered a little, packed a grip bag with some of her essential things and wrote a second note. 'Tom, it's your place, stop sleeping on a sofa in the premises. Come home. I'll go away if you want me to; all you have to do is tell me why. Face to face. I love you. Marcella.' Then she dialled Scarlet Feather.

Cathy went back to Waterview that evening, her head swimming with arrangements and plans for the wedding. They had come up with such inventive ideas, she and Tom. Marian would be delighted with them. Neil was home.

'You can't keep working these hours, you're not able to do it,' he said. He was very concerned for her.

'No, I'm fine, nothing a big mug of tea won't cure,' she said.

'Okay, I'll make one. Do you have a pain in your back?'

'A bit now and then, not much. Why do you ask?'

'I read a bit about it in a book.'

Her heart soared. The shock bit was wearing off; the father bit must be starting now. 'I went to Oaklands today.'

'You didn't tell them, did you?' Telling Hannah was going to be something that had to be planned, if anything had to be planned.

'Of course not, but I was looking at those pictures Mother had on the piano, of Manda and myself when we were children. She had so much help in the house then, and no job, and look at all you have to do. It's just not fair.'

'It's not important what she had back then.' Cathy couldn't care less about the past.

But he was persistent. 'And it was easier for men, the way privileged people lived then too. When my father came home from work he could just close himself away in a study to work, and whichever baby it was was brought off to a nursery not to disturb him. I'm only saying it's just the system some people have, everything dead easy for them, and others just don't.'

'Stop trying to rewrite history, and anyway, your father was never home to go to a study or a nursery. Wasn't he out on the first tee two minutes after he left the office?'

'But it's the principle of it,' Neil insisted.

'And my father had six of us crawling over him in the kitchen and it never distracted his mind for one minute from what was running next day at the Curragh.' Cathy kept it light.

Neil made the tea, but he was still brooding. He talked on about his mother and father, how they were totally accustomed to their lifestyle and thought it their right, how his mother had misunderstood Amanda and her partner being at a chalet on the lake, how

Sara had been on to say that some rich old man had died and left his Georgian house to an organisation for the homeless and all the neighbours were up in arms. The gross selfishness of this city was getting to him. Where he had been in Africa people had different priorities; he had come face to face with people who really did have generous and liberal attitudes and voted in socially responsible governments. There was this girl from Sweden he had met, and she would frighten you how she talked of how the rich paid taxes there to make sure that nobody would go without the best medical care . . . She looked at him for a long time as he talked.

'Scarlet Feather,' Tom said.
    'Tom, don't hang up, please.'
    'Marcella.' His voice was flat.
    'Can I come round there and talk to you?'
    'No, I'm just going out actually.'
    'Are you going home?'
    'No.'
    'I've left you a note there, it's on the table beside one I left you yesterday.'
    'It doesn't matter, Marcella.'
    'But we can't leave it like this . . .' she said in disbelief.
    'Why not?' he asked, and hung up. He sat and looked at the phone for a long time. What on earth did she expect him to say?
    In Stoneyfield Marcella sat and looked at the phone. He'd have to talk sometime, even to say goodbye. Why couldn't he talk now?

'Geraldine, that never came from a charity shop?' Lizzie Scarlet held the brand new outfit from Haywards up so that she could look at it again.
    'It *did*, Lizzie,' her sister lied straight to her face. 'You just don't know where to look. These dames wear something once, they think their bum looks big in it or their girlfriend sniggered at it and that's it. Out.'
    'It's gorgeous,' said Lizzie, stroking the dress and coat in a dark grey silky material. 'I could be the bride myself in that, not just the mother of the bride.'
    'You might meet a rich American, Lizzie, and then we'd never see you again,' Geraldine teased her.
    Muttie looked up from his newspaper. 'Lizzie doesn't want a rich American,' he said firmly. 'She wants Hooves and myself in all our

glory and with all our disadvantages, isn't that right, Hooves?' Hooves gave a bark of approval.

'Hooves says you're quite right,' said Lizzie. 'He says what more could a woman want than what I've got?' And for the first time in her whole life Geraldine felt a pang of envy for the sister who had married a no-hoper and scrubbed floors all her life.

Tom and Cathy had worked very hard on the wedding plans. They now had three events to cater for, and had hired many more staff. The Friday night was going to be a theme party: Ricky's basement would be done up as a speakeasy in Prohibition times. They would paint bars on the windows and arrange that there was something that looked like a peephole, a little door you pulled back to see who was there. Guests would be given a password to let them in. Then Ricky had big developing equipment which could have labels stuck on saying Bathtub Gin; there would be Al Capone pictures on the walls and reference to the St Valentine's Day massacre; they would have the Chicago greats in jazz on the music centre and everyone would be so pleased with the way they had been made to feel at home. The food itself would be delicious ribs of beef, Chicago-style, and some kind of chocolate-mint ice cream that the recipe books said was a real favourite in that city. It was so hard to learn about Chicago food, because any recipe book or website they looked up seemed to say it was an ethnic cuisine with strong Polish overtones.

'Polish cooking's nice,' Tom said. 'Lots of red cabbage and sour cream. Should we try some of that, do you think?'

'Maybe they want to get away from it,' Cathy said. 'We'll check when they ring back later on.'

'They were a bit silent about the menus,' Tom said after two days had passed and there was no response from America.

Cathy agreed. 'And there was I being called a saint, an angel, a genius, but now they don't even bother to acknowledge all our hard work.'

'Should we ring them?' Tom wondered. 'We'll have to get going on the props as soon as possible.'

'I almost hate drawing them on us, I know it's silly. In more normal times I'm all for doing the hard thing first and dealing with it,' Cathy said.

'Listen, you're allowed to have silly feelings – at least you haven't been eating lumps of coal as we make the food,' Tom said.

'No, I mustn't get any special treatment, it's a natural process – women years ago had their babies and just got on with it, no one indulged them.'

'Maybe,' Tom said. 'All this male solidarity, going to the pub and getting drunk to stay out of the way . . .'

'Oho, you're all fine and noble now because you don't have to be there, wait until you're going to be a father, we'll have a reality check.'

He flicked a spoon of dough at her and she threw a handful of raisins back at him.

'Now, look what you've done, I'll have to take them out of the tomato bread,' he complained.

'Could be the start of a world-class recipe,' Cathy laughed.

'Will Neil be at the birth?' Tom asked.

'Yes,' Cathy said firmly. 'Whether he knows it or not, he'll be there. Now which of us will ring Marian?'

'Since you're not having any special favours, then I think you should,' said Tom picking the last raisins out of his mixing bowl and eating them.

Talking to Marian was like talking to an entirely different person than the one she'd spoken to two days previously. She was alternately tongue-tied, confused, hissing in a whisper, or else she was speaking in a false, high-pitched tone about how grateful they all were for all that was being done.

'Here, I can't make head nor tail of this,' Cathy said eventually. 'Tom, will you talk to her, please.'

Tom didn't do much better; he kept shrugging at Cathy. 'Is she drunk, or high, do you think?' he wrote down on a pad beside the phone. Cathy had to get up and move away to hide her fit of laughing at the very thought. Finally Tom had a brilliant idea. 'Could I talk to Harry about it all, do you think? Maybe he and I could sort it out, man to man.'

'Harry's here,' said Marian in her normal voice. 'He came into my office to discuss the situation, I'll put him on now.'

'Harry, I'm Tom Feather. I'm no relation of anybody. If you don't like our menus, you tell me now and we'll send you more. I was wondering about Polish food myself, big soups, dumplings. Just say it, Harry.'

'Tom, I'm going to say it: everyone here has had to go and lie down even at the thought of a speakeasy party, at the mention of St Valentine's Day, and the whiff of bathtub gin.'

'I see. We thought you'd love it.'

'No, it would be like having the worst theme party you could dream up ... something about the IRA with bombs and things.'

'Or corned beef and cabbage,' Tom said quickly.

'I hear where you're coming from, Tom.'

'So we trade over this, okay? No speakeasy, no corned beef.'

'It's a done deal,' said Harry.

Sara called quite unexpectedly, and did an inspection of the house. Eyes watched as she opened the refrigerator, the washing machine, looked at the food shelves and checked the laundry in the airing cupboard.

'Maud and Simon, can I ask you to go out into the garden and practise your tennis for a little bit? I see you have a net set up out there; you could get ready for your next lesson.'

'We don't have lessons now,' Simon said.

'They were too dear,' Maud explained.

'And I think the tennis teacher went away, didn't she?' Kenneth Mitchell said.

'No, just for a weekend,' Maud explained.

Sara's mouth was in a hard line. 'All the more reason to practise then,' she said, in such a falsely cheerful voice that the twins recognised the hidden threat it involved to everyone and scurried out into the garden. Sara called out after them. 'When I'm finished here, I'll come out and play each of you separately. We'll do the best of seven points. Do me good to have a little exercise. Okay?'

They thought that sounded great, and in the silence of the house Kay and Kenneth Mitchell sat and listened to the children laughing and groaning over shots missed and shots achieved, and to the pit-pat of the tennis ball on the dry, uncared-for lawn.

'Correct me if I'm wrong, but I don't think anyone invited you to play tennis with my children in my house,' Kenneth Mitchell said, deciding to attack first.

'Correct *me* if I'm wrong, but you don't seem to have the remotest idea of how serious your position is, and how you are both on the verge of losing your children. If the fears that I have about their welfare form a substantial part of my report and are accepted, they could be out of your hands by the end of the month.'

*

341

'Can we dance at all three parties, do you think?' Simon asked Muttie back at St Jarlath's Crescent later that day.

'I have nothing to do with the arrangements, son; as you get older you learn to stay out of all that side of things. It's a kind of thing men do.'

'We'd have to have separate dances for each one – it might be very hard. But I wouldn't want to let them down, the Americans.'

'It's probably the kind of thing Cathy would know about,' Muttie said thoughtfully.

'Sure. Muttie, do you know why we got to come here to St Jarlath's Crescent as often as we like?'

'I don't, and I tell you that another thing I never do is question anything at all that turns out better than you expect. Remember that day last week when I lost my concentration down at the office, and I put an each-way instead of a win? I was so disappointed, and I'd nearly thrown away the ticket, when didn't one of my associates down at the office remind me I'd done it for a place as well? I couldn't believe it but I never questioned it; I think that's usually the best way to go.'

Simon thought about it. 'You're probably right, Muttie; it's just that if you knew *why* people do things, you'd be in a better position to make them do them again. You see, Father suddenly changed his mind about everything. I'd love to know what it was that Sara said which made everything different.'

'We never know half the things that go on in the world.' Muttie shook his head.

'But honestly, Muttie, Father brought a tray with lemonade out to the tennis court for us and Sara, and Mrs Barry is back again, so she must have been paid, and the tennis lessons are on, and we are in charge of washing our own clothes in the machine but Mrs Barry irons them, and Mother gets up and gets dressed. And we can come here on the bus whenever we want, like whenever you're free, I mean, and Maud and I think we must have done something right to make it all good, but we can't think what it could have been.'

Shona came into the Haywards kitchen long before the store opened officially.

'You're spying on me and trying to steal trade secrets.'

'Lord no, little microwave meals for one, that's me.'

'I doubt it.' He concentrated on his work as he talked. 'Pour us a coffee, will you, Shona?' he called.

They talked companionably about a lot of things. But neither of them asked the question they wanted to ask. Tom didn't enquire whether Marcella still worked in the nail salon, or if she had already gone across the water to start working on this new modelling contract that she had earned herself. She had left one more note before moving her things from the flat in Stoneyfield. Marcella had left behind her a watch, a bracelet and a leather-bound book of love poems. Her note was short.

'I still love you, and I cannot believe that you will let four years of our life end without a discussion. But then I cannot keep asking you the same question every day. If you want to tell me why we can't talk . . . then we both work at the moment in the same store. You might be able to tell me there, if not here. You owe me that much. Just one conversation.'

But it wouldn't be a conversation, it would only be two people sitting there, one saying that something mattered and one saying that something didn't. As the days went by Tom had steeled himself not to call the salon and discover whether she was there or not. It had become a matter of pride with him that he must not enquire. Shona for her part wanted to ask Tom to tell her every single thing he could about Mr James Byrne, retired chartered accountant and present-day part-time bookkeeper to Scarlet Feather. She would like to have asked was he a cheerful person or very intense, did he love music and go to concerts? Did he have many friends, or was he alone? Had they ever been in his apartment? Did he live alone or with anyone else? But she had kept her own counsel for so long it was hard to ask anyone else about such private things. Even someone as open and approachable as that Tom Feather, who was obviously broken-hearted over his silly girlfriend Marcella.

'What are you going to wear at the wedding?' asked Geraldine.

'A huge maternity tent with a white collar and flat shoes,' Cathy said.

'No, be serious; and talking of being serious, when are you going to tell your mother that she's going to be a granny again?'

'Soon, soon, just let her get the wedding out of her hair first,' Cathy pleaded. 'And let me get through that too, as it happens. We have so much work on nowadays, you just wouldn't believe it. I'm afraid to leave Tom out of my sight in case he takes on another booking.'

'He's desperately anxious to make up the money, isn't he,' Geraldine was sympathetic.

'Yes, and to work himself into the ground so that he doesn't have to think about Marcella,' Cathy added.

'No change of heart there?'

'He never says a word. He's not sleeping at the premises any more, so I gather she's moved out of the flat.'

'Silly little girl in many ways,' Geraldine said.

'Yes, but he adored her; still does, I think. Who knows anything about men and what they feel.'

'Who does?' Geraldine was slightly clipped.

Cathy opened her mouth and closed it again. They had been in touch with Freddie Flynn about another Villa Abroad reception: the Spanish and Italian ones had been such a hit, and he wanted something in the same style only different, of course. Cathy had asked should they liaise through her aunt as before; there had been a pause, and then he had said it would be simpler to deal with him directly. Geraldine hadn't mentioned it; she was still wearing her watch. Cathy would say nothing until she was told. As she had so often said to Maud and Simon, it was all part of being grown-up.

'Are Mother and Father being invited to the wedding?' Simon asked Maud.

'No, and don't ask why,' Maud warned.

'Why?' asked Simon.

'There, you asked,' Maud cried.

'I was only asking why must I not ask why?'

'Oh, it's got to do with Muttie's wife Lizzie. She's afraid of Aunt Hannah, and they couldn't ask one without the other.'

'It's very complicated,' Simon said disapprovingly. 'Is Walter coming?'

'No, we're going to be the only Mitchells apart from Neil.' Maud was very well informed. 'And we're going to all three parties, but we're only dancing at the actual wedding day one to make that special for them.'

'I'd say we should bring our shoes to the recovery party in the big apartment where Lizzie's sister lives. In case they ask for an encore.'

Maud considered it. 'I think you're right,' she said.

James Byrne went in and out of his basement a lot, trying to see it through the eyes of a visitor coming here for the first time. It was very difficult to know what she would make of it. But it was important because it would also affect the way she was going to think about him. If she saw the place as severe and cold, that would confirm a lot of her opinions; alternatively, if she found it fumbling and overcrowded and messy, that would make her think that this is how he was, which was almost as bad. For the first time James Byrne realised why there were so many magazine articles and television programmes about decor. It was when you came to think of it, more important than a lot of people ever believed.

'Will there be no Mitchells except us?' Simon wondered.

'Well, Neil will be there, of course,' Cathy replied.

'What about his sister, hasn't he a sister in America? Why isn't *she* coming over for a family wedding?'

'It's Canada she lives in, not the United States, and it's not exactly a family wedding for the Mitchells, you see . . .'

'Is she nice?'

'Yes, she's okay; she sent us a lovely wedding present,' Cathy said. For a moment she felt a wild urge to tell the twins about their cousin Amanda, to let them know she lived a happily gay life in Toronto with a woman called Susan. She would love to know exactly how much damage they could do with a piece of information like that. She smiled to herself.

'It's always dangerous when Cathy laughs to herself,' Muttie commented.

'What happens?' Simon asked anxiously.

'Anything could happen,' Muttie said.

'She could buy another building, a new van, take on more staff . . .'

The mobile phone rang. It was Tom. He had crashed into the back of some fool who had stopped without warning.

'Are you hurt?'

'No, but the bloody birthday cake I'm meant to be delivering is. I'm hopeless with cakes. Cathy, it looks like a bloody mess and I have to stay at the scene of the accident.'

'I'll get a taxi there. What should I bring with me?'

'Whatever you can lay your hands on: trays, cloths, icing sugar, cream, anything.'

'What! I'm meant to do all this, start from scratch in a taxi? Are you mad?'

'Well what am I to do, Cathy? It's running all over the van.'

'God,' said Cathy. 'Tell me where you are.'

They watched as she ran around her mother's kitchen, seizing this and that.

'Da, have you any very reliable associate who drives a cab, anyone who would like an exciting job for the afternoon?'

'Can we come? *Please*,' begged the twins when they heard what it was.

'Why not?' Cathy thought they couldn't make it any worse than it was.

They drove with Kentucky Jim, one of Muttie's very sound friends. He said he didn't believe that people got paid real money driving birthday cakes round to other people. It showed there was one born every minute.

'One what?' Simon wanted to know.

'A fool. They say there's a fool born every minute.'

'I wonder is there?' Maud said.

Cathy decided that she would never tell them that the philosopher Kentucky Jim had once owned a thriving business but his interest in Sandy Keane's betting shop had managed to reduce his circumstances to having a quarter share in a mini cab. It was doubtful if his views on fools being born every minute were necessarily very sound.

Tom was helpless when they found him.

'God, but you're a terrible driver, I've always said so,' she said, putting out a cloth and removing the silver paper-covered plinth and wiping it so she could reassemble the cake.

'Can you do it?'

'I'll have to do it, eejit. I brought the forcing bag so I could write the name again. Just as well, looking at what's left. Is this "Jackie"?'

'Yes, Jackie, that's right.'

'With an "ie" or a "y"?'

'Jesus, I don't know!'

'It's on the form, the order book, look it up!' Cathy cried as she glued back the crushed sides of the cake with a chocolate paste.

'You could ice in the two versions and eat one off when you find the right one,' Simon suggested helpfully.

'Shut up, Simon,' Tom and Cathy said together at exactly the same time.

'You're not turning my basement into a speakeasy after all?' Ricky said next day, and was disappointed. He had been looking forward to it.

'No, and Rick, be a mate and don't mention that little idea, will you? Real lead balloon *that* turned out to be.'

'Oh, dear,' Ricky said.

'Anyway, it's all calmed down now.'

'Which is more than you have, apparently,' Ricky smiled at him.

'Not quite sure what you mean.' Tom was too nonchalant, he knew exactly what Ricky meant.

'Just, they all tell me you and Marcella haven't been seen together since her show. I just happen to think it's a pity, that's all.'

Tom said, 'Yes, well.'

'And if I am in touch with her, Tom, do you want me to say anything to her?'

'No thanks, Ricky, it's all been said.'

Ricky left it. He shook his head because he had heard in three different weeping fits from Marcella that nothing had been said, nothing at all.

Cathy saw James Byrne carrying parcels in Rathgar and tooted the horn of the van.

'Do you want a lift? Are you going home, James?'

'Ah, how nice to see you, Cathy. Yes, I'd love a lift.'

When they got to the elegant house he turned to her. 'Can I ask you something very personal?' he began.

Oh, please God may it not be that he too had guessed she was pregnant. 'Anything you like,' she said wearily.

'Will you just come in the door with me, just walk in and tell me what you see?' he asked.

Cathy's heart sank. All they needed now was for their sane, calm accountant to lose all his marbles and go mad. 'And what do you think I *might* see, James?' she asked fearfully.

'I don't know, Cathy, but you will be honest, won't you.'

'I'll do my very best, James,' said poor Cathy, dragging herself out of the van.

Tom was expecting Cathy back at the premises, so he just buzzed the door without looking up.

Someone stood at the door.

It was odd, Cathy usually rushed in through their front room and into the kitchen. Hoping nothing was wrong, he came out to investigate.

Standing with her back to the light was Marcella. The cloud of dark hair surrounded her like a halo; her face was anxious and upset. She began to speak immediately.

'It's not fair to tell Ricky that we've talked it all out; we've done nothing of the sort.'

'That didn't take long to get back,' he said.

'Do you hate me, Tom?'

'Of course not, of course I don't hate you.' His voice was gentle.

'But what you said to Ricky . . .'

He felt terribly weary, suddenly. 'No, Marcella, I didn't tell Ricky that we'd talked it all out, I said that it had all been said, that's quite different . . . I meant there was nothing more to say.'

'But I wouldn't have walked out on you without saying why.'

'You know why.'

'It was just a stupid party.'

'Yes.'

'You don't want to know about it, it was just messing. I *told* you it would be like that. You don't want to know about it.'

'You're right, I don't want to know all about it, and why you didn't come home that night.'

'I told you, Tom, in advance that it was all meaningless. Unimportant.'

'To you, Marcella, and I told you in advance that it was hugely important to me.'

'But you *knew* there was a party, and that I had to go.' She was weeping now. He stood there, his hands by his sides. 'I was so honest, I really was. You're never going to meet anyone as honest as I am as long as you live.'

'No, Marcella, you weren't honest. People who are honest wouldn't do that to each other.'

'I told you the truth,' she sobbed.

'That's not the same at all,' said Tom.

'I'll go in first, put these things away and then come and open the door for you when you ring it,' said James Byrne. Cathy sighed as she rang the bell. She made a mental note not to give anyone she knew a lift again for the next four years. James came to the door, and she entered the apartment where she had already given cookery lessons. 'Look everywhere. What do you see?' he asked.

'James, for heaven's sake, what am I meant to be looking for? Is this a game?' Her voice was short with him.

'What does it look like to you? Who would you think lives here?' His eyes were clouded, waiting for the answer.

'James, you'll have to forgive me but I've had a long day. I *know* who lives here. *You* live here.'

'No, I mean if you just came in the door. . . ?'

'Like a burglar, do you mean?'

'No, I mean like someone coming to dinner.' He was crestfallen now, and very vulnerable. The cool James Byrne was so ashamed of himself and his raw, nervous state.

'Oh, I see what you mean,' Cathy recovered. 'What you're trying to do is to see what someone's first impressions would be, is that it?'

'Exactly.'

'I'm sorry, I didn't quite understand.' She bought time looking around the dark, lifeless apartment with its lack of colour and spirit.

'No, I didn't explain properly,' he apologised.

'Listen, I don't want to be too inquisitive, but in order for me to answer this question properly I'd have to know what kind of a guest it is.'

'I beg your pardon?'

'Well, like a businessman, or a lady you were inviting on a date, or a long-lost friend or something.'

'Why did you say long-lost friend?' he asked anxiously.

'Because if it was a regular friend, then he or she would *know* what the flat looked like already.' Cathy spoke as she would to Maud and Simon, very clearly but as if talking to an imbecile.

He thought about this for a while. 'Long-lost friend is about the nearest,' he said.

'Age?'

'About your age, as it happens, that's why—'

'Man or woman?'

'Well, a woman, as it happens.'

'A few flowers. You can come and borrow some of our potted plants if you like. Some brightly coloured cushions . . . and take all those papers off the desk there, and get your music centre out from under all those folded magazines or cuttings or whatever.'

'So what it needs is . . .'

'Some sense of colour, of light, a feeling of hope, of somebody actually living here.' She walked around the room as she spoke.

Then suddenly realised what she had just said. How she had been so destructive about the way he lived. Tears came to her eyes.

'James, I'm so very sorry,' she said, coming over and touching his arm.

'No, please.' He moved away. 'I asked your opinion and I got it; what is there to apologise for?' He spoke stiffly.

'I have to apologise for that totally unnecessary harangue about your place, which is perfectly fine except that it needs a little more colour.'

'Yes, quite.'

'James, I'm so nervy and anxious that I have upset almost everyone I know these days. *Please* let me believe that I didn't offer you a lift and then come in here and add you to the list.' He lost his stiffness and relaxed his shoulders. 'Would you trust me to make us some tea?'

'I'd love that.'

'Is it any one big problem, or a lot of middle-sized ones?'

'It's a lot of very big ones actually, James, but do you know the way that if you don't admit them or acknowledge them they sort of go away ... Well, not really go away, but you know ...'

'I know. They don't really go away but they do stay outside the door, at any rate.' He was sympathetic.

'You're very kind, James, a restful type of person to be with. I'm sure your dinner will be a big success.'

'I hope so, I really do. So much depends on it, you see.'

And they drank their tea peacefully, neither asking the other any more questions.

Back at the premises she found Tom curiously quiet. 'Anything more I should know about the wedding? Hit me with it if there is.'

'No.' He was far away.

'Right,' she said.

He didn't answer. It was very unlike him to be so taciturn. He had a lot of papers on the worktop.

'What are you working on?' she asked.

'This and that,' he said.

Marcella must have been in. She would go on as if nothing was wrong.

'I was talking to that priest who's going to marry them. He said we must never lose faith in prayer, even in the darkest hour.'

'Well let's hope he *would* say that; not much point in being in his particular line of business if he can't see a bit of light at the end of the tunnel.'

'No, you don't understand. He thinks *we* are the answer to his prayer.' Cathy laughed.

'Because we did up his mouldy old hall?'

'Exactly, he has an asset on his hands now: the community will get new life, money will roll in for good things.'

'Like statues, I suppose.' Tom was scornful.

'I think not ... He talked about old folks' outings, literacy classes.'

'Sorry,' Tom said.

'No, I'm just cheering myself up by saying that at least you and I are very important to *some* people, anyway.'

He understood. 'Yeah, let's list them: the dopey priest who didn't know he had a community hall until we showed it to him. That's one.'

'James Byrne is two. I had tea with him. The guest by the way is a woman my age, someone he hasn't seen for a long time.'

'Let's see,' said Tom. 'Mad Minnie, because we scrape bits of casserole into her dishes for her.'

'Nonsense, we give her gorgeous food and keep her marriage going, but you're right, that's three.'

'June. We keep her from killing Jimmy. Four,' Tom said.

'Con, or is that pushing it?'

'No,' Tom said, 'we are important to Con. That's five.'

'We could easily get to a dozen if we talked about satisfied clients. We could even get out a bit of paper and write them down,' Cathy said.

'Or we could do what you want me to do and get back to work,' he said with a laugh, and put the bits of paper away.

Cathy saw the words 'Dear Marcella' written on one of them. Things were very bad for poor Tom, much worse than they were for her. Without intending to, Cathy gave him a hug. She just came up behind him and threw her arms around his neck.

'See, we *are* important to lots of people,' she said.

To her surprise, he grasped her hands and held them to his chest.

'God, I hope so, Cathy, I hope so,' he said and his face moved around a little so that they were cheek to cheek.

Lizzie now had daily messages from Chicago about the upcoming visit and wedding. 'They sound very nice people, Harry's family. I hope they won't be disappointed in us,' she confided to her sister Geraldine. Apparently Marian had asked to see a video of the twins dancing. When she had asked for dancers she had really meant professional dancers, rather than children of Cathy's in-laws. She wanted to be sure that they were up to standard. Geraldine and Lizzie looked at each other in disbelief.

'Tell her they're brilliant and the video is on its way,' Geraldine said.

'But will we have to get one?'

'Certainly not, that's just today's worry. She'll have forgotten it tomorrow.'

'But suppose they're not good enough?'

'Lizzie, for God's sake, if they're like two blind elephants they're going to dance, you know that and I know it, and anyway Marian will be so crazed with excitement on her wedding day she'll think they're marvellous, believe me.'

'Cathy, you do realise you have taken on three weddings, not one, don't you?'

'It's under control, Neil.'

'It's not. If it were under control you would not be filling the freezer at eleven o'clock at night.'

'Only four more trays of these; I will rest when the wedding's over, I promise.'

'And the doctor, what does he say about it?'

'He's easy,' Cathy said, not exactly truthfully, but she *had* to do her bit; the others were working flat out.

Neil shook his head. 'Even Sara said you were doing too much in your condition.'

'You told Sara?' She was shocked.

'Hon, I *had* to tell her. She wanted me to join up for a big conference in England next year, I had to explain why I couldn't be a part of it.'

'Yeah, sure.'

'So she was concerned that you were working so hard.'

'What did she say when you told her the news?'

'She was very surprised, as it happens.'

'Why was she so surprised? It is something that happens to couples.'

'I know, Cathy, don't snap at me.'

'Sorry. It's just that I have to keep walking round you.'

'Oh, yes,' he moved slightly.

'Well she was surprised because I had told her a couple of weeks ago that we were never going to have children.'

'You talk about a lot of intimate things with Sara, don't you?'

'Not really, only when things have to be told, and talking about that, really, don't you think we should tell Mother and Father?'

'No, not until after the wedding, it's only a few days. Not until then, and ... Neil could you ever stand somewhere that's not directly in my path to the freezer, and if you do want to help, perhaps you could slide that in for me.' She smiled at him brightly. 'Thanks a million, this will speed us up no end,' she said.

'Drink that milk at your peril, Walter,' Kenneth Mitchell warned. 'Sergeant Sara could materialise at any moment to see if there's enough calcium in their diet.'

'Where are they?' Walter asked.

'Where do you think? Up with those people in that housing development, dancing like complete idiots for a crowd of halfwits.'

'Neil is going to make a speech at that wedding,' Walter said.

'Nonsense,' his father said.

'I'm only telling you what they said.'

'But what on earth would he be doing, visiting and speechifying with those Mutties and people like that?'

'They *are* his in-laws, I suppose.' Walter shrugged.

'She's a common, pushy girl that Cathy, not worth considering.'

'You shouldn't underestimate her, Father. Great mistake to underrate her because of her accent, believe me, I know.'

He did know. He had never believed that Cathy would go the distance that night when there had been the incident at the party. And he couldn't believe that her business was still up and running after his visit.

'Shona!'

'Lord, you look a busy shopper, Cathy. What have you got in all those bags?'

'You name it. Mainly material to make aprons; we're going to have to wear aprons with shamrocks on them, apparently; I keep waking up at night and seeing a great page of a calendar saying August Nineteen, August Nineteen in red neon lights. Will it ever be over, Shona, will it ever, ever be over?'

'August the nineteenth, you don't mean that you're going to be there?' She looked as white as a sheet.

'Of course I am, aren't I, cooking the whole damn thing.'

'He said there wasn't going to be anyone else, he wrote that he was cooking it all by himself.'

'Shona, what are we talking about?' Cathy asked her.

'What are *you* talking about?'

'My sister's wedding, three endless days of it. What were *you* talking about?'

'Sorry, I just thought for a moment ... No, it's nothing ... I've been invited out on August the nineteenth, and I thought you might be cooking for that.'

'Oh really, where?'

'No, just to a private house ... I thought that by some chance you might be doing the dinner.'

'No, I wish I were, it sounds nice and peaceful.'

'I wouldn't bet on that,' Shona said.

As Cathy left the store she wondered could Shona possibly be going to dinner with James Byrne? His party was on the nineteenth. He had said that his guest was about the same age as Cathy. But how could Shona be a long-lost friend? Anyway, this wasn't a village, this was Dublin, city of a million people. She was foolish to think that she knew everyone in the pond. And she had quite enough to worry about without drawing something still further on herself. Tonight, Wednesday, Marian and Harry were leaving Chicago, they would be here tomorrow morning. Their room was gleaming for them in St Jarlath's Crescent, Cathy remembered that nobody must sew the new aprons in front of them, or allow Simon and Maud anywhere near them. Tomorrow night, Thursday, the rest of the Chicagoans, dozens and dozens of them, were coming to various hotels near the city centre. They would all arrive on Friday morning. She felt dizzy thinking about it.

Harry was a small, round man with a head of dark curly hair and a great warm laugh.

'Muttie, I want you to know that I'm going to look after your little girl,' he said with a strong handshake.

'From all accounts you've been looking after her fine for a good while now,' said Muttie.

And the two men understood each other immediately. It turned out that Harry liked dogs and horses, and Muttie, who read more of the sports pages than people thought, knew all about the Chicago Bears. Marian was so excited she almost had to be tied to the table, she kept darting everywhere, saying she had no idea St Jarlath's Crescent was so small, so colourful, so elegant really. She couldn't believe the traffic, the number of posh cars parked outside the doors of the street where she had grown up. The fact that two of them, Geraldine's BMW and Cathy's Volvo, were connected with this house brought her further pleasure ... She was not at all the neurotic, hysterical sister who had plagued them for weeks and months by phone, e-mail and fax. Her wedding dress was unpacked and admired, her ring was tried on by all the women, her choice of husband praised to the skies.

'Where is he, by the way?' Cathy asked.

'He's gone off. Dad said he'd show him his office and get him a pint.'

'You know what your father means by his office.' Lizzie was still fearful of how all this would turn out.

'Oh, Mam, I've been away, that's true, but not so long that I don't know where my da's office is. Harry loves a bet just like the next man; he'd much prefer to be there than here talking about clothes.' Marian looked happy and relaxed; she looked younger than her thirty years, her hair was short, she was trim and fit, and her eyes were alight with happiness.

'Do you want me to take you on a tour, to show you where all the parties will be? Of course, they're not properly set up yet, but you'd get an idea,' Cathy offered.

'Not at all, Cathy, I can see you've got it all under control,' Marian said, and Cathy breathed normally for the first time in a few weeks.

'Tom Feather, my old friend, how are you?' Harry clenched Tom's hand at the pre-wedding party with a mighty grip.

'Look, not a sign of a speakeasy,' Tom hissed at him as he took the groom on a tour of Ricky's basement.

'And I got my folks to understand about the corned beef,' Harry whispered.

'Are there any pitfalls we should know about?' Tom asked him. He felt he could trust this man to the ends of the earth.

'My aunt over there, small, hatchet-faced, wearing purple – nothing has ever pleased her in this life ... Nothing ever will ...

Oh, and Cathy's eldest brother Mike's been put off the sauce recently, finds it very hard.'

'Thanks a lot. Let me see what I can tell you. Lizzie's not used to too much sherry, Muttie likes pints, the woman in the cardigan is a plain-clothes nun. And don't let the kids dance tonight or the party will be over, tomorrow is quite enough.'

'Fine. My card is marked, and Tom, do you have a significant other here that I should meet?'

'No, I've just broken up with my significant other,' Tom said ruefully.

'I'm sorry. Her doing or your doing?'

'Have you three hours and I'll tell you,' Tom grinned. 'No, seriously, a bit of both, I believe.'

'Right, then you'll survive,' Harry promised.

And for the first time since the night of the fashion show, Tom felt that somehow he might.

They were back at the premises, and Neil apologised for not being able to come back to help. There was something tomorrow, papers he had to go through.

'Where's Marcella? She should be on board for something like this.'

'Marcella's not on board at all these days,' Tom said.

'I'm very sorry.' Neil looked at Cathy accusingly, as if to say he should have been told this piece of information.

'Yes, I'm sorry, I should have told you, Neil, but then I didn't know if it was going to be a long-term or a short-term break . . .'

'None of us knew that,' June interrupted cheekily. 'But it's been a few weeks now, and no sign of her, so we think he's on the market again.' She winked at Lucy, the student who was working with them that night. 'What would you say, Lucy?'

'Oh, definitely open season on Tom, I'd say,' Lucy said. 'Why else do you think I agreed to work here?'

And as they worked on companionably to get everything done in readiness for the morning, Cathy glanced at Tom from time to time. He did seem to be less drawn and sad. Perhaps he was getting over her. But maybe it was an act. People who were as involved as Marcella and Tom didn't just part without a great deal of heartbreak. Wherever she was tonight, the silly girl would be thinking of big, handsome Tom Feather with his warm, loving ways. Cathy was thinking that she had never come across anyone so perpetually good-natured when she heard him saying, 'I wonder, has that aunt of Harry's got any allergies? Maybe we could feed her nuts or magic mushrooms or something tomorrow, and kill her before she does any more damage.'

'She asked me to bring her up and out into the fresh air, and then to bring her back down again,' Con said.

'She told me I needed a good girdle . . .' said June.

'She's lonely, and old and frightened, just be nice to her,' Cathy said.

They all looked at her in amazement.

'Why are you taking that attitude?' June was astounded.

'Because Tom, for once, isn't, and *somebody* round here has to play the role of angel if we're going to keep this company on the road,' Cathy said.

The wedding day, 19 August, was a beautiful sunny day, which nobody could have guaranteed. The priest was warm and welcoming, which might not have been the case in every single parish church in the country. The congregation had assembled in plenty of time, and all the women wore hats in honour of the occasion. Harry stood there beaming as Muttie and Marian walked up the aisle. Slow, measured steps, not scuttling. It was a miracle. Lizzie looked like someone who could have been photographed at the races for the Best-Dressed Lady, in an elegant grey silk outfit and a smart black hat. Geraldine, who had hired hats for all of them, wore an apricot suit, and Cathy stood beside her in the silk dress she had bought the week before in Haywards.

Neil had his best appearing-in-the-High-Court suit on to impress the in-laws. Soon, soon they would be finished with all this. He would take a day or two off and they would rest and talk about the future. He had promised this. Just as soon as Marian's wedding was over. In spite of herself, Cathy felt the tears come down her face when she saw Maud and Simon walking as solemnly as if their very lives depended on it behind the bride and Muttie. They were *so* good. Why had she thought they might behave stupidly and let everyone down? Their hair shining, their little kilts immaculate, their ordinary shoes polished to the highest degree. And she sniffed seriously when she heard Harry and Marian, who had been living together happily in Chicago for ages now, exchange their vows. For the first time she wished that she and Neil had organised something bigger and more celebratory themselves for their wedding day. But at that time to get married at all had been such a victory.

The church hall where they had the wedding feast looked magnificent, draped in ribbons and greenery and flowers. When the church was emptied June and Con were sent in to bring the flowers out quickly from the altar to the top table. There was a glass of champagne offered as soon as the guests came in the door. Tom took charge of Mike, the brother who found being on the dry a problem.

'Hi Mike, I'm Tom Feather, your sister's partner.'

'I thought she was married to Neil.' Mike glowered at him.

'Sure she is, I'm her work partner. Be nice to me, I'm in charge of the food and drink.'

'Drink, huh?' Mike said.

'I've got something here you'd love. Low-cal cranberry juice with freshly squeezed grapefruit whipped up with a little sugar syrup and white of egg.'

'What's it called?' Mike was still unwilling to thaw.

'It's called, "Let's not show it to the others, let's find something bearable for ourselves,"' Tom winked.

'You been put off alcohol too?'

'Hell, isn't it? Other people seem so stupid and go on so long and say the same thing over and over again.'

'And their elbows fall off tables,' Mike said in a fury.

'Oh, I know all about it . . .' said Tom. 'Still, we've got something here, you and I, that none of the others will have, and think how well we'll feel tomorrow.' Mike brightened up. 'And if *we* want to sing, we'll remember the words, unlike the rest of them.'

'Will there be singing?' Mike thought the day might not be so sepulchral.

'It's a wedding, isn't it? We have to sing the praises of My Kind Of Town Chicago Is, and then someone has to tell us about Dublin's Fair City, don't they?'

Mike was a much-cheered man when Tom left him. All Tom had to do now was make sure that there were a few singers in the hall. People who would be able to wrench the stage from Maud and Simon when their time came. There was a roar of conversation, and as they moved among the guests they realised that it was already a mighty success. The first of many weddings they would do in this hall. Next time, hopefully, wearing their smart Scarlet Feather uniform. Today, however, they were wearing their idiotic shamrock-decorated outfits which they had all finished sewing minutes before they put them on. They all reported conversations to each other as they flashed by in the kitchen, which was lit up by the late afternoon sun.

'Harry's aunt that you were being so nice about is fast asleep; that's how much she's enjoying it,' Tom said.

'I told them to let her sleep, not to wake her. It's jet lag. She can wake up for dessert and the entertainment,' Cathy said.

'Simon and Maud have asked us to hold their cake and ice cream, please, until after their dance,' June announced.

'Makes sense,' Con agreed. 'I'd hate to see them bringing up that lot on the floor, wouldn't you?'

In Rathgar, Shona stopped outside the house. She didn't have to go in. She had his phone number: she could call him now on her mobile and say that she didn't feel well. Which was actually true. She was an adult of twenty-eight years of age. She hadn't seen him for fourteen years. Nothing except a carefully written letter from an old man. Why had he said that he would cook for her? Somehow that had touched her. When she knew him almost a decade and a half ago, he couldn't cook. He had learned to cook especially to make her a meal, he said. It could be just a line he was taking in order to persuade her. But he had never been cunning enough or cared enough to do that in the past. Why should he begin now? And why on earth did he want to see her again? It was because she was so curious about this that she was here . . . And now that she was here, she would go in. Shona walked in and rang the doorbell of James Byrne's garden flat.

'Con, can you move that bottle of wine away from my mother and get my father another pint?' Cathy asked.

'They're devouring the salmon, will there be enough for second helpings?' Lucy asked.

'Yes, but fill the serving dish up with cress and dollops of sauce as well, to hide the fact that there ain't that much fish,' Tom advised, 'and carve another dish of lamb as well. Make it look nice; we can always use it again.'

And eventually there were the speeches, simple and straightforward, thanks being lavished everywhere and no awful best-man jokes. And finally, the moment was here for Maud and Simon.

Harry announced, 'When I first heard about this wonderful hospitable Irish wedding, I knew I would take my bride in my arms and dance around a flower-filled hall ... I never realised how beautiful both would look, but there are so many wonderful surprises today, including being introduced to Maud and Simon Mitchell, who are cousins by marriage of mine, now ... our beautiful flower girl and our elegant pageboy. Now they are going to dance for us, and I want you to give them the great big welcome they deserve.'

Maud and Simon strode out confidently in their cloaks, kilts and huge Tara brooches, as if they were totally accustomed to being greeted with such applause.

'My fellow guests at Marian and Harry's wedding,' Simon read from a piece of paper, 'I am Simon Mitchell. I want to welcome you all to Ireland, those who weren't here already, I mean. My partner Maud and I will dance a jig with the very suitable name of "Haste To The Wedding". Although in your case you're already here. *At* the wedding,' he beamed at them as an afterthought.

'Oh, loving God, let them start to dance before he thinks of any more asides,' Cathy breathed.

But she needn't have worried: Simon had nodded at the pianist, and they stood, arms high, hands joined and right foot pointed out until the introductory bars were played, and then they were away. There was thunderous clapping. And then Maud stepped forward.

'My fellow guests at this wedding, I hope you enjoyed the jig. Now my partner Simon and I will dance a reel with the name "Come West Along The Road". Which you haven't really done, since you came east to get here, but that's the name of the dance.'

She put away the paper and again they stood solemnly waiting for the music to start. They danced on, oblivious of the fact that the audience was fighting back tears at their eagerness and determination to explain everything and get it totally right, and fits of laughter at their pompous little ways. Cathy caught Tom's eye. He raised a glass to her. She smiled.

'You're smiling,' Tom said in mock surprise.

'I know, isn't it amazing? The muscles still work,' Cathy said.

'Come in, come in,' James Byrne fussed and led Shona into the room where he had carefully placed four brightly coloured cushions and two vases of flowers. She had brought him a bottle of wine. He made great play of looking at the label.

'My goodness, Australian Chardonnay, how wonderful. That looks very good, very interesting indeed.' He studied it as someone might look at a bottle of some vintage wine at a special wine auction. It set Shona's teeth on edge. It was a good, supermarket Australian white wine, no more, no less. Why did he have to keep taking off and putting on his glasses? Probably because he was nervous, she realised. As nervous as she was. Normally when you went into someone's place for the first time you found something to admire. Shona's eyes raked the room. She was at a total loss for words. She could see nothing she recognised, yet he could hardly have bought these things new. Perhaps it was just rented furnished accommodation. They sat down opposite each other, and she saw on the table the plate of fat olives plus a little basket of Tom Feather's bread. James Byrne was definitely making an effort. He had done all the talking so far ... about the wine, the weather, whether she had found the house easily. It was now up to Shona to bring up some subject.

'When did you come to live in Dublin?' she asked.

'Five years ago,' he said. 'Just after Una died.'

'She died? I'm sorry.' But the voice was cold.

'Yes. Yes, it was sad.'

Shona did not ask what happened, had it been peaceful, had she lingered a long time. None of the questions you ask when someone tells you that a wife has died. The silence hovered between them. Shona steeled herself not to speak again. She had asked one question, the ball was in his court, this invitation had come from him, let James Byrne be responsible for directing the conversation. Eventually he spoke.

'Una was never strong, you know, she found ordinary things like going upstairs or making the beds very difficult. Would you have known that now, when you were with us?'

'No, I didn't. I suppose, since it was the only life I knew, I thought everyone's home was like that. I didn't know what other homes were like until I lost the one I had.'

He looked at her with a face as sad as a bloodhound's. 'She was never the same after you left,' he said.

'I didn't leave, I was taken away, sent away.'

'Shona, I didn't ask you here to go over a war of words that did nothing except tear us to pieces half your lifetime ago.'

'Why did you ask me, then?' She realised that since she had come

361

in she had not addressed him by any name. But what name could she call him? Not Daddy, not Mr Byrne.

'I suppose I invited you because I wanted to tell you how great a gap you left in our lives, how nothing was ever, ever the same since the day you were taken away.'

'Since the day you handed me over without a struggle, saying it was the law,' Shona said, her face hard.

'But Shona, that's the terrible thing, it *was* the law,' he said with tears in his eyes.

In the church hall the pianist was playing the Anniversary Waltz and Harry led Marian onto the floor and everyone clapped.

'The bride will dance first with her father,' he announced.

Muttie, who had been explaining to his sons some of the finer parts of a horse that was going to make a killing next year, was startled. 'I'm not much of a dancer,' he whispered anxiously.

'Just relax, Dad, Marian will push you round as she does the rest of us,' they said to him.

They did two tours of the hall with everyone cheering them, and then the general dancing began. Tom had given the twins their cake and ice cream and a pound each, in return for their going to sit with the old lady in the purple suit and telling her about Ireland.

'What are *you* going to do, Tom?' Simon was suspicious.

'I'm going to circulate.'

'Does that mean dance?' Maud asked.

'*No*, just talk to people. I don't feel like dancing; anyway, what's all this after, you two?'

They were pleased. 'Would Marcella come back if you agreed to marry her, do you think?' Simon asked.

'No, I asked her lots of times and she wanted to have a career instead.'

'And did she have to choose? Couldn't you do both? Like Cathy, and Muttie's wife Lizzie?'

'There are women who can do both,' Tom explained, 'but modelling is a hard one, it involves travel.'

The twins shrugged. It was better that she went then. Tom said it was.

In the garden flat, they had managed to get to the point where a wooden and stilted conversation did manage to go backwards and forwards between them. He called her to the table and sat her down. She moved from being alternately touched at the trouble he had gone to, and enraged at the cold, clinical attitude to life that had guided him over years of silence and neglect. They talked of her school life after she had left the convent school in the country town. She spoke calmly about the home she returned to, the mother still lurching between drugs and rehabilitation, the father who had set up a new home with a more stable woman. Her older sisters who resented her return, claiming that she had been given airs and notions about herself. She told of her natural mother's death this year, and how she had dutifully gone to visit her in the hospital but felt nothing. He said that they had always known a foster child was only lent to them, and that if her home circumstances improved she would go back to them. They had unworthily hoped that this would never happen. He told of his wife's descent into the state of a permanent invalid, of the emptiness of the life they lived. He said it was impossible to stay in the house after her death, and he had come to Dublin and lost himself in work.

'Well I did that too,' Shona said as she finished the smoked fish and watched him put on his oven gloves to get the next course. 'I decided that work was the only answer, that and having something to show as a result. I wanted a place I could be proud of. Glenstar is far too expensive for me, but I like giving that address; I like coming home to a smart place like that each evening.'

'And what about love, Shona? Does that play any part in it?'

'No, I've never loved anyone.'

He smiled a little indulgently.

'Don't smile at me, James,' she said. 'The day you stood and let me go without telling me that you loved me and wanted me back, that day killed any thoughts of love that I would ever have.'

Chapter Nine

SEPTEMBER

After the wedding, life had to return to normal. And normal wasn't always easy. Tom never finished the letter to Marcella. He had been right; there was no more to say. She didn't say goodbye when she went across the water. He heard during one of his early morning sessions at Haywards that she had left her job in the salon. Two of the kitchen staff had heard she was going to be a model. Geraldine read in the property pages that Freddie Flynn and his wife Pauline had bought a country house with twenty-four rooms and eight acres, outside Dublin. June's husband Jimmy had a fall at work, naturally on a cash-in-hand job with no insurance, and was lying in bed for the duration. Joe Feather gave a great deal of his merchandise to a wide boy who managed to sell it off to all and sundry before leaving the country, all bills unpaid. Muttie needed the money to pay a vet's bill for Hooves, and borrowed some of Lizzie's savings for a sure thing which turned out not to be sure at all. James Byrne berated himself a dozen times a day for not taking that hurt, withdrawn girl into his arms and crying over the time lost and the pain endured. He had been so afraid that she would push him away. Old Barty wrote to say that he was on his way back and hoped he could come and stay again for a few days. Kenneth Mitchell wrote him a cold note saying that times were difficult, and that old Barty had left last time owing a great deal of money, so a visit would not be possible. Kenneth got by return of post an even colder note saying that Barty had now recovered his fortunes, but if he were no longer welcome there then so be it. Walter Mitchell got what was defined as a final warning from his uncle Jock. One more late morning or early leaving and he was out. Jock's face made it look as if this time it was meant. Neil and Cathy put off telling Jock and Hannah about the baby for a few more days. And so they didn't tell Muttie and Lizzie either.

Unexpectedly, Hannah rang and said she would like to invite Neil and Cathy to Oaklands.

'That sounds nice, Hannah, anything in particular?'

'No, should there be? I mean, it is my own son . . . and his wife, no need for an occasion or an excuse.'

'Of course not,' said Cathy, who had never been invited socially to dinner there before.

'Oh, and Cathy, do you do foods which people just serve in their own . . . I mean, the leaflet does say . . .'

'Of course we do, Hannah, tell me what you'd like.'

Hannah wanted a pheasant casserole, because Jock had been given a brace. It took forever, and they all cursed her back at the premises. But some things were more important than others, Cathy said, and not being fazed by Hannah Mitchell was top priority.

'Do we put in an invoice?' Tom asked.

'No,' Cathy said. Con was delivering it in the van later that afternoon; it would be bubbling merrily at Oaklands when they got there. Next week Hannah would telephone and fuss and waste more of their time.

They sat around the table that Lizzie had polished so often, and almost always to the dissatisfaction of Hannah. Cathy wondered did Hannah still think back on those days, or had she moved on? She was certainly an easier person to deal with now. Cathy would never really like her, but the hate was gone. Sometimes little waves of annoyance came back. Like when Hannah wondered why it was that Cathy and Neil never took a holiday abroad together, like normal people.

'Neil has to travel abroad a lot on work,' she said.

'Cathy is very tied up in her business,' he said.

She saw the look of triumph on Hannah Mitchell's face. For once the combined forces of Neil and Cathy were not ranged against her. She had managed to divide them at last. Over this, anyway. Cathy warned herself that it must not happen again. One of the many reasons she wanted to save her marriage was to prove Hannah Mitchell wrong.

*

'Tired?' Neil asked her when they were in the car driving home.

'Not really, why?'

'You're sighing,' he said.

'I'm always sighing,' Cathy said.

'The food was nice,' he said.

'Thanks,' she said innocently.

'Did you do it. . . ?' he asked surprised.

She looked at him thoughtfully, one of the brightest young men at the Bar, but not a lot of practical sense. Of *course* she had done the food, that was why it was not over-done beef followed by ice-cream with liqueur poured over it. But there was no point in saying any of that now.

He told her about the project for the homeless. Something he and Sara were proposing which other people on the committee were resisting. Cathy let her thoughts drift away, and wondered should she give cookery classes at the premises when she was too pregnant to go out on jobs. It might be a good idea. Little groups of eight or twelve, rich, lonely women like Hannah who hadn't a clue. She wondered how James Byrne's dinner party had gone, but she would never ask. Neil was still talking on, Sara had said this, he had said that. He seemed to see an awful lot of Sara, but never reported anything back about the twins. Still, Cathy reminded herself that they were mainly involved in this committee now; Simon and Maud were only a small item on Sara's busy caseload.

Geraldine asked Scarlet Feather if they could cater for a spur-of-the-moment supper party at Glenstar.

'Any theme?' Tom wondered.

'She's looking for a new sugar daddy; we *could* think up a few sugar-based dishes.'

'You're awful about her,' Tom said.

'No, I'm not, those are her own words. Freddie Flynn's gone back to his wife full-time, have you noticed, he even took his account away from her PR firm, which is going a bit far.'

'Well, maybe his wife wouldn't trust him around Geraldine's long legs and flashing smile,' Tom said with a grin.

'She was pleased with how well Glenstar looked for the recovery party after the wedding. She's decided to capitalise on it.'

'She's not going to have the dancers as a cabaret, by any chance,' he asked.

'No, she's drawn the line there. Tom, are we taking on too much, do you think?' she sounded worried.

'No, of course not, we've a load of terrific stuff for a buffet in the freezer already, and I'd say she'd like shellfish, don't you think?'

'Yes, but getting it ready, setting it up, serving it.'

'Cathy, June and I will do most of it. Does she need a barman as well, do you think?'

'Yes, she does, whether she knows it or not.' Cathy wanted every hand on deck.

'Relax, Cathy, there are bound to be times you're tired. Accept it, will you?'

She smiled wearily. It was great not to have to put on a brave face all the time.

Freddie Flynn's next rented-villa reception went very well. This time they had rum punch served in coconut shells, Bob Marley on the record player and June wearing a garland of flowers around her neck, which was, strictly speaking, more Hawaiian than Caribbean, but nobody cared.

'How's that marvellous aunt of yours?' Freddie asked.

'Wonderful. Will we be seeing you at her big party next week?' Cathy asked with an innocent smile. It had the desired effect of catching him off guard.

'Er . . . um . . . no, come to think of it, I believe I'm away next week, yes, I am, so that must be it,' he said.

'Oh well, next time then,' Cathy said brightly.

Sara came to The Beeches to ensure that the back-to-school process was going as planned. Kay looked at her bewildered. Sara explained slowly. Textbooks, exercise books, uniform, shoes to the mender's, haircuts. The kind of things normal people understood.

'There's always so much to do,' Kay Mitchell sighed. 'It's all quite endless, really, isn't it, Sara?'

'Endless, Mrs Mitchell. Shall we make a list of what has to be done?'

When he was taking Hooves for a healthy walk, Muttie met JT Feather by chance.

'Desperate business about the vandals destroying Tom and Cathy's premises,' Tom's father said.

'Never heard one single solitary word about it,' Muttie said.

They agreed that children these days were secretive and devious, and took risks and wouldn't tell you about anything unless they had to.

'They had to tell me *something* to get my men to try and build the place up again,' JT said grudgingly.

'Well, you're streets ahead of me in information anyway,' said Muttie, which pleased the other man greatly.

'Why didn't you tell me?' Lizzie demanded.

Cathy was nonplussed. There were so many things she hadn't told her mother. Which one could her mother mean?

'About what?' she asked.

'About your premises getting broken into.'

'Oh, Ma, I didn't want you going on like you're going to go on now.'

'And do they know who did it?'

'Nope, not a clue.'

'And were you insured?'

'Of course we were, Mam.'

'So this isn't the reason why you're killing yourselves and you're looking like a long wet week?'

'Mam.' She felt a surge of gratitude to her mother. She'd tell her about the baby this minute if there was any point, but it would be just one more worry. 'No, Mam, we're absolutely fine,' Cathy lied straight into her mother's anxious face.

James Byrne had been to the premises today and said that the hopes of getting the insurance company to pay up in the foreseeable future were very slim. They would be renting this expensive stuff for months down the line. Working flat out, they would see no profit, and quite possibly a massive loss at the end of the year.

The room was filling up at Geraldine's apartment. From the kitchen, Cathy saw James Byrne come in, wearing his best suit, and trying to find a background to stand in.

'Hey, he isn't your speed,' she warned her aunt. 'I've been in his flat; nothing you'd aspire to at all.'

'If I didn't have so much invested in you, Cathy Scarlet, I'd throw you off my balcony this minute. Mr Byrne's here because he advises our Residents' Association about our service contracts. One of the ladies here knew him years ago in Galway, and now that he's retired he does several of these little jobs. Most helpful and courteous he is, too.'

Cathy was pleased to see him. When it got quieter she might ask him about how the dinner party went.

June went up to Peter Murphy, hotelier and great friend of Geraldine's. 'Lovely party, isn't it, Mr Murphy?' she said to him.

'It is indeed, my dear,' he said distantly, giving the air of never having seen her before in his life.

'I'm no hit with that Peter Murphy,' June complained to Cathy.

'I think he still fancies the hostess,' Cathy said.

'Well, why doesn't she go back to him now that his wife's gone to Holy God and the other fellow back to his wife?' June grumbled.

'I don't know. I did ask her, but she gave me some crap about never revisiting things. I haven't an idea of what's she's talking about.'

'Look who's here now,' June said, nodding to the door. Joe Feather had just come in.

'Oh, God almighty,' said Cathy. This would be the first time the brothers had met since the night of the fashion show.

Shona walked straight over to the window, to where James was standing.

'I'm very sorry, I didn't know you'd be here,' she said.

'And I didn't know you'd be here either,' he said simply.

'I'd like to return your hospitality sometime soon,' she began.

'Oh, please, don't think you have to do . . .' he stammered.

'I don't think I *have* to, I'd like to. Would you like to have lunch with me at Quentin's one day next week?'

'But Shona, that's a very . . .' He spoke softly. But stopped. He had been about to say the restaurant was much too expensive. That might not have been tactful, or indeed sensitive.

She seemed to know what he had been going to say. 'I save my money to pay a posh rent and to have the odd meal in a posh place. I'd love you to be my guest. You pick a day.'

'I'd be proud and delighted to meet you there on Wednesday,' he said.

'I'll book the table for one o'clock,' she said, and left him.

'All right, Tom?' Joe said in a fake Cockney accent.

'All right, mate,' Tom answered in the same cheerful voice.

They looked at each other for a moment, not sure what to say next.

'Great place for a party,' Joe said eventually.

'Isn't it just? Have you a drink, or have you gone temperance on us?'

'I'm never going to drink again, Tom. Believe me.'

'Rough night, was it?'

'No, but I think I must have been drunk on the day when I gave that bloody gangster all that credit, he nearly wiped me out. Did you hear about it?'

'I heard something, yes.' Tom was vague.

'Listen, I won't interrupt you here at your work. Maybe we'll have a temperance lunch one day, and weep on each other's shoulders?'

'Okay, but I want somewhere with a pint, and I don't get to do any of the weeping, you do all that side of it. Okay?'

'Okay,' said Joe.

The telephone rang in Geraldine's apartment, and June answered.

'Please, June, could you put the call through to the bedroom, it's Frederick Flynn. Tell her I won't keep her long from her friends.'

'It's very busy here, Mr Flynn, do you think that you could—'

'Now, please, June,' he said.

Geraldine went into her bedroom and picked up the receiver. 'Yes, Freddie?' she asked pleasantly.

'I must have been mad. I tell you this, I must have been stark staring mad, I won't be without you, you mean too much to me.'

'I beg your pardon?'

'You heard me. I'm telling her.'

'What *exactly* are you telling Pauline?' she asked, her voice ice-cold.

'Well, I'm telling her that I have to spend some time in Dublin in the evening after work, that I can't be tied to coming home to the country every night, and . . . you know.'

'Oh, don't do all that, Freddie, it will upset Pauline and it won't mean anything in the end.'

'What do you mean? I love you, Geraldine, you're an exquisite woman. I'm such a fool to have said I'd give you up.'

'You didn't say that at all, Freddie, we agreed it had run its course.'

'But it hasn't . . . not for me.' There was a silence. 'Geraldine?'

'Yes, Freddie, I'm here, but I have people in so I must get back to my guests.'

'I *know* you have people in, half the bloody country, don't you think I want to be there too?' He sounded very upset. But she hardened her heart. He had made a decision. He had not called Geraldine with the news that he loved her so much that he would leave Pauline. Or even defy her. She was being asked to settle for a few more stolen nights until Pauline cracked the whip again. He had been the warmest, funniest of all her men, but still, he was a weak man, she wasn't going to get back into a muddled, uneasy compromise of a relationship where he would always be looking at his watch.

'You'll always be a special person to me, Freddie, but I have to go,' she said. She hung up, and straightened her bed. Geraldine went back to her party.

'Con, can you take this tray? I have to sit down,' Cathy said.

'Sure. You're very white, Cathy,' he said. 'Can I do anything for you, brandy, glass of water?'

'Yes, go and see which of Geraldine's posh bathrooms is free. I used to think she was mad to have two, but tonight we need one.'

He was back in seconds. 'The near one is free, lean on me, Cathy.'

'Thanks, Con, you're a trooper.' She went in and locked the door.

The first guests were beginning to leave. They had cleared a lot of things into the kitchen. June came in with a pile of plates.

'Cathy's in the loo, she doesn't look well,' Con reported.

'Right, you bring in the next lot of dishes, I'll go and check.' June went to the bathroom. 'Cathy, open up the door this minute.'

'June, go away, go to the other one.'

'I want this one, I'm going to keep knocking and shouting until you let me in.'

'You're mad, go away, get out of here.'

'CATHY,' June roared.

The bolt was drawn back, and Cathy sat there on the side of the bath, her face as white as the white porcelain around her.

'Go back, June,' she said in a weak voice. 'Go back, for Christ's sake, we can't afford to foul up on a good job like this, aunt or no aunt.'

'What's wrong? Just *tell* me,' June said.

'I felt a pain. Look, it's nothing, no bathroom full of blood, it's not a haemorrhage or anything, now will you go back.' She grimaced and held her middle.

'Have you passed any blood at all?' June snapped out the words.

'Literally a couple of drops, nothing you would notice unless you were looking for them.'

'You've got to lie down,' June insisted.

'Now? In the middle of the party? You're mad.'

'In the spare bedroom and now,' June said, scooping up all the towels she could see in the bathroom. 'Come on, Cathy, don't give me any trouble or I'll hit you in the jaw and knock you out.'

Cathy staggered to the spare room, very tasteful shades of lilac and mauve with a rich purple carpet and a wall-hanging in the same colours. 'Imagine, I'm probably the first person ever to sleep in this bed,' Cathy said dreamily as June put cushions under her feet and then went to collect what looked like an enormous amount of more towels from the hot-press beside the bathroom.

June approached Peter Murphy. 'Mr Murphy, I'm June. I wonder if you could tell me quietly whether anyone in this room might be a doctor?'

'Has there been an accident in the kitchen?'

'A sort of crisis, yes; I don't want to disturb Geraldine . . .'

They both looked over to where Geraldine stood talking animatedly to a tall man who seemed very taken with her.

'I don't know half the people here,' Peter Murphy said. 'I was just leaving. Perhaps her new friend is a consultant or something; he certainly dresses like one.'

'Why are you looking for a doctor?' Tom had amazing ears.

'Cathy. She's in the spare bedroom.'

He was in there in a flash. 'Tell me quickly, Cathy, what do we do?'

'There's a bit of blood . . . Tom, I don't know whether it's better to try and get to a hospital or to stay still.'

'Jesus, why didn't any of us qualify as doctors? Have you got your mobile?'

'In my bag in the kitchen, but don't go just yet, Tom.'

June was back in the room. 'There *was* a doctor, she's coming in.' She was one of the residents at Glenstar, a small Indian woman with an easy smile. She took in the situation immediately, sat down on the chair that June offered her and held Cathy's hand.

'How many weeks?'

'Fourteen or fifteen, I think.'

'And the pain? The cramps? The blood?' She asked the questions without any sense of rush. And nodded, as if pleased with all the answers. 'We'll keep you here and make you comfortable for a while, and then we'll think again,' she said.

'Please go back to the party,' Cathy begged. 'I'm all right now, you can see that.'

'They're coping fine,' Tom soothed her.

'God, Tom, there's only Con out there, and you know the panic people get into when they think the party's about to end. Go out and give him a hand, both of you.'

'Calm, calm,' the doctor said.

'You might as well try to turn back the tides as ask her to be calm,' Tom said resignedly.

'Are you her husband?'

'No, no, I've rung Neil but it's the answering machine. I didn't want to leave a message that would alarm him. Can you give me his mobile number, Cathy?'

'Not yet, let's see what we have to tell him first. Now please go, all of you,' she begged.

They left, and tears rolled down her face in the darkened room with its graceful design. She noticed that the doctor, helped by June, had put still more big bath towels beneath her. The good news was that Geraldine's elegant counterpane would not be stained or marked. The bad news was that the doctor must be expecting to see a lot more blood shortly.

Geraldine knew that something was wrong but that it was under control. She bade farewell to Nick Ryan, who owned a chain of dry-cleaning firms around the city. She murmured that she must not monopolise him; he really should circulate and meet everyone else. He murmured that he hated to go, but really he had no interest whatsoever in talking to anyone else. That was about as strong an indication as he could possibly give that he found her attractive. Geraldine saw Peter Murphy looking at her. But she would not go back on her tracks. No revisiting, as she had often told Cathy, not that the girl ever listened to anything. And where was she, by the way? This party was so strange, in a way. James Byrne and Shona Burke knowing each other from way back. That very nice neighbour, Doctor Said, who had said that she would drop in just for an hour, still here with the hard core. Freddie ringing to ask her to go back to him. Peter Murphy being utterly jealous and possessive. Wasn't bad for a girl about to turn forty. Geraldine was about to congratulate herself, when she saw Doctor Said moving quietly towards the spare room, and she suddenly realised why she hadn't seen Cathy for the last hour or so.

Only when she got to the hospital did Cathy tell them Neil's mobile number. And by the time he got there it was all over.

Back at the premises Tom, June and Con unpacked the van, washed up, tidied and stored everything. Geraldine said she would call them there when there was any news. They sat and drank coffee on the big sofas in their front room. It was the first place they had insisted on repainting and doing up after the break-in. Otherwise they would have been too depressed to face a day's work. They were trying to be practical; they would get Lucy, that bright little student, in again, and she might even have a couple of friends. It often worked that way. Con had a pal who was a good, reliable waiter. Whatever the news, they knew that Cathy wouldn't be able to work for a while. If she had kept the baby, she might have to lie down for weeks.

'One thing is sure . . . she's never going to recover her strength if she thinks *we* can't manage,' June said. What Cathy needed as much as any hospital care was the assurance that Scarlet Feather could survive her absence.

When the phone rang it seemed unnaturally loud. It was two in the morning and Geraldine was ringing from the hospital to say that Cathy had lost her baby. June sat there, and didn't even wipe away the tears. Tom and Con blew their noses loudly in great wads of kitchen paper. June, for the first time ever, rang a taxi and went without complaint or comment straight home to her husband. Con and Tom went to a club and had three Russian vodkas each.

'I thought it would make me feel better,' Tom said, disappointed.

'Me too, I don't even feel drunk,' Con said.

'What a terrible, terrible waste at those prices.'

'I know, we could have drunk vodka for free back at the premises, with no blaring noise and no strobe lights,' Tom said furiously.

And for some reason, they both found this funny, and they

laughed as they headed for their homes. Con to the flat he shared with three other guys, who might still be up and playing poker. Tom to Stoneyfield to sleep for a full two hours before he got up to make the bread at Haywards.

Neil came in and sat beside the bed to hold her hand.

'Well,' she said to him in a very tired voice.

'They say you're going to be fine,' he said.

'Yes,' she said.

'That's what matters. You're very precious to me.'

'Yes,' she said again.

'And Cathy, I'm very, very sorry. It could sound a little hollow, but I know it's a huge loss, and I *am* sorry that this should happen.'

'Thank you, Neil,' she said.

He stroked her forehead over and over saying, 'Poor Cathy. You'll be fine.' Eventually she closed her eyes and he thought she was asleep. He kissed her and she heard him speaking to the nurse, saying he'd come back before he went to work the next morning.

'How many days will you keep her here?' he asked.

The nurse thought it might be two nights, but she couldn't say definitely. Neil said that was great, because he didn't have to go out of town for another few days.

'Very considerate man, your husband, some fellows who come in are all over the place,' the nurse said.

'That's right,' said Cathym who realised that some fellows who came in here were heartbroken that they had lost an unborn child.

Cathy was adamant. She didn't want anyone else to know where she was. No point in telling four people that what might have been their grandchild had been lost. She knew too that she would have had to face the accusations that she had worked too hard, pushed herself too far. In other words, brought all this upon herself. Neil had been entirely supportive about this. It was her right to decide, he said, and only hers. Tom brought in a box of little home-made cakes for the nurses to have with their morning coffee.

Geraldine was also wonderful, she actually brought a file of work to Cathy's bed. 'Try to sleep, but I'm here if you want a chat,' she said.

It was very restful. Cathy dozed off several times, happy that Geraldine had plenty to do and didn't need to be entertained. Occasionally she would open her eyes and ask a question.

'Does Doctor Said like Ireland, do you think? When I'm better, Tom and I will make her a meal as a thank-you.'

'Was it a boy or a girl? In my mind I'll call the baby Pat, that could be either.'

'Do you really think I'm like you, Geraldine? You used to say I was once, but you haven't said it for ages.'

And finally, 'What would you do if you met that guy again, you know the first guy, the one you really loved?'

She never stayed awake enough to hear the bland, soothing answers that Geraldine murmured at her. But Geraldine thought about all the questions, and sat looking into the distance as Cathy lay there, white and weak, in the bed.

Neil drove her back to Waterview. He suggested that she go to bed; he would work and then bring her supper later. 'It's all right,' he reassured her. 'Tom brought round four little meals for two with instructions on them, so you won't be poisoned.'

The telephone rang. Cathy heard him telling someone that she wasn't there. They must work out a cover story for the next few days. She'd be on her feet again next week and back to work. But in the meantime, they must all say the same thing. Flu, virus or whatever.

'It was only Simon and Maud, some grouse, some whinge,' he said. 'I told them we'd ring in a couple of days.'

'Did that satisfy them?' Cathy asked.

'Satisfy those two? You must be joking, but I headed them off,' he said proudly.

'She *has* gone off us,' Maud said.

'But why? We haven't done anything. Not recently,' Simon said.

They went back over everything. Cathy had been great at the wedding, and had even said she was proud of them. Muttie and his wife Lizzie couldn't have told any tales. They washed all their own clothes, they kept their rooms tidy. They never complained when there was no meat or fish, only vegetables and rice. Sara had got them the money for school books. All they wanted to ask Cathy was could they do some more polishing for her at the premises because they wanted to earn some money for bus fares. Father had said that old Barty hadn't given him money that was owing, so there could be no pocket money this month.

*

'Miss Burke has booked a table for two,' James Byrne said as he came into Quentin's.

'This way, Mr Byrne.' Brenda Brennan was always amazed by the strange way people in Dublin turned up with the most unlikely companions. Whoever would have thought that these two would have known each other?

'I thought we'd be less likely to get emotional and shout at each other here,' Shona said.

'Not a restaurant known for its shouting, I agree,' James Byrne said.

They chose from the set lunch menu, and ordered a glass of wine each.

'I shouldn't have said that you taught me never to love again, that was going too far,' Shona began.

'If it was what you felt, and I pray God it will not always be this way, then you were perfectly right to say it,' he replied.

'Can you tell me exactly what happened? I won't interrupt.'

And in a soft voice, without looking for pity, he told her the story. How he and Una couldn't have children. They had been for every kind of test. All the fertility treatment they had thirty years ago wasn't like it is nowadays. Nothing worked. And then this was the time that more and more girls who had babies outside marriage were keeping them, which, though very admirable and right, did mean that there was no pool of children for those who wanted to adopt them. However, the social services were always willing to help, and there was fostering. You were always told that your foster child was on loan. You had to understand that you were minding her until it was possible for her to be returned to her parents. There had been a problem in Shona's home. Her parents had come from Dublin to the West to make a fresh start, but it hadn't worked. Her mother had found suppliers and dealers there as well as in Dublin, and in many ways it was worse for her because now she had no extended family to fall back on. Shona's father had not been a tower of strength. The Byrnes had been given the toddler Shona, aged three and a half. Other relations had taken her sisters and brother. They had loved her, no one could have asked for a more wonderful child. They had always told her about her real mother and father. But they had seemed shadowy figures to her, people much less real and exciting than *Goldilocks* or the *Turf-cutter's Donkey* or the other stories they told her. And the years went on, Shona went to school and made lots of friends.

'Carrie and Bebe,' Shona said. Remembering.

And she turned out to be very bright at school.

'You sat for hours and taught me,' Shona said. 'I was never bright, Carrie and Bebe weren't, my sisters weren't either in the homes they were in; it was only because you spent such a time there, looking things up for me, explaining over and over.'

'You remember?' He was pleased.

'Some of it, yes indeed,' she said.

The waiter arrived with their first course. They stopped talking to smile their thanks at him, and when he had gone they continued. He told her of the shopping trips, how they often went out intending to buy a winter coat for Una or a pair of shoes for himself, and they saw something for Shona which they bought instead.

'I'm not trying to tell you how much we spent as if I want to be thanked for it; we had plenty of money. Just want you to know that you were the centre of our lives, and no decision in that house, from what kind of cornflakes we ate right up to where we would go on holidays, was made without thinking of you. It's not looking for thanks; we wished we could have done more . . . I just wanted to know what a great hole you left in our lives when you had to go.'

The year they had to give her back, they had planned to take her to London to go to the Science Museum.

'I didn't know that,' she said. 'I've never been there.'

'It was to be a surprise, and well, obviously, when you had to go back we didn't tell you.'

'Did I really have to go back, James?'

'Oh, Shona, you did, and they told us that the best thing we could do for you was not to cry and tell you we'd miss you. They told us that you'd be with your family, and that it would be hard after ten years without us weeping and wailing and making it worse for you, so we were very strong and pretended that this was great news.'

'And I thought, always thought that you were relieved to be rid of me.' Her voice was flat.

'Ah, Shona, child, you *couldn't* have thought that. Not seriously?'

'What else could I think? No letters, I looked every day. You were both so good at writing to people, I couldn't believe you didn't write to me.'

'We were told not to, so as not to unsettle you.'

'I couldn't have been more unsettled than I was. I played it over and over in my mind that day. There were no tears when I went. I cried. I remember I said I wanted to stay, and you stood there like two stones saying that this was what we all wanted, and I was to tell my mother and sisters that I was delighted to see them.'

'I'll tell you about that day, and then you tell me. The car drove off and we watched it go down the drive. You never looked back.'

'I hated you so much for handing me over.'

'And we went back into the house, and I wondered would we have a cup of tea and Una said, "What for?". And the words hung there. What *was* the point of putting the kettle on, or indeed getting up in the morning, when you weren't there to share it? So the day went on, and Una sat in the kitchen looking out in the garden, and I sat in the hall looking at the door, for I suppose half an hour. Then she came out to the hall to me and said, "James, something odd has happened, all the clocks have stopped. They stopped at a quarter to six." And I said, but that *is* the time, it *is* a quarter to six. And then she wanted to know was that the morning or the evening. And that was the beginning of it, Shona, her mind started to go that afternoon, she thought you had been gone for five or six hours, she thought it must be nearly midnight. I brought her out and showed her the sky, I turned on the radio. She said you had left hours ago, you weren't forty minutes out of the house, and her mind started to go.'

'And she was so clever, so well read and everything,' Shona sighed.

'The last conversation we had was the night before you left. She wanted us to run away with you, change our names, go to England maybe, start again. I had to tell her that we couldn't, we would have nothing, we'd be on the run and we'd have to give you up eventually.'

'She wanted to do that?'

'So did I, Shona, but how could I sell the house, get another job, do anything to provide for you if we had to take false names? They'd be looking for us everywhere, people that stole a child. And since we couldn't do it, what we wanted to do, that's why it seemed right to go along with what had to be done.'

'I see,' she said.

'And we were allowed to write back if you wrote to us, but you never did. Tell me how the day turned out for you,' he asked.

She paused for a while and he didn't hurry her. She remembered that from the past, too. Dad would always wait until you got your thoughts together.

'It was a summer day, and the light was behind us all the way as we drove to Dublin because the sun was setting in the west. And I was in the back of the car and they talked to each other, the two women, I didn't know who they were, or that they were social workers. I suppose they were nice enough. We stopped in a town on the way and they bought me a burger and chips, and even though I was hungry I threw it away. Anyway, I got back to the house and the woman they said was my mother looked desperate. She had long, straggley hair that she hadn't washed for weeks, and she smoked all the time. She looked at me and said, "Will you look at the cut of you". That's all she said, she hadn't seen me for ten years and that was her greeting.'

'What did you say to her?' James asked.

'I was fourteen. I said nothing.'

The silence rested there between them, but it wasn't awkward. He simply waited for her to speak again.

'And then in a few days I knew what I had to do, I had to get out, you didn't want me . . . I thought, so I couldn't go back to you, I had to make my own way and maybe I could do it through school. So I began the life that I still lead, the life of a workaholic. My sisters were dossers, they did nothing except tell me I was full of airs and graces and I didn't like the milk carton on the table. "She wants a milk jug," they used to mock me. But I had great teachers. I told one, a Mrs Ryan, that things were bad at home, she was so nice. She said that things are always bad at home, that is the way the world runs, so I thought she had a lousy time too. It was only years later I learned that she had a great life. She taught me to type in lunch hours, and used to let me use the school machine to practise on. And there were others, too; it was a tough city school, so they loved someone who was making an effort to do something rather than shoplift or get pregnant at sixteen.'

'And when you left?'

'Ah, but before that I had to fight to stay and finish. They wanted me to work in the factory. I refused. I was sixteen. I wanted to get my Leaving Cert. and a life. My mother was using again, I didn't care any more. All I needed was somewhere to work, and I had my own room because the others left. I used to take a small amount of the welfare money every week, and tried to make an evening meal every night, potatoes, lentils, and you could get cheap, squashy tomatoes. Sometimes she was able to take a mug of soup, but mainly she didn't bother. And I'd love to have gone to university. I had enough points and everything, but the only way that I could get out of there was to get a job, so I went to work the day I finished my exams.'

'What did you do?'

'I moved out of home and worked in a travel agency as a junior. I learned everything I could in six months. I got a proper job in another travel agency. I got two holidays, one in Italy, one in Spain. The only holidays I ever had in my whole life. I've been to London on work a few times, but I never had another holiday. I remember the excitement of getting a passport. Then I worked in a dress shop, then a hotel and by the time the job came up at Haywards I was ready for it.'

'And your ... mother?'

'I went to see her every week ... You see, you did teach me manners after all. And how to behave. Sometimes she was so stoned she hardly knew who I was; other times she was depressed. I used to take her soup, some weeks she drank it, others I used to find it with mould on it. I wasn't the only martyr, my sisters went in too. We didn't fight, ever. They just sneered at me. Lady Muck, they called me in those early days. I said nothing; as time passed they got indifferent to me, as I to them. Now it's like meeting strangers. At the funeral I looked at them and I realised I knew nothing about them at all, or they about me.'

James took out a paper tissue and wiped his eyes.

'You finally realised you don't have to wash hankies. Mum and I used to say that you were the last of the folded-linen variety ...'

She stopped suddenly. She realised that she had called his dead wife Mum after all these years. She held out her hand at the same time as he did.

'What a waste,' he said.

'Of so many lives,' she agreed.

'We must make very sure it doesn't happen any more, Shona.'

'I'm more grateful than I can say that you got in touch,' she said.

'Well. I learned how to cook three dinners; you've only had one, there are still two to go,' he said, wondering had he gone too far.

'Saturday?' Shona suggested. 'I don't know when I last had something to look forward to on a Saturday night.'

*

'I'm going back to work tomorrow,' Cathy said. She sat in her dressing gown at the kitchen table in Waterview.

'No, it's too soon.'

'But they said when I felt well, and I feel well now.'

'No, it's too dangerous ... You're not fully better.'

'I've lost all I can lose. There are no bits of the baby left in there to lose any more.'

He winced at the phrase, the image. But she didn't mind. She wasn't going to pretend that this child had not existed.

'I still think you're not fully better,' he protested.

'I'm not fully better in my mind because I'm upset, but my body is fine and it needs to get back to working rather than sitting here all day on my own.'

'I'll be home early,' he promised.

'No, it's not that.'

'I know it's possibly not the right thing to say but there many ways—'

'Then don't say it.'

'You don't know what I'm going to say.'

'I do, and please don't say it,' she begged.

He laughed at her. 'You wouldn't get away with that kind of argument in court,' he said.

'We're not *in* court.'

'Please let me finish. I only wanted to say that in many ways all this sad business has shaken us up, made us have a proper look at ourselves and realise where we are going.'

'Yes.'

'And I will never assume again that you are willing to drop everything and follow me wherever *my* career takes me. Now that's all I was going to say. Is it all right?' He looked at her expectantly, waiting for a response.

'It's fine.'

'So after all you *didn't* know what I was going to say.' Again looking for the warm answer.

'Not precisely, no.'

'What do you mean?'

'I thought when you began you'd say it's all for the best, but you didn't, not in so many words.'

'I didn't say anything at all like that, and if you remember I called it a sad business. Where did I say it was all for the best?'

'But that's what you think, Neil,' she said sadly.

'So first I'm on trial for what I'm going to say and then when I don't say it, I'm on trial for what you believe I think.' He looked wounded.

'I'm sorry, Neil, when you put it like that, it sounds very harsh. I didn't mean to be that.'

'And neither do I mean to be insensitive. Rest more,' he said from the door.

Cathy wished things could get back to normal, but there seemed to be no way that she and Neil could talk about what had happened without her wanting to scream and rail. His cool, logical, lawyer's way of approaching it was driving her mad. She wanted them both to cry over the dead baby, to admit that it was a tragedy. But there was Neil going out purposefully to deal with other people's misfortunes, not realising that the biggest one was in his own home. If he could only give a tenth of that care and concern to the fact that they had lost a child, then it would be fine.

She mustn't sit around here indefinitely going over the same thing again and again. The only place things might be normal was back at work. She wouldn't even wait until tomorrow, she'd go today.

They were delighted to see her back, and made a great fuss. Nobody said anything about it all being for the best, they said how much they missed her and how hard they had worked.

'So what's new?'

'A couple aged about a hundred who want to get married next month and can't find a venue to suit them,' June said, taking out a file.

'How old are they really?'

'Ancient,' June said.

'Well, we can't all be seventeen-year-old brides,' Cathy laughed.

'Probably wiser not to be,' June sighed.

'How about the church hall?' Cathy asked.

'Too big for them, they don't know how many people they're going to invite. Fifty maybe; but they think it might only be about twenty-four.'

'They're not very flush with friends, are they?' Cathy asked.

'They were the nicest couple I ever met,' Tom said simply. 'They're coming in today, you'll love them.'

Tom was right. Stella O'Brien and Sean Clery were indeed the nicest people you could meet. Aged in their mid-fifties, they had met a year ago at a beginners' bridge class. They were both still utterly hopeless at bridge, but devoted to each other. There was a problem.

'Isn't there always a problem about a wedding,' Cathy said sympathetically.

This one centred around Sean's three children and Stella's two children. People who did not look forward to the nuptials. Stella's son and daughter assumed their mother would remain a widow, look after her grandchildren when they came along and leave them her house. Sean's three daughters had assumed that their father would remain a widower and would eventually move out of his house which could be sold and the money divided between the girls. They would move him from one of their homes to the other, none of them having him for more than four months a year. The couple didn't *tell* all this to Cathy, of course, it just emerged in the conversation. She nodded and listened and accepted what kind of places wouldn't do and why.

'This must seem very odd to you, Miss Scarlet. I mean, all you young people must live a normal, uncomplicated life where everything works like clockwork,' Stella apologised.

'Absolutely not, I didn't know on the morning of my wedding day if anyone except five friends and my aunt would turn up.'

'Tell us more than that did,' Sean begged.

'Yes, my mother and father came, and the few relations I had who didn't emigrate. Most of Neil's didn't, apart from his mother and father who were like two icebergs, but the friends made up for it. I look back on it and I think it was a fine day. You will too. Tell me where would you really *like* to have it, and we'll see if we can work out something around that.'

'Do you know Holly's hotel in Wicklow?' Stella began.

'Yes indeed,' Cathy said. It was where she had told Neil about the baby. What a long, long time ago that seemed now. 'They don't do weddings there, sadly, we did ask, but would you know somewhere a bit like that?' Cathy looked at Stella O'Brien, who had put a deposit on a dress at Haywards and who was so happy for the world to share her pleasure in meeting Sean Clery over a green-baize table. She looked at Sean Clery, who had bought her a gold ring with a Celtic design, and kept lifting her hand to admire it.

'I'll find you something like that hotel,' she promised.

'You are a very kind girl,' they assured her.

Cathy, who had shaken her head twice at the suggestion that she might talk to Maud and Simon on the phone, knew this wasn't true. A kind person would have spoken to those two children, but she really couldn't face them. Yet. She still felt a bit jittery, and wondered had she in fact come back to work too early.

'Anyone need the van for a couple of hours?' she asked.

She knew Tom's face so well, she could read on it that he was worried if she was fit to drive ... But if he thought it, he didn't show it.

'Sure ...' he said, and threw her the keys.

Cathy drove south to Wicklow. A beautiful autumn day, it was wonderful to get out of the city. She looked at the tape selection to see what was on offer. Pop groups she had never heard of, some Irish traditional music, a country and western tape and favourite arias. She put on the last one, and turned up the volume to lose herself and sang along to Pavarotti's swelling voice. The music made her sad. She thought again of the child who hadn't made it to getting born and the tears poured down her cheeks. Would she ever stop weeping? She sang louder to try and stop crying. At traffic lights, a man in the next car smiled at her.

'What are you singing?' he asked, looking at her admiringly.

'*Nessun dorma* ... None shall sleep,' she said. 'Possibly too true in terms of my singing.'

'You're lovely,' he said. 'Fancy a drink in Ashford?'

'No thanks, but you are sweet to ask,' she said.

She felt fifteen years younger, like a kid out of school. She drove on to Holly's hotel.

'I can't do it, Ms Scarlet, we don't have the resources,' Miss Holly said.

'They're the nicest people you ever met. You and I have to deal with such awful people in our work.'

'I know, Ms Scarlet, but I have three waitresses who are as old as myself, we can't take on weddings.'

'Let me do it, Miss Holly. We'll rent the place from you, we'll be in and out, you won't know we were ever here.'

'Are they family, or are they blackmailing you?'

'I never met them until this morning, but to tell you the truth I've not been well. I had a miscarriage, and in fact today's my first day back at work and I'm feeling a bit vulnerable. They were so bloody nice, and they said they wanted a place as like this as possible ... And you know I love it here, so I know what they mean.' She was afraid her voice sounded a bit choked.

'And you do like it here, you and your husband?'

'We love it, it's our great treat, it's a place that works magic for us.'

'It didn't last time,' Miss Holly said.

'What do you mean?'

'Last time you and your husband were talking about the baby at dinner. Betty, one of the waitresses told me.'

'Yes, that's true, but we haven't actually told anyone else ...'

'And neither have we. I'll let you have the place for the meal, Ms Scarlet.'

'You'll never regret it, Miss Holly.'

'Now all we have to do is think of the food for Stella and Sean,' Cathy said when she was back at the premises.

'What do you mean? We have to get a venue first, and it's so hard, given all the limitations.'

'Oh, that's all organised,' Cathy said, her eyes dancing.

'No, come on, I know you're superwoman, but we've been three days trying places ... Nowhere suits.'

'Miss Holly said yes.'

'You drove down there today?'

'Yup,' said Cathy.

'I thought we could manage without her, Tom, but it turns out I was wrong,' said June.

'Are you going on a honeymoon?' Cathy asked Stella O'Brien.

'We hadn't thought of it. The wedding itself is such a big thing. Once we have that sorted ...'

'I've sorted it all out, Stella. Miss Holly will let us do it in her place, so why don't you book in there for a honeymoon of three or four nights?'

'It's so peaceful, such a happy place to stay.' Stella O'Brien had tears in her eyes. 'It was a lucky day that we phoned your company,' she said.

'How *did* you hear of us, actually?' Cathy always liked to know.

'Last Easter I won a raffle at the school where I work, and the prize was to have a manicure at Haywards, and this very pretty girl said that her fiancé ran a catering company and gave me your card ... So when Sean and I decided to get married ... there you were in our address book. I'd really like to thank her.'

'Ah yes. Yes, indeed.'

'There's a problem about the girl, is there?'

'She and Tom aren't together any more ... that's all. Now, what kind of music would you like?'

'I beg your pardon?'

'For the wedding. Will we have a pianist or an accordionist ... Or would you prefer a music centre? Tom can organise that, no trouble, and put on all the CDs you want.'

Stella's voice dropped. 'I'm going to confide in you, I'd be afraid we might look silly if we had music. Sean had a very quiet wedding first time round, his wife was a kind of recluse I think. He's just dying for fun and excitement, he doesn't have an idea of how much his children resent us marrying. I don't think that any of those girls are going to come to the wedding.'

Cathy laid her hand on Stella's. 'They'll come just to see it. Believe me, they won't be able to let their father get married without coming to watch it. They'll be there ... Will yours?'

'My son will be there. My daughter, I don't know.'

'Bet you any money she will,' said Cathy.

'Not a word from those children,' Muttie said.

'I suppose they have such a great life up at The Beeches, they wouldn't have the time for us any more.' Lizzie was both humble and philosophical.

'Cathy said you wouldn't ask an ordinary rat to live at The Beeches,' Muttie grumbled.

'Yes, but you know the way Cathy goes on about the Mitchells in general,' Lizzie explained.

'They didn't come last Saturday, and never a solitary word out of them,' Muttie said, very upset.

'Well, I rang Cathy and she said they were grown-up enough to make up their own minds,' Lizzie said.

'There was so much we had to do, to arrange,' Muttie said. 'I don't believe it was anything to do with being grown-up at all, I think they didn't have their bus fare, that's what I think.'

'Well don't go saying that,' Lizzie ordered.

'Of course I won't,' said Muttie, who then sat down and wrote a letter to Master Simon and Miss Maud Mitchell at The Beeches.

'Just in case there's a problem about transport between our residences, I enclose £5 (five pounds). We are always here ... M. and L. Scarlet.'

'Walter?'

'Yes, Father?'

'Has that ... er ... social worker been in touch about anything?'

'Don't think so, why?'

'I realise the twins didn't go up to Mr Muttie, or whatever he's called, at the Jarlath's place last Saturday.'

'Well, I suppose they got tired of it.'

'I don't think they had any money for the fare, as it happened.'

'Did they just spend their pocket money, Father? Was that it?'

'They didn't really *get* any pocket money, you see, old Barty actually left me a bit short.'

'Oh, God, Father, be very, very careful. That Sara and Cathy, those two are real ball-breakers.'

'I know. Let's keep a watch.'

Walter picked up the mail. There was an odd-looking letter from someone to the children. Walter opened it carefully. It might be something about this ridiculous arrangement, he and his father should be forewarned. He found the fiver and pocketed it. He put the letter and envelope into the fire.

Jock Mitchell called at The Beeches. The twins were doing their homework at the table.

'Where's your dad?' he asked.

They told him that Father's friend old Barty had rung up and sorted out an old quarrel, and so Father had gone off to meet him in order to celebrate the fight being over.

'And your mother?'

Apparently Mother had got upset when Father went to meet old Barty. And she had gone down to the shops. Jock Mitchell didn't like the notion of his sister-in-law going down to the shops. That's how the drinking had started before, she just went to one particular section of the supermarket.

'And everything all right here, is it?'

The twins looked at each other and nodded their doubtful agreement that everything was all right. Uncle Jock didn't come to see them often; he might not come again for months. No point in hoping he'd come in regularly, as someone to keep an eye on things.

'Did you come to see Father, Uncle Jock?'

'No, I came to see where Walter keeps his computer, actually.'

The twins supposed it must be in his bedroom. But that was locked.

'He says he uses it every night, that's why he took it from the office.'

Maud and Simon looked at each other. They had never heard the sound of any computer, nor seen one coming into the house. But they knew it was better to give no information at all, so they looked blankly at their uncle. They were funny little things. He wished Hannah had taken to them more. They could have come to Oaklands and played on the swings around the big trees ... It didn't look as if that hard-working son of his and his equally career-minded wife were going to produce any grandchildren for them in a hurry, and Manda had told them that in her case it wasn't a starter either. But no point in complicating things; Kenneth had always been an odd fellow, and his wife very unstable from day one. Wiser to stay well away from them and their children. Jock sighed: he had definitely failed to do this in the case of Walter. There was no way of getting him into any kind of shape in the office now. Neil, always the champion of the underdog, had unexpectedly advised him to throw the boy out. Jock suspected that Walter had stolen the computer and sold it. But he had no proof, and it didn't look as if he were going to get any this evening from his visit to The Beeches.

'Will we say you called to see Walter?' Simon asked.

'Or should we just say nothing at all?' asked Maud.

'I think we should say nothing at all,' Jock said.

He contemplated giving them a couple of pounds each, as one had done to children long ago. But maybe it was patronising nowadays, and there was in operation a very firm agreement about everything, including pocket money. Maybe it would just throw things out of kilter. So he just rattled the coins as the children looked at him hopefully, and then said goodbye.

Geraldine had dinner at Quentin's with Nick Ryan. Brenda Brennan just nodded her head politely to her as they came in. No one would know that the women were friends. Some men felt threatened if they thought that their date was better known in the restaurant than they were. Geraldine admired that kind of professionalism. She practised it herself. Before this dinner she had read up a great deal about the dry-cleaning business in Ireland. He was a very pleasant man. Not afraid to pay a compliment. Also, he was upfront about everything, which she particularly liked. He said it was a treat for him to go out to dinner with a glamorous lady, normally at this time of the evening he was letting himself in the door at home and groaning to his wife about the day at the office and coping with two fairly difficult children. Geraldine nodded her understanding of this. *All* children were difficult, anyone who said otherwise wasn't a serious parent. This made him feel good, and also the way Geraldine seemed to accept the existence of a wife and family in the life of a man she was having dinner with. She looked, as always, perfectly groomed, and much younger than her years. She answered questions about herself in a practised, easy way, not giving very much away but still telling enough to make a picture of a woman with a working-class background who had worked hard to get where she had arrived. She made it very clear that she wasn't trying to get married and settle down. That she preferred a very independent life at this stage, and liked to see a great variety of friends.

'And you do have a lot of friends. I was very impressed at your party,' he said. 'Very pleasant gathering indeed.'

'I'm glad you enjoyed it, I hope you met a lot of people,' Geraldine said. It was far too soon in their relationship to tell him all that went on behind the scenes at the party, the bath towels, Doctor Said, Cathy being taken in an ambulance to the hospital.

'To be very honest, I wasn't all that interested in meeting other people,' he said.

'That's very flattering,' Geraldine said.

'And very sincere,' said Nick Ryan.

'I don't know how Geraldine does it,' Brenda Brennan said to her husband Patrick in the kitchen. 'She has yet another rich, handsome businessman out there purring at her and pawing the ground.'

'Ah, but she didn't get a safe and steady and reliable husband, like you did,' Patrick consoled her.

'I know.' Brenda's tone didn't seem to suggest somehow that she had won out in this comparison.

'Or a passionate, creative, temperamental chef like myself,' he suggested.

That was more like it. 'Indeed she did not,' said Brenda, pleased.

Mrs Barry wouldn't be at The Beeches for a while; she was going away to her daughter's for three weeks' holiday.

'The press is full of tins of things there for you, and the milkman is paid to the end of the month.'

'Thank you, Mrs Barry.'

'And you know ... you know your mother's not well. She should have a doctor. I'll ring Sara and let her know.'

'No, Mrs Barry, we'll ring Sara,' Maud said.

'We have other things to tell her, so we'll tell her about Mother not being well.'

'Good. That's all right then, she'll be round to see to things.'

Maud and Simon didn't ring Sara. It only upset everyone when Sara came in; it was fine for five minutes, but when she left everyone and everything got worse. Better for her not to come at all. And when she called to know was everything all right, they said it was all just fine.

Sara met Neil at the big public lecture on homelessness.

'Glad it's all going all right at The Beeches,' she said.

'Oh, is it? Good,' he said.

'You haven't been there recently, then?' she asked.

'No; there have been a few other things on our minds. Listen, I have to tell you because you're one of the few people that knew she was pregnant; Cathy had a miscarriage.'

'Oh, I am sorry,' Sara said.

'Yes, but nobody, least of all the twins or any of the family knows a thing about it so, of course ...'

'Of course not.'

'And in many ways, of course ...' Neil began.

'I know, in many ways it could be for the best at this particular time, you could still take that job abroad now.'

'I may not go forward for it,' Neil said.

'Still, there's an awful lot of work to be done at home,' Sara said, pleased that he was not going away. She looked at him with undisguised admiration.

He smiled at her. It was nice when someone thought you were great.

Cathy was going to ring the twins. She actually got as far as the phone, but then she thought of having to talk to Kenneth Mitchell, and she changed her mind. She tried to think back to the first days of her engagement to Neil. Had she really tried to please awful people like that, had she tried to get Kenneth and Kay on her side in the battle against Hannah? She hoped that she had not. That whole battle seemed so long ago, and in many ways so unimportant. What did points scored over her mother-in-law *mean*, anyway? Neil had been right in that, and how silly Cathy must have been to hug those little hard-won victories over her mother-in-law as if they were trophies. She'd ring the twins when this wedding was over, when she had some time to give to them.

Simon and Maud sat at the kitchen table. They had eaten sardines and cold tinned beans, which went well together. They had tied up the rubbish and left it outside the gates of The Beeches; the binmen came tomorrow. They rescued a newspaper, in case they should clean their shoes for school. It was full of a race meeting coming up shortly. Muttie had said he was going to take them to that, so they would get the feel of a real country race meet. He had told them how great it would be, but now there was no mention of it. They supposed he had gone off them, as people so often did.

'I can't understand those children not getting in touch with us. They were all over us at the wedding,' Muttie said.

'Maybe they have no money,' said Lizzie, who didn't know about the fiver he had sent to them.

'They don't need any money to pick up the phone,' said Muttie, who had sent them the very fiver he could well have put on a horse that he had liked the look of but not the sound of. It had won at thirty to one.

Stella O'Brien's daughter came to visit Scarlet Feather. Tall, pale, mid-twenties, discontented, they didn't like her on sight at the premises. Like almost every woman who came into the place, she looked at Tom Feather with admiration and a sly little smile. It did her no good.

'Cathy is mainly dealing with this wedding, perhaps you should talk to her.' Tom got them coffee in the front room, and with some relief left them to it.

This girl Melanie looked full of grievance, and she hadn't begun yet. 'I hope you know my mother isn't made of money.'

'Nor are any of us, Miss O'Brien, but we did go over the costs very carefully, and she and her fiancé seemed very satisfied.'

'It's not the cost of what you're providing that's wrong.' Melanie said.

'So what is upsetting you then?'

'The numbers. My poor mother thinks that there are fifty people coming to see her marry that little fortune-hunter she met at a poker party . . . She's off her head and throwing good money after bad.'

'Well, she did say that there was a certain fluidity about the numbers; we've taken that into account.'

'Fluidity my foot, there's twenty-eight invited from our side, and I can tell you that a good twenty of them won't be there, only eight at the very most . . . I don't know how many he's fielding, but from what I hear his lot don't want it either.'

Cathy felt a great urge to stand up, lean over the table and slap Melanie O'Brien so hard across the face and so often that she would fall to the floor. But she held it back.

'Dear me! Mr Clery's family object, too?'

'That's what I heard.'

'Why don't you go and see them?' Cathy suggested.

'I don't want to go near them, have anything to do with them.'

'No, I was thinking of your mother's money. Well, if *his* family isn't going to come and yours isn't, then you're quite right not to let her put up that much outlay.' It was a heavy risk, but Cathy decided it was worth it.

'I don't even know where they live,' Melanie grumbled.

'I could give you Mr Clery's address and phone number from the files. I think one of his daughters lives with him, so you could find them that way.'

'That's very helpful of you, Miss . . .'

'Scarlet . . . Cathy Scarlet.' She had about another forty seconds of good temper left.

'It's just, I don't see why you want to do this.'

'I liked your mother, I wouldn't want her to pay out a lot of money for people who were not going to turn up, this way you'll be able to get me the exact numbers and we can run it past Mrs O'Brien again.' She had written down Sean Clery's address as she was talking, and then she ushered Melanie out of the door. Cathy came back into the kitchen.

'Give me something to punch quickly,' she shouted.

June found the clean laundry bag that had just come back. Cathy sank her fists over and over in the tea towels, tablecloths and napkins. 'That's much better,' she said at last.

'What was that about?' Tom asked.

'I was just rearranging Melanie O'Brien's face without having to go to jail for it,' Cathy said, pleased.

'And dare we ask what you actually said to her out there?' Tom asked.

'I took a risk, Tom, and if it doesn't work I promise that I'll take all the blame.'

'Could you give us a vague clue ... just what area the risk was taken in?' He was laughing at her; he wasn't seriously worried. But then he didn't know what she had done. 'You're better off not knowing,' Cathy said.

Joe Feather took out the backgammon set. 'Come on, Dad, I'm one up, so get your revenge.'

'It's a silly game, that one,' Maura Feather said. 'I don't know why you play it. It's just like ludo for children.'

'No, it's not, you have to be able to guess and second-guess and gamble. You'd be good at it, Mam.'

'I would not.'

'Come on here, and you play against Dad. I'll sit beside you and see how you fare.'

Grumbling, she sat down and got into the game. Joe's mind drifted away. It wasn't nearly as bad as he had thought it would be, helping out with the old folk at home. He had begun this regular visiting to help Tom, take some of the burden off him, and had continued it out of guilt over Marcella. But oddly, he didn't mind it at all these days. The time there didn't hang so heavy on his hands, and he wasn't being interrogated about his lifestyle. Which actually was fairly monastic these days, until he got all that money back from the guy who had conned him. He would do it one of these days. Joe Feather knew that he was not going to let that smart guy get away with it. Just as he knew there was no great news on the modelling scene from across the water. Someone had met Marcella, who was very anxious to come home.

Melanie arranged to meet Sheila, who was Sean Clery's youngest daughter. They were about the same age. They agreed that the marriage was ridiculous and gross, and had come about out of sheer loneliness.

'Why else would she have gone to that poker club?' Melanie asked.

'I thought it was a whist drive, but it's all the same,' said Sheila.

'Suppose we told them that we'd be around more, make them less lonely. Do you think that would work?' Melanie asked.

'Do you know, I think it's too late for that,' said Sheila.

'So will you go or will you not?' Melanie was looking to get the numbers.

'I don't know, honestly. I'm not sure. I'm not saying a word against your mother; I'm sure she's a perfectly nice person, it's just that my father is great, and I don't want to see him doing anything foolish.'

'So you might go, is that what you're telling me?'

'Well, if he's going ahead, and it would make him happy to see us there, then we might well go – not with a good grace, but we'd go. What about you?'

'I'm not going, and again, nothing against your father personally, but my mother doesn't *need* to marry again.'

'And your brother?' Sheila asked.

'A real mammy's boy, he'd do anything to get a pat on the head.'

'So he *is* going, you think?'

'Probably,' Melanie said unwillingly.

'Well, if her side are going, then to be honest we wouldn't really want Dad to be standing there by himself,' Sheila said.

'So you will come to this wedding, then?'

'I think rather than hurt him I would.'

Melanie looked glum. 'And of course if you go, then others will, like your aunts and uncles and everything.'

'Sorry, Melanie, but you did ask, and I don't think we're going to stop them getting married,' Sheila said.

Cathy went to The Beeches.

'There was nothing about this constant visiting in the agreement,' Kenneth Mitchell said.

'I came to visit my cousins, is that a crime?'

'They're not your cousins.'

'No, but they *are* my husband's cousins, which is more or less the same thing.'

'Entirely different,' Kenneth Mitchell barked.

'Suit yourself,' Cathy said. 'But I would like to see them.'

'You've missed them, I'm afraid.'

'Oh, really, where are they?'

'I have no idea,' he said.

Cathy's eyes narrowed. 'Now we really *are* talking about the agreement. You're meant to know where they are at all times.'

'All right. They've gone to see their mother in hospital.'

'*What*? She's back in hospital?'

'Only momentarily. She's coming home tomorrow. They were just bringing her some clean clothes.' Cathy got out her mobile phone.

'What are you doing?'

'What you should have done, notifying Sara.'

'You're totally overreacting.'

'Where's the hospital?'

'It's none of your business,' Kenneth blustered.

'I wasn't going to go over there and torture the woman. I wanted to pick up the children, that's all.'

'You needn't do that, I hear them coming in,' he said sulkily.

Cathy thought their greeting was a little cool. 'I'm sorry your mother isn't well,' she said.

'We didn't tell her,' Simon said, looking guiltily at his father.

'Not a word,' Maud confirmed.

'But you were *meant* to tell Sara or me when things change here, you're meant to be grown-up enough to understand the agreement.'

They hung their heads.

'If the children made no complaint, then they were perfectly happy with the way things were,' Kenneth said smugly.

'I still have to let Sara know. That was the *deal*, Kenneth,' she said.

'Interfering, meddling . . .'

The twins couldn't bear to hear this, so they went out to the garden. Cathy followed them. They sat on a little bench beside the garden shed.

'You see, it gets worse if we tell,' Simon said.

'And better if we don't really,' Maud added.

'Why haven't you been to see Muttie and his wife Lizzie?' Cathy smiled to herself as she used the same form of words as the twins always did. They looked at her guiltily. Eventually she got it out of them; they just didn't have the fare.

'Dad told me that he sent you a fiver. Why didn't you use that?'

396

'A fiver?' said Maud.

'We didn't get it,' Simon said.

They looked at each other. It was so much money for anyone to send them. Cathy knew without a shadow of a doubt that they spoke the truth. They had never got that fiver. She reached into her handbag. 'He wanted you to have it, it must have got lost.' They looked at her innocently. They were still at the age when they believed things got lost in the post.

'Aren't they such total clowns?' Neil said that night.

'Who this time?'

It could have been anybody. The government, the insurance company, the law library, the judiciary, the newspapers.

'The eejits up at The Beeches. Dad told me that Walter's nicked the computer from his office and hidden it there, and Sara tells me the twins have been getting nothing to eat and no pocket money, and that Kay's back in the funny farm.'

'Not quite as bad as that, it was a check-up. They think she's coming home tomorrow.'

'Still.' He was annoyed.

She badly wanted to remind him that it was he who had fought for these hopeless people to get their children back. It was Neil Mitchell who had said that they must be restored to their flesh and blood instead of living happily between St Jarlath's Crescent and Waterview, where everyone could keep an eye on them. But it wasn't something to go to war over. So she left it. However, she did tell him about Muttie's missing fiver.

'I suppose that fool Walter can actually feel money through envelopes. I imagine he took it,' Neil said casually.

She felt a sense of rage against Walter rise in her. Muttie's money taken by that young brat. Admittedly it wasn't money that Muttie had in any sense gone out and worked for, but Lizzie had earned that money house-cleaning. And then it should go to line a Mitchell's pocket. She actually felt herself give a gasp of indignation.

'Do you feel all right?' Neil asked.

'Sorry, it's nothing.'

'You went back to work too early.'

'I didn't. I like it there, it's very busy, it takes my mind off things.'

'And talking about things . . .' he began.

She must not let him annoy her now. He meant so well, but everything was driving her mad. He might ask diffidently if she felt ready to think about love-making again, and she most certainly did not. He might go on about her work and it being too tiring and that would drive her wild – only at work could she keep her emotions under control. Neil could say any of a dozen things which would upset her, none of them intentionally.

It never used to be like this in the old days.

'I must tell you about this wedding we're doing,' she interrupted. She didn't want any more Meaning of Life. Whatever he said would be wrong. Neil shrugged. Cathy went into the tale about Stella and Sean, but he wasn't listening at all. There was a polite, attentive expression on his face. But he had opted out of the story.

'So what do you think I should do?' she asked him suddenly. It was mean. But she had to know that he really wasn't listening.

'About what, exactly?' he asked.

'About the music,' she smiled. She hadn't mentioned music yet in the story.

'You'll know it when you hear it,' he said. No wonder he was such a good lawyer, so quick on his feet.

'You're right, and I think you're right too about my being tired, Neil, I'm going to bed now.' She lay there, eyes open, for a long time. No one had told her that it would be like this. So empty.

'Cathy's late this morning,' June noted.

'She's gone to look for music for the wedding,' Tom said.

'Isn't she incredible? I wouldn't know where to start.'

'I don't think she does either, she just says that she'll know it when she hears it.'

'It'll be great doing a job all the way down the country. I wish we could stay longer,' June sighed.

'June, you'd die. You're such a Dub you would perish like a rare bird out of its environment if you were to stay in the country.'

'No I wouldn't. Jimmy and I once thought of living right out in the country. Honestly we did.'

'For about three minutes, you did. How is he, anyway?' June's husband was housebound since his fall.

'Like a weasel,' June said easily. 'The sooner I find myself a new one, the better. He doesn't know if I'm there or I'm not, Tom. I said to him the other day that I could go off for a month and he'd just ask me if I'd brought back the sausages when I got home.'

'I'm sure that's not true,' Tom said.

'What would you know, Tom, you didn't marry when you were a schoolkid like we did. We've had no life, either of us, and now Jimmy has a busted back. At least I have a great career.'

Cathy walked down Grafton Street without seeing anyone or anything. She had woken this morning with a heavy feeling of guilt. And yet what had she to be guilty about? The miscarriage wasn't her fault. Of course it wasn't. So why did she feel that she was somehow letting everyone in her life down quite badly? She could put it all right if only she had more time. Like she would insist on Tom taking a couple of days off; he looked very weary sometimes. She would take her mother off in the van for a day's shopping in the markets. She would invite Geraldine to a four-hour lunch at Quentin's. She would take the twins and Hooves for a weekend to Holly's; they had never stayed in a hotel, and Holly's had a guest-dog policy. And Neil? What would she do for Neil to make things better? It wasn't as easy as it was for everyone else. Then she heard the music, it was violins and accordions. Six men, a café orchestra playing on the street. They were refugees, they were collecting money. They would look perfect in the conservatory corner of Holly's hotel; they would be great for the party. She talked to Josef, the one with the best English, she explained everything, she wanted waltzes and old love songs.

'We do not have expensive clothes to play at a wedding in a hotel,' he said.

'That's not important. Do you know "A Kiss Is Just A Kiss"?' He said something to the group and they played it. And 'Smoke Gets In Your Eyes', and a Strauss medley.

'Would you have transport to Wicklow?' she asked, hardly daring to hope. It turned out that somebody had a van. 'You'll be perfect,' Cathy said. 'Where can I find you?' They gave her the name of a hostel, she gave them fifty pounds as a deposit.

'How do you know we may not take your money, pack our violins into their cases and go away before the wedding party?' Josef asked. 'Keep your fifty pounds.'

'No, how do you know that I'm not a madwoman and there's no wedding and no engagement at all? You must keep your fifty pounds.' She hugged herself and softly sang some of the songs they had played as she went down the street.

Shona called out to her, 'Hey, you're talking to yourself. That's a good sign.'

'Worse, I'm singing to myself. Better lock me up.'

Two days before the wedding, Melanie rang Cathy.

'My mother tells me you've booked a band, an entire band . . . Is she paying for this?'

'She and Sean agreed that the group sounded exactly what they wanted.'

'She went to a refugee hostel to listen to some deadbeats playing . . . And you're charging her to let those people into—'

'Melanie, excuse me, there's someone at the door, back in a second.' Cathy got up and walked three times round the premises, then went over to Tom.

'Sorry, Tom, I'm going to blow this, there are some people I can't talk to. It's Melanie saying that the orchestra is far too dear . . . Can you talk to her?'

'*No, no, no*, Cathy.'

'Yes, Tom, I beg you. She needs your dripping sensuality down the phone. Just say something sexy, she'll be putty in your hands like they all are.'

'I hate you, Cathy Scarlet.'

'And I hate you a lot of the time, Tom Feather, but for the good of the company I put up with a lot of—'

'What did you tell her. . . ?'

'That I had to answer the door.'

He picked up the receiver. 'Melanie O'Brien, how *are* you?' he said. 'Cathy got tied up with someone at the door. Tell me what I can do for you, but before you tell me something, tell me you'll keep me a dance on Wednesday night?'

Cathy watched Tom make a gesture as if he were stroking a cat.

'Piss artist,' Cathy said to June.

'But desperately good at it,' June said shrewdly. 'She's not bellyaching about the cost of the bloody orchestra *now*, is she?'

On the Tuesday Maud telephoned Cathy.

'Excuse me, I don't want to delay you,' she began.

'Good girl, Maud, I am quite busy,' Cathy said.

'It's just that you know you said we should be grown-up.'

'And you are being grown-up by saying we mustn't delay, so what can I do for you, Maud?'

'You don't want any treasure polishing, you say?'

'No, not at the moment, thank you.'

'But Cathy, when you gave us that fiver from Muttie, we went up to Muttie and his wife Lizzie, and they told us that some of your treasures were stolen . . .'

'Yes, but don't worry about that.'

'No, it's just I remember how much you liked the silver thing you called a punchbowl.'

'Yes, Maud?'

'Are they very dear?'

'I don't know, Maud, honestly, and if there isn't anything else . . .'

'It's just I saw one in our garden shed. It's usually locked, but I went in today and I thought maybe it might be nice for you instead of yours, and I could ask Father—'

'Don't ask anything for the moment, Maud, I beg you, we're up to our tonsils here and we'll get back to you.'

'You said that before, Cathy, and you never came back at all.'

'Jesus, Maud, don't nag, please, please don't nag, if you *knew* the kind of day we're having here.'

'Sorry.'

'And after we've done this wedding tomorrow, I really *will* come and see you. Promise. Okay?'

'Who was that?' Tom asked.

'Maud. I wasn't as patient as I might have been, but she was going on and on about some punchbowl.'

'What?'

'She says there's one hidden in their garden shed up at The Beeches.'

Suddenly they looked at each other.

'Oh, my God.' Cathy put her hand over her mouth.

'Walter,' said Tom.

It was a day when everything seemed to take twice the length it should have. They just didn't have the five minutes they needed to talk about the possibility of Walter being responsible.

'I can't believe he did all that damage,' Cathy said.

'You'd understand him nicking things, it's in his nature.'

'Maybe whoever was with him.'

'But how did he get *in*?' Tom worried

And that was it. They had to concentrate on the news from the fishmonger's that the catch had been bad last night and the fish they had ordered just hadn't turned up. So the platter that would have looked so well as a starter had to be rethought. Tom had forgotten to ask the butcher to cut and cube the meat, that meant another half-hour with knives. Cathy had arranged the wedding cake, but the confectioner didn't deliver to Wicklow. Yes, they delivered, they had snapped on the telephone, but to Dublin, not the wrong side of the moon. Con had a toothache and needed to go to the dentist. June said her husband Jimmy was behaving like a madman and insisting she be home by midnight, could Tom or Cathy ring him and tell him how far Wicklow was and how unpredictable the time a wedding ended. Lucy said she had had a row with her parents, who had asked were they paying university fees for her in order that she become a waitress. There had been a very firm demand that she spend more time at her lectures and less time working for Scarlet Feather. People who never rang them decided to call today. Joe Feather had rung to know would Tom come round tonight and help him beat the daylights out of the guy who had taken all his merchandise. Lizzie rang to say the photographs from Marian's wedding had arrived and they were beautiful. Did they want her to bring them into the premises? James Byrne rang about a final demand for a bill they thought they had paid, and they had to look up the records. Neil wanted to know which night could they invite this guy from Brussels to dinner. Cathy wondered would they maybe eat out, she didn't say since she was cooking all day it might be a treat. She hadn't time to tell him about Walter and the punchbowl.

Tom went ahead to Holly's with the others, and on the way dropped Cathy at the church. She wore a hat borrowed from Geraldine to honour the day, and a spray of flowers on her lapel. It didn't look promising, the gathering. Two very separate groups standing heads close together outside the church, each darting glances over at the other from time to time. Cathy went to the group that did not have Melanie O'Brien in. This was the family of Sean Clery on his big day, whispering and heads shaking. She introduced herself cheerfully and held a few names in her head, then she more or less backed over to the other group and made some introductions. Both sides were resisting it, but there was little they could do when this woman in the hat was more or less forcing them to shake hands. Then Sean arrived. There were no hugs from his family. Just a shrugging acknowledgement of his great beaming smile as he hurried into the church. Cathy felt an urge to kick them all. Then Stella arrived; she looked lovely in a blue and silver dress and jacket. She wore a little blue hat and huge silver earrings. Cathy felt a lump in her throat at the sight of this generous woman who wanted to spend her savings entertaining friends and family. Cathy looked over at the sour Melanie, who had barely bothered to wash her face or change her cardigan for the celebration, and she swore to herself that she would do everything in her power to make this day a great one, a memorable one for Stella and Sean.

Tom had everything under control when they got to Holly's. Trays of champagne greeted the guests as they came in.

'What was it like at the church?' Tom hissed.

'A bit grim. Is the orchestra here?'

'Yeah, they're a bit way-out-looking.'

'You haven't heard them play,' she pleaded.

'No, well, nobody might, go and talk to them, will you? I keep hitting on the ones that can't speak English.'

'Racist, how much of their language do you speak?'

'I don't know, what *is* their language?' Tom said with spirit.

'No idea, I'll go and talk to Josef,' she said cheerfully.

'And Cathy?'

'What is it now?'

'Take off your hat, put on your pinny, you're meant to be working here,' he laughed.

Josef understood weddings: in another life he had worked in a hotel, he said.

'Do you know what I mean when I say this one needs quite a lot of attention?' she asked.

'Like that music will be needed to replace conversation at the beginning?' Josef suggested.

'Let's hope and pray that it's only needed at the beginning,' said Cathy.

Because of the uncertainty as to who would or would not attend, they had arranged a buffet with open seating. All Sean's side sat at one end, all Stella's at the other. Lucy and Con poured the wine as liberally as they could, but reported a lot of hands placed firmly over glasses. They had even heard one of Sean's daughters saying she wouldn't give the other side the satisfaction of letting them see her drunk. The food went down well, they got some grudging compliments and plenty of requests for second helpings, The mazurkas and polkas and whatever else Josef's people were playing did indeed disguise the fact that this was not the most relaxed and happy of gatherings. Stella and Sean were so happy that everyone had come after all, they didn't seem to take in the degree of resentment around them. They were simple enough to believe that everyone had turned up today to wish them well. Lucy reported from the ladies' room that some of them were saying they'd try to escape before the speeches. So Tom nudged them towards the cake, and Josef's troupe gave a fanfare of anticipation. And Sean cleared his throat.

'When my wife Helen died, and when Stella's husband Michael died, we both thought our lives were over. And then we got a second chance. It's not going to be the same. Nobody can replace Helen and Michael, and no one is trying to, but we want to thank you for coming out with us this day to celebrate the happiness we had in the past and the happiness we hope is waiting for us in the future. This day would be nothing to Stella and myself if Helen and Michael's children and relations and friends didn't come to wish us well, so can I ask you to drink one toast to friendship and the future, and then to join us on the dance floor.'

They staggered to their feet and muttered the words. Josef struck up with a slow waltz, and turned round to beckon with flamboyant gestures that the group should dance. Sean led Stella onto the floor. It was a time when people should have applauded and looked at each other with warm smiles. But nobody joined them on the floor. Stella tried to encourage people.

'Don't beg them, don't beg them,' Cathy pleaded. She didn't realise she had spoken aloud.

'Take off your pinny,' Tom ordered.

He was ripping off the Scarlet Feather sweatshirt he wore over his ordinary white shirt. Then he dragged her out onto the dance floor. Josef and his friends had been playing something which might have been 'Tennessee Waltz', and now had turned into something that might have been 'Sailing Along On Moonlight Bay'. Cathy had never danced with Tom before. She had forgotten how very big he was, her head was way beneath his shoulder. When she danced with Neil they were the same size. Tom smelled of soap.

'I'm afraid to look, is anyone dancing?' she muttered into his chest.

'Con has Lucy out there, but I think it's time to change partners.' He released her suddenly and walked purposefully towards Melanie O'Brien. 'Now Melanie . . . you *promised*,' he called to her.

Melanie stood up and accepted his hand. Cathy had pulled a red-faced friend of Sean's from his group, June had joined in and got Stella's son on his feet, Con and Lucy had split up and asked other people. It was done with such authority that nobody could refuse. It happened very gradually, but it happened. They had got them on the dance floor. Tom danced with the bride. Stella smiled up at him.

'I'll simply never be able to thank you,' she said. 'Better than any son and daughter could have been. *My* wish is that you two will be blessed with your children in the future.' She looked over to where Cathy was dancing animatedly with the red-faced man. Like so many people, she assumed that Tom and Cathy were a couple.

'Cathy's married to a lawyer, and I'm, well, I'm still looking,' Tom said.

'I hope you find someone wonderful,' she said.

'I hope I'm as happy as you and Sean . . . Whenever I *do* get married, I'll think of this day, but I'm going to give you back to him now and go back to work.'

He passed round the cake, topped up the glasses and noticed that there actually *was* some conversation going on as well as dancing. It could never be voted the Party of the Year but the terrible freeze, the chilling silence when the bride and groom had danced alone was gone. He heaved a sigh of relief. If people started to go now it wouldn't be embarrassing. But of course, perversely, nobody now had a notion of leaving. They felt that they had to increase the sum they were giving Josef and his orchestra, since they were now an hour over the time agreed. They did their usual discreet clearing up, removing paper napkins, extra cutlery and coffee cups but without exactly wresting the glasses from people's hands. And soon the guests began to drift home. Tom decided to move the van nearer to the kitchen door of the hotel. It wouldn't start. Not a sound from the engine. They tried jump leads, without success. There wasn't a garage for miles. He moved quickly; Josef and his orchestra would drive June home.

'All my birthdays at once, I get to go home with the band,' June said, overjoyed.

Con could give Lucy a lift on the back of his motorbike, which she liked as an idea too. Miss Holly was hovering in the background supervising the departure, clucking with admiration at the spotless kitchen, thanking them for the gifts of food covered with cling film and neatly stacked in the hotel refrigerator. He made sure that the bride and groom knew nothing of what was happening. They sat down in the kitchen to have a badly needed glass of wine.

'You two are an example to the whole catering trade,' Miss Holly said approvingly. 'And if ever there's a chance of another wedding, I'd really be most anxious to do it, I can't tell you how—'

'Hold the praise, Miss Holly,' Tom said. 'We can't get the van to start, we have to stay the night here. I'm terribly sorry, it's never happened before . . .'

'Don't worry, you're in the right place, there are plenty of rooms free. Just take the keys from the rack in the hall.'

It was a feature of Holly's hotel, that old-fashioned key rack with the big tassels in different colours.

'Will you join us in a nightcap, Miss Holly?'

'No, I'm overexcited already by all this, I must go to bed. Stay as long as you like; you need to unwind,' she said, and went to her own quarters.

Tom and Cathy relaxed in the kitchen of Holly's. They talked on and opened another bottle. They could really expand once they had a place like this to do weddings; they must get Ricky to photograph it before the leaves had all left the trees. They talked about giving cookery classes on Wednesday afternoons back at the premises, about freezer packs for sale at the premises or even through stores. Tom would ring Haywards early tomorrow morning to get his emergency breads released from the freezer. How wise he had been to set up the system. 'I must ring Neil now,' Cathy took out her mobile. Tom made a move to give her some privacy, but she waved him back to sit down. It was only the answering machine.

'Neil, you'll never believe it but the van broke down, so I'm going to stay the night here at Holly's. I don't know what time we'll get it on the road tomorrow, but I'll give you a ring in the morning. Hope you're all right, *you're* out late but I expect the meeting went on a bit. The wedding down here went fine, by the way. I love you. Bye.'

'You're very independent, both of you.' Tom admired the way they could lead separate lives.

'It works, it usually works, but at the moment it's a bit up and down. He thinks I should go on a holiday with him.'

'Well go,' Tom said.

'I most certainly will not. What have we just been discussing? This is our very busiest time upcoming. I want *you* to take a couple of days off soon, but I'd be very pissed off if you decided to go off on a real holiday somewhere just now.'

'All right, I won't,' he grinned.

'We'll have one more glass of wine, Tom.'

'Sure, and a hangover, but why not.'

'Let's take it upstairs,' Cathy said.

They took one of the tasselled keys, and giggling like schoolchildren they went to open the bedroom door. Cathy picked one of the beds, kicked off her shoes and lay down, looking at him.

'We really should have a notebook to write all these things down. We won't remember anything tomorrow.'

'Write what down?' Tom sat on the other bed and poured the wine. 'Don't spill it, Cathy, you're very drunk.'

'Unlike you, who are stone-cold sober. Write down the ideas, the Wednesday cookery classes, the freezer-fillers, whatever.'

She put the glass down beside her and went straight to sleep. Just like a two-year-old would, or a puppy dog. One minute she was awake and talking about notebooks, the next she was fast asleep. Tom covered her with an eiderdown. He considered going down and getting a second key and finding another room. But they were talking about four hours, really. He lay down on the other bed and was asleep a few minutes later.

Walter Mitchell couldn't sleep. Those *stupid* twins had actually telephoned Cathy Scarlet and told her that half her stolen stuff was still in his garden shed. He couldn't believe it. Maud had been rooting around when he discovered her. Some cock and bull story that Cathy was going to call round after a wedding today and see them, and she wanted to see if there was anything else useful in the shed. Poor Cathy and Tom had this terrible burglary where vandals had got in and . . .

'I told you *never* to go into my shed, you promised me you wouldn't, but you are such liars, no wonder no one wants you.'

'People do want us,' Simon said.

'Name one.'

'Muttie does and his wife, that's two,' Simon said.

'They don't want you anywhere near them,' Walter said.

'They do, Cathy said that. He even sent us a five-pound note for bus fares, but it never got here.' Maud was stung. 'And Muttie is taking us to the races for our birthday.'

'And did you tell Cathy that you were rooting in *my* shed?'

407

'I told her that there was a punchbowl there like one of her treasures.'

Walter went white. 'And what did she say, tell me you little halfwit, before I have to beat it out of you.'

Maud was terrified. 'She didn't say anything, Walter, she only said she was busy but she'd come round after the wedding.'

'Go to your bedrooms at once,' he ordered.

'What are you going to do?' Maud asked.

'I'm leaving this house. I can't bear the sight of you, either of you, liars, messers, meddlers. No wonder nobody wants you anywhere near them.'

'But—'

They didn't wait. They peered out and saw him packing a suitcase in his bedroom, and then he went out to the garden. Out of the window they saw him filling black sacks full of things from the shed, then a taxi came and he stacked all the bags in it. He really was going. Father rang and said he had met old Barty, and wouldn't be home until very late tonight or possibly in the early morning, so not to send out a full-scale alert for him.

'You will be coming home tomorrow?' Simon asked.

'You really are the most tiresome child I ever met in my whole life,' Kenneth Mitchell said, and hung up.

'Walter's right,' Simon said. 'Nobody does want us. Nobody at all.'

Next morning Kenneth Mitchell came home at dawn from old Barty's club, where he had dozed in an armchair for a few hours and felt much revived. He found a note on the kitchen table. 'We are leaving home. Goodbye, Maud and Simon.'

He called his brother Jock. Jock was not well pleased to be woken at seven o'clock in the morning.

'Talk to Neil and Cathy, they'll know,' he said, and hung up.

Neil listened with no pleasure to the confused story.

'Shouldn't you ring Sara?' he suggested.

'I thought I'd talk to the family first,' Kenneth said.

'Okay, I'll contact Cathy for you. Doesn't Walter know anything?'

'He doesn't appear to be here either,' said Kenneth Mitchell.

Betty was on duty at Holly's hotel. She was full of praise for the way those young people had left the place, and treats in the fridge as well. The phone rang and she went to answer it. Very early for Holly's hotel. It was that nice young Neil Mitchell, looking for his wife. Apparently the van had broken down and she had stayed the night.

'I couldn't understand why that big van was still here. Hold on a moment, Mr Mitchell, she must be in Room Nine. I'll put you through.'

Neil waited, and then the phone was answered.

'Hallo,' the voice said. It was Tom Feather.

'Hallo?' Neil said again, puzzled. 'Is that Room Nine?'

'Yes, it is. Who's that?' Tom had a headache, he had woken an hour later than he intended to, he had to find a car mechanic, mend the van and get back to Dublin. Who was this ringing him and annoying him?

'I was looking for Cathy,' the voice said.

It was Neil. Tom was awake immediately. 'My God, Neil, what bloody bad luck we had last night, the van was dead as a dodo . . .' As he spoke, he began to shake Cathy into wakefulness in the next bed.

'Yes, I know, Cathy left a message. Where is she, by the way? I asked for her room.'

'Oh, she's down sorting out the van. I just came up here to her room to get her mobile for her, I think she was going to ring you on it.'

'I tried that first. She has it turned off.'

'No, I think the battery's dead, anyway, will I tell her to ring you on a real phone, a hotel phone I mean?' He was playing for time. Cathy had by now sat up, straightened herself and realised where she was.

'No, there's a bit of a crisis here. Will I hang on, or can you transfer me back down to the desk?'

'*No,*' Tom shouted. 'No, Neil, hang on, I see her coming up the stairs. Cathy, Cathy,' he shouted loudly. 'I found your phone here in your room, but the battery's down, but Neil is here on the hotel phone, come and speak to him.'

Cathy had understood much more quickly than he had thought she would. 'Sorry, Neil, I'm out of breath running up the stairs. Everything okay?'

He told her. 'Neil, I'm in the heart of the country with no transport, can't you ring Sara?'

'What about your parents?'

'They'd have phoned someone if the kids had turned up at St Jarlath's Crescent, but ring them anyway, please, Neil.'

'And of course no sign of Walter, the one time you'd need him.'

'*Neil*! Neil, I hadn't time to tell you. I think Walter was one of the vandals who broke into the premises. Something Maud saw in the shed, you must check the shed, they might be hiding things there. Listen, I'll charge this phone up and ring you later to know is there any news.' She hung up. They looked at each other.

'Quick thinking,' she said to him.

'Quickly taken up,' he praised her back.

'It wasn't really necessary, you know, we could have said what happened. Neil would have understood.'

'I know, but this way was easier,' he said.

'You're right. Less explaining. God, I feel terrible,' Cathy said, and went into the bathroom. 'And I look worse,' she screamed when she saw her reflection in the mirror.

'What's happened to the children?' Tom asked.

'They've run away. Of all the days out of the three hundred and sixty-five, they chose today.'

But the day was only beginning. When they had tidied up and splashed enough water to make themselves a bit respectable, they opened the door of the bedroom. Betty was in the corridor, bringing a breakfast tray to the newly-weds in Room Twelve. She paused to look at them. Betty, who had seen Cathy in the hotel just over a month ago telling her husband that she was pregnant, was utterly shocked. Miss Holly also seemed a lot less cordial today. She must have been informed.

It was an endless morning of negotiating with garages. The fault was identified, the part was found. She phoned Neil at the law library.

'Nothing at all, Sara's really worried. Can you call her? She wants to talk about Walter, apparently.'

'Do Mam and Dad know?' Cathy asked.

'They have the whole of St Jarlath's Crescent out with sticks beating bushes by the canal.'

'Not really?'

'No, but nearly. Are you all right, Cathy? You sound very ropy.'

'I have too much to do.'

'We choose our lives, Cathy. I've offered you a holiday.'

'We've been through that . . .'

'No, we've been through one poorly thought-out—'

'Neil, I'll ring you later,' she said.

They got back to Dublin in the early afternoon, in no humour to hear of June's fun with the orchestra, nor of Lucy's argument with her parents about her coming home on a motorbike with a man. They had no time for James Byrne about the final demand. Hannah Mitchell wittering on about a letter from Canada, or Peter Murphy who wanted to have a cocktail party to annoy Geraldine. They didn't want to hear where Freddie Flynn had bought villas nowadays, nor to discuss a Hallowe'en extravaganza with Shay and Molly Hayes. But they had to do all those things because that was what work was about. When the day was finally drawing to a close, two phones shrilled. Cathy looked at Tom with big, tired eyes.

'Why do I feel these are things we don't want to hear?' she asked him, and picked up the one nearest to her.

'Don't hang up on me, Cathy, it's Marcella, please try to get Tom to talk to me, *please*.'

Tom answered a call from Sara, saying it was all in the hands of the guards now and Maud and Simon were assumed to have spent one night sleeping rough and were heading into a second. Everyone was very worried indeed.

Chapter Ten

OCTOBER

Simon and Maud discussed telephoning Muttie and his wife Lizzie. If they really *had* sent a five-pound note that went astray, then they might not be as hostile as everyone else. They got Lizzie on the phone; she was cagey about Muttie's whereabouts, he had gone away for a day or two. This was puzzling. Muttie never went away anywhere. And what about the birthday treat?

'He's not refusing to talk to us or anything?' Maud asked.

'Child, aren't you the most extraordinary little thing, why would he do that?' Lizzie said. It sounded reassuring, but it wasn't a yes or a no.

Simon thanked her for the five-pound note. 'It was very kind of you, it's made a lot of difference,' he said.

Lizzie said they must be thinking of the wrong people; she and Muttie had sent no fiver. They explained how it had got lost in the post, and how Cathy had taken one from her handbag.

'Ah, there must have been some mistake.'

'I'm sorry, Lizzie,' Simon said politely. '*Do* you know when Muttie will be back?'

She sounded guarded. 'Hard to say, a day or two I think.'

'She's lying,' Maud said afterwards.

'Muttie never goes anywhere...'

'Except the races.'

Muttie Scarlet had spent a night in hospital ... an embarrassing matter of his private parts being examined by young doctors and unmentionable things being put into them. He wanted it neither discussed nor known. Lizzie was under strict instructions to say that he was away on business. He came home to find all hell had broken loose. The twins had disappeared. Sara, their social worker, was going mad and interrogating Lizzie. Poor Lizzie was going over every word of the conversation.

'I didn't know they were contemplating anything like this ... How was I meant to be inspired? They always said they were fine, I thought they were tired of coming here ... They didn't sound upset at all, they were full of old rubbish, thanking me for a fiver that we never sent them.'

It had been an endless day, with people going back over things, fruitlessly examining the note left in the kennel: 'We have taken Hooves with us.' It seemed somehow a very bleak little letter, giving no information, not even a hint of where they were heading. A search of possible places led nowhere: friends at school could reveal nothing. Kenneth had pulled himself together sharply and revealed with every sentence he spoke how little he knew of the life that went on at The Beeches. There seemed to be no trace of Walter. He had not shown up at work, so it was quite possible that the twins were with him. Kay, now frightened into sobriety by the amount of activity in the house said no, that Walter had left earlier, in a taxi with a lot of black bags. But since she was not considered a reliable witness, nobody took much notice of this memory. By the time the guards had been called and Maud and Simon were officially declared missing, Muttie had alerted many of his associates who said they would help to search for the children, who must have been in the neighbourhood of St Jarlath's Crescent at any time after ten p.m. when Lizzie went to bed. Neighbours who knew the children were drafted in. Every time the phone rang, everyone in St Jarlath's Crescent jumped. This time it was Cathy – she was on her way over to them. Muttie relaxed for the first time that day. Cathy would get it sorted.

'I have to go over there,' Cathy said.
    'Go straight away, take the van.'
    'Could you ring Marcella?' she said, too casually.
    'What?' he sounded shocked.
    'I've written down her number here, she's waiting by the phone.'
    'Thanks, but I'll pass on that.'
    'She was crying, Tom, I said I'd do my best.'

413

'And you have.' He was cold.

'I can't leave her standing in a phone box waiting for you to ring,' Cathy begged.

'Thanks, Cathy, take the keys and stop worrying. They'll turn up, those two, with some amazing explanation.'

'In the middle of a street in London, Tom, she deserves more than that.'

He turned away. Cathy dialled the number.

'Tom!' The excitement in Marcella's voice was almost hurtful to hear.

'No, Marcella, I'm sorry, it's Cathy again. I told him, and he's not going to phone you. No, I don't know why, but I didn't want you standing there waiting.'

There was a silence. 'Why won't he even talk?' Marcella sobbed.

'I'm so very sorry,' Cathy said, and she hung up and left the premises without even catching Tom's eye.

'It's all my fault, I was so short with poor little Maud,' Cathy wept at the kitchen table. 'I kept saying things like Hurry up, and If that's all, Maud . . .' Everyone was startled. This wasn't the Cathy they knew. Lizzie, Geraldine, Muttie and Sara all looked at each other helplessly. 'And the awful thing is that she was being so kind, she was trying to get me a punchbowl from the shed and she didn't even realise that it was stolen by her little shit of a brother.'

'Simon?' Muttie asked, totally bewildered.

'No, Walter, he has a shed full of things from our premises, I gather.'

Sara looked up sharply. 'You think Walter was your burglar?'

'Yes, he must have been. Maybe this has something to do with the children running away,' she said anxiously.

'Have you reported any of this? Does Neil know?'

'No, I only heard yesterday or the day before, and I've been up to my tonsils in a wedding in the country.'

Sara seemed to think this was odd. 'But if you thought that, surely you'd have told Neil?'

Cathy took no notice of her disapproving tone. 'Did you say that Walter has gone from The Beeches?'

'Yes, his mother thinks he went last night in a taxi . . . carrying a lot of bags,' Sara said somewhat doubtfully.

Then suddenly Sara and Cathy looked at each other as the

implication became clear. Sara took out her mobile phone and called the guards again.

At The Beeches, Kenneth and Kay waited for the guards to arrive. There was no news, but the guards needed to look in the garden shed and in Mr Walter Mitchell's bedroom. They said that Ms Cathy Scarlet would be joining them shortly.

'What does she want?' Kenneth asked.

'She is the daughter of the couple whose house the twins visited last night to collect their dog.'

'They don't *have* a dog,' Kay said.

'They think they do, madam, and Ms Scarlet is also married to your nephew, so could be considered family. I believe her husband is also joining her here.'

'Huh,' Kenneth said.

'Mr Neil Mitchell is a barrister, sir; if you have any objection to our looking though the house, please state it now.'

'And what would you do if I objected?' Kenneth asked.

'We'd get a search warrant,' the young guard said simply.

'I'm not saying he *did* steal the things, I'm only saying it's a pretty odd coincidence,' Cathy said to Neil as they drove to The Beeches.

'We must be very careful not to go in hurling accusations,' Neil warned. 'Dad did tell me that he nicked a computer from work *and* didn't turn up today, so it looks as if you're right, but . . .'

'And your drinky aunt thinks she heard him leaving with a lot of black plastic bags in a taxi last night . . .'

'I know. And if he took them, Cathy, no mercy, you understand?'

'No, I don't believe you, in the end you'll say he was a victim, he deserves our concern.'

'What have I done, hon? Why are you fighting with *me*?' Neil asked, aggrieved.

'I don't know, Neil, I really don't. I want to kill Walter and I want to kill myself. If I had only been just a bit nicer, those two foolish children wouldn't have run away.'

'You're working too hard. You just didn't have the time,' he said.

'No, Neil, I just didn't *make* the time, that's different.'

'But I have a surprise for you. I wasn't going to tell you before, but I think you need it now.'

'A surprise?' she looked at him warily.

'You *are* very tired, hon. I talked to Tom about it; he can spare you, he says, and I've booked us a week in Morocco!'

He waited to see her pleasure, but he was disappointed. 'Neil, it's kind of you, but no.'

'It's booked!' he said.

'I can't think of anything now except those children, and I don't really want to go away at all, we're too busy.'

'Tom said . . .'

'Tom is a kind man, he says what he thinks people want him to say. Most of the time,' she added, thinking of Marcella weeping down the phone. 'Can we talk about it another time, Neil?'

'Whenever you feel you'd like to give the time,' he said huffily.

'Well, not *now*, when we're worried sick about the kids.'

'Not any time, Cathy. There's no time to talk to you these days, and no way of talking to you, either.'

'I don't know what you mean.'

His face was very hard.

'If I talk about the miscarriage, I'm saying the wrong thing and upsetting you. If I don't talk about it I'm hard and unfeeling and I've forgotten it.'

'It's not like that.'

'Well, that's the way it looks from here. And when I do something, get us away from here for a bit of peace . . .'

'It's not peace trekking through Morocco seeing would I like Africa . . .'

'Oh, *shut up*, Cathy, there's no pleasing you. If I suggested a holiday on the Isle of Man you wouldn't want it either.' His face was set in a look she hadn't known before. He was very, very angry.

She spoke slowly. 'I would be perfectly happy to go on holiday but only if we discuss it, not when you *tell* me you've booked something . . .'

'Don't worry, a holiday with you is the last thing on my mind,' he said and they drove to The Beeches in silence.

The punchbowl was gone when the guards searched the shed, but there were a lot of other things that they asked Cathy to look at. At first she thought that she could see nothing that belonged to them. Then she saw some salad servers and a linen tablecloth.

'The salad servers were a present from Neil's parents last

Christmas, the cloth has our laundry mark on it,' she said in a small, flat voice.

Neil nodded gravely. The guards seemed entirely convinced. It would nail Walter when they found him.

Neil's father made a statement to the guards about the missing computer. 'And I want you to know that nephew or no nephew, we intend to go the distance on this one.'

They nodded, satisfied. 'Do you have any explanation of why he might have taken the children, sir?' The guards had long decided that there was little future in talking to the children's parents. They had higher hopes of Jock Mitchell, who seemed normal and articulate and capable of understanding that two nine-year-olds had left a note and vanished from their home.

'I can't understand it at all,' Jock Mitchell said. 'He never mentioned them at all, and if I ever asked about them he was vague, as if he really didn't know anything.'

'He didn't know they were there,' Cathy said. 'He never took them with him, I know that much for a fact. He high-tailed it out of here on his own because he thought we were onto him.'

'But it's too much of a coincidence that they should all go on the same day,' Neil argued.

'Neil, you never listened to him. I swear they didn't figure in his life, he didn't kidnap them or take them as hostages or anything.'

'I say,' Kenneth said disapprovingly, as if this kind of chat was going too far. They all looked at him, waiting to know what he was going to say. But he said nothing. 'Sorry,' he said eventually.

'They could still get in touch,' said Jock hopefully.

'But who would they ring?' Cathy asked. 'That's the thing that's breaking my heart, they rang everyone, and none of us listened.'

'They could be anywhere,' Muttie wailed.

'They're only nine, people will look at two kids and a dog and question them. And they're so distinctive, the guards will find them in no time,' Geraldine soothed them as best she could.

'No, the guards haven't a clue where they are, they keep asking us to think of likely places and known companions, and none of us knows anything about their lives, poor little devils. Why couldn't they have left them here with us instead of transplanting them to The Beeches?'

'They had to go,' Lizzie said because she believed it.

'And didn't they do really fine there,' Muttie scoffed. 'They did so fine that they ended up having to run away, come here by dead of night and take Hooves and head off the Lord knows where.'

'Do you remember them at Marian's wedding, they were so proud of themselves,' Lizzie said.

'And their speeches,' said Muttie, blowing his nose heavily.

'Oh, they're not *dead* for God's sake!' Geraldine said. 'Really and truly Lizzie, get a hold of yourself, those two are well able to look after themselves.'

'No, they're not, they're real babies,' Lizzie said.

'Wherever they are now, they're terrified,' said Muttie.

Tom was restless. He could settle to nothing. The idea of Marcella on a London street crying in a phone box wouldn't go away. He had been right not to speak to her; there were no more words to be said, only a circular argument going nowhere. But he wished that she hadn't called, she must have been desperate, particularly to admit it and plead with Cathy. Marcella was always so anxious to preserve an image of herself as confident. If he had answered the phone himself, would it have been different? Perhaps he could have said in his own normal voice that it hurt him too much to talk about what could not be changed. Then she might not have been left crying in a phone box. He could concentrate on nothing because of that image. He decided to go and see his parents. JT and Maura Feather were sitting at the kitchen table playing three-handed bridge with Joe. Joe looked as if a wall had fallen on him, his left eye was closed, his lip was swollen and part of his head had been shaved where he had stitches.

'Jesus!' said Tom.

'Wasn't it dreadful?' Maura Feather said. 'Poor Joe reversed into a wall, and it was the direct intervention of God that he didn't do himself any serious damage.'

Tom looked at the injuries which were obviously not the result of reversing into a wall.

'Was it the right wall?' he asked.

'Yes, it was,' Joe nodded painfully.

'And what happens now?' Tom asked.

'Bills are going to be paid,' Joe said with satisfaction.

'At some cost, though?' Tom looked at this brother's injuries sympathetically.

'No cost at all, considering,' Joe said.

And Tom realised that Joe the businessman had suffered much

more by being cheated than he had in a fist fight. His street cred was now restored, and to Joe that meant the injuries were irrelevant. His father frowned as if the conversation should change channels. So Tom told them that the twins had run away, and nobody knew where to start looking for them.

'Those two would be well able to speak up for themselves, aren't they Mitchells when all's said and done,' Maura sniffed.

'I'm worried about them, Mam, they're very odd, quaint kind of children, they take everything literally, anything could happen to them.'

'And tell me, is Marcella still on her holiday in London?' Maura asked.

'It's not a holiday, Mam, I told you that she's got contacts there and she wants to be a model, so she has to be in London for that.'

'And is it going well for her over there?' JT Feather asked kindly.

'I think so, Dad, I hear she's doing fine.'

'That's funny,' Joe said, 'I hear the very opposite.'

'No word?' Tom asked.

Cathy shook her head. 'No, and that's two nights out on their own somewhere; it's serious, and they all think that Walter has something to do with it, which is utter nonsense.'

'They'd only slow him down,' Tom agreed.

'It's some damn thing that they took literally, you know, like they thought that I was coming to see them on the night of the wedding, apparently I said, "after the wedding", I didn't mean that very day.'

'Would Muttie have said anything to upset them?'

'No; he was so embarrassed about having to go to hospital with his prostate, he hasn't said anything to anyone for days.'

They went through all the things it could be; some dancing engagement they thought they had got, some school project – a quest to find another punchbowl? Those two were so strange, they could have flown to Chicago. They jointed chickens and made sauces as they talked about the children. They never got around to mentioning the hunt for the man who had stolen their belongings and vandalised their premises. Or indeed, the confusion of spending a night, however innocently, in the same room. And just because that night wasn't mentioned, it seemed to take on a greater significance. The fact that Tom had lied to Neil on the phone. The knowledge that it had been seen and completely misconstrued by the hotel. It could easily have been one of the many things they laughed about, but because of the children they lost the moment, and now it was too late to go back to it.

Walter's friend Derek with the sports car wouldn't let him stay. 'You're too much trouble, Walter, and now you say the law is after you, I can't afford to have any policemen poking round this flat.' There was a fair chance they might find cocaine if they did, and black sacks of goods from the shed at The Beeches.

'Can I leave the stuff?'

'No, you can't . . . Take it up to the market,' Derek advised. 'You can unload it there in no time.'

'For peanuts.'

'Well, take the peanuts then and put them on a horse, *then* you're in the clear,' said Derek, who wanted Walter Mitchell miles from here.

Sara was tireless in her efforts to find them; she reread her notes over and over in case they might offer a clue. She came round to Waterview to ask Neil and Cathy what kind of interests the twins had.

'Well, they loved that dog, which is why they went and took him,' Cathy said.

'When they were here, what did they do in the evening?'

'We used to make them do homework for a bit, and they liked jigsaws . . . I don't know what else, Neil, do you?'

'Not really, they kept asking questions all the time . . . How much do you earn, how often do you mate.'

'Sara, nobody could have murdered them or anything?' Cathy's face was very anxious.

'She's very overwrought,' Neil said. 'Honestly, Cathy, you can't go on like this.'

'No, of course not,' said Sara, but her voice was shaky.

Cathy's eyes filled up and, unexpectedly, she leaned over and patted Sara on the arm.

'They'll be fine, they're a real pair of survivors, those two,' she said, consoling the white-faced social worker.

'Well, you'll be glad of the holiday,' Sara said.

'Holiday?'

Neil interrupted quite quickly. 'That's postponed now,' he said. Cathy was annoyed. He should *not* have told Sara all about the holiday as if it were settled before he had checked it with her. It wasn't important now, but it was very, very irritating all the same.

Geraldine couldn't settle down to work, thinking about the twins. There were two important jobs on hand, *and* her upcoming date with Nick Ryan. But the strange, troubled, pale faces of those children wouldn't go out of her mind. They had been so funny in her flat on the day of the recovery party, doing their encore because they thought people would expect it. She had kept cheering the others up, and mocking them for fearing the worst. But in her heart she was very worried. Two odd, unworldly children, and you heard the most awful things. Every day in the papers there was some horror. Geraldine shook herself firmly. She had a rule to stop herself brooding about things. When you can, you must concentrate feverishly on work, and if that doesn't work, concentrate feverishly on sex and social life. Geraldine and Nick Ryan were planning an evening which was going to involve his staying over at Glenstar. Both of them knew this, though neither of them had mentioned it. It was an elaborate ritual about the difficulty of finding somewhere they would like for a late dinner after the theatre. There were endless problems. Places to park, driving after a couple of glasses of wine, noisy people at other tables when you were trying to talk. Possibly they could bring some smoked salmon back to Geraldine's apartment. Indeed, what a good idea, and she had some of Tom Feather's wonderful bread in the freezer. And Nick would love to bring a bottle of wine. And did Nick have to leave at any specific time after the meal? Not at all, the night was his own, her own, their own. It was set up. The affair had begun.

Muttie went in just from sheer habit to Sandy Keane in the betting shop. 'Don't feel like having a bet today, my mind's distracted,' he said.

'Suit yourself, Muttie, but that was a nice little windfall you got yesterday,' Sandy said dourly.

'Yesterday, I didn't have a bet yesterday, I was preoccupied,' said Muttie.

'Internet Dream,' said Sandy.

'Never heard of it,' Muttie shrugged.

'Well, you won seventy pounds on it yesterday morning, which is good for a horse you never heard of,' Sandy said.

'Is one of us losing our minds, I wasn't near here yesterday.'

'I know, Muttie, they told me.'

'Who told you?'

'The twins,' said Sandy.

'Oh, my God, what time?'

'First race at Wincanton,' Sandy said.

'Can I have your phone? I must ring the guards.'

'You're going to bring the guards in here and tell them that I took a bet from minors? You're off your head, Muttie.'

'They won't be interested in that.'

'They won't like hell!'

'No, Sandy.' Muttie had begun to dial. 'You don't understand. The guards are out looking everywhere for these children. They've been missing for two days.'

It didn't in fact bring them very much further down the line. So the children had hung around the St Jarlath's Crescent area for the night with the dog, until the bookies' was open for bets.

'I feel a bit better that they had seventy pounds rather than just a fiver,' said Cathy.

'But it does mean they can stay away longer, like now they won't have to come home out of desperation,' Muttie said, biting his lip.

The hunt centred much more around St Jarlath's Crescent than The Beeches. This is where the children had been happiest, where they had collected Hooves and written their last note. Lizzie looked through the pictures she had of Maud and Simon. The guards had asked for a recent picture, which they would use if there was no news by tomorrow. They had obviously given up on the notion of getting anything helpful from Kenneth and Kay. Lizzie took out a big box; there were some lovely ones of them from Marian's wedding. But maybe they should use the one of the twins with Hooves. She must not let herself think that anything had happened to them. This was Ireland, not some dangerous place; nothing bad could happen to them here.

'I mean, nobody would *hurt* children, or anything?' she asked the guard fearfully as she showed him an endearing picture of Maud and Simon in their kilts outside the church at the wedding.

The guard looked at the two serious little faces and cleared his throat. He hated cases about children. 'We have to hope not, Mrs Scarlet.'

She had seen in his face the possibility that it might not end well, and the tears came down her face again. 'You see, you'd really have to know them to realise that they're such an odd little pair, not in the real world at all. They just get notions and follow them anywhere.'

'And would they trust strangers, do you think?' The big guard gave Lizzie a paper handkerchief.

'Of course they would, they'd go off with Jack the Ripper if he came to the door with a plan.' She put her head down on the table and wept aloud.

Muttie came and patted her shoulder awkwardly. 'If we could just think what mad thought was going through their little minds the moment they took off, then we'd find them in no time,' he said, shaking his head again and again.

All over Dublin people were trying to think what might have been going through their minds. To little avail. Maud and Simon, left so long surviving in a strange, troubled and changing lifestyle, had invented a little world of their own where no one could follow them.

'You know it will all be so obvious when we find them,' Cathy said to Neil.

'*If* we find them,' he said.

'Come on, you don't mean it. Why say something so frightening?'

'I'm only saying what the guards are saying, they don't like it at all,' he said.

The twins had no idea of the drama they had created. To them it had been utterly simple. Muttie had promised to take them to the races for their birthday. To hear the real thunder of hooves. *That's* where he had gone, to the country, to the races, and his wife Lizzie didn't want to admit it. And so they made their plans. They would go to the races and confront Muttie. Ask him straight out what they had done to annoy him. They had five pounds and eighty-three pence. It was a lot of money, but would it take them the hundred miles to County Kilkenny? They stayed up all night discussing it. There was nobody to object. Father was out with old Barty, Mother didn't get up these days at all and Walter had left home. They packed a plastic carrier bag each to take with them, extra shoes, a big sweater, pyjamas, a pot of jam, a loaf of bread and two slices of ham. There was an animated discussion about soap. Simon thought there might be soap already wherever they were going;

Maud said that since they were going to be sleeping in sheds and barns and in fields it might be mad to think there'd be any soap in those places. They took a small piece, just in case. Then shortly after dawn when the first bus passed the end of the road the twins ate into their savings and made their way to St Jarlath's Crescent. They weren't leaving without Hooves. Five pounds wouldn't take them to Kilkenny.

'What do people do when they need money desperately?' Maud wondered.

'They earn some or they steal, or they win the Lotto.'

'The Lotto isn't until Saturday,' Maud said.

'There's Muttie's office,' said Simon.

After that it had all been simple. They studied the paper for a long time before they went in, and they wrote out a slip of paper. Mr Keane knew them well.

'How's tricks?' he said, as he always did.

They told him tricks were great and placed the bet. Two pounds to win on a horse called Internet Dream.

'I break every rule in the book for the pair of you,' said Mr Keane. 'I let minors into my establishment and a small four-footed beast as well.'

'Muttie asked us to put it on for him.'

'Where's the man himself, he wasn't in yesterday either.'

They had planned for this one, too. They couldn't say he had gone to Gowran Park race meeting in Kilkenny, otherwise he should be putting on his own bets there.

'He has a whole lot of tiring things to do for his wife Lizzie today, so he asked us to put the bet on for him,' Simon said.

Sandy Keane nodded; this seemed entirely reasonable.

'And may we wait here to bring his winnings back to him?' Maud asked politely. 'Would you mind waiting outside, you're too young to be seen in here, strictly speaking.'

'It's cold outside, Mr Keane.'

'All right, but sit somewhere out of sight.'

They sat as quiet as mice until the race. Internet Dream won at thirty-five to one and they had their fare to Kilkenny. Hooves loved the train journey; he socialised with some of the other passengers by laying his head in their laps, and they seemed delighted with him.

'What will we do if he wants to pee?' Maud whispered.

'What do other people do with dogs on trains?' Simon whispered.

They looked around them. Nobody else had a dog.

'Maybe he'll know you can't go on a train,' Maud said optimistically. Hooves saw a nice leather briefcase and was about to relieve himself against it. Simon and Maud jumped up horrified and alerted the owner of the briefcase, who was reading a newspaper.

'Could you take it away? He thinks it's a lamp-post.'

'Easy mistake, often made,' the man said.

'Where should I take him? I can't hold him out the window,' Simon asked.

'Just out there where the two carriages sort of join, and look away as if you have nothing to do with it,' the man advised.

They came back and sat down to talk to him since he was so pleasant, and told him that they were going to the races.

'Aren't you a bit young to be going on your own?' he said.

'We'll be meeting a grown-up there, of course,' Simon said.

'Is that your Dad?'

'Yes,' said Simon.

'No,' said Maud at the same time.

'Sort of stepfather, foster father really.'

'And does he have any tips for today?'

'No, but he'll have been studying form all morning,' Maud explained.

'Great. The important thing is to feel lucky.'

'We've been quite lucky already today, we had Internet Dream,' Simon said proudly.

The man looked at him with more interest. 'You had? What odds?'

'Thirty-five to one,' Maud said.

'Well, maybe I should stick with the pair of you. How did you pick Internet Dream, anyway?'

'The name,' said Simon, as if it were self-evident.

'And who put the bet on for you?'

'We did it ourselves.'

'By God, I'll certainly stay with you, you could be the making of me,' said the man; who said his name was Jim, known to his friends as Unlucky Jim, and he'd be taking a taxi to the races if they'd like a lift.

'Thank you very much, Unlucky,' Maud said. 'But you know, all this business about not going in cars with strangers . . .'

'And we think there's going to be a bus to the racecourse anyway,' Simon said.

'Perhaps Unlucky could come on the bus with us?' Maud didn't want to let him go, they might need him to help them find Muttie.

'I don't think his name is Unlucky, I think it's Jim,' Simon whispered.

'Which is it?' Maud wanted a ruling.

'I think for a day at the races it had better be Jim,' the man said, bewildered.

Unlucky Jim came on the bus with them to the races. 'Where are you meeting your father?' he asked.

'Father?' Maud said alarmed.

'Muttie,' Simon hissed.

'Oh, just round and about, he'll be looking out for us.'

They realised that they must lose Unlucky Jim now. He was asking questions that were hard to answer.

'I think we'll take Hooves for a bit of a stroll before we go in,' Maud said.

'In case he tries to pee on someone else's briefcase,' Simon said.

'Have you the price of getting in?' Jim asked.

'Of course we do, we have a fortune,' Maud explained.

'You've been very good company. I wonder, would you let me buy you a drink after the third race, the bar beside the Tote? Your father too, if you've made contact.'

'We will, of course,' said Simon, as if at the age of nine he were used to travelling down the east coast of Ireland in a train and being invited to have a drink in the bar near the Tote.

Simon and Maud searched everywhere for Muttie, but with no success. They went in and out of bars, they stood near the winning post for one of the races, they went to the parade ring. If Muttie were here, then surely this is where he'd be. After the third race they went to meet Unlucky Jim.

'Did you have any winners?' they asked.

'What do you think? I'm here depending on you both.'

'We haven't studied form yet,' Maud said.

'And what about your da, did he come up with anything?'

'Not really,' Simon said.

They decided they would pretend they had met Muttie; people hated it if they thought you were on your own and lost or something. Better let people think they were being looked after.

'Where is he now?'

'He said he might drop in.'

'What do you fancy in the next one?' Jim asked.

'We're not experts, Jim,' Maud admitted.

'Well, you couldn't do worse than I've done.'

They looked at the race card carefully. 'Lucky Child,' said Maud. Jim peered at it for a while. 'It hasn't much going for it.'

'Look at the weight, and it didn't do badly last time out.' Muttie had taught them to read the vital signs.

'You're right, I'll put fifty each way on it,' said Unlucky Jim.

Maud and Simon went down and willed Lucky Child forward. It was a near thing, but he won.

'Thank God,' said Maud devoutly.

'It's very easy really, isn't it? I wonder why Father and old Barty and people who have money troubles don't do this all the time,' Simon said.

'I think they *do* do it all the time, which is why they have money troubles,' Maud said.

'You may be right.'

'Still, it's a pity we didn't put ten pounds on Lucky Child ourselves, look at what we'd have won.'

'But if it hadn't won we'd be in desperate trouble,' said Simon, who still had no plans on where they would stay for the night.

Unlucky Jim searched the place to give the twins a share of the biggest win he'd ever had. They were such quirky little things, dragging that dog round with them, so serious about everything and carrying stuffed plastic bags with them. He'd like to meet up with them again, and not only to mark his race card. Tipsters who could land Internet Dream and Lucky Child in one day were very few on the ground. Then he realised that he didn't even know their names.

'A lot of people don't come the first day, they come the second day,' Simon said wisely.

'Did Muttie *say* which day he had planned to take us?' Maud was tired, and a little worried about the night ahead.

'No, but if he's not here today he'll be here tomorrow.'

'So what do you think, should we try to sleep here in the racecourse, it would save us having to pay to get in again?'

'No, they must go round looking otherwise everyone would stay the three days,' Simon said.

So they got a bus back to Kilkenny. They walked and walked to find a suitable place, and then just by pushing a door they found it. It was a big shed with some broken agricultural machinery, tractors and things in it.

'It's like someone's boxroom,' Maud whispered.

It was ideal for them; there would be no problem with Hooves, and there was even a car seat ripped from some vehicle that they could sleep on. They gave Hooves one slice of ham, shared the other and had bread and jam. Tomorrow they'd find Muttie, no problem.

They slept very well because they were so tired, and woke only at the sound of Hooves barking. They had tied him to the door since he might well have found his way back to St Jarlath's Crescent. Maud looked around her. They had been sleeping in a shed full of broken machinery. She had hardly any clean clothes, they had stale bread and over half a jar of jam. They had to go out and find Muttie today.

Simon woke and rubbed his eyes. 'It's nearly ten o'clock,' he said.

'Do we have enough money for a breakfast?'

'You mean, go into a place and pay for it at a table?' Simon was horrified.

'We could have bacon and egg,' Maud said.

Simon was counting the money, they'd have to be very careful, he said, there was the bus to pay for, the entrance again, and then of course if they didn't find Muttie, the train fare home.

'But we're not *going* home, are we?' Maud asked.

Simon agreed this was so, and that under the circumstances they should go out and look for breakfast. Somewhere that would let Hooves in. They felt a great deal better after breakfast. They tidied themselves up as best they could and set off for the races again.

Unlucky Jim said to himself that he had never won so much money before as he had on Lucky Child. Perhaps there was a message here for him. Like quit when you're winning. Jim had never lived by this philosophy. He wondered should he try to do so now? But then he had never met two such odd children. Travelling on their own to the races, rescuing his briefcase, near-psychic powers about forecasting winners. There was something about that story of going to meet a father or a foster father that didn't sound right. Jim rang his wife and said he was coming home from the races.

'It's only day two,' she said in disbelief.

He alarmed her still further by suggesting that they go out for a meal somewhere posh tonight. She spent most of the day wondering what he could have done to make him feel so guilty.

The racecourse was becoming familiar to them now. They wondered if they would meet Unlucky Jim again. They realised and were almost ready to admit that they didn't really know *what* kind of a place they'd find Muttie in. Where would he be studying form? Would it be in a bar, or talking to the bookies? Up to now they had only seen him at work in what he called his office, Mr Keane's betting shop.

Maud sat down. 'I'm tired of looking,' she said.

'You can't be tired, you had an expensive breakfast,' Simon said.

'Suppose he's not here,' Maud said.

Now it was out in the open. Now it had been said and could never be taken back. Simon got such a shock that he let the lead go, and Hooves took off at a great rate through the crowds. The children were aghast. Hooves was a dog that could be allowed off a lead in a field or a park or on the beach, but never where there were crowds of people. He would do terrible damage out of sheer fright and a sense of unfamiliar freedom. They could hear him barking as he pushed his way through the crowds. They pushed their way after him ... People had staggered back as Hooves had come at them, bewildered and hysterically barking his head off. They saw him break for some space. The horses had left the parade ring and were lining up.

'Please, Hooves, please don't go on the racecourse, help, help, he'll be killed,' Maud cried, and fell over flat on her face, getting two very badly grazed knees and a cut forehead. But she picked herself up and ran on.

Simon was nearer. 'Please stop the dog,' he shouted.

From every side they were getting looks and indeed shouts of annoyance, no place to bring a dog, the horses might get frightened and rear up ... who let those children in here anyway with their damn dog? Hooves had decided against the actual racetrack and swerved to a reasonably empty area where there were some cars and horseboxes ... He looked around him, his eyes wild, and then ran straight under the wheels of a jeep that was reversing. The driver couldn't possibly have stopped in time. But the twins saw it all as if it were in slow motion. The way that Hooves was thrown right up in the air and then fell to the ground. He was very still when they got there.

Muttie was having a pint with some of his associates, and opinion was divided about Sandy Keane; should he have taken the children's bet? How could he have refused it? Might he not have thought something was amiss? Where *was* Muttie, anyway, for the last couple of days? That's what they'd all like to know. Muttie was vague about his overnight stay in hospital, and glossed over it easily. They couldn't live for ever on seventy pounds, they'd have to come out sooner or later. They could hardly go round all the betting shops in Dublin putting two quid on outsiders, or to a race meeting.

'Oh, my God,' said Muttie. 'I told them I'd take them to Gowran Park for their birthday. They could have gone there.'

Walter was going up to the bookmaker with the pittance he had got in the marketplace. He saw some disturbance in the distance, but didn't investigate what it was. The odds on Bright Brass Neck weren't good enough, he'd move around, get something better further down the course. Always stupid to put it on at the first place, and he had really good hopes of this one. He'd walk away today with a lot of the debt paid, not all, but a fair whack. And all the other things could then be sorted out. Walter was good at explaining.

Maud had fainted when she saw the accident, and a crowd had gathered. The children were taken into the offices. They were told that the dog was being looked after.

'Is he dead?' asked the boy with the tear-stained face.

'What's your name?' they asked him.

'Hooves,' said Simon.

They were bewildered, but they could get no more from Simon: he was too shocked to talk. Maud's cuts had been cleaned, she had been given hot sweet tea but she wouldn't stop shaking. Eventually they had managed to get the children's first names and an announcement was made.

'We have two children here at the information office in a state of considerable distress. Can the adults accompanying Maud and Simon please present themselves? They are particularly anxious to meet a Mister Muttie. The information office, please, as soon as you can. The children are very upset.'

Walter had gone down a line of bookies, there were better odds now on Bright Brass Neck than there were at the start. He had been wise to know they would lengthen. Then he heard the announcement. He couldn't believe it; those two devil children had followed him here. But they couldn't have. He had hitched in three stages. So what *were* they doing here? Then, beside him, he heard someone say that must be the same children who were in the accident with the dog and the jeep. Could he wait for a few minutes and go to the information office when he had placed his bet? There was the usual last-minute crowd around the bookies' stands, and the announcement was made again with a greater sense of urgency. Walter went to the information office.

Everything happened then at the same time. The guards in Kilkenny had heard from Dublin that there was a good chance of the missing children turning up at the race meeting. The race committee and its security staff, which were beginning to despair of ever discovering who these children were, were relieved at this news, which cast them all in the role of heroes. One of the many vets at the races said that Hooves would live. He would be lame and might have to have one paw amputated, but he would definitely live. The young woman who had been driving the jeep was comforted with so many brandies that she eventually couldn't drive at all and had to be taken home. Maud and Simon, already overjoyed with the good news about Hooves, could hardly believe it when Walter came to rescue them. Their faces lit up with delight because they knew now that they had been forgiven for all the awful things they had done: they hugged him tightly, and for the first time in his life he actually felt cheap and shabby.

'Are you Mr Muttie by any chance, sir?' one of the guards asked Walter.

Walter looked sadly at the guard's uniform.

'That's Walter, he's our brother,' said Maud proudly.

'He came to find us,' Simon said, pleased.

'There is a call for Simon and Maud, Mr Scarlet is on the line.'

'Muttie!' they cried in delight.

And outside, where the races still went on, the tannoy announced that Bright Brass Neck had won at eleven to one.

*

Muttie was being considered the hero of the hour, but he thought of himself as the villain. Of course he had told those children he'd take them. It was all his fault from start to finish. But he wasn't allowed to take the blame. Cathy insisted it was all *her* fault, she just hadn't realised how dependent they were on people, she should have let them into the vandalised premises, she should have given them a precise date when she was visiting them after the wedding rather than letting them sit there waiting, disappointed. How mean to break a promise to kids who had so little. And to forget their birthday was unforgivable. Neil said a lot of it was down to him, he had believed his father's brother and he really *had* thought the principle of blood being best was right. Sara said they were all mad, she had just lost the plot on this one, she had been too involved in the campaign for the homeless to see what was straight in front of her, the fact that Simon and Maud, who were her direct responsibility, had no home to speak of. Kenneth Mitchell said little. He had been told that his elder son was most probably guilty of a serious crime, of vandalism and theft. And that the relations intended to prosecute. Kay said even less than her husband did, she had been drinking vodka all day from a bottle which she claimed to be mineral water. Soon somebody would find out. But it didn't really matter because quite obviously Kenneth would be going on his travels again. And this time it might all be over and The Beeches would be sold.

Geraldine brought Nick Ryan back to her flat for the little supper, which would be much more convenient than going to a restaurant, mainly because it would let them start their affair nice and easily. She sat down while Nick opened the bottle of wine.

'You're a very restful person,' he said.

Geraldine thought about it. That's probably what she was, restful. Not making demands, not whining. Never seen in a dirty pinafore, or over a sink of dirty dishes. A woman who had time to listen, a woman who, because she wouldn't see him again for three or four days, had time to rest and go to the gym and restock the fridge and the bar. Not someone who had to bring up his children, entertain his boring work contacts, keep his house the way *he* liked it.

'Restful, that's a nice compliment,' she said, 'but will you excuse me until I see if there's any news of the children?' There was a message waiting. They had been found, safe and well. Lizzie and

Muttie had been driven down to Kilkenny to retrieve them. She closed her eyes with the relief of it all. You heard such terrible stories, anything could have happened to them. She came back to join Nick. 'Good news, they're on the way home,' she said, and then talked no more about it. Men didn't like people prattling on endlessly about people they didn't know. Geraldine knew a lot about men.

Sara drove Muttie and Lizzie down to collect the children.

'And you're sure the Mitchell family won't mind if they stay the night with us?' Lizzie asked fearfully. 'The agreement, and everything.'

'No, Mrs Scarlet, they'd be very pleased. All of them.'

'It's just, we don't want to make any trouble,' Lizzie said.

'And we're so sorry,' Muttie added.

'But no, there's nothing for *you* to be sorry about, and it all ended well,' she reassured him.

'Except for Hooves,' Muttie said.

'They're very pleased he's not dead,' Sara said.

'I know,' said Muttie.

'Simon has a theory that if we got him a roller skate for his bad foot, he'd be as good as new.'

'You love them, don't you?' Sara said suddenly.

'Ah, well, doesn't everyone love children, all of ours went off to Chicago apart from Cathy so we've nobody here, it was great to have children around the place again.'

'You must have been very upset after Cathy's news, then,' Sara said.

'What do you mean?' Muttie asked.

'If you love children so much.'

'What news?' Lizzie said.

With a feeling of lead in the bottom of her stomach, Sara realised that they didn't know about the miscarriage. Neil had told her it was low-key; she hadn't realised just how low.

'I thought it was Cathy who gave you the news that Maud and Simon were found,' she said helplessly.

'No, Muttie was there when the guards phoned,' Lizzie said.

'And why would we be upset? We were overjoyed.' Muttie was confused.

Sara bit her lip and told herself that she must be the worst social worker in the western hemisphere, as she drove on through the twilight to collect her charges.

'Cathy?' The call was late. Cathy was reading in the kitchen, Neil was working at his big table.

'Yes, who's that?'

'It's Walter.'

'Oh,' she said. The story that she heard had not been entirely clear, but it did appear that Walter had on this occasion managed to behave normally and had gone to the help of his little brother and sister.

'I'm still down here, they sort of thought I should wait until Maud and Simon were collected.'

'Good.' She was crisp.

'It's just, I was wondering, who is collecting them you know . . .'

'My mother, father and their social worker.'

'And will there also be . . . do you think?'

'Yes, I think there will . . .'

'I see,' he said. There was a silence between them. Then he spoke again. 'It's too late, I suppose, to ask you to—'

'Much too late, Walter, it's all in hand, your parents have been informed.'

'I see,' he said again.

'Would you like to talk to Neil, or will I just say goodbye, then?' she asked.

There was a pause. 'Goodbye then, Cathy,' Walter Mitchell said.

Tom Feather had been so pleased to hear the good news that he made a cake and delivered it round to St Jarlath's Crescent. He had attached a card with the words 'Happy Birthday and Welcome Home to Maud and Simon and Hooves' on it, and left it with Muttie and Lizzie's neighbours. He was delighted they had been found safe. Such funny little things. He had once said to Marcella that he hoped they'd have children like that one day, real individuals with their own personality through and through. He remembered she had smiled indulgently, as if he was saying that one day he'd fly his own spaceship to Mars. Perhaps Marcella had never intended to have children. He had been sorry to hear Joe's cryptic remark that things were not going well in London for her. He guessed that this must be so after her phone call to Cathy. It was not what he wanted to hear. The only thing that made sense out of all this hurtful, tragic business was if she got what she

434

wanted by doing what she had done. If she hadn't got a modelling career, then what on earth was the point of the whole thing?

Neil had wanted to make love that night, but Cathy said she was too tired.

'Well, now. Tired, is it?' he repeated.

'I *am* too tired actually, I have to get up very early, I'm going to pick up the kids from Mam and Dad's and take them to school, everyone thinks they should go straight back, it would cause the least disruption.'

'Certainly, whatever madam the educationalist thinks,' he said, hurt and annoyed at her rejection.

'Don't be so sneering and bitter,' she said.

'I'm not.'

'You're making fun of me,' she said, 'mocking me.'

'And you're keeping me at arm's length.'

'Goodnight, Neil,' she said.

And it was one of those increasingly frequent nights where they slept as far from each other as possible.

Nick Ryan left Glenstar discreetly half an hour before Geraldine did the next morning. It had been a memorable evening, 'a delightful and important evening,' he said. Geraldine murmured her agreement. Nick Ryan obviously felt slightly uneasy about the situation, and the fact that he would not be free to come back to this welcoming flat that evening.

'I really wish . . .' he began.

Geraldine stopped him. 'Let's not waste any time wishing,' she said as she poured the excellent coffee into beautiful china cups. 'Let's just look forward to another lovely evening, whenever it turns up.'

She knew when he left that he was already besotted with her. For all the good that that would do in the long run. She sighed and went to phone Lizzie. Everything was wonderful in St Jarlath's Crescent. The twins were going to stay there for the time being, Cathy was coming round to drive them to school, the dog's paw didn't need to be amputated, only a splint. And Sara, the nice social worker, who had been kindness itself, said that Muttie and Lizzie should apply to foster the children. She thought that they might have a very good chance of getting them.

*

Shona Burke rang James. 'Great news, those children have turned up.'

'I *am* pleased to hear that,' he said. 'Where are they now?'

'With Muttie and Lizzie Scarlet.'

'Well, please God that's where they'll stay,' James said, very aware of the issue that hung between them.

Simon and Maud were just ten. They were nearly five years younger than Shona was when the law said she must leave the place where she was happy.

'Please God indeed,' Shona said.

'The world is a saner place nowadays, Shona,' he said. There was a silence. 'Let's hope Muttie Scarlet has a lot more courage than I did,' James said.

'Let's hope he has just as much love as you did,' Shona said gently.

James Byrne felt better than he had done for a long time. A few minutes later, he got a call from Cathy.

'Good news for once.'

'I've just heard about the twins, isn't it wonderful?' he said.

'No, this good news is actually about their brother. The guards are looking for Walter Mitchell, they've retrieved enough items from The Beeches and they know now that he did the break-in.'

'I don't want to add a sour note . . .'

'But?' Cathy said.

'It wasn't technically a break-in, that has been the whole problem with the insurance company.'

'Well, that's what he did,' Cathy said impatiently.

'No, Cathy, look at it from their point of view . . . Your husband's cousin let himself in to your premises with a key. It won't make them think any less that the whole thing was an inside job.'

She thanked him politely and said goodbye. Then she crashed the receiver back and shouted at the phone. 'Thanks for ruining our day,' she yelled in a rage.

'Who did you just slam the phone down on *now*?' Tom asked mildly.

She told him.

'Walter's so slippery, he might even *say* that we were in on it all for the insurance money.' She sounded very upset.

'No, he's too stupid, he'd never think that one out for himself,' Tom soothed her.

'But much, much more serious is how *did* he get the keys?'

'He might have seen us doing the ceremony of the keys in the van and crept along to pick them up,' Cathy said.

'I've been over that, we didn't start doing it until Walter was sacked,' Tom said.

'You mean *you* thought they'd still think it an inside job even though we'd found the thief?'

'It's just bad luck his being a cousin,' Tom said.

'I know,' Cathy sighed. 'Oh, I really wonder where cousin Walter is, now this minute?'

Cousin Walter had made three phone calls since all the confusion at the races. There was the one to Cathy; then he phoned his father to say that he was sorry but the heat was on and he might not be home for a while.

'I know, I heard,' his father said gloomily.

'Still, it's good no harm came to the children,' Walter said.

His father was strangely distanced from this. 'They've brought all hell down around our ears over it all, social police, real police walking in and out of The Beeches as if it was their office, and that dreadful girl your cousin married, claiming you robbed her premises and getting people to search your room. And other people asking your mother how much she drinks really and truly.'

'I know, Father.'

'No, don't tell me about innocent, blameless children, they went to a licensed bookmaker and put on a bet at their age, they brought that Muttie's dog to a racecourse, the last place you should bring a dog, they all nearly got killed and somehow it's turned out to be *our* fault. Why they couldn't have stayed here like normal children is beyond me.'

Walter's third call was to Derek, to say that the guards would probably land there anyway, so to make sure there was no substance in the house that shouldn't be.

'Don't mind about that,' Derek said, 'I'm not going to be done for your stolen goods, am I?'

'No, it's all out of there.'

'And what are you doing?'

'I'll stay away for a few weeks until it all dies down. See you then, back in Dublin.'

'Take care of yourself, Walter, you're not the worst,' Derek said a trifle guiltily.

Walter caught the tone and went for a last throw. 'Oh, Derek, in about five hours' time you could report your credit card missing,' he said.

'You never took my credit card?' Derek roared down the phone.

'No, but I know its number and I'm going to book myself a one-way ticket.'

'To where?' Derek asked in a panic.

'Relax, just to London, I'll be out the other side of Heathrow airport in five hours, so that's when you call them and notice it's missing.'

'Walter, that's not fair.'

'Not fair, not fair? Just one measly air ticket? When I'm facing jail? Get real, Derek!'

'Okay, five hours from now I get a new credit card number, and it had better only *be* the air ticket,' said Derek.

Sara seemed very ill at ease when Cathy went to see her.

'You know your parents want to foster the twins?'

'Yes, and I want to know what are the chances of Muttie and Lizzie getting them. Realistically. They just adore them, I don't want them to have to go through all this again.'

'You know we're talking about fostering, not adopting.'

'I know that. Poor people foster, rich people adopt,' Cathy said cynically.

'That's actually not true, and you know it's not, it's because Maud and Simon's parents are alive and could easily put up a case to have them back, and the law says . . .'

'The law doesn't know its arse from its elbow about things like this,' Cathy said.

'Believe me, I'm with you on this, my work every day is saying what you just said, but not as succinctly.'

'I know you are. You are tireless about things, just like Neil. Did he tell you, by the way, that he will be free after all to go with you to that conference next February? Remember when I was pregnant, he told you that he couldn't?'

'But won't you be gone by then?' Sara asked.

'Gone?'

'By February?' Sara was surprised.

'Gone where?' Cathy asked. Sara made a big production out of looking for her mobile phone. 'Gone where?' Cathy repeated.

'No, I'm mixing it up with someone else who was going away to

438

... um ... to England around then. Take no notice of me, I'm in pieces these days.'

Cathy looked at her thoughtfully. Sara had gone quite pale.

She was very tired from the finicky work they had to do for Peter Murphy, a cocktail reception at his home with top-drawer finger food. The crème de la crème was there, he assured Cathy several times, and that she must tell her aunt. Cathy didn't believe people ever used phrases like that any more.

'He still fancies your aunt, you know!' June said, 'I hope we'll have as many people lusting after us when we turn forty.'

'I know it's not what you want to hear, but your husband is pretty anxious to put a stop to your gallop in the lusting department ... He was onto Tom this morning to know what kind of a do this was.'

'Don't mind him, he's mad.'

'He loves you,' Cathy said.

June laughed. 'God, he may have once for about twenty minutes when I was sixteen.'

'Don't put yourself down June, he *must* love you. Why else would he care and ring up about you?'

'I don't know, but I wouldn't put any money on it,' said June. 'Are you going straight home yourself when we're through?'

'Yes, tonight it's Tom and Con's turn to unload the van; you and I get home to our fellows.'

'Well you'll be delighted to see your fellow, and he'll be delighted to see you, there's the difference for a start,' June said. 'Be sure and keep a few of these prawn in filo pastry things for him, those will soften his cough.'

'I couldn't bear to look at any more of them, June.'

'But *he* hasn't been looking at them all day like we have,' June said with remorseless logic.

'Was it tiring tonight?' Neil asked.

'No, fine, sorry for grizzling about being tired last night.' Cathy was bright and cheerful.

'What are these?'

'I thought you'd like a few special prawns.'

He seemed pleased with them on their little plate. 'They're great, so light ... Did you make them?'

She felt a great urge to say no, they had picked them up in a takeaway, what did he think she *did* for a living? But she smiled and said that she had.

'They're really great.' He didn't ask about the do tonight, he never asked about any do, whether it was Peter Murphy's cocktails, a fashion show, a wedding or a funeral. It was always still Cathy's funny job.

'You met Sara today,' he began. He seemed uneasy.

'I wanted to ask about the twins. Like whether there was a real chance of Dad and Mam fostering them full-time.'

'And what did she say...?'

'Well, she told me that the law might come down heavy because of them being old and working-class, but I told her that was balls and she more or less agreed.'

'But did you talk about anything else?'

'Is this a guessing game, or what?' Cathy asked.

'Okay, straight out, she rang me and said she had put her foot in it.'

'About what?'

'You know, now it's you who's playing guessing games.'

'I *don't* know, tell me.'

'She said that she had let it slip to you that I was still interested in the refugee job.'

'Well of course you are,' she was perplexed. 'I assumed you wouldn't have thought of it so seriously and then suddenly just let it slip out of your mind, I supposed you'd be thinking about it, yes.'

'The thing is, they've put the offer to me again, with different terms.'

'And you're going to take it.'

'Of course I'm not going to take it just like that, but we need to talk about it seriously.'

'Meanwhile you talk to Sara about it seriously.'

'Cathy!'

'I'd love a nice long bath,' she said.

'Please don't be like that.'

'Look, Neil, of course we'll talk about it seriously, but not at this time of night. Now I'm going off to lie there and think about the world, and I'd prefer to do so as your friend than somebody having a silly pointless argument with you.'

'Enjoy your bath, friend,' he surrendered.

Tom Feather invited Shona Burke out to dinner. He meant it as a combination of a work dinner and a thank-you gesture. He took her to a small French place.

'I promise I won't spend the time examining and criticising the food,' he said with an apologetic smile. 'People tell me they see me cutting up things, analysing them and they spot me as a rival from a mile away.'

Shona said that she was exactly the same, she kept looking out for something that would be useful to her at work. And took notes. One man thought she was writing down what he was saying.

'And was he saying anything he didn't want written down?' Tom asked. He had been talking about motorcycles, apparently, and Shona had been writing down the name and address of an efficient air-conditioning system. 'And did you see him again?' Tom wondered.

'No, but I did learn something from the experience – I don't take my notebook on dates any more.'

'Very wise, I'd say. But then, what would I know. I haven't been out on a date myself for so long.'

'Do you miss her a lot?'

'Marcella?' he said, surprised.

'Sorry Tom, it's your business. I don't usually pry into other people's lives.'

He didn't seem offended. 'Well, the answer is yes and no. I miss what I thought we had rather than what we really had. Maybe that's the way it always is when something's over.'

After dinner, Tom took Shona back to Glenstar and refused coffee on the grounds that he had early-morning bread to make and needed his sleep. He drove home to Stoneyfield. As he parked he could see someone sitting on the steps outside in the cold night air. It was Marcella.

Chapter Eleven

NOVEMBER

'Come in, Marcella,' he said wearily.

They walked in silence up the stairs to the flat where they had lived together so happily once. She looked around her as if seeing it for the first time. Neither of them had spoken yet. Tom sat down at one side of the table, which still had the pink velvet cloth on it. And with his hand, made a gesture for her to sit at the other. There had never been any point in offering Marcella food or drink, she had taken none of it, so he didn't start now. He looked at her as he waited for her to speak. She looked very tired, beautiful, of course, with the tiny face and all that dark hair. She wore a black leather jacket and a white sweater, a red scarf tied around her long, graceful neck. She carried only a small leather handbag on a chain; she hadn't brought any luggage with her.

'Thank you for letting me in,' she said.

'Naturally I'd ask you in,' he said.

'But you don't talk to me on the phone?'

'It's late, I'm tired, I have to get up very early to bake bread, you and I don't want to go through it all again, now do we?' He spoke gently, trying to be reasonable rather than showing the hard, hurt side of himself as he must have done before.

'I just want to tell you something and then I'll go.' She sounded very beaten and down. Not pleading or sobbing, but just as if all the life had gone out of her.

'Then tell me,' he said.

There was a silence. 'It's quite hard. Do you think I could have a drink?'

He went to the kitchen and looked around him, confused about what to offer her. 'Anything at all,' she said. He took a can of lager from the fridge, picked up two tumblers and brought her an ashtray as well. She seemed to take ages lighting her cigarette. Eventually she began to speak.

'Paul Newton *does* have a model agency, and I know he does have quite well-known models that go through it. It's well established over there. But it wasn't what was going to work for me. It didn't work at all, not at all, not even from the start.'

She looked so bleak and sad that Tom felt he had to say something. 'Well you *tried* it, that's what you wanted to do.'

'No, I never got a chance to try. He didn't want me for that kind of modelling, not for shows and what I thought . . . Only glamour modelling. First he sent me to people who did lingerie pictures for catalogues . . . and they wanted what they called glamour shots, which is topless.' There was such shame and sadness in the story, Tom closed his eyes rather than see her face. 'It was terrible, so I said to them there had been a mistake, that I was a real model on Mr Newton's books and they only laughed, saying I could take it or leave it.' There was a silence. 'I left it, of course, and went back to Paul Newton to tell him. I thought that he'd be furious with these people.' She paused to sip the lager that he had never seen her touch before. 'He was very busy that day. I waited ages to see him. I remember all the people coming in and out, all the kind of people I had wanted to meet all my life, stylists and designers and other models. And then after a long time I got in to see him, and I told him and he said . . . he said . . .' She stopped, hardly able to repeat the words. 'He said what else did I expect at my age . . . and I said that he had promised to have me on his books as a model, and he got really impatient and said he *had* done that for God's sake, so what was I complaining about? And do you know what happened then? Joe called him about something and obviously asked after me, and Paul Newton said that not only was I fine but I was right here in the office, finding it all a bit strange in the beginning but getting to know the ropes.' Tom drank his beer in silence; he could sense how hurtful it must have been. 'Anyway, he finished with Joe and he said to me that now I must be a big grown-up girl, act my age and get on with it . . . But I said, "You promised," and then he got really annoyed. "I told you the truth," he said, over and over . . .'

Tom looked at her. 'And suddenly it was just like my sitting talking to you, where I told you that I had told you the truth but you said it wasn't the same as being honest, and that there was a difference. I didn't see it until then.'

'Oh, Marcella.'

'Yes, so anyway I had enough money for a month's rent, and then I didn't have any more. I took my portfolio around, and when I showed them the pictures of you and me that we did for Celebrity Couples, people asked what I was doing over there when I could be here. And I had no answer. And then the next month I didn't have the rent, so I did the topless pictures, and oddly enough it wasn't as disgusting as I thought. Everyone was quite professional and got the job done as quickly and as high-quality as possible, they were all quite respectful in an odd sort of way. And the money went through Paul Newton's office. I collected it at the end of each fortnight. I never saw him, except, except for the day . . . the day that I rang you . . .'

'What happened . . . tell me?' Tom asked.

'He was at the reception desk when I was picking up my envelope, and he asked me to come in. He said he was sorry we had parted bad friends, and that I was very good at what I was doing, and now he had something else to offer me. I was pleased because I thought he had a real job for me at last. And first he showed me magazines with me in them topless, I'd never seen the pictures before, and I felt upset when I saw them and then he said I didn't have to do this kind of thing all my life. I waited and he said that if I wanted to I could earn real money, and he showed me other magazines, hard-core porn ones, and I felt so sick when I saw where he thought my future lay.' She stopped again, shaking her head in memory of the shock. 'He said that these people were very detached about their job, and there would be no pawing or anything, that wasn't the way it was done, it was just a day's work for everyone in the end, and I thanked him and said I'd call him the next day and I moved flats and never saw him again.' A long pause. 'And then I came home.'

'And where. . . ?'

'I'm staying at Ricky's for the moment. I clean the place and help him around the studio. I've worked in bars a couple of nights too, and in a sandwich bar at lunchtime. You know that I'd be a real asset nowadays to Scarlet Feather?' The longing in her voice was almost too much to bear.

But he said what had to be said. 'No, believe me, this is not spite, nor sulking, but it's no.'

'I'm not saying we should get back together immediately ... I'd go on living at Ricky's for a while ...'

'No.'

'I'll ask you again, it's all I want to do. Be back the way we were. Suppose it were *you* that had made the mistake, and had upset me by stretching too far in some direction. And just suppose you realised it was the most stupid thing and begged me to start again, wouldn't you like me to say something hopeful rather than a cold, blank no?'

'It's not a cold, blank no, believe me it's not. There's nothing I'd like better in many ways than to wipe the past bit from our minds and start again ...'

'Then why can't we...?'

'It's just not the way things are. It would all be a pretence, an act, like playing at being in love again. Maybe I'm shallow and you're better off without me. I've told you that before.'

'I didn't believe it then, or now.'

'But I don't love you any more. I'll never forget all we had together, and if I do ever love someone else, that will always be special ...'

'Love me again, don't look for someone new. Love *me* all over again.'

He felt no desire for her, no memory of a love shared in this very flat. He felt nothing but pity. 'It wasn't a great summer for me, and after you left a lot of things went wrong and I was very unhappy,' he began. 'But compared to yours, mine was nothing. I'm more sorry than I can say.'

'You must be pleased that you were right,' she said.

'No, I was right about nothing. I didn't have an idea all this was going to happen to you, I thought you'd be a great success, you were, and are, so beautiful. And truly I hoped you would because you wanted it so much.'

She picked up her handbag. 'I'll always be here, always around, if you change your mind,' she said.

'No you won't, not a treasure like you.' He tried to make her smile. But her face was sad. 'Come on, I'll drive you back to Ricky's,' he said.

'Will we be friends from now on, anyway?' she asked.

'We'll be much more than friends; weren't we together for four years?' he said.

'That's true, and there's so much I want to know.'

But though he wanted to tell her all the adventures and dramas, and about the twins going missing and the guards looking for Walter for the break-in, he felt it wasn't the time for small talk, so they drove though the dark, empty, wet streets in silence.

'If you won't come on a holiday with me, will you come away for a weekend?' Neil asked.

'Sure, that would be nice,' Cathy said.

She didn't really like the sound of a weekend away. It sounded dangerously like a honeymoon and she wasn't ready for that yet. The doctor had said that Normal Married Life would of course resume, it took different people different times. But Cathy thought that in her case it might take a long time. It wouldn't really be fair to go away with Neil unless she felt ready. Then again, it wasn't something she could easily discuss.

If she said to him that she wasn't ready for love-making yet, he would reasonably say that he hadn't suggested it, he was only thinking of a weekend away. And in many ways a weekend would be nice. She would think about places to suggest to him. Not yet. In a few weeks time.

They had fallen into a disconcerting habit of one being out when the other was in. Breakfast was the only meal they shared, and even at weekends they were both out a lot of the time. Cathy was cooking less at home in Waterview now during the day, since the facilities had much improved back at the premises. In fact, she often spent time there in the evening, and found herself sitting to read and relax in the big comfortable sofa rather than going back home. If Tom noticed, he said nothing; sometimes he was there himself, other times out. Cathy knew that he occasionally took girls out on dates, but rarely anyone a second time. She knew that Marcella was back in town and staying with Ricky; that's all he had told Cathy. June, however, who heard everything, had it that Marcella had totally changed and was doing all kinds of jobs she would have turned her nose up at, and was aching to get back into Scarlet Feather. She had told someone that she would wash dishes all day if she could come back.

'Will he take her back, do you think?' June's eyes were round with interest.

'She never worked here to be taken back,' Cathy said defensively.

'No, stop playing games – you know what I mean.'

'He never, ever talks about it.'

'You surprise me. The pair of you have been through so much together, I thought he'd weep on your shoulder.'

'No, I think there's too much shoulder-weeping in this business as things are.' But she also knew that they needed their space from each other. She had been tempted to tell him how much Neil had upset her over the whole pregnancy thing. But she didn't even want to acknowledge it openly. And anyway, a lot of that hurt seemed less sharp now. She and Neil *did* get on very well on many levels. Only this morning he had said how he wished she were free to come to the big demonstration for the homeless, but he knew she had to work.

'Good luck, Neil,' she said. 'I hope you get a good crowd.'

'You never know, mid-week.' He sounded worried. 'But then, if it does take off it really will focus serious attention on everything.'

He had sounded so concerned, she was glad again that she hadn't decided to tell a whole self-pitying tale about him to Tom. Poor, tired Tom who had promised himself a nice quiet day at the premises when they were all out on this job.

'Oh, June, how are we going to get through this lunch today, this woman's a monster.'

'You say that about them all, and they turn out to be pussy cats.'

'Not this one: we are to use the back entrance to the house, and take the van and park it somewhere so the guests won't see it and be offended by it; we all have to have house shoes, which we put on when we come in the back door, only that way will she know that muck has not been walked in.'

'Oh, well, if it keeps her happy.'

'Wait till she sees your hair, June.'

'What's wrong with it?' June looked in the mirror and patted her head. She had never again been able to afford the outrageous purple streaks that she had got with the Haywards token, and they had grown out, leaving her with a slightly piebald appearance.

'Oh, Mrs Fusspot said that she hoped the staff would be decorous, because some of the guests are embassy wives.'

'Decorous? I wonder,' June made faces at her reflection.

'But if we're really good, then we might well get into a lot of embassies, that's what we must think throughout.'

Tom wasn't coming on this one, there would be Con as barman,

June and Cathy to prepare and serve the lunch. He urged them to leave in plenty of time, the lady seemed to think punctuality was highly important.

'Cathy, stop calling her Mrs Fusspot, will you? You'll say it to her face when you're there.'

'No I won't.'

'Do you know where the place is?'

'Yes, I looked it up just now.'

'Have you got your mobile?'

'*Yes* Tom, and let me tell you, *you* are rapidly becoming Mr Fusspot, perhaps the two of you are well met.'

He laughed and patted the van. 'Good luck,' he called after them.

The phone never stopped ringing.

'Hi Tom, Neil here, have I missed Cathy?'

'Yes, but she's got her phone in the van.'

'No, it's okay, just tell her I've booked us into Holly's for the weekend after next, that will cheer her up.'

'Simple question, Tom: I met Marcella, she said she'd like me to take her up to Fatima to see Mam and Dad, that you and she were good friends now. I just wanted an update.'

'She never wanted to go to see them in Fatima when she lived with me,' he said simply.

'You'd prefer not, then?'

'She must go where she pleases.'

'She's very broken, you don't know the kind of time she must have had over the water, she doesn't talk about it but it can't have been great.'

'No, and I do wish her well, and I really hope she finds happiness like I would for any friend.'

'Right Tom, matter dropped.'

'Tom, it's Muttie here. You see, the twins are making an Irish stew for Lizzie as a treat tonight, and they gave me a list...'

'You'd like us to make it for you ... Okay, Muttie...'

'I beg your pardon, they wouldn't *hear* of you making it. This is to be all their own work. I have all of the lamb and carrots and onions, but it's just that it says stock on the list. What's that?'

Tom told him what little cubes to ask for in the local supermarket, and what they looked like. Cathy's mother probably had plenty of excellent stock in her freezer, but this was no time for opening the wrong things.

'Is that Tom Feather? Nick Ryan here, I want to have a surprise birthday party for Cathy's aunt at her apartment, and for you both to cater it.'

'You know, Mr Ryan, we have a policy on surprise parties . . . we don't usually do them. They can go so very wrong.'

'But not with Geraldine, surely . . . she has so many friends?' He sounded uncertain.

'Could Cathy come back to you on this one? Please.'

'Well, all right then, I thought you'd be glad of the business.' He sounded huffy now.

'And indeed we are, Mr Ryan, as I say, Cathy will sort it all out as soon as she can.'

'Yes, well.'

'Tom?'

'Cathy, there's telepathy, I was just going to ring you.'

'Tom, have you her letter and the map there?'

'You mean you aren't *there* yet? Oh, my God!'

'Don't you panic, you're the one on dry land with the map, I've been to number twenty-seven, they never heard of Mrs Fusspot.'

'Well, if you called her—'

'Of course I didn't call her that, Tom, quick, will you.'

He ran to the desk and took down the file with that week's bookings in it. He came back to the phone and read out the address.

'That's where I am.'

'Well, it's on her writing paper printed there in front of me.' He read it aloud again, this time with the name of the suburb.

'*What?*' she screamed. There were two streets with the same name. People should be hanged for allowing this in any country. She was on the wrong side of Dublin.

'Tom, what will I do? If I ring her now she'll go to pieces. Tom, speak to me.'

'Just get there. I'm much nearer, I'll ring her and go round in a taxi with champagne and smoked salmon and hold them at bay until you get there. Drive carefully, don't take any risks. I don't want the entire company dead on arrival.'

He had a fairly horrific phone conversation with Mrs Fusspot,

449

where he had to hold the mobile far from his ear. The taxi man looked at him sympathetically.

'You know your job is nearly as bad as mine,' he commented, when Tom had put the phone down, exhausted.

'I don't think it's always as bad as this, but give me yours today, I beg you.'

'Not today, you wouldn't want it,' the taxi driver said gloomily. 'There's some kind of protest in the centre of Dublin, people marching from O'Connell Street to Stephen's Green. We'll be all day and all night getting to your one on the phone, and the one you were talking about with the van of food will be lucky to get there by next weekend.' Tom lay back and closed his eyes. He must stay calm. Somebody somewhere in this city must be calm.

Mrs Frizzell was around fifty, tiny in an unwise emerald-green wool dress. She had black hair scraped up into an angry-looking chignon and was very bad-tempered when he arrived. He saw with relief that there were no other cars, and noted from the high volume of abuse with which she greeted him that she must be alone, and that he had at least made it ahead of the guests.

'There, there, there.' Moving quickly into the kitchen and finding suitable glasses, he said, 'You see, I told you, the traffic was terrible, they'll all be delayed, it's exactly the same for everyone.' He hadn't said anything of the sort, but he was picking up what the taxi driver had said. 'I think it's some kind of protest march, Mrs Frizzell, it has totally disrupted the traffic and some streets are closed.' Her face was stony. Tom opened one bottle expertly and stood it in ice, then he swiftly arranged the smoked salmon pieces on the buttered brown bread, found a sharp knife and cut them into tiny pieces.

He had grabbed lemons and parsley to take with him, but he needed a plate. He looked around for one.

'I thought you said you provided all your own—'

'And indeed we do, and our china is on the way, it's just as I told you, the transport has been unavoidably delayed in this protest march.'

'Protest,' she scoffed.

'I know, it *is* inconvenient, but still, it's good that we live in a democracy, isn't it, and people can make their views known.'

Mrs Frizzell did not appear to think it was particularly good to live in a democracy, nor may ever have thought so. Meanwhile Tom had spotted a plain white platter. 'Let me use your lovely white plate, I'll take great care of it,' he soothed her, and produced in seconds an entirely acceptable dish of canapés. He noticed her beginning to thaw slightly.

'Let me take you back into the very nice sitting room I saw briefly on the way in, and give you a glass of champagne while you wait for your guests. They too will be anxious, being so late for you,' he said.

The guests were in fact not late at all, and to his annoyance he saw a big black car coming up the drive. He settled her down and ran back to the kitchen opening cupboards, fridges, drawers, anything to see was there any raw material from which he might make up a lunch, supposing Cathy never turned up. He did find a bottle of cheap brandy, and decided to add a few drops quietly to every glass of champagne he served. This was going to be the longest pre-luncheon drink in the history of catering: they might as well enjoy it.

'I don't *believe* this,' Cathy cried when the guard on traffic duty told her that the roads were closed. 'Has there been an accident?'

'Oh, no, it's only the homeless and those who care about them to the point of closing the city down,' he said, casting his eyes up to heaven. He was a weary man and he had little sympathy for those who made his job more difficult than it already was. 'Are you conjurers, the lot of you?' he asked them, interested. They had such a funny van with a red feather on it; they might be children's entertainers.

'*No*, Guard,' said Cathy before doing a perilous turn. 'But we may have to become conjurers before this day is over.'

'Who could have got them to close the streets?' Con asked in amazement.

'My husband,' Cathy said grimly.

Most of the women were very much at ease the moment they came in the door. They all signed a book on the hall table so that Mrs Frizzell could show her husband who had turned up ... Tom moved among them, easily smiling, reassuring that there were *no* calories in smoked salmon. He fought down his own panic. There were twelve women, two of the four bottles of champagne he had brought were empty, the plate of smoked salmon was nearly finished. It would take an hour to set up the table and serve the lunch, and there was no sign whatsoever of the van.

*

The television cameras covered the march, which was all the more impressive for being done in heavy rain. The banners were held high and the people were of all ages.

'I can't believe it, Neil,' Sara said. He squeezed her hand; it was better than any of them had ever believed possible. He wished Cathy could have come, but he'd tell her about it tonight, and some of the speeches might even be on the nine o'clock news.

Tom ripped open three tins of sardines, drained them and squeezed lemon juice and ground fresh black pepper into the mixture, and then like lightning he spread it over the contents of a packet of biscuits he had also unearthed.

'Very nice,' one woman said. 'What are they called?'

'Sardines au citron,' he said.

'They're good.' She smiled into Tom's eyes.

He smiled nervously and moved away.

He kept topping up the champagne with further drops of brandy, but never Mrs Frizzell's own glass, as he didn't want her to know why her guests seemed so animated. Tom tried to keep a mental note of all he had taken from Mrs Frizzell's stores; if this day ever ended he would have to restore as well as half a bottle of brandy many more items. He had opened jars of gherkins, chopped a cucumber and made a little bowl of dip out of various yoghurts he found in the fridge. Oh, please God, remember that Mrs Maura Feather of Fatima prayed night and day to Him, and surely there must be some credit in the prayer bank now which God could use to make the van turn up.

'I'm afraid to go in,' Cathy said at the gate. 'They're here; and the place is full of cars. God, there are even chauffeurs.'

'Drive in, Cathy,' said June.

'Will I ring first?'

'Drive in,' Con begged.

Cathy drove right up to the front door, then remembered and reversed to go to the back door. Tom saw them coming, and thanked God and his mother for having answered the prayer.

'I've seen her somewhere before. I know her, and that dress,' Cathy said.

'Of course you haven't, you're hallucinating . . .' Tom hurried them on.

'Cold canapés of any kind – no time to heat anything, I have the ovens on, just fling the main course in,' he hissed to Cathy.

'And open more champagne, Con, they've drunk my lot. Quick, June, start the tables.'

There were twelve in total: she was going to have two tables of six, do her best. Cathy went into the dining room, stunned that Tom had been able to make these people stay so long without anything to eat. She urged them to have the little asparagus tips with Parma ham, and insisted that Mrs Frizzell have just one of the tiny caviar and sour-cream blinis . . . All the other guests seemed to be enjoying them. To her amazement, Mrs Frizzell said she was very sorry about those dreadful protesters who had delayed her; a lot of the guests had been upset by the traffic diversions too. Mr Feather had explained all about the march and had been marvellous. Cathy said she was delighted to hear it, and scooped up some really revolting-looking things on plates which were on the tables and the piano.

'God, what on earth are these?' she said scraping them into a bin.

'Those were my best efforts, and they loved them until you arrived with the cavalry,' he said. 'I'll go home now, and leave you to cope.'

'You *can't* go.'

'But there's three of you here!'

'Tom, our nerves have gone, you *must* stay and help.'

'Of course I won't, I'm off now to lie down for a month.'

'You don't understand, they love you, they can't stand the rest of us, you *have* to stay and help us get on with it.'

She saw he had only been joking. 'Of course I'll stay, you clown, anyway, I don't have the strength to walk down that avenue. I have to get a lift home in the van.'

And so it all went into its well-tried routine. They all moved around the kitchen, helping each other, passing things, getting rid of rubbish, totting up the number of wine bottles on the calculator, covering little delicacies in some of Mrs Frizzell's dishes for her to discover later in her fridge. Con gave them the word, the ladies were leaving, the van was loaded. Three of the eleven guests had been interested enough in the food to ask for cards. They were ready to roll. Tom had listed the sardines, brandy and other items he had taken, so there would be no misunderstandings. Mrs Frizzell thanked them grudgingly. It had, of course, been very distressing that everyone was so late, and extra precautions really should have been taken on a day when everyone knew that the city traffic would be difficult.

'Ah, but *did* they know,' Tom said. In about eight minutes they would be out of here. Cathy had promised to buy them all a pint to apologise for having got the address wrong.

'Well, apparently they did, or should have; some of the ladies were telling me that that good-looking lawyer son of Jock and Hannah Mitchell you always see spouting on about causes was on breakfast television this morning warning everyone, so really you should have known. Still, in the end it had turned out all right, and you needn't pay for the items you used, just regard that as a tip.'

'You know the Mitchells then, Mrs Frizzell?' Tom said innocently.

'My husband plays golf with Jock. We were at their house once. Oaklands – big place, very nice.'

Cathy remembered her then, and the dress, from New Year's Eve. But mercifully Mrs Frizzell had no similar memory. They smiled until their faces hurt, until they got in their van. Then when they had driven out through the gate they played the scene out over and over for Con and June.

'. . . that good-looking lawyer . . .' Tom said.

'. . . spouting about causes . . .' Cathy giggled.

They told Tom that the guard had thought they were conjurers. And Tom said if that guard had seen him scraping Mrs Frizzell's bits and pieces onto biscuits he would know that conjurors was exactly what they were. He told Cathy she was to call Nick Ryan sometime about a surprise fortieth birthday for Geraldine.

'That's a non-starter, she'd flay us alive,' Cathy said. 'Anything else happen when I was driving the wrong way round Dublin?' she asked.

'Yes, the handsome spouting lawyer rang and said he'd booked you both into Holly's the weekend after next.'

'Well, that's another non-starter for a variety of reasons,' said Cathy, looking straight ahead and not catching Tom's eye as he drove to the pub.

Neil came home just in time for the news.

'It was a huge success, I gather,' Cathy said.

'Yes, people can't pretend any more that they don't know about the problem, and that's good.'

'Let's turn on the television and see what they say.'

She handed him a glass of wine and put a plate of warm Stilton tartlets on the table between them.

'These are nice,' he said. 'Leftovers?'

She was annoyed. She had saved them specially for him in waxed paper. 'Well, I suppose they are in a way, but I didn't see them like that.'

'Stop being prickly, hon.' She shrugged. The news hadn't yet begun. 'How did it go anyway, *your* do?'

'Fine. She knew your parents, as it happens . . .'

The signature tune for the news came on. 'Shush. Here we go,' he said. The march got very full coverage, and there were aerial pictures too of the way Dublin transport had been brought to a halt. Somewhere in that television footage was the Scarlet Feather van, turning and twisting like a wounded animal. She half hoped they would see it. It would be hard to miss with its distinctive logo. Instead they saw Neil. About twenty seconds worth of him, young and eager, his hair blowing in the wind, his face wet from the rain, but there as always with the one short, telling phrase.

'Thank you for coming out on the streets today to say that in a country of plenty we are ashamed that people will sleep without a home tonight.' He looked straight at the camera. 'Let nobody's conscience feel easy by saying that the homeless have sought out their lifestyle. Which one of us here would choose to spend this November night in a doorway or under a bridge in the cold and rain?'

As he got down from the platform, supporters grasped him and hugged him in solidarity. One of the people reaching out to him was Sara. Cathy watched wordlessly.

And then the report went on to a politician saying what was being done, and a member of the opposition saying that not nearly enough was being done. Neil had stood out above them all. These were just grey people in a studio, without the passion of the young man standing in the rain.

'You were great,' Cathy said admiringly. And she meant it.

'It just might help to change things.' He was talking about the whole demonstration, not about his own little excerpt. 'It was great out there, Cathy; I *wish* you had been able to come, be a part of it.'

Cathy thought how she and June and Con had sat for what seemed like hours in their van, and cursed him to the pit of hell. 'In a way I *was* a part of it,' she said.

And then the phone began to ring. People congratulating him, further tactics to be agreed, newspapers and radio programmes wanting him to do more interviews. He was adept at passing the requests on to other people. He was only one person of a very big committee, and perhaps they should talk to this person or that; he could give them a phone number, an e-mail address. Neil knew too well the pitfalls in being seen as the only voice; he made sure that there was no danger of his taking the whole thing over. When people called him on his mobile, Cathy answered the ordinary phone. She was indeed kept fully busy for the evening as the assistant and helpmate he wanted her to be.

'Cathy, it's Sara.'

'Oh, Sara, good to hear from you. Did it all go well?'

'Well, sure it did, didn't you see, don't you know?'

'I haven't had time to ring my mam yet, but I hear that they're making an Irish stew to mark the day.'

'Who are? I don't understand.' Sara sounded totally confused.

'The twins, you know, all their belongings have gone into a lock-up shed, my dad told me all about it. The Beeches is being boarded up today.'

'Oh, the *twins*,' Sara said. Cathy was silent. 'Sorry, Cathy, of course you meant the twins. Sorry.'

'And *you* meant the march?'

'Yes, I was walking a bit of the way with Neil. Wasn't he wonderful on television!' Sara said.

'He was indeed, will I put you on to him?' and she passed the phone to Neil. Cathy felt very tired, and out of things. In fact, she wanted to go to bed. These calls could go on all night. Yet it looked dismissive and cold to Neil on his big day to show so little interest. In something that meant so much. She would have been very happy to curl up on a sofa and hear all about it. But these weren't sofas you could curl up on; slim, clean lines, and there wasn't any chance of hearing anything except one end of a telephone conversation. A few months ago she would have told him all about Mrs Frizzell and they would have laughed at his being called a spouting lawyer. Tonight it would have been out of place. Things had changed a lot. They really did need to spend some time away from everything. Which reminded her that she must tell him that she wouldn't go to Holly's with him, but tonight was not a night for a row so she would leave that until tomorrow. So Cathy sat there, listening enthusiastically to Neil's side of phone calls. He waved away any offers of food, the adrenalin was enough. 'It will be real food, not leftovers,' she said. And immediately wished she hadn't.

'Oh, Cathy, you *are* getting very petty about a silly remark. Sorry if it offended you, anyway, I don't want any more, thanks all the same.'

The phone rang again and he seemed to take the call with some relief. Well why not? Cathy asked herself. The rest of Ireland thought he was a hero. His wife just made petty remarks about leftovers. Which would anyone prefer?

Next morning Neil was rushing, he had to get into the radio studio to do an interview on *Morning Ireland* before anything else. Cathy didn't tell him about Holly's then. It seemed inappropriate.

'See you at eleven,' she called as he was leaving. 'You'll knock them dead on the radio.'

'Eleven?' he said.

'Remember, the meeting.'

'Meeting?' He looked blank.

'Oh, Neil, at our premises, the bad guys are coming, and James.'

'God yes, of course, I'll be there,' he said.

James Byrne had asked for another meeting with the insurance company. He had been told that the position was still very unsatisfactory; apparently a cousin of one of the partners had let himself into the premises and destroyed everything for no apparent reason. This said cousin had now disappeared, and the insurance company was expected to pay up as if this in fact had been a de facto breaking and entering by criminals who were strangers. Neil hadn't turned up at eleven when they were meant to begin. Coffee was served in the front room, the phones put on the answering machine and James began. He would like the representatives of the company to look around the place, which had shown all the signs of two people trying to get their business back to where it had been. And until Neil Mitchell, barrister-at-law who was advising them arrived . . . perhaps James could step in and bring them up to date with the way things were progressing. He showed them the meticulous books he kept, the receipts for the equipment they rented, the ongoing calendar for work planned and booked. He explained that they were now not in any position to take on a job that meant large financial outlay, they didn't dare to accept anything which would not be paid for within the traditional ninety days that big companies insisted on. He painted a picture of a decent, hard-working, struggling pair who were anxious only for what was theirs by right and law.

'Law has to be interpreted, defined,' one of the insurance men said.

Cathy wished with a passion that Neil was here to answer him. *Why* did he have to be late on this of all days? Then her mobile rang.

'Neil?'

'Sorry, hon, you've no idea the impact all this has made, I'm literally besieged . . .'

'They're here for the consultation, and we need you . . .'

'I'm really sorry, and please give my sincerest regrets to—'

'*No* Neil.' Tears had sprung to her eyes. He did this too often. Everyone had been looking at the door for the last half an hour waiting for him, and now it turned out that he wasn't anywhere near them.

'If I could . . .'

'They've just said law has to be interpreted and defined, you *should* be here to do that for us.'

Tom and James started to talk loudly, at exactly the same moment, to gloss over what was obviously a husband-and-wife quarrel and the slightly humiliating non-appearance of their legal adviser. But Cathy had turned her phone off.

'Neil wasn't able to make it, he said to apologise to you all, so even though I'm furious with him for not being here, I'm passing on his regrets.'

Tom let his breath out. Slowly. She was in control again. They pointed out that Walter was not Cathy's cousin, merely a cousin of her husband, that they were most certainly not in touch with him, the guards believed that he was in London, and they had no idea where. The fact that Cathy's parents were hoping to foster Walter Mitchell's brother and sister did not mean a close and continuing relationship. Walter had nothing to do with anything at all. The meeting ended indecisively, the insurance men left saying that they would not come to another meeting or consultation until there was something new to put on the table. Meanwhile, investigations and negotiations would go on at their usual pace.

Tom, James and Cathy sat in silence after they had left.

'I could kill him,' Cathy said.

'Don't,' said Tom. 'We're in enough trouble already.'

'We are in trouble,' James said. 'Unless the insurance pays before Christmas, you won't be able to carry on.'

Sandy Keane wouldn't let those two children near his betting office again, so Simon and Maud had to wait outside when Muttie went to his office to meet his associates there.

'I'm calling the guards if they come in the door,' he said.

'You're a very extreme person, Sandy,' Muttie said.

'You're not the one who got grilled by the entire Garda station ... They said a man who could take a bet off children under ten years of age was capable of doing anything, even abducting them.' Sandy shivered at the memory.

'Well why *did* you take their bet then?' Muttie wondered. 'I'd never sent them in before with money to you.'

'But you weren't there, you hadn't been seen for two days. Where were you, anyway?'

'I was about my business,' Muttie said. He wanted no mention or indeed memory of the hospital examination.

'Muttie, you don't *have* any business except coming in here tormenting me,' cried Sandy in despair.

There was a loud knocking on the door. The twins stood outside.

'No,' cried Sandy.

'We're not coming in, thank you, Mr Keane, it's just to tell Muttie that Cathy came by in her van and is going to take us for a drive, and as we were getting a bit wet out here ...'

'Good, good, go on the drive, goodbye,' he shouted.

'We didn't want Muttie to think we'd gone missing again.'

'No, we'd all hate that,' Sandy Keane said drily.

'Thank you, Mr Keane,' Maud said.

Muttie came out to them. 'Man has a head like a block of wood. What harm on earth would two well-behaved children and a pedigree Labrador do to his betting shop? They'd raise its tone. He has no judgement whatsoever.'

Cathy brought the van up beside them. 'I needed a bit of nice company, so I thought of Hooves, and of course that means taking Simon and Maud too.'

'That's a joke,' Maud said to Muttie.

'Cathy was always a great one for the jokes when she was young,' Muttie said. 'She used to come home from school with a new one every day.'

'You don't have many jokes nowadays, Cathy,' Simon said.

'Oh, I'm full of them,' she said.

'When do you tell them and laugh at them?'

Cathy paused to think. She had laughed properly in the van when they were coming away from Mrs Frizzell's house. 'At work, at home, everywhere.'

'Does Neil like jokes?' Maud asked.

'He loves them. Dad, we can't tempt you. . . ?'

'No, I have a lot of work ahead of me. Will see you at supper, maybe; there's still some of that great Irish stew the twins made.'

'We made far too much, I'm afraid,' Simon said.

'No, you can never make too much, that's what God invented freezers for . . .'

'But God didn't actually . . .' Simon began. 'I see,' he said.

They went to an Internet café and the twins sat at a machine, while Cathy drank too much coffee and planned what she would say to Neil tonight. His presence there today would have alerted those people; things might have been moved forward. He must be made to understand that. Without nagging, whingeing and being . . . what was that word he used about her recently? Prickly. And even though she hated doing it, she felt it only fair to tell him about James's very dire forecast. Perhaps it might make him feel more guilty about letting them down today. And of course she hadn't had time to tell him that she wouldn't go to Holly's. It would be a conversation with very few jokes in it, she realised. At that moment Simon came back from the computer.

'We've found a really good website, Cathy, could we have another half an hour of it, or is that greedy?'

'No, that's fine.' She gave them the money.

'It's not too dear, is it, what with you being poor again after the robbery?'

So far the twins didn't really understand Walter's part in it all, and she kept it from them. Their mother and father had abandoned them yet again; there was no point in taking away the only remaining member of their immediate family, the one who *had* stood by them that time.

'No, we can afford another half an hour, and don't forget, you might well get a computer at Christmas. You'd never need to come to a place like this again.'

'Imagine, having it at home.' Simon's eyes were shining.

Cathy had arranged that Jock and Hannah give them this as a

present. She would arrange for a good basic computer to be delivered to St Jarlath's Crescent. Neil had said that strictly speaking, since it was educational, the funds should come out of whatever trust there was for the twins. He might talk to Sara about it all. Cathy had sighed.

'Let your parents do something for them, Neil, they did so damn little that they were full of guilt. This will get them off the hook.'

He had been startled, but agreed.

'And you don't mind sitting here?' Maud asked.

Cathy didn't. She was in no hurry to go back to Waterview.

There was news when they got back to St Jarlath's Crescent. Marian had been on the phone. It was early days, but she and Harry were expecting a child, wasn't it wonderful? They would have the christening in Chicago in April, and everyone must come over.

'Do they dance at christenings?' Simon asked.

And Cathy found herself reaching out to squeeze her mother's hand at the same time as Lizzie reached for hers. Neither of them trusted themselves to speak.

Cathy was still putting off going home. She went to one of the new places hidden among the foodie streets in Temple Bar for a snack. Neil wasn't eating these days, it appeared, and there were plenty of what he called leftovers to offer him. To her great surprise she was served by Marcella. She looked very beautiful in a smart black trouser suit and a red necklace around her throat. They stared at each other in disbelief.

'You look lovely, Marcella, but then you always did.'

'For all the good it did me,' Marcella said. There was a sudden awkward silence. 'Are you meeting anyone?' Marcella asked.

'No, I was ... Well, I just wanted a glass of wine and something small.'

'We have a lovely plate of mixed tapas,' Marcella suggested.

Cathy nodded dumbly. 'That would be fine,' she said in a choked voice.

'And Cathy, I'm just on my break now. Would it annoy you if I sat down with you for ten minutes? I'd love that.'

'So would I,' said Cathy insincerely. Please may Marcella not want to cry and tell the whole story about just wanting to talk to Tom all over again. But in fact it was quite different. Marcella asked about Scarlet Feather and what had happened since she left. There was a lot to tell. Cathy told her about Marian's wedding, and her own pregnancy and miscarriage; she told about the twins' disappearance, about June's husband Jimmy being housebound, about Geraldine's new chap, how Con was now working almost full-time with them and about Walter being the thief. She left some things out. Like their very poor financial future. Like Tom looking like a ghost for so long that they all worried, and just now beginning to show signs of recovery. She didn't tell either about having grown so distant from Neil that she dreaded going home to see him tonight. Which was why she was sitting here eating tapas.

'I've been rabbiting on about myself. You can tell me or ask anything you like, Marcella, Tom and I never talk about personal things at all, it's just like an unwritten rule.'

'Do you think there's a chance he'd have me back?' It was so naked, humble and sad.

'I haven't an idea, Marcella, I really don't. I know one side of him so well, and nothing at all about the other.'

'And does he have anyone in particular. . . ?'

'No, no one in particular. I know he does take girls out, but I don't hear anything.'

'Thank you, Cathy.' She looked at her watch and got up.

'I'd better go, too.' Cathy took out her wallet.

'On me, Cathy.'

She knew that the wages in these places were not good, and there would be no tip. But dignity was also important. 'Thank you. It was delicious, and I'll send people here.'

A group of people had just come in. Marcella went to greet them, tall and beautiful, with that assured smile.

She called Neil at the town house. He wasn't home yet. She didn't want to sit there waiting. Where else could she go? It was eight o'clock on a winter's evening. It was tempting to go and sit in the premises for an hour, put on some music, sit in one of those deep sofas and close her eyes. But she might fall asleep. She would go back to Waterview. Funny how she hardly ever called it home now. Just Waterview.

They arrived together, her van pulling in beside the Volvo.

'There's timing,' he said, pleased. He had a lot of documents under his arm and a briefcase over his shoulder. He walked ahead of her and looked at the number of times the little red light flashed. 'Only three messages. Good,' he said.

'Leave them, Neil.'

He laughed. 'What on earth are you talking about, hon, you don't have a message machine, unless you want—'

'Please leave them. If you listen to them, you'll have to do something about them,' she said.

'Ah, Cathy, what *is* this?'

'An attempt to talk before we are both too exhausted and have to crash into bed,' she said simply.

'I *told* you, I booked us into Holly's. We'll talk all weekend there.' He was moving towards the phone.

'I'm not going to Holly's with you,' she said, her voice unexpectedly loud.

'You really are coming on very strong. You won't come on the holiday which I cleared with Tom, I told Tom how tired you were and he said they'd cover for you, I took the time off myself which was hard, cancelled a whole lot of things I now have to refix. Then you agreed to go to Holly's, now you change your mind. Honestly . . .'

'I said I'd like a weekend, I didn't ask you to go ahead and book it without discussion.'

'But you *like* Holly's.'

'I don't want to go there,' she said.

'Why on earth. . . ?' he looked at her, bewildered.

'The last time you and I went there I was telling you about how we were going to have a baby. You don't think I want to go back there again, Neil?' She felt guilty as she said it. It was valid, but only half the reason. Still, she had nothing to be ashamed of, no real secret. She would have told Neil that she had fallen asleep in Tom's room, had she been given a chance.

He looked at her, embarrassed. 'I'm afraid I didn't think of that. I'll book us somewhere else tomorrow.'

'Or maybe we could do it after some discussion between us,' she said.

Neil gave up thoughts of checking the telephone. 'Is this what this is about? My not running everything past you before we do it? Is that it?'

'No, it's about much, much more. It's about your not turning up today when we really needed you so badly,' she said.

He had forgotten. It had been such a busy day for him. If they turned on the nightly current affairs programme he would be mentioned in it. How could he have thought to recall a conference with some insurance people, long agreed and then totally abandoned? 'Look, I told you at the time . . .' he began.

'You weren't there, Neil.'

'You knew how much in demand I was today after the march, for God's sake, you were there last night when the calls came in.'

'Then you should have cancelled our meeting.'

'But Cathy, it wasn't . . .' he began.

This time she didn't interrupt him, she waited. He said nothing. 'It wasn't what, Neil?' she asked, almost defying him.

'It was a matter of priorities,' he said eventually. 'We all have to make decisions every day about what to do and what not to do.' He was still calm, reasonable.

'And you decided at the last minute not to come to a very important meeting about your wife's company? Leaving the three of us looking so foolish you wouldn't believe it?'

He stopped being calm now. 'Cathy, please. There were things that had to be done, a joint committee is being set up, they needed someone to advise about the terms of reference . . .'

'*We* needed you at the premises, you had promised to come. You don't know what happened, they ran rings around us, they were supercilious and . . . And you won't believe this, but if they don't pay up in time we could be out of business before the New Year.' She waited for the shock on his face, but it wasn't there yet. 'Like go out of business, permanently cease trading,' she said, afraid that he hadn't understood.

'Cathy, I know this is a blow for you and Tom, and I'm sorry of course, but seriously, in terms of what else is going on . . . It's not something I could run away from everything else for. It's only a business, after all, it's only a small business, cooking food for rich people, giving them upmarket food.'

'What?' She looked at him astounded.

'You know I've always been very proud of you, and you've done very well. Very well . . .' He paused.

'Sorry, I don't understand. This is my job, Neil, this is what I do.'

'I know, hon, but you can't compare what you're doing . . . You know, all these discussions about canapés and finger food, with what I had to do today.'

'There were no discussions about finger food today, there were people, big companies whose job it is not to pay up until they have to. You told me that yourself when we had the robbery.'

'I know, I know.'

'So what are we talking about then? Tell me, Neil, tell me now why we, who had booked you for a consultation couldn't have you, couldn't rely on your being there as you had promised?'

'That is such a grossly unfair—'

'Tell me.'

'Because it was not as important as the setting up of a joint committee. Don't get carried away with the importance of a business, Cathy. They come, they go.'

'Even if you've slaved for them and played everything by the book like we've done all the way?'

'What are we talking about . . . You despise these people, you just make money out of them, I've heard you over and over groaning and pouring scorn on them, but you still take their fees.'

'And is that immoral, to do a service and get paid for it?'

'No, Cathy, it's not, but it seems to me that you are trying for a very high moral ground saying that I should have given up good work in defence of the homeless in order to protect what we all agree is something which in the end is fairly unimportant.'

'Just say that again, Neil.'

'Stop playing games, you heard me.'

'You think Scarlet Feather is unimportant.'

'Not in itself. It is filling a need, but in terms of—'

'Did you always think this, like, say, a year ago when I was so busy setting it up?' she asked. He sighed heavily.

'I need to know.' She was calm.

'Well, I thought it pleased you, you know, because of all this nonsense about your mother and mine, which never mattered to anyone.'

'It mattered to everyone except you,' she said.

'So you say. . .'

'So you always thought it was a fairly trivial enterprise, something that started and could close.'

'That's what happens to businesses.' He shrugged. Uncaring.

'So why did you even bother to get involved when we had a break-in . . . a robbery that was actually masterminded by your own first cousin, as it happens?'

'I wondered when we'd get to that,' he said.

'No, Neil, why did you bother taking it up if you weren't going to follow through?'

'I was going to follow through, and I am going to, but today was not the day. Anyone in Ireland could have told you, I had other things to do today.' He looked very hurt.

'But you thought it a Mickey Mouse, rich people's enterprise. Why then did you bother at all . . .'

'It was the principle of the thing, they should not be allowed to get away with it,' he said. There was a long silence. 'Cathy?'

'What?'

'Do you . . . um . . . um . . .' he asked.

She looked at him for a long time. 'Do I think you should listen to the phone messages now? Yes, I think that's a great idea,' she said.

'Don't piss me about.'

'I'm not. Believe me.'

'You wanted to talk,' he said.

'And we did,' she said.

'Is there anything I could say or do to make you feel better?' he asked.

'No, no, there's not, Neil.'

'I know I'm very insensitive, like that thing about Holly's hotel.'

'Again, I tell you, it's not important, believe me there, too.'

'I love you,' he said.

'Maybe, Neil.'

'No, really and truly, and we have always been honest with each other, always.'

'Yes,' she said thoughtfully.

'And I don't want anyone else in the world but you. So yes, I annoyed you today and maybe also a bit over the past months by not being here enough. I admit this. But I've come to a decision.'

'Yes?' She looked at him.

'I honestly didn't realise how much that whole baby thing meant to you.' He leaned forward and held both her hands. 'Cathy, I want to say it straight out. If you'd like us to try for another child, then I wouldn't mind, I really wouldn't mind at all.'

Chapter Twelve

DECEMBER

One of Muttie's associates went to have acupuncture and his back straightened up; in fact he wondered had he been to Lourdes, so great was the transformation. Cathy told June about it just in case it would help her husband.

'Nothing will help Jimmy, he's like Interpol these days, what time did the job end, why was I so long coming home. It would drive you right up the walls and down again.'

Cathy took Jimmy's side. 'To be fair, now you gave him a bit of reason to be jealous ... going off to parties and clubs.'

'I never slept with anyone else since I married him a hundred years ago, more than you can say for most people, but there's no telling him that. He's put a halt to my gallop recently, and me the only blameless soul left in Dublin.'

Cathy wondered was that right. Were most people unfaithful? She never had been. And Neil? Hard to know, very hard to know nowadays. The thought shocked her, that he could be in bed with red-haired Sara, for example, saying the same things that he said to her, doing the same things. It was unthinkable. But then, so were so many other things.

'*Cathy*. You've put seventy into that box, not sixty ...' June snatched it from her. They were doing their Christmas freezer order, flat boxes of canapés. Sixty per box.

'You're miles away,' June grumbled.

'You're right.' She pulled herself together sharply. 'And we must finish quickly because we're having Power Elevenses, remember?'

'All right, I'll speed up if you put your mind on them.'

'All right. I'll keep my mind on them if you give Jimmy the name of the acupuncture man. He deserves a crack at it.'

And with that they went into fast mode, laughing as they bumped into each other, but the boxes got filled and labelled and filed deep in the heart of the rented freezers. By eleven o'clock Tom was well back from Haywards and the cash and carry. Con and Lucy had turned up as requested to, and they were all sitting in the front room, five Scarlet Feather mugs of coffee and a plate of shortbread on the table that used to hold Cathy's beloved punchbowl.

'Now this is like a council of war. Cathy and I thought it only fair that you all realise how near the edge of the precipice we are. Our only hope is to work the arses off ourselves this month. There will be nothing whatsoever to do in January, there will be no money out there, so our only hope is in the next four weeks. Now what we have to do is to know how many days and nights we can all work, otherwise we'll be taking on more than we can handle and we'll fall on our faces.'

'I can work every night except Christmas Day,' Con said.

'But Con, the pub?' Tom gasped.

'I've asked for the day shifts there. I prefer it. Anyway, it's messy in December.'

'If you're sure?'

'I'm sure. I'm going skiing with a bird in January, so I need all the dough I can get.'

'And you, Lucy?'

'Any night except Christmas Day, most lunchtimes too.'

'Lucy, have you given up university?'

'No, but there's not much on between now and February when we have to put our heads down and study, anyway, I'm going skiing with a fellow so I'll need to buy a few clothes.' She laughed conspiratorially with Con.

'June?' Tom said.

'Every night including Christmas night,' she said.

'But Jimmy?' Cathy began.

'Isn't bringing in any money, and will be glad of my wages.'

'Cathy?' Tom asked.

'Any night, obviously, and any day. This is our last throw.'

'But won't you have to. . . ?'

'No,' she said.

'The holiday, the weekend?' He was mystified.

'Won't happen. I'll be here for the duration.'

'And I'll be here all the time, so there was hardly any need for a Power Elevenses at all.' The team would be there, every one of them, every night. They were going to do it, all five of them; they would see that Scarlet Feather didn't go under. All they had to do now was go out and get the bookings.

It was a matter of leaflets; they'd put them up everywhere, in Lucy's university, in Con's pub, on the food counter in Haywards, in Geraldine's friend Mr Ryan's chain of dry-cleaners. Geraldine and Shona would deliver them around Glenstar, Lizzie would leave them in the apartment blocks where she cleaned. Stella and Sean, still starry-eyed from their wonderful wedding, would give them out in their area. Tom was to go to the printer's that morning. Cathy would go to the market and see if any of the stallholders might put them up. Geraldine was on the phone; she was delighted to hear they were all so enthusiastic, she would call in a favour from Harry, a journalist she knew, and ask him to give Scarlet Feather a mention in one of those Countdown to Christmas columns. They agreed to report progress to each other before the day was out.

Their progress was strange. When Tom went to the printer's the man remembered him.

'You lot were in a year ago, you bought Martin Maguire's place.'

'That's right.' Tom was surprised.

'Any word on how the poor divil is getting on these days? Terrible business that was, terrible.'

'I think he's fine. Cathy, my partner, met him during the summer; he was going to come and see us, but at the last moment he didn't.'

'Ah, you couldn't expect the man to set foot in that place again after all that happened in there.'

'I'm afraid that I don't know. What *did* happen?' Tom said eventually.

'Don't mind me, I talk too much,' the printer said.

'Please tell me.' Tom was gentle but insistent.

'His son Frankie went and hanged himself there, right in the premises. They never did another day's work in that place.'

Cathy went to the market, it was gearing up with Christmas gifts, and there would be huge crowds passing through. But most of the stalls and stands didn't look suitable places to advertise their party service. Perhaps there was a community noticeboard on that building at the end; she walked towards it, and on her way she saw a bric-a-brac stall, and noticed a silver punchbowl just like hers. She picked it up and looked at the base.

There it was. 'Awarded to Catherine Mary Scarlet for Excellence.'

'How much?' she asked the stallholder in a whisper.

'Not sterling silver or anything, but a nice piece.'

'Please?' she asked again.

'Thirty?' he said doubtfully.

'Twenty?' she suggested, and got it for twenty-five pounds.

'It doesn't matter to me in the slightest, but would you have any idea where you got it?' she asked.

'Not an idea in the world,' he said.

'It's not important now,' she said, and totally forgot about finding a place for their advertisement.

Geraldine dropped into the newspaper and gave in the little piece about Scarlet Feather that she had typed out. It was ready to run. Harry was an old mate. She had known him for ever, and had recently given him the telephone numbers of two politicians, so he owed her.

'Will you come and have a drink, Ger, it does me good to be seen with a young dishy piece like yourself, makes my street cred go up.'

It was flattering to be called a dishy young piece, but then Harry was considerably older than she was. Everything was relative.

'I won't, Harry, thanks all the same, I've a lot to do.'

'Pity, I'm a bit down. I needed to be cheered up.'

'I'm sorry, what has you down?'

'All my old friends dying off like flies, poor Teddy's the latest, I suppose you heard.'

Geraldine had heard not a word about the one man she had ever loved, the man who had left Ireland for Brussels with his wife and family twenty-two years ago. She felt faint, but she hid it. 'I heard something,' she murmured. 'But tell me . . .'

'Oh, the usual, he's not going for the chemo this time. Wants to come back to Ireland to die. Funny, he hardly came back at all over all that time, and he must be gone about fifteen years.'

'Longer, I think,' she said.

'Maybe. Did you know him at all back then?'

'A bit,' she said, and got out into the fresh air before her legs went from under her in the warm office.

'Do you get enough money to make it all right for us to live here, Muttie?' Simon asked.

'Cathy said you're not to ask people about what money they get,' Maud was reproving.

'I didn't ask how much Muttie got, I just wanted to make sure it was enough.' Simon was outraged to be misunderstood.

'We have plenty, son, we lack for nothing,' Muttie said.

'You lack a good coat, Muttie, yours is very thin.'

'But I have a great thick jumper,' Muttie said cheerfully.

'Father always had a good coat with a velvet collar, and I'm sure they got a lot of money for The Beeches.' Simon was distressed at the unequal nature of things.

'Ah, but now remember, your poor father lost his house and your mother lost her health, so not everyone has everything, that's the most important thing to remember,' Muttie said.

'There are new people going into The Beeches after Christmas,' Maud said.

'Will that upset you, child? Will you miss the place?'

'No, Muttie, I mean there's no one there any more, Mother's going to be in a home mainly, Father's travelling with old Barty and Walter's gone away. There's no one there any more to miss.'

'And this is your home for as long as you like. For ever, really. I know it's not a grand place like you are used to, but we'd miss you to bits if you weren't here ... We did, you know.'

'We know you did,' Simon reassured him. 'Didn't you come all the way down to Kilkenny to find us?'

'I wonder where Walter is,' Maud said. 'He never sends a postcard or anything.'

'I'm sure he will one day,' Muttie reassured them.

'I hope he has a good job,' Maud said. 'He was so nice to come and find us too, the day you did; I didn't expect him to.'

'No, I thought he wouldn't bother with us, but he must have been worried about us,' said Simon.

'We thought he had gone away himself that night, I don't really remember it all clearly,' Maud said with a troubled face.

Muttie decided it was time to change the subject. 'They always say you should never look back. Do I look back to the day I meant to put the tenner on Earl Grey, and I wasn't seeing things clearly,

471

so didn't I mix up the names and put it on to King Grey instead? A dark day that was, but do I look back on it? I do not.'

'Tom, don't hang up, it's Marcella.'

'I'm not going to hang up,' he said.

'Listen, I can't talk long, there's this television game giving dream prizes, you know, a flight in a helicopter, someone to cook a dinner party for you . . .'

'I know.' Tom sighed. 'Geraldine tried to get us in there, but . . .'

'I'm having dinner with the director, I'm actually at Quentin's with him now. Why don't you and Cathy get down here, and I'll introduce you, and Brenda will praise you to the skies. Wouldn't it be a great chance—'

'You're very good to think of it, but . . .'

'But what, Tom, it's eight o'clock at night. I'll be here with this guy for at least another hour and a bit. Go on, get Cathy, I bet she'd think it was worth it.' She was gone.

They met at Quentin's. Tom was wearing a dark suit and white shirt.

Cathy looked at him with admiration. 'You scrub up very well,' she said. She wore her blue velvet trouser suit, and her hair hung loose on her shoulders.

'And you've put on make-up!' he said.

'Let's only have a starter, we can't afford a whole meal,' she said, looking at the menu anxiously.

Tom was looking over at Marcella, smiling up at a square-jawed man with glasses. The director who had the power to make Scarlet Feather's name. He realised with a sense of loss that he really didn't love Marcella any more.

Brenda came to the table. 'I know what this is about,' she said. 'They're having their coffee now, don't order anything yet and they can sit with you for five minutes on their way out; you don't want the table covered with food.'

'You're a genius,' Cathy whispered.

'No, it's just that I love these kind of dramas, trying to change people's lives, it's what makes the business worthwhile. You should know, you do it yourselves.'

It worked like a dream. Marcella showed surprise to see them, Tom begged them to sit down for five minutes. Douglas, the director who seemed a nice sort of fellow, the only one in the dark about the whole thing, talked easily. Nobody mentioned the television show.

'What are you doing nowadays, Marcella?' Tom asked.

'I hope she'll decorate our television programme as one of the prize-givers,' Douglas said, smiling.

At that point Brenda arrived and congratulated Douglas on having discovered Scarlet Feather, the best-kept catering secret in Ireland. 'Patrick and I always quiver when they come in here, they have such high standards,' Brenda said.

'Tell me, what kind of a dinner party would you cook for eight people. . . ?' Douglas began. And they knew it was theirs. Under the table, they squeezed each other's hands very tightly.

Kay Mitchell was in a nursing home. It was thought that she would never be able to look after herself fully; sheltered accommodation was mentioned as a long-term plan. The nursing home had been chosen with a view to easy access for the children, who could get there on one bus journey from school or from St Jarlath's Crescent. There was a cheerful sitting room where she could come and meet them every week. And would, of course, meet her husband Kenneth if he ever came back from his travels with old Barty. And Walter, if anyone could tell her where he was and when he was coming back. Sometimes she asked the twins, but they didn't know. Sometimes she forgot that The Beeches had been sold and asked about the garden. There were even days when she wasn't sure who Maud and Simon were, exactly. But the twins remained good-tempered throughout.

'I expect if you've got bad nerves people sort of slip out of your mind like down through a grating,' Simon said as they went home after a visit where their mother had constantly asked them who they had come to see.

'And then when the nerves get better, she finds them again,' Maud agreed, as they went back to the comfort of St Jarlath's Crescent, where everyone knew who they were and welcomed them home for supper.

Geraldine did not take long to find which hospital Teddy was in, and learned that he had a private room. Twice she went to the hospital with the intention of visiting him, twice she left without doing so. She had even got as far as the corridor and seen that there was nobody else with him . . . But still something stopped her. Why had he come back to Ireland? He hardly knew anyone here now, his family had grown up in Brussels, he wasn't close to his brother and sister. Did she want to see him now, when he was so very ill? Did he want her to see him this way? Was there a wild possibility that now, in this last part of his life, he had wanted to see her again, but did not dare to ask her to visit. On her third visit she was determined not to run away. The door of his room was slightly open; she could see the end of a bed and a nurse talking to him. But still she couldn't go in. She had the phone number of the hospital and her mobile . . . She moved further down the corridor and made the call; they put her through to his room. She could hear the phone ringing beside his bed and then he answered.

'Teddy, it's Geraldine O'Connor,' she said.

'I'm sorry?' His voice was frail, he sounded confused.

'You know . . . Geraldine,' she said, and paused.

'Have you got the right person?' he asked.

'Teddy, it's Geraldine, for God's sake, Geraldine.' She moved nearer to the room. He was not going to forget her or pretend that he had forgotten her. This was not going to happen. She had behaved so well for over half of her life, she only wanted to say goodbye, tell him that she had never stopped loving him.

'I'm sorry,' he apologised. 'I'm on a lot of medication and I'm afraid I don't recall everyone's names.'

'So why did you come back here, then, Teddy, if you don't remember anyone?' She knew her voice sounded hard.

'Please forgive me,' he said, and put the phone down.

She saw the nurse moving around his bed. Geraldine didn't go into the room. She stood without moving in the corridor and watched the pleasant-looking girl go back to the nurses' station at the corner. Geraldine didn't know how long she stood there. One or two people asked her if she was all right, and she must have answered satisfactorily. She saw people going into the various rooms, but nobody went into Teddy's. Eventually she turned away and went to the elevator. She was too shaky still to drive her car, so she had a cup of tea in the restaurant downstairs. It was all for the best, she told herself. What could she have talked about with him, anyway? How he had ruined her life, how his doctor friend had ruined her chances of ever having a child? Would she have told him about all the men who had replaced him in her life, but none of them loved as he had been loved? A man about to die would not want to hear such tragedy. She wiped away the tears that were falling into her cup of tea. It had all been for the best that he hadn't remembered her.

It had been such a wonderful night at Quentin's that Tom had not wanted to darken the mood by telling the story of young Frankie Maguire, who had killed himself at the premises. Sometimes he looked around wondering which room it might have happened in. But it wasn't something Cathy had to know now, nor indeed any of the others. And anyway, there wasn't a free moment for anyone to tell anything. The television dinner party was on ... Tom and Cathy would be in the studio ... The leaflets were beginning to yield some results, the five of them worked non-stop, cooking, packing and unpacking the van, delivering, serving and clearing up, taking more bookings. So much was happening that Tom couldn't sleep. It was no effort to get up and go to bake bread at Haywards at a time when most people were asleep.

Shona wasn't asleep; she was letting herself in at the same time. 'I'll make you breakfast,' he offered.

'Done.' She came and sat in the kitchen and watched as he got the place to life, prepared his doughs and got them both coffee and toast.

'What on earth has you in so early, Shona, they work you too hard?'

'No, this is my own life. I'm in because I want an uninterrupted hour on the Internet. I'm the one in charge of booking a holiday and I'm not very used to it.'

'How many of you are there going?' Tom asked absently.

'Two,' she said.

He looked up with a smile. 'That's nice,' he said.

'Not what you think, Tom.'

'Nothing's what you think,' he said. 'The older I get, the more I realise that.'

Cathy went into the hairdressing salon at Haywards. 'I want a totally new image for a television show tomorrow,' she said.

'What kind of an image?' asked Gerard, the senior stylist.

'I want to dazzle everybody,' she said.

Gerard had been given better guidelines in his life. 'What will you be wearing?' he asked.

'A red T-shirt, black trousers and a white pinafore. I have to have my hair sort of hidden in a hat I think, or something to make it look as if it isn't falling onto the food.' Gerard asked not unreasonably why, if her hair was going to be hidden by a hat, she needed a new hairstyle or any hairstyle, in fact. Maybe it was a hat she needed, a smart, white hat. 'I have to have a nice hairstyle because months ago my mother-in-law gave me a token here,' she said, as if it was the most obvious thing in the world.

'What did you do with it?'

'I gave it to my friend June who got purple streaks,' Cathy said.

'I see,' said Gerard.

'And I only have three-quarters of an hour, Gerard, so could you think of something quick.' Gerard sent down to the store for a white hat so that they could examine the situation more clearly. 'This will take for ever!' Cathy wailed.

'You're a pro and I'm a pro. You wouldn't let your food go out looking like swill. I don't want you going on the television with my hairdo looking like a bird's nest after a party.'

Cathy's saw the point; he had to protect his reputation too. Gerard fixed on the white cap at a jaunty angle, and then proceeded to cut her hair to just above her shoulders.

'I look like a simpleton in a pantomime,' Cathy said, staring at herself.

'Thanks a bundle, and I bet your food tastes like shit too,' said Gerard, insulted.

They caught each other's eye in the mirror, and both began to laugh. The sedate clientele of Haywards was startled to see the near hysteria as Cathy and Gerard laughed until they thought they would never stop.

'Tom, you know we wouldn't annoy you in a million years,' Maud said on the telephone.

'I *know* that, like you know I wouldn't offend you in a million years, but it's just that we're so busy now, you wouldn't believe it.'

'I would believe it. I heard Muttie tell his wife Lizzie that the two of you will be in your coffins before St Patrick's Day with the amount of hours you're working . . .'

'He said that?' Tom reached over and grabbed a saucepan just before it began to burn.

'He did, he said if ever he got a lot of money that he'd go out and he'd invest it in your company.'

'Well, that was very kind of him, Maud, and it *is* nice to have a chat from time to time, but—'

'We have a day off school on Friday, we wondered could we come and polish your treasures, we want to earn money to buy Muttie a coat.'

'I don't think you'd earn enough in an afternoon, to be honest.' Poor Tom was desperate.

'There's a coat in the thrift shop for three pounds,' said Maud.

'Oh, well then, we'll see you Friday,' Tom said, and hung up.

'I don't believe you,' Cathy said.

'I had to,' Tom said. 'You would have had to if you'd been here. Well, come on, take off your hat. Let's see the new you ...'

'I look like a plough boy with a straw in his mouth,' Cathy said.

'I know, you've always looked like that, but let's see the hair.'

'Come on,' June said. 'Why else do you think I hung about?'

'Did Jimmy go to the acupuncturist?' Cathy fought to buy time.

'We've had this discussion, he did and he feels a bit better, now let's see your hair.' June was giving no quarter.

She took off her hat. Unlike other women who cared about their appearance, she didn't go to a mirror to fluff it up, and explain that it was probably a bit flat by now.

Tom, June, Lucy and Con looked at her in silence.

'Oh, Jesus, is it as bad as that?'

'You look beautiful,' June said simply.

'Beautiful,' Tom agreed.

Con and Lucy clapped and beat saucepan lids on the work surfaces.

'That's enough, I will not be mocked,' she threatened them. But they could see she was pleased, and when she got a chance she went into the cloakroom and looked at it herself. It wasn't at all bad; it looked as if it were meant to be that way. It was shiny and sort of glamorous, not scraped back out of the way as if it were an embarrassment. She must send a postcard to Gerard to thank him. Now all she had to do was cook a dinner in front of half a million people.

The day in the studio passed in a horrible blur. Hot lights melted things, the food had to be pinned together eventually, sprayed with a terrible kind of starchy substance so that it would keep a shine. Over and over they were told that it didn't *matter* what it tasted like, the audience was not going to eat it, only to see what Tom and Cathy could prepare for the winner. They had to unpack things from refrigerated boxes so that the viewers could imagine them turning up in simple kitchens anywhere in Ireland and producing this gourmet meal. Douglas, the director looked not at all hassled in the studio. Tom and Cathy watched him admiringly; they had never been so alarmed and so self-conscious, yet this man was as cool as anything. Oddly, he seemed equally admiring of them that they could cook under such circumstances.

'You're naturals,' he said. 'I wouldn't be at all surprised if you are invited back. Nice little earner that, the new celebrity cooking couple. Have you been long together?'

'We've been working together as Scarlet Feather for a while, but we've only had the premises for under a year.' Cathy said.

She knew he thought they were a real couple, as so many people did.

'I bet your guests get well fed in your home,' he said.

They hadn't the energy to disabuse him. They nodded glumly as the make-up girl came to powder their faces again.

'She's a lovely girl, your friend Marcella, isn't she?' Douglas said.

Tom and Cathy's eyes met.

'Lovely,' Tom said. 'Very special.'

'She's been a friend of ours always,' said Cathy.

And then they were back into countdowns, and settle down studio and good luck everyone for the final rehearsal before they went out live.

The phone hardly stopped ringing the next day. In the front room Lucy sat coping with the requests, taking details and sending out brochures all morning. It had done exactly what they had hoped – brought them right out there into the public eye.

'You'll never be able to thank Marcella enough,' June said.

'I'm going to send her a bunch of flowers from all of us,' said Cathy. 'Here's the card, let's all sign it now and we'll get it delivered round to Ricky's.'

They let Tom be the last to sign before it went into the envelope. He wrote, 'Marcella, you have been a very generous and good friend, love from Tom.'

Cathy noticed that Lucy was stretching her muscles. 'Here, I'll take over the phone for a while, go and move around the kitchen for a bit,' she said. It was peaceful there in the front room. Her punchbowl back on the table, a little Christmas tree in the window, their coloured box files filling up with more and more addresses, contacts, customers. And it was quiet. It gave her a chance to think between calls. Think about Neil. Last night when she got home, Neil had been working as usual. He had smiled, glad to see her. And then suddenly a look of guilt came over his face.

'Oh, my God, it was tonight, the television thing.'

'You didn't see it?'

'I'm so sorry . . .'

'Or record it. . . ?'

'I can't tell you . . .'

She had gone straight to bed. And she had left this morning before he had got up. Things had never been so bad. He would call sometime today to say he was sorry; she needed time to think what she would say. It wasn't a matter of sulking or refusing to forgive him. Because in many ways it didn't really matter all that very much. Not in itself; more what it seemed to say about them both.

'Geraldine, Neil Mitchell here. Did you by any chance make a video recording of Cathy's thing yesterday?'

'Yes, I did, wasn't she great? They were marvellous, the pair of them.'

'Could I see it?'

'You don't have one yourselves, there's casual,' she laughed.

'Can I have a loan of it please, Geraldine?'

'No, sorry, I gave it into a place to adapt it for America, you see, I thought Cathy's sister Marian would like—'

'Muttie, did you see Cathy last night on the television?'

'Wasn't half St Jarlath's Crescent in here watching.'

'Do you have a video of it?' Neil sounded urgent.

'Neil lad, the children took it to school today.'

'What in the name of God for?' He sounded almost angry now.

'For a project, they have a project every Thursday where the children have to stand up and present something. So Simon and Maud are going to show seven minutes of Cathy and Tom, then they're going to talk about the food industry. Aren't they gas little tickets,' Muttie said proudly.

'Gas tickets, yeah,' said Neil, and hung up.

'Mother, did you record Cathy last night on television?'

'No dear, why should I?'

'I just thought you might. Did you see it?'

'Yes, they were surprisingly good, don't you think?'

'Yes, yes, very,' Neil said.

'I'm delighted she finally did something about her hair, used that token I gave her, makes a lot of difference, don't you think?'

'Great difference, goodbye, Mother,' Neil said.

Sara rang him to arrange about a meeting later in the day. 'Hey, wasn't that a great plug for Scarlet Feather?' she said.

'You saw it?'

'Well, of course I did.'

'But how could you have seen it, you were in the café with us all when it was on.'

'I know, but I videoed it.'

'You did? That's great. Can I have the video?'

'No, I've recorded over it, a horror film later last night.'

'Sara, was Cathy's hair different?'

'Yeah, I hardly recognised her,' said Sara with her usual tact.

'What?'

'Well, I don't mean that, but it's pretty good, you have to admit.'

'I didn't notice it,' he said.

'Really?' Sara said, her spirits lifting.

Some of the calls that came in were of congratulation, clients who were proud of them, the Riordans, Molly Hayes, Stella and Sean, Mrs Ryan who had the apple strudels way back, even Mrs Fusspot. June's husband Jimmy rang to say they had been stars, and that he was also dead grateful about the acupuncture, some mad heathen kind of superstition but you wouldn't believe it, it seemed to be working. And then Neil rang.

'There's nothing I can say except I am so ashamed.'

'It's all right, Neil,' she said wearily, and she actually meant it. It *was* all right. Compared to the much bigger picture, the fact that the programme had slipped his mind was no big deal.

'Look, I know lunch wouldn't make it all right.'

Cathy wasn't going to keep up the dark mood. It was no life living in a perpetual sulk. She knew he was devastated.

'I don't have time for lunch today, Neil, I'm not being cold, it's just a fact. The phone is jumping off the hook – you wouldn't believe it.'

'Congratulations, I'm very proud of you. I'll try to see it today.'

'No, don't, honestly, you're too busy, we'll get a copy of the video from Mam and Dad later on. Leave it, Neil, it's all right, believe me.'

'And your hair, Cathy?'

'Yes?'

'It's very nice.'

'You told me that.'

'When did I tell you?'

'On Tuesday. I asked you did you think it suited me, and you said yes.'

'And I do,' he said. 'When will you be home if you don't want lunch?'

'About seven,' she said. 'But you're going out.'

'I won't tonight,' he promised. 'I'll cancel that meeting.'

Shona Burke was having lunch with James in his flat. He had discovered that soups were very easy to make; he didn't know why nobody had ever told him this before. They talked about the great television programme, and how it could be the turning point for them.

'If only the insurance would pay up,' James said. 'I don't want to be the spectre at the feast, but it's serious, you know. How did that horrible boy gain entrance? We need to know, and he's unlikely to tell us.'

'There's five of them working flat out there today. I called in to congratulate them on my way here . . .'

'What do they think of us going to Morocco for Christmas?' he asked.

'I didn't tell them.'

'Why ever not?'

'Well, you're such a private person, you never talk about your own business. Neither do I. I didn't think you'd want them, or indeed anyone, to know . . . about us having found each other and everything . . .' she looked awkward.

'I used not to be a private person, Shona, I used to tell everyone everything, I brought your essays to the office to show my colleagues, that's how outgoing I used to be, once.'

'Me too. I just learned to be private. But I suppose we could unlearn it. Will I tell them, or will you?'

'We could even tell them together,' he suggested.

Cathy came in at exactly seven o'clock. She looked tired, he thought, and her hair was beautiful, very soft and feminine; how had he failed to notice it before, or admire it only in a perfunctory way on Tuesday night?

'I have turned the answering machine down, we won't even *hear* anyone if they call.' His infectious smile didn't get a response. 'I got oysters,' he said. 'To try to make amends ... They aren't open. I don't know how to open them, actually, but I thought you might like ...'

'To come home from eleven hours in a catering kitchen and open oysters?' she asked.

'No, perhaps not. Not a great idea.'

'It's beyond gestures now, isn't it, Neil?'

'What do you mean... ?'

'We're much too far apart, there's nothing left. Weekends, feasts, surprises, talk, oysters ... It would only be acting.'

'It's a bad patch, certainly ... We are missing each other a lot in a way that we never did before, but I *did* say that I was perfectly willing to try for another child.'

'That's the one thing that has driven us further apart than anything else.'

'What do you mean?'

'Neil, you can't say you'll *give* me a baby and *put up* with a baby just to shut me up.'

'I never used any of those words, nor felt them. Don't put things into my mouth.'

'It's what you were offering me as a last chance.'

'You're imagining it,' he said.

'You and I used to be able to talk about everything. It was the greatest thing in the world.'

'We can get it back, can't we?' He sounded unsure of himself.

'I don't think so.'

'You're not serious,' he said.

'I am. What you want is a different kind of wife entirely. Someone who idolises you, someone who will stay at home with you and have nice dinner parties for your colleagues....'

'I never said ...'

'No, you didn't, and I'm not saying it's wrong to want that, but you don't need someone independent with a career, you need someone who will throw up everything and follow you. I'm not that person, but there are many of them out there. Sara, for example.'

'Sara? What are you talking about?'

'You have that ability to talk with her that you and I used to have once.'

'Sara ... you're not suggesting?'

'I'm just saying she's very young, she hero-worships you ...'

'She's very concerned ...'

'She's got a crush on you, but that's not the point, that's not what we're talking about.'

'What *are* we talking about?'

'I suppose about what we do now.' She felt exhausted and fatigued, almost defeated. Somehow once she had said the words they seemed less frightening. It was out in the open. They were admitting that things between them were very bad indeed.

'You still care about what I do, the work that has to be done, don't you?'

'Yes, I do, I really do. But I think you've forgotten about you and me in the whole thing. We don't talk ... It's not that we have no time, it's just that we make no time. And much as I admire you, it seems to me that you bleed for everyone in the world and for big global problems, but you can't see the hurts and hopes and dreams on your own doorstep.'

'Now that's not really fair, you *said* you supported the same things as I did, then you suddenly went off on a tangent trying to be the world's biggest caterer. You *said* that you didn't want children, just like me, and then you got pregnant and I was the worst monster in the world because I wasn't suddenly delighted. Then you *said* you were sad and lonely and tired, and I said okay, let's have another baby, and apparently that was the worst thing I ever said in my whole life. So don't throw all the accusations at me.'

Cathy looked at him as if for the first time. He really and truly felt that she had totally misjudged him in all this. They were further apart than she had thought.

'I don't want a slanging match, Neil, I just said that you are so involved in everything else you don't see what's happening to us. There's nothing out there that you wouldn't fight for, but we are missing each other every step of the way.'

'No, that's not so, I won't have this. I've done everything I can, you're trying to put a label on me – it's not fair to say I'm Mister Rent-a-Cause. I just won't accept it.'

'What will you accept then?' she asked. 'Are you going to accept that things are very, very bad between us.'

'I can't believe this is happening,' he said, shaking his head as if to get a buzzing noise out of his ears.

She sat very still and said nothing.

'This is all a total mess. It's brought about by us both working too hard,' he began. 'Cathy, don't let us lose it, it's up to us . . . you know that . . . If we want something we can get it. We did it before.'

She was about to say that she thought it was too late, but the words didn't come out.

'Listen to me, Cathy, we can start again, leave here, leave all the pressures, start all over. I'll take the job, we can go away, put everything behind us, we'll have space and peace to work everything out, have our baby when we want to. We can put all this unhappy year behind us.'

She looked at him open-mouthed.

'That's what we'll do, they're on to me every day to make up my mind. We'll tell them that we'll go. We'll go together.'

'Please, Neil, no, please.'

But she couldn't stop him, he was in full flight now.

'It's what we've needed, to get out of here . . . People do get bogged down by things, you're right, we have been missing each other. What with rushing between the twins and the break-in and your parents and my parents and the American wedding and the insurance and the late nights and the never having time to talk . . .'

'It's got nothing to do with all that,' she attempted.

'It has everything to do with it. Once we're on our own far way from everything here . . .'

'There is no way that . . .'

'We've been working too hard, we haven't given ourselves time to pause and think . . .'

'No, Neil.' Suddenly she snapped.

'Will you stop shaking your head at me and talking like a nanny. Honestly, even my mother wasn't as certain and definite as you are. I'm offering us the chance to save our marriage, we love each other. We fought hard to get each other, against a lot of opposition, we're not going to throw it all away just after one bad year are we?'

She said nothing.

'Are we? Don't just sit there looking at me reproachfully as if I were Maud and Simon. This is serious, this is our future for God's sake.'

'It's your future.'

'I want it to be ours, I want us to do it together . . .'

'But. . . ?' she said.

'But I don't know what you want, I really don't. If I did know what you want, I'd try to do it.'

'I've always wanted the same thing,' she said.

'No, that's not true, you want to be out all hours with stupid, vain, rich people making them ever more ludicrous food.'

'I see.'

'It's not a life, it's not a way to live. This was never our plan. Come away with me, come on, we can make it work.'

'No.'

'You're just being stubborn, you're making a point.'

'Not true.'

'We've been through this over and over. This is important. I am at the point that I can't bear us to go on having these endless rows. I'll go without you if you won't come. I mean it. They're on to me every day. I've only been stalling them for you. Now if you're not going to come, what's the point of stalling them any more?'

'No point,' she said blankly.

'I don't want to go without you.'

'No, no I see that.'

'But I will, I mean this is what I've always wanted. I thought it was what we had always wanted. I would turn sour, be very bitter, we'd have nothing left at all if I were to stay.'

'You have a very good career at the Bar, you do a lot of good for a lot of people, people like Jonathan.'

'I can do more on a bigger canvas.'

'And you'll go alone?'

'Yes, if I have to. I'm going to go now, before Christmas if I can, and leave it open for you to join me.'

'That's a non-starter. You know that. I know that. You can't railroad people into things.'

'Would you ever have come with me?' he asked.

She thought for a while.

'I might have, but not until the business was up and running, I had paid back my debts, found someone to replace me.'

'It mattered as much as that?'

'Did you think it was a game?'

'I thought it was something to show my mother you could be a person in your own right. I never thought you needed to prove that to anyone, but honestly, that's all I thought it was.'

'We'll have to tell her, you know.'

'Tell her what?'

'That your plans have changed, that you'll be abroad – we were going there for Christmas.'

'Yes, I suppose so.'

'Funny, I think that's something that's going to stick in my throat badly, the fact that she was right all those years ago when she said I wasn't right for you.'

'Cathy . . .'

'If you don't mind I won't stay for us both to get more upset. We can talk better in the daylight.'

'Please don't go,' he begged.

'It's for the best,' said Cathy Scarlet as she packed a bag and left.

She knew Tom was out with Con doing a rugby club party. There were kitchens at the club, so they would not be coming back here tonight. Before she lay down on the chintz-covered sofa, she left a message on Tom's phone back at his flat.

'Hope the company doesn't mind, I'm spending a couple of nights on its sofa.'

Then she went to sleep. When she woke to get a drink of water in the night she saw that a fax had arrived. It said simply, 'The company wishes you sweet dreams.' She knew he would never ask her a question any more than she had ever asked him. Somehow it was very restful.

She had every sign of her overnight stay carefully removed before anyone came. And as she knew there wouldn't be, there was no comment from Tom Feather. Once or twice he lifted a pot for her, or passed her oven gloves as if he feared she would do herself an injury.

'Shona said that she wanted to come and have coffee this morning,' she said. 'James will drop by too, and it won't take long.'

'God, what a morning to choose, we have the heavenly help force with us today.'

'What?'

'Had you forgotten? A team of highly skilled polishers have a half-day from school and are heading in this direction, on the invitation of someone who is Just a Boy Who Can't Say No.'

'Oh, God, Simon and Maud.' She had forgotten.

'Doesn't matter, the day will end sometime.'

The twins arrived early. They were wearing their oldest clothes, they said, and could do heavy work. Muttie's wife Lizzie had given them wire scrubbing pads and old toothbrushes for getting into the crevices of things which might have legs.

'I didn't know what she meant, exactly,' Simon said. 'Like chicken carcases or something.'

'No, like sauce boats or the handles of things,' Cathy explained.

'Oh, look, you've got another punchbowl,' Maud said, pleased.

'It's the same one, actually, look, my name is on the bottom,' Cathy said.

'How did you find it?' Simon asked. 'Was it here all the time?'

'No, no, it made a weary journey around the place from black plastic bag to garden shed to one market stall and then another. I bought it back.'

Then she remembered the twins didn't know of Walter's part in the burglary. She hoped they hadn't made the connection between the garden shed and their brother storing things there. But they were too happy and eager to start their work to notice anything at all. Cathy told them their duties, and stressed the need to keep out of people's way in the kitchen because there was a rush on.

'Do we have the relaxing hot drink and a scone like we had before when we came?' Simon wondered.

'Why not?' Cathy said. 'Come on, Tom, let's take five minutes to relax with Maud and Simon.'

The four of them sat in the front room while the twins told what a success the project had been at school. Everyone loved it, and was very impressed that Cathy was their aunt. Aunt! She would not be their aunt for much longer, when she and Neil divorced. The thought hardly seemed real; she had to run it past herself again. The children chattered on.

'Do you still have the same code to get in, nineteen and then six?' Maud asked.

'How on earth did you know that was our code?' Cathy asked, quietly.

'You told us. Remember, one day when you were driving us back to The Beeches in the van. You were doing a party, and you told us about the ceremony of the keys. What you did each time in the van and where you put them.'

Cathy could hardly breathe.

'And did you tell anyone else about it, do you think?'

'I don't think so,' Simon said. 'No point in telling your code to everyone we meet, some of them might be robbers and come in.'

'We did tell Walter that night,' Maud said.

Tom and Cathy let their breath out very slowly.

'You did?' Tom said, in a deceptively light tone.

'Yes, you see we had been telling him all about your treasures and polishing them and things, and he said we knew nothing about your business, so just to show him . . .' explained Maud.

'It doesn't matter, does it?' Simon felt uneasy.

'No, it doesn't matter,' Cathy said. 'In fact, it's very good to know that, because a lot of things fall into place.'

'No, Cathy, you can't ask them,' Tom began.

'We can, we'll explain,' she said.

'It's too tough on them. Leave them something to hold onto.'

'Do you think Walter was your burglar?' Simon asked suddenly.

'And then that really was your punchbowl in our garden shed?' Maud said, horrified.

'But Muttie said everything was all broken into little pieces, why would Walter do that?' Simon said.

'Do you think he did it, Cathy?' Maud asked straight out.

'I do, yes, Maud.'

'Why?' she asked.

'I don't know, maybe he was short of money.'

'He was always very nice to us, except when we were stupid,' Maud said.

'I know, I know,' said Cathy.

'And he did come to find us that time.'

'Of course he did.' They must be allowed to believe that, at least.

'Are you very cross with him?' Maud asked.

'No, not now, but there *is* something which would help us a lot without getting Walter into any more trouble.'

'What's that?' They looked at her with anxious eyes.

Gently Cathy explained that the guards already knew Walter had taken the goods, but didn't know how he had found the code and the keys.

'You won't get into any trouble,' Tom promised. 'It's my fault, I didn't tell you it was a secret.'

'And Walter isn't in Ireland anyway, so they can't find him, but it will mean that the insurance company might pay us. Do you mind doing that, telling people? If you do mind, then we'll leave it, but it would be such a great help.'

They looked at each other. 'We'll tell,' they said.

And in the middle of one of the busiest mornings that Scarlet Feather had ever known, hours were spent while Maud and Simon Mitchell told James Byrne, then the guards and then an insurance official about the night they had wanted to prove to their brother they knew all about the business. And everyone softened at the obviously true story and the mixed feelings about their big brother, who had crossed Ireland to find them because he knew they were in trouble.

'It's going to help a great deal, believe me, this is what we needed,' James said.

'What were you going to tell us, Shona?' Tom asked.

'James?'

'Hold on a minute. Simon, Maud, do you want to make an extra pound? Could you go down to the newsagent, it's at the end of the street, and buy me an *Irish Times*?'

'A whole pound?' Simon said.

'Should I go on polishing, do you think?' Maud wondered.

'No, go with him for company,' James said.

When they were gone, Shona spoke immediately. 'When I was young I was fostered with James and his wife Una in Galway, but I was taken away and brought back to my own home when I was fourteen. We've only just got to know each other again.'

Cathy and Tom exchanged glances. What else would this day throw at them?

James spoke in a different voice than usual. 'We were told it was for the best that we didn't make contact. I didn't question it; that's what I blame myself for, not questioning something that felt so wrong, like letting the child we loved go away without begging to have her back.'

'So now we're making up for lost time, meal after gourmet meal . . .' She laughed at the teachers who had taught her lost father to cook.

'And we're going to go away together for a three-week holiday,' James said proudly.

Tom blew his nose loudly. 'If I hadn't another ten hours' work ahead of me today. I'd say that we all went out and got drunk on this.'

'In the New Year,' promised James. 'You come round to my flat, I'll cook a Moroccan speciality for you.'

'Oh, be sure to buy those Tajine dishes and we'll make chicken and prunes and almonds,' Cathy's eyes danced at the thought.

'Weren't you and Neil going to go there?' James asked.

'No, that's not going to happen now,' Cathy said, and at that moment the children came back with the paper.

'Mam, can I have my Christmas dinner here?' Cathy asked.

'Well, of course you can, but I thought the pair of you were going to Oaklands.'

'Neil is, Mam, I'm not.'

'Ah, now, don't tell me you've fought with Mrs Mitchell again, that is very silly at this season of the year.'

'Mam, sit down, I have to tell you something,' Cathy said.

'Geraldine, will you be coming to Mam and Dad's on Christmas Day, as usual?' Cathy asked.

'Yup, that's what us naughty ladies never get to have, Christmas Day with a man. They have this habit of going back to base for the turkey.'

'I'll be joining you there on my own, and I'm relying on you to keep it all going.'

'A bad row?'

'No, a separation. Oddly enough, there have been very few rows.'

'Well then, why in the name of God? Why don't all those men I know who are in the middle of perfectly dreadful marriages not break up? Why leave it to you and Neil, who fought everything to get married and are so suited in every way.'

'Not any more, Geraldine. I need him to care about home and us and having a child and about Maud and Simon, and about maybe a dozen or two dozen people; he wants me to care about millions of people and principles and ... issues.'

'You can do both.'

'Not the way we've been going at it, Geraldine.'

'Do you love him?'

'I thought I did, but I don't really. I'm very fond of him, though.'

'And is there someone else?'

Cathy laughed aloud. 'Me? I don't have enough time to keep one relationship going, how would I have time for two?'

'I just wondered.'

'Well, you wondered wrong.'

'You're being dangerously calm about it all,' Geraldine said. 'When I think of how you fought Hannah Mitchell and the world to marry Neil.'

'I know, I think about that too; it's hard to explain, but I get the feeling that I loved the idea of him rather than him himself. Does that make any sense at all?'

'I know exactly what you're talking about, as it happens.' Cathy looked at her doubtfully. 'You remember the man I told you about, the man from long ago?'

'Yes?' Cathy said.

'He doesn't remember me.' She told the story.

'Of course he remembers you,' Cathy said defensively. 'He just pretended, that's all. How could he not remember you at eighteen, and what happened? Tell me where he is. I'll go in and see him, beat the truth out of him.'

Geraldine's face was very sad. 'No, dear Cathy, thank you for the vote of confidence. I've said all that to myself over and over. But the truth is he doesn't. I was loving the idea of him, not the reality. I've thought about him for twenty-two years, and he must have hardly thought of me at all.'

'We'll help each other through Christmas Day,' Cathy promised.

'Not that it will be hard with that cast,' Geraldine said.

It wasn't really all that much easier to talk in the daylight, but then Cathy had never really thought it would be. Yet they managed a very creditable performance between them. They spent a few hours sitting peacefully in Waterview and made a list of who would take what.

'Live here, if you won't come with me. Stay here, it's your home.'

'It never felt like home. I have too much of St Jarlath's in me to like it. It's too minimalist.' She smiled ruefully when she said it, and so did he.

In so many ways it seemed quite natural to be sitting there, talking, making mugs of tea. But there was nothing natural, it was like reading lines in a play. They decided to put the house on the market in January; that would give them plenty of time to find a destination for the furniture they wanted. Neil said that there would be no problem in putting his share in a warehouse. Cathy said she would have found somewhere to stay by then. They looked at the pictures. There was the one they'd bought in Greece.

'Please take it,' she said.

'No, it was painted for you,' he said.

'Let's neither of us have it,' she said and it went into the great number of personal items which would find a home with neither Cathy nor Neil. He promised to finish off the insurance business for them and she assured him she didn't want the Volvo, the van was fine. Neither one of them could believe it was real sometimes. Yet they knew that there was no going back.

'Have you told many people?' Neil asked.

'Just my Mam and Geraldine really,' she said. 'And you?'

'Nobody.'

'The one thing we should really do together is go and see your parents. We owe it to them,' Cathy said. 'I'd really like to go tomorrow evening, about six.'

'That's fine for me. I will be there, I promise,' he said.

But of course he wasn't. They had arranged to call in for a visit at six o'clock the following evening. At five, she got a call to say that the meeting was going on.

'We can't have them sitting there wondering what it is,' she said.

'You don't have to go today, you can wait until I'm able to come with you.'

She hung up. She saw Tom looking at her.

'Thanks,' she said.

'What for...?'

'You know what for, for not asking.'

'Oh, *that*'s no trouble,' he said, smiling at her. 'You know how dim men are, they wouldn't even know if there was anything to ask about.'

'Oh, you came in the van,' Hannah said as she answered the door.

'Neil has the Volvo, he's been held up,' Cathy said, walking straight in the hall door, leaving her scarf and gloves on the hall table and hanging up her coat. She moved into the den, where Jock and Hannah had been sitting.

'Ah, Cathy, a drink?'

'Yes please, Jock, a small brandy would be nice. Lovely fire, it's very cold out.'

'And is Neil not with you?'

'No, you know the way he always gets tied up at things. Well, today there's a meeting and he sent his apologies.'

Hannah rushed to defend him. 'He has *so* many responsibilities, he couldn't drop them for a social call.'

'It's more than a social call, Hannah, we had something to tell you, but now I'll tell you myself.'

Jock looked alarmed. 'Nothing wrong, is there?' he asked suddenly.

Hannah's hand went to her throat. 'I know what you're going to tell us, you've come to tell me that you and Neil are going to have a baby!'

Walter rang the premises, and Tom answered.

'Er, it was really Cathy I wanted,' he said.

'I'm sure she'll be overjoyed that you called, Walter,' Tom said. 'But sadly she's not here.'

'Stop pissing about, Tom, this isn't a joke.'

'You'd better believe it isn't a joke, Walter.' Tom looked around the premises that the boy had so nearly permanently destroyed.

'I wanted to ask her a couple of things.'

'Ask away,' Tom said agreeably.

'Can you put me on to her?'

'No, she's not here.'

'Has The Beeches been sold?'

'Yes. What else did you want to ask?'

'The twins, are they okay?'

'Much more okay than when they had you to keep an eye on them.'

'Are they with Cathy's parents?'

'Why?'

'I wanted to send them a Christmas present. I didn't know the address.'

'Send them to this address, this is one address you certainly know.'

'You think you're a comedian.'

'No, I think I'm a poor fool who actually goes out and works for a living to be able to buy Christmas presents, rather than steal and smash places up for them.'

'Tell Cathy I rang, anyway.'

'I will. I don't suppose you'd like to leave a number where she can call you back?'

'She and half the guards in Ireland,' Walter said.

'Could happen,' Tom said agreeably.

'Wise guy,' said Walter, and hung up.

Cathy sat for a moment and looked at her parents-in-law. It wasn't fair to keep them dangling, waiting about something as big as this.

'It's nothing like that at all. I came to tell you that Neil and I will not be spending Christmas here. He is taking this overseas job that he mentioned to you before and I'm not going with him, so he won't even be in Ireland for Christmas and under the circumstances I will go to my parents in St Jarlath's.'

They looked at her open-mouthed.

'Are you serious?' Jock asked eventually.

'I'm afraid so. Neil promised he would be here to tell you with me, but it hasn't turned out that way.' It's a matter of us both wanting different things . . .'

'Well, by heavens, you wanted him badly enough some years ago when we all told you that you were different people with different backgrounds.'

'I don't think the background has anything to do with it, it's more the future. Neil wants to go abroad and has his mind on a big job in Europe. I don't want to leave my business . . .'

'But surely your business isn't as important as . . .' Hannah began.

'Unfortunately, Neil didn't think it was important either, so we differed about that too.'

'A bit drastic, isn't it?' Jock said. 'It sounds a bit more like a tiff to me.'

'No, it's much, much more than that.'

'So what's going to happen?' Hannah asked. She didn't look triumphant and superior. She actually looked frightened. A now familiar world was changing.

'We're taking it slowly.'

'Have you someone else?'

'I have nobody else in my life, Hannah.'

'You're not suggesting that Neil does, I hope? Does Poor Lizzie know about all this?'

'Yes Hannah, *Poor* Lizzie knows.'

'You're so quick to take offence, you always were, when there's absolutely no need.'

'Well I'm sure you'll be glad that you were right about me all along,' Cathy said.

Jock interrupted. 'Now none of that, we're both very shocked at your news. It's out of the blue.'

Hannah spoke slowly. 'And no matter what you think, I am *not* pleased. I think you did make Neil happy. I get no joy of saying I told you so, no joy at all.'

'I've made your Christmas cake and plum pudding. Con will deliver them whenever it suits, and anything else you want, of course.'

'And when will Neil come and tell us all about it, what time will his meeting end?' Hannah looked bewildered, a little lost.

Cathy spoke gently. 'I really don't know, you see, he doesn't have to tell me his plans, his schedule any more. I know he'll come and tell you everything, I know he will.'

'It's really all very sad,' Hannah said flatly.

There was a silence. And then Cathy got up. 'You'll want to talk, and Neil will get in touch with you. I'll go now. You can always get me at work, and I've left the number I'll be staying at for the next three weeks, it's at Glenstar apartments. I'm minding Shona Burke's flat.' She paused at the door of the den. 'I'll see myself out, I don't think there's any real etiquette over all this, except to say that I hope we can always keep in touch. I really mean that. Even if Neil is abroad, we might meet through Maud and Simon.' And she left them to digest the news that they would have loved to hear half a decade ago. That she and their son might not have a future together.

'Ricky's having people in on Christmas Day, buffet all afternoon,' Marcella said to Tom.

'I know, we gave him a load of stuff for his freezer,' Tom said, pleased.

'At least they'll get something to eat. It's mainly for people who are on their own, people who don't want to sit down to endless turkey.'

'I'll be up in Fatima for the day,' Tom said.

'There's no strings attached, just a lot of nice people.'

'I know, but I'm still going to be in Fatima.'

'You're very stubborn, can't Joe go for once?'

'He'll be there too,' Tom said.

'And I don't suppose that...'

'I know, I don't suppose that either of us will stay awake for the whole afternoon, but it's something we've agreed to do, to have just the four of us,' he said, intent on heading her off at the pass. He knew Marcella wanted to come to Fatima. But it was too late for her to visit there now. He thought back on all the times he would have loved her to have been there.

On Christmas Eve they opened a bottle of champagne at the Scarlet Feather premises. And then another and another. It was a celebration that they had done what they hoped.

The insurance had paid up, they had been booked to do another television show, there was vague talk of a whole series of thirteen programmes. Between them they had worked all day and all evening for twenty-four days. Even James Byrne had begun to smile before he went off to Morocco. So they deserved a party. Jimmy was there, his back magically straightened by the man with all the mad needles. Geraldine sent her apologies, she was having a little drink with Nick Ryan as he made the excuse of last-minute shopping. Lucy's mother and father were there, disapproving at the start and thawing out gradually. Con was there with his mother, who watched Lucy steadily for the first two drinks and then relaxed considerably. Muttie and Lizzie came with the twins. Only Tom and Cathy had no one to field.

'There's a parcel for you two,' Tom said cheerfully to the twins.

'Is it from you?' they asked.

'No, my present is under your tree in St Jarlath's Crescent.'

They asked could they open it, and Lizzie thought definitely they could.

They tugged at it and produced two watches. Watches that you could use underwater, watches that would give you the time in America if you wanted it. They immediately worked out Chicago time, and set the little dial for that. They had never seen watches like that before. The card said, 'Love from Walter.' This was greeted by a total silence.

'Very nice of him,' Cathy said loudly, and they all murmured that it was.

'Hot?' Tom whispered to her.

'As the hob of hell, I imagine,' she said.

'But we'll leave it, won't we?' he pleaded.

'Of course we will, eejit.' She smiled at him.

'Will you come to Christmas Dinner in St Jarlath's Crescent tomorrow, Tom?' Simon offered graciously.

'Thanks, but I have to arm-wrestle my mother over the turkey, she's inclined to put packet stuffing in it and burn it to a crisp if I'm not there to fight her all the way.'

'It won't be very much the season of peace and goodwill, will it?' Maud said, worried.

'He's joking, Maud,' Cathy said.

'Not altogether,' Maud said.

'Sharp girl,' Tom said.

They were all off now until New Year's Day, when there was a big lunch and the team would gather again, but the main thing they were celebrating was that they had refused eleven bookings on New Year's Eve. They wanted to consider it an anniversary ... one whole year since they had found the premises. Everyone went home. Tom and Cathy insisted that they do the clearing up.

'It's only putting things in a machine, don't our arms do that automatically?' Tom said.

The twins were going back to the best Christmas of their lives.

'Have you got a present for Hooves?' Maud asked Cathy.

'Would I forget Hooves?' asked Cathy, who had.

'I didn't see it under the tree,' Simon said.

'That's because he might have smelled it under the tree,' Tom intervened.

Their eyes lit up.

'She's got him a *bone*!' Simon said, excited.

'Or something in that area,' Cathy said.

They went off down the lane from the premises arm in arm with Lizzie. Tom and Cathy waved them goodbye.

'Get me something out of the freezer for Hooves, for God's sake. You're an utter genius, did you know that?' Cathy said.

'I could thaw a fillet steak if you like,' he suggested. 'We froze them in threes, remember. Well, I might eat one myself, I'm not going anywhere,' Tom Feather said.

'Neither am I,' said Cathy Scarlet.

The day passed as Christmas Day passes for so many people, in a sea of paper and presents and fuss about cooking.

Maura Feather asked them all to kneel down for the papal

blessing, and to please her they did because she had given in on everything else, including the turkey.

Neil had an awkward lunch at Oaklands, where nobody was able to talk about the situation, and where Amanda rang from Toronto to wish them all well. It seemed very artificial.

Muttie was delighted with his new red overcoat that they had got him in the thrift shop, and said he would wear it everywhere. Including tomorrow, when they watched the races on television. He said that he had the accumulator of a lifetime on tomorrow at the races, everything he won on the first race would go onto this horse in the second race, and all the way through the card. It could be millions. And for a very small stake.

Simon and Maud planned spending the millions. They would get their mother a dressing gown like another lady had in the home. Mother hadn't known it was Christmas Day. It had been a bit sad, but Lizzie had said that the poor lady was in a bit of a dream and she was quite happy. Father had sent them five pounds to buy gifts, and said he and old Barty would be home to see them sometime. And of course Walter had sent them the marvellous watches. They could hardly believe that Uncle Jock and Aunt Hannah had given them the computer of their dreams. They had been sure that Aunt Hannah hated them. Neil had left presents under the tree for them: they were marvellous computer games.

Cathy had got Hooves a wonderful steak wrapped up in silver paper with a big pink bow, and she even cooked it for him herself. She was smiling a lot, even when there was nothing particular to smile at. They had been warned by everyone to be particularly nice to her because of this separation thing. But she hadn't been cranky at all. It was a mystery.

The next day, as he sat in his new red coat in front of the television, Muttie's first horse won and so did his second. They were all standing behind his chair watching the television, willing the horses to win for him. When the third horse won they all began to get chest pains. Even Hooves began to howl at the tension in the air. Geraldine's face was contorted by the time the chosen horse started to pull away from the rest in the fourth race.

'I didn't know the meaning of the word stress until this moment,' she said in a strangled voice.

Lizzie said over and over that he should have done the races individually, then they'd have been fine. *Why* had he to do it this way and give them all heart failure? They were fairly short odds, some of them were even favourite, and his associates said he was as mad as a hatter, but Muttie said he had been studying form seriously. This time he really knew what he was doing, Sandy Keane up at the bookies' wouldn't know what hit him this time. The phone rang just as the fourth horse won. Tom answered it. It was Marian from Chicago. He spoke in clipped tones.

'Marian, no one in this house is able to speak now, including myself, so just hang up will you, like a good girl, and we'll call you back later.'

Then he left the phone off the hook. During the fifth race he had his arm so tightly around Cathy's neck she thought she was going to choke. When it won, they all leaped up and hugged each other; only one race to go.

Lizzie said, 'If he hadn't included the last race he'd have walked away with ten thousand pounds, Mother of God, imagine putting ten thousand pounds that would have solved our problems for ever onto a horse. Muttie, *nobody* puts that kind of money on a horse ... I can't believe this is happening.'

'Lie down, Mam.' Cathy got her a footstool and a cold towel for her forehead. Hooves, sensing illness, laid his head in her lap ...

'What are the odds on the next one?' Maud and Simon were screaming with excitement as they tried to work it out.

Tom got Muttie a glass of water, he got Geraldine a whiskey and then he drew up two chairs for himself and Cathy – they no longer had the strength to stand. Muttie's face was ashen, it was within his grasp. Tom and Cathy clutched each other's hands like people on a life raft. The horse was in the last three. One of the others fell.

'I can't *bear* it,' screamed Geraldine.

'Come on, Muttie. Come on, Muttie,' shouted the twins. There had been so many horses to cheer for in the afternoon, they had forgotten the name of this one.

'Listen, God, I'll give you another try if it wins,' Tom said.

'Please, please horse, win for my dad, please win for him, he's never done a bad thing in his life,' Cathy begged the horse, with tears streaming down her face.

'Ten thousand pounds that could have set us up for life thrown away on a horse.' Lizzie had her eyes closed, so she didn't see Muttie's horse, the only long shot on the list, come in at thirteen to one.

'That's thirteen thousand pounds, not bad for a day's work,' said

Muttie with a beatific smile on his face, well satisfied with his efforts.

'No, Muttie, it's a hundred and thirty thousand,' said everyone in the room, except Lizzie and Hooves, at exactly the same time.

Nobody remembered much about what happened after that. Tom reminded them to ring Marian, and they told her that they would all be over for the baby's christening. Muttie took some of his associates for a drink, and told them firmly that the money would be invested by Lizzie, who was good at this sort of thing, and he would still get an allowance, though perhaps an increased allowance. All things considered. And some of the savings would be used to go to Chicago, and some to help finance Scarlet Feather, and some to buy a second-hand van in case Lizzie and himself wanted to go on outings or take the children somewhere educational.

'And what about yourself, Muttie?' everyone asked.

'Haven't I got everything a man could want?' Muttie would say with such sincerity that people got an odd feeling in their noses and eyes.

Tom said he'd drive Cathy back to Shona's apartment in Glenstar. Geraldine was going to stay the night in St Jarlath's Crescent; she said that someone had to mind this family, which had now gone totally insane.

She kissed Cathy goodnight. 'What a year,' she said.

'It had its moments, certainly.' Cathy tried to be light; then she saw Geraldine's face and remembered that Teddy had died, Freddie Flynn had gone and the future with Nick Ryan was uncertain. Cathy had been trying to put a brave face on it for herself and all that had happened to her.

'Next year will be better for all of us, I have a real feeling about that,' she said as she got into the van.

Just before the turn to Glenstar, Tom said, 'You know we never had any Christmas cake tonight.'

'After all the trouble we took icing it,' Cathy said.

'We could drop by the premises, maybe, and have tea and a slice of cake there?'

She thought it was a great idea. Neither of them wanted to go home to empty flats, but it hadn't been their custom to invite the other in at night. The premises had always been neutral ground.

They settled into the front room, drank their tea, and talked about Muttie's win.

'I think he's more pleased about beating Sandy Keane into the ground than actually getting the money,' Cathy said.

'I know, it's personal. We can't take any of his money though,' Tom said.

'We can let him invest,' Cathy said. 'At least that way it's here, rather than in Sandy's hot little hand.'

'I do wonder which is the sounder investment,' Tom said.

'Stop that at once, Tom Feather. We won. We've had a hard year, but in terms of the business, anyway, we won, didn't we?'

'Sure we did. It was a worse year for you than me, but we did win in the end.'

The phone rang.

At this time of night?

'Leave it,' Cathy said.

'I hadn't a notion of answering it,' he said.

They listened as the twins spoke their message. They were thanking them for the best Christmas ever. It had been magic, they said, pure magic. And Muttie's wife Lizzie, and Lizzie's sister Geraldine had said they could stay up until they were so tired that they fell down.

Tom and Cathy sat side by side on the sofa and listened while the twins talked on. They moved very slightly closer to each other and realised that they were holding hands. It seemed very natural so neither of them moved away.

'Goodnight, Tom. Goodnight, Cathy,' the twins said eventually when they thought the tape might be running out.

'They knew we were here,' Cathy said in surprise.

'Imagine,' said Tom Feather as he stroked her hair.